Lawrence Block was awarded the (
2004. He is also a Grand Master of t
is the author of many novels and sl
awards for his mystery writing. He
To find out more, visit: www.lawrenceblock.com

Lawrence Block's

This omnibus edition first published in Great Britain in 2011
by Orion Books,
an imprint of The Orion Publishing Group Ltd
Orion House, 5 Upper Saint Martin's Lane
London WC2H 9EA

An Hachette UK Company

1 3 5 7 9 10 8 6 4 2

A CIP catalogue record for this book is
available from the British Library.

ISBN 978 1 4091 3089 5

Typeset at The Spartan Press Ltd,
Lymington, Hants

Printed in Great Britain by
CPI Mackays, Chatham ME5 8TD

The Orion Publishing Group's policy is to use papers that are natural,
renewable and recyclable products and made from wood grown in sustainable
forests. The logging and manufacturing processes are expected to
conform to the environmental regulations of the country of origin.

www.orionbooks.co.uk

Contents

Burglars Can't Be Choosers

For Steve and Nancy Schwerner

1

A handful of minutes after nine I hoisted my Bloomingdale's shopping bag and moved out of a doorway and into step with a tall blond fellow with a faintly equine cast to his face. He was carrying an attaché case that looked too thin to be of much use. Like a high-fashion model, you might say. His topcoat was one of those new plaid ones and his hair, a little longer than my own, had been cut a strand at a time.

'We meet again,' I said, which was an out-and-out lie. 'Turned out to be a pretty fair day after all.'

He smiled, perfectly willing to believe that we were neighbors who exchanged a friendly word now and then. 'Little brisk this evening,' he said.

I agreed that it was brisk. There wasn't much he might have said that I wouldn't have gladly agreed with. He looked respectable and he was walking east on Sixty-seventh Street and that was all I required of him. I didn't want to befriend him or play handball with him or learn the name of his barber or coax him into swapping shortbread recipes. I just wanted him to help me get past a doorman.

The doorman in question was planted in front of a seven-story brick building halfway down the block, and he'd been very nearly as stationary as the building itself during the past half-hour. I'd given him that much time to desert his post and he hadn't taken advantage of it, so now I was going to have to walk right past him. That's easier than it sounds, and it's certainly easier than the various alternatives I'd considered earlier – circling the block and going through another building to get into the airshaft behind the building I wanted, doing a human fly act onto the fire escape, torching my way through steel grilles on basement or first-floor windows. All of those things are possible, I suppose, but so what? The proper method is Euclidean in its simplicity: the shortest route into a building is through its front door.

I'd hoped that my tall blond companion might be a resident of the building himself. We could have continued our conversation, such as it was, right through the lobby and onto the elevator. But this was not to be. When it was clear that he was not going to turn from his eastward course I said, 'Well, here's where I get off. Hope that business in Connecticut works out for you.'

This ought to have puzzled him, as we hadn't talked about any business in Connecticut or elsewhere, but perhaps he assumed I'd mistaken him for someone else. It hardly mattered. He kept on walking toward Mecca while I turned to my right (toward Brazil), gave the doorman a quick unfocused nod and smile, warbled a pleasant 'Good evening' at a gray-haired woman with more than the traditional number of chins, chuckled unconvincingly when her Yorkie made snapping sounds at my heels, and strode purposefully onto the self-service elevator.

I rode to the fourth floor, poked around until I found the stairway, and walked down a flight. I almost always do this and I sometimes wonder why. I think someone must have done it in a movie once and I was evidently impressed, but it's really a waste of time, especially when the elevator in question is self-service. The one thing it does is fix in your mind where the stairs are, should you later need them in a hurry, but you ought to be able to locate stairs without scampering up or down them.

On the third floor, I found my way to Apartment 311 at the front of the building. I stood for a moment, letting my ears do the walking, and then I gave the bell a thorough ring and waited thirty thoughtful seconds before ringing it again.

And that, let me assure you, is not a waste of time. Public institutions throughout the fifty states provide food and clothing and shelter for lads who don't ring the bell first. And it's not enough just poking the silly thing. A couple of years back I rang the bell diligently enough at the Park Avenue co-op of a charming couple named Sandoval, poked the little button until my finger throbbed, and wound up going directly to jail without passing Go. The bell was out of order, the Sandovals were home scoffing toasted English muffins in the breakfast nook, and Bernard G. Rhodenbarr soon found himself in a little room with bars on the windows.

This bell was in order. When my second ring brought no more response than my first, I reached a hand beneath my topcoat – last year's model, not plaid but olive – and drew a pigskin case from my trouser pocket. There were several keys in the case and several other useful things as well, these last made of the finest German steel. I opened my case, knocked on the door for luck, and set to work.

A funny thing. The better your building, the higher your monthly rental, the more efficient your doorman, why, the easier it's going to be to crack your apartment. People who live in unattended walk-ups in Hell's Kitchen will fasten half a dozen deadbolt locks to their doors and add a Segal police lock for insurance. Tenement dwellers take it for granted that junkies will come to kick their doors in and strong-arm types will rip the cylinders out of their locks, so they make things as secure as they possibly can. But if the building itself is so set up as to

6

intimidate your garden variety snatch-and-grab artist, then most tenants make do with the lock the landlord provides.

In this case the landlord provided a Rabson. Now there's nothing tacky about a Rabson lock. The Rabson is very good. But then so am I.

I suppose it took me a minute to open the lock. A minute may be long or short, significant or inconsequential. It is long indeed when you are spending it inserting burglar's tools into a lock of an apartment manifestly not your own, and when you know that during any of its sixty seconds another door down the hallway might open and some Nosey Parker might want to know just who you think you are and just what you think you are doing.

No one opened a door, no one got off the elevator. I did creative things with my finely-tempered steel implements, and the tumblers tumbled and the lock mechanism turned and the deadbolt drew itself deliberately back and disengaged. When that happened I let out the breath I'd been holding and drew a fresh one. Then I wiggled my picks a little more and opened the spring lock, which was child's play after the deadbolt, and when it snicked back I felt that little surge of excitement that's always there when I open a lock. It's a little like a roller coaster ride and a little like sexual triumph, and you may make of all that what you will.

I turned the knob, eased the heavy door inward half an inch or so. My blood was really up now. You never know for certain what's going to be on the other side of the door. That's one of the things that makes it exciting, but it also makes it scary, and it's still scary no matter how many times you've done it.

Once the lock's open, though, you can't do it an inch at a time like an old lady slipping into a swimming pool. So I pushed the door open and went inside.

The room was dark. I closed the door behind me, turned the bolt, dug a penlight flash out of my pocket and played the beam around. The drapes were drawn. That explained the room's utter darkness, and it meant I might as well turn the lights on because no one could see in from the building across the street. Apartment 311 fronted on Sixty-seventh Street but with the drapes drawn it might as well have been fronting on a blank wall.

The wall switch near the door turned on a pair of table lamps with leaded glass Tiffany-type shades. They looked like reproductions to me but they were nice ones. I moved around the room, taking time to get the feel of it. I've always done this.

Nice room. Large, about fifteen by twenty-five feet. A highly po-lished dark oak floor with two oriental rugs on it. The larger one was Chinese and the smaller one at the far end of the room might have been a Bokhara, but I couldn't tell you for sure. I suppose I ought to know more about rugs but I've never taken the time to learn because they're too much trouble to steal.

Naturally I went over to the desk first. It was a nineteenth-century rolltop, oaken and massive, and I'd probably have been drawn to it simply because I like desks like that, but in this case my whole reason for being in this apartment was tucked away in one of its drawers or cubbyholes. That's what the shifty-eyed and pear-shaped man had told me, and who was I to doubt his word?

'There's this big old desk,' he had said, aiming his chocolate eyes over my left shoulder. 'What you call a rolltop. The top rolls up.'

'Clever name for it,' I'd said.

He had ignored this. 'You'll see it the minute you walk in the room. Big old mother. He keeps the box in the desk.' He moved his little hands about, to indicate the dimensions of the box we were discussing. 'About like so. About the size of a box of cigars. Maybe a little bigger, maybe a little smaller. Basically I'd call it cigar-box size. Box is blue.'

'Blue.'

'Blue leather. Covered in leather. I suppose it's wood under the leather. Rather than being leather straight through. What's under the leather don't matter. What matters is what's inside the box.'

'What's inside the box?'

'That don't matter.' I stared at him, ready to ask him which of us was to be Abbott and which Costello. He frowned, 'What's in the box for you,' he said, 'is five thousand dollars. Five kay for a few minutes' work. As to what's actually inside the box we're talking about, see, the box is locked.'

'I see.'

His eyes moved from the air above my left shoulder to the air above my right shoulder, pausing en route to flick contemptuously at my own eyes. 'Locks,' he said, 'prolly don't mean too much to you.'

'Locks mean a great deal to me.'

'This lock, the lock on the box, you prolly shouldn't open it.'

'I see.'

'Be a very bad idea for you to open it. You bring me the box, you get the rest of your money, and everybody's happy.'

'Oh,' I said. 'I see what you're doing.'

'Huh?'

'You're *threatening* me,' I said. 'How curious.'

The eyes widened but only for a moment. 'Threats? Not for the world, kid. Advice and threats, there's a world of difference. I wouldn't dream of threatening you.'

'Well, I wouldn't dream of opening your blue leather box.'

'Leather-covered.'

'Right.'

'Not that it makes a difference.'

8

'Hardly. What color blue?'

'Huh?'

'Dark blue, light blue, robin's egg blue, Prussian blue, cobalt blue, powder blue. What color?'

'What's the difference?'

'I wouldn't want to bring the wrong blue box.'

'Don't worry about it, kid.'

'If you say so.'

'Just so it's a blue leather box. Unopened.'

'Gotcha.'

Since that conversation I'd been whiling away the hours trying to decide whether I'd open the box or not. I knew myself well enough to recognize that any lock constitutes an immediate temptation for me, and when I've been cautioned against opening a particular lock that only increases the attraction of it.

On the other hand, I'm not a kid anymore. When you've been inside a couple of times your judgment is supposed to improve, and if it seemed likely that there was more danger than profit in opening the elusive blue box . . .

But before I came to terms with the question I had to find the box, and before I did that I had to open the desk, and I wasn't even ready to tackle that project yet. First I wanted to get the feel of the room.

Some burglars, like some lovers, just want to get in and get out. Others try to psych out the people they're thieving from, building up a whole mental profile of them out of what their houses reveal. I do something a little different. I have this habit of creating a life for myself to suit the surroundings I find myself in.

So I now took this apartment and transformed it from the residence of one J. Francis Flaxford to the sanctum sanctorum of yours truly, Bernard Grimes Rhodenbarr. I settled myself in an oversized wing chair upholstered in dark green leather, swung my feet up on the matching ottoman, and took a leisurely look at my new life.

Pictures on the walls, old oils in elaborate gilded frames. A little landscape that clearly owed a lot to Turner, although a lesser hand had just as clearly held the brush. A pair of old portraits in matching oval frames, a man and a woman eyeing each other thoughtfully over a small fireplace in which not a trace of ash reposed. Were they Flaxford's ancestors? Probably not, but did he attempt to pass them off as such?

No matter. I'd call them my ancestors, and make up outrageous stories about them. And there'd be a fire in the fireplace, casting a warm glow over the room. And I'd sit in this chair with a book and a glass, and perhaps a dog at my feet. A large dog, a large *old* dog, one not given to yaps or abrupt movements. Perhaps a stuffed dog might be best all around . . .

Books. There was a floor lamp beside my chair, its bulb at reading

9

height. The wall behind the chair was lined with bookshelves and another small case of books, one of those revolving stands, stood on the floor alongside the chair. On the other side of the chair was a lower table holding a silver cigarette dish and a massive cut-glass ashtray.

All right. I'd do a lot of reading here, and quality stuff, not modern junk. Perhaps those leather-bound sets were just there for show, their pages still uncut. Well, it would be a different story if I were living here. And I'd keep a decanter of good brandy on the table beside me. No, two decanters, a pair of those wide-bottomed ship's decanters, one filled with brandy, one with a vintage port. There'd be room for them when I got rid of the cigarette dish. The ashtray could stay. I liked the size and style of it, and I might want to take up smoking a pipe. Pipes had always burned my tongue in the past, but perhaps as I worked my way through the wisdom of the ages, feet up on the hassock, book in hand, port and brandy within easy reach, a fire glowing on the hearth . . .

I spent a few minutes on the fantasy, figuring out a little more about the life I'd lead in Mr Flaxford's apartment. I suppose it's silly and childish to do this and I know it wastes time. But I think it serves a purpose. It gets rid of some tension. I get wired very tight when I'm in someone else's place. The fantasy makes the place my own home in a certain way, at least for the short time I'm inside it, and that seems to help. I'm not convinced that's why I started doing it in the first place, or why I've continued.

The time I wasted couldn't have amounted to very much, anyway, because I looked at my watch just before I put my gloves on to go to work and it was only seventeen minutes after nine. I use sheer skin-tight rubber gloves, the kind doctors wear, and I cut out circles on the palms and backs so my hands won't perspire as much. As with other skintight rubber things, you don't really lose all that much in the way of sensitivity and you make up for it in peace of mind.

The desk had two locks. One opened the rolltop and the other, in the top right-hand drawer, unlocked that drawer and all the others at once. I probably could have found the keys – most people stow desk keys very close to the desk itself – but it was faster and easier to open both locks with my own tools. I've never yet run into a desk lock that didn't turn out to be candy.

These two were no exception. I rolled up the rolltop and studied the usual infinite array of pigeonholes, tiny drawer upon tiny drawer, cubicle after cubicle. For some reason our ancestors found this an efficient system for the organization of one's business affairs. It's always seemed to me that it would have to be more trouble keeping track of what bit of trivia you stowed in what arcane hiding place than it would be to keep everything in a single steamer trunk and just rummage through it when there was something you needed. But I suppose there are plenty of people who get enormously turned on by the notion of a place for everything and everything in its place. They're the people who line up their shoes in the closet according to height. And they remember to rotate their tires every three months, and they set aside one day a week for clipping their fingernails.

And what do they do with the clippings? Stow 'em in a pigeonhole, I suppose.

The blue leather box wasn't under the rolltop, and my pear-shaped client had so positioned his little hands as to indicate a box far too large for any of the pigeonholes and little drawers, so I opened the other lock and released the catches on all the lower drawers. I started with the top right drawer because that's where most people tend to put their most important possessions – I've no idea why – and I worked my way from drawer to drawer looking for a blue box and not finding one.

I went through the drawers quickly, but not too quickly. I wanted to get out of the apartment as soon as possible because that's always a good idea, but I had not committed myself to pass up any other goodies the apartment might contain. A great many people keep cash around the house, and others keep traveler's checks, and still others keep coin collections and readily salable jewelry and any number of interesting things which fit neatly enough into a Bloomingdale's shopping bag. I wanted the four thousand dollars due me upon delivery of the blue box – the thousand I'd received in advance bulged reassuringly in my hip pocket – but I also wanted whatever else might come my way. I was standing in the apartment of a man who did not evidently have to worry about the source of his next meal, and if I got lucky I might very well turn a five-thousand-dollar sure thing into a score big enough to buy my groceries for the next year or so.

Because I no longer like to work any more than I have to. It's a thrill, no question about it, but the more you work the worse the odds get. Crack enough doors and sooner or later you are going to fall down. Every once in a while you'll get arrested and a certain number of arrests will stick. Four, five, six jobs a year – that ought to be plenty. I didn't think so a few years ago when I still had things to prove to myself. Well, you live and you learn, and generally in that order.

I gave those drawers a fast shuffle, down one side and up the other, and I found papers and photograph albums and account ledgers and rings full of keys that probably didn't fit anything and a booklet half-full of three-cent stamps (remember them?) and one of a pair of fur-lined kid gloves and one of a pair of unlined pigskin gloves and one earmuff of the sort that your mother made you wear and a perpetual calendar issued in 1949 by the Marine Trust Company of Buffalo, New York, and a Bible, King James version, no larger than a pack of playing cards; and a pack of playing cards, Tally-Ho version, no larger than the Bible, and a lot of envelopes which probably still had letters in them, but who cared, and stacks of canceled checks bearing various dates over

11

the past two decades, held together by desiccated rubber bands, and enough loose paper clips to make a chain that would serve as a jump rope for a child, or perhaps even for an adult, and a postcard from Watkins Glen, and some fountain pens and some ball pens and some felt pens and no end of pencils, all with broken tips, and . . .

And no coin collections, no cash, no traveler's checks, no bearer bonds, no stock certificates, no rings, no watches, no cut or uncut precious stones (although there was a rather nice chunk of petrified wood with felt glued to the bottom so it could be used as a paperweight), no gold bars, no silver ingots, no stamps more precious than the three-cent jobs in the booklet, and, by all the saints in heaven, no blue box, leather or otherwise.

Hell.

This didn't make me happy, but neither did it make me throw up. What it made me do was straighten up and sigh a little, and it made me wonder idly where old Flaxford kept the Scotch until I reminded myself that I never drink on a job, and it made me think about the cigarettes in the silver dish until I recalled that I'd given up the nasty things years ago. So I sighed again and got ready to give the drawers another look-see, because it's very easy to miss something when you're dealing with a desk that is such a reservoir of clutter, even something as substantial as a cigar box, and I looked at my watch and noted that it was twenty-three minutes of ten, and decided that I would really prefer to be on my way by ten, or ten-thirty at the very latest. Once more through the desk, then, to be followed if necessary by a circuit of other logical hiding places in the living room, and then if need be a tour of the apartment's other rooms, however many there might be of them, and then adieu, adieu. And so I blew on my hands to cool them as they were beginning to sweat a bit, not that blowing on them did much good, encased in rubber gloves as they were, and this may well have led me to sigh a third time, and then I heard a key in the lock and froze.

The apartment's tenant, J. Francis Flaxford, was supposed to be off the premises until midnight at the very least.

By the same token, the blue box was supposed to be in the desk.

I stood facing the door, my hip braced against the desk. I listened as the key turned in the lock, easing back the deadbolt, then turning further to draw back the spring lock. There was an instant of dead silence. Then the door flew inward and two boys in blue burst through it, guns in their hands, the muzzles trained on me.

'Easy,' I said. 'Relax. It's only me.'

2

The first cop through the door was a stranger, and a very young and fresh-faced one at that. But I recognized his partner, a grizzled, gray chap with jowls and a paunch and a long sharp nose. His name was Ray Kirschmann and he'd been with the NYPD since the days when they carried muskets. He'd collared me a few years earlier and had proved to be a reasonable man at the time.

'Son of a gun,' he said, lowering his own gun and putting a calming hand upon the gun of his young associate. 'If it ain't Mrs Rhodenbarr's son, Bernard. Put the heat away, Loren. Bernie here is a perfect gentleman.'

Loren holstered his gun and let out a few cubic feet of air. Burglars are not the only poor souls who tend to tense up when entering doors other than their own. And trust Ray to make sure his young partner cleared the threshold ahead of him.

I said, 'Hi, Ray.'

'Nice to see ya, Bernie. Say hello to my new partner, Loren Kramer. Loren, this here is Bernie Rhodenbarr.'

We exchanged hellos and I extended a hand for a shake. This confused Loren, who looked at my hand and then began fumbling with the pair of handcuffs hanging from his gunbelt.

Ray laughed. 'For Chrissake,' he said. 'Nobody ever puts cuffs on Bernie. This ain't one of your mad dog punks, Loren. This is a professional burglar you got here.'

'Oh.'

'Close the door, Loren.'

Loren closed the door – he didn't bother to turn the bolt – and I did a little more relaxing myself. We had thus far attracted no attention. No neighbors milled in the hallways. And so I had every intention of spending what remained of the night beneath my own good roof.

Politely I said, 'I wasn't expecting you, Ray. Do you come here often?'

'You son of a gun, you.' He grinned. 'Gettin' sloppy in your old age, you know that? We're in the car and we catch a squeal, woman hears

13

suspicious noises. And you was always quiet as a mouse. How old are you, Bernie?'

'Be thirty-five in April. Why?'

'Taurus?' This from Loren.

'The end of May. Gemini.'

'My wife's a Taurus,' Loren said. He had liberated his nightstick from its clip and was slapping it rhythmically against his palm.

'Why?' I asked again, and there was a moment of confusion with Loren trying to explain that his wife was a Taurus because of when she was born, and me explaining that what I wanted to know was why Ray had asked me my age, and Ray looking sorry he'd brought the whole thing up in the first place. There was something about Loren that seemed to generate confusion.

'Just age making you sloppy,' Ray explained. 'Making noises, drawing attention. It's not like you.'

'I never made a sound.'

'Until tonight.'

'I'm talking about tonight. Anyway, I just got here.'

'When?'

'I don't know, a few minutes ago. Maybe fifteen or twenty minutes at the outside. Ray? You sure you got the right apartment?'

'We got the one's got a burglar in it, don't we?'

'There's that,' I admitted. 'But did they specify this apartment? Three-eleven?'

'Not the number, but they said the right front apartment on the third floor. That's this one.'

'A lot of people mix up left and right.'

He looked at me, and Loren slapped the nightstick against his palm and managed to drop it. There was a leather thong attaching it to his belt but the thong was long enough so that the nightstick hit the floor. It bounced on the Chinese rug and Loren retrieved it while Ray glowered at him.

'That's more noise than I made all night,' I said.

'Look, Bernie—'

'Maybe they meant the apartment above this one. Maybe the woman was English. They figure floors differently over there. They call the first floor the ground floor, see, so what they call the third floor would be the floor three flights up, which you and I would call the *fourth* floor, and—'

'Jesus.'

I looked at Loren, then back at Ray again.

'What are you, crazy? You want me to read you your rights and all so you'll remember you're a criminal caught in the act? What the hell's got into you, Bernie?'

'It's just that I just got here. And I never made a sound.'

14

'So maybe a cat knocked a plant off a shelf in the apartment next door and we just got lucky and came here by mistake. It's still you and us, right?'

'Right.' I smiled what certainly ought to have been a rueful smile. 'You got lucky, all right. I'm nice and fat tonight.'

'That so?'

'Very fat.'

'Interesting,' Ray said.

'You got the key from the doorman?'

'Uh-huh. He wanted to come up and let us in but we told him he ought to stay at his post.'

'So nobody actually knows I'm here but you two.'

The two of them looked at each other. They were a nice contrast, Ray in his lived-in uniform, Loren all young and neat and freshly laundered. 'That's true,' Ray said. 'Far as it goes.'

'Oh?'

'This'd be a very good collar for us. Me'n Loren, we could use a good collar. Might get a commendation out of it.'

'Oh, come on,' I said.

'Always possible.'

'The hell it is. You didn't nail me on your own initiative. You followed up a radio squawk. Nobody's going to pin a medal on you.'

'Well, you got a point there,' Ray said. 'What do you think, Loren?'

'Well,' Loren said, slapping the stick against his palm and nibbling thoughtfully on his lower lip. The stick was beat up and scratched in contrast to the rest of his outfit. I had the feeling he dropped it often, and on surfaces more abrasive than Chinese carpets.

'How fat are you, Bernie?'

I didn't see any point in haggling. I generally carry an even thousand dollars in walkaway money, and that was what I had now. Coincidentally enough, the ten hundreds in my left hip pocket were the very ones I'd taken as an advance on the night's work, so if I gave it all to my coppish friends I'd break even, with nothing lost but my cab fare and a couple of hours of my time. My shifty-eyed friend would be out a thousand dollars but that was his hard luck and he would just have to write it off.

'A thousand dollars,' I said.

I watched Ray Kirschmann's face. He considered trying for more but must have decided I'd gone straight to the top. And there was no dodging the fact that it was a satisfactory score since it only had to be cut two ways.

'That's fat,' he admitted. 'On your person right now?'

I took out the money and handed it to him. He fanned the bills and gave them a count with his eyes, trying not to be too obvious about it.

'You pick up anything in here, Bernie? Because if we was to report

15

there was nobody here and then the tenant calls in a burglary complaint, we don't look too good.'

I shrugged. 'You could always claim I left before you got here,' I told him, 'but you won't have to. I couldn't find anything worth stealing, Ray. I just got here and all I touched is the desk.'

'We could frisk him,' Loren suggested. Ray and I both gave him a look and he turned a deeper pink than his usual shade. 'It was just a thought,' he said.

I asked him what sign he was.

'Virgo,' he said.

'Should go well with Taurus.'

'Both earth signs,' he said. 'Lots of stability.'

'I would think so.'

'You interested in astrology?'

'Not particularly.'

'I think there's a lot to be said for it. Ray's a Sagittarius.'

'Jesus Christ,' Ray said. He looked at the bills again, gave a small shrug, then folded them once and found them a home in his pocket. Loren watched this procedure somewhat wistfully. He knew he'd get his share later, but still . . .

Ray gnawed a fingernail. 'How'd you get in, Bernie? Fire escape?'

'Front door.'

'Right past the clown downstairs? They're terrific, these doormen.'

'Well, it's a large building.'

'Not that large. Still, you do look the part. That clean-cut East Side look and those clothes.' I live on the West Side myself, and usually wear jeans. 'And I suppose you carried a briefcase, right?'

'Not exactly.' I pointed to my Bloomie's bag. 'That.'

'Even better. Well, I guess you can pick it up and walk right out again. Wait a minute.' He frowned. '*We'll* leave first. I like it better that way. Otherwise, why are we taking so much time here, et cetera, and et cetera. But don't get light-fingered after we split, huh?'

'There's nothing here to take,' I said.

'I want your word on it, Bernie.'

I avoided laughing. 'You've got it,' I said solemnly.

'Give us three minutes and then go straight out. But don't hang around no more'n that, Bernie.'

'I won't.'

'Well,' he said. He turned and reached for the door, and then Loren Kramer said he had to go to the bathroom. 'Jesus Christ,' Ray said.

Loren said, 'Bernie? Where is it, do you know?'

'Search me,' I said. 'Not literally.'

'Huh?'

'I never got past this desk,' I said. 'I suppose the john must be back there somewhere.'

16

Loren went looking for it while Ray stood there shaking his head. I asked him how long Loren had been his partner. 'Too long,' he said.

'I know what you mean.'

'He ain't a bad kid, Bernie.'

'Seems nice enough.'

'But he's so damn stupid. And the astrology drives me straight up the wall. You figure there's anything in that crap?'

'Probably.'

'But even so, who gives a shit, right? Who cares if his wife's a Taurus? She's a good-looking bitch, I'll give her that much. But Loren, shit, he was ready to search you. Just now when you said "Search me." The putz woulda done it.'

'I had that feeling.'

'The one good thing, he's reasonable. They gave me this straight arrow a while back and you couldn't do nothing with him. I mean he even paid for his coffee. At least Loren, when somebody puts money in his hand he knows to close his fist around it.'

'Thank God for that.'

'That's what I say. If anything, he likes the bread too much, but I guess his wife is good at spending it fast as he brings it home. You figure it's on account of she's a Taurus?'

'You'd have to ask Loren.'

'He might tell me. But you can put up with a lot of stupidity in exchange for a little reasonableness, I have to say that for him. Just so he don't kill hisself with that nightstick of his, bouncing it off his knee or something. Bernie? Take the gloves off.'

'Huh?'

'The rubber gloves. You don't want to wear those on the street.'

'Oh,' I said, and stripped them off. Somewhere in the inner recesses of the apartment Loren coughed and bumped into something. I stuffed my gloves into my pocket. 'All the tools of the trade,' Ray said. 'Jesus, I'd always rather deal with pros, guys like you. Like even if we had to bag you tonight. Say I had the doorman backing my play and there was no way to cool it off. No money in it that way but at least I'm dealing with a professional.'

Somewhere a toilet flushed. I resisted an impulse to look at my watch.

'You feel comfortable about it,' he went on. 'Know what I mean? Like tonight, coming through that door. I didn't know what we was gonna find on the other side of it.'

'I know the feeling,' I assured him, and started to reach for my shopping bag. I caught a glimpse of Ray's face that made me turn to see what he was staring at, and what he was staring at was Loren at the far end of the room with a mouth as wide as the Holland Tunnel and a face as white as a surgical mask.

'In . . .' he said. 'In . . . In . . . In the bedroom!' And then, all in a rush: 'Coming back from the toilet and I turned the wrong way and there's the bedroom and this guy, he's dead, this dead guy, head beaten in and there's blood all over the place, warm blood, the guy's still warm, you never saw anything like it, Jesus, I knew it, you can never trust a Gemini, I knew it, they lie all the time, oh God—'

And he flopped on the rug. The one that may very well have been a Bokhara.

And Ray and I looked at each other.

Talk about professionalism. We both went promptly insane. He just stood there with his face looming, not going for his gun, not reaching for me, not even moving, just standing flatfooted like the flatfoot he indisputably was. And I, on the other hand, began behaving wholly out of character, in a manner neither of us ever expected I might be capable of.

I sprang at him. He went on gaping at me, too astonished even to react, and I barreled into him and sent him sprawling and bolted without waiting to see where he landed. I shot out the door and found the stairs right where I'd left them, and I raced down two flights and dashed through the lobby at the very pace the word *breakneck* was coined to describe.

The doorman, obliging as ever, held the door for me. 'I'll take care of you at Christmas!' I sang out. And scurried off without even waiting for a reply.

3

It's a good thing the sidewalks were fairly clear. Otherwise I probably would have run straight into somebody. As it was, I managed to reach the corner with a simple stretch of broken-field running, and by the time I took a left at Second Avenue, logic and shortness of breath combined to take the edge off my panic. No one seemed to be pelting down the street behind me. I slowed to a rapid walk. Even in New York people tend to stare at you if you run. It may not occur to them to do anything about it, but it gets on my nerves when people stare at me.

After a block and a half of rapid walking I stuck out a hand and attracted the attention of a southbound cab. I gave him my address and he turned a couple of corners to transform himself into a northbound cab, but by that time I'd changed my mind. My apartment was nestled high atop a relatively new high-rise at West End and Seventy-first, and on a clear day (which comes up now and then) you can see, if not forever, at least the World Trade Center and selected parts of New Jersey. And it's a perfect refuge from the cares of the city, not to mention the slings and arrows of outrageous fortune, which is why I automatically spoke the address to the driver.

But it was also the first place Ray Kirschmann and his fellows would come looking for me. All they had to do was check the phone book, for God's sake.

I pressed myself back into my seat and patted my left breast pocket in a reflexive hunt for the pack of cigarettes that hadn't been there in several years. If I lived in that apartment on East Sixty-seventh, I thought, I could sit in the green leather chair and knock dottle from my pipe into the cut-glass ashtray. But as things stood . . .

Relax, Bernard. Think!

There were several things to think about. Like, just who had invested a thousand dollars in setting me up for a murder charge, and just why the oddly familiar pear-shaped man had chosen me for the role of imbecile. But I didn't really have time for that sort of long-range thinking. I'd gotten a break – one cop collapsing in a providential faint, the other reacting slowly even as I was reacting with uncharacteristic speed. That break had given me a head start, but the head start probably didn't amount to more than a handful of minutes. It could vanish before I knew it.

I had to go to ground. Had to find a bolt hole. I'd shaken the hounds from my trail for a moment or two and it was up to me to regain the safety of my burrow before they recaptured the scent. (It didn't thrill me that all the phrases that came to me were from the language of fox hunting, incidentally.)

I shrugged off the thought and tried to get specific. My own apartment was out; it would be full of cops within the hour. I needed a place to go, some safe and sound place with four walls and a ceiling and a floor, all of them reasonably close together. It had to be a place that no one would think to connect with me and one where I could not be readily discovered or observed. And it had to be in New York, because I'd be a lot easier to run down once I was off my home ground.

A friend's apartment.

The cab cruised northward while I reviewed my list of friends and acquaintances and established that there was not a single one of them whom I could drop in on. (In on whom I could drop? No matter.) My problem, you see, was that I had always tended to avoid bad company. Outside of prison – and I prefer to be outside of prison as often as possible – I never associate with other burglars, hold-up men, con artists, swindlers or miscellaneous thieves and grifters. When one is within stone walls one's ability to pick and choose is circumscribed, certainly, but on the outside I limit myself to people who are, if not strictly honest, at least not the felonious sort. My boon companions may pilfer office supplies from their employers, fabricate income tax deductions out of the whole cloth, file parking tickets in the incinerator, and bend various commandments perilously close to the breaking point. But they are none of them jailbirds, at least as far as I know, and as far as they know neither am I.

It should consequently not surprise you to learn that I have no particularly close friends. With none of them knowing the full truth about me, no genuine intimacy has ever really developed. There are chaps I play chess with and chaps I play poker with. There are a couple of lads with whom I'll take in a fight or a ball game. There are women with whom I dine, women with whom I may see a play or hear a concert, and with some of these ladies fair I'll now and then share a pillow. But it's been quite a while since there was a male companion in my life whom I'd call a real friend, and almost as long since I'd been involved with a woman on more than a casual basis. That modern disease of detachment, I suppose, augmented by the solitary nature of the secretive burglar.

I'd never had occasion to regret all of this before, except on those once-in-a-while bad nights everybody has when your own company is the worst company in the world and there's nobody you know well enough to call at three in the morning. Now, though, what it all meant was there was no one on earth I could ask to hide me. And if there was it wouldn't help, because if I had a close friend or a lover that's the first place the cops would look, and they'd be on the doorstep an hour or two after I was through the door.

Problems . . .

'You want me to turn around?'

My driver's voice shook me out of my reverie. He had pulled to a stop and had turned around to blink at me through the Plexiglas partition that kept him safe from homicidal fares. 'Senny-first 'n' Wes' End,' he announced. 'You want this side or the other?' I blinked back, turned up my coat collar, shrank down inside it like a startled turtle. 'Mac,' he said patiently, 'want I should turn around?'

'By all means,' I said.

'That means yes?'

'That means yes.'

He waited while traffic cleared, then arched the cab in the traditional illegal U-turn, braking smoothly to a stop in front of my very own building. Could I spare a minute to duck inside, grab some clothes and my case money, be out in no time at all . . .

No.

His hand reached to throw the flag shutting off the meter. 'Hold it,' I said. 'Now drive downtown.'

His hand hovered over the flag like a hummingbird over a flower. Then he withdrew it and turned again to look querulously at me. 'Drive downtown?'

'Right.'

'You don't like this place no more?'

'It's not as I remembered it.'

His eyes took on that wary New York look of a man who realizes he's dealing with a lunatic. 'I guess,' he said.

'Nothing's the same anymore,' I said recklessly. 'The neighborhood's gone to hell.'

'Jesus,' he said, cab in motion now, driver at ease. 'Lemme tell you, this here is nothin'. You oughta see where I live. That's up in the Bronx. I don't know if you're familiar with the Bronx. But you're talking about a neighborhood on the skids—'

And talk about a neighborhood on the skids is precisely what he did, and he did it all the way down the western edge of Manhattan. The best thing about the conversation was its utter predictability. I didn't have to listen to it. I just let my mind go wherever it wanted while my mouth filled in with the appropriate grunts and uh-huhs and izzatsos as the occasion demanded.

So I sent my mind on a tour of my friends, such as they were. The woodpushers I whipped routinely at chess, the card sharps who just as

21

routinely trimmed me at poker. The sports fans. The drinking companions. The disconcertingly short list of young ladies with whom I'd been lately keeping the most cursory sort of company.

Rodney Hart.

Rodney Hart!

His name popped into my mind like a fly ball into shallow right field. A tall fellow, spare of flesh, with high and prominent eyebrows and a longish nose, the nostrils of which tended to flare when he was holding anything much better than two pair. I'd first met him at a poker game perhaps a year and a half ago, and since then I'd seen him precisely two times away from the card table – once in a Village bar when we happened to run into each other and chatted our way through a couple of beers, and another time when he had the second lead in a short-lived off-Broadway show and I went backstage after the performance with a young lady I was trying to impress. (It didn't work.)

Good old Rodney Hart!

What, you may well ask, was so wonderful about Rodney? Well, in the first place, I happened to know that he lived alone. More important, he wasn't home now and wouldn't be back in town for a couple of months. Just the other week or so he'd turned up at the poker game and announced we wouldn't have him to kick around any more. He'd just signed for the road company of *Two If By Sea* and would be traveling the length and breadth of these United States, bringing Broadway's idea of culture to the provinces. And he'd even dropped the gratuitous information that he wasn't subletting his apartment. 'Not worth it,' he'd said. 'I've had the place for years and I pay a hot ninety a month in rent. The landlord doesn't even bother getting increases he's entitled to. He likes renting to actors, if you can believe it. The roar of the greasepaint and all that. He eats it up. Anyway, it's worth ninety a month not to have some sonofabitch sitting on my toilet and sleeping in my bed.'

Ha!

He didn't know it, but the sonofabitch who would be sitting on his potty seat and lolling between his percales was none other than Bernard Rhodenbarr. And I wouldn't even pay him ninety a month for the privilege.

But where the hell did he live?

I seemed to remember that he lived in the Village somewhere, and I decided that was as much as I had to know while I was in this particular cab. Because I had unquestionably made myself a memorable passenger, and the papers would shortly be full of my face, and the driver might, for the first time in his unhappy life, actually go so far as to put two and two together.

'Right here is fine,' I said.

'Here?'

22

We were somewhere on Seventh Avenue now, a couple of blocks from Sheridan Square. 'Just stop the cab,' I said.

'You're the boss,' the driver said, using a phrase which has always seemed to me to be the politest possible way of expressing absolute contempt. I dug out my wallet, paid the man, gave him a tip designed to justify his contempt, and while so doing began to regret bitterly the thousand dollars I'd paid to Ray and Loren. Hardly the best investment I had ever made. If I had that thousand now it might give me a certain degree of mobility. But all I had, after squaring things with the cabbie, was seventy dollars and change. And it seemed somehow unlikely that Rod would be the sort to leave substantial quantities of cash around his empty apartment.

And where was that apartment, anyway?

I found that answer in a phone booth, thinking as I turned the directory how providential it was that Rod was an actor. It seems as though everyone else I know has an unlisted number, but actors are another breed; they do everything but write their numbers on lavatory walls. (And some of them do that.) Good old Rod was listed, of course, and while Hart is a reasonably common name Rodney is reasonably uncommon, and there he was, praise be to God, with an apartment on Bethune Street deep in the bowels of the West Village. A quiet street, an out-of-the-way street, a street the tourists never trod. What could be better?

The book gave not only his address but his phone number as well, as telephone books are wont to do, and I invested a dime and dialed the number. (One does this sort of thing before breaking and entering.) It rang seven times, which I thought was probably enough, but I'm compulsive; I always let phones in potentially burglarable apartments go through a tedious twelve rings. But this one rang only seven before someone picked it up, at which point I came perilously close to vomiting.

'Seven-four-one-nine,' a soft female voice said, and my risen gorge sank and I calmed down. Because just as actors have listed phones so do they have services to answer them, and that was what this voice represented; the number which had been spoken to me was nothing other than the last four digits of Rodney's phone number. I cleared my throat and asked when Rodney would be back in town, and the lady with the dulcet tones obligingly informed me that he would be on tour for another fifteen weeks, that he was in St Louis at the moment, and that she could supply me with the number of his hotel there if I wished. I didn't wish. I suppressed an infantile urge to leave a comic message and returned the phone to its cradle.

It took a little doing but I managed to find Bethune Street and walked west on it until I located Rod's building. It was half a block west of Washington Street in a neighborhood that was half brownstones and the other half warehouses. The building I wanted was a poor but honest five-story brownstone indistinguishable from its neighbors on either side but for the rusty numerals alongside the front door. I stayed on the street a moment to make sure there was no one taking obvious notice of me, then slipped into the front vestibule. I scanned the row of buttons on the wall, looking for names of illustrious actors and actresses, but Helen Hayes wasn't listed and neither were the Lunts. Rod was, however; one R. Hart was inked in as occupying Apartment 5-R. Since there were five floors and two apartments to a floor, that meant he was on the top floor at the rear of the building, and what could be less obtrusive than that?

Because old habits die hard, I gave his bell a good ringing and waited for anyone who might be in his apartment to buzz me back. Happily no one did. I then thought of ringing other bells at random. This is what I would do on a job. People buzz you on through the locked front door without a qualm, and if they happen to pop out into the hallway to see who you are you just smile apologetically and say that you forgot your key. Works like a charm. But Rod lived on the top floor, which meant I'd have to walk past all the other floors, and anyone who noticed me might notice again when the papers saw fit to print my picture, and I might be holed up here for a while, if not forever, and . . .

Didn't seem worth the risk, small though the risk might be. Especially since it took me less than fifteen seconds to let myself through that front door. A strong wind could have opened that lock.

I scampered up four flights to the top floor and took deep breaths until my heartbeat returned to normal. Rod's door had 5-R on it and I went and stood in front of it and listened. The door at the other end of the hallway, 5-F, had no light shining underneath it. I knocked on Rod's door, and waited, and knocked again, and then I took out my burglars tools.

Rod had three locks on his door. Sometime in the past an amateur had dug at the frame around one of them with a chisel or screwdriver, but it didn't look as though he'd accomplished anything. Rod's locks included a fancy Medeco cylinder, a Segal police lock with a steel bar wedged against the door from within, and a cheap piece of junk that was just there for nuisance value. I knocked off the third lock first to get it out of the way, then tackled the Segal. It's good insurance against a junkie kicking the door in and it's not easy to pick but I had the tools and the touch and it didn't keep me waiting long. The tumblers fell into place and the steel bar slid aside in its channel and that left the Medeco.

The Medeco's the one they advertise as pickproof and of course that's errant nonsense, there is no such thing, but it's a pardonable exaggeration. What it meant was that I had to do two jobs at once. Suppose you're a cryptographer and you're given a message which was encoded from an original in Serbo-Croat, a language you don't happen to speak. Now you have to crack the cypher and learn the language at the same time. That's not exactly what I had to do with the Medeco but it's as close an explanation as I can give you.

It was tricky and I made some mistakes. At one point I heard a door open and I almost had a seizure but the door was on the floor below and I relaxed again. Sort of. Then I tried again and screwed up again, and then I just plain hit it right and the message turned out to be 'Open sesame.' I popped inside and locked all three locks, just like the old maid in all the stories.

The first thing I did was walk through the whole apartment and make sure there weren't any bodies in it but my own. This wasn't that much of a chore. There was one large room with a bookcase set up as a sort of room divider screening off a sleeping alcove. The kitchen was small and uninviting. The bathroom was smaller and less inviting, and roaches scampered when I turned the light on. I turned it off again and went back to the living room.

A homey place, I decided. Well-worn furniture, probably purchased secondhand, but it was all comfortable enough. A scattering of plants, palms and philodendrons and others whose names I did not know. Posters on the walls, not pop posters of Bogart and Che but the sort printed to herald gallery openings, Miró and Chagall and a few others as unknown to me as some of the plants. I decided, all in all, that Rod had fairly good taste for an actor.

The rug was a ratty maroon carpet remnant about twelve feet square, its binding coming loose on one side and entirely absent on another, its threads quite bare in spots and patches, its overall appearance decidedly unwholesome. Next time, I thought, I'll bring along the bloody Bokhara.

And then I started to shake.

The Bokhara wasn't bloody, of course. Loren had merely fainted upon it. But the rug, in the bedroom I had not seen, presumably was. Bloody, that is.

Who had killed the man in the bedroom? For that matter, who was the man in the bedroom? J. Francis Flaxford himself? According to my information he was supposed to be away from home from eight-thirty at the latest to midnight at the earliest. But if the whole point of that information had been to put me on the spot where I could get tagged for homicide, well, I couldn't really put too much stock in it.

A man. Dead. In the bedroom. And someone had beaten his head in, and he was still warm to the touch.

Terrific.

If I'd only had the sense to give the whole apartment a looksee the minute I went into it, then it would have been an entirely different

25

story. One quick reconnaissance mission and I'd have seen the late lamented and been on my way. By the time the illustrious team of Kirschmann and Kramer made their entrance I'd have been back in my own little tower of steel and glass, sipping Scotch and smiling southward at the World Trade Center. Instead I was a fugitive from what passes for justice these days, the very obvious murderer of a murderee I'd never even met in the first place. And, because my presence of mind had been conspicuous by its absence, I'd reacted to things by (a) using brute force and (b) scramming. So that if there'd ever been any chance of convincing people I'd never killed anything more biologically advanced than cockroaches and mosquitoes, that chance had vanished without a trace.

I paced. I opened cupboards looking for liquor and found none. I went back, tested another chair, decided the one I'd already sat in was more comfortable, then rejected both chairs and stretched out on the couch.

And thought about the curious little man who'd gotten me into this mess in the first place.

4

He was a thick-bodied man built rather like a bloated bowling pin. While he wasn't terribly stout, they'd been out of waists when he reached the front of the line that day. He must have had to guess where to put his belt each morning.

His face was round and jowly, with most of its features generally subdued. His eyes came closer to prominence than anything else. They were large and watchful and put me in mind of a pair of Hershey's Chocolate Kisses. (With the foil removed.) They were just that shade of brown. His hair was flat black and perfectly straight and he was balding in the middle, his hairline receding almost to the top of his skull. I suppose he was in his late forties. It's good I'm a burglar; I could never make a living guessing age and weight at a carnival.

I first met him on a Thursday night in a drinking establishment called The Watering Whole. (I'm sure whoever named it took great pride in his accomplishment.) The Whole, which in this instance is rather less than the sum of its parts, is a singles joint on Second Avenue in the Seventies, and unless you own a piece of it and want to inspect the register receipts there's really only one reason to go there. I had gone for that very reason, but that evening the selection of accessible young ladies was as dazzling as the dinner menu on a lifeboat. I'd decided to move on as soon as my wineglass was empty when a voice at my elbow spoke my last name softly.

There was something faintly familiar about the voice. I turned, and there was the man I've described, his eyes just failing to meet my own. My first thought was that no, he was not a cop, and for this fact I was grateful. My second thought was that his face, like his voice, was familiar. My third thought was that I didn't know him. I don't recall my fourth thought, though it's possible I had one.

'Want to talk to you,' he said. 'Something you'll be interested in.'

'We can talk here,' I said. 'Do I know you?'

'No. I guess we can talk here at that. Not much of a crowd, is there? I guess they do better on weekends.'

'Generally,' I said, and because it was that sort of a place, 'Do you come here often?'

'First time.'

'Interesting. I don't come here too often myself. Maybe once or twice a month. But it's interesting that we should run into each other here, especially since you seem to know me and I don't seem to know you. There's something familiar about you, and yet—'

'I followed you.'

'I beg your pardon?'

'We coulda talked in your neighborhood, one of those joints on Seventy-second where you hang out, but I figure the man's gotta live there. You follow me? Why shit where the man eats, that's the question I ask myself.'

'Ah,' I said, as if that cleared things up.

Which it emphatically did not. You doubtless understand, having come into all this in roundabout fashion, but I had not the slightest idea what this man wanted. Then the bartender materialized before us and I learned that what my companion wanted was a tall Scotch and soda, and after that drink had been brought and my own wineglass replenished I learned what else he wanted.

'I want you to get something for me,' he said.

'I don't understand.'

'See, I know who you are, Rhodenbarr.'

'So it would seem. At least you know my name, and I don't know yours, and—'

'I know how you make your money. Not to beat against the bush, Rhodenbarr, but what you are is a burglar.'

I glanced nervously around the room. His voice had been pitched low and the conversational level in the bar was high, but his tone had about it the quality of a stage whisper and I checked to see if our conversation had caught anyone's interest. Apparently it had not.

I said, 'Of course I don't know what you're talking about.'

'I suggest you cut the shit.'

'Oh,' I said, and took a sip of wine. 'All right. Consider it cut.'

'There's this thing I want you to steal for me. It's in a certain apartment and I'll be able to tell you when you can get in. The building's got security, meaning a doorman around the clock, but there's no alarm system or nothing. Just the doorman.'

'That's easy,' I said, responding automatically. Then I gave my shoulders a shake-shake-shake. 'You seem to know things about me,' I said.

'Like what you do for a living.'

'Yes, just that sort of thing. You should also know that I work alone.'

'I didn't figure to go in there with you, kid.'

'And that I find my own jobs.'

He frowned. 'What I'm doing is handing you a piece of cake, Rhodenbarr. I'm talking about you work an hour and you pick up five thousand dollars. That's not bad for an hour's work.'

'Not bad at all.'

'You do that forty hours a week, just go and figure the money you'd make.'

'Two hundred thousand a week,' I said promptly.

'Whatever the hell it comes to.'

'That's what it comes to, all right. Annually, let me think now, annually that would come to ten million dollars a year. That's with two weeks off in the summer.'

'Whatever.'

'Or a week in the summer and a week in the winter. That's probably the best way to do it. Or I could take my vacation in the spring and fall to avail myself of low off-season rates. Though I suppose the savings wouldn't be significant if I was earning ten million dollars a year. Hell, I'd probably start blowing the bucks left and right. Flying first class. Taking cabs all the time. Buying the Mondavi zinfandel by the case instead of a niggling bottle at a time, and of course you save ten percent by the case but it's not a true savings because you always find yourself drinking more than you would otherwise. You've probably noticed that yourself. Of course the pressure might get to me, anyway, but then I'd have those two weeks of vacation to let it all out, and—'

'Funny,' he said.

'Just nerves.'

'If you say so. You done talking for a minute? I want you to do this thing for me. There's something I need and it's a cinch for you to get it for me. And my price is fair, don't you think?'

'That depends on what you want me to steal. If it's a diamond necklace worth a quarter of a million dollars, then I'd have to say five thousand is coolie's wages.'

His face moved into what I suppose was meant as a smile. It failed to light up the room. 'No diamond necklace,' he said.

'Fine.'

'What you'll get for me is worth five grand to me. It's not worth nothing to nobody else.'

'What is it?'

'A box,' he said, and described it, but I've told you that part already. 'I'll give you the location, the apartment, everything, and for you it's like picking up candy in the street.'

'I never pick up candy in the street.'

'Huh?'

'Germs.'

He waved the thought away with one of his little hands. 'You know what I mean,' he said. 'No more jokes, huh?'

'Why don't you get it yourself?' He looked at me. 'You know the apartment, the layout, everything. You even know what you're looking for, which is more than I know and more than I want to know. Why don't you keep the five thousand in your pocket?'

'And pull the job myself?'

'Why not?'

He shook his head. 'Certain things I don't do,' he said. 'I don't take out my own appendix, I don't cut my own hair, I don't fix my own plumbing. Important things, things that need an expert's touch, what I do is I go and find an expert.'

'And I'm your expert?'

'Right. You go through locks like grease through a goose. Or so I'm told.'

'Who told you?'

An elaborate shrug. 'You just never remember where you hear a thing these days,' he said.

'I always remember.'

'Funny,' he said. 'I never do. I got a memory with holes in it you could fall through.' He touched my arm. 'Place is filling up. What do you say we take our business outside. We'll walk up and down the street, we'll work everything out.'

So we walked up and down the street, and though we didn't pick up any candy we did work everything out. We settled our terms and established that I would keep my schedule flexible for the next week or so. It wouldn't go more than that, he assured me.

He said, 'I'll be in touch, Rhodenbarr. Next time I see you I'll give you the address and the time and everything you gotta know. Plus I'll have your thousand in front.'

'I sort of thought you might let me have that now.'

'Haven't got it on me. You never want to carry heavy cash on the street at night. All these muggers, these junkies.'

'The streets aren't safe.'

'It's a jungle.'

'You could let me have the address now,' I suggested. 'And the name of the man who won't be home when I crack his crib. Give me that much time to check things out.'

'You'll have all the time you need.'

'I just thought—'

'Anyway, I don't happen to have the name or address at the moment. I told you about my memory, didn't I?'

'Did you?'

'I coulda sworn I did.'

I shrugged. 'It must have slipped my mind.'

Later that night I spent some time wondering why I'd agreed to do the job. I decided I had two motives. The money was first, and it was certainly not trivial. The certainty of five thousand dollars, plus the security of having the job already cased, outweighed the two-in-the-bush of setting up a job cold and then having to haggle with a fence.

But there was more to it than money. Something about my shmoo-shaped friend suggested that it would be unwise to refuse him. It's not that there was anything in particular I feared would happen to me if I told him to go roll his hoop. It just seemed unlikely to be a good idea.

And then there was curiosity. Who the hell *was* he? If I didn't know him, why did he seem so damned familiar? More important, how did he know about me? And what was his little game all about in the first place? If he was a pro, recognizing me as another pro, why were we circling each other like tropical birds in an involved mating ritual? I didn't necessarily expect ever to learn the answers to all these questions, but I felt they might turn up if I saw the thing through, and I didn't have any other work I was dying to do, and the money I had in reserve wouldn't last forever, and . . .

There's a luncheonette I go to once or twice a month on Amsterdam Avenue between Seventy-fourth and Seventy-fifth. The owner is a Turk with an intimidating moustache and the food he serves is every bit as Turkish, if less intimidating. I was sitting at the counter two days after my first meeting with my new-found friend. I'd just finished polishing off an exceptional bowl of lentil soup, and while I waited for my stuffed grape leaves I glanced at a selection of meerschaum pipes in a glass case on the wall. The man with the moustache goes home to Turkey every spring and returns with a satchel full of pipes which he insists are better than anything you can buy over the counter at Dunhill's. I don't smoke a pipe so I'm not really tempted, but whenever I eat there I look at the pipes and try to figure out if there's a pipe smoker on earth I'm a close enough friend to so that I can buy him one of these beauties. There never is.

'My old man used to smoke a meerschaum,' said a familiar voice beside me. 'Only pipe he owned and he musta smoked it five, six times a day. Over the years the thing turned as black as the deuce of spades. He had this special glove he always wore when he smoked it. Just on the one hand, the hand he held the pipe in. He'd always sit in the same chair and just smoke that pipe real slow and easy. Had a special fitted case he kept it in when he wasn't smoking it. Case was lined in blue velvet.'

'You do turn up at odd times.'

'Then one day it broke,' he went on. 'I don't know whether he dropped it or set it down hard or it just got too old or whatever the hell happened. My memory, you know.'

'Like a sieve.'

'The worst. What's funny, the old man never got hisself a new pipe. Not a meerschaum, not a briar, not anything. Just quit the habit like it was no habit at all. When I think about it what I always come up with is he just never believed anything would happen to that pipe, and then when it did he realized that nothing on earth lasts forever, and if that was the case he figured the hell with it and he wouldn't smoke anymore. And he didn't.'

'There's a reason you're telling me this story.'

'No reason at all. Just that it came to mind looking at those pipes there. I don't want to interrupt your meal, Rhodenbarr.'

'One might say you've already done that.'

'So I'll be on the corner gettin' my shoes shined. I don't guess you'll be too long, will you?'

'I guess not.'

He left. I ate my grape leaves. I hadn't intended to have dessert but I decided the hell with it and ate a small piece of too-sweet baklava and sipped a thick cup of inky Turkish coffee. I thought about having a second cup but figured it would keep me awake for four years and I didn't want that. So I paid the man with the moustache and walked to the shoeshine stand on the corner.

My friend told me everything I'd always wanted to know about J. Francis Flaxford and his blue leather box. If anything, he told me more than I wanted to know without answering any of my more important questions.

At one point I asked him his own name. He slid his soft brown eyes across my forehead and treated me to a look of infinite disappointment.

'Now I could tell you a name,' he said, 'but then what would you know that you don't know now? Not too much chance that it would be a real name, is there?'

'Not too much, no.'

'So why should we make complications for ourselves? All you got to know is where and when to get the box, which we just went over, and how and where to give it to me so you can get the other four grand.'

'You mean we'll plan that in advance? I thought I'd just go about my business and one of these days you'd turn up breathing over my shoulder at the delicatessen. Or maybe you'd be in the basement laundry room when I went down to throw my socks in the dryer.'

He sighed. 'You'll be inside Flaxford's place nine, nine-thirty. You'll be outta there by eleven, eleven-thirty the latest. Can't take too long to take a box out of a desk. You'll want to go home, have a drink, take a shower, change your clothes, that kind of thing.' And drop off burglar tools and such, along with whatever sundry swag I might happen to acquire. 'So you take yourself some time, and then what you do, you go to a place nice and convenient to your apartment. There's a bar on Broadway and I think it's Sixty-fourth Street, called Pandora's. You know it?'

'I've passed it.'

'Nice quiet place. Get there, say, twelve-thirty and take a booth at the back. There's no waitress so what you do is you get your drink at the bar and carry it back to your table.'

'Sounds as though I'd better wear a suit.'

'It's private and it's quiet and they leave you alone. You'll get there at twelve-thirty and you might have to sit there half an hour.'

'And then you'll turn up around one?'

'Right. Any problem, you wait until half past one and then you take the box and go home. But there won't be no problems.'

'Of course not,' I agreed. 'But suppose someone tries to take the box away from me?'

'Well, take cabs, for Chrissake. You don't want to walk around at that hour. Oh, wait a minute.'

I didn't say anything.

'You think I'd knock you over for a lousy four thousand dollars? Why would I do that?'

'Because it might be cheaper than paying me.'

'Jesus,' he said. 'Then how could I use you some other time? Look, carry some heat if it's gonna make you feel better. Except all you do then is get nervous and shoot your own foot off. I swear you got nothing to worry about from me. You bring me the box and you get your four gees.'

'Gees,' I said.

'Huh?'

'Thou, kay, gees. Grand.'

'Huh?'

'Four big ones.'

'What's the point?'

'You've got so many nicknames for money, that's all. You're like a thesaurus of slang.'

'Something wrong with the way I talk, Rhodenbarr?'

'No,' I said. 'Nothing. It's just me. My nerves, I guess. I get all keyed up.'

'Yeah,' he said thoughtfully. 'I just bet you do.'

And now I sat up on Rod's couch and looked at my watch. It was getting on for midnight. I'd gotten out of the Flaxford apartment with plenty of time to spare, but all the same it didn't look as though I'd be in Pandora's by twelve-thirty. My thousand dollars in front money was but a memory and the remaining four big ones were never to be mine, and at one o'clock my nameless friend would be sipping his Scotch and wondering why I'd decided to stand him up.

Oh, sure he would.

5

I don't know just when I got to sleep. A little after midnight a wave of exhaustion hit me and I got out of my clothes and into Rod's bed. I was just on the verge of sleep when I sensed an alien presence hovering at the bedside. I told myself I was being silly, and you know how well that sort of thing works, and I opened my eyes and saw that the alien presence was a split-leaf philodendron on a small stand by the side of the bed. It had as much right to be there as I did, if not more, but by the time we'd taken each other's measure I was awake again, my mind spinning around in frenzied circles and not getting anywhere.

I switched on the radio part of Rod's stereo, set the volume low, and perched in a chair waiting for the music to end and the news to come on. You know how when you want music there's a newscast every fifteen minutes? Well, the reverse is just as true. Cops, taxis, newscasts, nothing's ever there when you want it.

Ultimately there *was* a newscast, of course, and I listened intently to any number of items in which I had no interest whatsoever, and the round-voiced announcer did not have Word One to say about a burglary and murder on East Sixty-seventh Street. Nada. Zip.

I switched to another station but of course I had half an hour to wait for their newscast, having just missed it, and they were playing a bland sort of folk-rock. When the singer started telling me that his girl's voice was a stick of chalk drawn across the blackboard of his soul (I swear I'm not making this up) I remembered I was hungry. I went to the kitchen and opened drawers and cabinets and peered inside the fridge, and you'd have thought Old Mother Hubbard lived there. I managed to turn up half a box of Uncle Ben's Converted Rice (formerly Buddhist and now Presbyterian, I suppose), a discouraging-looking can of Norwegian sardines in mustard sauce, and a lot of little jars and tins of herbs and spices and sauces which could have perked up food if there had been any around. I decided I'd make myself some rice, but a look into the box showed me that I was not the first uninvited guest to take note of it, and Uncle Ben had been further converted, this time from rice to roach shit.

In another cupboard I found an unopened box of spaghetti, which I decided might be palatable with olive oil provided that the oil wasn't rancid, which it was. At this stage I began to think that perhaps I wasn't hungry after all, and then I opened another cupboard and discovered that Rodney Hart was a soup fiend. There were sixty-three cans of Campbell's soup in that cupboard, and I know the exact number because I counted them, and I counted them because I wanted to know just how long I could stay alive without leaving the apartment. At the concentration-camp rate of a can a day I was good for two months, and that was plenty of time, I told myself, because long before my soup ran out the police would arrest me and in no time at all I'd be serving a sentence for first-degree murder, and feeding me would be the state's problem.

So there was really nothing to worry about after all.

I started to shake a little but forced myself to concentrate on the process of opening the can. Rod's can opener was pretty primitive, considering that soup was the mainstay of his existence, but it did the job. I dumped concentrated Chicken With Stars soup into a presumably clean saucepan, added water, heated the mess on the stove, pepped it up with a little thyme and a dash of soy sauce, and was sitting down to eat it just as the folk-rock station came through with a five-minute news summary. It repeated some of the items I'd already heard on the jazz station, told me far more than I needed to know about the weather, since I didn't dare go out in it anyway, and had nothing to say about the late J. F. Flaxford or the murderous burglar who had done him in.

I finished my soup and tidied up in the kitchen. Then I went through some more cupboards until I found Rod's booze collection, which consisted in the main of things like a bottle of ancient blackberry brandy with perhaps an ounce of the crud left in the bottom of it. That sort of treasure. But there was, incredibly, a fifth of Scotch about two-thirds full. Now this particular Scotch was some liquor store's private label, and it had been bottled over in Hackensack, so what we had here was not quite in the Chivas and Pinch class.

But burglars can't be choosers. I sat up for what was probably a long time, sipping Scotch and watching the really late movies on Channel 9, switching every half hour (when I remembered) to check out the radio news. Nothing about J. Francis, nothing about me, though after a while I probably could have heard the item and not paid any attention to it.

In one of those drab hours just before dawn I managed to kill the television set (having already done as much for the bottle) and insert myself a second time between Rodney's sheets.

The very next thing I knew there was a crashing noise and a girl's voice saying, 'Oh, *shit!*'

No one ever returned more abruptly to consciousness. I had been deep in dreamless sleep and now I was jarringly awake. And there was someone in the apartment with me, someone female, and judging by her voice she was in rather close proximity to my no-longer-sleeping form.

I lay very still, trying to go on breathing as one breathes in sleep, hoping that she had not noticed my presence even as I realized that this was impossible. Who was she, anyway? And what the hell was she doing here?

And how was I going to get out of this mess?

'Shit,' she said again, taking the word right out of my mouth. This time the syllable was addressed not to the Fates but to me. 'I woke you up, didn't I? I was trying not to. I was being so quiet, just slipping around watering the plants, and then I had to go and knock the stupid thing over. I hope I didn't hurt the plant. And I'm sorry I disturbed you.'

'It's all right,' I told my pillow, keeping my face to it.

'I guess my plant-watering talents won't be needed anymore,' she went on. 'Will you be staying here for a while?'

'A couple of weeks.'

'Rod didn't mention anything about anyone staying here. I guess you just got in recently, huh?'

Damn her, anyway. 'Late last night,' I said.

'Well, I'm terribly sorry I woke you up. I'll tell you what I'll do. I'll make us a cup of coffee.'

'There's just soup.'

'Soup?'

I rolled reluctantly over and blinked at her. She was at the side of the bed. She had the split-leaf philodendron back on its perch and she was pouring water at its roots. The plant didn't look any the worse for wear and she looked terrific.

Hair short and dark, a high forehead, and very precisely measured facial features with just the slightest upward tilt to her nose and just the right amount of determination in her jawline. A well-formed mouth that, if not generous, was by no means parsimonious. Little pink ears with well-defined lobes. (I'd recently read a paperback on determining character and health from ears, so I was noticing such things. Her ears, according to my source, would seem to be ideal.)

She was wearing white painter's pants which showed good judgment by hugging her tightly. They were starting to go thin at the knees and in the seat. Her shirt was denim, one of those Western-style numbers with pearlish buttons and floral print trim. She had a red bandanna around her neck and deerskin moccasins upon her little feet.

The only thing I could think of that was wrong with her was that she was there in my apartment. (Well, Rod's apartment.) She was watering his plants and jeopardizing my security. Yet when I thought of all the mornings I had awakened alone and would have been delighted to have had this very person in the room with me – ah, the injustice of it all.

Women, policemen, taxis, newscasts, none of them on hand when you want them.

'Soup?' She turned her face toward me and smiled a tentative smile. Her eyes were either blue or green or both. Her teeth were white and even. 'What kind of soup?'

'Almost any kind you'd want. Black bean soup, chicken noodle soup, cream of asparagus soup, tomato soup, cheddar cheese soup—'

'You're kidding about the cheddar cheese soup.'

'Have I ever lied to you? It's in the cupboard if you don't believe me. If Campbell's makes it, Rod stocks it. And nothing else except for some roach-ridden rice.'

'I guess he's not terribly domestic. Have you known him long?'

'We're old friends.' A lie. 'But I haven't seen very much of him in the past few years.' A veritable truth.

'College friends? Or back in Illinois?'

Damn. What college? Where in Illinois? 'College,' I ventured.

'And now you've come to New York and you're staying at his place until—' the blue or green eyes widened '—until what? You're not an actor, are you?'

I agreed that I wasn't. But what in hell was I? I improvised a quick story, sitting up in bed with the sheet covering me to the throat. I told her how I'd been in the family feed business back home in South Dakota, that we'd been bought out at a good price by a competitor, and that I wanted to spend some time on my own in New York before I decided what turn my life should take next. I made the story very sincere and very dull, hoping she'd lose interest and remember a pressing engagement, but apparently she found my words more fascinating than I did because she hung on every one of them, sitting on the edge of my bed with her fingers interlaced around her knees and her eyes wide and innocent.

'You want to find yourself,' she said. 'That's very interesting.'

'Well, I never even suspected that I was lost. But now that I'm really at loose ends—'

'I'm in the same position myself, in a way. I was divorced four years ago. Then I was working, not a very involving job, and then I quit, and now I'm on unemployment. I paint a little and I make jewelry and there's a thing I've been doing lately with stained glass. Not what everybody else does but a form I sort of invented myself, these three-dimensional free-form sculptures I've been making. The thing is, I don't know about any of these things, whether I'm good enough or not. I mean, maybe they're just hobbies. And if that's all they are, well, the hell with them. Because I don't want hobbies. I want something to do and I don't have it yet. Or at least I don't think I do.' Her eyelashes fluttered at me. 'You don't really want soup for breakfast, do you?

Because why don't I run around the corner for coffee, it won't take me a minute, and you can put on some clothes and I'll be right back.'

She was on her way out the door before I had any chance to object. When it closed behind her I got out of bed and went to the toilet. (I would avoid mentioning this, but it was the first time in a long time that I knew what I was doing.) Then I put on yesterday's clothes and sat in my favorite chair and waited to see what came through my door next.

Because it might well be the plant-watering lady with the coffee come to serve breakfast to the earnest young man from South Dakota.

Or it might be the minions of the law.

'I'll just run around the corner for coffee,' Sure. Meaning she'd just recognized the notorious murdering burglar, or burgling murderer (or bungling mumbler, or what you will), and was taking this opportunity to (a) escape his clutches and (b) let Justice be done.

I thought about running but couldn't see any real sense in it. As long as there was a chance she wasn't going to the cops, then this apartment was a damn sight safer than the streets. At least that's how my reasoning went, but I suspect the main factor was inertia. I had a bloodstream full of last night's lousy Scotch and a head full of rusty hardware and it was easier to sit than to run.

I could drag this out, but why? I didn't have to wait for the door to open to know she'd come back alone. I heard her steps on the stairs, and there is just no way that a herd of cops can ascend a staircase and sound in the process like a diminutive young lady. So I was relaxed and at ease long before the door opened, but when it did in fact open and her pert and pretty face appeared, I must confess it pleased me. Lots.

She had bought real coffee, astonishingly enough, and she now proceeded to make a pot of it. While she did this we chatted idly and easily. I'd had a chance to practice my lies during her absence, so when she told me her name was Ruth Hightower I was quick to reply that I was Roger Armitage. From that point on we ruthed and rogered one another relentlessly.

I said something about the airlines having lost my luggage, tossing the line in before it could occur to her to wonder at my lack of possessions. She said the airlines were always doing that and we both agreed that a civilization that could put a man on the moon ought to be able to keep track of a couple of suitcases. We pulled up chairs on either side of a table and we drank our coffee out of Rod's chipped and unmatched cups. It was good coffee.

We talked and talked and talked, and I fell into the role so completely that I became quite comfortable in it. Perhaps it was the influence of the environment, perhaps the apartment was making an actor out of me. Rod had said the landlord liked actors. Perhaps the whole building

swarmed with them, perhaps it was something in the walls and woodwork . . .

At any rate I was a perfect Roger Armitage, the new boy in town,
and she was the lady I'd met under cute if clumsy circumstances, and
before too long I found myself trying to figure out an offhand way
to ask her just how well she knew Rod, and just what sort of part he
played in her life, and, uh, shucks Ma'am—

But what the hell did it matter? Whatever future our relationship had
was largely in the past. As soon as she left I'd have to think about
clearing out myself. This was not a stupid lady, and sooner or later she
would figure out just who I was, and when that happened it would
behoove me to be somewhere else.

And then she was saying, 'You know, I was trying so hard to take
care of those plants and get out before I woke you, and actually what I
should have done was just leave right away because you would have
taken care of the plants yourself, but I didn't think of that, and you
know something? I'm glad I didn't. I'm really enjoying this conversation.'

'So am I, Ruth.'

'You're easy to talk to. Usually I have trouble talking to people.
Especially to men.'

'It's hard to believe you're not at ease with everyone.'

'What a nice thing to say!' Her eyes – I'd learned by now that they
ranged from blue to green, varying either with her mood or with the
way the light hit them – her eyes, as I was saying way back at the
beginning of this sentence, gazed shyly up at me from beneath lowered
lashes. 'It's turned into a nice day, hasn't it?'

'Yes, it has.'

'It's a little chilly out but the sky is clear. I thought about picking up
some sweet rolls but I didn't know whether you'd want anything
besides just coffee.'

'Just coffee is fine. And this is good coffee.'

'Another cup? Here, I'll get it for you.'

'Thanks.'

'What should I call you, Bernie or Bernard?'

'Whichever you like.'

'I think I'll call you Bernie.'

'Most people do,' I said. 'Oh, sweet suffering Jesus,' I said.

'It's all right, Bernie.'

'God in Heaven.'

'It's all right.' She leaned across the table toward me, a smile flickering at the corners of her mouth, and she placed a small soft-palmed
hand atop mine. 'There's nothing to worry about,' she said.

'There isn't?'

'Of course not. I know you didn't kill anybody. I'm an extremely

39

intuitive person. If I hadn't been pretty sure you were innocent I wouldn't have gone to the trouble of knocking the plant over in the first place, and—'

'You knocked it over on purpose?'

'Uh-huh. The stand, anyway. I picked up the plant itself so nothing would happen to it, and then I kicked the stand so that it bounced off the wall and fell over.'

'Then you knew all along.'

'Well, your name's all over the papers, Bernie. And it's also all over your driver's license and the other papers in your wallet. I went through your pockets while you were sleeping. You're one of the soundest sleepers I've come across.'

'Do you come across that many?'

Incredibly enough, the minx blushed. 'Not all that many, no. Where was I?'

'Going through my pockets.'

'Yes. I thought I recognized you. There was a photo in the *Times* this morning. It's not a very good likeness. Do they really cut a person's hair that short when they send him to prison?'

'Ever since Samson pushed the temple down. They're not taking any chances.'

'I think it's barbaric of them. Anyway, the minute I looked at you I knew you couldn't have murdered that Flaxford person. You're not a murderer.' She frowned a little. 'But I guess you're a genuine burglar, aren't you?'

'It does look that way.'

'It certainly does, doesn't it? Do you really know Rod?'

'Not terribly well. We've played poker together a few times.'

'But he doesn't know what you do for a living, does he? And how come he gave you his keys? Oh, I'm being dull-witted now. What would you need with keys? I saw your keys in your pants pocket, and all those other implements. I must say they look terribly efficient. Don't you need something called a jimmy to pry doors open with?'

'Only if you're crude.'

'But you're not, are you? There's something very sexual about burglary, isn't there? How on earth did you get into a business like that? But the man's supposed to ask the girl that question, isn't he? My, we have a lot to talk about, and it should be a lot more interesting than all that crap about Roger Armitage and the feed business in South Dakota, and I'll bet you've never even been to South Dakota, have you? Although you do string out a fairly convincing pack of lies. Would you like some more coffee, Bernie?'

'Yes,' I said. 'Yes, I think I would.'

6

By six twenty-four that evening the chaps at Channel 7 had said all they were likely to say about the five-state manhunt now under way for Bernard Rhodenbarr, gentleman burglar turned blood-crazed killer. I set one of the foxy old Colonel's better chicken legs on my plate and crossed the room to turn off Rod's Panasonic. Ruth sat cross-legged on the floor, a chicken leg of her own unattended while she muttered furiously about the perfidy of Ray Kirschmann. 'The gall of that man,' she said. 'Taking a thousand dollars of your hard-earned money and then saying such horrible things about you.'

In Ray's version of the proceedings, I'd crouched in the shadows to take him and Loren by surprise; only his daring and perseverance had enabled him to identify me during the fracas. 'I've felt for years that Rhodenbarr was capable of violence,' he'd told the reporters, and it seemed to me that his baleful glower had been directed not at the TV cameras but through them at me.

'Well, I let him down,' I said. 'Made him look foolish in front of his partner.'

'Do you think he really believed what he said?'

'That I killed Flaxford? Of course he does. You and I are the only people in the world who think otherwise.'

'And the real killer.'

'And the real killer,' I agreed. 'But he's not likely to speak up and nobody's going to take my word for anything, and you can't do much in the way of proving your case. As a matter of fact, I don't see why you believe me to begin with.'

'You have an honest face.'

'For a burglar, maybe.'

'And I'm a very intuitive person.'

'So I've been given to understand.'

'J. Francis Flaxford,' she said.

'May he rest in peace.'

'Amen. You know, I can never bring myself to trust men who turn their first name into an initial that way. I always feel they're leading some sort of secret life. There's just something devious about the way they perceive themselves and the image they present to the world.'

'That's quite a generalization, isn't it?'

'Oh, I don't know. Look at the record. G. Gordon Liddy, E. Howard Hunt—'

'Fellow burglars, both of them.'

'Do you have a middle name, Bernie?'

I nodded. 'Grimes,' I said. 'My mother's maiden name.'

'Would you ever call yourself B. Grimes Rhodenbarr?'

'I never have. Somehow I doubt I ever shall. But if I did it wouldn't mean I was trying to hide something. It would mean I had taken leave of my senses. B. Grimes Rhodenbarr, for God's sake! Look, plenty of people have first names they're not nuts about, and they like their middle names, so—'

'Then they can drop their first names entirely,' she said. 'That's open and aboveboard enough. It's when they keep that sneaky little initial out in front there that I don't trust them.' She showed me the tip of her tongue. 'Anyway, I like my theory. And I wouldn't dream of trusting J. Francis Flaxford.'

'I think you can trust him now. Being dead means never having to do anything sneaky.'

'I wish we knew more about him. All we really know is that he's dead.'

'Well, it's the most salient fact about him. If he weren't dead we wouldn't have to know anything at all about the sonofabitch.'

'You shouldn't call him that, Bernie.'

'I suppose not.'

'*De mortuis* and all that.'

De mortuis indeed. She gnawed the last of the meat from her chicken bone, then gathered together all of our leavings and carried them to the kitchen. I watched her little bottom as she walked, and when she bent over to deposit the chicken bones in the garbage I got a lump in my throat, among other things. Then she straightened up and set about pouring two cups of coffee and I made myself think about the late Francis Flaxford, with a J. in front of his name and an R.I.P. after it.

The night before I'd wondered idly if the dead man was actually Flaxford. Maybe some other burglar had been working the same side of the street, taking advantage of Flaxford's scheduled absence and arriving there before me. Then he'd managed to get his head dented and had been there when I showed up.

But who would have killed him? Flaxford himself?

No matter. The corpse was truly Flaxford, a forty-eight-year-old entrepreneur and dabbler in real estate, a producer of off-off-Broadway theatrical ventures, a *bon vivant*, a man about town. He'd been married and divorced years and years ago, he'd lived alone in his plush East Side apartment, and someone had smashed his skull with an ashtray.

'If you were going to kill somebody,' Ruth said, 'you wouldn't use an ashtray, would you?'

'He liked substantial ashtrays,' I told her. 'There was one in the living room that would have felled an ox. A big cut-glass thing, and they say the murder weapon was a cut-glass ashtray, and if it was a mate to the one I saw it would have done the job, all right.' I looked at the *Post* story again, tapped a fingernail against his picture. 'He wasn't bad-looking,' I said.

'If you like the type.'

He had a good-looking, high-browed face, a mane of dark hair going gray at the temples, a moustache that his barber had taken pains to trim.

'Distinguished,' I said.

'If you say so.

'Even elegant.'

'Try sneaky and shifty while you're at it.'

'*De mortuis*, remember?'

'Oh, screw *de mortuis*. As my grandmother used to say, if you've got nothing good to say about someone, let's hear it. I wonder how he really made his money, Bernie. What do you suppose he did for a living?'

'He was an entrepreneur, it says here.'

'That just means he made money. It doesn't explain how.'

'He dabbled in real estate.'

'That's something you do with money, like producing plays off-off-Broadway. The real estate may have made money for him and the plays must have lost it, they always do, but he must have done something for a living and I'll bet it was faintly crooked.'

'You're probably right.'

'So why isn't it in the paper?'

'Because nobody cares. As far as everybody's concerned, he only got killed because he was in the wrong place at the wrong time. A mad-dog burglar happened to pick his apartment at random and he happened to be in it, and that was when J. Francis kept his appointment in Samarra. If he'd been wearing ladies' underwear at the time of his death he'd make better copy and the reporters would take a longer look at his life, but instead he was just wearing a perfectly ordinary Brooks Brothers dressing gown and that made him dull copy.'

'Where does it say he was wearing a Brooks Brothers robe?'

'I made that up. I don't know where he bought his clothes. It just says he was wearing a dressing gown. The *Times* says dressing gown. The *Post* calls it a bathrobe.'

'I had the impression he was naked.'

'Not according to the working press.' I tried to remember if Loren had blurted out anything about his dress or lack of it. If he did, I didn't remember it. 'He'll probably be naked in tomorrow morning's *Daily News*,' I said. 'What difference does it make?'

'It doesn't.'

We were sitting side by side on the Lawson couch. She folded the paper and put it on the seat beside her. 'I just wish we had someplace to start,' she said. 'But it's like trying to untie a knot when both ends of the rope are out of sight. All we've got are the dead man and the man who got you mixed up in this in the first place.'

'And we don't know who he is.'

'Mr Shmoo. Mr Chocolate Eyes. A man with narrow shoulders and a large waistline who avoids looking people right in the eye.'

'That's our man.'

'And he looks vaguely familiar to you.'

'He looks specifically familiar to me. He even sounded familiar.'

'But you never met him before.'

'Never.'

'Damn.' She made fists of her hands, pressed them against her thighs. 'Could you have known him in prison?'

'I don't think so. That would be logical, wouldn't it? Then of course he would have known I was a burglar. But I can't think of any area of my life in or out of prison that he fits into. Maybe I've seen him on subways, passed him in the street. That sort of thing.'

'Maybe.' She frowned. 'He set you up. Either he killed Flaxford himself or he knows who did.'

'I don't think he killed anybody.'

'But he must know who did.'

'Probably.'

'So if we could just find him. I know you don't know his name, but did he give you a fake name at least?'

'No. Why?'

'We could try paging him at that bar. I forget the name.'

'Pandora's. Why page him?'

'I don't know. Maybe you could tell him you had the blue leather box.'

'*What* blue leather box?'

'The one you went to – oh.'

'There isn't any blue leather box.'

'Of course not,' she said. 'There never was one in the first place, was there? The blue leather box was nothing but a red herring.' She wrinkled up her forehead in concentration. 'But then why did he arrange to meet you at Pandora's?'

'I don't know. I'm sure he didn't bother to show up.'

'Then why arrange it?'

'Beats me. Unless he planned to tip the police if I showed up there,

44

but I don't think that makes any sense either. Maybe he just wanted to go through the motions of setting up a meeting. To make the whole thing seem authentic.' I closed my eyes for a moment, running the scene through my mind. 'I'll tell you what's funny. I have the feeling he kept trying to impress me with how tough he was. Why would he do that?'

'So you'd be afraid to double-cross him, I suppose.'

'But why would I cross him in the first place? There's something funny about the guy. I think he was pretending to be tough because he's not. Not tough, I mean. He talked the talk but he didn't walk the walk. I suppose he must have been a con artist of some sort.' I grinned. 'He certainly conned me. It's hard to believe there was no blue box in that apartment. He had me convinced that it was there and that he really didn't want me to open it.'

'You don't remember him from jail. Do you think he's ever been arrested?'

'Probably. It sort of comes with the territory. However good you are, sooner or later you step in the wrong place. I told you about my last arrest, didn't I?'

'When the bell was out of order.'

'Right, and I wound up tossing an apartment while the tenants were home. And I had to pick a man with a gun and an air of righteous indignation, and then when I told him how we ought to be able to be reasonable about this and pulled out my walking money, he turned out to be the head of some civic group. I'd have had about as much chance of bribing a rabbi with a ham sandwich. They didn't just throw the book at me, they threw the whole library.'

'Poor Bernie,' she said, and put her hand on mine. Our hands took a few minutes to get acquainted. Our eyes met, then slipped away to leave us with our private thoughts.

And mine turned, not for the first time, to prison. If I gave myself up they'd undoubtedly let me cop a plea to Murder Two, maybe even some degree of manslaughter. I'd most likely be on the street in three or four years with good time and parole and all that. I'd never served that much time before, but my last stretch had been substantial enough, eighteen months, and if you can do eighteen months you can do four years. Either way you straighten up and square your shoulders and do your bit one day at a time.

Of course I was older now and I'd be crowding forty by the time I got out. But they say it's easier to do time when you're older because the months and the years seem to pass more rapidly.

No women inside. No soft cool hands, no taut rounded bottoms. (There are men inside with taut rounded bottoms, if you happen to like that sort of thing. I don't happen to like that sort of thing.)

'Bernie? I could go to the police.'

'And turn me in? It might make sense if there was a reward, but—'

'What are you talking about? Why would I turn you in? Are you crazy?'

'A little. Why else would you go to the cops?'

'Don't they have books full of pictures of criminals? I could tell them I was taken by a con man and get them to show me pictures.'

'And then what?'

'Well, maybe I'd recognize him.'

'You've never seen him, Ruth.'

'I feel as though I have from your description.'

'A mug shot would just show his face. Not his profile.'

'Oh.'

'That's why they call it a mug shot.'

'Oh.'

'I don't think it's a viable approach.'

'I guess not, Bernie.'

I turned her hand over, stroked the palm and the pads of her fingers. She moved her body a little closer to mine. We sat like that for a few minutes while I got myself all prepared to put my arm around her, and just as I was about to make my move she stood up.

'I just wish we could *do* something,' she said. 'If we knew the name of the man who roped you in we would at least have a place to start.'

'Or if we knew why somebody wanted to kill Flaxford. Somebody had a reason to want him dead. A motive. If we knew more about him we might know what to look for.'

'Don't the police—'

'The police already know who killed him. There won't ever be any investigation, Ruth, because as far as they're concerned I'm guilty and the case is closed. All they have to do is get their hands on me. That's why the frame works so perfectly. It may be that there's only one person in the world with a motive for killing Flaxford, but no one will ever know about it because Flaxford's murder is all wrapped up and tied with a ribbon and the card has my name on it.'

'I could go to the library tomorrow. I'll check *The New York Times Index*. Maybe they ran something on him years ago and I can read all about it in the microfilm room.'

I shook my head. 'If there was anything juicy they'd have dug it up and run it in his obit.'

'There might be something that would make some kind of connection for us. It's worth a try, isn't it?'

'I suppose so.'

She walked half a dozen steps in one direction, then retraced them, then turned and began the process anew. It was a reasonably good Caged Lion impression. 'I can't just sit around,' she said. 'I get stir crazy.'

46

'You'd hate prison.'

'God! How do people stand it?'

'A day at a time,' I said. 'I'd take you out for a night on the town, Ruth, but—'

'No, you have to stay here,' she said. 'I realize that.' She picked up one of the papers, turned pages. 'Maybe there's something on television,' she said, and it turned out that there was a Warner Brothers gangster thing on WPIX. The whole crew was in it – Robinson, Lorre, Greenstreet, and a ton of great old character actors whose names I've never bothered to learn but whose faces I'd never forget. She sat on the couch next to me and we watched the whole thing, and eventually I did manage to put an arm around her and we sort of cuddled, doing a little low-level necking during the commercials.

When the last villain got his and they rolled the final credits she said, 'See? The bad guys always lose in the end. We've got nothing to worry about.'

'Life,' I announced, 'is not a B picture.'

'Well, it ain't no De Mille epic either, boss. Things'll work out, Bernie.'

'Maybe.'

The eleven o'clock news came on and we watched it until they got to the part we were interested in. There were no new developments in the Flaxford murder, and the report they gave was just an abbreviated version of what we'd seen a few hours earlier. When they cut to an item about a drug bust in Hunts Point Ruth went over to the set and turned it off.

'I guess I'll go now,' she said.

'Go?'

'Home.'

'Where's that?'

'Bank Street. Not far from here.'

'You could stick around,' I suggested. 'There's probably something watchable on the tube.'

'I'm pretty tired, actually. I was up early this morning.'

'Well, you could, uh, sleep here,' I said. 'As far as that goes.'

'I don't think so, Bernie.'

'I hate to think of you walking home alone. At this hour and in this neighborhood—'

'It's not even midnight yet. And this is the safest neighborhood in the city.'

'It's sort of nice having you around,' I said.

She smiled. 'I really want to go home tonight,' she said. 'I want to shower and get out of these clothes—'

'So?'

'—and I have to feed my cats. The poor little things must be starving.'

'Can't they open a can?'

'No, they're hopelessly spoiled. Their names are Esther and Mordecai. They're Abyssinians.'

'Then why did you give them Hebrew names?'

'What else would I call them, Haile and Selassie?'

'That's a point.'

I followed her to the door. She turned with one hand on the knob and we kissed, and it was very nice. I really wanted her to stay, and she made a rather encouraging sound down deep in her throat and ground herself against me a little.

Then I let go of her and she opened the door and said, 'See you tomorrow, Bernie.'

And left.

7

The subway wasn't doing much business by the time I got onto it. I caught an uptown Eighth Avenue local at Fourteenth Street and there was only one other person in the car with me. That was the good news. The bad news is that he was a Transit Authority cop with an enormous revolver on his hip. He kept looking at me because there was nobody else for him to look at, and I just knew that he was going to figure out why I looked familiar. At any moment a light bulb would form in the air over his head and he would spring into action.

Except he never did. At Times Square we picked up some fellow travelers – a pair of off-duty nurses, an utterly wasted junkie – and that gave the cop someplace else to focus his eyes. Then at Fifty-ninth Street he got off, and a stop later it was my turn. I climbed the stairs and emerged into the early morning air at Seventy-second and Central Park West and wondered what the hell I thought I was doing.

Earlier that evening I'd been completely comfortable sitting around Rod's apartment with my eyes on the television set and my arm around Ruth. But once she was gone I began finding the place unbearable. I couldn't sit still, couldn't watch the tube, kept pacing around and getting increasingly twitchy. A little after midnight I took a shower, and when the prospect of putting on the same clothes seemed as appalling as you might imagine it would, I went through Rod's closet and dresser to see what he'd left behind.

There wasn't much I could use. Either he tended to take an awful lot of clothing on the road with him or he didn't own much in the first place. I found a shirt I could wear, although I didn't much want to, and a pair of navy blue stretch socks, but that was about the extent of it.

Then I came across the wig.

It was a blondish wig, long but not quite hippie in style. I put it on and checked myself out in the mirror and I was astonished at the transformation. The only problem was that it was a little too garish and drew a little too much attention, but that problem was solved when I found a cloth cap on a shelf in the closet. The cap softened the effect of the wig and made it less of an attention-getter.

Anyone who knew me personally would recognize me, I decided. But a stranger passing me on the street would just see yellow hair and a cloth cap.

I told myself I was crazy. I took off the cap and the wig and sat down in front of the television set. After a few minutes the phone started to ring, and it went on ringing twenty-two times by actual count before the caller gave up or the service did what it was supposed to do. The phone had rung periodically during the day – Ruth almost answered it once – but it had never gone so long unattended.

At a quarter to one I put on the wig and the cap and got out of there.

From the subway I walked over to my apartment building. I'd taken the subway instead of a cab because I hadn't wanted to talk to anyone on a one-to-one basis. Maybe on some level or other I was worried that I'd run into the cabbie who'd driven me around the night before. But once I had to walk those few blocks to my building I began wishing I'd done things the other way around. There were a lot of people on Seventy-second Street and it was brightly lit, and I'd lived in that neighborhood for several years. In the course of a short walk I saw several people whom I recognized. I didn't know their names but I'd seen them on the streets at one time or another, and it was logical to assume they'd seen me and could recognize me if they took a good long look at me. I tried to assume a posture and a rhythm of walking that was not my usual style. Maybe it helped. In any event, nobody seemed to notice me.

Finally I was standing in the shadows on the corner diagonally across the street from where I lived. I gazed up and found my window up there on the sixteenth floor facing south. My apartment. My little chunk of private space.

God knows it wasn't much, two small rooms and a kitchen, an overpriced cubicle in a sterile modern building. The view was the only charm the place had. But it was home, dammit, and I'd been comfortable here.

All that was over now. Even if I got out of this mess (and I couldn't really imagine how that could happen) I didn't see how I could go on living here. Because now they all knew the horrible truth about that pleasant chap in 16-G. He was a burglar, for God's sake. A criminal.

I thought of all the people I nodded to daily in the elevator, the women I'd exchanged pleasantries with in the laundry room, the door-men and hall porters, the super and the handyman. Mrs Hesch, the chainsmoking old lady across the hall from whom I could always borrow a cup of detergent. She was the only person there that I really knew, and I don't suppose I knew her very well, but I was on amicable terms with all those people and I'd liked living among them.

Now I couldn't go back there. Bernard Rhodenbarr, burglar. I'd have to move somewhere else, have to use some sort of alias to rent an apartment. Jesus, it's hard enough functioning as a professional criminal, but when you have the added burden of notoriety you're really up against it.

Could I possibly risk going upstairs? The midnight-to-eight doorman, a stout old fellow named Fritz, was on his post. I didn't really think the cap and the wig would fool him. It was possible that a couple of bucks would blind him to his civic duty, but it was also possible that it would not, and the downside risk seemed disproportionate to the possible gain. On the other hand, there was a side entrance, a flight of stairs leading to the basement. They kept that entrance locked; you could get out through it from inside, and the super would unlock it for deliveries, but you couldn't get in.

You couldn't get in. *I* could.

From the basement I could catch the self-service elevator straight upstairs, past the lobby to the sixteenth floor. And I could let myself out the same way, and I could carry with me a suitcase full of clothes and my five thousand dollars in case money. If I did turn myself in, or if they grabbed me, I had to have money for a lawyer. And I wanted to have the money on me, not tucked away in an apartment that I wouldn't be allowed to go to.

I fingered my ring of keys and picks, stepped out of the shadows and started to cross Seventy-first Street. Just as I reached the opposite corner a car pulled up in front of my building and parked at a hydrant. It was an ordinary late-model sedan but there was something about the nonchalance with which the driver dumped it next to the hydrant that shouted *cop* to me.

Two men got out of the car. I didn't recognize them and there was nothing obviously coppish about their appearance. They were wearing suits and ties, but lots of people do that, not just plainclothes detectives.

I stayed on my side of West End Avenue. And sure enough they showed something to Fritz, and I stayed where I was, backing away from the curb, as a matter of fact, and placing myself alongside the stoop of a brownstone where I wouldn't be noticeable. Anyone who noticed me would take me for a mugger and give me a wide berth.

I just stood there for a minute. Then it occurred to me that I'd like to have a look at my window, so I crossed back to the corner I'd occupied originally and counted up to the sixteenth floor and over to the G apartment, and the light was on.

I stayed there for fifteen long minutes and the light went right on blazing away. I scratched my head, a dumb thing to do when you're wearing a loose-fitting wig. I rearranged the wig and the cap and wondered what the bastards were doing in my apartment and just how long it would take them to do it.

Too long, I decided. And they'd be noisy, there being no reason for them to toss my place in silence, so that if I went in after them my neighbors might very well be sensitive to sounds, and . . .

The hell with it.

I walked for a while. I kept to residential streets and stayed away from streetlights, walking around and trying to figure out what to do next. Eventually I found myself just half a block from Pandora's. I found a spot where I could watch the doorway without being terribly noticeable myself and I stood there until I got a cramp in my calf and became very much aware of a dryness in my throat. I don't know just how long I stood there but it was long enough for eight or ten people to enter the saloon and about as many to leave. None of them was my little pear-shaped friend.

Maybe I'd seen him around the neighborhood. Maybe that was why he looked familiar to me. Maybe I used to pass him regularly on the streets and his face and figure had registered on some subliminal level. Maybe he'd mentioned Pandora's because it was his regular hangout and the first place that came to mind, even though he'd had no intention whatsoever of keeping our appointment.

Maybe he was inside there right now.

I don't honestly think I believed this for a minute. But I was thirsty enough to grab at a straw if it meant I could grab at a beer. The faint possibility of his presence in the place enabled me to rationalize going inside myself.

And of course he wasn't there, but the beer was good.

I didn't stay there long, and when I left I had a bad couple of minutes. I was convinced someone was following me. I was heading south on Broadway and there was a man twenty or thirty yards back of me who I was sure had come out of the bar after me. I turned right at Sixtieth Street and so did he, and this didn't do wonders for my morale.

I crossed the street and went on walking west. He stayed on his side of the street. He was a smallish chap and he wore a poplin windbreaker over dark slacks and a light shirt. I couldn't see much of his face in that light and I didn't want to stop and stare at him anyway.

Just before I reached Columbus Avenue he crossed over to my side of the street. I turned downtown on Columbus, which becomes Ninth Avenue at about that point, and to the surprise of practically no one he turned the corner and followed me. I tried to figure out what to do. I could try to shake him, I could pop into a doorway and deck him when he came by, or I could just keep walking and see what he did.

I kept walking, and a block farther on he ducked into a saloon and that was the end of him. He was just another poor bastard looking for a drink.

I walked to Columbus Circle and took a subway home. Well, to my home away from home, anyway. This time I had less difficulty finding Bethune Street. It was right where I left it. I opened the downstairs door about as quickly as I could have managed if I had a key to it, scampered up the four miserable flights of stairs, and was in Rod's apartment in no time at all. I had no trouble with the three locks because I hadn't had a key to lock them with when I left. Only the spring lock was engaged, and I loided it with a strip of flexible steel, an operation that honestly takes less time than opening it with a key.

Then I fastened all the locks and went to bed. I hadn't accomplished a thing and I'd taken any number of brainless chances, but all the same I lay there in Rod's bed and felt pleased with myself. I'd gone out on the street instead of hiding, I'd gone through the motions of taking some responsibility for myself.

It felt good.

8

She didn't have to knock any plants over the next morning. I was awake and out of bed a few minutes after nine. I took a shower and looked around for something to shave with. Rod had left his second-string razor behind. I found it in the medicine chest hiding behind an empty Band-Aid box. It was an obsolete Gillette that hadn't been used in at least a year and hadn't been cleaned in at least a year and a day. The old blade was still in it and so was the crud and whiskers from Rod's last shave with it. I held it under the faucet stream, but that was like trying to sweep out the Augean stables with a child's toy broom.

I decided to call Ruth and ask her to bring things like toothpaste and a toothbrush and shaving gear. I looked up Hightower in the Manhattan white pages and found it was a commoner name than I would have guessed, but none of the Hightowers were named Ruth or lived on Bank Street. I called Information and an operator with a Latin accent assured me that there were no listings in that name or on that street. After I'd put the phone down I told myself there was no reason to question the competence of a telephone operator just because English looked to be her second language, but all the same I dialed 411 again and put another operator through the same routine. Her accent was pure dulcet Flatbush and she didn't do any better at finding Ruth's number.

I decided she was probably unlisted. What the hell, she wasn't an actress. Why should she have a listed phone?

I turned on the television set for company, put up a pot of coffee, and went back and looked at the phone some more. I decided to dial my own number to see if there were any cops in the place at the moment. I picked up the phone, then put it down when I realized I wasn't sure of my number. It was one I never called, since when I was out there was never anybody home. This sort of surprised me; I mean, even if you never call your own number you have to know it to give it out to people. But I guess that doesn't happen often in my case. Anyway, I looked it up and there it was, and I'm happy to say I recognized it once I saw it. I dialed and nobody answered, which stood to reason, and I put the phone back in its cradle.

I was on my second cup of coffee when I heard footsteps ascending

54

the staircase and approaching the door. She knocked but I let her use her keys. She came in, all bright-eyed and buoyant, carrying a small grocery bag and explaining that she'd brought bacon and eggs. 'And you've already got coffee made,' she said. 'Great. Here's this morning's *Times*. There's not really anything in it.'

'I didn't think there would be.'

'I suppose I could have bought the *Daily News* too but I never do. I figure if anything really important happens the *Times* will tell me about it. Is this the only frying pan he owns?'

'Unless he took the others on tour with him.'

'He's not very domestic at all. Well, we'll have to deal with the material at hand. I'm relatively new at harboring fugitives but I'll do my best to harbor you in the style to which you are accustomed. Is it called harboring a fugitive if you do it in somebody else's apartment?'

'It's called accessory after the fact to homicide,' I said.

'That sounds serious.'

'It ought to.'

'Bernie—'

I took her arm. 'I was thinking about that earlier, Ruth. Maybe you ought to bail out.'

'Don't be ridiculous.'

'You could wind up buying a lot of trouble.'

'That's crazy,' she said. 'You're innocent, aren't you?'

'The cops don't think so.'

'They will when we find the real killer for them. Hey, c'mon, Bern! I've seen all the old movies, remember? I know the good guys always come through in the end. We're the good guys, aren't we?'

'I'd certainly like to think so.'

'Then we've got nothing to worry about. Now just tell me how you like your eggs and then get the hell out of here, huh? There's room for me and the roaches in this kitchen and that's about all. What are you doing, Bernie?'

'Kissing your neck.'

'Oh. Well, that's okay, I guess. Actually you could do it some more if you'd like. Hmmmm. You know, that's sort of nice, Bernie. I could learn to like that.'

We were polishing off the eggs when the phone rang. The service was on the ball and picked up midway through the fourth ring.

Which reminded me. 'I tried to call you earlier,' I said, 'but your numbers unlisted. Unless you've got it listed in your husband's name or something like that.'

'Oh,' she said. 'No, it's unlisted. Why were you trying to call?'

'Because I need a shave.'

55

'I noticed. Your face is all scratchy. Actually I sort of like it, but I can see where you'd want to shave.'

I told her about the lack of shaving cream and the state of Rod's razor. 'I thought you could pick them up on your way over here.'

'I'll go get them now. It's no trouble.'

'If I'd had your number I could have saved you a trip.'

'Oh, it's no trouble,' she said. 'I don't mind. Is there anything else you need?'

I thought of a few things and she made a small list. I took a ten out of my wallet and made her take it. 'There's really no rush,' I said.

'I'd just as soon go now. I was just thinking, Bernie. Maybe it's not a good idea to use the telephone.'

'Why not?'

'Well, couldn't the people at the service tell if it was off the hook or if you were talking to someone? I think they could even listen in, couldn't they?'

'Gee, I don't know. I've never understood just how those things work.'

'And they know Rod's out of town, and if they knew someone was in his apartment—'

'Ruth, they usually let the phone ring twenty times before they get around to answering it. That's how efficient they are. The only time they pay attention to a subscriber's line is when it's ringing, and even then their attention isn't too terribly keen.'

'The last time it rang they got it right away.'

'Well, accidents happen, I suppose. But you don't really think there's any risk in using the phone, do you?'

'Well—'

'There can't be.'

But when she went out I found myself standing next to the phone and staring at it as if it were a potential menace. I picked up the receiver and started dialing my own apartment – I remembered the number this time – but halfway through I decided the hell with it and hung up.

While she shopped I did up the breakfast dishes and read the paper. All the *Times* had to tell me was that I was still at large and I already knew that.

This time I hadn't bothered locking the door, and when she knocked I went over and opened it for her. She handed me a paper bag containing a razor, a small package of blades, shaving cream, a toothbrush and a small tube of toothpaste. She also gave me forty-seven cents change from my ten-dollar bill. Every once in a while something like that comes along to demonstrate that all this talk about inflation is not entirely unwarranted.

'I'll be going out in a few minutes,' she said. 'You can shave then.'

'Out? You just got here.'

'I know. I want to go to the library. And check the *Times Index* – we talked about that last night. I don't know how else we're going to learn anything about Flaxford unless I go track down his ex-wife and talk to her.'

'That sounds like more trouble than it's likely to be worth.'

'The *Times?* I just go to Forty-second and Fifth—'

'I know where the library is. I mean the ex-wife.'

'Well, it might not be any trouble at all, actually. Do ex-wives come to memorial services for their ex-husbands? Because that's where I'm going this afternoon. There's a memorial service for him at two-thirty. What's the difference between a memorial service and a funeral?'

'I don't know.'

'I think it's whether or not you have the body around. I guess the police are probably hanging onto the body for an autopsy or something. To make sure he's really dead.'

'They already established cause and time of death.'

'Well, maybe they just aren't releasing the body, or maybe it's being shipped somewhere. *I* don't know. But that's the difference, isn't it? You can't have a funeral without a corpse, can you?'

'Tell that to Tom Sawyer.'

'Funny. Maybe I'll go over to that bar. Pandora's Box.'

'Just Pandora's. Why would you go there?'

'I don't know. The same reason I'm going to the memorial service, I suppose. On the chance that I might run into the little man who wasn't there.'

'I don't see why he would be at the memorial service.'

She shrugged. 'I don't either. But if he's a business acquaintance of Flaxford's he might have to go, and anything's possible, isn't it? And if he's not at the service he might be drowning his sorrows at Pandora's.'

And she went on to explain her reasons for thinking Pandora's might be our friend's regular hangout, and they were pretty much the same reasons which had led me to drop in there for a beer the night before. If he was at the bar or the memorial chapel, she felt certain she'd recognize him from my description.

We sat around talking about this and other things for perhaps another hour before she decided it was time for her to head uptown. Several times I was on the point of mentioning that I'd gone to Pandora's myself just a matter of hours ago, but for one reason or another I never did get around to it.

Once she was gone, the day sagged. She was out doing things, pointless or otherwise, and all I had to do was hang around and kill time. I decided I should have put on the wig and the cap and tagged along after her, and I decided that would have been pretty stupid, since the cops would certainly have a man on duty at the service just as a matter of routine. I found myself wondering if Ruth was aware of this possibility, and if she knew enough not to attract attention there or to be followed when she left.

When you have nothing better to worry about, you make do with what you've got. I decided I ought to let her know about this danger. But I couldn't call her because I didn't have her number and anyway she was going straight to the library. Of course I could call the library and have her paged, except I was by no means certain that they would page people, although I could always claim it was a matter of life and death . . .

No, all that would do was draw attention. So I could put on the wig and the cap and go up to the library and tell her, and no doubt I would corner her in a room where three cops were browsing at the moment, and she'd call me by name, and my cap and wig would fall off.

So instead I went and shaved. I took as much time as possible doing this, soaping and rinsing my face four or five times first, then shaving very carefully and deliberately. I treated myself to the closest shave I'd had in years – unless you count my departure from the Flaxford apartment, heh heh – and I left my moustache unshaven, figuring that it might become a useful part of my disguise, no doubt combining nicely with wig and cap.

Then I dragged the cap and the yellow wig out of the closet and tried them on, and I scrutinized the patch of eighth-of-an-inch fur on my upper lip, and I returned wig and cap to closet shelf and lathered up again and erased the attempted moustache altogether.

And that was about the size of it. I had done as thorough a job of shaving as I possibly could, and the only way to invest more time in the process would be to shave my head. It's an indication of my state of mind that there was a point when I actually considered this, thinking that my wig would fit much better if I had no hair of my own underneath it. Fortunately the notion passed before I could do anything about it.

At one point I did dial my own apartment again, just out of boredom. I got a busy signal and it spooked me until I realized that it didn't necessarily mean my phone was off the hook. It could mean that the circuits were busy, which happens often enough, or it could mean that someone else was trying to call me and he'd gotten connected first. I tried a few minutes later and the phone rang and no one answered it.

I went back to the television set and hopped around the channels. WOR had some reruns of *Highway Patrol* and I sat back and watched Broderick Crawford giving somebody hell. He's always been great at that.

I took out my little ring of keys and picks and weighed it in my hand, while weighing in my head the possibility of giving some of the other apartments in the building a quick shuffle. Just to keep my hand in, say. I could check the buzzers downstairs, get the names, look them up in the phone book, determine over the phone who was home and who wasn't, and go door to door to see what would turn up. Some clothing in my size, say, or some cat food for Esther and Mordecai.

I never really gave this lunacy *serious* consideration. But I was so desperate for things to think about that I did give it some thought.

And then somewhere along the line I dozed off in front of the television set, paying token attention to the story until some indeterminate point where it faded out and my own equally uninspired dreams took over. I don't know exactly when I fell asleep so there's no way of saying just how long I slept, but I'd guess it was more than an hour and less than two.

Maybe a noise outside woke me. Maybe my nap had simply run its course. But I've always thought it was the voice itself; I must have heard and recognized it on some subconscious level.

Whatever the cause, I opened my eyes. And stared. And blinked furiously and stared again.

It was a few minutes after five when Ruth got back. I'd very nearly worn out the rug by then, pacing back and forth across its bare threads, scuttling periodically to the phone, then backing away from it without so much as lifting the receiver. At five o'clock the TV news came on but I was too tautly wired to watch it and could barely pay attention while a beaming chap rattled on and on about something hideous that had just happened in Morocco. (Or Lebanon. One of those places.)

Then Ruth's step on the stairs and her key in the lock, and I opened the door before she could turn the key and she popped energetically inside and spun around to lock the door, the words already spilling from her lips. She seemed to have no end of things to tell me about the weather outside and the facilities at the public library and the service for J. Francis Flaxford, but she might as well have been speaking whatever they speak in Morocco (or Lebanon) for all the attention I was able to pay her.

I cut in right in the middle of a sentence. 'Our fat friend,' I said. 'Was he there?'

'No, I don't think so. Not at the service and not at Pandora's. That's a pretty crummy bar, incidentally. It—'

'So you didn't see him.'

'No, but—'

'Well,' I said. '*I* did.'

59

9

'An actor!'

'An actor,' I agreed. 'I slept through most of the movie. I was just lucky that I woke up for his scene. There he was, looking back over the seat of his cab and asking James Garner where he wanted to go. "*Where to, Mac?*" I think that was the very line I came in on, word for precious word.'

'And you recognized him just like that?'

'No question about it. It was the same man. The picture was filmed fifteen years ago and he's not as young as he used to be, but who do you know that is? Same face, same voice, same build. He's put on a few pounds since then, but who hasn't? Oh, it's him, all right. You'd know him if you saw him. As an actor, I mean. I must have watched him in hundreds of movies and TV shows, playing a cabdriver or a bank teller or a minor hoodlum.'

'What's his name?'

'Who knows? I'm rotten at trivia. And they didn't run the list of credits at the end of the movie. I sat there waiting, and of course Garner never happened to hail that particular cab a second time, not that I really expected him to, and then there were no credits at the end. I guess they cut them a lot of the time when they show movies on television. And they don't always have them in the first place, do they?'

'I don't think so. Would he be listed anyway? If he didn't say more than "*Where to, Mac?*"'

'Oh, he had other lines, Maybe half a dozen lines. You know, talking about the weather and the traffic, doing the typical New York cabbie number. Or at least what Hollywood thinks the typical New York cabbie number ought to be. Did a cabdriver ever say "*Where to, Mac?*" to you?'

'No, but not that many people call me Mac. It's funny. You said he seemed familiar to you and you couldn't figure out where you saw him before.'

'I saw him on the screen. Over and over. That's why even his voice was familiar.' I frowned. 'That's how I recognized him, Ruth. But how in the hell did he recognize me? I'm not an actor. Except in the sense that all the world's a stage. Why would an actor happen to know that Bernie Rhodenbarr is a burglar?'

'I don't know. Maybe—'

'Rodney.'

'Huh?'

'Rod's an actor.'

'So?'

'Actors know each other, don't they?'

'Do they? I don't know. I suppose some of them do. Do burglars know each other?'

'That's different.'

'Why is it different?'

'Burglary is solitary work. Acting is a whole lot of people on a stage or in front of a camera. Actors work with each other. Maybe he worked with this guy.'

'I suppose it's possible.'

'And Rodney knows me. From the poker game.'

'But he doesn't know you're a burglar.'

'Well, I didn't think he did. But maybe he does.'

'Only if he's been reading the New York papers lately. You think Rodney happened to know you were a burglar and then he told this actor, and the other actor decided you'd be just the person to frame for murder, and just to round things out you went from the murder scene to Rodney's apartment.'

'Oh.'

'Just like that.'

'It does call for more than the usual voluntary suspension of disbelief,' I admitted. 'But there are actors all over this thing.'

'Two of them, and only one of them's all over it.'

'Flaxford was connected with the theater. Maybe that's the connection between him and the actor who roped me in. He was a producer, and maybe he had a disagreement with this actor—'

'Who decided to kill him and set up a burglar to take a fall for him.'

'I keep blowing up balloons and you keep sticking pins in them.'

'It's just that I think we should work with what we know, Bernie. It doesn't matter how this man found you, not right now it doesn't. What matters is how you and I are going to find him. Did you notice the name of the picture?'

'*The Man in the Middle*. And it's about a corporate takeover, not a homosexual *ménage à trois* as you might have thought. Starring James Garner and Shan Willson, and I could tell you the names of two or three others but none of them were our friend. It was filmed in 1962 and whoever the droll chap is who does the TV listings in the *Times*, he

61

thinks the plot is predictable but the performances are spritely. That's a word you don't hear much anymore.'

'You wouldn't want to hear it too often.'

'I guess not,' I said. She picked up the phone book and I told her she'd want the Yellow Pages. 'I thought of that,' I said. 'Call one of those film rental places and see if they can come up with a print of the picture. But they'll be closed at this hour, won't they?'

She gave me a funny look and asked me what channel the movie had been on.

'Channel 9.'

'Is that WPIX?'

'WOR.'

'Right.' She closed the phone book, dialed a number. 'You weren't serious about renting the film just so we could see who was in it, were you?'

'Well, sort of.'

'Someone at the channel should have a cast list. They must get calls like this all the time.'

'Oh.'

'Is there any coffee, Bernie?'

'I'll get you some.'

It took more than one call. Evidently the people at WOR were used to getting nutty calls from movie buffs, and since such buffs constituted the greater portion of their audience they were prepared to cater to them. But it seemed that the cast list which accompanied the film only concerned itself with featured performers. Our Typical New York Cabdriver, with his half-dozen typical lines, did not come under that heading.

They kept Ruth on the phone for a long time anyway because the fellow she talked to was certain that an associate of his would be sure to know who played the cabdriver in *Man in the Middle*. The associate in question was evidently a goldmine of such information. But this associate was out grabbing a sandwich, and Ruth was understandably reluctant to supply a callback number, and so they chatted and killed time until the guy came back and got on the line. Of course he didn't remember who played the cabdriver, although he did remember some bit taking place in a cab, and then Ruth tried to describe the pear-shaped man, which I felt was slightly nervy since she'd never seen him, either live or on film. But she echoed my description accurately enough and the conversation went on for a bit and she thanked him very much and hung up.

'He says he knows exactly who I mean,' she reported, 'but he can't remember his name.'

'Sensational.'

'But he found out the film was a Paramount release.'

'So?'

Los Angeles Information gave her the number for Paramount Pictures. It was three hours earlier out there so that people were still at their desks, except for the ones who hadn't come back from lunch yet. Ruth went through channels until she found somebody who told her that the cast list for a picture more than ten years old would be in the inactive files. So Paramount referred her to the Academy of Motion Picture Arts and Sciences, and L.A. Information came through with the number, and Ruth placed the call. Someone at the Academy told her the information was on file and she was welcome to drive over and look it up for herself, which would have been a time-consuming process, the drive amounting to some three thousand miles. They gave her a hard time until she mentioned that she was David Merrick's secretary. I guess that was a good name to mention.

'He's looking it up,' she told me, covering the mouthpiece with her hand.

'I thought you never lie.'

'I occasionally tell an expeditious untruth.'

'How does that differ from a barefaced lie?'

'It's a subtle distinction.' She started to add something to that but someone on the other side of the continent began talking and she said things like *yes* and *uh-huh* and scribbled furiously on the cover of the phone book. Then she conveyed Mr Merrick's thanks and replaced the receiver.

To me she said, 'Which cabdriver?'

'Huh?'

'There are two cabdrivers listed in the complete cast list. There's one called Cabby and another called Second Cabby.' She looked at the notes she had made. 'Paul Couhig is Cabby and Wesley Brill is Second Cabby. Which one do you suppose we want?'

'Wesley Brill.'

'You recognize the name?'

'No, but he was the last cabby in the picture. That would put him second rather than first, wouldn't it?'

'Unless when you saw him he was coming back for an encore.'

I grabbed the directory. There were no Couhigs in Manhattan, Paul or otherwise. There were plenty of Brills but no Wesley.

'It could be a stage name,' she suggested.

'Would a bit player bother with a stage name?'

'Nobody sets out to be a bit player, not at the beginning of a career. Anyway, there might have been another actor with his real name and he would have had to pick out something else for himself.'

'Or he might have an unlisted phone. Or live in Queens, or—'

'We're wasting time.' She picked up the phone again. 'SAG'll have

addresses for both of them. Couhig and Brill.' She asked the Information operator for the number of the Screen Actors Guild, which saved
me from having to ask what SAG was. Then she dialed another ten
numbers and asked someone how to get in touch with our two actor
friends. She wasn't bothering to be David Merrick's secretary this time.
Evidently it wasn't necessary. She waited a few minutes, then made
circles in the air with her pen. I gave the phone book back to her and
she scribbled some more on its cover.

'It's Brill,' she said. 'You were right.'

'Don't tell me they described him for you.'

'He has a New York agent. That's all they would do is give me the
agents' names and numbers, and Couhig's represented by the West
Coast William Morris office and Brill has an agent named Peter Alan
Martin.'

'And Martin's here in New York?'

'Uh-huh. He has an Oregon 5 telephone number.'

'I suppose actors would tend to be on the same coast as their agents.'

'It does sound logical,' she agreed. She began dialing, listened for a
few minutes, then blew a raspberry into the phone and hung up. 'He's
gone for the day,' she said. 'I got one of those answering machines. I
hate the damn things.'

'Everyone does.'

'If my agent had a machine instead of a service I'd get a new agent.'

'I didn't know you had an agent.'

She colored. 'If I had one. If we had some ham we could have ham and
eggs if we had some eggs.'

'We've still got some eggs. In the fridge.'

'Bernie—'

'I know.' I looked again in the phone book. No Wesley Brill, but there
were a couple of Brill, W's. The first two numbers answered and
reported that there was no Wesley there. The third and last went
unanswered, but it was in Harlem and it seemed unlikely that he'd
live there. And telephone listings with initials are almost always
women trying to avoid obscene calls.

'We can find out if he has an unlisted number,' Ruth suggested.
'Information'll tell you that.'

'An actor with an unlisted number? I suppose it's possible. But even
if we find out that he does, what good will it do us?'

'None, I suppose.'

'Then the hell with it.'

'Right.'

'We know who he is,' I said. 'That's the important thing. In the
morning we can call his agent and find out where he lives. What's
really significant is that we've found a place to start. That's the one
thing we didn't have before. If the police kick the door in an hour from

now it'd be a slightly different story from if they'd kicked it in two hours ago. I wouldn't be at a complete dead end, see. I'd have more than a cockeyed story about a round-shouldered fat man with brown eyes. I'd have a name to go with the description.'

'And then what would happen?'

'They'd put me in jail and throw the key away,' I said. 'But nobody's going to kick the door in. Don't worry about a thing, Ruth.'

She went around the corner to a deli and picked up sandwiches and beer, stopped at a liquor store for a bottle of Teachers. I'd asked her to pick up the booze, but by the time she came back with everything I'd decided not to have any. I had one beer with dinner and nothing else.

Afterward we sat on the couch and drank coffee. She had a little Scotch in hers. I didn't. She asked to see my burglar tools and I showed them to her, and she asked the name and function of each item.

'Burglar tools,' she said. 'It's illegal to have them in your possession, isn't it?'

'You can go to jail for it.'

'Which ones did you use to open the locks for this apartment?' I showed her and explained the process. 'I think it's remarkable,' she said, and gave a delicious little shiver. 'Who taught you how to do it?'

'Taught myself.'

'Really?'

'More or less. Oh, once I was really into it I got books on locksmithing, and then I took a mail-order course in it from an outfit in Ohio. You know, I wonder if anybody but burglars ever sign up for those courses. I knew a guy in prison who took one of those courses with a correspondence college and they sent him a different lock every month by mail with complete instructions on how to open it. He would just sit there in his cell and practice with the lock for hours on end.'

'And the prison authorities let him do this?'

'Well, the idea was that he was learning a trade. They're supposed to encourage that sort of thing in prison. Actually the trade he was learning was burglary, of course, and it was a big step up for him from holding up filling stations, which was his original field of endeavor.'

'I guess there's more money in burglary.'

'There often is, but the main consideration was violence. Not that he ever shot anybody but somebody took a shot at him once and he decided that stealing was a safer and saner proposition if you did it when nobody was home.'

'So he took a course and became an expert.'

I shrugged. 'Let's just say he took the course. I don't know if he became an expert or not. There's only so much you can teach a person, through the mails or face to face. The rest has to be inside him.'

'In the hands?'

65

'In the hands and in the heart.' I felt myself blushing at the phrase. 'Well, it's true. When I was twelve years old I taught myself how to open the bathroom door. You could lock it from inside by pressing this button on the doorknob and then the door could be opened from the inside but not from the outside. So that nobody would walk in on you while you were on the toilet or in the tub. The usual privacy lock. But of course you can press the button on the inside and then close the door from the outside and then you've locked yourself out of it.'

'So?'

'So my kid sister did something along those lines, except what she did was lock herself in and then just sit there and cry because she couldn't turn the knob. My mother called the Fire Department and they took the lock apart and rescued her. What's so funny?'

'Any other kid who went through that would decide to become a fireman. But you decided to become a burglar.'

'All I decided was I wanted to know how to open that lock. I tried using a screwdriver blade to get a purchase on the bolt and snick it back, but it didn't have the flexibility. I could almost manage it with a table knife, and then I thought to use one of those plastic calendars insurance men pass out that you keep in your wallet, you know, all twelve months at a glance, and it was perfect. I figured out how to loid that lock without even having heard of the principle involved.'

'Loid?'

'As in celluloid. Any time you've got a lock that you can lock without a key, you know, just by drawing the door shut, then you've got a lock that can be loided. It may be hard or easy depending on how the door and jamb fit together, but it's not going to be impossible.'

'It's fascinating,' she said, and she gave that little shivery shudder again. I went on talking about my earliest experiences with locks and the special thrill I'd always found in opening them, and she seemed as eager to hear all this as I was to talk about it. I told her about the first time I let myself into a neighbor's apartment, going in one afternoon when nobody was home, taking some cold cuts from the refrigerator and bread from the bread drawer, making a sandwich and eating it and putting everything back the way I'd found it before letting myself out.

'The big thing for you was opening locks,' she said.

'Opening locks and sneaking inside. Right.'

'The stealing came later, then.'

'Unless you count sandwiches. But it didn't take long before I was stealing. Once you're inside a place it's a short step to figuring out that it might make sense to leave with more money than you brought with you. Opening doors is a kick, but part of the kick comes from the possibility of profit on the other side of the door.'

'And the danger?'

'I suppose that's part of it.'

'Bernie? Tell me what it's like.'

'Burglary?'

'Uh-huh.' Her face was quite intense now, especially around the eyes, and there was a thin film of perspiration on her upper lip. I put a hand on her leg. A muscle in her upper thigh twitched like a plucked string.

'Tell me how it feels,' she said.

I moved my hand to and fro. 'It feels very nice,' I said.

'You know what I mean. What's it like to open a door and sneak into somebody else's place?'

'Exciting.'

'It must be.' Her tongue flicked at her lower lip. 'Scary?'

'A little.'

'It would have to be. Is the excitement, uh, sexual?'

'Depends on who you find in the apartment.' I laughed a hearty laugh. 'Just a joke. I suppose there's a sexual element. It's obvious enough on a symbolic level, isn't it?' My hand moved as I talked, to and fro, to and fro. 'Tickling all the right tumblers,' I went on. 'Stroking here and there, then ever so gently easing the door open, slipping inside little by little.'

'Yes—'

'Of course your crude type of burglar who uses a pry bar or just plain kicks the door in, he'd be representative of a more direct approach to sex, wouldn't he?'

She pouted. 'You're joking with me.'

'Just a little.'

'I never met a burglar before, Bernie. I'm curious to know what it's like.'

Her eyes looked blue now and utterly guileless. I put a finger under her chin, tipped her head up, placed a little kiss upon the tip of her nose. 'You'll know,' I told her.

'Huh?'

'In a couple of hours,' I said, 'you'll get to see for yourself.'

It made perfect sense to me. She was remarkably good at getting people to tell her things over the phone, and maybe she could worm Wesley Brill's address out of his agent first thing in the morning, but why wait so long? And why chance the agents passing the word to Wesley? Or, if the agent was in on the whole thing, why set his teeth on edge?

On the other hand, Peter Alan Martin's office was located on Sixth Avenue and Sixteenth Street, and if there was anything easier than knocking off an office building after hours I didn't know what it was. At the very least I'd walk out of the building with Brill's address a few hours earlier than we'd get it otherwise, and without arousing suspicions. And if I got lucky – well, it had the same attraction as any burglary. You didn't know what you might find, and it could always turn out to be more than you'd hoped for.

'But you'll be out in the open,' Ruth said. 'People might see you.'

'I'll be disguised.'

Her face brightened. 'We could get some make-up. Maybe Rod has some around. I'll make you up. Maybe a false moustache for a start.'

'I tried a real moustache this afternoon and I wasn't crazy about it. And make-up just makes a person look as though he's wearing make-up, and that's the sort of thing that draws attention instead of discouraging it. Wait here a minute.'

I went to the closet, got the wig and cap, took them into the bathroom and used the mirror to adjust them for the best effect. I came out and posed for Ruth. She was properly appreciative, and I bowed theatrically, and when I did so the cap and wig fell on the rug in front of me. Whereupon she laughed a little more boisterously than I felt the situation absolutely required.

'Not that funny,' I said.

'Oh, nonsense. It was hysterical. A couple of bobby pins will make sure that doesn't happen. It could be embarrassing if your hair fell off on the street.'

Nothing happened last night, I thought. But I didn't say anything. I hadn't mentioned that I'd gone out on my own and I felt it would be awkward to bring it up now.

It was around nine when we left the apartment. I had my ring of tools in my pocket along with my rubber gloves and a roll of adhesive tape I'd found in the medicine cabinet; I didn't think I'd have to break any windows, but adhesive tape is handy if you do and I hadn't cased Martin's office and didn't know what to expect. Ruth had found some bobby pins lurking in the bottom of her bag and she used them to attach the blond wig to my own hair. I could bow clear to the floor now and not worry about dislodging the wig. Of course I'd lose the cap, and she wanted to pin the cap to the wig as well, but I drew the line there.

Outside the door I took Rod's spare keys from her and locked all three locks, then gave them back to her. She looked at them for a moment before dropping them back into her bag. 'You opened all those locks,' she said. 'Without keys.'

'I'm a talented lad.'

'You must be.'

We didn't run into anyone on the way out of the building. Outside the air was fresh and clear and not a touch warmer than it had been the night before. I almost said as much until I remembered I hadn't been out the night before as far as she was concerned. She said it must feel good to be outside after spending two days cooped up, and I said yeah, it sure did, and she said I must be nervous being on the streets with every cop in the city gunning for me, which was something of an exaggeration, and I said yeah, I sure was, but not too nervous, and she took my arm and we headed north and east.

It was a lot safer with her along. Anybody looking at us saw a guy and a girl walking arm in arm, and when that's what meets your eye it doesn't occur to you to wonder if you're eyeballing a notorious fugitive from justice. I was able to relax a good deal more than I had the past night. I think she was edgy at first, but by the time we'd walked a few blocks she was completely at ease and said she couldn't wait until we were inside the agent's office.

I said, 'What you mean *we*, kemosabe?'

'You and me, Tonto. Who else?'

'Uh-uh,' I said. 'Not a chance. I'm the burglar, remember? You're the trusted confederate. You stay on the outskirts and guard the horses.'

She pouted. 'Not fair. You have all the fun.'

'Rank has its privileges.'

'Two heads are better than one, Bernie. And four hands are better than two, and if we're both checking Martin's office things'll go faster.'

I reminded her about too many cooks. She was still protesting when we reached the corner of Sixteenth and Sixth. I figured out which was Martin's building and spotted a Riker's coffee shop diagonally across the street from it. 'You'll wait right there,' I told her, 'in one of those cute little booths with a cup of what will probably not turn out to be the best coffee you ever tasted.'

'I don't want any coffee.'

'Maybe an English muffin along with it if you feel the need.'

'I'm not hungry.'

'Or a prune Danish. They're renowned for their prune Danish.'

'Really?'

'How do I know? You can hold up lanterns in the window. One if by land, two if by sea, and Ruth Hightower'll be on the opposite shore. What's the matter?'

'Nothing.'

'*Two If By Sea*. That's the show Rod's in, did you know that? Anyway, I'll be on the opposite shore, and I won't be terribly long. Get in and get out, quick as a bunny. That's my policy.'

'I see.'

'But only in burglary. It's not my policy in all areas of human endeavor.'

'Huh? Oh.'

I felt lighthearted, even a little lightheaded. I gave her a comradely kiss and steered her toward the Riker's, then squared my shoulders and prepared to do battle.

The building was only a dozen stories high, but the man who built it had probably thought of it as a skyscraper at the time. It was that old, a once-white structure festooned with ornamental ironwork and layered with decades of grime. They don't build them like that anymore and you really can't blame them.

I looked the place over from across the street and didn't see anything that bothered me. Most of the streetside offices were dark. Only a few had lights on – lawyers and accountants working late, cleaning women tidying desks and emptying trashbaskets and mopping floors. In the narrow marble-floored lobby, a white-haired black man in maroon livery sat at a desk reading a newspaper which he held at arm's length. I watched him for a few minutes. No one entered the building, but one man emerged from the elevator and approached the desk. He bent over it for a moment, then straightened up and continued on out of the building, heading uptown on Sixth Avenue.

I slipped into a phone booth on the corner and tried not to pay attention to the way it smelled. I called Peter Alan Martin's office and hung up when the machine answered. If you do that within seven seconds or so you get your dime back. I must have taken eight seconds because Ma Bell kept my money.

When the traffic light changed I trotted across the street. The attendant looked up without interest as I made my way through the revolving doors. I gave him my Number 3 smile, warm but impersonal, and let my eyes have a quick peek at the building directory on the wall while my feet carried me over to his desk. He moved a hand to indicate the ledger and the yellow pencil stub I was to use to sign my name in it. I wrote *T. J. Powell* under Name, *Hubbell Corp.* under Firm, *441* under Room, and *9:25* under Time In. I could have written the Preamble to the Constitution for all the attention the old man gave it, and why not? He was an autograph collector and not a hell of a lot more, a deterrent for people who deterred easily. He'd been posted in the lobby of a fifth-rate office building where the tenants probably had an annual turnover rate of thirty percent. Industrial espionage was hardly likely to occur here, and if the old man kept the junkies from carting off typewriters, then he was earning the pittance they paid him.

The elevator had been inexpertly converted to self-service some years back. It was a rickety old cage and it took its time getting up to the fourth floor, which was where I left it. Martin's office was on six, and I didn't really think my friend in the lobby would abandon his tabloid long enough to see if I went to the floor I'd signed in for, but when you're a professional you tend to do things the right way whether you have to or not. I took the fire stairs up two flights – and they were unusually steep flights at that – and found the agent's office at the far end of the corridor. There were lights burning in only two of the offices I passed, one belonging to a CPA, the other to a firm called Notions Unlimited. No sound came from the accountant's office, but a radio in Notions Unlimited was tuned to a classical music station, and over what was probably a Vivaldi chamber work a girl with an Haute Bronx accent was saying, '. . . told him he had a lot to learn, and do you know what he said to that? You're not going to believe this . . .'

The door to Peter Alan Martin's office was of blond maple with a large pane of frosted glass set into it. The glass had all three of his names on it in black capitals, and *Talent Representative* underneath them. The lettering had been done some time ago and needed freshening up, but then the whole building needed that sort of touch-up work and you knew it wasn't ever going to get it. I could tell without opening the door that Martin wasn't much of an agent and Brill couldn't have much of a career these days. On the outside the building still retained an air of faded grandeur, but in here all of the grandeur had faded away.

The door's single lock had both a snap lock and a deadbolt, and Martin had taken the trouble to turn his key in the lock and put the deadbolt to work. It was hard to figure out why, because locking a door like that is like fencing a cornfield to keep the crows out. Any idiot could simply break the glass and reach inside, and I had adhesive tape that would enable me to break the glass without raising the dead; a few strips crisscrossed on the pane would keep the clatter and tinkle to a minimum.

A broken pane of glass is a calling card, though, especially if they find it with tape on it. Since I didn't expect to steal anything, I had the opportunity to get in and out without anyone ever knowing I'd existed. So I took the time to pick the lock, and there was precious little time involved. I knocked off the deadbolt easily, and loiding the snap lock was more than easy. There was a good quarter-inch of air between the wooden door and its wooden jamb, and a child with a butter spreader could have let himself in.

'What's it like, Bernie?'

Well, there was a little excitement in turning the knob and easing the door open, then slipping inside and closing the door and locking up.

I had my pencil light with me but I left it in my pocket and switched on the overhead fluorescents right away. A little flashlight winking around in that office might have looked strange from outside, but this way it was just another office with the lights on and I was just another poor bastard working late.

I moved around quickly, taking the most perfunctory sort of inventory. An old wooden desk, a gray steel steno desk with typewriter, a long table, a couple of chairs. I got the feel of the layout while establishing that there were no corpses tucked in odd places, then went over to the window and looked out. I could see Riker's but couldn't look inside. I wondered if Ruth was at a front table and if she might be looking up at my very window. But I didn't wonder about this for very long.

I checked my watch. Nine thirty-six.

Martin's office was shabby and cluttered. One entire wall was covered with dark brown cork tiles which had been inexpertly cemented to it. Thumbtacks and pushpins held glossy photographs in place. The greater portion of these photos showed women, who in turn showed the greater portion of themselves. Most of them showed their legs, many showed their breasts, and every one of them flashed a savage mechanical smile. I thought of Peter Alan Martin sitting at his cluttered desk and gazing up at all those teeth and I felt a little sorry for him.

There were a few head and shoulders shots in among the sea of tits and legs, a couple of male faces in the crowd. But I didn't see the face I was looking for.

Next to the white touchtone phone on the desk stood a Rolodex wheel of phone numbers and addresses. I flipped through it and found Wesley Brill's card. This didn't really come as a surprise, but all the same I felt a little thrill when I actually located what I was looking for. I tried a couple of Martin's Flair pens, finally found one that worked, and copied down *Wesley Brill, Hotel Cumberland, 326 West 58th, 541-7255.* (I don't know why I wrote down his name, I don't know why I wrote down anything, come to think of it, because all I had to do was remember the name of the hotel and the rest would be in the phone book. Listen, nobody's perfect.)

I put my rubber gloves on at about this point and wiped the surfaces I remembered touching, not that any of them seemed likely to take a print and not that anyone would be looking for prints in the first place. I checked the Rolodex for Flaxford, not really expecting to find his name, and was not vastly surprised when it wasn't there.

There were three old green metal filing cabinets on the opposite side of the window from the cork wall. I gave them a quick look-through and found Brill's file. All it held was a sheaf of several dozen 8 by 10 glossies. If Martin had any correspondence with or about Brill he either threw it out or kept it elsewhere.

But it was the pictures that interested me. Only when I saw them did I know for certain that Wesley Brill was the man who had set me up for a murder rap. Until then there was still some room for doubt. All those long-distance phone calls had had us operating in something of a vacuum, but here was Brill in living black and white and there was no doubt about it. I flipped through the pictures and picked out a composite shot, half a dozen head-and-shoulders pics arranged to show various facial expressions and attitudes. I knew it wouldn't be missed – mostly likely the whole file wouldn't have been missed, and possibly the entire filing cabinet that contained it – and I folded it twice and put it in a pocket.

Martin's desk wasn't locked. I went through it quickly, mechanically, without finding anything to tell me much about Wesley Brill. I did come upon a mostly-full pint of blended whiskey in the bottom drawer and an unopened half-pint of Old Mr Boston mint-flavored gin snuggled up next to it. Both of these were infinitely resistible. In the wide center drawer I found an envelope with some cash in it, eighty-five dollars in fives and tens. I took a five and two tens to cover expenses, put the rest back, closed the drawer, then changed my mind and opened it again and scooped up the rest of the money, leaving the empty envelope in the drawer. Now if I left any evidence of my presence, if the clutter I left behind struck him as different from the clutter he'd left there himself, he'd simply think it was the work of some hot-prowl artist who'd made off with his mad money.

(Then why was I disguising my presence in every other respect? Ah, you've spotted an inconsistency, haven't you? All right, I'll tell you why I took the eighty-five bucks. I've never believed in overlooking cash. That's why.)

But I *was* careful to overlook what I found in the top left-hand drawer. It was a tiny little revolver with a two-inch barrel and pearlized grips, and tiny or not it looked very menacing. I leaned into the drawer to sniff intelligently at the barrel the way they're always doing on television. Then they state whether or not the gun's been fired recently. All I could state was that I smelled metal and mineral oil and what you usually smell in a musty desk drawer, a drawer which I was now very happy to close once I got my nose out of it.

Guns make me nervous, and you'd be surprised how many times a burglar will run across one. I only once had one pointed at me and that was one I've mentioned, the gun of good old Carter Sandoval, but I've found them in drawers and on night tables and, more than once, tucked beneath a pillow. People buy the hateful things to shoot burglars with, or at least that's what they tell themselves, and then they wind up shooting themselves or each other accidentally or on purpose.

A lot of burglars steal guns automatically, either because they have a use for them or because it's a cinch to get fifty or a hundred dollars for a nice untraceable handgun. And I knew one fellow who specialized in suburban homes who always took guns with him so that the next burglar to hit that place wouldn't be risking a bullet. He took every gun he encountered and always dropped them down the nearest sewer. 'We have to look out for each other,' he told me.

I've never stolen a gun and I didn't even contemplate stealing Martin's. I don't even like to touch the damned things and I closed the drawer without touching this one.

At nine fifty-seven I let myself out of the office. The corridor was empty. Faint strains of Mozart wafted my way from the Notions Unlimited office. I wasted a minute relocking the door, though I could have let him figure he'd forgotten to lock up. Anybody with Peter Alan Martin's taste in booze probably greeted the dawn with a fairly spotty memory of the previous day.

I even walked down to the fourth floor before I rang for the elevator. Nobody was home at Hubbell Corp. I rode the elevator to the lobby, found my name in the ledger – three people had come in since my arrival, and one of them had left already. I penciled in *10 P.M.* under Time Out and wished the old man in the wine-colored uniform a pleasant evening.

'They all the same,' he said. 'Good nights and bad nights, all one and the same to me.'

I caught Ruth's eye from Riker's doorway. The place was fairly de-serted, a couple of cabbies at the counter, two off-duty hookers in the back booth. Ruth put some coins on her table next to her coffee cup and hurried to join me. 'I was starting to worry,' she said.

'Not to worry.'

'You were gone a long time.'

'Half an hour.'

'Forty minutes. Anyway, it seemed like hours. What happened?'

She took my arm and I told her about it as we walked. I was feeling very good. I hadn't accomplished anything that remarkable but I felt a great sense of exhilaration. Everything was starting to go right now, I could feel it, and it was a nice feeling.

'He's in a hotel in the West Fifties,' I told her. 'Just off Columbus Circle, near the Coliseum. That's why he didn't have a listed phone. I never heard of the hotel and I have a feeling it's not in the same class with the Sherry-Netherland. In fact I think our Mr Brill has had hard times lately. He's got a loser for an agent, that's for sure. Most of Peter Alan Martin's clients are ladies who came in third in a county-wide beauty contest a whole lot of years ago. I think he's the kind of agent you call when you want someone to come out of the cake at a bachelor party. Do they still have that sort of thing?'

'What sort of thing?'

'Girls popping out of cakes.'

'You're asking me? How would I know?'

'That's a point.'

'I never popped out of a cake myself. Or attended a bachelor party.'

'Then you wouldn't want Martin to represent you. I wonder why he's representing Brill. The guy's had tons of work over the years. Here, you'll recognize him.' We moved under a street light and I unfolded the composite sheet for her. 'You must have seen him hundreds of times.'

'Oh,' she said. 'Of course I have. Movies, TV.'

'Right.'

'I can't think where offhand but he's definitely a familiar face. I can even sort of hear his voice. He was in – I can't think exactly what he was in, but—'

'*Man in the Middle*,' I suggested. 'Jim Garner, Shan Willson, Wes Brill.'

'Right.'

'So how come he's on the skids? He's got two last names, his agent's got three first names, and he's living in some dump across from the Coliseum and consorting with known criminals. Why?'

'That's one of the things you'll want to ask him tomorrow.'

'One, of several things.'

We walked a little farther in silence. Then she said, 'It must have been a new experience for you, Bernie. Letting yourself into his office and not stealing anything.'

'Well, when I first started my criminal career all I stole was a sandwich. And I haven't stolen anything from Rod outside of a little Scotch and a couple cans of soup.'

'Sounds as though you're turning over a new leaf.'

'Don't count on it. Because I did steal something from Whatsisname. Martin.'

'The photograph? I don't think that counts.'

'Plus eighty-five dollars. That must count.' And I went on to tell her about the money in the desk drawer.

'My God,' she said.

'What's the matter?'

'You really *are* a burglar.'

'No kidding. What did you think I was?'

She shrugged. 'I guess I'm terribly naive. I keep forgetting that you actually steal things. You were in that man's office and there was some money there so you automatically took it.'

I had a clever answer handy but I left it alone. Instead I said, 'Does it bother you?'

'I wouldn't say that it bothers me. Why should it bother me?'

'I don't know.'

'I guess it confuses me.'

'I suppose that's understandable.'

'But I don't think it bothers me.'

We didn't talk much the rest of the way home. When we crossed Fourteenth Street I took her hand and she let me keep it the rest of the way, until we got to the building and she used her key on the downstairs door. The key didn't fit perfectly and it took her about as long to unlock the door as it had taken me to open it without a key. I said as much to her while we climbed the stairs and she laughed. After we'd climbed three of the four flights she walked up to 4-F and started to poke a key in the lock.

'It won't fit,' I said.

'Huh?'

'Wrong apartment. That one's unfit for military service.'

'What?'

'Four-F. The draft classification. We're looking for 5-R, remember?'

'Oh, for God's sake,' she said. Her face reddened. 'I was thinking I was at my place. On Bank Street.'

'You're in the fourth floor front?'

'Well, fourth floor at the top of the stairs. There are four apartments to a floor; it's not as narrow a building as this one.' We walked to the final flight of stairs and began climbing them. 'I'm glad no one opened the door while we were there. It would have been embarrassing.'

'Don't worry about it now.'

In front of Rod's apartment she fished her keys out again, paused for a moment, then turned and deliberately dropped them back into her bag.

'I seem to have misplaced my keys,' she said.

'Come on, Ruth.'

'Let's see you open it without them. You can do it, can't you?'

'Sure, but what's the point?'

'I guess I'd like to see you do it.'

'It's silly,' I said. 'Suppose someone happens to come along and sees me standing there playing lock-smith. It's an unnecessary risk. And these locks are tricky. Well, the Medeco is, anyhow. It can be a bitch to open.'

'You managed before, didn't you?'

'Sure, but—'

'I already fed the cats.' I turned and stared at her. 'Esther and Mordecai. I already fed them.'

'Oh,' I said.

'This afternoon, on my way back here. I filled their water dish and left them plenty of dried food.'

'I see.'

'I think it would excite me to watch you open the locks. I told you I felt confused about the whole thing. Well, I do. I think watching you unlock the locks, uh, I think it would get me, uh, hot.'

'Oh.'

I took my ring of picks out of my pocket.

'I suppose this is all very perverted of me,' she said. She put an arm around my waist, leaned her hot little body against mine. 'Kinky and all.'

'Probably,' I said.

'Does it bother you?'

'I think I can learn to live with it,' I said. And went to work on those locks.

Quite a while later she said, 'Well, it looks as though I was right. I'm a kinkier bitch than I realized.' She yawned richly and snuggled up close. I ran a hand lazily over her body, memorizing the contours of hip and thigh, the secret planes and valleys. My heart was beating normally again, more or less. I lay with my eyes closed and listened to the muffled hum of traffic in the streets below.

She said, 'Bernie? You have wonderful hands.'

'I should have been a surgeon.'

'Oh, do that some more, it's divine. No wonder all the locks open for you. I don't think you really need all those curious implements after all. Just stroke the locks a little and they get all soft and mushy inside and open right up.'

'You're a wee bit flaky, aren't you?'

'Just a wee bit. But you have got the most marvelous hands. I wish I had hands like yours.'

'There's nothing wrong with your hands, baby.'

'Really?'

And her hands began to move.

'Hey,' I said.

'Something the matter?'

'Just what do you think you're doing, lady?'

'Just what do *you* think I'm doing?'

'Playing with fire.'

'Oh?'

The first time had been intense and urgent, even a bit desperate. Now we were slow and lazy and gentle with each other. There was no music on the radio, just the sound of the city below us, but in my head I heard smoky jazz full of blue notes and muted brass. At the end I said *'Ruth Ruth Ruth'* and closed my eyes and died and went to Heaven.

I awoke first in the morning. For a moment something was wrong. The ghost of a dream was flickering somewhere behind my closed eyelids and I wanted to catch hold of it and ask it its name. But it was gone, out of reach. I lay still for a moment, taking deep breaths. Then I turned on my side and she was there beside me and for this I was grateful. At first I did nothing but look at her and listen to the even rhythm of her breathing. Then I thought of other things to do, and then I did them.

Eventually we got out of bed, took our turns in the bathroom, and put on the clothes we'd thrown off hastily the night before. She made the coffee and burned the toast and we sat down in silence and had breakfast.

There was something wrong with this particular silence. Ray Kirschmann's young partner Loren would have slapped his battered nightstick against his palm and said something inarticulate about vibrations, and maybe that would have been as good an explanation as any. Perhaps I read something in the tilt of her head, the set of her chin. I didn't know exactly what it was but something was not at all right.

I said, 'What's the matter, Ruth?'

'Ruth,' she said.

'Huh?'

'*Dear Ruth.* That's a play.'

'Baby Ruth,' I said. 'That's a candy bar.'

'Ruth Ruth Ruth. You said that last night. And this morning, too. At the very end.'

'*You* said "Sweet fucking shit I'm coming," but I hadn't planned on throwing it in your face for breakfast. If you don't like your name why don't you change it?'

'I like my name fine.'

'Then what's the trouble?'

'Shit. Look, Bernie, if you keep calling me Ruth I'm going to start calling you Roger.'

'Huh?'

'As in Armitage.'

'Oh,' I said. Then my eyes widened a bit and my jaw slackened and I said *Oh* again, but with a little more conviction, and she gave a slow nod.

'Your name isn't Ruth Hightower.'

'Too true.' She averted her eyes. 'Well, *you* were calling yourself Roger and I knew that wasn't *your* name and I thought we ought to start on an equal footing. And then we got it straightened out who you were and it just seemed easier for me to go on being Ruth. There was never a convenient time to tell you.'

'Until now.'

'If you're going to murmur a name into my ear at intimate moments I'd just as soon you got the name right.'

'I guess I can understand that. Well?'

'Well what?'

'Well, what's your name? Take plenty of time, kid. Make sure you come up with one that'll sound nice in a husky whisper.'

'That's not nice.'

'Not nice! Here I am feeling like an utter zip, cooing some alias into your pink shell-like ear, and you tell me I'm not nice?' I turned her face so that I could see her eyes. There were tears welling up in their corners. 'Hey,' I said. 'Hey, come on now.'

She blinked furiously but the tears did not go away. She blinked some more, then erased the tears with the back of her hand. 'I'm all right,' she said.

'Of course you are.'

'My name's Ellie.'

'For Eleanor?'

'For Elaine, but Ellie'll do just fine.'

'Ellie what? Not Hightower, I don't suppose.'

'Ellie Christopher.'

'Pretty name.'

'Thank you.'

'I think it suits you. But then I thought Ruth Hightower suited you pretty well, so who am I to say? What do I know? Is Christopher your married name?'

'No. I took my maiden name back after the divorce.'

'What was your husband's name?'

'What's the difference?'

'I don't know.'

'Are you angry with me, Bernie?'

'Why should I be angry?'

'You didn't answer my question.'

I went on not answering it and finished my coffee, then got to my feet. 'We've both got things to do,' I said. 'I want to go to my apartment.'

'I don't know if that's safe.'

I didn't either but I didn't feel like talking about it. I couldn't believe the cops would have my place staked out, not at this point, and a phone call would let me know if there was anyone on the premises at the moment. And I really wanted clean clothes, and I had the feeling it would be nice to have my case money on hand. Things were almost ready to come to a head and the five grand I'd tucked away at my place might turn out to be useful.

'Things to do,' I said. 'You want to go back to your place and change your clothes, freshen up, that sort of thing. And feed your cats.'

'I suppose so.'

'And empty the catbox and put out fresh kitty litter, all those things. Take the garbage out to the incinerator. The little day-to-day chores that eat up so much of a person's time.'

79

'Bernie—'

'Do you really have cats? Abyssinians? And are their names really Esther and Ahasuerus?'

'Esther and Mordecai.'

'There's a lot I don't know about you, isn't there?'

'Not so very damned much. I don't see what you're so thoroughly pissed about.'

I didn't either, exactly. But I glared at her anyway.

'Give me a little room, huh? I'm just a neighborhood kid who wandered in one morning to water the plants.'

'Well, you don't owe me anything, that's for sure.'

'Bernie—'

'I'll meet you at the Childs on Eighth Avenue and Fifty-eighth Street,' I said. 'That'll be a few doors from his hotel. Do you still want to come along?'

'Of course. And I'll dress up like we said last night? Nothing's changed, Bernie.'

I let that pass and looked at my watch. 'It's a quarter after ten,' I said. 'Figure two hours to do everything we have to do plus a margin for error, so that makes what? I'll meet you at the restaurant at twelve-thirty. How does that sound?'

'It sounds fine.'

I got the wig and cap and she came around and helped me with the bobby pins. I wanted to do it myself but I forced myself to stand still while she poked around there. 'If I'm not there by one o'clock,' I said, 'you can assume I got arrested.'

'That's not funny.'

'Lots of things aren't. Don't forget to lock up. The streets are full of burglars.'

'Bernie—'

'I mean it. It's a jungle out there.'

'Bernie—'

'What?'

'Just be careful.'

'Oh, I'm always careful,' I said, and let myself out.

11

In the taxi heading uptown I thought about Ellie (whom I found myself
still thinking of as Ruth) and wondered why I'd gotten so steamed with
her. She told me a lie or three, but so what? On balance she'd placed
herself in jeopardy to help a total stranger who looked to be a murderer
in the bargain. On the strength of her vaunted intuition she'd put
herself on the line for me. So what if she kept her name to herself?
That seemed like no more than a sensible precaution – if I got nailed by
the long arm of the law, I wouldn't be able to drag her into it. Not so
long as I didn't know who she was.

And then, when the old animal passions began to churn, she felt bad
about the deception. So she told me her name and everything was right
out in the open where it belonged.

So what was my problem?

Well, for openers, I'd been honest with her. And that was a new
experience for me. In all my previous relationships with women, a
central fact was always kept secret. Whatever else women learned
about me – what I ate for breakfast, what I wore to bed, how I like to
make love, whether I preferred the smooth or the crunchy peanut
butter – they never got to find out what I did for a living. I would
explain that I was between positions or that I had a private income or
was in investments. Occasionally, if we were not likely to be more to
each other than two ships passing in the night, I would equip myself
with an interesting business or profession for the duration. At one time
or another I had been a magazine illustrator, a neurosurgeon, a com-
poser of modern classical music, a physical education instructor, a
stockbroker, and an Arizona land developer.

And I'd always been comfortable playing one of these roles. I'd
always told myself that I did this sort of thing because I couldn't afford
to let a lady friend know what I really did to support myself, but now I
wondered if that was true after all. The more I thought about some of
those ladies, the more I got the feeling that they might have reacted
pretty much the way Ellie did. Burglary, after all, is the sort of career people are apt to perceive as exciting, the moral implications

notwithstanding, and it's been my observation that most women have highly adaptable moral systems.

I'd kept my career a secret because I liked being secretive. Because I didn't want anyone to know me all that well.

With Ruth – no, dammit, Ellie, the woman's name is Ellie, at least until she tells me different – with Ellie, I had no choice. And as a result she'd gotten very close to the real Bernard Rhodenbarr, and at the same time I'd found out what it was like to be intimate with a girl without holding so much of myself in reserve.

And all along I was whispering the wrong name into her ear. The shoe was on the other foot. That's what it was. All those years of automatically lying to women and now one of them had turned the tables, and I didn't seem to like it much.

I let the cab drop me right at my door. Not the front door, though, but the service entrance around the corner. I gave the driver one of Peter Alan Martin's limp five-dollar bills and sent him on his way. Easy come, easy go.

I'd been prepared to pick the service entrance lock in broad daylight, that being safer on the balance than slipping past the doorman, but I didn't have to exert any of my special talents because the door was wide open when I got to it. Two enormous men were carrying a small spinet piano through it. I stood aside while they cleared the doorway and went on to load the thing into an unmarked half-ton panel truck. Either they were unlicensed gypsy movers or they'd gone into the business of stealing pianos, which seemed unlikely but by no means impossible, New York being New York. Whatever they were doing was clearly no concern of mine, so I went on into the basement and took the elevator up to the sixteenth floor without attracting any attention whatsoever.

The long narrow corridor was happily empty. I hurried down its length to my very own door, dug my personal key ring out of my pocket, and was about to indulge myself in the unaccustomed luxury of opening a door with a key. Then I got a sudden flash that there was someone in the apartment and cursed myself for not calling up first. I extended a finger to ring my bell, then withdrew it. Either the person inside would just freeze and not answer the bell or he'd yank it open and slap cuffs on me.

I hesitated. I glanced down at my hand, the hand that held the key, and my fingers were trembling. I told myself this was silly and I told my fingers to cut it out and they did. Then I stopped looking at my fingers and looked instead at my lock, or more accurately looked where it had been the last time I'd been home.

There was a neat round hole in the door where my Rabson cylinder belonged. Above it, the Yale springlock the landlord supplied was still in place, but my key wouldn't go into it. I dropped to one knee and had a look at it and it wasn't the original equipment. I could see marks around it where someone had scratched and gouged the door in the process of demolishing the old lock, and now they'd put on a new one to keep people from walking in at will.

I peered through the hole where my sixty-dollar Rabson had been, but the apartment was dark and I couldn't see anything, so I went through the rather absurd ritual of picking my own lock to let myself in. By then I had a feeling I knew what I would find, because it was already clear to me that I'd had more than one set of visitors. The cops might have drilled the Rabson out if they didn't have anyone on hand who could pick it, but they'd have had the super use his key on the other lock, the one that came with the apartment. They certainly wouldn't have employed brute force to kick it in, not after they'd taken the trouble to drill the Rabson. So someone else had come along afterward, someone not inclined to be gentle and painstaking, and that gave me an idea of what my apartment would look like.

But I still wasn't prepared for what lay within. I let myself inside, closing the door and flicking on the light in a single motion, and just like that I was transported to Dresden after the bombing. The place had been turned upside-down and inside-out, and after what had been done to it I couldn't imagine why the super had put a new lock on the door, because no future intruder could have made things any worse than they already were.

Everything I owned was in the middle of the living room floor. Chair cushions had been slashed and the stuffing torn out. Every book had wound up off the shelves and on the floor after having first been taken by the covers and shaken so that anything tucked between its pages would fall out. The wall-to-wall broadloom, imperfectly installed in the first place, had been yanked up so that whatever I might have secreted between it and the padding, or between padding and floor, could be discovered.

God, what a mess! I have always been the neatest of burglars, having nothing but respect for the private property of others, whether I intended to leave that property in their hands or transfer it into my own. The utter lack of consideration my visitors had shown literally sickened me. I had to sit down, but I couldn't find a place to sit. There was not a single inviting surface in that apartment. I managed to put an unupholstered (hence unslashed) chair on its feet and planted myself on it.

What was the point of all this?

The police, of course, would have searched the apartment if only to assure themselves that I wasn't in it. They might have made off with an address book in the hope that it would lead them to possible associates and friends of mine. But the cops, however much they

83

might dislike me for having made them look fairly foolish, would not react by waging total war on my apartment. This carnage was clearly the work of whoever had kicked the door in.

But *why?*

Someone had been looking for something. While no pack of adolescent vandals could have been more destructive, there was too much method to this particular madness for it to be simple vandalism. I was perfectly willing to believe the bastards had enjoyed their work, but all of their efforts had been undertaken with the aim of finding something.

What?

I walked from room to room, trying to figure it out. The little kitchen, never my favorite room at the best of times, had been sacked. I hadn't kept anything in it more valuable than canned ravioli, so there was no reason to waste time looking at the mess. They'd even dumped the contents of the refrigerator, so *mess* was the right word for it.

The bedroom had received similar treatment. I ignored the disorder as much as I could and waded through it to the bedroom closet. I'd built a false back wall into that closet just above the overhead shelf, giving myself a space five feet wide and three feet high and some fifteen inches deep that the building's own architect couldn't have found unless he knew what he was looking for. I used that space to stow whatever I might bring back from a midnight shopping spree, holding it there until I'd made arrangements to fence it. I'd had no end of swag tucked away there at one time or another, though never for terribly long. There'd been nothing in it when I was last in the apartment except for a passport and the sort of personal papers other people keep in safe deposit boxes, but I wanted to see if my visitors, thorough as they'd been, had found my hiding place.

They'd been in the closet, certainly. They had thrown all my clothing onto the bed, pausing only to rip out an occasional jacket lining. But they hadn't found my hiding place and that made me feel a little better. I opened it up, easing the panel out of its moorings, and there were my passport and high school diploma and class picture and sundry treasures. I found myself wishing I'd left a satchel full of emeralds in there just so the bastards could have missed them.

Then I went back to the living room and began sifting through the pile of books. At least half of them had their bindings wholly or partially demolished by the treatment they'd been given. I paid as little attention to this as possible, merely going through the heap until I'd found three individual volumes. These were the book-club edition of *The Guns of August*, the second volume of the three-volume Heritage Press edition of Gibbon's *Decline and Fall of the Roman Empire*, and something called *The Romance of Beekeeping*, which I'd bought because the title struck me as a contradiction in terms. All three books had seen much better days and the cover of the beekeeping book was now attached to the text by a thread and a prayer, but that was all right. I didn't care. I toted the three books into the bedroom and put them on top of my dresser. There was plenty of room there because my visitors had tipped everything that used to be on the top of the dresser onto the floor. Considerate of them to make room for the books.

There was a smallish canvas suitcase in the closet. My leather suitcase had been carved up by a lunatic looking for a secret compartment, I suppose, but the canvas bag was so flimsy that it was obviously hiding nothing. I put my three books in it and added clean clothing from the pile on my bed and the other pile on the bedroom floor. I left myself a change of clothes, packed enough socks and shirts and underwear to last a few days, zipped up the suitcase, then took off the clothes I'd been wearing. I dropped them on the floor along with everything else and went into the bathroom to take a shower.

It was a sloppy shower because my good friends had pulled down the rod that holds the shower curtain in place. They'd also yanked the towel bars loose from their moorings. Some of these bars are hollow and some people hide things in them. I've never been able to understand why; the stash winds up being hard for its owner to get at, while a prowler or cop can reach it in a second by ripping the bar off the wall.

I've noticed over the years that your average person is not terribly good at hiding things.

Anyway, I had to shower without the benefit of shower curtain, which meant that an awful lot of water wound up on the floor. There were clothes and things there to absorb most of it as it landed. Somehow I just couldn't bring myself to care what happened to the floor or the clothes or the whole apartment, because I was never going to have anything to do with any of them again. I couldn't live in the apartment even if I wanted to, and now I no longer wanted to, so the hell with all of it.

I finished my shower, kicked clothing aside until I found a couple of towels to dry myself with, put on my clean clothes and slid my feet into my best pair of scotch-grain loafers. Then I added a few more things to my suitcase – my own razor, some other toilet articles, a vial of hay fever pills (although it wasn't the season) and a rabbit's foot key chain with no keys on it that I'd given up for lost ages ago. It must have been hiding out in the back of a dresser drawer or something and my guests had located it for me in the process of dumping the drawer. An ill wind that blows no good, said I to myself, and paused in my labors to transfer the rabbit's foot from the suitcase to my pocket, then paused again and attached it to my little ring of picks and keys and such. As little good as the foot may have done its original rabbit owner, it had always been lucky for me, and nowadays I seemed to need all the help I could get. I took a last look around; wondering what I hoped to find. I picked up my telephone, wondered if it was tapped, decided that it probably wasn't. But who was I going to call? I hung up and found the phone book, which had received the dump and shake treatment like every other book in the apartment. I picked it up and looked for Elaine Christopher without success. There were several E Christophers listed but none on Bank Street. I decided that the lady's listing or lack thereof was one of an ever-increasing number of things I couldn't be bothered to think about.

So I hefted my suitcase, killed the lights, opened the door, stepped out into the hallway, and there was Mrs Hesch.

She was wearing a shapeless housedress with faded flowers on it. (Printed on it, that is. Not pinned to it or anything like that.) She had cloth slippers on her feet and her gray hair was pinned up in a sort of sloppy chignon. An unfiltered cigarette with a good half-inch of ash hung from the right corner of her wide mouth. I'd seen her in this outfit before, or in one very much like it. I'd also seen her dressed to the nines, but I'd never seen her without a cigarette smoldering in the corner of her mouth. She never took it out to talk and I'm not positive she removed it when she ate.

'Mr Rhodenbarr,' she said. 'I thought I heard you moving around in there. Meaning I thought I heard somebody. I didn't know it was you.'

'Uh,' I said. 'Well, it was.'

'Yeah.' Her bright little eyes took in the suitcase. 'Going someplace? Not that I blame you. Poor boy, you got some kind of trouble for yourself, huh? The years we live across the hall from each other, you and me, and whoever would guess a nice boy like you would be a burglar? You never bothered anybody in this building, did you?'

'Of course not.'

'Exactly what I said. You know the kind of conversations you hear in the laundry room. There are crazy women in this building, Mr Rhodenbarr. One the other day, she's running off at the mouth like a broken record. "We ain't safe in our own beds!" I said to her, "Gert," I said, "in the first place you'd be safe in anybody's bed, believe me." And I said to her, I said, "When did Mr Rhodenbarr ever hurt anybody? Who did he ever rob in this building, and who cares what he does over on the East Side, where the rich *momsers* deserve whatever happens to them?" You might as well be talking to a wall.' Ashes spilled from her cigarette. 'We shouldn't stand here like this,' she said, her voice pitched lower. 'Come on into my place, I got coffee on the stove.'

'I'm really in sort of a rush, Mrs Hesch.'

'Don't be ridiculous. You always got time for a cup of my coffee. Since when are you in such a rush?'

I followed her into the apartment as if hypnotized. She poured me a cup of really excellent coffee and while I sipped it she stubbed out her cigarette and replaced it immediately with a fresh one. She went on to tell me how I'd brought no end of excitement to the building, how the police had been in and out of my apartment, and how there had been other visitors as well.

'I didn't see them,' she said, 'but the door was wide open when they left. It was yesterday afternoon when Jorge put the new lock on it. I saw what they did to your apartment. Like animals, Mr Rhodenbarr. Except an animal wouldn't do nothing like that. Who was it? Cops?'

'I don't think so.'

'You know who it was?'

'No, I wish I did. You didn't see them?'

'I don't even know when they were there. Such a mess they made you'd think I'd of heard them, but when I got the set going I don't hear nothing. You don't know who did this thing? Is it mixed up with the man you killed?'

'I never killed anybody, Mrs Hesch.'

She nodded thoughtfully, neither buying nor rejecting the statement. 'I can imagine you a burglar,' she said slowly. 'But killing somebody is something else again. I said as much to the cop that questioned me.'

'They questioned you?'

'They questioned the building, believe me. Listen, I didn't tell them a thing. I'll be honest with you, I got no use for the *momsers*. The time my niece Gloria was raped all they did was ask her stupid questions. What I told them about you was you're a nice boy who would never hurt a cockroach. I wouldn't tell a cop if his pants was on fire, believe me. But what he told me, the cop, he told me you ran into this Flaxford – that's his name?'

'Flaxford, right.'

'He says when Flaxford discovered you, you panicked, but I thought about this, Mr Rhodenbarr, and I don't know if I can see you killing somebody in a panic. You didn't do it?'

'Definitely not, Mrs Hesch. In fact I'm trying to find out who did.'

'If you say so.' She was still keeping an open mind on the subject. 'Though to be frank, those *momsers* on the East Side, what do I care if you did or didn't? They got it coming is how I look at it. This is good coffee, isn't it?'

'The best.'

'Coffee's one thing I make a fuss about. You got to take the trouble or you're drinking dishwater. Maybe you're hungry, I didn't think to ask. You like cinnamon buns?'

'I just had breakfast, Mrs Hesch, but thanks.'

'Sit anyway. Where are you going? Sit, you'll have another cup. You don't have to be in such a hurry. One more cup of coffee ain't gonna kill you. Sit!'

I sat.

'So you're a burglar,' she said. 'You mind a personal question? You make a pretty decent living at it?'

I manage.

She nodded. 'Exactly what I told Whatsername in 11-J. I said a bright boy like that, clean-cut and a good dresser, always a smile or a nice word for a person, I said if he ain't making a living he'll get into something else. But it's like talking to a wall, believe me, and then the other one, Gert, she starts in how she's not safe in her bed. The people in this building, Mr Rhodenbarr, take it from me, it's like talking to a wall.'

12

Most people who checked into the Cumberland had either a suitcase or a girl in tow. I was unusual in that I had one of each with me. My canvas suitcase looked slightly disreputable, but then so did my girl. She was wearing skintight jeans and a bright green sweater a size too small for her with no bra under it. And she'd done something moderately sluttish to her hair, and she was wearing dark lipstick and several pounds of eye shadow. She looked remarkably tawdry.

The clerk looked her over while I registered us as Mr and Mrs Ben G. Roper of Kansas City, which might have made more sense had my luggage been monogrammed. I gave him back the registration card along with a pair of ten-dollar bills, and while he was finding my change Ellie slid an envelope onto the counter. The clerk gave me $6.44 or thereabouts, then spotted the envelope with Brill's name printed on it and blinked. 'Where'd this come from?' he wondered.

I shrugged and Ellie said she thought it was there all along. The clerk didn't seem terribly interested in this or much of anything else. He stuck it in a pigeonhole numbered 305.

Our own key was numbered 507. I grabbed my bag – there was no bellhop at the Cumberland – and Ellie walked with me to the elevator, her behind swaying professionally to and fro. The old man in the elevator cage chewed his cigar and took us up to the fifth floor without a word, then left us to let ourselves into our room.

It wasn't much of a room. The bed, which took up most of it, looked as though it had had hard use. Ellie sat lightly on the edge of it, removed make-up, did something to her hair to make it as it had been originally.

'A lot of trouble for nothing,' she said.

'You enjoyed the masquerade.'

'I suppose so. I still look like a tramp in this sweater.'

'You certainly look like a mammal, I'll say that much.'

She glowered at me. I checked my wig and cap in the bathroom mirror. They hadn't made much of an impression on Mrs Hesch, who never even noticed that my hair had changed color.

'Let's go,' I said, then did a Groucho Marx thing with my eyebrows. 'Unless you'd like to make a couple of dollars, girlie.'

'Here? Ugh.'

'A bed is a bed is a bed.'

'This one's no bed of roses. Do people actually have sex in rooms like this?'

'That's all they do. You don't think anyone would sleep here, do you?'

She wrinkled her nose and we left, taking our suitcase with us. A call from Childs had established that Wesley Brill was out, and a knock on his door established that he hadn't come back yet. I could have picked his lock in a couple of seconds but it turned out that I didn't have to, because I stuck our room key in on a hunch and oddly enough it worked. Quite often the rooms on a particular line will respond to the same key – 305 and 405 and 505, for instance – but now and then in older hotels the locks loosen up with age and a surprising number of keys turn out to be interchangeable.

Brill's room was nicer than the ones they used for the hot sheets trade. It still wasn't much but at least there was a piece of carpet covering some of the floor and the furniture was only on its penultimate legs. I put my suitcase on a chair, rummaged idly through Brill's closet and dresser, then took my suitcase off the chair, put it on the floor, and sat on the chair myself. There was another chair with arms and Ellie had already taken it.

'Well,' she said, 'here we are.'

'Here we are indeed.'

'I wonder when he's coming back.'

'Sooner or later.'

'Good thinking. I don't suppose you thought to bring along a deck of cards?'

'I'm afraid not.'

'That's what I thought.'

'Well, I never thought of playing cards as proper equipment for a burglar.'

'You always worked alone.'

'Uh-huh. You'd think he'd have a deck of cards here. You'd think anyone who spent a lot of time in this room would play a lot of solitaire.'

'And cheat.'

'Most likely. I'd pace the floor if there was room. I find myself remembering bad stand-up comics. "The room was so small . . ."'

'How small was it, Johnny?'

'The room was so small you had to go out in the hall to close the door.'

'That small, eh?'

'The room was so small the mice were hunchbacked. I have to admit I've never understood that line. Why would mice be hunchbacked in a small room?

'I think you've got an overly literal mind.'

'I probably do.'

She smiled. 'You're nice, though. Just the same, literal mind or not, you're nice.'

We would talk, fall silent, talk some more. At one point she asked me what I would do when it was all over.

'Go to jail,' I said.

'Not once we find the real killer. They'll drop the other charges, won't they? I bet they will.'

'They might.'

'Well, what'll you do then? After it's all over?'

I thought about it. 'Find a new apartment,' I said at length. 'I wouldn't be able to stay where I am, not even if those visitors hadn't turned it into a slum. All this publicity, the whole building knows about me. I'll have to move someplace else and take the apartment under another name. It'll be a nuisance but I guess I can live with it.'

'You'll stay in New York?'

'Oh, I think so. I think I'd go crazy anywhere else. This is home. Besides, I'm connected here.'

'How do you mean?'

'I know how to operate in New York. When I steal something I know who'll buy it and how to negotiate the sale. The cops know me, which in the long run does you more good than harm, although you might not think so. Oh, there's any number of reasons why a burglar is better off operating in territory that he knows in and out. I don't even like to work outside of Manhattan if I can avoid it. I remember one job I went on up in Harrison, that's in Westchester—'

'You're going to go on being a burglar.'

I looked at her.

'I didn't realize that,' she said. 'You're going to keep on opening locks and stealing things?'

'What else?'

'I don't know.'

'Ellie, on some level or other I think you think you're watching all of this on television and I'm going to reform right in time for the final commercial. That may keep the audience happy but it's not terribly realistic.'

'It isn't?'

'Not really, no. I'm almost thirty-five years old. Opening locks and stealing things is the only trade I know. There's a lot of ads in *Popular Mechanics* telling me about career opportunities in meatcutting and taxidermy but somehow I don't think they're being completely honest with me. And I don't figure I could cut it by raising chinchillas at home or growing ginseng in my backyard, and the only kind of work I'm qualified for pays two dollars an hour and would bore the ass off me before I'd earned ten dollars.'

'You could be a locksmith.'

'Oh, sure. They break their necks running around handing out licenses to convicted burglars. And the bonding companies are just standing in line to do business with locksmiths with criminal records.'

'You must be qualified for something, Bernie.'

'The state taught me how to make license plates and sew mailbags. This is going to stun you but there's very little call for either of those skills in civilian life.'

'But you're intelligent, you're capable, you can think on your feet—'

'All important qualifications that help me make it as a burglar. Ellie, I've got a very good life. That's something you don't seem to realize. I work a couple of nights a year and I spend the rest of my time taking things easy. Is that such a bad deal?'

'No.'

'I've been a burglar for years. Why should I change?'

'I don't know.'

'Nobody changes.'

We didn't have too much to say after that exchange. The time passed about as quickly as the Middle Ages. While we waited, the management kept renting out the room next door to us. Several times we heard footsteps in the hallway and sat motionless, thinking it might be Brill, and then the door next to us would open, and before long bedsprings would creak. Soon the bedsprings would cease creaking and shortly thereafter the footsteps would return to the elevator.

'True love,' Ellie said.

'Well, it's nice the hotel serves a purpose.'

'It does keep them off the streets. That last chap was in rather a hurry, wouldn't you say?'

'Probably had to get back to his office.'

Then at last footsteps approached from the elevator but did not stop at the room next door. Instead they stopped directly in front of the door behind which we lurked. I drew a quick breath and got to my feet, padding soundlessly into position at the side of the door.

Then his key turned in the lock and the door opened and it was him all right, Wesley Brill, the man with the soft brown eyes that had never quite met mine, and I stood with my hands poised waist-high at my sides, ready to catch him if he fainted, ready to grab him if he tried to bolt, ready to hang a high hard one on his chin if he decided to get violent.

What he did was stare. 'Rhodenbarr,' he said. 'This is utterly incredible. How on earth did you manage to find me? And they didn't tell me anyone was waiting for me.'

'They didn't know it.'

'But how did you – oh, of course. You're a burglar.'

'Everybody's got to be something.'

'Indeed.'

His voice and his whole manner of speaking were completely different. The Runyonesque diction was gone and he no longer bit off his words at their final consonants. There was an archness to his inflections, a lilt that was either theatrical or slightly faggoty or both.

'Bernie Rhodenbarr,' he said. Then he caught sight of Ellie, broadened his grin, raised a hand and lifted a brown trilby hat from his head. 'Miss,' he said, then turned his attention to me once more. 'Just let me close this door,' he said. 'No need to share our business with a whole neighborhood of buyers and sellers. There. How on earth did you ever find me, if you don't mind my asking?'

'I saw you on television.'

'Oh?'

'An old movie.'

'And you recognized me?' He preened a bit. 'Which film?'

'*The Man in the Middle.*'

'Not that dog with Jim Garner? I played a cab driver in that one. I played a lot of cabdrivers.' His eyes misted up at the memory. 'No question about it, those were the days. Last year, God help us all, I *drove* a cab for a couple of weeks. Not in a film, but in what we call real life.' He swung his arms back and forth, then put his little hands together and rubbed his palms as if to keep warm. 'Those days are dead and gone. Let us live in the present, eh? The important thing is that she still wants the box.'

I looked at him.

'That's why you looked me up, isn't it? The infamous blue leather box.'

'Leather-covered,' I said. Don't ask me why.

'Leather, leather-covered, whatever. Just so you've got it. As far as killing Flaxford, well, that certainly wasn't what she had in mind, but it's my impression she figures it couldn't have happened to a nicer guy. What she didn't know was whether you'd managed to pick up the box before you had to get out of there, but if you did she definitely wants it and she'll be glad to pay for it.'

I stared at him, but of course his eyes didn't meet mine. They were aimed over my shoulder, as usual.

'Look, Bernie—' He grinned suddenly. 'You don't mind if I call you Bernie, do you? You know who I am and I don't have to play the heavy any longer, do I? And you can call me Wes.'

'Wes,' I said.

'Excellent. And I don't think I've met the little lady.'

'C'mon, Wes. You're slipping back into character. Wesley Brill wouldn't say that. "The little lady." '

'You're absolutely right.' He faced Ellie and made a rather courtly bow. 'Wesley Brill,' he said.

'Ruth Hightower,' I said.

He smiled. 'Not really.'

'That's a private joke,' Ellie said. 'I'm Ellie Christopher, Wes.'

'My pleasure, Miss Christopher.'

She said he could call her Ellie, and he told her to call him Wes, which she'd already done, and he added that no one called him Wesley, that indeed his name had originally been John Wesley Brill, his mother having seen fit to name him for the founder of Methodism, a move she might not have dared had she suspected he was destined for an actor's life. He'd dropped his first name entirely the first time he trod the boards. (That was his phrase, trod the boards.) Ellie assured him that she thought dropping a first name altogether was perfectly all right but that when you retained an initial out in front it was a sign of a devious character. Good ol' Wes said he couldn't agree more. Ellie mentioned G. Gordon Liddy and E. Howard Hunt and Wes chimed in with J. Edgar Hoover. While they were at it I thought of F. Scott Fitzgerald and decided there might be a few weak spots in Ellie's theory.

'Wes,' I cut in, 'the purpose of our call wasn't entirely social.'

'I'd guess not. You're up to your neck in it, aren't you? Killing old J. Francis. That really surprised her because she said you never impressed her as violent. I told her it must have been self-defense. Although I don't suppose the law calls it self-defense when it happens in the middle of a burglary.'

'The law calls it first-degree murder.'

'I know. It doesn't seem entirely fair, does it? But the big question, Bernie, is have you got the box?'

'The box.'

'Right.'

I closed my eyes for a minute. 'You never actually saw the box yourself,' I said. 'Because you described it very precisely but you didn't know what color blue it was. And you didn't make up an answer when I asked.'

'Why would I make up an answer?'

'You'd make one up if there was no box in the first place. But there really is a box, isn't there?'

He peered intently at me and his forehead developed a single vertical line just above the nose like the one David Janssen has in the Excedrin commercial, the one that makes you certain he really does have one rat bastard of a headache.

'The box exists,' I said.

'You mean you thought—'

'That's what I thought.'

'Which means you don't—'

'Right. I don't.'

'Shit,' he said, pronouncing the word as emphatically as if he'd just stepped in it. Then he remembered that the little lady was present. 'I beg your pardon,' he said.

She told him not to worry about it.

There really was a box. In fact he'd been waiting for me in Pandora's that first night, sitting in a back booth with four thousand dollars on his hip, stretching out his drinks until they closed the place. It wasn't until the following day that he found out what had gone wrong.

'And you didn't kill Flaxford,' he said, after I'd done some recapping on my own.

'And neither did you.'

'Me? Kill the man? I never even met him. Oh, *I* see what you mean. You thought I set you up. But if *you* didn't kill Flaxford—'

'Somebody else did. Because beating your own head in with a blunt instrument is no way to commit suicide.'

'I wish I knew more about this,' he said. 'I'm not really in the center of things. There's a lot happening I don't know about.'

'I know how you feel.'

'All I am is an actor, really. And that career's not going too well. One thing leads to another, and I had this drinking situation that's over with now, thank God, but I reached a point where I couldn't remember lines. I still have trouble. I can improvise, which is what I was doing the two times I saw you, building a role around a framework, but you can't do that in the movies unless you're directed by Robert Altman or something. The jobs stopped coming, and this agent I'm with now, I'd have to say he's more pimp than agent.'

'I know. I was in his office.'

'You met Pete?'

'I was in his office,' I repeated, 'but he wasn't. Last night. To get your address.'

'Oh,' he said. He looked for a moment at his own door, no doubt reflecting on its failure to keep us out of his room. 'The point is, I'm in this because I'm an actor. I used to play a lot of heavies and that's what she hired me for, to hire you to get the box and then to pay you off and take the box to her.'

'How did you know to hire me?'

'She told me to.'

'Right, sure,' I said. 'She told you to hire a burglar. But how did you happen to know that I happened to be one?'

He frowned. 'She told me to hire you,' he said. 'You specifically,

95

Bernard Rhodenbarr. I'm an *actor*, Bernie. How would I go about finding a burglar on my own? I don't know any burglars. I can *play* crooks but that doesn't mean I hang around with them.'

'Oh.'

'I used to know a bookie but since off-track betting came in I couldn't tell you if he's alive or dead. As far as burglars are concerned, well, I now know one burglar, or—' with a nod to Ellie '—or possibly two, but that's all.'

'The woman who hired you,' Ellie said. 'She knew Bernie was a burglar.'

'That's right.'

'And she knew where he lived and what he looked like, is that right?'

'Well, she took me over there and pointed him out to me.'

'How did she know him?'

'Search me.'

Loren the cop would have frisked him. I just said, 'What's her name, Wes?'

'I'm supposed to keep her name out of this.'

'I'm sure you are.'

'That's why she hired me in the first place.'

Ellie's eyes flashed. 'Now you just wait a damned minute,' she said. 'Don't you think Bernie has a right to know who got him into this mess? He's wanted for a murder he didn't commit and he's taking a chance every time he sets foot outside, and he has to go around wearing a disguise—'

'The hair,' Wes said. 'I knew something was different. You dyed your hair.'

'It's a wig.'

'Really? It looks remarkably natural.'

'God *damn* it,' Ellie said. 'How can you have the nerve to tell us the woman doesn't want her name mentioned?'

'Well, she doesn't.'

'Well, that's too bad. You'll just have to tell us who she is or else.'

'Or else what?' he asked. Reasonably, I thought.

Ellie frowned, then glanced at me for help. But I was getting flashes and the tumblers were beginning to drop. Brill hadn't known me, hadn't even known I was a burglar. But this woman had hired him to rope me in, selecting him because he was an actor who had made a career out of playing underworld types. She didn't know any real underworld types, nor did she know any real burglars except for me, but she did know who I was and where I lived and what I looked like and how I kept the wolf away from my door.

I said, 'Wait a minute.'

'You can't let him get away with it, Bernie.'

'Just hold it for a minute.'

'You can't. We found him and we trapped him and now he's supposed to tell us what we want to know. Isn't that the way it's supposed to go?'

I closed my eyes and said, 'Cool it, will you? Just for a minute.' And the last tumbler tumbled and the mental lock eased open so sweetly, so gently, like the petals of a flower, like a yielding lady. I opened my eyes and beamed at Ellie, then turned the warmth of my smile on Wesley Brill.

'He doesn't have to tell me a thing,' I said to Ellie. 'It's enough that he told me it was a woman. That triggered it, really. A woman who doesn't know anything about crime except that a guy named Bernie Rhodenbarr burgles for a living. I know who she is.'

'Who?'

'Does she still live in the same place, Wes? Park Avenue, right? I don't remember the address offhand but I could draw you a floor plan of the apartment. I tend to remember the layout of places where I've been arrested.'

Brill was perspiring. Beads of sweat dotted his forehead and he wiped them away not with his whole hand but with an extended index finger. The gesture was very familiar. I must have seen him do it dozens of times in movies.

'Mrs Carter Sandoval,' I said. 'Didn't I tell you about the Sandovals, Ellie? Of course I did. Her husband had a monster coin collection that I'd taken an interest in. He also had a monster of a gun and his doorbell was out of order and he and his wife were home when I came a-calling. I'm sure I told you about this.'

'Yes, you did.'

'I thought so.' I grinned at Brill. 'Her husband was head of CACA. That's not a bathroom word, it stands for the Civic Anti-Crime Association or something like that. It's a group of high-minded pests who push for everything from more foot patrolmen on the beat to investigations of political and judicial corruption. The sonofabitch held a gun on me and I tried to buy my way out, and he was the wrong man to offer a bribe to. He even wanted to prosecute me for attempted bribery but he wasn't a cop, for God's sake, and there's no law against trying to bribe a private citizen. At least I don't think there is, but come to think of it I'm probably wrong. There's a law against just about everything, isn't there? Of course I didn't know he was the head CACA person. All I knew was that he did something terribly profitable on Wall Street and thought rare coins were a hell of a hedge against inflation. Does he still have the coins, Wes?'

Brill just stared at me.

'I remember them well,' I said. I was enjoying this. 'And they would remember me, Wes. I saw them the night I was arrested, of course, but they were also on hand when I went before the judge. They didn't have to be. I copped a plea to a lesser charge, and don't think that didn't take some doing. Carter Sandoval wasn't nuts about the idea of that. But somebody must have taken him aside and explained that the courts would never get anything done if every criminal went through the ritual of a jury trial, and he must have decided it would get more of us evildoers off the streets if the system was allowed to go along as usual, so he and his wife showed up to watch me stand up and plead guilty and get sent away to the license plate factory. I suppose he figured it would be good publicity for his cause with him there to watch justice triumph. And I think he got a personal kick out of it, too. He seemed pretty attached to those coins and thoroughly steamed at the thought of me violating the sanctity of his home.'

'Bernie—'

'She was a lot younger than him. She must have been around forty or close to it, so I guess she's around forty-five now. Good-looking woman. A little too much jawline for my taste, but maybe she was just setting her jaw with determination the times I saw her. Is her hair still the same color, Wes?'

'I never told you her name.'

'That's true, Wes, and I wish you would. It's on the tip of my tongue. It's not Carla and it's not Maria and what the hell is it?'

'Darla.'

Something made me glance at Ellie. Her shoulders were set and her head cocked forward. She looked to be concentrating intently. 'Darla Sandoval,' I said. 'Right. That ring any kind of a bell for you, Ellie?'

'No. I don't think you mentioned her name before. Why?'

'No reason. Why don't you call her, Wes?'

'She calls me. I'm not supposed to call her.'

'Call her and see if she wants the box back.'

'But you don't *have* the box, Bernie.' He eyed me in his oblique fashion. 'Or do you? I'm getting more confused by the minute. Do you have the box or don't you?'

'I don't.'

'I didn't think so because you didn't even believe there *was* a box. You didn't get the box from Flaxford's apartment, then. Did you see it there and—'

'No.'

'You went through the desk? There *was* a desk there, wasn't there? A large rolltop?'

'There was, and I went through it pretty carefully. But I couldn't find any kind of blue box in it.'

'Shit,' he said, and this time he didn't think to apologize to Ellie. I don't think she minded. I'm not even sure she heard him. She seemed to have something else on her mind.

'That means they got it,' he said.

'Who?'

'Whoever killed him. You didn't commit the murder or steal the box, so somebody else did both those little things and that's why the box was gone when you got there. So that's the end of everything.'

'Call Darla.'

'What's the point?'

'I know where the box is,' I said. 'Call her.'

13

Her hair was still blond, and if she had changed much in any other respect I didn't notice it. She was still slim and elegant, with strength in her face and assurance in her carriage. Wes and I met her as arranged over the phone at a brownstone apartment a few blocks from the one I'd been caught burgling a few years back. She opened the door, greeted me by name, and told Wes his presence would not be necessary.

'You run along, Wesley. It's quite all right, Mr Rhodenbarr and I will work things out.' It was the dismissal of a servant, and whether he liked it or not he took it without a murmur. She was swinging the door shut even as he was turning. She bolted it – with the burglar already inside, I thought – and favored me with a cool and regal smile. She asked if I'd like a drink and I said Scotch would be fine and told her how to fix it.

While she made the drinks I stood around thinking of Ellie. She'd decided rather abruptly that she wouldn't come along to meet Darla Sandoval. A quick glance at her watch, a sudden realization that it was much later than she'd thought, an uncertain bit of chatter about an unspecified appointment for which she was already late, a promise to meet me back at Rodney's apartment later on, and away she went. I'd see her later, after her appointment had been kept, after her legendary cats had been fed, after her legendary stained-glass sculpture had been assembled . . .

I was running various thoughts through my mind when Darla Sandoval came back with drinks for both of us. Hers was a darker shade of amber than mine. She raised her glass as if to toast, failed to hit on a suitable phrase, and looked slightly less than certain for the first time in our acquaintance. 'Well,' she said, which was toast enough, and we took sips of our drinks. It was excellent Scotch and this did not much surprise me.

'Nice place you've got here.'

'Oh, this? I borrowed it from a friend.'

'Still live at the same spot? Where we met?'

'Oh, yes. Nothing's changed.' She sighed. 'I want you to know I'm sorry about all this,' she said, sounding apologetic if not devastated. 'I never expected to get you involved in anything so complicated. I thought you'd do a very simple job of burglary for me. I remembered how skillfully you opened our locks that night—'

'That was skill, all right. Hitting the place with you two in it.'

'Accidents do happen. I thought you'd do perfectly, though, and of course you're the only person I know who could possibly do the job. I remembered you, of course, your name, and I just glanced through the telephone book on the chance that you might be in it, and there you were.'

'There I was,' I agreed. 'They charge extra for an unlisted number and I've always considered it a waste of money. The idea of paying them for an unperformed service. Goes against the grain.'

'I never thought Fran would be home that night. There was an opening downtown.'

'An opening?'

'An experimental play. He was supposed to be in the audience and at the cast party afterward. Carter and I were there, you see, and when Fran didn't turn up I got very nervous. I knew you were going to be burgling his apartment and I didn't know where he could be, whether he'd gone somewhere else or stayed home or what. Wesley says you didn't kill him.'

'He was dead when I got there.'

'And the police—'

I gave her a quick summary of what had happened in Flaxford's apartment. Her eyes widened when I mentioned how I'd arranged to buy my way out. Here her husband was battling police corruption and she didn't seem to know that cops took money from crooks. I guess civilians just don't understand how the system works.

'Then someone else actually killed him,' she said. 'I don't suppose it could have been accidental? No, of course it couldn't. But you did look in the desk before the police came? I saw Fran put the box in the desk. It was a deep blue, a little darker than royal blue, and the box itself was about the size of a hardcover novel. Maybe larger, perhaps as big as a dictionary. And I saw him put it in the desk.'

'Where in the desk? Under the rolltop?'

'One of the lower drawers. I don't know which one.'

'It doesn't matter. I went through those drawers.'

'Thoroughly?'

'Very thoroughly. If the box was there I would have found it.'

'Then someone else got it first.' Her face paled slightly beneath her make-up. She drank some more of her drink, sat down in a straight chair with a needlepoint seat. 'Whoever killed Fran took the box,' she said.

'I don't think so. That desk was locked when I found it, Mrs

Sandoval. Desk locks are always easy to open but you have to know what you're doing.'

'The killer could have had a key.'

'But would he have bothered to lock up afterward? With a corpse in the bedroom? I don't think so. He'd have thrown things all over the place and left a mess behind him.' I thought of my own ravaged apartment. 'Besides,' I went on, 'somebody's still looking for the box and you don't go on looking for something you already have. I went back to my own place a couple of hours ago and it looked as though Attila had marched his Huns through it. You didn't have anything to do with that, did you?'

'Of course not.'

'Well, you could have hired someone. No hard feelings if you did, but you'd better tell me or we'll be wasting our time chasing wild geese.'

She assured me she had had nothing to do with looting my place and I decided she was telling the truth. I hadn't really figured she'd been involved in the first place. It was more logical to assume it had been tossed by the same person who had scrambled Flaxford's brains.

'I think I know where the box is,' I said.

'Where?'

'Where it's been all along. Flaxford's apartment.'

'You said you looked.'

'I looked in the desk, but that's as far as I got. I'd have kept on looking if the Marines hadn't landed and I think I probably would have found it. It could have been anywhere in the apartment. Just because you saw him put it in the desk doesn't mean he left it there forever. Maybe he had a wall safe behind a picture. Maybe he stuck it in a drawer in the bedside table. It could even be in the desk but not in a drawer. Those old rolltops have secret compartments. Maybe he put the box in one of them after you left. Anyway, I'll bet it's still there, right where he put it, and the killer assumes I've got it, and the apartment's all locked up with a police seal on the door.'

'What can we do?'

An idea began heating up in the back of my mind. I let it simmer there while I took a different tack with her. 'This blue box,' I said. 'I think it's time I knew what was inside it.'

'Is it important?'

'It's important to you and it's important to the man who killed Flaxford. That makes it important to me. Whatever it is must be pretty valuable.'

'Only to me.'

'He was blackmailing you.'

A nod.

'Photographs? Something like that?'

'Photographs, tape recordings. He showed me some pictures and

102

played part of a tape for me.' She shuddered. 'I knew he didn't love me any more than I loved him. But I thought he enjoyed what we did.' She stood up, took a few steps toward the window. 'My life with my husband is quite conventional, Mr Rhodenbarr. Some years ago I learned that I'm not all that conventional myself. When I met Fran some months ago we learned we had certain, uh, tastes in common.' She turned to face me. 'I never expected to be blackmailed.'

'What did he want from you? Money?'

'No. I don't have any money I had a hard time raising enough cash to hire you and Wesley. No, Fran wanted me to influence my husband. You know he's involved with CACA.'

'I know.'

'There's a man named Michael Debus. He's the District Attorney of Brooklyn or Queens, I can never remember which. Carter's spearheading some sort of investigation which threatens to expose this Debus.'

'And Flaxford wanted you to pull the plug on it?'

'Yes. As if I could, incorruptible as Carter is.'

'What was Flaxford's interest?'

'I don't know. I can't figure out how he fits into it all. He and I became involved long before Carter began this investigation, so he didn't start seeing me with an ulterior motive in mind. And I always understood that he was involved with the theater. He produced some shows off-off-Broadway, you know, and he moved in those circles. That's how I met him.'

'And that's how you met Brill also?'

'Yes. He didn't know Fran or any of my other theater friends, which made me feel safer about using him. But Fran must have been involved with crime in some way that I never knew about.'

'He must have been some kind of a fixer,' I said. 'He was obviously trying to fix things for Debus.'

'Well, he certainly fixed me.' She came over, sat down on a love seat, took a cigarette from a box on the coffee table, lit it with a butane table lighter. 'He must have known just what he was doing when he started up with me,' she said levelly. 'Even if the Debus investigation hadn't started. He knew who Carter was and he must have decided that it would come in handy sooner or later to have a hold on me.'

'Did your husband ever meet him?'

'Two or three times when I dragged Carter to an opening or a party. I'm interested in the theater the way Carter is interested in collecting coins. With those small companies you can have the excitement of being a backer and the thrill of being an insider for a couple of hundred deductible dollars. It's an inexpensive way to delude yourself into thinking you're involved in creative work with creative people. Oh, you meet the most interesting people that way, Mr Rhodenbarr.'

She took our empty glasses into the kitchen. I think she may have helped herself to a slug from the bottle while she was at it because when she came back her face had softened and she seemed more at ease.

I asked her when Flaxford had shown her the contents of the blue box.

'About two weeks ago. It was only the fourth time I'd been to his apartment. We generally came here. This isn't a friend's apartment, you see. I rented it myself some years ago as a convenience.'

'I'm sure it's convenient.'

'It is.' She drew on her cigarette. 'Of course he took me to his apartment so he could make the tapes and photographs. And then he invited me up to show me his work and make his pitch.'

'He told you to get your husband to drop the Debus investigation?'

'Yes.'

'But you couldn't do that?'

'Tell Carter to discontinue a CACA project?' She laughed. 'You ought to remember just how high-principled a man my husband is, Mr Rhodenbarr. You tried to bribe him, remember?'

'I do indeed. Didn't you say as much to Flaxford?'

'Of course I did. He said he was just trying to give me a chance to work things out on my own. For the sake of our friendship, he said.' She gritted her teeth. 'But if I couldn't sway Carter myself, then he'd go to him directly, threaten to circulate the photos.'

'What would Carter have done?'

'I don't know. I'm not certain. He couldn't have allowed the photographs to circulate. Carter Sandoval's wife doing perverted things? No, he could hardly have tolerated that, no more than he could have tolerated remaining married to me. I'm not sure just what he would have done. He might have tried something dramatic, something like leaving a detailed note implicating Fran and Debus and then diving out a window.'

'Would he have tried killing Flaxford?'

'Carter? Commit murder?'

'He might not have thought of it as murder.'

Her eyes narrowed. 'I can't imagine him doing it,' she said. 'Anyway, he was with me at the theater.'

'The whole night?'

'We had dinner together and then we drove downtown.'

'And you were together the entire time?'

She hesitated. 'There was a one-act curtain raiser before the main production. An experimental extended scene written by Gulliver Shane. I don't know if you're familiar with his work.'

'I'm not. Is Carter?'

'Pardon?'

'He missed the curtain-raiser, didn't he?'

104

She nodded. 'He dropped me in front of the theater and then went to park the car. The curtain was at eight-thirty and I had time for a cigarette in the lobby so he must have dropped me at twenty after eight. Then he had trouble finding a parking place. He won't park by a hydrant even though they don't tow cars away that far downtown. He's so disgustingly honest.'

'So he missed the curtain.'

'If you're not seated when the lights go up you have to watch from the back of the theater. So he couldn't sit next to me during the Shane play. But he said he watched from the back, and he was sitting beside me by nine o'clock, or maybe nine-fifteen at the outside. That wouldn't have given him enough time to rush all the way uptown and kill Fran and get back to me that quickly, would it?'

I didn't say anything.

'And Carter wouldn't even have known about Fran. Fran hadn't gone to him yet, I know he hadn't. I was supposed to have until the end of the week. And Carter wouldn't kill anyone by striking him. He'd use a gun.'

'Does he still have that cannon of his?'

'Yes. It's a horrible thing, isn't it?'

'You don't know the half of it. You didn't have it pointed at you. But suppose Carter didn't plan any murder. Suppose Flaxford confronted him with the photos and he reacted on the spur of the moment. He wouldn't have had the gun with him, and—'

I left it right there because it didn't make any sense. It wasn't just that Sandoval would have been acting completely out of character. Beyond that, there was no reason for Flaxford to have met him at that hour or to have been wearing a dressing gown during the confrontation. And if a man like Carter Sandoval did kill anyone in a blind rage, which was hard enough to believe, he certainly would have given himself up and taken his punishment afterward.

'Forget all that,' I said. 'Carter didn't do it.'

'I didn't see how he could have.'

'It keeps coming back to the blue box,' I told her. 'We have to get our hands on it. You want those photos and tapes before some opportunist gets his hands on them. And I want to find out what's in the box besides tapes and pictures.'

'You think there's something else?'

'I think there has to be. You and your husband are the only people who'd be interested in the tapes and pictures. But if neither of you killed Flaxford and neither of you sacked my apartment then there has to be something else for somebody else to be looking for. And once we know what it is we'll have a shot at knowing who's looking for it.'

She started to say something but I tuned her out. An idea was beginning to glimmer. I picked up my glass, then put it down without

105

drinking anything. No more liquor tonight, not for Bernard. He had work to do.

'Money,' I said.

'In the blue box?'

'That's always possible, I suppose. But that's not what I'm talking about. You were going to pay me another four thousand dollars. Have you still got it?'

'Yes.'

'At home?'

'Here, as a matter of fact. Why?'

'Can you raise any more?'

'Maybe two or three thousand over the next few days.'

'No time for that. Your four thousand and my five thousand is nine thousand – isn't it impressive the way I can work out these sums in my head – nine thousand might be enough. Ten thousand would be a lot better. Could you dig up an extra thousand dollars in the next couple of hours if you put your mind to it?'

'I suppose I could. I'm thinking who I could ask. Yes, I could manage a thousand dollars. Why?'

I opened my suitcase, took out the three books. I gave Gibbon to Darla Sandoval and kept Barbara Tuchman and beekeeping for myself. 'Every thirty pages or so,' I said, talking as I riffled pages, 'you will find two pages glued together. Tear them open—' I suited action to words '—and you'll find a hundred-dollar bill.'

'Where did you get these books?'

'Mostly on Fourth Avenue. Not *Guns of August*, that came from Book-of-the-Month Club. Oh, you thought I stole them. No, this is my stash, my case money. I may have stolen the money but the books are all my own. They've been shaken and riffled and all but they've refused to give up their secret. Come on, now. If we both work we'll get the money that much faster.'

'But what are we going to do with it?'

'We are going to put your five thousand and my five thousand together,' I said, 'and that will give us ten thousand dollars, and we're going to use it to get me into J. Francis Flaxford's apartment, past the doorman and through the police evidence seal and everything. We're going to do it in the most expedient way possible. We're going to hire a police escort.'

106

14

I sat back in my chair and watched Ray Kirschmann count hundred-dollar bills. He performed his operation in silence but he did move his lips as he counted so it was easy for me to keep up with him. When he was all done he said, 'Ten thousand, all right. That's what you said.'

'Ten thousand two hundred, Ray. I must have had some bills stuck together. Careless of me. Leave two of them on the table there, huh? The price we set was ten even.'

'Jesus,' he said, but he put a pair of hundreds on the glass-topped coffee table before shuffling the remaining ten thou into a neat if bulky roll. 'This is crazy,' he said. 'Dizziest damn thing I ever did. Dizziest damn thing I ever heard of, to tell you the truth.'

'It's also the easiest money you ever made in your life.'

'I'm takin' a hell of a risk, Bernie.'

'What risk? You've got every right in the world to want to have another look at the Flaxford apartment, you and Loren. You were the two cops who caught the original squeal and you were right in the middle of everything.'

'Don't remind me.'

'So there's something you have a feeling you may have missed, so you pick up the keys and get a warrant or permission slip or whatever the hell you get, and you and Loren go let yourselves into Flaxford's place.'

'Except it ain't Loren.'

'So instead of one skinny guy in a blue uniform you have a different skinny guy in a blue uniform. All cops look alike, you know that.'

'Jesus.'

'If you want to put the money back on the table—'

He gave me a sour look. I was in the same apartment where I'd met Darla Sandoval but I was drinking instant Yuban now instead of Scotch and Darla herself was tucked away behind a pair of louvered doors in the kitchen. Since half of the ten grand was hers I figured she had every right in the world to listen in on our arrangements, but I also figured she'd be better off not meeting Ray Kirschmann face to face. If he'd even bothered to wonder whose apartment we were using he'd kept his

curiosity to himself. Outside of a conventional *Nice place you got here,
Rhodenbarr* we might as well have been meeting over hot dogs at
Nedick's.

'I just don't know,' he said now. 'A fugitive from justice, an escaped
murderer—'

'Ray, all I ever killed is time. I already told you that.'

'Yeah.'

'You don't honestly think I killed Flaxford, do you?'

'I got no opinion on the subject, Bernie. You're the same fugitive
from a homicide charge whether you killed him or he died of an in-
grown toenail.' He frowned at an irksome memory. 'If you *didn't* do it,'
he said, 'why in the hell did you jump me the way you did? Made me
feel like seven different kinds of an asshole.'

'I was stupid, Ray. I got spooked.'

'Yeah, spooked.'

'If I'd already known Flaxford was dead on the floor I wouldn't have
gone nuts like that, but it shocked me, same as it shocked Loren, and
I—'

'When Loren gets shocked he faints. It's a lot less hostile, just closing
your eyes and hitting the rug.'

'Next time I'll faint.'

'Yeah.'

'I'm going to find something in that apartment that'll point straight
at the real killer. Because I *know* I didn't kill anybody, Ray, and I'll find
out who did, and when I've got it worked out I'll hand it to you and
look what a hero you'll be. "The resourceful cop who dug beneath the
surface to get at the real truth." You're a safe bet to make plainclothes
on the strength of that.'

'Yeah, plainclothes. When you tell it I come out of it with a promotion. When I work it out on my own I see myself winding up stepping
on my cock.'

'Forget that, Ray. A promotion and ten grand, that's how you'll wind
up.'

'Don't forget I got to split with Loren.' I shot him a doubtful look and
he gave me back an injured expression in exchange. 'Right down the
middle,' he said. 'It's the same fuckin' risk for the both of us. You'll be
wearin' his badge and twirlin' his nightstick, for Chrissake. Be his gun
on your hip. If the shit hits the fan he'll be right there in front of it, arm
in arm with me. So it's five grand for him and five grand for me.'

'Sounds fair to me.'

He looked at me for a moment, then let out air in a soundless
whistle. He patted the bulky package on the sofa beside him. 'Size
thirty-eight long,' he said. 'That's what you ordered, right?'

'That's what I take.'

'Loren's smaller'n you so I picked this up new. Maybe you better try it on.'

I unwrapped the parcel, got out of my own clothes, donned a pair of regulation police blues over a blue shirt. There was no cap; I would wear Loren's. When I was dressed Ray inspected me, tugged here and there on the uniform, frowned, stepped back, shrugged, shook his head doubtfully and turned aside.

'I don't know,' he said. 'You don't look like New York's Finest to me.'

'Just so I'm not a disgrace to the uniform.'

'I guess it ain't too bad of a fit. It don't look tailor-made, you got to admit that, but then you also got to admit that neither does Loren's.'

I took a moment to picture Loren. 'No,' I agreed, 'he doesn't look as though the uniform was stitched together around him.' I patted my trousers, pressed out imaginary wrinkles. 'So I guess I'll do,' I said.

'Yeah,' he said. 'I guess you'll do.'

I was still in uniform when he left. After the door closed behind him Darla Sandoval emerged from the kitchen. She looked me up and down and raised her eyebrows.

'Well?'

'I think you look like a policeman. There's a mirror on the bedroom door if you want to see yourself.'

I wouldn't have been surprised if there had been a mirror on the bedroom ceiling. (Well, maybe I would have.) But I went and checked my reflection on the mirrored door and decided I cut a reasonably dashing figure. I returned to the living room and agreed with Darla that I looked like a cop.

'He took all our money,' she said. 'Do you think that was wise?'

'I think it was inevitable. You can't pay cops half in advance and the balance upon delivery. You ought to be able to but they don't like to work that way.'

'He's picking you up here tonight.'

I nodded. 'At twenty-one hundred hours. That's nine o'clock in English but he said it in cop talk because I was wearing the uniform.'

'So you'll just wait for him here?'

I shook my head. 'I'll go back to where I'm staying downtown. I didn't want to complicate things by having him meet me there. I'd just as soon he didn't know where I'm staying.'

'Suppose he doesn't show up, Bernard? Then what?'

'He'll show. He'll even make sure he's on time because he doesn't want anything to go wrong. He'll bring Loren and I'll equip myself with all of Loren's paraphernalia, the badge and the cap and the gun and the nightstick and the cuffs, all that crap, and Loren'll curl up here with an astrology magazine while Ray and I go and do the dirty deed. Then Ray'll drop me back here and pick up Loren and that's the end of it.'

'But suppose he keeps the ten thousand dollars and forgets all about you?'

'Oh,' I said, 'he won't do that.'

'How can you be sure?'

'He's honest,' I said, and when she stared at me I explained. 'There's all kinds of honest. If a cop like Ray makes a deal he'll stick with it. He's that kind of honest. And you heard him carry on when I showed some doubt about his giving Loren an even split. He was genuinely offended at the implication. What's so funny?'

'I was thinking of Carter. He wouldn't understand a syllable of this.'

'Well, he's a different kind of honest.'

'He certainly is. Bernard, I think I can have one more drink without harming myself any. Can I get you one?'

'No thanks.'

'You're sure?'

'Positive.'

'More coffee, then?'

I shook my head. She went back to the kitchen and returned with drink in hand. She sat down on the sofa, sipped her drink, set it down on the coffee table and noticed the pair of hundred-dollar bills I'd convinced Ray to leave behind. 'I guess these are yours,' she said.

'Well, one of us counted wrong, Mrs Sandoval.'

'Darla.'

'Darla. Why don't we each take one of them?'

That struck her as fair. She kept a bill and passed its brother to me. Then she said, 'You said he was honest. That policeman. But he would have kept the extra two hundred dollars.'

'Oh, sure. He was steamed when I called him on it.'

'There really are all kinds of honesty, aren't there?'

'There really are.'

It was time to change back into mufti, time to pack up the uniform and cart it downtown. But for the moment I didn't feel much like moving. I sat in a chair across from Darla and watched her nibble at her drink.

'Bernard? I was thinking that it's a waste of time for you to chase downtown and back. And it's an added risk, isn't it? Being out on the street that much?'

'I'll take cabs both ways.'

'Even so.

'A small risk, I suppose.'

'You could stay here, you know.'

'I'd like to drop my suitcase at the place where I'm staying.'

'Oh?'

'And there's someone I'll want to see before I meet Ray this evening. And a stop or two I'll want to make.'

110

'I see.'

Our eyes met. She had a lot of presence, this lady did. And something more than that.

'You really look effective in that uniform,' she said.

'Effective?'

'Very effective. I'm just sorry I won't be able to be here tonight when you have all the accessories. The nightstick and the handcuffs and the badge and the gun.'

'Well, you can imagine how I'll look with the props.'

'Yes, I certainly can.' She ran the tip of her tongue very purposefully over her lips. 'Costumes can be very useful, you know. I sometimes think that's what I like most about theater. Not that the actors wear costumes physically, although they often do, but that the whole character which an actor puts on is a sort of costume.'

'Do you do any acting yourself, Darla?'

'Oh, no, I'm just a dabbler. I told you that, didn't I? Why should you think I might have acted?'

'The way you were using your voice just then.'

She licked her lips again. 'Costumes,' she said, and ran her eyes over my uniform. 'I think I told you that I used to consider myself a very conventional person.'

'I think you did.'

'Yes, I'm quite sure I said that.'

'Yes.'

'Conventional in sexual matters.'

'Yes.'

'But in recent years I've found out otherwise. I may have told you that.'

'Uh, yes. I think you did.'

'In fact I'm positive I did.'

'Yes.'

She got to her feet and stood in such a way as to make me very much aware of the shape of her body. 'If you were to wear that uniform,' she said, 'or one rather like it, and if you were to have handcuffs and a nightstick, I think I would find you quite irresistible.'

'Uh.'

'And we might do the most extraordinary things. Imaginative persons could probably find interesting things to do with handcuffs and a nightstick.'

'Probably.'

'And with each other.'

'Very probably.'

'Of course you might be too conventional for that sort of thing.'

'I'm not all that conventional.'

'No, I didn't really think you were. Do you find me attractive?'

'Yes.'

'I hope you're not saying that out of politeness.'

'I'm not.'

'That's good. I'm older than you, of course. That wouldn't bother you?'

'Why should it?'

'I've no idea. It wouldn't?'

'No.'

She nodded thoughtfully. 'This is not the right time for us,' she said.

'And I don't have the cuffs or the stick.'

'No, you don't. But as an experiment, why don't you come kiss me?'

It was a stirring kiss. We were standing, her arms around my neck, and midway through the kiss I dropped my hands to her buttocks and took hold of them and squeezed with all my strength, whereupon she made some extraordinary sounds and quivered a bit. Eventually we let go of each other and she stepped backward.

'After all of this is over, Bernard—'

'Yes. Definitely.'

'The uniform wouldn't even be all that important. Or the other paraphernalia.'

'No, but it might be fun.'

'Oh, it would definitely be fun.' She licked her lips again. 'I want to wash up. And you'll want to change, or do you plan to wear the uniform downtown?'

'No, I'll change.'

I was in my own clothes by the time she returned from the bathroom, the heat flush gone from her face, the lipstick replenished on her mouth. I put on my silly yellow wig and fixed my cap in place over it. She gave me keys for the front door and the door to the apartment so that I would be able to let myself in when I returned. I didn't remind her that I could manage without them.

She said, 'Bernard? That two hundred dollars the policeman was going to keep?'

'What about it?'

'Would he have divided it with his partner?'

I had to think about it, and finally I told her I just didn't know.

She smiled. 'It's a good question, isn't it?'

'Yes,' I said. 'It's a very good question.'

I got back to Rod's place before Ellie did. While I waited for her. I tried my cop suit on again and frowned at my shoes. Did cops wear scotch-grain loafers? It seemed to me that they always wore square-toed black oxfords, occasionally switching to black wing tips. But did they ever wear loafers?

I decided it didn't matter. Nobody was going to be staring at my feet.

When Ellie walked in my outfit gave her a giggling fit. This didn't do wonders for my self-confidence. 'But you can't be a cop,' she said. 'You're a crook!'

'The two aren't mutually exclusive.'

'You just don't look like a cop, Bernie.'

'Cops don't look like cops anymore,' I pointed out. 'Oh, older bulls like Ray still look the part, but the younger generation's gone to hell. Ray's partner's a good example. Bumping his nightstick into his knee, asking me what my sign was, then collapsing in a dead faint. I look as much like a cop as he does. Anyway, the only person I have to convince is a doorman. And I'll be with Ray and he'll do all the talking.'

'I guess,' she said.

'Don't you think it's a good idea?'

'I suppose so. You really think it's still there? The blue box?'

'If it was there in the first place it's there now. I think I know who turned my apartment inside out. I think it was a couple of people from Michael Debus's office.' Probably the two men I'd seen going into my building two nights ago, I thought. While I'd stood on the corner looking up at my lighted windows they'd been busy turning order into chaos. 'He's a DA in Brooklyn or Queens and he was connected to Flaxford.'

'Flaxford was blackmailing him, too?'

'I don't think so. I think he was Debus's fixer. Carter Sandoval was making things hot for Debus and Flaxford was putting pressure on Mrs Sandoval to call her husband off. Debus must have been worried that something incriminating was left on the premises. But he probably didn't know it was in a blue box or anything like that, just that Flaxford had it and he couldn't let it fall into the wrong hands. At any rate, he sent over a pair of oafs to toss my place. If he did that, then he didn't get the box himself. And that means no one did.'

'What about the killer?'

'Huh?'

'Flaxford had a visitor at his apartment that night. Someone he knew. Probably someone else he was blackmailing. Who knows how many people he had his hooks into? And he could have kept all the evidence in that box of his.'

'Keep talking.'

She shrugged. 'So he met with his victim and the victim demanded to see the evidence and Flaxford showed it to him, and then the victim killed Flaxford, smashed his head in, and scooped up the box and ran like a thief.'

'Like a murderer, too.'

'Exactly. Seconds later you went in – it's a miracle you and the killer didn't bump into each other in the hallway, actually – and meanwhile someone heard the struggle and called the police, and while you were riffling desk drawers they came through the door and there you were.'

'There I was,' I agreed.

'This Debus would still think the box was either at Flaxford's apartment or at your place. Because he wouldn't know about X.'

'About who?'

'X. The killer.' I looked at her. 'Well, that's how they always say it on television.'

'I hate seeing my whole life reduced to an algebraic equation.'

'Well, call him whatever you want. Just because Debus thinks you have the box doesn't mean a third person couldn't have it, so if you don't find it in the apartment it may be because it isn't there in the first place.'

I felt slightly angry, the way people must have felt a few centuries back when Galileo started making waves. I said, 'The box is in Flaxford's apartment.' And the earth is flat, you bitch, and heavy objects fall faster than light ones, and quit raining on my parade, damn you.

'It's possible, Bernie, but—'

'The killer may have panicked and ran out of the apartment without the box. Maybe Flaxford never showed him the box in the first place.'

'Maybe.'

'Maybe the blue box has been in Flaxford's safe deposit box all along. Safe in the bowels of some midtown bank.'

'Maybe.'

'Maybe Michael Debus killed Flaxford. He got the box and then Darla Sandoval and Wesley Brill ransacked my apartment.'

'You don't think—'

'No, I don't. Maybe Brill killed Flaxford because he couldn't remember his lines. He gave the box to Carter Sandoval to keep his coin collection in. That's not what I think, either. I'll tell you what I think. I think the blue box is in Flaxford's place.'

'Because you want it to be there.'

'That's right, because I want it to be there. Because I'm a fucking intuitive genius who plays his hunches.'

'Which is largely responsible for the fantastic success you've made of your life.'

We were by this point managing the neat trick of screaming at each other without raising our voices. In a portion of my mind – the portion that wasn't screaming – I wondered just what we were really mad about. I knew that on my part there was at least a little sexual agitation involved. Darla Sandoval had started fires that had not yet been properly extinguished.

Ultimately the fighting died down as pointlessly as it had started. We looked at each other and it was over. 'I'll make coffee,' she offered. 'Unless you'd rather have a drink.'

'Not when I'm working.'

'But you'll have keys, won't you? And you'll be with an authorized representative of the law.'

'It's still burglary as far as I'm concerned.'

'So just coffee for you. Fair enough. He's picking you up at her place? Are you going uptown dressed like that?'

'Don't you think I'll be warm enough? Sorry. I don't know if I'll change or not. Frankly I'm getting sick of putting this uniform on and taking it off. But with my luck somebody'll stop me en route uptown and expect me to shoot it out with a holdup man.'

'Or investigate a burglary.'

'Or that. And without the cap the uniform looks incomplete. I guess I'll change.'

'After you take your uniform off,' she said, 'would you have to put your other clothes on right away?'

'Huh?'

She turned toward me, gave me a slow smile.

'Oh,' I said, and began undoing buttons.

15

I beat the cops to Darla's place, but not by more than a few minutes. I had barely finished changing into my basic blue when the doorbell rang. I opened the door to admit Ray and Loren. Ray looked sour, Loren uncertain. Ray came in first, pointing over his shoulder with his thumb. 'He's been driving me nuts, Bernie,' he said. 'You want to tell him why he can't come along with us?'

I looked at Loren, who in turn looked at my scotch-grain loafers, not because he disapproved of them but because they were where he wanted to point his eyes. 'I just think I should go, too,' he said. 'Suppose something happens. Then what?'

'Nothing's gonna happen,' Ray said. 'Me and Bernie, we're gonna visit a place, then we're gonna leave the place, then we come back here and Bernie gives you your stuff back and you and me, we get the hell outta here and go home and count our money. You bring some magazines along?'

'I brought a book.'

'So you sit on the couch there and read your book. It's a nice comfortable couch. I sat on it earlier myself. You usually pick up this kind of dough reading a book?'

Loren breathed in and out, in and out. 'Suppose something happens. Suppose this Gemini here pulls something and you and I are on opposite ends of town, Ray. Then what?'

'Flaxford's apartment's on the East Side,' I pointed out. 'Just like this one.'

No one responded to this. Loren began describing things that could go wrong, from traffic wrecks to sudden civil defense alerts. Ray replied that having three cops along, two legitimate and one not, was more awkward than having one real one and one ringer.

'I don't like this,' Loren said. 'I'm not nuts about it, if you want to know the truth.'

'If you came along, you and Bernie'd only have one gun between the two of you. And one badge and so on. Just one hat, for Chrissakes.'

'That's another thing. I'm going to be sitting here without my badge, without my gun. Jesus, I don't know, Ray.'

'You'll be sittin' behind a locked door in an empty apartment, Loren. What in the hell do you need a gun for? You scared of cockroaches?'

'No roaches,' I said. 'This is a class building.'

'There you go,' Ray said. 'No roaches.'

'Who cares about roaches?'

'I thought maybe you did.'

'I just don't know, Ray.'

'Just sit down, you asshole. Give Bernie your stuff. Bernie, maybe a drink would help him unwind, you know?'

'Sure.'

'You got any booze around?'

I went into the kitchen for the Scotch. I brought the bottle and a glass and some ice. 'I better not,' Loren said. 'I'm on duty.'

'Jesus Christ,' Ray said.

I said, 'Well, it's here if you want it, Loren.' He nodded. I buckled on his gun belt and made sure the holster was snapped shut so that the gun wouldn't fall out and embarrass us all. I reached back, patted the cold steel on my hip, and thought what a horrible thing it was. 'Damned thing weighs a ton,' I said.

'What, the gun? You get used to it.'

'You'd think it'd be hard to walk straight, all that weight.'

'No time at all you get used to it. You get so you feel naked without it, you know.'

I took the shiny black nightstick from Loren and gave it an experimental whack against my palm. The wood was smooth and well-polished. Ray showed me how to hook it to my belt and fix the stick so it wouldn't swing loose and wallop me in the shin. Then I pinned on my badge, set my cap on my head and straightened it. I went to the bedroom and looked at myself in the mirrored door, and this time I decided that I really did look like a cop.

The cap helped, certainly, and I think the badge and gun and stick and cuffs made a subtle difference too, changing my own attitude, making me feel more comfortable in my role. I took the nightstick from its grip, giving it a tentative twirl, then tucking it back where it belonged. I even considered practicing getting the gun out of the holster but rejected the idea, confident that I would only succeed in shooting off a toe. Miraculous enough that I'd pinned my badge to my uniform blouse, I thought, and not to my skin.

But by the time I returned to the living room I felt enough like a cop to tell someone to move on, or hold up traffic, or get a free meal at a lunch counter. And I guess Ray noticed the difference. He looked me over from cap to shoes and back again and gave a slow nod. 'You'll pass,' he said.

Even Loren had to agree. 'They're natural actors,' he said.

'Burglars?'

'Geminis.'

'Jesus,' Ray said. 'Let's get the hell outta here.'

In the black-and-white he said, 'We're cleared to enter the apartment. It's sealed as evidence but what we do is break those seals and affix new ones when we leave. It'll all be recorded that way so nothing'll be screwed up.'

'Is that standard?'

'Oh, sure. The seals are to prevent unauthorized entry. They can't really keep anybody out who wants in but you can't go through the door without you break the seal. This particular apartment, it's been opened up and resealed a couple times already. I saw the sheet on it.'

'Oh? Who's been inside?'

'The usual. The photographer and the lab crew went through it before it was sealed up in the first place, but then the photographer went back for seconds later on. Maybe some of his pictures didn't turn out or maybe somebody from the DA's office wanted him to get establishing shots of the other rooms. You never know what those monkeys'll want to show to a jury and label it Exhibit A. Then there was another visit from an Assistant DA, probably to get the feel of the place firsthand, and there were a couple of bulls from Homicide, even though this is the precinct's case all the way and we're not letting those pricks from Homicide take it away from us, but of course they have to get a look all the same, maybe figuring the MO'll fit a case they're already carryin' on the books. Then, and it musta been the same kind of thing, there was a visit from another DA's office, not even Manhattan but some clowns from across the river—'

'When was that?'

'I dunno. What's the difference?'

'Which office was it? Brooklyn? Queens?'

'Brooklyn.'

'Who's the Brooklyn DA?'

'Kings County DA is – shit, I forget the name.'

'Is it Michael Debus?'

'That's it. Yeah, Debus. Why?'

'When were his men there?'

'Sometime between the murder and tonight. What's it matter?' He looked at me thoughtfully, almost sideswiping a parked car in the process. 'They park right in the middle of the fuckin' street,' he complained. 'How do you connect up with this Debus character, Bernie?'

'I don't. I think Flaxford did.'

'How?'

I thought for a moment. If I knew precisely when my own apartment had been visited, and precisely when Debus had had the Flaxford apartment searched, then . . . Then what? Then nothing. It might help

118

my theory in my own mind if I could establish that Debus had sent men to East Sixty-seventh Street before he sent them to West End Avenue, but it wouldn't really prove anything, nor would it demolish my theory if the timing was the other way around.

When all was said and done, the only really important variable was the box. Either I could find it or I couldn't.

'It might eventually be important,' I said, 'to know just who Debus sent to the apartment and when they were there.'

'Well, it's a matter of record.'

'You could find out?'

'Not right this minute, but later on. Sure.'

'It'll be there anyway,' I said.

'Huh?'

'Nothing.'

I recognized the doorman. But he didn't recognize me, and I decided that I would definitely have to remember him at Christmas. He held the door for us as he'd held it for me twice before, and while Ray chatted with him he paused twice to challenge people on their way into the building. Evidently he'd been reprimanded for letting me in, but at least they hadn't taken his job away and I was happy for him.

I didn't even get a second glance from him. I was wearing a uniform and I was standing there next to Ray, so why should he pay any attention to me?

We rode up on the elevator with a man dressed as a priest. I suppose he probably *was* a priest, but he looked less like a priest than I looked like a cop, so why should I take anything for granted? It occurred to me that clerical garb would make a good cover for a burglary. It would certainly get you past most doormen in a hurry. Of course it wouldn't do you too much good in the suburbs where the object was to avoid getting noticed in the first place, but apartment houses were something else.

Now in the suburbs a mailman's uniform would be ideal. Of course, a lot of people know their route man, but if you could pass yourself off as the guy who delivers parcels or special delivery letters or something like that—

'Something on your mind, Bernie?'

'Just thinking about business,' I said. We got off at the third floor and left the alleged priest to ascend alone. I stood aside while Ray broke the seals on Flaxford's door. Then, while he was fishing in his pocket for the keys, I extended a finger and poked the doorbell. He gave me a look as the bell sounded within the apartment.

'Just routine,' I explained.

'Police seals on the door and you think there's somebody inside the place?'

'You never know.'

'That's crazy.'

'Everybody has a routine,' I said. 'That's mine.'

'Jesus,' he said. He found the keys, poked one at the lock. I could see it wasn't going to fit and it didn't. He tried the other and it slid in.

'Must seem funny to you,' he said. 'Using a key.'

Just a little earlier I'd used Darla's key and now we were using Flaxford's. The only place I had to break into these days was the place where I was living.

'Last time I opened this door,' he said, 'there was a burglar on the other side of it.'

'Last time I opened it there was a corpse in the bedroom.'

'Let's hope tonight's a new experience for both of us.'

He gave the key a half-turn clockwise and pushed the door open. He said something I didn't catch and went on inside, reaching to flick on the light switch. Then he turned and motioned me inside but I stayed where I was.

'Come on,' he said. 'Whattaya waitin' for?'

'The door wasn't locked.'

'Of course it was. I unlocked it.'

'Just the snaplock. All you had to do was turn it halfway around and it opened. A lock like that has a deadbolt, too, and if the deadbolt's engaged you have to turn it one and a half times around to open it.'

'So?'

'So the last person out didn't bother locking it with the key. He just closed it on his way out.'

'What's it matter? Maybe his partner's got the key and he's halfway to the elevator so he doesn't bother. Maybe he never thinks to lock it with the key. A lot of people always leave their doors like that. They never take the trouble to use the whatchamacallit, the deadbolt.'

'I know. They make my life a lot easier.'

'So here we got somebody who it's not his apartment in the first place and he's gonna be slapping an evidence seal on it anyway, and what does he care about deadbolts? It don't mean a thing, Bernie.'

'Right,' I said. I poked at my memory, trying to catch something small and quick that kept darting around corners. '*I* put the deadbolt on,' I said.

'How's that?'

'Once I was inside. I closed the door and I turned this gizmo here, this knob. That's how you engage the deadbolt from inside the apartment.'

'So?'

'And when you and Loren got here with the key from the doorman, you had to turn it around a full turn to undo the bolt and then another half turn to draw back the spring lock.'

'If you say so,' Ray said. He was a little impatient now. 'If that's what you say I'll take your word for it, Bernie, because I frankly don't make a point of noticing how many times I turn a key in a lock, especially when I don't know what the fuck's on the other side of the door, which I didn't at the time. None of this makes the slightest fucking difference and I don't know what the hell you're rattling on about. I thought you wanted to get into this place, but if all you want is to stand outside talking about bolts like a nut—'

'You're absolutely right,' I said. I came all the way inside and closed the door behind me. And turned the bolt.

The apartment didn't look different from when I'd seen it last. If the wrecking crew at my apartment had been Michael Debus's responsibility, he'd clearly assigned a gentler crowd altogether to the task of searching J. Francis Flaxford's digs. Of course the search of my place had been unauthorized and unrecorded while the visit here had been made with official permission and was duly noted in some official log. So Flaxford's books remained on Flaxford's shelves and Flaxford's clothes remained in Flaxford's closets and drawers. No one had slashed open his furniture or taken up his rugs or cast pictures down from his walls.

All of this seemed wildly unfair. Flaxford, who had gone to whatever reward awaits fixers and blackmailers, would never wear these clothes or read these books or inhabit this apartment again, yet everything was shipshape for him. I, on the other hand, had a use for the contents of my apartment. And I had been sorely mistreated.

I tried to put this inequity out of my mind and concentrate instead on searching the place. I began in the bedroom, where chalkmarks on the oriental rug (I've no idea what kind) indicated the position of the body. He had been lying just to the left of the foot of his bed, his outspread feet reaching toward the doorway. There were dark brown stains on the carpet where his head had been outlined and similar stains on the unmade bed.

I said, 'Blood?' Ray nodded. 'You always think of blood as red,' I said.

'Brown when it dries, though.'

'Uh-huh. He must have flopped on the bed when he was hit. And slid down onto the floor.'

'Figures.

'The paper said he was killed with an ashtray. Where is it?'

'I thought it was a lamp. You sure it was an ashtray?'

'The paper said.'

'A lot they know. Whatever it was, somebody musta tagged it and took it the hell outta here. Murder weapon, you don't go and leave something like that behind. It gets tagged and run through the lab sixteen different ways and photographed a couple hundred times and then locked up somewhere.' He cleared his throat. 'Even if something

like that was here, Bernie, there's no way I could let you do nothin'
about it. No tamperin' with evidence.'

'I just wondered what happened to it.'

'Just so you understand.'

I brushed past him and moved around the bed to where an oil painting of a ramshackle barn hung in a heavy gilded frame. I realized that if
there was a wall safe in the place fifteen people had already gone
through it since the murder, but I moved the picture anyway and the
only thing behind it was a wall.

I said, 'Funny. You'd think he'd have a safe. A man like him would
have cash around the house frequently. Maybe he just didn't worry.'

'What cash? He owned property and he was in the theater, Bernie.
Where does cash come into it? The only thing is the theater receipts
and nobody brings those home nowadays. They go straight into the
bank's night depository. Plus the little theaters he messed around with,
how much money'd be involved in the first place?'

I thought, *Why bother going into it?* But all the same I said, 'He was
mixed up with a lot of characters. I think he operated as some kind of
bagman or fixer. I know he was tied into some political heavies, but
whether he just free-lanced for them I can't be sure. Plus he screwed
around with blackmail and extortion.'

'I thought you didn't know him?'

'I didn't.'

'Then where do you get off knowing all this?'

'The Shadow knows,' I said. 'The Department must know something
about it, too, as far as that goes. Didn't you hear anything about
Flaxford's secret life?'

'Not a word. But I don't guess anybody looked to find out. Seein' we
knew who killed him and we got an airtight case, why futz around with
details? What's the percentage?'

'Airtight,' I said hollowly.

'Bernie, if you want to tell me what we're looking for—'

'*We* are not looking for anything. *I* am looking for something.'

'Yeah, but what?'

'I'll know it when I see it.'

'Suppose I see it?'

I made my way past him again, stepping gingerly over the chalkmarks as if the body itself were still there, an ectoplasmic presence
hovering just above the carpet. I walked down the hallway, stopping to
check out the bathroom. It was large in proportion to the rest of the
apartment, suggesting the building had been divided into smaller rental
units somewhere along the line. There was a massive claw-footed tub,
an antique survivor that contrasted with the modern sink and toilet. I
ran water in the sink, gave the toilet a flush, turned to see Ray looking
at me with his eyebrows raised.

122

'Just remembering,' I said. 'If Loren hadn't taken a wrong turn after he flushed the toilet we'd have all been on our way.'

'It's a fact. Who knows when somebody'd have finally discovered the poor sonofabitch?'

'Not for days, maybe.'

'You'da been clear, Bernie. Even if we make the connection, what the hell can we do? Walk in with our caps in our hands and say we had you but we let you go? Besides, by the time it all comes together we wouldn't know if you were there the same night he got it, because with all that time gone you can't fix the time of death all that close.'

'But Loren walked right in on him.'

I stood for a moment in the bathroom doorway, turned toward the bedroom, then turned again and went back to the living room. I could check Flaxford's closet for false backs and bottoms but that just didn't seem like his style.

The desk.

I went over and stood next to it, started tapping it here and there. Darla Sandoval had seen him take the blue box from this desk and put it back in the desk when he was done showing its contents to her. And the desk had still been locked after Flaxford lay dead in his bedroom. I'd been through it once but those old fossils were loaded with secret compartments, drawers lurking behind drawers, pigeonholes in back of pigeonholes. The desk was where I'd been told to look in the very beginning, and it was where I was looking when Ray and Loren walked in on me, and it was where I would look now.

I got out my ring of burglar tools. 'Sit down,' I told Ray. 'This may take a while.'

It took close to an hour. I removed each drawer in turn, checked behind them, turned them upside down and very nearly inside out. I rolled up the roll-top and probed within and I found more secret compartments than you could advertise on the back of a cereal box. Most of them were empty, but one held a collection of raunchy Victorian pornography which had evidently been secreted there by a raunchy Victorian. I passed the half-dozen booklets to Ray, who'd complained earlier that Flaxford's shelves contained nothing more salacious than Motley's *Rise of the Dutch Republic* in two leather-bound volumes.

'This is better,' he reported. 'But I wish to hell they could write it in plain English. By the time you figure out exactly what the guy's doing to the broad you could lose interest.'

I went on performing exploratory surgery on the desk. Now and then I removed an interior panel knowing I'd never be able to put it back later, and I felt sorry about this, but not sorry enough to cry about it. Eventually I realized that, however more secret compartments the desk might contain, Flaxford wouldn't have used any of them for the blue box. It would have taken him too long to put it away and get it out again.

I stepped back and looked down at the desk and wanted to wash my hands of the whole damned thing. The thought of washing my hands made me think of running water, which led me back to the bathroom in short order. While I stood there doing my Niagara Falls impression I found myself studying the elaborately inlaid tile floor beneath my feet. Old fashioned clay tiles about an inch square, most of them white, with a geometric pattern traced in light blue tiles. When I got to where I was actually toying with the idea of taking up the floor I knew I was skating dangerously close to the edge. I gave the toilet a flush, rinsed my hands, looked without success for a towel, dried my hands on my blue pants, took Loren's nightstick from its clasp, slapped it briskly against my palm, and got out of there.

And turned left instead of right, tracing Loren's route into the bedroom. I went over to the closet and went through it very quickly, knowing I'd find nothing but clothes, and that was all I did find.

I was on my way out of the room when I happened to see it out of the corner of my eye, just a little scrap of something that had wedged itself between the bedpost and the wall.

I got down on one knee and examined it. I took a very careful look and I did some thinking, and it all fit with some thoughts I'd already had. I got up and left it where it was and went back to the living room.

I was sliding the final drawer back into the desk when Ray said, 'What in the hell does *gamahouche* mean?'

I made him spell it, then took the book away from him and looked for myself. 'I think it means to go down on a girl,' I said.

'That's what I figured. Why the fuck can't they just *say* that?'

'Other times, other customs.'

'Shit.'

I left him squinting at antique filth and did some pacing, then dropped into the green wing chair where I'd planted myself before tackling the desk in the first place. I swung my feet onto the hassock, took a deep breath, and again tried to put myself into the mood of the apartment. *Your name is J. Francis Flaxford*, I told myself, *and you're sitting here comfortably in your bathrobe, except it's such a nice one you call it a dressing gown. You're supposed to be at the theater but you're hanging around with a drink at your elbow and a book in your lap and a cigar in your mouth and* . . .

'That's weird,' I said.

'What is?'

'They must have taken both ashtrays.'

'Huh?'

'There used to be a heavy cut-glass ashtray on this table.'

'They found it in the bedroom. The one he was killed with, I told you they'd take that along and lock it up.'

'No, there was a second ashtray,' I said. 'It was on this table here. I suppose it was a mate to the murder weapon. Why would they take both ashtrays?'

'Who knows?'

'Just super-efficient.'

'Bernie, we're runnin' outta time.'

'I know.'

'And you didn't find what you were lookin' for.'

'I found something.'

'In the desk?'

'In the bedroom.'

'What?' I hesitated and he didn't press. 'Not what you're lookin' for, anyway. What *are* you lookin' for? Maybe I seen it myself.'

'It's not very likely.'

'You never know.'

'A blue box,' I said. 'A blue leather-covered box.'

'How big?'

'Jesus,' I said. 'Either you saw it or you didn't, Ray. What's the difference how big it is?'

'You say a box, hell, it could be the size of a pack of cigarettes or the size of a steamer trunk.'

'About so big,' I said, moving my hands in the air. 'About the size of a book.' I remembered Darla's words. 'The size of a hard-cover novel. Or maybe as large as a dictionary. Oh, for Christ's sake.'

'What's wrong?'

'I'm an idiot,' I said. 'Aside from that, nothing's wrong.'

It took perhaps three minutes to find it, another five minutes to establish that all the other leather-bound volumes were what they purported to be. Flaxford's blue leather-covered box was nothing but a dummy book, a neat wooden lockbox that had been passing itself off as Darwin's *Origin of Species*. When it was open it wouldn't have looked like a book at all, just like a rather elaborate box which one might keep on a dresser top as a repository for tie tacks and cuff links and that sort of thing. Closed and locked and tucked away on a lower shelf, it looked no different from all of the real books which surrounded it.

The goons who went through my apartment would have found the box. When they shook each book in turn they would have found one that didn't flip open and that would have been that. But Flaxford's apartment never got that kind of a search.

'Aren't you gonna open it, Bernie?'

I glanced pointedly at Ray. I was in the green wing chair again and he was hovering beside me, gazing down over my shoulder. 'You go back to your book,' I said, 'and I'll concentrate on mine.'

'I guess that's right,' he said, returning to his own chair and book. I kept my eyes on him and saw him peek over his porn at me, then resume the charade of reading.

'Back in a minute,' I said. 'Nature calls.'

I walked right on past the bathroom and into Flaxford's bedroom, blue box in hand. Whether they look like books or not, those little home strongboxes are about as hard to get into as a stoned nymphomaniac. This one had a combination lock concealed behind a leather flap. You lined up the three ten-digit dials and you were home free. You pried the thing open with a chisel.

I wasn't in quite that much of a hurry and I did want the box to look as though it hadn't been opened, so I did a little poking and probing for a few seconds until the lock yielded. I had a look at everything that was in the box, then transferred all of it to my own person. My uniform had enough room in the pockets so that none of them wound up sporting an unseemly bulge.

When the box was properly empty I took hold of the bed and tugged it an inch or two away from the wall. The small rectangle that had caught my eye earlier was where I had left it, and it was a good deal more visible now that I had moved the bed. I used Loren's nightstick to coax it out into the open, then took it ever so carefully between thumb and forefinger, holding it by its edges and placing it into the legendary blue box.

And closed the box, and locked it.

On my way back to the living room I encouraged history to repeat itself, giving the toilet a convincing flush. Ray looked up when I returned to where I'd left him. 'Nervous stomach?'

'Guess so.'

'Nervous myself,' he said. 'What say we get outta here?'

'Fine. I can open this back at my place.'

'I'd think you'd be in a hurry.'

'Not that much of a hurry,' I said. 'I'm more anxious to get out of here. And Loren was unhappy about missing' out on all this, so let's give him a chance to see what's in the box. I already have a pretty good idea what we'll find.'

'And you think it'll get you off the hook?'

'It'll get me off,' I said, 'and it'll get somebody else on.'

We gave the place a lightning once-over to make sure we'd left everything more or less as we'd found it. The internal damage I'd done to the beautiful old desk didn't show, and the bookshelves looked quite undisturbed. Outside, Kirschmann affixed a seal to the door, noted date and time and added his signature. Then he gave me a deliberate smile and used the key to turn the deadbolt.

And, as the lock turned, the last piece fitted into place for me.

16

By the time we got back to Darla Sandoval's little love nest, Loren Kramer was a nervous wreck. I let us in with my key and when we came through the door Loren was behind it. Since we hadn't thought he might have chosen that spot for himself, we inadvertently hit him with the door. When he groaned Ray yanked the door forward and stared unhappily at his partner. 'I don't believe this,' he said. 'I thought I told you to stay on the couch.'

'I didn't know it was you, Ray.'

'Hiding behind doors. Jesus.'

'I got nervous, that's all. You were gone a long time and I started worrying about it.'

'Well, Bernie here had to look for a box that wasn't there. It was sort of fun to watch him. He took a desk apart and everything. Then the box he was looking for turned up on a bookshelf. That's it right there. It was pretendin' to be a book.'

'*The Purloined Letter*,' Loren said.

'Huh?'

'Edgar Allan Poe,' I said. 'A short story. But that's not exactly right, Loren. Now if you were to hide a book on a bookshelf, that would be like the story. Except this was a box that was disguised as a book.'

'It sounds like pretty much the same thing to me,' Loren said. He sounded sulky about it.

While we puzzled over all of this, Ray went to the kitchen and made himself a drink. He came back, took a large swallow of it, and suggested that it was time to open the box.

'And time I had my gun back,' Loren said. 'And my stick and my badge and my cuffs and my cap, the whole works. Nothing against you, Bernie, but it bothers me seeing them on someone who's not really a cop.'

'That's understandable, Loren.'

'Plus I don't feel dressed without them. The gun, we even have to carry them off-duty, you know. When you think of all the holdups foiled by off-duty patrolmen you understand the reason behind the regulation.'

What I mostly thought of was all the off-duty cops who tended to shoot one another in the course of serious discussions of the relative merits of the Knicks and the Nets, but I decided not to raise this point. I didn't think it would go over too well.

'The box,' Ray said.

'Couldn't I get my stuff back and then he opens the box?'

'Jesus,' Ray said.

I hefted the box in my hands. 'Surprisingly enough,' I said, 'this box isn't all that important.'

Ray stared at me. 'It was worth ten thousand dollars to you, Bernie. That sounds pretty important. And it's supposed to get you off a murder charge, though I'll be damned if I see how it's gonna do that. For the sake of argument I'll buy that you didn't kill Flaxford. But I don't see you comin' up with a dime's worth of proof in that direction, let alone ten grand's worth.'

'It must look that way,' I admitted.

'Unless the proof's in the box.'

'The box was a personal matter,' I said. 'Call it a favor for a friend. The important thing was for me to get into the apartment, Ray. I didn't even realize it at the time, in fact I actually thought that the box was the important thing, but just being in the apartment told me what I wanted to know.'

'I don't get it,' Loren said. He looked as though he expected a trick, as though when I opened the blue box I'd be likely to extract a white rabbit. 'What did you find in the apartment, Bernie?'

'For openers, the door wasn't locked completely. The deadbolt wasn't on.'

'Oh, Jesus,' Ray said. 'I told you some cop just shut the door and didn't bother locking it. What's it matter?'

'It doesn't. What does matter is that the deadbolt *was* locked when I let myself into Flaxford's apartment the other night. If it had just been the spring lock I'd have opened it faster, but that's a good Rabson lock and I had to work the cylinder around for one and a half turns. It didn't take me too long because I happen to be outstanding in my chosen field—'

'Jesus, what we gotta listen to.'

'—but I had to turn the bolt first, then go on to knock off the spring lock. Which I did.'

'So?'

'So either the murderer happened to take a key with him on his way out of the apartment and then happened to take the time to use the key to lock Flaxford's corpse inside, or else Flaxford engaged that deadbolt himself by turning the knob from the inside. And I somehow can't see the murderer having the key in the first place or bothering to use it if he did.'

I had their attention now but they didn't know quite what to make of it. Slowly Ray said, 'You're sayin' Flaxford locked hisself in, right?'

'That's what I'm saying.'

'Jesus, Bernie, all you're puttin' is your own neck in the noose. If he locked hisself in and the door's locked when you get there, then the bastard was alive when you let yourself in.'

'That's absolutely right.'

'Then you killed him.'

'Wrong.' I slapped Loren's stick against the palm of my hand. 'See, I have an advantage here,' I went on. 'I happen to know for a fact that I didn't kill Flaxford. So knowing he was alive when I got there means something different to me. It means I know who killed him.'

'Who?'

'It's obvious, isn't it?' I pointed with the nightstick. 'Loren killed him. Who else?'

I watched Loren's right hand. Interestingly enough, it went to where his gun would have been if I hadn't been wearing it at the time. He dropped his hand to his side and saw me looking at him and flushed.

'You're out of your mind,' he said.

'I don't think so.'

'If that's not typical for Gemini I don't know what is. Just try on any kind of a wild lie and see how it goes over. Ray, I think we better take him in. This time put cuffs on him, will you? He already escaped from us once.'

Ray was silent for a moment. Then to me he said, 'Are you just snowballing this one, Bernie? Puttin' it together as you go along?'

'No, I think it's fairly solid, Ray.'

'You want to run it by me once just for curiosity?'

'Ray, you're not going to listen to this maniac—'

'Shut up,' Ray Kirschmann said. And to me he added, 'Go ahead, Bernie, you got me interested. Go through it once for me.'

'Sure,' I said. 'It's pretty simple, actually. J. Francis Flaxford was supposed to go to the opening of a play that night. It was all set. That's why I picked that particular time to hit his apartment. I had inside information and my source knew for a fact he'd be out.

'Well, he was all set to go. He was in his dressing gown, ready to get dressed, and then he had an accident. I don't know if it was a stroke or a fainting spell or a minor heart attack or an accidental fall or what, but the upshot of it is he wound up passed out on his bed wearing his robe. Somewhere along the line he probably knocked the lamp off the bed-side table or bumped into something and maybe that was the noise that prompted some neighbor to call the cops. It doesn't matter. The signifi-cant thing is that he was unconscious in his bedroom with the door locked from inside when I entered the apartment.'

'This is crazy,' Loren said.

'Let him talk.' Ray's voice was neutral. 'So far you're just spinnin' your wheels, Bernie.'

'All right. I got into the apartment and went right to work. I never left the living room and did nothing but go through the desk because that was where the box was supposed to be. My informant didn't know the box was disguised as a book. I was still playing around with the desk when you arrived. We had our conversation, made our financial arrangements, and we were all set to leave when Loren got a call of nature.'

'So?'

'So according to his story, he went to the bathroom, used the toilet, then made a wrong turn on his way back and walked to the bedroom by mistake. There he discovered Flaxford's corpse. So he turned and rushed all the way back to the living room where we were waiting for him, finally sounded the alarm far and wide, turned a little green around the gills and flopped over in a faint.'

'Well, we both saw him do that, Bernie. And then you sandbagged me and took off like a bat outta hell.'

I shrugged off that last charge. 'Loren saw Flaxford right off the bat,' I said, 'speaking of bats. He had to. That's a short hallway. If you walk toward the bathroom from the living room you can see those chalk-marks on the bedroom carpet before you reach the bathroom door. Of course there were no chalkmarks at the time. But there was a body there, sprawled out on the bed, and that was interesting enough so that Loren passed right by the john and checked out the bedroom.'

'And?'

'He was in there for a few minutes. Then the body – Flaxford, that is – came to life. I don't know whether Loren originally thought he was dead or unconscious, but either way the man was suddenly alive and awake and staring at him, and Loren reacted automatically. He swung his trusty nightstick and cracked Flaxford over the head.'

'Crazy,' Loren said. His voice was trembling but that might have been rage and indignation as easily as guilt. 'He's out of his mind. Why would I do anything like that?'

'For money.'

'What money?'

'The money you were filling your pockets with when Flaxford blinked his baby blues at you. There was money all over his lap and all over the floor when you found him.' To Ray I said, 'Look, Flaxford was a fixer, a bagman, a guy with a lot of angles going for himself. He may have bank accounts and safe deposit boxes and secret stashes but he also would have had cash on hand. Every operator like that does, whether his operations are legal or not. Look, I'm just a small-time burglar myself but I was able to put my hands on ten grand tonight.' I saw no point in adding that only half of it had been mine.

'Now the one thing that never turned up in Flaxford's apartment was money. Not in his drawers or closets, not in any wall safe, not in that fantastic desk. With all the searches that place got, including the search I gave it tonight, the one thing that never turned up was cash.'

'So you're saying that because there was no cash Loren here must have taken it?'

'It's crazy,' Loren said.

'It's not crazy,' I said. 'Whatever knocked Flaxford unconscious, it got him suddenly. A fall, a stroke, whatever – all of a sudden he was unconscious. It's my guess he had a recent visitor bringing him a payoff that he was supposed to transfer from one person to another. The payoff was big enough to make him delay his trip to the theater. He got the cash, his visitor left, and he took it to his bedroom to count it before he passed out. Loren walked in and found this unconscious man in a room full of hundred-dollar bills.'

'You're guessing.'

'Am I? My apartment got ransacked, Ray. Every drawer turned upside down, every book shaken open, the most complete search you can imagine. There's nothing in the blue box that could inspire that kind of a search. But somebody knew Flaxford had a lot of money on him when he was killed, and the person who would have made that assumption was the person who gave him the money. I think it was probably Michael Debus or someone associated with him. Either the money was being channeled to Debus or Debus was spreading it through Flaxford to head off an investigation into his office. But that explains why Flaxford's visitor couldn't have killed him, in addition to the business with the locks. That person – say Debus for convenience – left Flaxford alive and left the money with him. And the sum was large enough so that Debus wasn't willing to write it off after Flaxford was killed. It was even large enough so that Loren thought it was worth killing for.'

'Ray, he's crazy. This man is crazy.'

'I don't know, Loren,' Ray said.

'You've got to be kidding.'

'I don't know. You always liked money.'

'You sound like you're starting to believe this fairy story.'

'You always took what was handed to you, Loren. As green as you were I was a little surprised. Usually it'll take a while before a guy learns to stick his hand out. Then he sees how it's part of the system and he gets hardnosed in various ways and little by little he develops an appetite. But you, Loren, you were hungry right outta the box. You were hungry without ever gettin' hip. You're still mopin' around with your moon in fuckin' Capricorn or whatever it is and you're the hungriest sonofabitch I ever saw.'

'Ray, you know I'd never kill anybody.'

'I'm not sure what I know.'

'Ray, with a nightstick? Come on.'

I was glad he'd brought that up. I swung Loren's nightstick and slapped it ringingly against my palm. 'Nice club,' I said. 'Smooth and shiny. A person would swear you never hit anybody with it, Loren.'

'I never did.'

'No, you never did. Or bumped it into anything or dropped it on the pavement or scraped it against a brick wall. Or even wore it until a couple of days ago.' I pointed it at him in a shamelessly theatrical gesture. 'It's new, isn't it, Loren? Brand new. Positively virginal. Because you had to replace your old one. It wasn't brand new and it had been knocked around a lot because you liked to play with it and you tended to drop it a lot. The surface was chipped and there were a few cracks in it. And you knew Flaxford's blood could have soaked into the cracks – blood or skin fragments or something – and you have to know what a crime lab can do with something like that and that all the scrubbing in the world isn't always enough to get rid of the evidence. You got rid of the whole nightstick.'

Loren opened his mouth but didn't say anything. Ray took the stick out of my hand and examined it. 'It does look pretty cherry,' he said.

'Ray, for God's sake.'

'Very fuckin' new, Loren. This ain't the club you been carryin' around. When'd you get this one?'

'Oh, maybe a week, two weeks ago.'

'Before the Flaxford murder, huh?'

'Of course before the burglary. Ray—'

'What was the matter with the old one?'

'I don't know. I just liked the heft of this one better. Ray—'

'You throw the old one away, Loren?'

'I probably got it around somewheres.'

'You figure you could come up with it if you had to?'

'I guess so. Oh, come to think of it, I think I maybe left it out in the backyard. Of course one of the neighbors' kids might have run off with it but there's still a chance it's there.'

The two of them looked at each other. I might as well not have been in the room. They held each other's gaze for a long time before Loren averted his eyes and examined his shoes. They were black oxfords, incidentally, polished to a high sheen and far more suitable for a uniformed patrolman than my scotch-grain loafers.

Ray said, 'The toilet. He went to the bathroom and we heard him flush the toilet and then just a few seconds later he was back in the living room. How'd he have time to do everything you said?'

'He flushed the toilet on the way back, Ray. He walked right past the bathroom originally and he just stopped on the way back to flush the toilet.'

'As a cover?'

'Right.'

'Yeah, I guess that would fit. What about the ashtray? Flaxford got killed with an ashtray.'

'From the living room.'

'How do you figure that?'

'You remember when I asked about the ashtray? There was one in the living room on the table next to where I was sitting. It wasn't there tonight and I thought at first that it was the mate to the murder weapon, one of a pair, and the lab crew took both of them for some reason. But there was only the one ashtray. It was in the living room when I entered the apartment and by the time the lab crew got there it was in the bedroom.'

'How'd it get there? He took it?'

'Sure. He came back to the living room and did his fainting act. It seemed strange the way that happened. It was the damnedest delayed reaction ever, if you think about it. Of course if he never saw a corpse before—'

'He's seen a few.'

'Well, maybe this was the first one he was ever responsible for. So he probably did feel a little weak in the knees, but he managed to get all the way back to where we were and then flop on the rug. It wasn't a real faint. A minute later I was out the door, and then when you got yourself together you ran right out after me, didn't you?'

'So?'

'He was still on the rug when you took off. As soon as you cleared the door your buddy here grabbed the glass ashtray off the table and went back to the bedroom with it. Then he parted Flaxford's hair with it. Maybe he'd only stunned him with the nightstick. Maybe Flaxford was already dead but Loren wanted to supply, a convenient murder weapon. I think he was probably still alive, but a couple of swipes with a heavy hunk of glass would finish the job. Then he could recover consciousness and rush out and join you on the street. He'd have the rest of the money picked up by then and he'd be home free, leaving me with a murder rap hanging around my neck.'

I don't know exactly when Ray Kirschmann knew I was telling the truth, but somewhere in the course of that speech the last of his doubts vanished. Because I heard him unsnap his own holster so that he'd be able to get to his gun if he needed it. The gesture was not lost on Loren, who looked as though he was about to take a step forward, then changed his mind and sat down on the couch.

Ray said, 'How much money, Loren?' And when Loren didn't answer he asked me.

'He'll tell you sooner or later. My guess is it's better than twenty thou and probably double that. It would have to be quite a bit to account for the way Debus is pressing to recover it. Of course Loren wouldn't have known just what it added up to until he got home and counted it, but he could see right away that there was enough there to kill for.'

There was a long silence. Then Loren said, 'I thought he was already dead.'

We looked at him.

'He was sprawled out like a corpse. I thought for sure this guy killed him. I don't know what I thought. I started picking up the money. It was automatic. I don't know what came over me. Then he opened his eyes and started to get up and – see, all along I thought he was dead, and then he opened his eyes.'

'And then you went back with the ashtray just to make sure, huh?'

'Oh, God,' Loren said.

'How much did it finally come to, partner? Twenty grand? Forty?'

'Fifty.'

'Fifty thousand American dollars.' Ray whistled softly. 'No wonder you weren't crazy about our deal tonight. Why take chances for ten grand when you already had fifty salted away, especially when you'd have to split the ten in half and the fifty was yours free and clear.'

'Half's yours, Ray. You think I would hold out?'

'Oh, you're real cute, Loren.'

'I was just waiting until I could find a way to explain it to you. I wouldn't hold out on you.'

'Of course not.'

'Twenty-five thousand tax-free dollars is your end of it, Ray. Jesus, here we have the murderer standing right next to you. It's open and shut and all he is is a fucking burglar, Ray. See how sweet it is?'

'Oh, I get it. You think we should hang it all on Bernie here.' Ray scratched his chin. 'Thing is, what happens when he tells his story? They'd lean on you and do some checking and you'd crack wide open, Loren.'

'He could get shot trying to escape. Ray, he escaped once, right? He's a dangerous man. Listen to me, Ray. Think about twenty-five thousand dollars. Or maybe you should get more than half. Is that it? Ray, listen to me—'

Ray hit him. He used his open hand and slapped Loren across the face. Loren put his hand to his cheek and stood there looking properly stunned while the slap went on echoing in the silent apartment.

'You have the right to remain silent,' Ray said after a moment. 'You have the right to – oh, fuck this noise. Bernie, if the question ever comes up you'll recall that I read this cocksucker his rights.'

'No question about it.'

'Because I want this to be airtight. I never liked the little shit but you'd think he'd know the difference between clean and dirty, between taking money and killing for it. You know what I'd like? I'd like something hard, some piece of evidence that would nail his ass to the wall. Like his nightstick with Flaxford's blood on it, but it's a sure bet that already went down the incinerator.'

'You'll find the money. With blood on some of it.'

'Unless he stashed it.' He glared at Loren. 'But I suppose he'll tell me where it is.'

'He doesn't have to.'

'What do you mean?'

'I don't think he actually picked up fifty thousand dollars. I think he picked up forty-nine thousand nine hundred.'

'You lost me, Bernie.'

I held out the blue box. 'Now I didn't open this box yet,' I said, 'because I don't know the combination. But I could probably pick the lock, and when I do I have a feeling I know what we'll find inside. I think we'll find a hundred-dollar bill and I think there'll be a bloodstain on the bill and I even think there'll be a fingerprint on the bloodstain. Now it could conceivably be Flaxford's fingerprint if he did some bleeding before Loren got to him. Maybe he cut himself on the lamp as he knocked it over. But I have a hunch it'll be Loren's fingerprint, and it certainly ought to be a good piece of evidence, don't you think?'

Ray gave me a long look. 'That's what you *think* you'll find in the box.'

'Call it a hunch.'

'So why not open the box and see for ourselves?' And when I'd done so he said, 'Beautiful, Just beautiful. When'd you set this up, anyway? Oh, sure, the time you went to the toilet. You faked flushing it same as Loren did. That's cute. And the bill was there all the time? The lab boys missed it? Amazing.'

'It must have been in the blue box all along.'

'Uh-huh. I don't suppose I'll ever learn what was really in the blue box, and I don't really suppose I give a shit. I like what's in there now. That's a beautiful print, all right, and I'll bet it does turn up to be yours, Loren, and I'll also bet that blood turns out to be the right type.' He sighed heavily. 'Loren,' he said, 'I think you're in a lot of trouble.'

17

'That's fantastic,' Ellie said. 'Just incredible. You actually solved the murder.'

'That's what I did, all right.'

'It's amazing.' She drew up her legs and tucked her feet underneath herself. She was wearing the outfit she'd had on the morning she knocked the plant over, the white painter's pants and the Western-style denim shirt, and she looked as fetching as ever. 'I don't see how you figured it out, Bernie.'

'Well, I told you how it went. The main thing was realizing that the deadbolt had been locked originally. At the time I assumed that Flax-ford had locked it on his way out, but of course he was in the bedroom then. Once I made the connection, there were two possibilities. Either the murderer was someone with a key, or Flaxford had locked it him-self from the inside. And if Flaxford had locked up, then he was alive when I was in the apartment, and if that was the case only one person could have killed him.'

'Loren.'

'Loren. And if Loren killed him it was for money, and money was the one thing that wasn't turning up. And there just had to be money in the case.'

'And you figured all this out while you were opening the door.'

'I had it pretty much figured out before then. I wanted it to look like it was coming to me while Ray was around so it would be easier for him to follow the reasoning.'

'And then you had the luck to find the hundred-dollar bill on the floor.'

I let that pass. It *was* luck, but I'd been prepared to make my own luck. There was a hundred-dollar bill in my wallet right now, one of the pair Darla and I had split, and there was a little blood on it for decor-ation, and it would have gone into the blue box if the genuine article hadn't turned up behind the bed. I'd needed something to take Ray's mind off what was originally in the box and a piece of bloody currency had looked to have the right sort of dramatic value, something Perry Mason might wave about in a courtroom. Maybe that was why I happened to notice the bill Loren had actually left behind. Well, this way I could keep my own bill, at least until I found something to spend it on.

Ellie got up and went to the kitchen for more coffee. I stretched out and put my feet up on the coffee table. I was bone-tired and tightly wired all at once. I wanted to lie down and sleep for six or seven days, but the way I felt I might have to stay awake about that long.

It was getting late now, almost one-thirty. Once Ray and Loren had gotten out of Darla's apartment I'd called her at home as we'd arranged, ringing twice and hanging up. A few minutes later she rang me back and I reported that I'd found the box and had the tapes and pictures in hand. 'You don't have to worry about negatives,' I said. 'They're Polaroid shots. One thing, whoever took them had a nice sense of composition.'

'You looked at them.'

'I had to know what they were and I didn't trust myself to identify them by touch.'

'Oh, I'm not complaining,' she said. 'I just wondered if you found them interesting.'

'As a matter of fact, I did.'

'I thought you might. Have you listened to the tapes?'

'No. I'm not going to. I think there should be a certain amount of mystery in our relationship.'

'Oh, are we going to have a relationship?'

'I rather thought we might. Does your fireplace work or is it just for decoration?'

'It works. I've never had a relationship in a fireplace.'

'I had something else in mind for it. I'm going to burn the pictures and tapes before I leave. They're half mine anyway. I spent all my case money getting them back and I want them out of the way as soon as possible.'

'They might make interesting souvenirs.'

'No,' I said. 'It's too dangerous. It's like keeping a loaded gun around the house. The possible benefit is infinitesimal and the downside risk is enormous. I want to destroy them tonight. You can trust me to do it, incidentally. I'm not a potential blackmailer, just in case you were wondering.'

'Oh, I trust you, Bernard.'

'I still have my cop suit. I thought I might leave it here. It would save dragging it back downtown.'

'That's a good idea.'

'And I still have the handcuffs and the nightstick, strangely enough. The cop they belonged to had to leave in a hurry and he won't have any further use for them. I'll leave them here, too.'

'Lovely. If it weren't so late already—'

'No, it's too late. And I have some other things to do. But I'll be in touch, Darla.'

'Oh, good,' she said. 'That will be nice.'

I looked up the number of the Cumberland and called Wesley Brill to tell him that the whole thing was wrapped up and tied with a ribbon. 'You're completely out of it,' I said. 'The case is solved, I'm in the clear, and neither you nor Mrs S. ever got mentioned. In case you were worried.'

'I was,' he admitted. 'How'd you pull it off?'

'I got lucky. Look, have you got a minute? Because I've got a couple of questions.'

I asked my questions and he answered them. We chatted for a minute or two, agreed we ought to meet for a drink one of these days, albeit at someplace other than Pandora's, and that was that. I found Rodney Hart's number in the book, dialed it, heard it ring upwards of fifteen times, then got a cooperative girl at the answering service. She told me where to reach Rod – he was still in St Louis – but when I got through to his hotel there he hadn't come in yet. I suppose the play was still on the boards.

I changed back into my own clothes and stowed my cop gear in Darla's closet. She had some interesting gear of her own there, some of which I'd seen in the Polaroid shots, but I didn't really have time to inspect it. In the living room I flipped through the photographs and piled all but one of them in the wood-burning fireplace, which I now transformed into a film-burning fireplace. I added the cassettes, which smoldered and stank a bit, stirred the ashes when ashes there were, put on the air conditioner and left.

I took a cab downtown to Bethune Street and had a lot of fun telling the driver how to find it. I looked up at the building. There were no lights on in the fourth-floor apartment. I stood in the vestibule and checked the buzzer at 4-F. No name beside the button. I poked the button and nothing happened, so I opened the downstairs door in my usual fashion and went up three flights.

The locks were easy to pick. I let myself in and didn't have to spend too much time in there. After ten minutes or so I left, picked the locks shut behind me, and climbed another flight to Rod's apartment where Ellie was waiting.

And we were both there now, sipping cups of coffee laced with Scotch and working everything out. 'You're completely in the clear,' she said. 'Is that right? The cops don't even want to talk to you?'

'They'll probably want to talk to me sooner or later,' I said. 'A lot depends on what Ray ultimately decides to do. He wants Loren out of that uniform for good and he wants him to do some time in prison, but at the same time he'd probably like to avoid a full-scale investigation and court battle. I figure they'll probably work out some kind of compromise. Loren'll plead guilty to some kind of manslaughter charge. If he's inside for more than a year I'll be surprised.'

'After he killed a man?'

'Well, it would be hard to prove all that in court, and it would be impossible to do without dragging in errant burglars and bribe-taking cops and corrupt district attorneys and other politicians, so you might say the system has a vested interest in putting a lid on this one. And Loren has fifty thousand silent arguments in his favor.'

'Fifty thousand – oh, the money. What happens to the money now?'

'That's a good question. It belongs to Michael Debus, I think, but how is he going to come around and claim it? I can't see anybody letting Loren keep it, and I don't think Ray'll be able to grab it all for himself. I wish there was a way I could cut myself in for a piece of it. Not out of greed but just so that I could wind up close to even. This whole business is costing me a fortune, you know. I got a thousand dollars in front and gave it to Ray. Then Debus's men did a few thousand dollars' damage to my apartment and its contents, and finally my five grand case money went to Ray so that I could clear myself. It all adds up to a hell of a depressing balance sheet.'

'Can you get part of the fifty thousand?'

'Not a chance. Cops don't give money to crooks. I'm the one person in the world who won't get a sniff of the fifty thou. I'll have to go steal some money in a hurry, though. I'm as broke as I've ever been.'

'Oh, Bernie. Look what happened the last time you tried to steal something.'

'That was stealing-to-order. From now on I'm strictly freelance.'

'Oh, you're incorrigible.'

'That's the term, all right. Rehabilitation is wasted on me.'

She put down her coffee cup, snuggled up close, nestled her little head on my shoulder. I breathed in her perfume. 'What's really amazing,' she said, 'is that the box was empty all along.'

'Except for the hundred-dollar bill inside it.'

'But before you put the bill in the box was empty.'

'Uh-huh.'

'I wonder what happened to the pictures.'

'Maybe there never were any pictures,' I suggested. 'Maybe he threatened Mrs Sandoval but never actually showed her any pictures. Because in order to take photographs there would have had to be a third person there, wouldn't there? And no extra person ever did turn up in this case.'

'That's true. But I thought you said he showed the pictures to her.'

'That's the impression I had, but maybe he just showed her the box and talked so smoothly that she was left with the impression he'd proved there were pictures in the box? That's possible, isn't it?'

140

'I guess so.'

'So there probably were never any pictures or tapes in the first place. And if there were, it's academic because they're gone now.'

'Gone where?'

'Up in smoke – that would be my guess.'

'That's amazing.'

'It certainly is.'

'And everything's all cleared up? That's the most amazing thing of all. The police don't want to lock you up anymore?'

'Oh, there are a few charges they could bring,' I said. 'But I talked to Ray about that and he's going to get them quashed without any noise. They could charge me with resisting arrest and unlawful entry, but they're not really interested in that and they'd probably have trouble making the charges stick. Besides, however they decide to wrap all this up, the last thing they want is my testimony getting in the way.'

'That makes sense.'

'Uh-huh.' I draped an arm around her, curled my fingers around her shoulder. 'It all wound up nice and neat,' I said. 'I didn't even have to bring you into it. You're completely in the clear.'

The silence was devastating. Her whole body went rigid under my hand. I kept that hand on her shoulder and reached into my back pocket for the book I'd found in Apartment 4-F. I had the page marked and flipped right to it.

I read, ' "I was divorced four years ago. Then I was working, not a very involving job, and then I quit, and now I'm on unemployment. I paint a little and I make jewelry and there's a thing I've been doing lately with stained glass. Not what everybody else does but a form I sort of invented myself, these three-dimensional free-form sculptures I've been making. The thing is, I don't know about any of these things, whether I'm good enough or not I mean, maybe they're just hobbies. And if that's all they are, well, the hell with them. Because I don't want hobbies. I want something to do and I don't have it yet. Or at least I don't think I do." '

'Shit,' she said. 'Where'd you get the script?'

'In your apartment.'

'Double shit.'

'Just one flight down. Fourth-floor front. Very conveniently located. I dropped in on my way up here. I thought your cats might be hungry but old Esther and Haman were nowhere to be found.'

'Esther and Mordecai.'

'Since you don't have any cats it seems silly to argue about their names.' I tapped the little paper-bound book. *Two If By Sea,* I said. 'The very play our mutual friend's traveling around the country with.

And the speech I read comes trippingly from the lips of a character named Ruth Hightower.'

'Who told you?'

'Wesley Brill told me which play Ruth Hightower's a character in. But I thought to ask him the question in the first place. When I introduced you to him as Ruth Hightower he thought that was amusing. I suppose he thought it might be coincidental, but you were quick to switch the conversation around and give your real name. And the night before when we hit Peter Alan Martin's office I was mumbling some doggerel about one if by land and two if by sea and Ruth Hightower on the opposite shore will be, some Paul Revere crap, and you got very edgy. You must have thought I had everything figured out and I was just babbling. Then this morning you decided to tell me your real name.'

'Well, it doesn't mean anything, does it?' Her eyes met mine. 'I just got into a role and it took me a little time to get back to being me.'

'It's more complicated than that.'

'Oh, it's not so complicated.'

'Oh, I think it is. You got into a role, all right. And it was easy for you to get into a role because you're an actress. That should have been obvious to me earlier than it was. Look how neatly you ran down Brill yesterday. You knew just who to call – first Channel 9, then the Academy in Hollywood, then SAG. I didn't even know what SAG was, I thought it was something women tend to do after a certain age, and there you were on the phone with them, dropping little bits of shoptalk left and right.

'The thing is, the whole business was lousy with actors and theater buffs from the beginning. Flaxford dabbled as a producer and real estate operator while he made his money in less respectable areas. Rod's an actor who talked about the great deal he had on an apartment because the landlord has a soft spot for actors. Darla Sandoval's hobby is theater; that's how Flaxford got his hooks into her in the first place, and that's how she found Brill and used him to hire me. And you're an actress, and that's how you knew Rod.'

'That's right.'

'But it's only the beginning. It's also how you happened to know Flaxford, and he was the one who introduced you to Darla. You didn't meet her downtown or you would have known her last name. But you didn't. It wasn't until you heard her first name this afternoon at Brill's hotel room that you realized how it all tied together. Once you knew that the Mrs Sandoval we were talking about was a lady named Darla, then you decided you had a previous engagement and couldn't tag along to her apartment. Because she would recognize you and you wouldn't just be the nice young thing who dropped by to water the plants.'

'What do you mean?'

'You know what I mean, honey.' I stroked her hair, smiled down at her. 'The blue box wasn't empty.'

'Oh.'

I reached into my pocket, took out the one photograph I'd kept. I looked at it for a moment, then showed it to Ellie. She took a quick look at it, shuddered and turned away.

'That's Darla,' I said. 'The one on the left. The other one is you.'

'God.'

'I burned the rest of the pictures. And the tapes. You don't have to hold out on me, Ellie. I know you were involved with Flaxford. I don't know whether you met him through the theater or because he was your landlord. He owned this building, didn't he? He was the legendary landlord with the soft spot for actors?'

'Yes. He found me this apartment. I didn't even realize at the time that it was his building.'

'And he had you on the hook one way or another. I don't know what he had on you and I don't care, but it was enough so that you cooperated with Darla. Then the other night you were over at his place. The night he was killed.'

'That's not true.'

'Of course it is. Look, Ellie, Ray Kirschmann bought my explanation about how Flaxford locked himself in his apartment. But that doesn't mean *I* bought it. I was the one selling it. You were in the apartment with him. You had a key to the place, and not because he wanted you to water his plants. You were sleeping with J. Francis often enough to have a key of your own.

'And you were in bed with him that night. That's why you were confused when the papers described him as wearing a dressing gown. You said you thought you'd heard he was discovered nude. Well, that wasn't what you thought you heard. It was how he was when you left him.' I took a sip of my coffee. 'There was a time when I thought you might have been in the apartment while I was searching the desk. It seemed possible. You could have heard me at the door and ducked into a closet or something. Then you'd have stayed put until I got out of there and both cops went tearing after me, and then you could have gotten out yourself. That possibility occurred to me because I couldn't figure out how else you knew about me and knew I was at Rod's place. But that didn't make sense either, and I was sure you'd left Flaxford with his clothes off. But then how did you happen to turn up here? It was enough of a coincidence that you and Rod lived in the same building and I picked his apartment to hide out in. But how did you know I was here and how did you recognize me? You must have called Rod and asked to borrow his apartment and picked up his keys from some other neighbor. But how did you know to do that?'

'Hell.'

'I kept you out of it, Ellie. The cops don't know you exist and they'll never have reason to find out. But I'd like to know how it all fits together.'

'You know most of it.'

'I'd like to know the rest.'

'Why?' She drew further from me, turned her head to the side. 'What difference does it make? I'll go back to my life and you'll go back to yours. I can leave now. There's a whole pot of coffee and most of a bottle of Scotch left so you'll be all right.'

'I want to know the story first, Ellie. Before anybody goes anywhere.'

She turned to look at me, a challenge in the blue-green eyes. Then she said, 'Well, you figured out most of it. I don't know where to start, really. I was at his apartment that evening. You know that much. He had an opening to attend and he wanted me to go with him.'

'The Sandovals were going to be there.'

'That wouldn't have mattered. I'd seen her around, actually, and we'd talked once or twice before he put us together for the photography session. I just never heard her last name. There must be hundreds of people I know on a first-name basis only.'

'Go on.'

'I was up there and we went to bed. He was an awful man, Bernie. He was extremely cruel and manipulative. I didn't want to go to bed with him. I hadn't wanted to go to bed with Darla, as far as that goes. He was . . . I would have killed him if I were capable of killing anybody. I tried to do the next best thing. I tried to let him die.'

'What do you mean?'

'We were . . . we were in bed, and I guess he had a heart attack or something. He gasped and collapsed on the bed. I thought he was dead, and it was horrible, but at the same time I felt a great rush of relief.'

'But he was alive. Did you know that?'

She nodded. 'I checked his pulse and his heart was beating, and then I saw that he was breathing, and I knew that I ought to call the fire department or an ambulance or something. Then I realized that I wanted him to be dead. I even felt cheated because he was breathing and his heart was beating. I thought of killing him, smothering him with a pillow while he lay there unconscious, but I couldn't do that.'

'So you left him there.'

'Yes. I just . . . left him there. I got dressed in a hurry. There were a few things of mine in his closet. I packed them in a shopping bag, put my clothes on and left. I figured maybe he would live and maybe he would die and he would just have to take his chances. I wouldn't call an ambulance. I'd leave it up to fate.'

'Where did you go?'

'Home. My apartment downstairs.'

'What time was that?'

'I don't know exactly. Probably around seven or seven-thirty.'

'That early?'

'It must have been. We hadn't started to get dressed and we had to be at the theater in time for an eight-thirty curtain.'

I thought about it. 'All right,' I said. 'He was collapsed on the bed naked around seven or seven-thirty. Somewhere along the line he came back to consciousness. He got up, picked up a robe and put it on. He looked around for you and you were gone. Where was the money?'

'What money?'

'The fifty thousand dollars Loren found.'

'I don't know anything about it. There was no money in sight when I was with him. I don't know who brought him the money or where he got it.'

'But you locked the door when you went out.'

She hesitated, then nodded. 'I didn't want anyone just walking in and saving him. I couldn't actually kill him but I could make it easy for him to die. Was that horrible of me, Bernie? I guess it was.'

I left the question unanswered. 'He probably, already had the money,' I said. 'Sure. He realized you were gone and he looked in the closet and your things were gone, too, and he wanted to make sure you didn't decide to take along the fifty thousand bucks that Debus had passed on to him, or that he had picked up on Debus's behalf. Whatever. So he went to wherever he'd put the money and it was there, and then he got a little woozy and he went back to the bedroom and sat there with the money in his hand, and he felt rotten and he tried to get up and he knocked a lamp over or something, made a noise, maybe cried out in desperation, and then he collapsed on the bed again. That could have happened any time before my arrival a little after nine. Then he was unconscious while I riffled his desk. He'd have lapsed into regular sleep by the time Loren went in and started picking up what must have looked like all the money in the world. Then the commotion woke him and Loren went nuts and smacked him with his nightstick, and Flax-ford closed his eyes for the third and final time that night, and after Ray and I had done our little pas de deux Loren went back and beat him to death with the ashtray.'

'God.'

'But how did you come into it again? How did you know I was in this apartment?'

'I saw you come in.'

'How? You couldn't have followed my cab, and how would you know to follow it anyway? Besides you were down here all along. All right, you could have seen me from your window, you've got an apartment that fronts on the street. But how would you recognize me?'

'I saw you uptown, Bernie.'

'What?'

'I went back uptown. I sat in my apartment for a while and then I started to worry about him. If he was dead, well, then he was dead and that was that. But if not I really had to do something for him. I took a cab back up there and tried to decide what to do. I didn't want to call him up and I didn't want to send an ambulance before I knew whether he was all right or not, and I just didn't know what to do. I sent the cab away and I was walking back and forth on the sidewalk in front of his building, trying to get up my courage to go inside. I had my key, of course, and the doorman would have let me in because he knew me. But I was afraid Fran would be furious with me if he was all right and knew I'd left him, and if he was dead I didn't want to walk in on him, and – God, I just didn't know what to do.'

'And then you saw me go into the building? But you wouldn't have recognized me.'

'It was later than that. I saw you come *out* of the building. You were moving at the speed of light and you almost ran right into me. You sort of dodged me and went tearing off down the street, and a few minutes later a policeman came tearing out after you, and then the doorman told me you were a burglar who'd been in Mr Flaxford's apartment.'

'And then what?'

'Then the other policeman came downstairs a few minutes later and they talked about how Fran was dead and you had killed him. I didn't know what had happened. I came back here and stayed in my apartment, and I was convinced the police would find out that I had been responsible, although I don't think I really was responsible, but I was getting increasingly paranoid. I kept going to the window and looking out for cops, and then I saw you walk right into the building and I thought I was going to die. I didn't know who you were or how you knew about me and I was sure you were coming after me to kill me.'

'Why would I be after you?'

'How did I know? But why else would you be coming into the building? I locked all my locks and I stood at the door shaking like a leaf and listening to you come up the stairs. When you reached the fourth floor I nearly died, and when you went on up to the fifth floor I thought you'd made a mistake and you'd be back down in a minute. When you didn't come back down I couldn't figure out what had happened. Finally I went upstairs and listened at the two doors up here, and when I heard sounds in this apartment I knew you must be in here because Rod was out of town and the apartment was empty. I couldn't figure out what you were doing here but I went back to my own apartment and knocked myself out with a Seconal, and in the morning I bought the papers and found out what had happened and who you were.'

'And then you called Rod and arranged to pick up his keys.'

'I also found out that he knew you. I said I'd run across a fellow named Bernie Rhodenbarr and hadn't he mentioned that name to me once? And

146

he said he might have, though he didn't recall, but that the two of you had played poker together a few times. So I figured that was why you'd picked this apartment.' She took a deep breath. 'Then I decided to come up here. I didn't know whether you had killed Fran or not. I figured he must have been dead before you got there, that he died because he didn't receive prompt medical attention and it was my fault. But then there was all that business about the ashtray and I wondered if maybe you had killed him after all. And then you and I met, and I guess it's obvious I was drawn to you and fascinated by you, and I got involved more deeply than I probably should have. And at the same time I had to play a part. I couldn't give you my real name or address at the beginning because if you really were the killer and I wanted to bail out, then I was better off if you didn't know who I was or where to get hold of me. And if the police caught you, you wouldn't be able to drag me into it.'

'And then you told me your right name because you were afraid I'd catch you in the lie.'

She shook her head. 'That's not it. I just couldn't stand it when you called me Ruth. I hated it, and when we went to bed and you kept saying my name at critical moments it was absolutely horrible. And I figured you'd find out my real name anyway. By then I knew you hadn't killed anybody, I was really fairly sure of that from the beginning—'

'Your famous intuition. I knew you had to be involved to some degree, Ellie. Nobody trusts her intuition that much. You had to have something else to go on.'

'Anyway, you'd find out my name sooner or later. Unless I just disappeared one day. But I wasn't sure I wanted to. And everything happened so quickly.'

'Right.'

'So now you know the truth. I did a fair job of blowing the whole thing when I almost let us into the wrong apartment, didn't I?'

'I'd have put it all together anyway.'

'I suppose so.' She looked off into the middle distance, and I guess I did, too. A silence descended and hung around for quite a while. Finally she broke it.

'Well,' she said, 'things worked out pretty well after all, didn't they?'

'In every way but financially, yes. You're clear, Darla's clear, and I am no longer wanted for homicide. I'd say things worked out beautifully.'

'Except that you must hate me.'

'Hate you?' I was genuinely surprised at the thought. 'Why on earth should I hate you? You may have come up here originally out of curiosity and to make sure you weren't in danger, but after that you helped me a lot. Not as much as if you had told me all the truth at the beginning, but what kind of fool goes through life expecting honesty in interpersonal relationships?'

'Bernie—'

'No, seriously, I don't blame you. Why should you have opened up to somebody who might turn out be a murderer after all and who was certainly a convicted felon to begin with? And you did help me a great deal. I couldn't have straightened things out without your help and I probably wouldn't have tried. I'd have gotten in touch with a lawyer and tried to work some kind of a deal through Ray. So I'd have to be a complete moron to hate you.'

'Oh.'

'To tell the truth,' I said, 'I'm kind of fond of you. I think you're a little bit nuts, but who the hell isn't?'

'You know I was involved with Flaxford.'

'So?'

'And you saw that picture.'

'So?'

'It didn't bother you?'

'Not in the way you mean.'

'How else could it have bothered you?'

'In the sense of hot and bothered,' I said.

'Oh. I see.'

'Yeah.'

'Oh.'

I tipped up her chin and kissed her, and that lasted for a time, and then she sighed and nestled in my arms and said it was funny how things turned out. 'And now what happens?' she wanted to know.

'Things keep on keeping on, baby. You go on being an actress and I go on being a burglar. People don't change. Both of our careers may be slightly disreputable but I think we're stuck with them. And we'll see each other, and we'll see how it goes.'

'I'd like that.'

And I'd see Darla Sandoval, and I'd try to figure out a way to knock off her husband's coin collection without Darla guessing who did it. And I'd probably try to put my apartment back together again, and maybe the neighbors would overlook my alleged occupation in view of the fact that I confined my operations to the East Side where the *momsers* had it coming. And I'd probably go on playing poker and watching an occasional baseball game and pulling jobs when I had to. It wouldn't be perfect, but who leads a perfect life? We're all imperfect creatures leading imperfect lives in an imperfect world, and all we can do is the best we can.

I said some of this to Ellie, if not all of it, and we cuddled together, and at first it was just nice and comfy and gentle, and then it got to be a little more than that.

'Let's go to bed,' she said.

I thought that was a great idea. But first I went and made sure the doors were locked.

Burglar's Choice

In January of 1976 I was in a motel on the outskirts of Mobile, Alabama, trying to write a book. Six months earlier I'd left New York in a rusted-out Ford wagon, bound for California and in no rush to get there. I was going through what the British call a bad patch. I kept starting books and abandoning them after thirty or forty or fifty pages, unable to think of a reason for the characters to Go On.

In Mobile I wrote about a burglar who gets in touch with the detective who arrested him years ago. The burglar's out now, and up to his old tricks, and has had the ill fortune to happen on a murder scene, at once becoming its leading suspect and a fugitive from justice. He wants the detective to clear him. I wrote the opening chapter, took a good look at what I'd written, tore it up and threw it out and drove to Sardis, Mississippi. Don't ask why.

Two months later I was in LA, finally, living in a place called the Magic Hotel. I couldn't figure out what the hell to do. For over fifteen years I'd made my living writing, and now I seemed unable to do that.

Don't rule out crime, a little voice said.

Crime had much to recommend it. You didn't have to cobble up a resumé or provide references. There were no forms to fill out, no taxes and Social Security withheld from your pay. You just took money and ran.

And suppose you got caught? Well, for heaven's sake, they fed you and clothed you and housed you. Not the worst thing that could happen to a person, was it?

Hmmm.

But what kind of crime could I possibly commit? Nothing violent, certainly. Nothing where I might be called upon to hurt somebody, or, worse yet, where somebody might be called upon to hurt me. Nothing with guns or sharp objects. Nothing like con games, either, that involved duplicitous interaction with others. Indeed, nothing that involved *any* interaction with others. I didn't seem to be all that good at interaction just then.

Burglary, I thought. Go in when nobody's home, get out before they return. You work alone, and in pleasant surroundings – Robin Hood, after all, had just shown good sense in stealing from the rich. You avoid all human contact. You don't shoot anyone, and no one shoots you.

How seriously did I entertain the notion? Beats me. I did go so far as to try to learn to open my hotel-room door without the key, utterly ruining a credit card in the process. (No great loss, that. That card had long since ceased to open any doors for me.)

Then I thought about the plot notion I'd gotten nowhere with back in Mobile. Maybe if I lost the detective and just told the burglar's story, maybe something would come of it.

So I sat down at the typewriter to see what would happen.

I never thought it would come out funny. The notion I had in mind seemed like pretty serious business, but on the very first page Bernie appeared full-blown, like Athena from the brow of Zeus. (Well, maybe not much like Athena. And maybe from somewhere other than the brow . . .)

I wrote three or four chapters and a vague outline. All I needed was a title, and I found that while I was proofreading. Burglars can't be choosers, Bernie mused, and I looked up, startled. I didn't remember writing the line, but I knew a title when I saw one.

I sent it to my agent, who sent it to Lee Wright at Random House, who sent me a contract. I went back to work on the book. In July my kids came out to LA to spend the summer with me. They joined me for a month at the Magic Hotel, and then we spent August driving back east. Now and then we'd stay someplace for several days in a row so that I could get in some work on the book. One place we stopped was Yellow Springs, Ohio, where we stayed with my friends Steve and Nancy Schwerner. I talked to them about the book and said I was having problems with the solution. 'Oh, that's easy,' Steve said, and told me who he figured had dunnit. I decided he was right.

I dropped the girls with their mother in New York and wound up finishing the book in Greenville, South Carolina. (Don't ask why.) I was very pleased with the way the book had turned out, but I never thought I'd be writing anything else about Bernie.

Shows what I know.

– Lawrence Block
Greenwich Village
July 1994

The Burglar
in the Closet

For Mary Pat,
who opened the right door

Sir, he who would earn his bread writing books must have the assurance of a duke, the wit of a courtier, and the guts of a burglar.

– Dr Samuel Johnson

1

'Gramercy Park,' said Miss Henrietta Tyler, 'is an oasis in the middle of a cruel sea, a respite from the slings and arrows of which the Bard has warned us.' A sigh escaped her lips, the sort of sigh that follows upon the contemplation of an oasis in the middle of a sea. 'Young man,' she said, 'I do not know what I would do without this blessed green plot. I simply do not *know* what I would *do*.'

The blessed green plot is a private park tucked into Manhattan's East Twenties. There is a fence around the park, a black wrought-iron fence seven or eight feet high. A locked gate denies access to persons who have no legal right to enter. Only those persons who live in certain buildings surrounding the park and who pay an annual fee toward its maintenance are issued keys that will unlock the iron gate.

Miss Henrietta Tyler, who was seated on the green bench beside me, had such a key. She had told me her name, along with much of her personal history, in the fifteen minutes or so we'd been sitting together. Given time, I was fairly sure she'd tell me everything that had occurred in New York since her birth, which I calculated had taken place just a year or two after Napoleon's defeat at Waterloo. She was a dear old thing, was Miss Henrietta, and she wore a sweet little hat with a veil. My grandmother used to wear sweet little hats with veils. You don't see them much anymore.

'Absence of dogs,' Miss Henrietta was saying. 'I'm ever so glad they don't allow dogs in this park. It's the only spot left in the city where one may walk without constantly scanning the pavement beneath one's feet. A disgusting animal, the dog. It leaves its dirt anywhere at all. The cat is infinitely more fastidious, isn't it? Not that I would care to have one underfoot. I've never understood this compulsion people have to bring animals into their houses. Why, I wouldn't even care to have a fur coat. Let that sort of thing stay in the forest where it belongs.'

I'm sure Miss Henrietta wouldn't have talked thus to a stranger. But strangers, like dogs, are not to be found in Gramercy Park. My presence in the park indicated that I was decent and respectable, that I had a rewarding occupation or an independent income, that I was one of Us and not one of Them. My clothes had certainly been chosen to reinforce that image. My suit was a tropical worsted, a windowpane check in light and dark gray. My shirt was light blue with a medium-length button-down collar. My tie carried stripes of silver and sky blue on a navy field. The attaché case at my feet was a slim model in cocoa Ultrasuede that had cost someone a pretty penny.

I looked, all in all, like a bachelor taking a breather in the park after a hard day in a stuffy office. Perhaps I'd stopped somewhere for a bracing brace of martinis. Now I was taking some air on this balmy September evening before I trotted on home to my well-appointed apartment, there to pop a TV dinner in the microwave oven and inhale a beer or two while the Mets dropped a squeaker on the tube.

Well, not quite, Miss Henrietta.

No hard day, no stuffy office. No martinis, because I do not permit myself so much as a sniff of the cork when I am about to go to work. And there's no microwave oven in my modest apartment, and no TV dinners either, and I stopped watching the Mets when they traded Seaver. My apartment's on the Upper West Side, several miles from Gramercy Park, and I didn't pay a cent for the Ultrasuede attaché case, having appropriated it some months ago while liberating an absent gentleman's coin collection. I'm sure it had cost *him* a pretty penny, and God knows it contained any number of pretty pennies when I waltzed out the door with it in hand.

Why, I didn't even have a key to the park. I'd let myself in with a cunning little piece of high-tempered German steel. The lock on the gate is a shockingly simple one to pick. It's surprising more people don't let themselves in when they want to spend an hour away from dogs and strangers.

'This business of running around the park,' Miss Henrietta was saying. 'There goes one of them now. Look at him, won't you?'

I looked. The chap in question was around my age, somewhere in his middle thirties, but he'd lost a good deal of his hair. Perhaps he'd run out from under it. He was running now, or jogging, or whatever.

'You see them day and night, winter and summer. There's no end to it. On cold days they wear those suits, sweating suits I believe they're called. Unbecoming gray things. On a warm night like tonight they wear cotton shorts. Is it healthy to carry on like that, do you suppose?'

'Why else would anyone do it?'

Miss Henrietta nodded. 'But I can't *believe* it's good for one,' she said. 'It looks so *unpleasant*. You don't do anything of the sort, do you?'

'Every once in a while I think it might be good for me. But I just take two aspirin and lie down until the thought passes.'

'I believe that's wise. It appears ridiculous, for one thing, and nothing that looks so ridiculous can possibly be good for you.' Once more a sigh escaped her lips. 'At least they're constrained to do it *outside* the park,' she said, 'and not *inside* the park. We've that to be thankful for.'

'Like the dogs.'

She looked at me, and her eyes glinted behind the veil. 'Why, yes,' she said. '*Quite* like the dogs.'

By seven-thirty Miss Henrietta was dozing lightly and the jogger had run away somewhere. More to the point, a woman with shoulder-length ash-blond hair and wearing a paisley print blouse and wheat-colored jeans had descended the stone steps in front of 17 Gramercy Park West, glanced at her watch, and headed around the corner on Twenty-first Street. Fifteen minutes had passed and she had not returned. Unless the building had held two women of that description, she was Crystal Sheldrake, the future ex-wife of Craig Sheldrake, the World's Greatest Dentist. And if she was out of her apartment it was time for me to go into it.

I let myself out of the park. (You don't need a key to do that, or even a piece of high-tempered German steel.) I crossed the street, attaché case in hand, and mounted the steps of Number Seventeen. It was four stories tall, an exemplary specimen of Greek Revival architecture thrown up early in the nineteenth century. Originally, I suppose, one family had sprawled over all four floors and stowed their luggage and old newspapers in the basement. But standards have crumbled, as I'm sure Miss Henrietta could have told me, and now each floor was a separate apartment. I studied the four bells in the vestibule, passed up the ones marked Yalman, Porlock, and Leffingwell (which, taken as a trio, sounds rather like a firm of architects specializing in industrial parks) and poked the one marked Sheldrake. Nothing happened. I rang again, and nothing happened again, and I let myself in.

With a key. 'The bitch changed the lock,' Craig had told me, 'but she couldn't hardly change the one downstairs without getting the neighbors steamed at her.' Having the key saved me a couple of minutes, the lock being a rather decent one. I pocketed the key and walked to the elevator. It was in service though, the cage descending toward me, and I decided I didn't much want to meet Yalman or Porlock – Leffingwell lived on the first floor, but I decided it might even be he in the elevator, returning to base after watering his rooftop garden. No matter; I walked on down the hallway to the stairs and climbed two flights of carpeted steps to Crystal Sheldrake's apartment. I rang her bell and listened to two-tone chimes within, then knocked a couple of times, all in the name of insurance. Then I put my ear to the door and listened for a moment, and then I retrieved my ear and went to work.

Crystal Sheldrake's door had not one but two new locks, both of them Rabsons. The Rabson's a good lock to begin with, and one of these was equipped with their new pickproof cylinder. It's not as pickproof as they'd like you to think but it's not a plate of chopped liver either, and the damn thing took me a while to get past. It would have taken even longer except that I have a pair of locks just like it at home. One's in my living room, where I can practice picking it with my eyes closed while I listen to records. The other's on my own door, keeping out burglars less industrious than I.

I picked my way in, albeit with my eyes open, and before I even locked the door behind me I took a quick tour of the apartment. Once upon a time I didn't bother to do this, and it later turned out that there was a dead person in the apartment, and the situation proved an embarrassment of the rankest order. Experience is as effective a teacher as she is because one does tend to remember her lessons.

No dead bodies. No live bodies except my own. I went back and locked both locks, plopped my attaché case upon a Victorian rosewood love seat, slipped my hands into a pair of skintight sheer rubber gloves, and went to work.

The name of the game I was playing was Treasure Hunt. 'I'd like to see you strip the place to the four walls,' Craig had said, and I was going to do my best to oblige him. There seemed to be more than four walls – the living room I'd entered, a full dining room, a large bedroom, a small bedroom that had been set up as a sort of den and television parlor, and a kitchen with a fake brick floor and real brick walls and a lot of copper pots and pans hanging from iron hooks. The kitchen was my favorite room. The bedroom was all chintzy and virginal, the den angular and uninspired, and the living room an eclectic triumph featuring examples of bad taste down through the centuries. So I started in the kitchen and found six hundred dollars in the butter compartment of the refrigerator door.

Now the refrigerator's always a good place to look. A surprising number of people keep money in the kitchen, and many of them tuck it into the fridge. Cold cash, I suppose. But I didn't pick up the six hundred by playing the averages. I had inside information.

'The slut keeps money in the refrigerator,' Craig had told me. 'Usually has a couple hundred stashed in the butter keeper. Keeps the bread with the butter.'

'Clever.'

'Isn't it just? She used to keep marijuana in the tea canister. If she lived where people have lawns she'd probably store it with the grass seed.'

I didn't look in the tea canister so I don't know what kind of tea it contained. I put the cash in my wallet and returned to the living room to have a shot at the desk. There was more money in the top right-hand drawer, maybe two hundred dollars at most in fives and tens and twenties. It wasn't enough to get excited about but I was getting excited anyway, the automatic tickle of excitement that starts working

160

the instant I let myself into someone else's abode, the excitement that builds every time I lay hands on someone else's property and make it my own. I know this is all morally reprehensible and there are days when it bothers me, but there's no getting around it. My name is Bernie Rhodenbarr and I'm a thief and I love to steal. I just plain love it.

The money went in my pocket and became my money, and I started slamming through the other drawers in the little kneehole desk, and several in a row contained nothing noteworthy and then I opened another and right on top were three cases of the sort that good watches come in. The first one was empty. The second and third were not. One of them was an Omega and the other was a Patek Philippe and they were both gorgeous. I closed the cases and placed them in my attaché case where they belonged.

The watches were choice but that was it for the living room and it was actually more than I'd expected. Because the living room like the kitchen was just a warm-up. Crystal Sheldrake lived alone, although she often had overnight guests, and she was a woman with a lot of valuable jewelry, and women keep their jewelry in the bedroom. I'm sure they think they do it so it's handy when they're getting dressed, but I think the real reason is that they sleep better surrounded by gold and diamonds. It makes them feel secure.

'It used to drive me crazy,' Craig had said. 'Sometimes she left things lying out in plain sight. Or she'd just toss a bracelet and a necklace in the top drawer of the bedside table. She had the bedside table on the left-hand side, but I suppose they're both hers now so check 'em both.' No kidding. 'I useta beg her to keep some of that stuff in a safe-deposit box. She said it's too much trouble. She wouldn't listen to me.'

'Let's hope she didn't start listening recently.'

'Not Crystal. She never listened to anybody.'

I took my attaché case into the bedroom with me and had a look for myself. Earrings, finger rings, bracelets, necklaces. Brooches, pendants, watches. Modern jewelry and antique jewelry. Fair stuff, good stuff, and a couple things that looked, to my reasonably professional eye, to be very good indeed. Dentists take in a certain amount of cash along with the checks, and hard as it may be to believe this, some of that cash doesn't get reported to the Internal Revenue people. Some of it gets turned quietly into jewelry, and that jewelry could now get turned just as quietly right back into cash again. It wouldn't bring in what it had cost in the first place, since your average fence is a rather more careful customer than your average dentist, but it would still amount to a fairly impressive sum when you consider that it all started out with nothing but a whole lot of toothaches and root-canal work.

I searched very carefully, not wanting to miss anything. Crystal Sheldrake kept a very neat apartment on the surface, but the interiors of her drawers were a scandal, with baubles and beads forced to keep company with rumpled panty hose and half-full make-up jars. So I took my time, and my attaché case grew heavier as my fingers grew lighter. There was plenty of time. She had left the house at seven-fifteen and would probably not return until after midnight, if indeed she returned before dawn. Her standard operating procedure, according to Craig, called for a drink or two at each of several neighborhood watering holes, a bite of dinner somewhere along the way, and then a few hours devoted to a combination of serious drinking and even more serious cruising. Of course there were nights that got planned in advance, dinner engagements and theater dates, but she'd left the house dressed for a casual night's entertainment.

That meant she'd either bring home a stranger or go to a stranger's home, and either way I'd be long gone before she recrossed her own threshold. If they settled on his place, the jewels might be fenced before she knew they were missing. If she brought the guy home and they were both too sloshed to notice anything was missing, and if he in turn let himself out before she woke up, she might just tag the crime on him. Either way I looked to be in the clear, and enough thousands of dollars ahead so that I could coast for the next eight or ten months, even after I gave Craig his share. Of course it was hard to tell just what the attaché case contained, and it's a long, long way from jewelry to cash, but things were looking good for Mrs Rhodenbarr's boy Bernard, no question about it.

I remember having that thought. I can't begin to tell you what a comfort it was a little later when Crystal Sheldrake locked me in the bedroom closet.

2

The problem, of course, derived from an offshoot of Parkinson's Law. A person, be he bureaucrat or burglar, tends to take for a task as much time as is available for it. Because I knew Crystal Sheldrake would be absent from her apartment for hours on end, I was inclined to spend several of those hours divesting her of her possessions. I've always known that burglars should observe the old *Playboy* Philosophy – i.e., Get In and Get Out – but there's something to be said for making use of the available time. You can miss things if your work is rushed. You can leave incriminating evidence behind. And it's a kick, going through another person's things, participating vicariously (and perhaps neurotically) in that person's life. The kicks involved are one of the attractions of burglary for me. I can admit that, even if I can't do anything much about it.

So I lingered. I could have tossed the Sheldrake *pied-à-terre* in twenty efficient minutes if I put my mind to it. Instead I took my precious time.

I'd finished picking the second Sheldrake lock at 7:57 – I happened to note the time before easing the door open. At 9:14 I closed my attaché case and fastened the snaps. I picked it up and noted its increased weight with approval, trying to think of the avoir-dupois more in terms of carats than ounces.

Then I set the case down again and gave the premises another careful contemplative toss. I don't even know if I was really looking for anything at this point. A person younger than I might have said I was trying to pick up vibrations. Come to think of it, I might have said that myself, but not aloud. What I was probably trying to do, in truth, was prolong the delicious feeling of being where I wasn't supposed to be and where no one knew I was. Not even Craig knew I was there. I'd told him I would go in a night or two later, but it was such a pleasant evening, such a propitious night for breaking and entering . . .

So I was in the bedroom, examining a pastel portrait of a youngish woman elegantly coiffed and gowned, with an emerald at her throat that looked to be head and shoulders above anything I'd stolen from Crystal Sheldrake. The painting looked early nineteenth century and the woman looked French, but she might simply have cultivated the art of looking French. There was something fetching about her expression. I decided she'd been disappointed so many times in life, largely by men, that she'd reached a point where she expected disappointment and decided that she could live with it, but it still rather rankled. I was between women myself at the time and told her with my eyes that I could make her life a joy and a fulfillment, but her chalky blues met mine and she let me know that she was sure I'd be just as big a letdown as everybody else. I figured she was probably right.

Then I heard the key in the lock.

It was a good thing there were two locks, and it was another good thing I'd relocked them upon entering. (I could have bolted them as well, so that they couldn't be opened from outside, but I'd given up doing that a while ago, figuring that it just let citizens know there was a burglar inside and moved them to come back with a cop or two in tow.) I froze, and my heart ascended to within an inch or two of my tonsils, and my body got damp in all those spots the antiperspirant ads warn you about. The key turned in the lock, and the bolt drew back, and someone said something inaudible, to another person or to the empty air, and another key found its way into another lock, and I stopped being frozen and started moving.

There was a window in the bedroom, conventionally enough, but there was an air conditioner in it so there was no quick way to open it. There was another smaller window, large enough so that I could have gotten through it, but some spoilsport had installed bars on it to prevent some rotten burglar from climbing in through it. This also prevented rotten burglars from climbing out, although the installer had probably not had that specifically in mind.

I registered this, then looked at the bed with its lacy spread and thought about throwing myself under it. But there wasn't really a hell of a lot of room between the box spring and the carpet. I could have fit but I could not have been happy about it. And there's something so undignified about hiding under a bed. It's such a dreary cliché.

The bedroom closet was every bit as trite but rather more comfortable. Even as the key was turning in the second Rabson lock, I was darting into the closet. I'd opened it before to paw through garments and check hatboxes in the hope that they held more than hats. It had then been quaintly locked, the key stuck right there in the lock waiting for me to turn it. I don't know why people do this but they do it all the time. I guess if they keep the key somewhere else it's too much trouble hunting for it every time they want to change their shoes, and I guess locking a door provides some sort of emotional security even when you leave the key in the lock. I'd taken nothing from her closet earlier; if she had furs they were in storage, and I hate stealing furs anyway, and I certainly wasn't going to make off with her Capezios.

At any rate, I hadn't bothered relocking the closet and that saved unlocking it all over again. I popped inside and drew it shut after me, slipped between a couple of faintly perfumed gowns and adjusted them again in front of me, took a deep breath that didn't even begin to fill my aching lungs, and listened carefully as the door opened and two people entered.

It was not hard to know that there were two of them because I could hear them talking, even though I could not yet make out their conversation. From the pitch of their voices I could tell that one was female and one was male, and I assumed the female was Crystal Sheldrake, wheat jeans and paisley blouse and all. I had no idea who the man might be. All I knew was that he was a fast worker, having hustled her back here so swiftly. Maybe he was married. That would explain his hurry, and why they'd wound up here rather than at his place.

Sounds of ice clinking, sounds of liquid pouring. I breathed in the closet smells of Arpège and Shalimar and antique perspiration and thought wistfully of the two before-dinner martinis I'd neglected to have. I never drink before I work because it might impair my efficiency, and I thought about that policy, and I thought about my efficiency, and I felt rather stupider than usual.

I hadn't had the before-dinner drinks and I hadn't had the dinner either, preferring to postpone that pleasure until I could do it in style and in celebration. I'd been thinking in terms of a latish supper at a little hideaway I know on Cornelia Street in the Village. Those two marts first, of course, and then that cold asparagus soup they do such a good job with, and then the sweetbreads with mushrooms, God, those sweetbreads, and a salad of arugola and spinach with mandarin orange sections, ah yes, and perhaps a half bottle of something nice to go with the sweetbreads. A white wine, of course, but what white wine? It was something to ponder.

Then coffee, lots of coffee, all of it black. And of course a postprandial brandy with the coffee. No dessert, no point in overdoing it, got to watch the old waistline even if one's not quite obsessive enough to jog around Gramercy Park. No dessert, then, but perhaps a second snifter of that brandy just to take the edge off all that coffee and reward oneself for a job well done.

A job well done indeed.

In the living room, ice continued to clink in glasses. I heard laughter. The radio or the record player was pressed into service. More ice clinking. More laughter, a little more carefree now.

I stood there in the closet and found my thoughts turning inexorably in the direction of alcohol. I thought about the martinis, cold as the Klondike, three hearty ounces of crystal-clear Tanqueray gin with just the most fleeting kiss of Noilly Prat vermouth, a ribbon of twisted lemon peel afloat, the stemmed glass perfectly frosted. Then my mind moved to the wine. Just what white wine would be ideal?

'. . . beautiful, beautiful evening,' the woman sang out. 'Know something, though? I'm a little warmish, sweetie.'

Warmish? I couldn't imagine why. There were two air conditioners in the apartment, one in the bedroom and one in the living room, and she'd left them both running in her absence. They'd kept the apartment more than comfortable. My hands are always warm and sweaty inside my rubber gloves, but the rest of me had been cool and dry.

Until now, that is. The bedroom air conditioner was having no discernible effect on the air in the closet, which was not what you'd call conditioned. My hands were getting the worst of it and I peeled my gloves off and stuck them in my pocket. At the moment fingerprints were my least pressing concern. Suffocation probably headed the list, or at least it seemed to, and close behind it came apprehension and arrest and prison, following one upon the other in a most unpleasant way.

I breathed in. I breathed out. Maybe, I thought, just maybe, I could get away with this one. Maybe Crystal and her gentleman friend would be sufficiently involved in one another so as not to notice the absence of jewelry. Maybe they'd do whatever they'd come to do, and having done it perhaps they'd leave, or lapse into coma, and then maybe I could let myself out of the closet and the apartment. Then, swag in hand, I could return to my own neighborhood and—

Hell!

Swag in hand indeed. My swag, all of it neatly packed in the Ultra-suede attaché case, was not by any means in hand, not in hand and not at hand either. It was resting on the opposite side of the bedroom from me, propped against the wall under the pastel portrait of the disappointed mademoiselle. So even if Crystal didn't notice the absence of her jewelry she seemed more than likely to notice the presence of the case, and that would indicate not merely that she had been burgled but that the burglar had been interrupted while at work, and that would mean she would put in an urgent phone call to 911, and cop cars would descend upon the scene of the crime, and some minion of the law would be bright enough to open the closet, and I, Bernard Grimes Rhodenbarr, would be instantly up the creek, and in no time at all, up the river as well.

Hell!

'Something more comfortable,' the woman said. I could hear them better now because they were en route to the bedroom, which I can't say astonished me. And then they were in the bedroom, and then they did what they'd come to the bedroom to do, and that's all you're going to hear from me on that subject. It was no fun listening to it and I'm certainly not going to try to re-create the experience for you.

As a matter of fact, I paid them the absolute minimum of attention myself. I let my mind return to the question of the perfect wine as accompaniment to the sweetbreads. Not a French white, I decided, for all that the sweetbreads were a French dish. A German white might have a little more oomph. A Rhine? That would do, certainly, but I decided after some thought that a choice Moselle might carry a wee bit more authority. I thought about a Piesporter Goldtröpfchen I'd had not long ago, a bottle shared with a young woman with whom, as it turned out, that was all that was to be shared. That would be acceptable with the sweetbreads, certainly. One wouldn't want anything too dry. And yet the dish did call for a wine with a slight lingering sweetness, a fruity nose—

Of course! My mind summoned up memories of a '75 Ockfener Bockstein Kabinett, with a full, lovely flowery scent, a tart freshness of flavor like a bite out of a perfect Granny Smith apple, the merest hint of spice, just a trace of tongue-tickling spritz. There was no guarantee that the restaurant I'd chosen would have that particular wine, but neither was there any guarantee that I'd be having dinner there instead of doing five-to-fifteen at Attica, so I might as well give my imagination free rein. And what was that nonsense about a half bottle of wine? Any wine worth drinking was worth having a full bottle of, surely.

I rounded out my meal somewhat by guessing what the vegetable *du jour* might chance to be. Broccoli, I decided, steamed *al dente*, uncomplicated with Hollandaise – just dotted lightly with sweet butter. Or, failing that, some undercooked zucchini sauced very lightly with tomato and basil and dusted with grated Parmesan.

My thoughts then jumped sensibly enough to the after-dinner brandy. A good Cognac, I thought. Any good Cognac. And I let myself dwell on various good Cognacs I'd had at one time or another and the ever-more-comfortable circumstances than the present in which I'd relished them.

A drink, I thought, would help. It might not *really* help, but it would seem to help and I'd settle for that just now. A well-equipped burglar, I told myself, really ought to be supplied with a hip flask. Or even a square flask. A thermos, perhaps, to keep the martinis properly chilled . . .

Nothing lasts forever. The lovemaking of Crystal Sheldrake and her latest friend, which certainly seemed eternal to me if not to them, lasted by actual measurement twenty-three minutes. I can't say when Crystal's key turned in her lock, having had more urgent matters on my mind at the time. But I did glance at my watch not too long after and noted that it was 9:38. I glanced again when the two of them entered the bedroom. 10:02. I checked again from time to time while the performance was in progress, and when the finale descended with a crash my glow-in-the-dark watch told me it was 10:25.

There was a spate of silence, a chorus of *Gee, you were terrific* and *You're sensational* and *We've got to do this more often*, all the things good up-to-date people say instead of *I love you*. Then the man said, 'Christ, it's later than I thought. Half-past ten already. I better get going.'

'Running back home to what's-her-name?'

'As if you didn't remember her name.'

'I prefer to forget it. There are moments, my sweet, when I actually manage to forget her existence altogether.'

'You sound jealous.'

'Of course I'm jealous, baby. Does that come as a surprise to you?'

'Oh, come on, Crystal, you aren't really jealous.'

'No?'

'Not a chance.'

'Think it's just a role I play? Maybe you're right. I couldn't say. Your tie's crooked.'

'Mmm, thanks.'

They went on like this, not saying anything I had any enormous need to hear. I had trouble keeping all of my mind on their conversation, not only because it was duller than a Swedish film but because I kept waiting for one or the other of them to stub a toe on the attaché case and wonder aloud how it happened to be there. This, however, did not happen. There was more chitchat, and then she walked him to the door and let him out and locked up after him, and I think I heard the sound of her snicking the sliding bolt shut. Fine precaution to take, lady, I thought, with the burglar already tucked away in your clothes closet.

Then I heard nothing at all for a while, and then the phone rang twice and was answered, and there was a conversation which I couldn't make out. More silence, this time followed by a temper tantrum of brief duration. 'Stinking sonofabitch bastard,' Crystal roared, out of the blue. I had no way of knowing whether she was referring to her recent bedmate, her ex-husband, her telephone caller, or someone else altogether. Nor did I too much care. She yelled out just once, and then there was a thudding sound, perhaps of her heaving something at a wall. Then calm returned.

And so did Crystal, retracing her steps from living room to bedroom. I guess she had replenished her drink somewhere along the way, because I heard ice cubes clinking. By now, however, I no longer actively wanted something wet. I just wanted to go home.

The next thing I heard was water running. There was a lavatory in the hallway off the living room, a full bathroom off the bedroom. The bathroom had a stall shower and that's what I was hearing. Crystal was going to erase the patina of love-making. The man had left and Crystal was going to take a shower and all I had to do was pop out of the closet and scoop up my jewel-laden attaché case and be gone.

168

I was just about to do this when the shower became suddenly more audible than it had been. I shrank back behind the rack of dresses and sundry garments, and footsteps approached me, and a key turned, neatly locking me in the closet.

Which of course was not her intent. She wanted to unlock the door, and she had left it locked and assumed it was still locked, so she'd turned the key, and—

'Funny,' she said aloud. And paused, and then turned the key in the opposite direction, this time unlocking the closet, and reached in to take a hooded lime-green terry-cloth robe from a hanger.

I did not breathe while this was happening. Not specifically to escape detection but because breathing is impossible when your heart is lodged in your windpipe.

There was Crystal, ash-blond hair stuffed into a coral shower cap. I saw her but she didn't see me, and that was just fine, and in the wink of an eye (if anyone's eye winked) she was closing the door again.

And locking it.

Wonderful. She had a thing about closets. Some people can't leave a room for five minutes without turning off the lights. Crystal couldn't walk away from an unlocked closet. I listened as her footsteps carried her back to the bathroom, listened as the bathroom door closed, listened as she settled herself under her pulsating massagic shower head (no speculation; I'd looked in the bathroom and she had one of those jobbies).

Then I stopped listening and poked between the dresses and turned the doorknob and pushed, and when the door predictably refused to budge I could have wept.

What an incredible comedy of errors. What a massive farce.

I stroked the lock with my fingertips. It was laughable, of course. A good kick would have sent the door flying open, but that would involve more noise than I cared to create. So I'd have to find a gentler way out, and the first step was to get the damned key out of the lock.

Which is easy enough. I supplied myself with a scrap of paper by tearing one of the protective garment bags that was protecting one of Crystal's garments. I scrunched down on hands and knees and slipped the paper under the door so that it was positioned beneath the keyhole. Then I used one of my little pieces of steel to poke around in the silly-ass lock until the key jiggled loose and fell to the floor.

Back on my hands and knees again, tugging at the paper. Tugging gently, because a swift tug would have the effect of a swift yank on a table-cloth, removing the cloth but leaving the dishes behind. I didn't just want the paper. I wanted the key that was on it as well. Why pick a lock if the key's just inches from your grasp? Easy does it, take your time, easy, that's right—

And then the door buzzer buzzed.

I swear I wanted to spit. The damned buzzer made a sound loud enough to make hens stop laying. I froze where I was, praying fervently that Crystal wouldn't hear it under the shower, but evidently my prayer wasn't quite fervent enough. Because the thing sounded again, a long horrible piercing blurt, and while it was so doing Crystal shut off the water.

I stayed where I was and I went on tugging at the scrap of paper. The last thing I wanted was for her to spot the key on the floor on her way to the door. The key cleared the door and came into view, and while this was happening the bathroom door opened and I heard her footsteps.

I stayed where I was, crouched on the floor as if in prayer. If she noticed that the key was missing, well, at least she wouldn't be able to open it because I had the key. That, I told myself, was something.

But she didn't even slow down as she passed the closet. She swept right on by, presumably in her lime-green terry-cloth robe. I suppose she poked the answering buzzer to unlatch the downstairs door. I waited, and I suppose she waited, and then the doorbell sounded its two-tone chime. Then she opened the door.

By this time I had gotten to my feet again and was standing behind the rack of dresses. I was also paying close attention to what was happening, but it was hard for me to get a clear picture of what was going on. The door opened. I heard Crystal saying something. Part of what she said was inaudible, but I could make out *'What is it? What do you want?'* and similar expressions. It seems to me that there was panic in her voice, or at the least a whole lot of apprehension, but I may have just filled that in after the fact.

Then she said *'No, no!'* very loud, and there was no missing the terror. And then she screamed, but it was a very brief scream, chopped off abruptly as if it were a recording and someone lifted the tone arm from the record.

Then a thudding sound.

Then nothing at all.

And there I was, standing snugly in my closet like the world's most cautious homosexual. After a moment or two I thought about using the key in my hand to unlock the door, but then once again I heard movement outside. Footsteps, but they sounded different from Crystal's. I couldn't say that they were lighter or heavier. Just a different step. I'd grown used to Crystal's footsteps, having spent so much time lately listening to them.

The footsteps approached, reached the bedroom. The source of the footsteps began moving around the bedroom, opening drawers, moving furniture around. At one point the doorknob turned but of course the door was still locked. Whoever had turned the knob was evidently not proficient at picking locks. The closet was abandoned and I was safe inside it.

More movement. Then, after what couldn't really have been an eternity, the footsteps passed me again and returned to the living room. The apartment's outer door opened and closed – I'd learned to recognize that sound.

I looked at my watch. It was eleven minutes to eleven, and thinking of it that way made it more memorable than 10:49. I looked at the key I was holding and I slipped it into the lock and turned it, and then I hesitated before opening the door. Because I had all too good an idea what I'd find there and it wasn't anything I was in a rush to look at.

On the other hand, I was really sick of that closet.

I let myself out. And found, in the living room, pretty much what I'd expected. Crystal Sheldrake, sprawled out on her back, one leg bent at the knee, the foot cramped beneath the opposite thigh. Blond hair in shower cap. Green robe open so that most of her rather spectacular body was exposed.

An ugly purple welt high on her right cheekbone. A thin red line, sort of a scratch, reaching from just below her left eye to the left side of her chin.

More to the point, a gleaming steel instrument plunged between her noteworthy breasts and into her heart.

I tried to take her pulse. I don't know why I made the attempt because God knows she looked deader than the Charleston, but people are always taking pulses on television and it seemed like the thing to do. I spent a long time taking hers because I wasn't sure I was doing it right, but finally I gave up and said the hell with it.

I didn't get sick or anything. My knees felt weak for a moment, but then the sensation lifted and I was all right. I felt rotten because death is a rotten thing and murder is particularly horrible, and I felt vaguely that there should have been something I could have done to prevent this particular murder, but I was damned if I could see what it was.

First things first. She was dead and I couldn't help her, and I was a burglar who certainly did not want to be found at the scene of a far more serious crime than burglary. I had to wipe off whatever surfaces might hold my fingerprints and I had to retrieve my attaché case and then I had to get the hell out of there.

I didn't have to wipe Crystal's wrist. Skin doesn't take fingerprints, any number of inane television programs notwithstanding. What I did have to wipe were the surfaces I'd been near since I took off my rubber gloves (which I now put back on, incidentally). So I got a washcloth from the bathroom and I wiped the inside of the closet door and the floor of the closet, and I couldn't think what else I might have touched but I wiped around the outside closet knob just to make sure.

171

Of course the murderer had touched that knob. So maybe I was wiping away *his* prints. On the other hand, maybe he'd been wearing gloves.

Not my concern.

I finished wiping, and I went back to the bathroom and put the washcloth back on its hook, and then I returned to the bedroom for a quick look at the disappointed pastel lady, and I gave her a quick wink and dropped my eyes to look for my attaché case.

To no avail.

Whoever killed Crystal Sheldrake had taken her jewelry home with him.

3

It never fails. I open my mouth and I wind up in hot water. But in this case the circumstances were special. After all, I was only following orders.

'Open, Bern. A little wider, huh? That's right. That's fine. Perfect. Just beautiful.'

Beautiful? Well, they tell me it's in the eye of the beholder and I guess they're right. If Craig Sheldrake wanted to believe there was beauty in a gaping mouthful of teeth, that was his privilege and more power to him. They weren't the worst teeth in the world, I don't suppose. Twenty-some years ago a grinning orthodontist had wired them with braces, enabling me to shoot those little rubber bands at my classmates, so at least they were straight. And since I'd given up smoking and switched to one of those whiter-than-white toothpastes, I looked somewhat less like a supporting player in *The Curse of the Yellow Fangs*. But all of the molars and bicuspids sported fillings, and one of the wisdom teeth was but a memory, and I'd had a wee bit of root-canal work on the upper left canine. They were respectable teeth for one as long in the tooth as I, perhaps, and they'd given me relatively little trouble over the years, but it would be an exaggeration to call them either a thing of beauty or a joy forever.

A stainless-steel probe touched a nerve. I twitched a little and made the sort of sound of which one is capable when one's mouth is full of fingers. The probe, relentless, touched the nerve again.

'You feel that?'

'Urg.'

'Little cavity, Bern. Nothing serious but we'll tend to it right now. That's the importance of coming in for a cleaning three or four times a year. You come in, we shoot a quick set of X-rays just as a routine measure, we have a look around, poke the old molars a bit, and we catch those little cavities before they can grow up into big cavities. Am I right or am I right, keed?'

'Urg.'

'All this panic about X-rays. Well, if you're pregnant I suppose it's a different story, but you're not pregnant, are you, Bernie?' He laughed at this. I've no idea why. When you're a dentist you have to laugh at your own jokes, which might be a hardship but I suspect it's more than balanced by the fact that you remain blissfully unaware of it when your precious wit goes over like a brass blimp. Since the patient can't laugh anyway, his silence needn't be interpreted as a reprimand.

'Well, we'll just take care of it right away before I turn you over to Jillian for a cleaning. First molar, lower right jaw, that's a cinch, we can block the pain with Novocaine without numbing half your head in the process. Of course some practitioners of the gentle art would wind up depriving you of sensation in half your tongue for six or eight hours, but you're in luck, Bern. You're in the hands of the World's Greatest Dentist and you have nothing to worry about.' Chuckle. 'Except paying the bill, that is.' Full-fledged laugh.

'Urg.'

'Open a little wider? Perfect. Beautiful.' His fingers, tasting as though they'd been boiled, deftly packed my mouth with cylinders of cotton. Then he took a curved piece of plastic tubing attached to a long rubber tube and propped it at the root of my tongue, where it commenced to make slurping noises.

'This is Mr Thirsty,' he explained. 'That's what I tell the kids. Mr Thirsty, come to suck up all your spit so it doesn't gum up the works. Of course I don't put it quite so crudely for the little tykes.'

'Urg.'

'Anyway, I tell the kids this here is Mr Thirsty, and when I whack 'em out with nitrous oxide I tell 'em they're going for a ride in Dr Sheldrake's Rocket Ship. That's 'cause it gets 'em so spacy.'

'Urg.'

'Now we'll just dry off that gum there,' he said, peeling back my lower lip and blotting the gum with a wad of cotton. 'And now we'll give you a dab of benzocaine, that's a local that'll keep you from feeling the needle when we jab a quart of Novocaine into your unsuspecting tissue.' Chortle. 'Just kiddin', Bernie. No, you don't have to give a patient a liter of the stuff if you have the skill to slip the old needle into the right spot. Oh, thank your lucky stars you've got the World's Greatest Dentist on your team.'

The World's Greatest Dentist shot me painlessly with Novocaine, readied his high-speed drill, and began doing his part in the endless fight against tooth decay. None of this hurt. What was painful, albeit not physically, was the patter of conversation he directed my way.

Not at first, though. At first everything was fine.

'I'll tell you something, Bernie. You're a lucky man to have me for a dentist. But that's nothing compared to how lucky *I* am. You know why? *I'm* lucky to *be* a dentist.'

'Urg.'

'Not just because I make a decent living. Hell, I don't have any guilt on that score. I work hard for my money and my charges are fair. I give value for value received. The thing about dentistry is it's very rewarding in other ways. You know, most of the dentists I know started off wanting to be doctors. I don't know that they had any big longing for medicine. I think half the time the attraction was that their parents thought it was a great life. Money, prestige, and the idea that you're helping humanity. Anybody'd be happy to help humanity with all that money and prestige there as an added incentive, right?'

'Urg.'

'Speak up, Bern, I can't hear you.' Chuckle. 'Just joking, of course. How we doing? You in any pain?'

'Urg.'

'Of course you're not. The WGD strikes again. Well, all these guys went to dental school instead. Maybe they couldn't get accepted at medical school. A lot of bright guys can't. Or maybe they looked at all that education and training stretching out in front of them, four years of med school and two years internship and then a residency, and when you're a kid a few years looks like a lifetime. Your perspective on time changes when you get to be our age, but by then it's too late, right?'

I guess we were about the same age, getting a little closer to forty than thirty but not quite close enough to panic about it. He was a big guy, taller than me, maybe six-two or six-three. His hair was a medium brown with red highlights, and he wore it fairly short in a deliberately tousled fashion. He had an open honest face, long and narrow, marked by warm brown eyes and a long down-curving nose and sprinkled with freckles. A year or two back he'd grown a mustache of the macho variety sported by male models in men's cologne ads. It was redder than his hair and didn't look quite bad enough for me to counsel him to shave it off, but I sort of wished he would. Beneath the mustache was a full mouth overflowing with the nicest teeth you could possibly imagine.

'Anyway, here you've got a load of dentists who secretly wish they were doctors. Some of them don't even keep it a secret. And you've got others who went into dentistry because, hell, a man has to go into something unless he wants to go on welfare, and it looked like a decent deal, set your own hours, a steady buck, no boss over you, some prestige, and all the rest of it. I was one of this group, Bern, but in my case something wonderful happened. Know what it was?'

'Urg?'

'I fell in love with my work. Yep, that's what happened. One thing I recognized right off the bat is dentistry's about solving problems. Now they're not problems of life and death, and I'll tell you, that's fine with me. I sure as hell don't want patients dying on me. The doctors are welcome to all that drama. I'd rather deal with smaller life questions, like Can This Tooth Be Saved? But a man comes in here, or a woman, and I look around and take X-rays, and there's a problem and we deal with it then and there.'

No *urg* this time. He was rattling along too well to need encouragement from me.

'I'm just so damn lucky I wound up in this line of work, Bern. I remember my best friend and I were trying to decide what we wanted to do with our lives. I picked dental school and he went into pharmacy school. His educational route looked easier and his potential income was certainly much higher. You own your own store, you branch out and open other stores, hell, you're a businessman, you can make a ton. For a little while there I wondered if maybe I shouldn't have taken the road he took. But just for a little while. Jesus, can you picture me standing behind a counter selling Kotex and laxatives? I couldn't be a businessman, Bern. I'd be rotten at it. Hey, open a little wider, huh? Perfect, beautiful. I'd be rotten at it and I'd go out of my bird with boredom. I read somewhere that pharmacists get more action than any other occupational group. Some study out of California. I wonder if it's true or not? What woman would want to ball a druggist, anyway?'

He went on with this line of thought and my mind drifted off a ways. I was a captive audience if there ever was one, and I had to sit there and take it but I didn't, by God, have to pay attention.

And then he was saying, 'So I sure as hell wouldn't want to be a pharmacist, and I swear I wouldn't want to be anything but what I am. Satisfied Sam, huh? True, though.'

'Urg.'

'But I'm normal, Bernie. I have fantasies just like everybody else in this world. I try to think what I'd be if dentistry just didn't happen to be an option for me. Just asking myself the hypothetical question, like. And because it's hypothetical and I *know* it's hypothetical, why, I can feel free to indulge myself. I can pick something that would call for someone a lot more adventurous than I actually know myself to be.'

'Urg.'

'I try to have fantasies of being a professional athlete, for instance. I play a lot of squash and a fair amount of tennis, and I'm not absolutely lousy, in fact I'm getting so I shape up pretty decent on the squash court, but there's such an obvious gulf between my game and the pro game that I can't even fantasize about playing that role. That's the trouble with reality. It gets in the way of the best fantasies.'

'Urg.'

'So I've settled on something I'd like to be, and I can enjoy it on a fantasy level because I know virtually nothing about it.'

'Urg?'

'It's exciting, it's adventurous, it's dangerous, and I can't say I don't have the skills or temperament for it because I don't know exactly what they are. I gather it pays a whole lot and the hours are short and flexible. And you work alone.'

'Urg?' He had me interested by now. It sounded like the sort of thing I might be interested in.

'I was thinking about crime,' he went on. 'But nothing where you have to point guns at people or where you wind up with them pointed at you. In fact I'd want a criminal career with no human contact involved in it at all. Something where you work alone and don't have to be a part of a gang.' Chuckle. 'I've pretty much narrowed it down, Bernie. If I had it to do all over again, and if dentistry was just out of the picture, I'd be a burglar.'

Silence.

'Like you, Bernie.'

More silence. Lots of it.

Well, of course it rocked me. I'd been set up with considerable skill. Here was ol' Craig Sheldrake, Mr Laid Back and World's Greatest Dentist, just running pleasantly off at the mouth about how much he loved his work, and the next thing I knew he'd dropped this brick into my open mouth and all the Novocaine in the world couldn't have numbed the shock.

You see, I've always kept my personal and professional lives as separate as possible. Except during my blessedly infrequent stays as a guest of the state, at which times one's freedom of association is severely proscribed, I don't hang out with known criminals. My friends may swipe stationery from the office or buy a hot color TV. They almost certainly fiddle a bit on their income tax returns. But they don't make their livings lifting baubles from other people's apartments, or knocking over liquor stores and filling stations, or writing checks drawn on the Left Bank of the Wabash. Their moral caliber may be no greater than mine but their respectability quotient is infinitely higher.

And as far as any of them know, I'm as respectable as the next fellow. I don't talk much about my work, and in the sort of casual friendships toward which I gravitate there's nothing remarkable about that. It's generally understood that I'm in investments, or living on a small but apparently adequate private income, or doing something dull but earnest in import-export, or whatever. Sometimes I'll assume a more colorful role to impress a youngish person of the interesting sex, but for the most part I'm just Good Old Bernie, who always has a buck in his pocket but never throws it around recklessly, and you can always count on him for a fifth at poker or a fourth at bridge, and he probably does something like sell insurance but hasn't thank God tried to sell it to *me*.

Now my dentist evidently knew I was a burglar. The fact that my cover was blown wasn't horrible – there were people in my apartment building who knew, and a few other folks around town. But the whole thing was startling, so was the manner in which it had all been brought to my attention.

'Couldn't resist that,' Craig Sheldrake was saying. 'Damn if you didn't just about drop your lower incisors on my linoleum. Didn't mean to shake you up but I couldn't help myself. Hell, Bern, it don't make no never mind to me. You had your name in the paper when they were trying to hang a murder charge on you a year or so ago and I happened to notice it. Rhodenbarr's not the most common name in the world, and they even gave your address, which I of course have in the files, so it looked to be you all right. You've been in a few times since then and I never said anything because there was never any need.'

'Urg.'

'Right – but there is now. Bernie, how'd you like to rack up a really nice score? I guess different burglars like to steal different things but I never heard of a one who doesn't like to steal jewelry. I'm not talking about crap from the costume counter at J. C. Penney. I'm talking about the real stuff. Diamonds and emeralds and rubies and lots of fourteen- and eighteen-carat golderoo. Stuff any burglar would be proud to stash in his swag bag.'

I wanted to tell him not to use what he evidently thought was thieves' argot. But what I said was 'Urg.'

'You betcha, Bern. But open a little wider, huh? That's the ticket. Let me get to the point. You remember Crystal, don't you? She worked for me, but that was before your time. Then I made the mistake of marrying her and lost a great dental hygienist who put out and gained in return a slovenly wife who also put out – for half the world. But I know I've told you my troubles with that bitch. I poured that tale into any ear that would stand still for it.'

How could any ear escape it when it shared a head with a mouth with Mr Thirsty slurping up the saliva?

'Bought her all the jewelry in the world,' he went on. 'Sold myself on the idea that it was a good investment. I couldn't just hold onto money, Bern. Not built that way. And she gave me this song and dance about investing in jewelry, and I had all this undeclared cash I couldn't invest in stocks and bonds, it had to go into something where you can pay cash and keep the whole thing off the books. And you can get good bargains in the jewelry line if you'll do business that way, believe me.'

'Urg.'

'Thing is, then we went and got divorced. And she got all the pretties, and I couldn't even pitch a bitch in court or the IRS might stand up and start wondering where the cash for those pretties came from in the first place. And I'm not hurting, Bern. I make a good living. But here's this bitch sitting on a couple hundred thousand dollars in jewelry, plus she got the house and everything in it, the co-op apartment on Gramercy

Park with a key to the fucking park and everything, and I got my clothes and my dental equipment, and on top of that I pay her a healthy chunk of alimony every month, which I have to pay until she dies or remarries, whichever comes first, and personally I wish that what comes first is her death and that it comes yesterday. But she's healthy, and she's smart enough not to remarry, and unless she drinks and screws herself to death I'm on the hook forever.'

I'm not divorced, never having gotten married in the first place, but it seems to me that everyone I know is either divorced or separated or thinking of moving out. Sometimes, when they all carp about alimony and child-support payments, I feel vaguely out of it. But most of the time what I feel is grateful.

'You could knock her off easy,' he went on, and then he began explaining just how I could go about it and when she was apt to be off the premises and all the rest. He went into greater detail than you have to know about, with me supplying the *urgs* whenever he stopped for air or zeroed in for some serious work on the old molar. When the drilling was done he had me rinse and then he set about putting in a filling, and throughout the whole process I heard just what an easy score it would be and how profitable I would find it, and more than anything else, what a bitch she was and how she had it coming. I suppose a lot of this last part was rationalization. Evidently he figured I would be happier stealing from a bad person than a good one. In point of fact I've found that it doesn't make much difference to me, and that what I really prefer is to burgle a victim about whom I know absolutely nothing. This business works best when you keep it as impersonal as you can.

He went on, did Craig Sheldrake, World's Greatest Dentist, and so did the elaborate process of filling my tooth. And finally his conversation was finished and so was my tooth, and Mr Thirsty made his exit and so did all the now-sodden wads of cotton, and there was a spate of rinsing and spitting, a bit of opening wide a final time while the great man checked the results of his handiwork, and then I sat back in the chair while he stood beside me, I examining my remodeled tooth with the inquisitive tip of my tongue, he holding one hand with another and waiting to ask the urgent question.

'Well, Bern? Have we got a deal?'

'No,' I said. 'Absolutely not. Out of the question.'

I wasn't just fencing. I damn well meant it.

See, I like to find my own jobs. There are a lot of burglars who love to work on the basis of inside information, and God knows there's a lot of such information to be had. Fences are a prime source of this sort of data. A fence will oftentimes contact a thief, not merely with a request for a particular item but with the specs and location of the item all

179

written out for him. This is an easy way to work and a lot of burglars are crazy about it.

And the jails are full of them.

Because what do you really know when you're dealing with a fence? Receivers of stolen goods are a curious breed, and there's something unquestionably slimy about the greatest portion of them. If I had a daughter, I certainly wouldn't want her to marry one. A fence does something manifestly illegal but he rarely does a single hour behind bars for his sins, partly because it's hard to nail him with the evidence, partly because his crime is the sort there's little public outcry against, and partly because he's apt to be pretty clever at playing both sides against the middle. He may pay off cops, and if paying them off with cash and furs doesn't work, he may turn to paying them off by setting up other criminals for them. I don't say that you're likely to get set up if you take jobs a fence hands you, but I've managed to dope out one thing in my time. If you're the only one who knows you're going to pull a particular job, then nobody's in a position to rat on you. Any trouble you fall into is either your own damn fault or the luck of the draw.

Now I certainly wasn't worried about Craig setting me up. There was little chance of that. But he liked to talk, accustomed as he was to all those immobile ears, and who could say when it would seem like a good idea to talk about the clever job he and good old Bernie Rhodenbarr had pulled on sluttish Crystal?

Ahem.

Then how did I wind up in the very same Crystal's apartment while someone was stopping her heart?

Good question.

Greed, I guess. And perhaps a portion of pride. Those were two of the seven deadly sins and between them they'd done me in. The Gramercy Park apartment sounded as though it would yield a sizable score with minimal risk and no special security equipment to overcome. There are no end of apartments every bit as easy to get into but most of them contain nothing more valuable or portable than a color TV. Crystal Sheldrake's place was a prime grade-A target, the only drawback being that Craig would know about my role in the deal. With the state of my bankroll what it was, which is to say slim indeed, this objection gradually paled to the point of invisibility.

Pride came into it in a curious way. Craig had gone to great lengths to talk about what a groovy thing it was to be a burglar, how it was adventurous and all, and while that may have been largely a buildup to that *Like you, Bernie* punch line, it still was not without effect. Because, damn it all, I guess I see what I do as glamorous and adventurous and all the rest of it. That's one reason I find it impossible to stop making surreptitious visits to other people's residences, that plus the fact that the only job for which I have any training is making license plates, and you have to be behind bars to pursue that career.

A thought occurred to me, although not until later. I may have known all along I was going to go for the deal. I may have acted reluctant in order to keep the World's Greatest Dentist from expecting too much in the way of a finder's fee. I don't think I was aware of that aim, but aware or not it worked pretty well. I don't know what Craig may have had in mind to ask, but in the course of talking me into changing my mind his percentage dropped to a fifth of whatever I netted when the take was fenced. Now that was eminently fair, considering that Craig got to sit home in front of the television set, never fearful of being shot or arrested in the name of justice. But he was an amateur, and amateurs rarely have a sense of proportion about these matters, and he could easily have wanted as much as half if I'd been eager from the start.

No matter. When he got down to twenty percent I suppressed an urge to see just how far down he'd go – he obviously wanted her to lose the jewels more than he wanted his own share of the proceeds. And I caved in and told him I'd do the dirty deed.

'Fantastic,' he said. 'Super. You'll never regret it, Bern.'

Even then, I wished he hadn't said that.

I stayed in the dental chair. Craig went off, doubtless to boil his hands before facing another patient, and in no time at all Jillian took over. I was encouraged to lean back in my chair again while she picked and poked at my teeth and gums, liberating tartar, scaling, and doing all the unpleasant chores that come under the heading of dental cleaning.

Jillian didn't talk much, and that was really all right. Not that I had anything against her conversation, but my ears were due for a rest and my mind had thoughts to play with. At first the thoughts centered upon the Crystal Sheldrake apartment and how I would endeavor to knock it off. I was not entirely certain that I should have said yes, and so I did a certain amount of arm-twisting on myself, building up my resolve, telling myself it was like finding money in the street.

These thoughts, while undoubtedly useful, ultimately gave way to thoughts about the comely young lady who was probing my oral cavities – which, come to think of it, sounds a damn sight more appealing than it actually was. I don't know why one would be inclined to have reprehensible fantasies about a dental hygienist but I've never been able to avoid it. Maybe it's the uniform. Nurses, stewardesses, usherettes, nuns – the male chauvinist mind will go on weaving its smarmy webs.

But Jillian Paar could have been a laundress or a streetsweeper and she'd have had the same effect on me. She was a slender slip of a girl, with straight dark brown hair cut as if with a soup bowl over her head, but clearly by someone who knew what he was doing. She had that spectacular complexion associated with the British Isles – white porcelain illuminated with a rosy glow. Her hands, unlike her employer's, were small, with narrow fingers. They did not taste boiled. Instead they smelled of spice.

She tended to lean against one while working on one's mouth. There was nothing objectionable in this. Quite the contrary, truth to tell.

So the cleaning seemed to pass in no time at all. And when it was all done and my teeth had that wonderfully shiny feel to them that they only have the first few hours after they've been cleaned, and after we'd exchanged a few pleasantries and she'd shown me for what seemed like the thousandth time the proper way to brush my teeth (and every damned dental hygienist shows you a different way, and each swears it's the *only* way) she batted an eyelash or two at me and said, 'It's always good to see you, Mr Rhodenbarr.'

'Always a pleasure for me, Jillian.'

'And I'm so glad to hear you're going to help Craig out and burglarize Crystal's jewels.'

'Urg,' I said.

I suppose I should have bailed out there and then. It was the right time for it – the plane was still in the air and I had a parachute.

But I didn't.

I wasn't happy about things. My tight-lipped dentist had managed to break security within five minutes. Presumably Jillian was his trusted confidante, and quite likely she received a good number of his confidences while both parties were in a horizontal position, an hypothesis I'd entertained earlier in light of her obvious attractions and Craig's historic predilection for diddling the help.

This didn't butter no parsnips, as my grandmother would never have dreamed of saying. (Granny was a strict grammarian who wouldn't have said *ain't* if she had a mouthful.) As far as I was concerned, if one person knew a burglar's plan, that was awful. If two people knew, that was ten times as awful. It didn't matter if the two people were sleeping together. Hell, maybe it was *worse* if they were sleeping together. They could have a falling-out and one of them could go about blabbing resentfully.

I did take time to speak to Craig, assuring him that it would be in everybody's interest for him to give his errant tongue a Novocaine hit. He apologized and promised to be properly silent in the future, and I decided to let it go at that. I wouldn't bail out. I'd see if I couldn't fly the damn plane to safety.

Pride and greed. They'll do you in every time.

That was on a Thursday. I got out to the Hamptons for the weekend, spent half a day out on a bluefish boat, worked on my tan, sampled the bar scene, stayed at a fine old place called the Huntting Inn (spelling it with two *T*'s was their idea), agreed with everyone that the place was a damn sight better now that the season was over, and in the course of things struck out with an impressive number of otherwise charming young ladies. By the time I was back in Manhattan where I belong, I'd eaten up a little more of my case money and was almost glad I'd decided to hit the Sheldrake residence. Not wild about it but, oh, let's say sanguine.

I spent Tuesday and Wednesday casing the joint. Wednesday night I called Craig at his East Sixty-third Street bachelor digs to get another report on Crystal's routine. I told him, not without purpose, that Saturday night sounded like the best time for me to make my move.

I didn't intend to wait until Saturday. The very next night, Thursday, I had my conversation with Miss Henrietta Tyler and cracked Crystal's crib.

And languished in her closet. And probed for a pulse in her lifeless wrist.

4

Around ten the next morning I was spreading rhubarb preserves on a piece of whole-wheat toast. I'd bought the preserves, imported from Scotland at great expense, because I figured anything in an octagonal jar with a classy label had to be good. Now I felt an obligation to use them up even though my figuring seemed to be wrong. I had the piece of toast nicely covered and was about to cut it into triangles when the phone rang.

When I answered it Jillian Parr said, 'Mr Rhodenbarr? This is Jillian. From Dr Craig's office?'

'Oh, hi!' I said. 'Beautiful morning, isn't it? How are things in dental hygiene?'

There was a funereal pause. Then, 'You haven't heard the news?'

'News?'

'I don't even know if it was in the papers. I haven't even *seen* the papers. I overslept, I just grabbed coffee and Danish on my way to the office. Craig had a nine-thirty appointment booked and he's always at the office on time and he didn't show up. I called his apartment and there was no answer, and I figured he must be on his way in, and then I had the radio on and there was a newscast.'

'Jesus,' I said. 'What happened, Jillian?'

There was a pause and then the words came in a rush. 'He was arrested, Bernie. I know it sounds crazy but it's true. Last night some-one killed Crystal. Stabbed her to death or something, and in the middle of the night the police came and arrested Craig for her murder. You didn't know about this?'

'I can't even believe it,' I said. I wedged the phone between ear and shoulder so that I could quarter the toast. I didn't want it to get cold. If I have to eat rhubarb preserves I can damn well eat them on warm toast. 'It wasn't in the *Times*,' I added. I could have added that it wasn't in the *News* either, but that it was all over the radio and television newscasts. But for some curious reason I didn't mention this.

'I don't know what to do, Bernie. I just don't know what I should do.'

I took a bite of toast, chewed it thoughtfully. 'I suppose the first step is to close the office and cancel his appointments for the day.'

'Oh, I already did that. You know Marian, don't you? The receptionist? She's making telephone calls now. When she's done I'll send her home, and after that—'

'After that you can go home yourself.'

'I suppose so. But there has to be something I can *do*.'

I ate more toast, sipped some coffee. I seemed to be developing a definite taste for the rhubarb jam. I wasn't positive I'd go running out for another jar when this one was finally finished, but I was beginning to like it. Coffee, though, was not quite the right accompaniment. A pot of strong English breakfast tea, that would be more like it. I'd have to remember next time.

'I can't believe Craig would kill her,' she was saying. 'She was a bitch and he hated her but I can't believe he would kill anyone. Even a rotten tramp like Crystal.'

I tried to remember that Latin phrase for speaking well of the dead, then gave it up. *De mortuis ta-tum ta-tum bonum*, something along those lines.

'If only I could *talk* to him, Bernie.'

'You haven't heard from him?'

'Nothing.'

'What time did they pick him up?'

'They didn't say on the radio. Only that he'd been arrested for questioning. If it was just a matter of questioning they wouldn't have had to arrest him, would they?'

'Probably not.' I paused, chewed rhubarb-laden toast, considered. 'When was Crystal killed? Did they happen to say?'

'I think they said the body was discovered shortly after midnight.'

'Well, it's hard to say when they would have gotten around to picking Craig up. They might have questioned him without charging him for a while. He could have insisted they charge him, but he might not have thought of that. And he might not have bothered insisting on having a lawyer present. In any event, somewhere along the way he must have called an attorney. He wouldn't have a criminal lawyer but his own lawyer would have referred the case to somebody and he's almost certainly got counsel at hand by now.' I thought back to my own experiences. I used a couple of mouthpieces over the years before I finally settled on Herbie Tannenbaum. He's always straight with me, I can call him at any hour, and he knows he can trust me to come up with his fee even if I don't have anything in advance. He also knows how to reach the reachable judges and how to work trade-offs with the DA's people. But I somehow doubted he'd be the kind of lawyer Craig Sheldrake would wind up with.

'You could get in touch with Craig's lawyer,' I added. 'Find out from him how things stand.'

'I don't know who he is.'

'Well, maybe he'll call you. The lawyer. If only to tell you to cancel the appointments. He shouldn't take it for granted that you happened to catch the newscast.'

'Why hasn't he called yet? It's almost ten-thirty!'

Because you're on the phone, I wanted to say. Instead I swallowed some food and said, 'They may have waited until a decent hour before they arrested him. Don't panic, Jillian. If he's been arrested he's certainly in a safe place. If the lawyer doesn't call you sometime this afternoon, make some calls and find out where he's being held. They might even let you see him. If not, at least they'll give you the name of his attorney and you can take it from there. Don't expect Craig to call you. They'll let him call his lawyer and that's generally the extent of his phone privileges.' Unless you bribe a guard, but he wouldn't know how to go about doing that. 'You don't really have anything to worry about, Jillian. Either you'll hear from the lawyer or you'll get in touch with the lawyer and either way things'll work out. If Craig's innocent—'

'Of course he's innocent!'

'—then things'll get straightened out in no time at all. They always pick up the husband when the wife gets murdered. But Crystal led a rather loose life, from what I've heard—'

'She was a slut!'

'—so it's likely there were any number of men with a good motive and opportunity to kill her; and she might even have brought home a stranger—'

'Like *Looking for Mr Goodbar*!'

'—so I'm sure there are more suspects in this case than cockroaches on Eldridge Street, and the World's Greatest Dentist ought to be back drilling and filling in no time at all.'

'Oh, I *hope* so!' She took a breath. 'Can't he get out on bail? People always get out on bail, don't they?'

'Not when the charge is Murder One. There's no bail allowable in first-degree murder cases.'

'That doesn't seem fair.'

'Few things are.' More toast, more coffee. 'I think you should just sit tight, Jillian. Either where you are or at your apartment, wherever you'll be more comfortable.'

'I'm scared, Bernie.'

'Scared?'

'I don't know why or what of but I'm terrified. Bernie?'

'What?'

'Could you come over? It's crazy, maybe, but I don't know who else to ask. I just don't want to be alone by myself now.' I hesitated, at least partly because I had some unswallowed food on my tongue, and she

186

said, 'Forget I said all that, okay? You're a busy man, I know that, and it's an imposition, and—'

'I'll be right over.'

There's something to keep in mind. I didn't agree to bop on over to Craig's Central Park South office just because I have a penchant for sticking my head in the lion's mouth, or into whatever orifice the beast chooses to present to me. Nor was I making the trip because I couldn't help remembering how nice it felt when Jillian leaned against me during a cleaning, or how nice her fingers tasted.

On the surface, it might look as though I had a vested interest in staying uninvolved. I was after all a burglar, and am hence regarded generally as a Highly Suspicious Person. And I was, further, no more than a dental patient and casual acquaintance of Craig Sheldrake, nor was my relationship with Jillian such that she'd be likely to turn to me before all others for solace in time of stress. Why, she'd never called me anything but Mr Rhodenbarr until this morning. So at first glance it certainly looked as though I ought to keep a low profile.

On the other hand – and there's always another hand – whoever jammed Crystal's pump had taken a caseful of jewels along with him. I had taken to thinking of those jewels as my own, and I still thought of them as my own, and I damn well wanted to get them back.

I didn't just want the jewels, as far as that goes. The precious pretties, you may recall, were in an attaché case I'd brought into the apartment with me. I was reasonably certain no one could trace that case to me – I, after all, had stolen it in the first place. But I couldn't begin to be sure that the inside of the damn thing wasn't covered with my fingerprints. The outside was Ultrasuede and would no more take a print than Crystal Sheldrake's wrist would, but the inside was some sort of vinyl or Naugahyde, which might or might not take prints, and there was a lot of metal trim in the interior, and it wasn't at all hard to conjure up scenarios in which a cadre of cops kicked my door in and sought to learn what a case with my prints on it, loaded with Crystal's jewelry, was doing in the apartment of a murder suspect.

So if they caught him I might be in trouble. And if they didn't catch him he'd be getting away with my loot. And if there was no one to catch because the World's Greatest Dentist had indeed gone and committed the world's dumbest murder, well, that was less than super for me, too. Because in that case Craig would hand me to them on a platter. '*I was talking to him about all this jewelry she had around, see, and he seemed to be taking quite an interest, and later it dawned on me that I'd read something about him being a burglar and once being mixed up in a murder, and I never dreamed he'd actually burglarize poor Crystal's apartment—*'

I could just about write the script for him, and after the way he'd set me up a week ago, I didn't doubt he had the acting talent to read his lines properly. It might not be enough to get him out of the soup but it would certainly put me in the kettle alongside of him.

In fact, even if he wasn't guilty he might try that approach. If no other suspect turned up he could panic. Or he could have the same doubts about me that I was having about him, and he could decide I might have hit Crystal's apartment two days earlier than I said I would – which in fact I did – and that I happened to kill her accidentally in a moment of panic. He might simply have figured that our arrangement might come out so he'd better put the best possible light on it in advance.

What it came down to was that there were far too many ways that I could wind up in trouble.

And there was the fact that I liked Craig Sheldrake. When you are a patient of the World's Greatest Dentist you don't readily give him up and walk in off the street to any clown with a sign in his window advertising painless extractions. The man was taking good care of my mouth and I wanted him to carry on.

And Jillian was certainly a charming young lady. And it was much nicer to be called *Bernie* by her than *Mr Rhodenbarr*, which had always struck me as overly formal. And her fingers did have that nice spicy taste to them, and it seemed reasonable to assume that this was characteristic of more of her than her fingers alone. Jillian was Craig's personal love interest, of course, and that was fine with me, and I had no intention of horning hornily in on another chap's romance. That's not my style. I only steal cash and inanimate objects. All the same, one needn't have designs on a young lady to find her company enjoyable. And if Craig should prove to be guilty, Jillian would be out of a job and a lover just as I would be out of a dentist, and there was no reason for us to do other than console each other.

But why build sand castles? Some evil bastard had not stopped at killing Crystal Sheldrake. He'd gone on to steal jewels I'd already stolen.

And I intended to make him pay for that.

5

'You're fantastic, Bernie.'

I must admit I'd had fantasies in which Jillian spoke those very words to me, and in approximately that tone of voice, but I hadn't been hanging up a telephone when it happened. I'd planned on being in a horizontal position at the time. Instead I was vertical, and I was replacing the receiver of the phone that perched on the desk of Marian the Receptionist. Marian was out for the day. Craig Sheldrake, on the other hand, was not. He was still behind bars – which was what my phone conversation had just determined.

A few other calls had revealed a few other things. Craig's regular attorney was a man by the name of Carson Verrill, with offices some-where downtown. Verrill had engaged a criminal lawyer named Errol Blankenship to represent Craig in this particular matter. (The choice of phrasing was that of someone in Verrill's office.) Blankenship had an office listed in the phone book on Madison Avenue in the thirties. I tried his phone and no one answered it. If he had a home phone, either his home was outside of Manhattan or the number was unlisted. I let it go. I figured he was in court or something and his secretary had decided to celebrate by taking a long lunch hour.

Craig had been arrested in his own Upper East Side apartment around six-thirty in the morning. Not many good things happen at that time of day and being arrested certainly isn't one of them. They'd let him shave and change from his pajamas into something more suitable for street wear. I hoped he'd known to wear loafers, but how many straight-arrow citizens would think of that? They don't always take your shoelaces away from you in jail, but periodically some Yo-Yo decides you look like the suicidal sort, and there you are clumping around with your shoes falling off your feet.

Well, probably that was the least of his worries.

He was in a cell now in a hostile building downtown on Centre Street. I don't suppose he was happy about it. I've never known anyone who was. I'd asked if he could have visitors and the person I talked to didn't seem to be the voice of authority on the subject. He said he thought so, but why didn't I drop around and make sure?

Whatever the ruling, the last thing I wanted to do was drop around that grim establishment myself. My previous visits had not been the sort to make me anxious to return for old times' sake.

'*You're fantastic, Bernie.*'

Actually, she didn't say it again. I'm repeating it so as to preserve the thread of this narrative. What I said in reply was that she shouldn't be silly, that I was not fantastic, and even if I did happen to be moderately sensational in certain unspecified other areas, nevertheless I'd done nothing remarkable in her presence. Yet.

'You could have made the same calls and found out the same information,' I said. 'You just don't have experience with this sort of thing.'

'I wouldn't have had any idea what to do.'

'You could have figured it out.'

'And I would have gotten all rattled on the phone. I sometimes get terribly nervous. I'm not very good at talking to people. Sometimes I think there's too much silence when I'm working on a patient. They can't talk, obviously, and I just can't manage to open my mouth.'

'Believe me, it's a release after Craig does his Motormouth number.'

She giggled. It was a charming giggle, which surprised me about as much as that the sun had picked the east to rise in that morning. 'He does talk a lot,' she acknowledged, as if painfully admitting that the Liberty Bell had a crack in it. 'But that's only with patients. When he's alone he's very shy and quiet.'

'Well, I wouldn't expect him to talk to himself.'

'Pardon me?'

'Everybody's quiet when they're alone.'

She thought about it, then blushed prettily. I'd come to think of that as a lost art. 'I meant he's quiet when he's alone with me.'

'I knew what you meant.'

'Oh.'

'I was being a smart-ass. Sorry.'

'Oh, that's all right. I just – my mind's not working too brilliantly this morning. I wonder what I should do. Do you think I can go see Craig?'

'I don't know whether or not he can have visitors. You could go down there and find out, but I think it would be a good idea for us to learn a little more about what's going on first. If we had a better idea of just how good a case they've got against Craig, we might be in a better position to figure out what to do next.'

'Do you think they've got a good case?'

I shrugged. 'Hard to say. It would help if he has an alibi for last night, but I guess if he had a good one he'd be back on the street by now. I, uh, gather he wasn't with you?'

She blushed again. I guess there was no avoiding it. 'No,' she said.

'We had dinner together last night but then we each had some things to do so we went our separate ways. I guess it was about nine o'clock that I saw him last. I went home and so did he.'

'Uh-huh.'

'Oh!' She brightened. 'I talked to him before I went to bed. It was during the Carson show, I remember that. It wasn't much of a conversation, we just said goodnight to each other, but he was home then. Would that help give him an alibi?'

'Did you call him?'

'He called me.'

'Then it wouldn't help his alibi a whole lot. You've only got his word as to where he was when he called you. And the police are likely to take the position that a murderer wouldn't draw the line at lying to a pretty lady.'

She started to say something, then gnawed a little scarlet lipstick from her lower lip. It was a becoming shade and a most attractive lower lip. I wouldn't have minded gnawing it myself.

'Bernie? You don't think he did it, do you?'

'I'm pretty certain he didn't.'

'Why?'

I had a reason but I preferred to keep it to myself. 'Because of the kind of guy he is,' I said instead, and that was evidently just what she wanted to hear. She started enlarging on the topic of Craig Sheldrake, World's Greatest Guy, and I'll be damned if she didn't make him sound like someone I'd have really liked to meet.

I decided to change the subject. 'The fact that we know he's innocent doesn't do him much good,' I said, by way of transition. 'The cops have to know he's innocent, and the easiest way for that to happen is if they've got someone else they know is guilty. Unless you're on the Orient Express, one murderer per corpse is all anybody could possibly ask for.'

'Do you mean we should try to solve the crime ourselves?'

Did I? 'Well, I wouldn't go that far,' I said, backpedaling. 'But I wish I knew more than I do. I'd like to know just when the murder was committed, and I'd like to know what men Crystal was involved with lately, and where all of them were when somebody was busy killing her. And I'd like to know if anybody had a particularly strong reason for wanting her dead. Craig had a ton of reasons, and you and I know that and so does the long arm of the law, but a woman who led as active a life as Crystal Sheldrake did must have made a few enemies along the way. Maybe some lover of hers had a jealous wife or girlfriend. There's a whole world of possibilities out there and I hardly know where we should start.'

She looked at me. 'I'm so glad I called you, Bernie.'

'Well, I don't know how much help I can really be—'

'I'm really so glad.' Her eyes did a little number, and then suddenly her forehead crinkled up and her gaze narrowed. 'I just thought of something,' she said. 'You were going to burglarize Crystal's apartment on Saturday night, weren't you? Imagine if the killer had picked that time to strike!'

Let's imagine no such thing, Jillian. 'But Crystal was home last night,' I reminded her, carefully shifting her gears and pointing her in a safer direction. 'I would never have gone in if she was home.'

'Oh. Of course. I just thought—'

Whatever she just thought will be forever unrecorded because she didn't get to the end of the sentence. There was a brisk rat-tat-tat, a loud knock on the clouded glass panel of the outer door. 'Open up in there,' said a professionally authoritative voice. And added, quite unnecessarily in my opinion, 'It's the police.'

Jillian blanched.

I, in turn, did the only possible thing under the circumstances. Without the slightest hesitation I grabbed her by the shoulders, drew her close, and brought our mouths together in a passionate embrace.

The knock was repeated.

Well, what the hell. So was the kiss.

6

I don't know if Jillian was nonplussed, but she certainly wasn't plussed. Her face held an expression somewhere between bemusement and astonishment, with pronounced overtones of shock. Have I mentioned her eyes? They were the faded blue of well-washed denim, and they were large, and I had never seen them larger.

Rat-tat-tat.

'Bernie!'

'Police. Open up there.'

I was still gripping her shoulders. 'I'm your boyfriend,' I whispered urgently. 'You're not Craig's girl, you're my girl, and that's why you happened to ask me to drop over, and we've been doing a little innocent smooching.'

Her mouth made an O, her eyes showed instant comprehension, and her head bobbed in affirmation. Even as I was pointing at the door she was moving toward it. I snatched a Kleenex from the box on Marian's desk, and as the door opened to reveal a pair of plainclothes cops, I was in the process of dabbing at Jillian's scarlet lipstick.

'Sorry to interrupt you,' said the taller of the two. He had bigger shoulders than most people, and very widely spaced eyes, as if while in the womb he'd toyed with the idea of becoming Siamese twins and decided against it at the last minute. He did not sound at all sorry to interrupt us.

'We're police,' the other one said. During the July blackout someone said *'Dark out, isn't it!'* That was as unnecessary a sentence as I've ever heard uttered, and *'We're police'* came a close second.

For one thing, they'd told us as much through the locked door. For another, they damn well looked the part. The shorter one was slender rather than broad. He had black curly hair and a small, inexpertly trimmed black mustache, and no Hollywood casting director would pick him for a cop. He looked more like the member of the gang who turns stool pigeon in the second-to-last reel. But standing there in front of us he looked like a cop and so did the one with all the shoulders. Maybe it's the stance, maybe it's the facial expression, maybe it's just some aspect of the inner self they manage to project, but cops all look like cops.

This pair introduced themselves. The block of granite was Todras, the stoat was Nyswander. Todras was a detective and Nyswander was a patrolman, and if they had first names they were keeping them a secret. We furnished our names, first and last, and Todras asked Jillian to spell her first name. She did, and Nyswander wrote all this down in a little dog-eared notebook. Todras asked Jillian what people called her for short and she said they didn't.

'Well, it's just routine,' Todras said. He seemed to be the natural leader of the two, the offensive guard clearing a path for Nyswander to weasel through. 'I guess you heard about your boss, Miss Paar.'

'There was something on the radio.'

'Yeah, well, I'm afraid he's gonna have his hands full for a while now. You got the office closed up, I see. You call around and cancel his appointments yet?'

'For the rest of the day.'

The two of them exchanged glances. 'Maybe you should cancel them for the rest of the month,' Nyswander suggested.

'Or the rest of the year.'

'Yeah, because it really looks as though he stepped in it this time.'

'Maybe you better close the office for good,' Todras said.

'Maybe you should.'

'And find somebody else to work for.'

'Somebody who figures divorce is enough and stops short of murder.'

'Or someone who when he kills a former spouse finds a way to get away with it.'

'Yeah, that's the idea.'

'Right.'

It was really something, the way the lines came back and forth from the two of them. It was as though they had a vaudeville act they were working on, and they wanted to break it in in the smaller rooms before they took it on the road. We were a sort of warm-up audience, and they were making the most of us.

Jillian didn't seem to think they were all that hysterical. Her lower lip, which now carried less than its usual quantity of lipstick, trembled slightly. Her eyes looked misty. *I'm your boyfriend*, I thought, trying to beam the thought her way. *Craig's just your boss. And don't for God's sake call him Craig.*

'I can't believe it,' she said.

'Believe it, Miss Paar.'

'Right,' came the echo from Nyswander.

'But he wouldn't do something like that.'

'You never know,' Todras said.

'They'll fool you every time,' said Nyswander.

194

'But Dr Sheldrake couldn't kill anyone!'

'He didn't kill just anyone,' Todras said.

'He killed somebody specific,' Nyswander said.

'Namely his wife.'

'Which is pretty specific.'

Jillian frowned and her lip quivered again. I had to admire the way she was using that lip-quiver. Maybe it was real, maybe she wasn't even conscious of it, but she was fitting it into a generally effective act. It might not stun 'em in Peoria the way Todras & Nyswander might, but she got her point across.

'He's such a good man to work for,' she said.

'Been working for him long, Miss Paar?'

'Quite a while. That's how I met Bernie. Mr Rhodenbarr.'

'You met Mr Rhodenbarr here through the doc?'

She nodded. 'He was a patient of the doctor's. And we met here and started seeing each other.'

'And I suppose you had an appointment for some more dental work this morning. That right, Mr Rhodenbarr?'

It wasn't right. Tempting, perhaps, but not right, and if they checked the appointment book they'd know as much. Why tell an obvious lie when a less obvious one will do?

'No,' I said. 'Miss Paar called me and I was able to get over to comfort her. She was anxious and didn't want to be here alone.'

They nodded to each other and Nyswander wrote something down. The time and temperature, perhaps.

'I guess you been a patient of the doc's for some time, Mr Rhodenbarr.'

'A couple of years now.'

'Ever meet his former wife?'

Well, we were never formally introduced. 'No,' I said. 'I don't think so.'

'She was his nurse before they got married, wasn't she?'

'His hygienist,' Jillian corrected. The two of them stared at her. I said that I understood Mrs Sheldrake had retired upon marrying her employer, and that by the time I became his patient she was no longer working at the office.

'Nice deal,' Nyswander said. 'You marry the boss, that's even better'n marrying the boss's daughter.'

'Unless the boss kills you,' Todras suggested.

The conversation drifted on in this fashion. I slipped in a tentative question now and again of the sort they could have fun doing macabre Smith-and-Dale routines with, and I managed to pick up an item here and an item there.

Item: The Medical Examiner had fixed the time of death at somewhere between midnight and one in the morning. Now you know and I know that Crystal Sheldrake died at 10:49, eleven minutes of eleven, but I couldn't find a way to supply that bit of information.

Item: There were no signs of forced entry, no indication that anything had been removed from the apartment, and everything pointed to the supposition that Crystal had admitted her killer herself. Since she was rather informally attired, even to the bathing cap on her head, it was logical to suppose that the murderer was a close acquaintance at the very least.

No argument there. No signs of forced entry, certainly, because when I bamboozle the tumblers of a lock I don't leave tracks. No indication of burglary if only because there was no mess, no drawers turned inside-out, none of the signals left behind by either an amateur at the game or a pro in a hurry. Whoever killed Crystal might well have left the apartment looking as though the Hell's Angels had sublet it for a month, but I'd made things uncommonly easy for him, gathering all the loot in advance of his call and packing it up for him. God, that rankled!

Item: Craig couldn't account for his time while his ex-wife was getting herself murdered. If he'd mentioned anything about having dinner with Jillian, the news didn't seem to have found its way to Todras & Nyswander. It would eventually, of course, and sooner or later they'd know Jillian was the boss's girlfriend and I was nothing more than your friendly neighborhood burglar. Which would, sooner or later, constitute a problem, a thorn in the side, a pain in the neck. But not yet, thank you. Meanwhile, Craig was telling them that he'd spent a quiet evening at home. A lot of people spend a lot of their evenings quietly at home, but those are the hardest sort of evenings to prove.

Item: Someone, some neighbor I suppose, had seen a man answering Craig's description leaving the Gramercy building at around the time the murder was supposed to have been committed. I couldn't tell just what time the person had been seen, or whether he'd been leaving merely the building or the specific apartment, or just who had seen him or just how certain the witness was about the time and the identification. Someone or anyone could have spotted the man who'd made love to Crystal, or the man who killed her, or even Bernard Rhodenbarr himself, beating a hasty retreat from the premises after the horse was stolen.

Or it could have been Craig. All I knew about the killer was he had two feet and he didn't talk much. If Gary Cooper were still alive he could have done it. Maybe it was Marcel Marceau. Maybe it was Craig, uncharacteristically silent.

'Wondered if we could just go into the office,' Todras said. And when Jillian explained that that's where we were, in the office, he said, 'Well, I don't know the name for it, maybe. The room where he does what he does.'

'I beg your pardon?'

'With the chair that goes back,' Nyswander said.

'And all the drills.'

'And the instruments, those cute little mirrors on the ends of sticks, and the things for picking the crud out from underneath your gums.'

'Oh, right,' Todras said, smiling at the memory. His own teeth were large and white and even, like the snow when Good King Wenceslas looked out. (That's not exactly right, but you must know what I mean.) His wide-set eyes gleamed like high-beamed headlights over the grill-work of his smile. 'And that slurpy thing that sucks up all your spit. Don't forget the slurpy thing.'

'That's Mr Thirsty,' I said.

'Huh?'

Jillian led us to the room where Craig did his handiwork, solving people's problems and sending them out to do battle with tough steaks and nougat-centered chocolates. The two cops amused themselves by tilting the chair to and fro and making Dr Kronkheit passes at each other with the drill, but then they got down to serious business and opened the cabinet with the drawers of steel implements.

'Now these here are interesting,' little Nyswander said, holding a nasty little pick at arm's length. 'What's this called, anyway?'

Jillian told him it was a pick for scraping tartar from the teeth. He nodded and said it must be important to do that, huh? She said it was vital; otherwise you got irritation and bone erosion and periodontal disease, and you wound up without any teeth. 'People think cavities are the big thing,' she explained, 'but your teeth can be in perfect shape and you'll lose them anyway because of the gums.'

'Those teeth are beauties,' Todras said heartily, 'but I'm afraid those gums have to come out.'

We all laughed it up over that one. Nyswander and Todras took turns holding up implements and wanting to know what they were. This one was another pick, that one was a dental scalpel, and there were no end of others, the names and functions of which have mercifully slipped my mind.

'All these gizmos,' Todras said, 'there's a basic similarity, right? Like they're all part of a set, but instead of being in a case or something so you can be sure they're all here, they're just sort of lined up in the drawer. The doc buy 'em all in a set or something?'

'You can buy them in sets.'

'Is that what he did?'

Jillian shrugged. 'I wouldn't know. He had the office set up a good many years before I came to work for him. Of course the individual implements are available singly. These are fine-quality steel, but accidents happen. Picks drop and get bent. Scalpels get nicks. And we keep several of each implement on hand because you have to have the right tool for the job. I'm the hygienist, I don't handle paperwork, but I know we reorder individual items from time to time.'

'But they're all the same,' Nyswander said.

'Oh, they may look it, but the picks will be angled in slightly different ways, or—'

She stopped because he was shaking his head, but it was Todras who spoke. 'They all have these six-sided handles,' he said. 'They all come from the same manufacturer is what he means.'

'Oh. Yes, that's right.'

'Who's the manufacturer, Miss Paar? You happen to know?'

'Celniker Dental and Optical Supply.'

'You want to spell that, Miss Paar?' She did, and Nyswander wrote something in his notebook, capped his pen, turned a page. While he was doing this Todras brought a large hand out of his pocket and opened it to disclose yet another dental implement. It looked to me quite like the one Jillian had identified as a dental scalpel. I'd had something similar in appearance once, though undoubtedly inferior in quality. It had been part of an X-acto knife kit I had as a boy, and I'd used it to whittle sad little wingless birds from balsa blocks.

'You recognize this, Miss Paar?'

'It's a dental scalpel. Why?'

'One of yours?'

'I don't know. It's possible.'

'You wouldn't know how many of this model the doc happens to have on hand?'

'I wouldn't have any idea. Quite a few, obviously.'

'He ever carry them with him when he leaves the office?'

'Whatever for?'

Again they exchanged presumably meaningful glances.

'We found this one in Crystal Sheldrake's apartment,' Nyswander said.

'Actually it was some other cop found it. He's using "we" in the departmental sense.'

'Actually it was found in Crystal Sheldrake herself.'

'Actually it was in her heart.'

'Actually,' said Todras (or perhaps it was Nyswander), 'this pretty much frosts the cupcake, don't it? Looks to me like your boss is up every creek in town.'

It rattled Jillian. It didn't do a thing to me or for me, as I'd seen that hexagonal handle protruding from between Crystal's breasts while I was fumbling mindlessly for a pulse. I'd more or less known it would turn out to be one of Craig's tools, or a reasonable facsimile thereof, and I'd even toyed with the idea of carrying it off with me.

But there had been abundant reasons for not doing so. The most obvious one was that it would have been just my luck to pocket the deadly device and walk straight into the arms of a cop. It's bad enough when they catch you with burglar's tools. When you're carrying murderer's tools as well they take a dim view indeed.

Besides, as far as I was concerned the scalpel proved Craig was innocent, not guilty, and that someone had only succeeded in setting up the world's clumsiest framing job. Why would Craig use a dental scalpel to kill his wife, knowing it would point immediately to him? And why, if he did have a sufficient lapse of taste and sense to do so, would he leave the scalpel sticking out of her instead of retrieving it and carrying it away with him? Whatever line they took officially, the cops would have to reason along these lines themselves sooner or later, whereas if I had removed the scalpel and some brilliant lab work had later proved that a dental scalpel had inflicted the wound, well, then Craig would really be in a bind.

So I'd left it there, and now I was doing my best to appear as though I was seeing it for the first time. 'Gee,' I said, mouth agape. 'That was the murder weapon?'

'You bet it was,' Todras said.

'Plunged right into her heart,' Nyswander added. 'That's a murder weapon, all right.'

'Death musta been instant.'

'Hardly any bleeding. No muss, no fuss, no bother.'

'Gee,' I said.

Jillian was on the edge of hysteria, and I was hoping she wouldn't overreact. It was logical to assume she'd be shocked at the idea of her boss committing murder, but if their relationship was just that of dentist and hygienist there was a limit to the extent of her shock.

'I just can't believe it,' she was saying. She reached out her hand to touch the scalpel, then drew back at the last moment, her fingertips just avoiding contact with the bright metal. Todras smiled fiercely and returned the scalpel to his pocket, while Nyswander drew a manila envelope from his inside jacket pocket and commenced selecting other dental scalpels from a tray of implements. He put four or five of them into the envelope, licked the flap, sealed it, and wrote something on its outside.

Jillian asked him what he was doing. 'Evidence,' he said.

'The DA'll want to show how the doc's got other scalpels the same size and shape as the murder weapon. You get a good look at it, Miss Paar? Maybe there's something about it, some nick or scratch you'll recognize.'

'I saw it. I can't identify it, if that's what you mean. They all look alike.'

'Might notice something if you give it a close look. Todras, let Miss Paar here have another look at it, huh?'

Jillian didn't much want to look at it. But she forced herself, and after a careful glance announced that there was nothing specifically familiar about the instrument, that it seemed identical to ones they used in the office. But, she added, dentists all over the country used Celniker tools, they were very common, and a search of the offices of dentists throughout New York would turn up thousands of them.

Nyswander said he was sure that was true but that only one dentist had a clear motive for killing Crystal Sheldrake.

'But he cared for her,' she said. 'He was hoping to get back together with her again. I don't think he ever stopped loving her.'

The cops looked at each other, and I couldn't say I blamed them. I don't know what had prompted her to start off in this direction but the cops dutifully followed it up, questioning her about this desire of Craig's for a reconciliation. Then, after she'd improvised reasonably well, Todras took the wind out of her sails by explaining that this just furnished Craig with yet another motive for murder. 'He wanted to get back together,' he said, 'and she spurned him, so he killed her out of love.'

' "Each man kills the thing he loves," ' Nyswander quoted. ' "By each let this be heard. The coward does it with a kiss. The brave man with a sword." And the dentist with a scalpel.'

'Pretty,' Todras said.

'That's Oscar Wilde.'

'I like it.'

'Except that part about a dentist doing it with a scalpel. Oscar Wilde never said that.'

'No kidding.'

'I just put that in on my own.'

'No kidding.'

' 'Cause it seemed to fit.'

'No kidding.'

I thought Jillian was going to scream. Her hands had knotted themselves into little fists. Just hang in there, I wanted to tell her, because this comedy routine of theirs takes their minds off more important things, and in a minute they'll bow and scrape themselves offstage and out of our lives, and then we can work up an act of our own.

But I guess she wasn't listening.

'*Wait a minute!*'

They turned and stared at her.

'Just one damn minute! How do I know you actually brought that thing with you? That scalpel? I never saw you take it out of your pocket. Maybe you picked it up off a tray while I was looking the other way. Maybe all those things you hear about police corruption are true. Framing people and tampering with evidence and—'

They were still staring at her and at about this point she just ran out of words. Not, I'd say, a moment too soon. I wished, not for the first time in my life, that there were a way to stop the celestial tape recorder of existence, rewind it a bit, and lay down a substitute track for the most recent past.

But you can't do that, as Omar Khayyam explained long before tape recorders. The moving finger writes and all, and dear little Jillian had just gone and given us the moving finger, all right.

'This dental scalpel,' said Todras, showing it to us yet again. 'This particular one wasn't found in the chest of Crystal Sheldrake, as a matter of fact. Rules of evidence and everything, we don't ever carry murder weapons around with us. The actual scalpel that snuffed the lady, it's in the lab right now with a tag on it while the men in the white smocks check blood types and do all the things they do.'

Jillian didn't say anything.

'The scalpel my partner's showing you,' Nyswander put in, 'was picked up on the way here when we stopped at Celniker Dental and Optical Supply. It's an exact twin of the murder weapon and useful for us to carry around in the course of our investigation. That's why my partner can keep it in his pocket and take it out when the spirit moves him. It's not evidence so there's no way he can be tampering with it.'

Todras, grinning furiously, made the scalpel disappear again. 'Just for curiosity,' he said, 'maybe you'd like to tell us how you spent the evening, Miss Paar.'

'How I—'

'What did you do last night? Unless you can't remember.'

'Last night,' Jillian said. She blinked, gnawed her lip, looked beseechingly at me. 'I had dinner,' she said.

'Alone?'

'With me,' I put in. 'You're writing this down? Why? Jillian's not a suspect, is she? I thought you had an open-and-shut case against Dr Sheldrake.'

'We do,' said Todras.

'It's just routine,' Nyswander added. His weasel face looked craftier than ever. 'So you had dinner together?'

'Right. Honey, what was the name of that restaurant?'

'Belevedere's. But—'

'Belvedere's. Right. We must have been there until nine o'clock or thereabouts.'

'And then I suppose you spent a quiet evening at home?'

'Jillian did,' I said. 'I headed on over to the Garden myself and watched the fights. They already started by the time I got there but I saw three or four prelim bouts and the main event. Jillian doesn't care for boxing.'

'I don't like violence,' Jillian said.

201

Todras seemed to approach me without actually moving. 'I suppose,' he said, 'you can prove you were at the fights.'

'Prove it? Why do I have to prove it?'

'Oh, just routine, Mr Rhodenbarr. I suppose you went with a friend.'

'No, I went alone.'

'That a fact? But you most likely ran into somebody you knew.'

I thought about it. 'Well, the usual ringside crowd was there. The pimps and the dope dealers and the sports crowd. But I'm just a fan, I don't actually know any of those people except to recognize them when I see them.'

'Uh-huh.'

'The fellow who sat next to me, we were talking about the fighters and all, but I don't know his name and I don't even know if I'd recognize him again.'

'Uh-huh.'

'Anyway, why would I have to prove where I was?'

'Just routine,' Nyswander said. 'Then you can't—'

'*Oh*,' I said brightly. 'Hell. I wonder if I have my ticket stub. I don't remember throwing it out.' I looked at Jillian. 'Was I wearing this jacket last night? You know, I think I was. I probably dropped the stub in the garbage, or when I was cleaning out my pockets before I went to bed. Maybe it's in a wastebasket at my apartment. I don't suppose – oh, here's something.'

And, amazingly enough, I showed Nyswander an orange stub from last night's fight card at Madison Square Garden. He eyed it sullenly before passing it to Todras who didn't seem any happier to see it, his smile notwithstanding.

The ticket stub cooled things. They didn't suspect us of anything, they knew they already had the murderer in a cell, but Jillian had irritated them and they were getting a little of their own back. They returned to a less intimidating line of questioning, just rounding out things in their notebooks before moving on. I could relax now, except that you can't relax until they're out the door and gone, and they were in the process of going when Todras raised a big hand, placed it atop his big head, and scratched diligently.

'Rhodenbarr,' he said. 'Bernard Rhodenbarr. Now where in the hell have I heard that name before?'

'Gee,' I said, 'I don't know.'

'What's your line of work, Bernie?'

A warning bell sounded. When they start calling you by your first name it means they've pegged you as a criminal. As long as you're a citizen in their eyes it's always Mr Rhodenbarr, but when they call you Bernie it's time to watch out. I don't think Todras even knew what he'd said, but I heard him, and the ice was getting very thin out there.

'I'm in investments,' I said. 'Mutual funds, open-end real-estate trusts. Estate planning, that's the real focus of what I do.'

'That a fact. Rhodenbarr, Rhodenbarr. I know that name.'

'I don't know where from,' I said. 'Unless you grew up in the Bronx.'

'How'd you know that?'

By your accent, I thought. Anybody who sounds like Penny Marshall in *Laverne and Shirley* could have grown up nowhere else. But I said, 'What high school?'

'Why?'

'What school?'

'James Monroe. Why?'

'Then that explains it. Freshman English. Don't you remember Miss Rhodenbarr? Maybe she's the one who had you reading Oscar Wilde.'

'She's an English teacher?'

'She was. She passed on – oh, I don't know exactly how many years ago. Little old lady with iron-gray hair and perfect posture.'

'Relative of yours?'

'My dad's sister. Aunt Peg, but she'd have been Miss Margaret Rhodenbarr as far as her students were concerned.'

'Margaret Rhodenbarr.'

'That's right.'

He opened his notebook, and for a moment I thought he was going to write down my aunt's name, but he wound up shrugging his great shoulders and putting the book away. 'Must be it,' he said. 'A name like that, it's distinctive, you know? Sticks in the mind and rings a bell. Maybe I wasn't in her class myself but I just have a recollection of the name.'

'That's probably it.'

'It woulda come to me,' he said, holding the door for Nyswander. 'Memory's a funny thing. You just let it find its own path and things come to you sooner or later.'

7

Jillian and I left the office together ten or fifteen minutes after Todras and Nyswander. We joined the lunch crowd at a coffee shop around the corner on Seventh Avenue. We had coffee and grilled-cheese sandwiches, and I wound up eating half of her sandwich along with my own.

'Crystal Sheldrake,' I said between bites. 'What do we know about her?'

'She's dead.'

'Beside that. She was Craig's ex-wife and somebody killed her, but what else do we know about her?'

'What difference does it make, Bernie?'

'Well, she was killed for a reason,' I said. 'If we knew the reason we might have a shot at figuring out who did it.'

'Are we going to solve the murder?'

I shrugged. 'It's something to do.'

But Jillian insisted it was exciting, and her blue eyes danced at the prospect. She decided we would be Nick and Nora Charles, or possibly Mr and Mrs North, two pairs of sleuths she had a tendency to confuse. She wanted to know how we would get started and I turned the conversation back to Crystal.

'She was a tramp, Bernie. Anybody could have killed her.'

'We only have Craig's word that she was a tramp. Men tend to have strict standards when it comes to their ex-wives.'

'She hung out in bars and picked up men. Maybe one of them turned out to be a homicidal maniac.'

'And he just happened to have a dental scalpel in his pocket?'

'Oh.' She picked up her cup, took a delicate sip of coffee. 'Maybe the guy she picked up was a dentist and – but I guess most dentists don't carry scalpels around in their pockets.'

'Only the ones who are homicidal maniacs in their off hours. And even if she was killed by a dentist, he wouldn't have left the scalpel sticking in her. No, somebody swiped a scalpel from the office deliberately to frame Craig for the killing. And that means the murderer wasn't a stranger and the murder wasn't a spur-of-the-moment thing.

It was planned, and the killer was someone with a motive, someone who was involved in Crystal Sheldrake's life. Which means we ought to learn something about that life.'

'How?'

'Good question. Do you want some more coffee?'

'No. Bernie, maybe she kept a diary. Do women still keep diaries?'

'How would I know?'

'Or a stack of love letters. Something incriminating that would let us know who she was seeing. If you could break into her apartment – What's the matter?'

'The horse has already been stolen.'

'Huh?'

'The time to break into an apartment,' I said, 'is before someone gets killed in it. Once a murder takes place the police become very efficient. They put seals on the doors and windows and even stake the place out now and then. And they also search whatever the killer left behind, so if there was a diary or a pile of letters, and if the killer didn't have the presence of mind to carry it away with him' – like a caseful of jewels, I thought with some rancor – 'then the cops already have it. Anyway, I don't think there was a diary or a love letter in the first place.'

'Why not?'

'I don't think Crystal was the type.'

'But how would you know what type she was? You never even met her, did you?'

I avoided the question by catching the waitress's eye and making the usual gesture of scribbling in midair. I wondered, not for the first time, what diner had invented that bit of pantomime and how it had gone over with the first waiter who was exposed to it. Monsieur desires the pen of my aunt? *Eh bien?*

I said, 'She had a family somewhere, didn't she? You could get in touch with them, pass yourself off as a friend from college.'

'What college?'

'I don't remember, but you can get that from the newspaper article, too.'

'I'm younger than she was. I couldn't have been at college the same year.'

'Well, nobody's going to ask your age. They'll be too overcome with grief. Anyway, you can probably do this over the phone. I just thought you could poke around the edges of her life and see if any male names come into the picture. The point is that she probably had a boyfriend or two or three, and that would give us a place to start.'

She thought about it. The waitress came over with the check and I got my wallet out and paid it. Jillian, frowning in concentration, didn't offer to pay her half of the check. Well, that was all right. After all, I'd polished off half her sandwich.

'Well,' she said, 'I'll try.'

'Just make some phone calls and see what happens. Don't give your right name, of course. And you'd better stay pretty close to home in case Craig tries to get hold of you. I don't know if he'll be able to make any calls himself, but his lawyer may be getting in touch with you.'

'How will I get ahold of you, Bernie?'

'I may be hard to reach. I'm in the book, B. Rhodenbarr on West Seventy-first, but I won't be hanging out there much. What I'll do, I'll call you. Is your phone listed?'

It wasn't. She searched her wallet and wrote her number and address on the back of a beautician's appointment card. Her appointment had been nine days ago with someone named Keith. I don't know whether or not she kept it.

'And you, Bernie? What'll you be doing?'

'I'll be looking for someone.'

'Who?'

'I don't know. But I'll know her when I find her.'

'A woman? How will you know her?'

'She'll be doing some serious drinking,' I said, 'in a very frivolous bar.'

The bar was called the Recovery Room. The cocktail napkins had nurse cartoons all over them. The only one I remember featured a callipygian Florence Nightingale asking a leering sawbones what she should do with all these rectal thermometers. There was a list of bizarre cocktails posted. They had names like Ether Fizz and I-V Special and Post Mortem and were priced at two or three dollars a copy. Assorted props of a medical nature were displayed haphazardly on the walls – Red Cross splints, surgical masks, that sort of thing.

For all of this, the place didn't seem to be drawing a hospital crowd. It was on the first floor of a brickfront building on Irving Place a few blocks below Gramercy Park, too far west of Bellevue to be catching their staff, and the clientele looked to be composed primarily of civilians who lived or worked in the neighborhood. And it was frivolous, all right. If it had been any more frivolous it would have floated away.

Frankie's drinking, on the other hand, was certainly serious enough to keep the Recovery Room anchored in grim reality. A stinger is always a reasonably serious proposition. A brace of stingers at four o'clock on a weekday afternoon is about as serious as you can get.

I made several stops before I got to the Recovery Room. I'd started off with a stop at my own place, then cabbed down to the East Twenties and began making the rounds. A little gourmet shop on Lexington sold me a teensy-weensy bottle of imported olive oil, which I rather self-consciously opened and upended and drained around the corner. I'd read about this method of coating the old tumtum before a night of heavy drinking. I'll tell you, it wasn't the greatest taste sensation I ever experienced, and no sooner had I knocked it back than I began bar-hopping, hitting a few joints on Lexington, drifting over to Third Avenue, then doubling back and ultimately finding my way to the Recovery Room. In the course of this I had a white wine spritzer in each of several places and stayed long enough to determine that no one wanted to talk about Crystal Sheldrake. I did run into two fellows who would have been glad to talk about baseball and one old fart who wanted to talk about Texas, but that was as much conversation as I could scrape up.

Until I met Frankie. She was a tallish woman with curly black hair and a sullen, hard-featured face, and she was sitting at the Recovery Room's bar sipping a stinger and smoking a Virginia Slim and humming a rather toneless version of 'One for My Baby.' I suppose she was around my age, but by nightfall she'd be a lot older. Stingers'll do that.

I somehow knew right away. It just looked like Crystal's kind of place and Frankie looked like Crystal's kind of people. I went up to the bar, ordered my spritzer from a bartender with a sad, hung-over look to him, and asked Frankie if the seat next to her was taken. This was forward of me – there were only two other customers at the bar, a pair of salesmen types playing the match game at the far end. But she didn't mind.

'Welcome aboard, brother,' she said. 'You can sit next to me long as you like. Just so you're not a goddamned dentist.'

Aha!

She said, 'I'll tell you what she was, Bernie. She was the salt of the fucking earth is what she was. Well, hell, you knew her, right?'

'Years ago.'

'Years ago, right. 'Fore she was married. 'Fore she married that murdering toothpuller. I swear to God I'll never go to one of those bastards again. I don't care if every tooth I got rots in my head. The hell with it, right?'

'Right, Frankie.'

'I don't have to chew anything anyway. The hell with food is what I say. If I can't drink it I don't need it. Right?'

'Right.'

'Crystal was a lady. That's what she was. The woman was a fucking lady. Right?'

'You bet.'

'Damn right.' She crooked a finger at the bartender. 'Rodge,' she said. 'Roger, honey, I want another of these, but let's make it plain brandy and let's cool it with the crème de menthe, huh? Because it's beginning

207

to taste like Lavoris and I don't want to be reminded of dentists. Got that?'

'Got it,' Roger said, and took her glass away and hauled out a clean one. 'Brandy, right? Brandy rocks?'

'Brandy no rocks. Ice cracks your stomach. Also it shrinks your blood vessels, the veins and the arteries. And the crème de menthe gives you diabetes. I oughta stay away from stingers, but they're my downfall. Bernie, you don't want to be drinking those spritzers all night.'

'I don't?'

'First of all, the soda water's bad for you. The bubbles get into your veins and give you the bends, same as the sandhogs get when they don't go through decompression chambers. It's a well-known fact.'

'I never heard that, Frankie.'

'Well, you know it now. Plus the wine rots your blood. It's made out of grapes and the enzymes from the grapes are what screw you up.'

'Brandy's made from grapes.'

She gave me a look. 'Yeah,' she said, 'but it's distilled. That purifies it.'

'Oh.'

'You want to get rid of that spritzer before it ruins your health. Have something else.'

'Maybe a glass of water for now.'

She looked horrified. 'Water? In this town? You ever see blow-up photos of what comes out of the tap in New York City? My God, they got these fucking microscopic worms in New York water. You drink water without alcohol in it, you're just asking for trouble.'

'Oh.'

'Let me look at you, Bernie.' Her eyes, light brown with a green cast to them, fought to focus on mine. 'Scotch,' she said authoritatively. 'Cutty rocks. Rodge, sugar, bring Bernie here a Cutty Sark on the rocks.'

'I don't know, Frankie.'

'Jesus,' she said, 'just shut up and drink it. You're gonna drink to Crystal's memory with a glass of wormy water? What are you, crazy? Just shut up and drink your scotch.'

'Now take Dennis here,' Frankie said. 'Dennis was crazy about Crystal. Weren't you, Dennis?'

'She was an ace-high broad,' Dennis said.

'Everybody loved her, right?'

'Lit up the joint when she walked in the door,' Dennis said. 'No question about it. Now she's deader'n Kelsey's nuts and ain't it a hell of a thing? The husband, right?'

'A dentist.'

'Wha'd he do, shoot her?'

'Stabbed her.'

'A hell of a thing,' Dennis said.

We had left the Recovery Room a drink or two ago at Frankie's insistence and had moved around the corner to Joan's Joynt, a smaller and less brightly lit place, and there we had met up with Dennis, a thickly built man who owned a parking garage on Third Avenue. Dennis was drinking Irish whiskey with small beer chasers, Frankie was staying with straight Cognac, and I was following orders and lapping up the Cutty Sark on the rocks. I was by no means convinced of the wisdom of this course of action, but with each succeeding drink it seemed to make more sense. And I kept reminding myself of the little bottle of olive oil I had swigged earlier. I imagined the oil coating my stomach so that the Cutty Sark couldn't be absorbed. Drink after drink would slide down my throat, hit the greased stomach and be whisked on past into the intestine before it knew what hit it.

And yet it did seem as though a wee bit of the alcohol was getting into the old bloodstream after all . . .

'Another round,' Dennis was saying heartily. 'And have something for yourself, Jimbo. And that's another brandy for Frankie here, and another Cutty for my friend Bernie.'

'Oh, I don't—'

'Hey, I'm buying, Bernie. When Dennis buys, everybody drinks.'

So Dennis bought and everybody drank.

In the Hen's Tooth, Frankie said, 'Bernie, want you to meet Charlie and Hilda. This is Bernie.'

'The name's Jack,' Charlie said. 'Frankie, you got this obsession my name's Charlie. You know damn well it's Jack.'

'The hell,' Frankie said. 'Same thing, isn't it?'

Hilda said, 'Pleasure to meetcha, Bernie. You an insurance man like everybody else?'

'He's no fucking dentist,' Frankie said.

'I'm a burglar,' said six or seven Cutty Rockses.

'A what?'

'A cat burglar.'

'That a fact,' said someone. Jack or Charlie, I suppose. Perhaps it was Dennis.

'What do you do with them?' Hilda wanted to know.

'Do with what?'

'The cats.'

'He holds 'em for ransom.'

'There any money in it?'

'Jesus, lookit who's askin' if there's any money in pussy.'

'Oh, you're terrible,' said Hilda, clearly delighted. 'You're an awful man.'

'No, seriously,' Charlie/Jack said. 'What do you do, Bernie?'

'I'm in investments,' I said.

'Terrific.'

'Thank God my ex was an accountant,' Hilda said. 'I never thought I'd hear myself saying that and just listen to me. But you never have to worry about an accountant killing you.'

'I don't know,' Dennis said. 'My experience is they nickel and dime you to death.'

'But they don't stab you.'

'You're better off with a stabbing. Get the damn thing over and done with. People look at a parking garage, all they see is that money coming in every day. They don't see the constant headaches. Those kids you gotta hire, they scrape a fender and you hear about it, believe me. Nobody appreciates the amount of mental strain in a parking garage.'

Hilda put a hand on his arm. 'They think you got it easy,' she said, 'but it's not that easy, Dennis.'

'Damn right. And then they wonder why a man drinks. A business like mine and a wife like mine and they wonder why a man needs to unwind a little at the end of the day.'

'You're a hell of a guy, Dennis.'

I excused myself to make a phone call, but by the time I got to the phone I couldn't remember who I'd intended to call. I went to the men's room instead. There were a lot of girls' names and phone numbers written over the urinal but I didn't notice Crystal's. I thought of dialing one of the numbers just to see what would happen. I decided it was not the sort of thought to which a sober man is given.

When I got back to the bar Charlie/Jack was ordering another round. 'Almost forgot you,' he said to me. 'Cutty on the rocks, right?'

'Er,' I said.

'Hey, Bernie,' Frankie said. 'You okay? You look a little green around the gills.'

'It's the olive oil.'

'Huh?'

'It's nothing,' I said, and reached for my drink.

8

There were a lot of bars, a lot of conversations, a lot of people threading their separate ways in and out of my awareness. My awareness, come to think of it, was doing some threading of its own. I kept going in and out of gray stages, as if I were in a car driving through patches of fog.

Then all at once I was walking, and for the first time all night I was by myself. I'd finally lost Frankie, who'd been with me ever since the Recovery Room. I was walking, and there in front of me was Gramercy Park. I went over to the iron gate and held onto it. Not exactly for support, but it did seem like a good idea.

The park was empty, at least as much of it as I could see. I thought of picking the lock and letting myself in. I wasn't carrying anything cumbersome like a pry bar, but I did have my usual ring of picks and probes and that was sufficient to get me inside, safe from dogs and strangers. I could stretch out on a nice comfortable green bench and close my eyes and count Cutties sailing over rocks, and in only a matter of time I'd be . . . what?

Under arrest, in all likelihood. They take a dim view of bums passing out in Gramercy Park. It's frowned on.

I maintained my grip on the gate, which did seem to be swaying, although I knew it wasn't. A jogger ran by – or a runner jogged by, or what you will. Perhaps he was the same one who'd run or jogged around the park while I'd been talking with Miss Whatserface. Taylor? Tyler? No matter. No matter whether it was the same jogger or not, either. What was it she'd said about jogging? 'Nothing that appears so ridiculous can possibly be good for you.'

I thought about that, and thought too that I probably looked fairly ridiculous myself, clinging desperately to an iron gate as I was. And while I thought this the jogger circled round again, his canvas-clad feet tapping away at the concrete. Hadn't taken him long to circle the park, had it? Or was it a different jogger? Or had something bizarre happened to my sense of time?

I watched him jog away. 'Carry on,' I said, aloud or otherwise, I'm afraid I'll never know. 'Just so you don't do it in the street and frighten the horses.'

Then I was in a cab, and I must have given the driver my address because the next thing I knew we were waiting for a traffic light on West End Avenue a block below my apartment. 'This is good enough,' I told the driver. 'I'll walk the rest of the way. I can use the fresh air.'

'Yeah,' he said. 'I'll bet you can.'

I paid him and tipped him and watched him drive away, and all the while I was sorting through my brain, trying to think of a snappy retort. I finally decided the best thing would be to yell, 'Oh, yeah?' but I told myself he was already several blocks distant and was thus unlikely to be suitably impressed. I filled my lungs several times with reasonably fresh air and walked a block north.

I felt lousy, full of booze I hadn't wanted in the first place, my brain numb and my body shaky and my spirit sagging. But I was homing in on my own turf and there's a comfort in getting back home, even when home is an overpriced couple of rooms designed to give you a good case of the lonelies. Here, at least, I knew where I was. I could stand on the corner of Seventy-first and West End and look around and see things I recognized.

I recognized the coffee shop on the corner, for instance. I recognized the oafish Great Dane and the willowy young man who was walking or being walked by the beast. Across the street I recognized my neighbor Mrs Hesch, the inescapable cigarette smoldering in the corner of her mouth, as she passed the doorman with a sandwich from the deli and a *Daily News* from the stand on Seventy-second Street. And I recognized the doorman, Crazy Felix, who tried so hard all his life to live up to the twin standards of his maroon uniform and his outsized mustache. And in earnest conversation with Felix I recognized Ray Kirschmann, a poor but dishonest cop whose path has crossed mine on so many occasions. And near the building's entrance I recognized a young couple who seemed to be stoned on Panamanian grass twenty hours out of twenty-four. And diagonally across the street—

Wait a minute!

I looked again at Ray Kirschmann. It was him, all right, good old Ray, and what on earth was he doing in my lobby, talking to my doorman?

A lot of cobwebs began to clear from my mind. I didn't get struck sober but it certainly felt as though that was what had happened. I stood still for a moment, trying to figure out what was going on, and then I realized I could worry about that sort of thing when I had the time. Which I didn't just now.

I moved back across the sidewalk to the shelter of shadows, glanced back to make sure Ray hadn't taken notice of me, started to walk east on Seventy-first, keeping close to the buildings all the while, glanced back again a few times to see if there were any other cops around, reminded myself that this business of glancing back all the time simply gave me the appearance of a suspicious character, and what with look-ing back in spite of this realization, ultimately stepped smack into a souvenir left on the pavement by the galumphing Great Dane or an-other of his ilk. I said a four-letter word, a precise description indeed of that in which I had stepped. I wiped my foot and walked onward to Broadway, and a cab came along and I hailed it.

'Where to?'

'I don't know,' I said. 'Drive downtown a little ways, it'll come to me.' And then, while he was saying something I felt no need to attend to, I dug out my wallet and managed to find the little card she'd given me.

'My appointment's with Keith,' I said. 'But what good is this? It was almost two weeks ago.'

'You okay, Mac?'

'No,' I said. I turned the card over and frowned at what was writ-ten on it. 'RH-seven-one-eight-oh-two,' I read. 'Let's try that, all right? Drive me there.'

'Mac?'

'Hmmm?'

'That's a phone number.'

'It is?'

'Rhinelander seven, that's the exchange. My phone is all numbers, but some people still got letters and numbers. I think it's more classy, myself.'

'I agree with you.'

'But I can't drive you to a phone number.'

'The address is right under it,' I said, squinting. 'Right under it.' The letters, I did not add, were squirming around before my very eyes.

'Wanta read it to me?'

'In a minute or so,' I said, 'that's just what I'm going to do.'

She lived in a renovated brickfront on East Eighty-fourth, just a block and a half from the river. I found her bell and rang it, not expecting anything to happen, and while I was preparing to let myself in she asked who I was via the intercom. I told her and she buzzed me in. I climbed three flights of stairs and found her waiting in the doorway, clothed in a blue velour robe and a frown.

She said, 'Bernie? Are you all right?'

'No.'

'You look as if – did you say you're *not* all right? What's the matter?'

'I'm drunk,' I said. She stepped aside and I walked past her into a small studio apartment. A sofa had converted itself into a bed and she had evidently just emerged therefrom to let me in.

'You're drunk?'

'I'm drunk,' I agreed. 'I had olive oil and white wine and soda and

Scotch and rocks. The soda water gave me the bends and the ice cracked my stomach.'

'The ice—?'

'Cracked my stomach. It also shrinks the blood vessels, the veins and the arteries. Crème de menthe gives you diabetes but I stayed the hell away from it.' I took off my tie, rolled it up, put it in my pocket. I took off my jacket, aimed it at a chair. 'I don't know what the olive oil does,' I said, 'but I don't think it was a good idea.'

'What are you doing?'

'I'm getting undressed,' I said. 'What does it look like I'm doing? I found out a lot about Crystal. I just hope I remember some of it in the morning. I certainly can't remember it now.'

'You're taking your pants off.'

'Of course I am. Oh, hell, I better take my shoes off first. I usually get the order right but I'm in rotten shape tonight. Wine's made out of grapes and it poisons the blood. Brandy's distilled so that purifies it.'

'Bernie, your shoes—'

'I know,' I said. 'I've got a cop in my lobby and something even worse on my shoe. I know all that.'

'Bernie—'

I got into bed. There was only one pillow. I took it and put my head on it and I pulled the covers over my head and closed my eyes and shut out the world.

9

After six or seven hours' sleep, after the fourth aspirin and the third cup of coffee, the fog began to break up and disperse. I looked over at Jillian, who sat in a sling chair balancing a coffee cup on her knee. 'I'm sorry,' I said, not for the first time.

'Forget it, Bernie.'

'Bursting in on you like that in the middle of the night. Jumping out of my clothes and diving into your bed. 'What's so funny?'

'You make it sound like rape. You had too much to drink, that's all. And you needed a place to stay.'

'I could have gone to a hotel. If I'd had the brains to think of it.'

'You might have had trouble finding one that would rent you a room.'

I lowered my eyes. 'I must have been a mess.'

'Well, you weren't at your best. I cleaned off your shoe, incidentally.'

'God, that's something else for me to apologize for. Why do people keep dogs in the city?'

'To protect their apartments from burglars.'

'That's a hell of a reason.' I drank some more coffee and patted my breast pocket, looking for a cigarette. I quit a few years ago but I still reach for the pack now and then. Old habits die hard. 'Say, where did you, uh, sleep last night?'

'In the chair.'

'I'm really sorry.'

'Bernie, stop it.' She smiled, looking remarkably fresh for someone who had spent the night in a sling chair. She was wearing jeans and a powder-blue sweater and she looked sensational. I was wearing last night's outfit minus the tie and jacket. She said, 'You said you found out some things about Crystal. Last night.'

'Oh. Right.'

'But you didn't seem to remember what they were.'

'I didn't?'

'No. Or else you were just too exhausted to think straight. Do you remember now?'

It took me a few minutes. I had to sit back and close my eyes and give

215

my memory little nudges, but in the end it came through for me. 'Three men,' I said. 'I got most of my information from a woman named Frankie who was evidently a pretty good drinking buddy of Crystal's. Frankie was drunk when I met her and she didn't exactly sober up as the night wore on but I think she knew what she was talking about.

'According to her, Crystal was just a girl who liked to have a good time. All she wanted out of life was a couple of drinks and a couple of laughs and the ever popular goal of true love.'

'Plus a million dollars worth of jewelry.'

'Frankie didn't mention jewelry. Maybe Crystal didn't wear much when she went bar-hopping. Anyway the impression I got from her was that Crystal didn't make a policy of picking up strangers. She went to the bars primarily for the booze and the small talk. Now and then she got half in the bag and went home with somebody new at the end of the evening, but as a general rule she limited herself to three guys.'

'And one of them killed her?'

I shrugged. 'It's a reasonable assumption. At any rate, they were the three men in her life.' I picked up that morning's *Daily News*, tapped the story we'd read. The Medical Examiner had told them what I'd already known. 'Somebody was intimate with her the evening she was killed. Either the killer or someone else. And that would have been early in the evening so it's not likely that she'd already gotten smashed and dragged a stranger home with her.'

'I don't know, Bernie. According to Craig, she was more of a tramp than this Frankie seemed to think she was.'

'Well, Craig was prejudiced. He was paying alimony.'

'That's true. Do you know who the three men are?'

I nodded. 'This is where it gets tricky. I had trouble questioning Frankie because I couldn't let her think I was too interested or she'd wonder what it was all about. Then as the night wore on I was too smashed to do a good job as Mr District Attorney. And I'm not sure how much Frankie really knew about Crystal's boyfriends. I think two of them were married.'

'Almost everybody is.'

'Really? I thought everybody was divorced. But two of Crystal's three were married.' Including, I thought, the one who'd been rolling around with her while I'd languored in her closet, the one who had to hurry on home to What's-Her-Name. 'One of them's a lawyer. Frankie referred to him as the Legal Beagle when she wasn't calling him Snoopy. I think his first name may be John.'

'You think it may?'

'Uh-huh. Frankie did an Ed McMahon imitation a couple of times in reference to him. "And now, heeeeeeeere's Johnny!" So I assume that's his name.'

216

'A married lawyer named Johnny.'

'Right.'

'That sure narrows it down.'

'Doesn't it? Married Boyfriend Number Two is a little easier to get a line on. He's a painter and his name is Grabow.'

'His last name?'

'I suppose so. I suppose he has a first name to go with it. Unless he's very artsy and he just uses the one name. Frankie was pretty vague on the subject of Grabow.'

'It sounds to me as though she was pretty vague about everything.'

'Well, she was, but I don't think she ever met Grabow. At least that's the impression I got. She saw a lot of the Legal Beagle because Crystal used to drink with him in the bars. I gather Frankie found him amusing, but I don't know whether she laughed with him or at him. But I have the feeling all she knew about Grabow was what Crystal told her, and that may not have amounted to very much.'

'What about the third man?'

'He's easy. Maybe because he's not married, or at least I don't think he's married, which would mean he'd have nothing to hide. Anyway, Frankie knows him. His name is Knobby and he tends bar at Spyder's Parlor. That's one of the places I hit last night.'

'So you met him?'

'No. We went there looking for him but he'd switched shifts with Lloyd.'

'Who's Lloyd?'

'The guy who was tending bar at Spyder's Parlor last night. I'll tell you one thing, he pours a hell of a drink. I don't know Knobby's last name. I don't know Frankie's last name, come to think of it, or anybody's last name. None of the people I met last night had last names. But I don't suppose it'll be hard to find Knobby, not if he hangs onto his job.'

'I wonder why he didn't work last night.'

'Beats me. I gather the bartenders switch shifts with each other all the time. Maybe there was something on television Knobby didn't want to miss. Or maybe he had to sit up washing Crystal's blood out of his official Spyder's Parlor T-shirt. Not really, because there wasn't any blood to speak of.'

'How do you know that, Bernie?'

Brilliant. 'She was stabbed in the heart,' I said. 'So there wouldn't have been much bleeding.'

'Oh.'

'So here's what we've got,' I said, changing the subject back where it belonged. 'The Legal Beagle, Grabow the Artist, and Knobby the Bartender. I think we'll have to concentrate on the three of them for the time being.'

217

'How?'

'Well, we can find out who they are. That would be a start.'

'And then what?'

And then I could see who had the jewels, but I couldn't tell Jillian that. She didn't know anything about my Ultrasuede attaché case filled with twice-stolen pretties, nor did she know B. G. Rhodenbarr had been on the premises when Crystal got hers.

'And then,' I said, 'we can see if one of them had a reason for killing Crystal, and if there was any link between any of them and Craig, because the killer didn't just happen to turn up with a dental scalpel because the local hardware store was fresh out of javelins. If it turns out that Grabow's got a partial plate that Craig made for him, or – God, I'm stupid today. You're really seeing me at my worst, Jillian. Drunk last night and hungover this morning. I've got a brain underneath it all, honest I do. A small one, but it's stood me in good stead over the years.'

'What are you talking about?'

'Your files. Well, Craig's files, actually. Knobby and Grabow and the Beagle. Craig has a record of everyone he's seen professionally, doesn't he? Grabow'll be a cinch if he was ever a patient, unless Frankie got his name wrong. Knobby'll be harder until I learn what his legal name is, but that shouldn't take long and then you can see if there's any connection between him and Craig. As far as Johnny the Lawyer is concerned, well, there we've got a problem. I don't suppose you have your patients listed by occupation.'

She shook her head. 'There's blanks for business address and employer on the chart, but when they're self-employed they don't usually specify what they're self-employed at. I know what I could do.'

'What?'

'I could go through and pull all the Johns who aren't obviously something other than lawyers, and then I can check the ones who are left against the listings of attorneys in the Yellow Pages. Not all lawyers are listed, of course. I guess most of them aren't. But does it sound as though it might be worthwhile?'

'It sounds like a long shot. And a lot of hard work.'

'I know.'

'But every once in a while somebody sifts through a haystack and actually comes up with a needle. If you don't mind taking the time—'

'I don't have anything else to do. And it'll at least give me the feeling that I'm doing something to help.'

'You're harboring a fugitive,' I said. 'That's something.'

'Do you really think you're a fugitive? Just because you recognized a policeman in your lobby doesn't mean he was there waiting for you. He might have been checking on some other tenant.'

'Mrs Hesch, say. Maybe he came to arrest her for smoking in the elevator.'

'But he wasn't even one of the cops we saw before, Bernie. Why would he be the one to go looking for you? I could understand if it was . . . I forget their names.'

'Todras and Nyswander. Todras was the block of granite with the menacing smile. Nyswander was Wilbur the Weasel.'

'Well, if they were waiting for you, then you'd have something to worry about. But I don't think – who's that?'

The doorbell sounded again, right on cue.

I said, 'I came here last night around one. I left about an hour ago. You don't know anything about my being a burglar. I never really talk much about my work and we haven't been going together that long. You've been seeing other men besides me, see, although you haven't let me know that.'

'Bernie, I—'

'Pay attention. You can answer the bell in a minute. They're downstairs and they're not about to kick the door in. You're Craig's girlfriend, it might even be a good idea to volunteer that, but you like to play the field a bit and neither Craig nor I knows you're seeing the other one. You'd better use the intercom now. I'll have time to get out before any New York cop can drag his ass up three flights of stairs.'

She walked to the wall, depressed the switch to activate the intercom. 'Yes?' she said. 'Who is it?'

'Police officers.'

She looked at me. I nodded and she poked the buzzer to let them in. I went to the door, opened it, put one foot out into the hallway. 'It's official,' I said, 'you've been harboring a fugitive, but you didn't know it so it's not your fault. For that matter, nobody told me I was a fugitive. I lied to the cops about my line of work, but why not, since I didn't want *you* to know about it? I think we'll both be all right. I'll get in touch with you later, either here or at the office. Don't forget to go through the files.'

'Bernie—'

'No time,' I said, and blew her a kiss and scampered.

I had ample time to climb one flight of stairs while Todras and Nyswander were climbing three. I loitered on the top step and listened while their feet led them to Jillian's door. They knocked. The door opened. They entered. The door closed. I gave them a minute to get comfortable, then descended a flight and stood beside the door, listening. I heard voices but couldn't make them out. I could tell there were two of them, though, and I'd heard both pairs of feet on the stairs, and I didn't want to hang around until one of them got psychic and yanked the door open. I went down three more flights of stairs and took my tie out of my pocket and put it right back when I saw how wrinkled it was.

The sun seemed brighter than it had to be. I blinked at it, momentarily uncertain, and a voice said, 'If it ain't my old pal Bernie.'

Ray Kirschmann, the best cop money can buy, stood with his abundant backside resting upon the fender of a blue-and-white police cruiser.
He had a lazy smile on his broad face. A smile of insupportable smug-
ness.

I said, 'Oh, hell, Ray. Long time no see.'

'Been ages, hasn't it?' He drew the passenger door open, nodded at
the seat. 'Hop in,' he said. 'We'll have us a ride on a beautiful morning
like this. It's no kind of a day to be inside, like in a cell or anything like
that. Hop in, Bern.' I hopped.

10

Every block in New York sports several fire hydrants spaced at intervals along the sidewalk. These have been installed so that the police won't have to circle the block looking for a parking space. Ray pulled away from one of them and told me I'd just missed a couple of friends of his. 'A couple of fellows in plainclothes,' he said. 'Myself, I'm happy wearin' the uniform. These two, you musta missed each other by a whisker. Maybe they were in the elevator while you was on the stairs.'

'There's no elevator.'

'That a fact? Just plain bad luck you didn't run into them, Bernie. But I guess you made their acquaintance yesterday. Here they missed you, and now they'll come downstairs and find that I took a powder my own self. Not that they'll be sorry to see me gone. They come here on their own, you know, in their own blue-and-white, and I tagged along and I had the feelin' they wanted to tell me to get lost. You take a cop and put a business suit on him and he develops an attitude, you know what I mean? All of a sudden he thinks he's a member of the human race and not your ordinary flat-foot. You want a smoke, Bernie?'

'I quit a few years ago.'

'Good for you. That's strength of character is what it is. I'd quit myself if I had the willpower. What's all this crap about your aunt teaching school in the Bronx?'

'Well, you know how it is, Ray.'

'Yeah, that's the truth. I know how it is.'

'I was trying to impress this girl. I just met her fairly recently, and one of those cops must have recognized my name and I didn't want her to find out I've got a criminal past.'

'A criminal past.'

'Right.'

'But that's all behind you, that criminal past. You're Stanley Straight-arrow now.'

'Right.'

'Uh-huh.' He puffed on his cigarette. I rolled down my window to let some smoke out and some New York air in, a pointless exchange if there ever was one. He said, 'How do you tie in with this Sheldrake character?'

'He's my dentist.'

'I got a dentist. They say to see him twice a year and that's plenty for me. I don't hang out at his office, I don't try slipping it to his nurse.'

'Hygienist.'

'Whatever. You a big fight fan, Bernie?'

'I get to the Garden when I can.'

'This used to be a real fight town. Remember when they had a Wednesday card at St. Nick's Arena? And then you had your regular fights out at Sunnyside Gardens in Queens. You ever used to get out there?'

'I think I went two, three times. That was some years ago, wasn't it?'

'Oh, years and years,' he said. 'I love it that you showed Todras and Nyswander a ticket stub. Just happened to have it with you. Jesus, I really love it.'

'I was wearing the same jacket.'

'I know. If it was me and I was settin' up an alibi I'd have the stub in a different jacket and I'd take 'em back to my apartment and rummage through the closet until I came up with the stub. It looks better that way. Not so obvious, you know?'

'Well, I wasn't setting up an alibi, Ray. I just happened to go to the fights that night.'

'Uh-huh. But if you just happened to stop there on your way home to pick up a stub that somebody else just happened to throw away, well, that would be interesting wouldn't it? That would mean you were tryin' to set up an alibi before the general public knew there was anythin' to need an alibi for. Which might mean you knew about Sheldrake's wife gettin' bumped while the body was still warm, which would be a damned interestin' thing for you to know, wouldn't it?'

'Wonderful,' I said. 'The only thing worse than not having an alibi is having one.'

'I know, and it's a hell of a thing, Bern. You get suspicious when you've had a few years in the Department. You lose the knack of takin' things at face value. Here all you did was take in a fight card and it looks for all the world like I'm fixin' to tag you with a felony.'

'I thought it was open and shut. I thought you people figured the husband did it.'

'What, the murder? Yeah, it looks as though that's how they're writin' it up. A man kills his ex-wife and leaves his own personal scalpel in her chest, that's as good as a signature, isn't it? If it was my case I might think it was a little too good, the way that ticket stub in your pocket was a little too good, but it ain't my case and what does an ordinary harness bull in a blue uniform know about something fancy like homicide? You got to wear a three-piece suit in order to be up on the finer points of these things, so I just keep my own nose clean and let the boys in suits and ties take care of the homicides. I mind my own business, Bernie.'

'And what's your business exactly, Ray?'

'Now there's another good question.' A light turned and he hung a right turn, his fleshy hands caressing the wheel. 'I'll tell you,' he said. 'I think there's a reason I'm still wearin' a uniform after all these years on the force, and I think the reason's I never been a subtle guy. My trouble is I notice the obvious first and foremost. I see a ticket stub happens to be in somebody's pocket and what comes to mind is a planned alibi. And I look at the guy in question and he's a fellow that's spent his whole life liftin' things out of other people's houses, what comes to mind is a burglary. Here we got a burglar who went to some trouble settin' hisself up with an alibi, and the next morning we find him in the office of the dentist who just cooled out his wife, and the morning after that one he's tiptoein' out of the dentist's nurse's bedroom, and I don't know what a subtle plainclothes man would make of all that, but old Ray here, he gets right down to cases.'

Ahead of us, a UPS van had traffic tied up. Some of the other drivers around us were using their horns to ventilate their feelings. But Ray was in no hurry.

I said, 'I'm not sure what you're getting at.'

'Well, what the hell, Bernie. Here we are, just you and me and a traffic jam, so let's us get down to carpet tacks. The way I figure it, you decided the Sheldrake dame looked like an easy score. Maybe you kept your ears open when you were gettin' your teeth drilled, or maybe you got hipped by the nurse that you been havin' a romance with, one way or another, but you decided to drop over to Gramercy and open a couple of locks and see what was loose. Now maybe you were in and out before Sheldrake came callin', but then how would you know you needed an alibi? No, I'll tell you the way I figure it. You got there and opened the door and found her with her heart stopped. You took a minute to fill your pockets with pretty things and then you got the hell out, and on the way home you stopped at the Garden and picked a stub off the floor. Then first thing the next mornin' you hopped over to Sheldrake's office to keep in touch with what was happenin' and make sure your own neck wasn't on the block.'

'What makes you think something was stolen?'

'The dead woman had more jewelry than Cartier's window. There's nothin' in the apartment but prizes out of Cracker Jack boxes. I don't figure it walked away.'

'Maybe she kept it in a bank vault.'

'Nobody keeps it all in a bank vault.'

'Maybe Sheldrake took it.'

'Sure. He remembered to turn the place inside out and carry off all the jewels but he was so absentminded that he left his whatchacallit, his scalpel, he left it in her heart. I don't think so.'

'Maybe the cops took it.'

'The investigatin' officers?' He clucked his tongue at me. 'Bernie, I'm surprised at you. You think a couple of guys checkin' out a homicide are gonna stop to rob the dead?'

'It's been known to happen.'

'Honestly? I think it's a hell of a thing. But it didn't happen this time because the downstairs neighbor was on hand when they cracked the Sheldrake woman's door. You don't steal when somebody's watchin' you. I'm surprised you didn't know that.'

'Well, you don't go ahead and commit a burglary if you have to step over a corpse to get to the jewels, Ray. And I'm surprised *you* didn't know *that*.'

'Maybe.'

'More than maybe.'

He gave his head a dogged shake. 'Nope,' he said. 'Maybe's as far as I'd go on that one. Because you know what you got? You got the guts of a burglar, Bernie. I remember how cool you were when me and that crud Loren Kramer walked in on you over in the East Sixties, and there's a dead body in the bedroom and you're actin' like the apartment's empty.'

'That's because I didn't *know* there was a body in the bedroom. Remember?'

He shrugged. 'Same difference. You got the guts of a burglar and all bets are off. Why else would you fix yourself an alibi?'

'Maybe I actually went to the fights, Ray. Ever think of that?'

'Not for very long.'

'And maybe I set up an alibi – which I *didn't* because I really *was* at the fights—'

'Yeah, yeah.'

'—because I was working some other job. I'm not that crazy about jewels. They're getting tougher and tougher to sell, the fences are turning vicious, you know that. Maybe I was out lifting somebody's coin collection and I established an alibi just as a matter of course, because I know you people always come knocking on my door when a coin collection walks out of its owner's house.'

'I didn't hear nothin' about a coin collection stolen the other night.'

'Maybe the owner was out of town. Maybe he hasn't missed it yet.'

'And maybe what you robbed was a kid's piggy bank and he's too busy cryin' to tell the cops about it.'

'Maybe.'

'Maybe shit don't stink, Bernie. I think you got the Sheldrake woman's jewels.'

'I don't.'

'Well, you gotta say that. That don't mean I gotta believe it.'

'It's the truth.'

'Yeah, sure. You spent the night with Sheldrake's nurse because you didn't have no better place to stay. I believe everything you tell me, Bernie. That's why I'm still in a blue uniform.'

I didn't answer him and he didn't say anything more. We drove around for a while. The UPS truck had long since gotten out of the way and we were drifting in the stream of traffic, turning now and then, taking a leisurely ride around the streets of midtown Manhattan. If all you noticed was the weather, then you might have mistaken it for a nice fall day.

I said, 'Ray?'

'Yeah, Bern?'

'There's something you want?'

'There always is. There's this book, they ran a hunk of it in the *Post*, *Looking Out for Number One*. Here's a whole book tellin' people to be selfish and let the other guy watch out for his own ass. Imagine anybody has to buy a book to learn what we all grew up knowin'.'

'What is it you want, Ray?'

'You care for a smoke, Bernie? Oh, hell, you already told me you quit. It bother you if I smoke?'

'I can stand it.'

He lit a cigarette. 'Those jewels,' he said. 'Sheldrake's jewels that you took from her apartment.'

'I didn't get them.'

'Well, let's suppose you did. Okay?'

'Okay.'

'Well,' he said, 'I never been greedy, Bern. All I want is half.'

11

Spyder's Parlor was dark and empty. The chairs perched on top of the tables. The stools had been inverted and set up on the bar. A menu in the window indicated that they opened for lunch during the week, but today was Saturday and they wouldn't turn the lights on until mid-afternoon. I stayed with Lexington a block or two uptown to a hole in the wall where the counterman mugged and winked and called his female patrons dear and darling and sweets. They ate it up. I ate up a sandwich, cream cheese on date-nut bread, and drank two cups of so-so coffee.

Grabow, Grabow, Grabow. In a hotel lobby I went through the Manhattan telephone directory and came up with eight Grabows plus two who spelled it without the final letter. I bought dimes from the cashier and tried all ten numbers. Six of them didn't answer. The other four didn't know anything about any artist named Grabow. One woman said her husband's brother was a painter, exteriors and interiors, but he lived upstate in Orchard Park. 'It's a suburb of Buffalo,' she said. 'Anyway he didn't change his name, it's still Grabowski. I don't suppose that helps you.'

I told her I didn't see how it could but thanked her anyway. I started to leave the hotel and then something registered in my mind and I went back to the directory and started calling Grabowskis. It would have been cute if it worked but of course it didn't, it just cost me a lot of dimes, and I called all seventeen Grabowskis and reached I don't know how many, fourteen or fifteen, and of course none of them painted anything, pictures or interiors or exteriors, none of them even colored in coloring books or painted by number, and that was the end of that particular blind alley.

The nearest bank was a block east on Third Avenue. I bought a roll of dimes – you can still get fifty of them for five dollars, it's one of the few remaining bargains – and I carried all fifty of them to another hotel lobby. I passed some outdoor phone booths on the way but they don't have phone books anymore. I don't know why. I called Spyder's Parlor to make sure it was still closed and it was. I hauled out the Yellow Pages and looked up Attorneys. See Lawyers, said the book, so I did. I don't know what I expected to find. There were eighteen pages of lawyers and plenty of them were named John, but so what? I couldn't see any reason to call any of them. I sort of flipped through the listings, hoping something would strike me, and a listing for a firm called Carson, Kidder and Diehl made me flip to the V's. I called Carson Verrill, Craig's personal attorney, and managed to get through to him. He hadn't heard anything since he'd referred Craig to Errol Blankenship and he wanted to know who I was and what I wanted. I told him I was a dentist myself and a personal friend of Craig's. I didn't bother inventing a name and he didn't press the point.

I called Errol Blankenship. He was out, I was told, and would I care to leave a name and a number?

Grabow, Grabow, Grabow. The listing for artists filled a couple of pages. No Grabow. I looked under art galleries to see if he happened to own his own gallery. If he did, he'd named it something other than Grabow.

I invested a dime and called Narrowback Gallery, on West Broadway in SoHo. A woman with a sort of scratchy voice answered the phone just when I was about to give up and try somebody else. I said, 'Perhaps you'll be able to help me. I saw a painting about a month ago and I haven't been able to get it out of my mind. The thing is, I don't know anything about the artist.'

'I see. Let me light a cigarette. There. Now let's see, you saw a painting here at our gallery?'

'No.'

'No? Where did you see it?'

Where indeed? 'At an apartment. A friend of a friend, and it turns out they bought it at the Washington Square Outdoor Art Show a year ago, or maybe it was the year before. It's all sort of vague.'

'I see.'

She did? Remarkable. 'The only thing I know is the artist's name,' I said. 'Grabow.'

'Grabow?'

'Grabow,' I agreed, and spelled it.

'Is that a first name or a last name?'

'It's what he signed on the bottom of the canvas,' I said. 'For all I know it's his cat's name, but I suppose it's his last name.'

'And you want to find him?'

'Right, I don't know anything about art—'

'But I'll bet you know what you like.'

'Sometimes. I don't like that many paintings, but I liked this one, so much so that I can't get it out of my mind. The owners say they don't want to sell it, and then it occurred to me that I could find the artist and see what else he's done, but how would I go about it? He's not in

227

the phone book, Grabow that is, and I don't know how to get hold of him.'

'So you called us.'

'Right.'

'I wish you could have waited until late in the day. No, don't apologize, I should be up by now anyway. Are you just going through the book and calling every gallery you can find? Because you must own stock in the phone company.'

'No, I—'

'Or maybe you're rich. Are you rich?'

'Not particularly.'

' 'Cause if you're rich, or even semi-rich, I could show you no end of pretty pictures even if Mr Grabow didn't paint them. Or Ms Grabow. Why don't you come on down and see what we've got?'

'Er.'

'Because we haven't got any Grabows in stock, I'm afraid. We've got a terrific selection of oils and acrylics by Denise Raphaelson. Some of her drawings as well. But you probably never heard of her.'

'Well, I—'

'However, you're talking to her. Impressed?'

'Certainly.'

'Really? I can't imagine why. I don't think I ever heard of a painter named Grabow. Do you have any idea how many millions of artists there are in this city? Not literally millions, but tons of 'em. Are you calling all the galleries?'

'No,' I said, and when she failed to interrupt me I added, 'You're the first one I called, actually.'

'Honest? To what do I owe the honor?'

'I sort of liked the name. Narrowback Gallery.'

'I picked it because this loft has a weird shape to it. It skinnies down as you move toward the rear. I was beginning to regret not calling it the Denise Raphaelson Gallery, what the hell, free advertising and all, but calling it Narrowback finally paid off. I got myself a phone call. What kind of stuff does Grabow paint?'

How the hell did I know? 'Sort of modern,' I said.

'That's a surprise. I figured he was a sixteenth-century Flemish master.'

'Well, abstract,' I said. 'Sort of geometric.'

'Hard-line stuff?'

What did that mean? 'Right,' I said.

'Jesus, that's what everybody's doing. Don't ask me why. You really like that stuff? I mean, once you get past the fact that it's interesting shapes and colors, then what have you got? As far as I'm concerned it's waiting-room art. You know what I mean by that?'

'No,' I said, mystified.

'I mean you can hang it in a waiting room or a lobby and it's great, it won't offend anybody, it goes nice with the décor and it makes everybody happy, but what *is* it? I don't mean because it's not representational, I mean artistically, what the fuck is it? I mean if you want to hang it in a dentist's office that's sensational, and maybe you're a dentist and I just put my foot in my mouth. Are you a dentist?'

'Christ, no.'

'You sound like you're the direct opposite of a dentist, whatever that could be. Maybe you knock people's teeth out. I'm a little flaky this morning, or is it afternoon already? Jesus, it is, isn't it?'

'Just barely.'

'Gag.'

'I beg your pardon?'

'That's how you can find your Grabow, though I don't think you should bother, to tell you the truth. What I think you should do is buy something beautiful by the one and only Denise Raphaelson, but failing that you can try Gag. That's initials, G-A-G, it's Gotham Artists' Guild. They're a reference service, you go there and they have slides of everybody's work in their files, plus they have everything indexed by artists' names, and they can tell you what gallery handles an artist's work or how to get in touch with him directly if he doesn't have any gallery affiliation. They're located somewhere in midtown, I think in the East Fifties. Gotham Artists' Guild.'

'I think I love you.'

'Honest? This is so sudden, sir. All I know about you is you're not a dentist, which is a point in your favor, truth to tell. I bet you're married.'

'I bet you're wrong.'

'Yeah? Living with somebody, huh?'

'Nope.'

'You weigh three hundred pounds, you're four-foot-six, and you've got warts.'

'Well, you're wrong about the warts.'

'That's good, because they give me toads. What's your name?'

Was there any way on earth the cops were going to interrogate this lady? There was not. 'Bernie,' I said. 'Bernie Rhodenbarr.'

'God, if I married you I'd still have the same initials. I could keep on wearing all my monogrammed blouses. And yet we'll never meet. We'll have shared this magic moment over the telephone and we'll never encounter each other face to face. That's sad but it's okay. You told me you loved me and that's better than anything that happened to me all day yesterday. Gotham Artists' Guild. Got it?'

'Got it. 'Bye, Denise.'

' 'Bye, Bernie. Keep in touch, lover.'

*

Gotham Artists' Guild was located on East Fifty-fourth Street between Park and Madison. They told me over the phone to call in person, so I took a bus uptown and walked over to their office. It was two flights up over a Japanese restaurant.

I'd been winging it with Denise Raphaelson, inventing my story as I went along, but now I was prepared and I gave my spiel to an owlish young man without any hesitation. He brought me a half dozen Kodachrome slides and a viewer.

'This is the only Grabow we have,' he said. 'See if it looks like the painting you remember.'

It didn't look anything like the painting I'd described to Denise, and I almost said as much until I remembered that the painting I'd been talking about had never existed in the first place. Grabow's work turned out to involve bold amorphous splashes of color applied according to some scheme which no doubt made considerable sense to the artist. It wasn't the kind of thing I usually liked, but I was looking at it in miniature, and maybe it would blow my mind if I saw it life-size.

As if it mattered. 'Grabow,' I said positively. 'The painting I saw was like these, all right. It's definitely the same artist.'

I couldn't get an address or a phone number. When the artist is represented by a gallery that's all they'll tell you, and Walter Ignatius Grabow was represented by the Koltnow Gallery on Greene Street. That was also in SoHo, quite possibly no more than a stone's throw from Denise Raphaelson. And possibly rather more than that; my grasp of geography south of the Village is limited.

I found a pay phone – the Hotel Wedgeworth, Fifty-fifth just east of Park. I called the Koltnow Gallery and nobody answered. I called Jillian's apartment and nobody answered. I called Craig's office and nobody answered. I called 411 and asked the Information operator if there was a listing in Manhattan for Walter Ignatius Grabow. She told me there wasn't. I thanked her and she said I was welcome. I thought of calling Denise back and telling her I'd managed to get in touch with my Grabow, thanks to her good advice, but I restrained myself. I called Koltnow again, and Jillian, and Craig's office, and nothing happened. Nobody was home. I dialed my own number and established that I wasn't home either. The whole world was out to lunch.

Ray Kirschmann had staked his claim to half of Crystal's jewels and I hadn't even stolen them yet. He'd figured things wrong but he'd come scarily close to the truth. Todras and Nyswander knew the story about my aunt was a lot of crap and that I was a burglar. I had no idea if they knew there was a lot of jewelry involved in the case, and I couldn't begin to guess what they had told Jillian or what Jillian had said to them. Nor did I know anything much about Craig's situation. He was probably still in jail, and if Blankenship was any good he'd told his client to button his lip, but how many lawyers are any good? At any moment Craig might decide to start singing a song about Bernie the Burglar, and where would that leave me? I had a ticket stub between me and a homicide charge, and I couldn't make myself believe it amounted to an impregnable shield.

I walked around. It was a medium-nice fall day. The smog had dimmed the sun somewhat but it was still nice and bright out, the kind of day you don't take the trouble to appreciate until the only fresh air you get to breathe is out in the exercise yard.

Damn it, who killed the woman? W. I. Grabow? Knobby? Lawyer John? Had the murderer and the lover been one and the same? Or had the murderer killed her because he was jealous of the lover, or for an entirely different reason? And where did the jewels fit in? And where did Craig fit in? And where, damnitall, did *I* fit in?

What I kept fitting in was phone booths, and the next time I tried the Koltnow Gallery a woman answered on the second ring. She sounded older than Denise Raphaelson, and her conversation was less playful. I said I understood she represented Walter Grabow, that I was an old friend and wanted to get in touch.

'Oh, we used to have some paintings of his, though I can't remember that we ever made a sale for him. He was trying to get together enough grade-A material for a show and it never materialized. How did you know to call us?'

'Gotham Artists' Guild.'

'Oh, Gag,' she said. 'They've still got us listed as Wally's gallery? I'm surprised. He never really caught on with anybody, you know, and then he got involved with graphics and became more interested in print-making techniques than anything else. And he stopped painting, and I thought that was insane because his forte was his color sense, and here he was wrapping himself up in a strait-jacket of detail work. Are you an artist yourself?'

'Just an old friend.'

'Then you don't want to hear all this. You just want to know where he's *at*, as the children say. Hold on a moment.' I held, and after a little while the operator told me to put in another nickel. I dropped a dime in the slot and told her to keep the change. She didn't even thank me, and then the woman at Koltnow Gallery read off a number on King Street. I couldn't remember where King Street was at. As the children say.

'King Street.'

'Oh, I'll bet you're from out of town. Are you?'

'That's right.'

'Well, King Street is in SoHo, but just barely. It's one block So of Ho.' She laughed mechanically, as if she used this little play on words frequently and was getting sick of it. 'South of Houston, that is.'

'Oh,' I said. I now remembered where King Street was, but she went on to explain just what subways I should take to get there, all that crap, none of which I needed to hear.

'This is the most recent address I have for him,' she said. 'I couldn't swear that he's still there, but we've kept him on our mailing list for invitations to gallery openings and the mail doesn't come back, so if you write to him the Post Office'll forward it, but—'

She went on and on. She didn't have a telephone number listed, but I could look in the phone book, unless of course I'd already done so, and maybe he had an unlisted number, and of course if I went to the King Street address and he wasn't there I could always check with the super, that was occasionally helpful, and all of this stupid advice that any fourth-grader could have figured out by himself.

The operator cut in again to ask for more money. They're never satisfied. I started to drop yet another dime in the slot, then came abruptly to my senses. And hung up.

I still had the dime in my hand. I started to put it in my pocket. Then, without any real thought involved, I began making a phone call instead. I dialed Jillian's apartment, and when a male voice answered I said, 'Sorry, wrong number,' and hung up. I frowned, checked the number on the card in my wallet, frowned again, fished out another dime – I still had an ample supply – and dialed once more.

'Hello?'

The same voice. A voice I'd heard often over the years, saying not *Hello* but *Open wider, please.*

Craig Sheldrake's voice.

'Hello? Anybody there?'

Nobody here but us burglars, I thought. And what are *you* doing *there*?

12

King Street lies just below the southern edge of Greenwich Village, running west from Macdougal Street toward the Hudson. SoHo's a commercial district that's been turned into artists' housing, but the stretch of King where Grabow lived had always been primarily residential. Most of the block was given over to spruced-up brownstones four and five stories tall. Here and there an old commercial building newly converted to artists' lofts reminded me I was south of Houston Street.

Grabow's building was one of these. It stood a few doors off Sixth Avenue, a square structure of dull-red brick. It was four stories tall but the height of its ceilings put its roofline even with the five-story brownstones on either side. On all four floors the building sported floor-to-ceiling industrial windows extending the full width of the building, an unarguable boon to artists and exhibitionists.

A boon, too, to the veritable jungle of plants on the second floor, a tropical wall of greenery that was positively dazzling. They were soaking up the afternoon sun. The building was on the uptown side of the street so the windows faced south, which was probably terrific for the plants but less desirable for artists, who prefer a north light. On the first and third and top floors, drapes prevented the south light from screwing up masterpieces. Or perhaps the tenants were sleeping, or out for the day, or watching home movies—

I opened the door and stood in a small areaway facing another door, and this one was locked. The lock looked fairly decent. Through a window in the door – glass with steel mesh in it, they weren't kidding around here – I could see a flight of stairs, a large self-service freight elevator, and a door that presumably led into the ground-floor apartment. This last was probably a safety requirement, as the ground-floor place had its own entrance in front from the days when it had been some sort of store. The downstairs tenant got his mail through a slot in his front door, because there were only three mailboxes in the hall where I stood, each with a buzzer beneath it, and the middle box was marked Grabow. Nothing fancy, just a scrap of masking tape with the name printed in soft pencil, but it did get the message across.

So his loft figured to be the middle one of the three, which would put it two flights up. I reached for the buzzer and hesitated, wishing I had a phone number for him. After all, I had a whole pocket full of dimes. If I could call him I'd know whether or not to open his door. Hell, if I called him anything could happen. His wife could answer the phone. Craig Sheldrake could answer the phone. He was answering all sorts of phones these days—

But I didn't want to think about that. I'd cabbed downtown trying not to think at all about Craig and his surprising presence in Jillian's apartment. If I started thinking about that I'd start wondering why he was there instead of in a cell, and just when they had started letting persons charged with homicide go dancing out on bail. I might even wonder what had led the cops to drop charges against Craig, and who they were looking for to take his place.

God, why would *anyone* want to think about that?

I pushed Grabow's button. Nothing happened. I pushed it again. Nothing happened again. I gazed thoughtfully at the lock and touched the ring of cunning implements in my trouser pocket. The lock didn't scare me, but how did I know there was nobody home upstairs? Grabow was an artist. They keep odd hours in the first place, and this guy didn't have a listed phone, he might not have any phone at all, and maybe he was a temperamental bastard, and if he was sleeping or working he might just let the bell ring and say the hell with it, and then if I came hopping into his place he might be as tickled by the interruption as a hibernating bear.

'Help you?'

I hadn't even heard the door open behind me. I made myself take a breath and I turned around, arranging my face in what was supposed to be a pleasant smile. 'Just looking for someone,' I said.

'Who?'

'But he doesn't seem to be home, so I'll—'

'Who you looking for?'

Why hadn't I noticed either of the other tenants' names? Because I somehow knew who this man was. I had no logical reason for assuming the specter looming before me was Walter Ignatius himself, but I'd have bet all my dimes on it.

And he certainly did loom. He was immensely tall, a good six-six, and while that might make him a backcourt man in pro basketball it certainly placed him squarely in the forecourt of life. He had a broad forehead beneath a mop of straight blondish hair cut soup-bowl style. His cheekbones were prominent and the cheeks sunken. His nose had been broken once and I felt sorry for the idiot who'd done it, because Grabow looked as though he'd known how to get even.

'Uh, Mr Grabow,' I said. 'I'm looking for a Mr Grabow.'

'Yeah, right. That's me.'

I could see him attacking a canvas, dipping a three-inch brush in a quart can of porch paint. His hands were enormous – a little dental scalpel would have disappeared in them. If this man had wanted to kill Crystal, his bare hands would have been more lethal than any weapon they might have held.

I said, 'That's odd, I expected an older man.'

'I'm older'n I look. What's the problem?'

'You're Mr William C. Grabow?'

A shake of the head. 'Walter. Walter I. Grabow.'

'That's odd,' I said. I should have had a notebook to look in, a piece of paper, something. I got my wallet out and dug out Jillian's hair appointment card, holding it so Grabow couldn't see it. *'William C. Grabow,'* I said. 'Maybe they made a mistake.'

He didn't say anything.

'I'm sure they made a mistake,' I said, and referred again to the card. 'Now you had a sister, Mr Grabow. Is that right?'

'I got a sister. Two sisters.'

'You had a sister named Clara Grabow Ullrich who lived in Worcester, Massachusetts, and—'

'No.'

'I beg your pardon?'

'You got the wrong party after all. I got two sisters, Rita and Florence, Rita's a nun, Flo's out in California. What's this Clara?'

'Well, Clara Grabow Ullrich is deceased, she died several months ago, and—'

He moved a large hand, dismissing Clara Grabow Ullrich forever. 'I don't have to know this,' he said. 'You got the wrong party. I'm Walter I. and you're looking for William.'

'William C.'

'Yeah, whatever.'

'Well, I'm sorry to bother you, Mr Grabow.' I moved toward the door. He stepped aside to let me pass, then dropped a hand on the doorknob, just resting it there.

'Wait a minute,' he said.

'Is something wrong?' Had the hulk suddenly remembered a long-lost sister? Oh, God, had he decided to try to glom onto some non-existent legacy?

'This address,' he said.

'Pardon me?'

'Where'd you get this address?'

'My firm supplied it.'

'Firm? What firm?'

'Carson, Kidder and Diehl.'

'What's that?'

'A law firm.'

'You're a lawyer? You're not a lawyer.'

'No, I'm a legal investigator. I work for lawyers.'

'This address isn't listed anywhere. How'd they get it?'

'There are city directories, Mr Grabow. Even if you don't have a phone, all tenants are—'

'I sublet this place. I'm not the tenant of record, I'm not in any directories.' His head jutted forward and his eyes burned down at me.

'Gag,' I said.

'Huh?'

'Gotham Artists' Guild.'

'They gave you this address?'

'That's how my firm got it. I just remembered. You were listed with Gotham Artists' Guild.'

'That's years back,' he said, wide eyed with wonder. 'Back when I was painting. I was into color then, big canvases, I had scope, I had vision—' He broke off the reverie. 'You're with this law firm,' he said, 'and you're coming around here on a Saturday?'

'I work my own hours, Mr Grabow. I don't follow a nine-to-five routine.'

'Is that a fact.'

'Now if you'll just excuse me I'll let you go on about your business.'

I made to take a step toward the door. His hand stayed on the knob.

'Mr Grabow—'

'Who the fuck *are* you?'

God, how had I gotten myself into this mess? And how was I going to get myself out? I started running the same tape again, babbling that I was a legal investigator, repeating the name of my firm, and it was all just hanging in the air like smog. I made up a name for myself, something like John Doe but not quite that original, and then I looked at that hair appointment card again as if something on it would inspire me, and he extended a hand.

'Let's see that,' he said.

It didn't have any of the information I'd been making up. All it had was Jillian's address and number on one side and some crap about an appointment with Keith on the other. And there was his great paw, beckoning.

I started to hand him the card. Then I stopped, and let out a horrible groan, and clapped my hand, card and all, to my chest.

'What in—'

'Air!' I croaked. 'Air! I'm dying!'

'What the hell is—'

'My heart!'

'Look—'

'My pills!'

'Pills? I don't—'

236

'Air!'

He held the door open. I took a step outside, doubled over, coughing, and then I took another step, and then I straightened up and ran like a sonofabitch.

13

Happily, Walter Ignatius Grabow wasn't in the habit of spending his evenings loping around Gramercy Park. If I'd had a long-distance runner chasing after me I wouldn't have stood a chance. As it was, I don't think he even made an effort. I had a few steps on him and took him utterly by surprise, and while I didn't stop to see whether he was pounding the pavement after me, I did hear his yells of 'Hey!' and 'What the hell?' and 'Where you going, damn it?' trailing off behind me. They trailed rather sharply, suggesting that he merely stood in place and hollered while I ran, appropriately enough, like a thief.

Unhappily, I wasn't a jogger either, and by the time I'd managed a couple of blocks on sheer adrenaline stimulated by rank cowardice, I was clutching my chest in earnest and holding onto a lamppost with my other hand. My heart was hammering in a distinctly unhealthy fashion and I couldn't catch my breath, but the old master painter was nowhere to be seen, so that meant I was safe. Two cops wanted me for murder and another cop wanted half the jewels I hadn't stolen, but at least I wasn't going to get beaten to death by a crazy artist, and that was something.

When I could breathe normally again I found my way to a bar on Spring Street. There was nothing artsy about the place or the old men in cloth caps who sat drinking shots and beers. It had been doing business long before SoHo got a face-lift, and the years had given it a cozy feel and a homey smell that was composed of equal parts of stale beer, imperfect plumbing, and wet dog. I ordered a glass of beer and spent a long time sipping it. Two gentlemen a few stools over were remembering how Bobby Thompson's home run won the 1951 pennant for the Giants. They were the New York Giants then, and as far as my fellow drinkers were concerned it all happened the day before yesterday.

'It was Ralph Branca threw that pitch. Bobby Thompson, he hit it a ton. What I always wondered is how Ralph Branca felt about it.'

'Made himself immortal,' the other said. 'You wouldn't be remembering Ralph Branca but for that pitch he served up.'

'Oh, go on.'

238

'You wouldn't.'

'Me forget Ralph Branca? Now go on.'

When my beer was gone I went to the phone at the back and tried Jillian's number. While it rang I thought of things to say to Craig when he answered, but he didn't and neither did anybody else. After eight or ten rings I retrieved my dime and got Craig's home number from Information. It rang three times and he picked it up.

'Hi,' I said. 'I got a toothache. Let me talk to Jillian, will you?'

There was a long and thoughtful pause. Pensive, you might say. Then he said, 'Sheesh, Bern, you're really cool.'

'Like a burpless cucumber.'

'You're something else, Bern. Where are you calling from? No, don't tell me. I don't want to know.'

'You do not want de information?'

'Who are you supposed to be?'

'Peter Lorre. I know it's not very good. I do a pretty good Bogart, shweetheart, but my Peter Lorre's strictly Amateur Night. Let me talk to Jillian.'

'She's not here.'

'Where is she?'

'Home, I suppose. How should I know?'

'You were over there before.'

'How did you – oh, you were the wrong number. Listen, Bernie, I don't think we should be having this conversation.'

'You figure the line is tapped, eh, shweetheart?'

'Jesus, cut it out.'

'It's not a bad Bogart impression.'

'Just cut out the whole thing, will you? I've been in jail, I've been hassled by cops, my whole life's been spread all over the fucking news-papers, and my ex-wife is dead, and—'

'Well, it's an ill wind, right?'

'Huh?'

'You were praying Crystal would die, and now—'

'*Jesus!* How can you talk like that?'

'I've got the guts of a burglar. When did they let you out, anyhow?'

'Couple of hours ago.'

'How did Blankenship manage that?'

'Blankenship couldn't manage the Bad News Bears. All Blankenship wanted was for me to sit tight. I kept sitting tight and I'd have gone on sitting tight while they shaved my head and attached the electrodes. Then they'd have thrown the switch and I'd have sat even tighter.'

'They don't do that anymore.'

'With my luck it'll come back into style. I got rid of Blankenship. The prick wouldn't believe I was innocent. How could he do me any good if he thought I was guilty.'

'My lawyer's done me loads of good over the years,' I said, 'and he *always* thought I was guilty.'

'Well, you always were, weren't you?'

'So?'

'Well, I was innocent, Bern. I dumped Blankenship and got my own lawyer in my corner. He's not a criminal lawyer but he knows me, and he also knows his ass from a hole in the ground, and he heard me out and told me how to open up to the cops a little, and by ten o'clock this morning they were unlocking the cell door and treating me like a human being again. It made a nice change, let me tell you. Being locked up isn't my idea of a good time.'

'Tell me about it. What did you give them?'

'Who?'

'The cops. What did you say that made them let you off the hook?'

'Nothing important. I just leveled a little, that's all.'

'Leveled about what?'

Another pause, not as long as the first one. Not so much pensive this time as, well, evasive. Then, 'Jillian says you've got an alibi anyway. You were at the fights.'

'You bastard, Craig.'

'I just told them about the jewels, that's all. And about the conversation we had.'

'You told them you talked me into going after her jewels?'

'That's not what happened, Bernie.' He spoke carefully, as if for the benefit of eavesdropping ears. 'I was talking about Crystal's jewelry, bitching about it more or less, and you seemed very interested, and of course at the time I had no idea you were a burglar, and—'

'You're a real son of a bitch, Craig.'

'You're really steamed, aren't you? Sheesh, Bern, *don't* you have an alibi? Wait a minute. *Wait. A. Minute.*'

'Craig—'

'You actually did it,' he said. Maybe he believed it, maybe he was still talking to an electronic listener, maybe he was trying to rationalize blabbing my name to the law. 'You went in Thursday night. She interrupted you and you panicked and stabbed her.'

'You're not making much sense, Craig.'

'But why would you use one of my dental scalpels? How come you just happened to have one of them in your pocket?' He was thinking his way along as he spoke and I guess he wasn't used to the process. 'Wait. A. Minute! You had the whole thing planned, burglary and murder rolled into one, with me set up for it. You must have been making a pitch for Jillian, that's what it was, and you wanted me out of the way so you could have a clear field with her. *That's* what it was.'

'I don't believe I'm hearing this.'

'Well, you just better start believing it. Jesus, Bernie. And then you

240

call up here and ask to speak to her. You're incredible, that's all I've got to say.'

'I've got the guts of a burglar.'

'You can say that again.'

'I don't particularly want to. Craig, I—'

'I don't think we should be having this conversation.'

'Oh, grow up, Craig. I want to—'

Click!

He'd hung up on me. First he handed me to the cops and now he had gone and hung up on me. I stood there holding the dead phone and shaking my head at the inhumanity of man to man. Then I fed it another dime and tried him again. It went unanswered for eight rings. I broke the connection, put the dime back in the slot, dialed again. And got a busy signal.

When Jillian's number didn't answer on a second try, I wondered if I'd gotten a couple of digits switched around. I looked through my wallet for the card she'd given me but of course I hadn't put it back after the go-round with Grabow. I checked my pockets. No luck – it was gone. She'd said the number was unlisted. I tried Information and sure enough, there was no listing for her. I dialed the number again as I remembered it and got no answer, and then I looked up and dialed the number of Craig's office and while it rang I asked myself why I was wasting my time, and before I could answer myself she picked up the phone.

She said, 'Oh, thank God! I've been trying your number for hours.'

'I haven't been home.'

'I know. Listen, everything's going crazy. Craig's out of jail. They released him.'

'I know.'

'What he did, he gave them your name, told them you probably took Crystal's jewels or something like that. He sort of glossed over what he told them.'

'I'll just bet he did.'

'That's why those policemen came up this morning. They must have known he was going to be released and they wanted to talk to me before he did. I guess. Plus they were looking for you. I told them what you said to tell them, at least I tried to get it all right. I was nervous.'

'I can imagine.'

'It's good you were at the boxing matches and can prove it. I think they're trying to frame you for murder.'

I swallowed. 'Yeah,' I said. 'It's lucky I've got an alibi.'

'Craig says they'll be looking for witnesses who saw you in Crystal's neighborhood the night she was killed. But how are they going to find anybody since you weren't there? I told him he was awful to do what he did but he said his lawyer told him it was the only way to get out of that cell.'

'Carson Verrill.'

'Yes, he said the other man wasn't doing him any good at all.'

'Well, thank God for old Carson Verrill.'

'He's not old. And I'm not very thankful for him, to tell you the truth.'

'Neither am I, Jillian.'

'Because I think the whole thing was really rotten all the way down the line. I mean, here you were trying to do him a favor and now look what he's done in return. I tried to tell him you were after the real killer and I don't even think he paid any attention to what I was saying. He was over at my apartment and we had a fight about it and he wound up storming out. Actually he didn't storm exactly. Actually I asked him to leave.'

'I see.'

'Because I think it stinks, Bernie.'

'So do I, Jillian.'

'And I came here because I wanted to look in the files, but so far all I've done is waste time. There's no patient anywhere in the files named Grabow.'

'Well, I found Grabow. He may be a hell of a painter but he can't run worth a damn.'

'If you've learned Knobby's name I'll look him up right now. I didn't happen to see anybody listed as working at Spyder's Parlor. That's the name of the place, isn't it?'

'Uh-huh.'

'But I didn't look at all the cards. I also was looking for people named John and then checking to see if they were lawyers, but that's really beginning to seem hopeless.'

'Forget it,' I said. 'That's not how this is going to get solved anyway. Look, I want to check Knobby, and there are a couple of other things I ought to see about. Where are you going to be tonight?'

'My place, I guess. Why?'

'Will you be alone?'

'As far as I know. Craig won't be coming over, if that's what you mean. Not if I have anything to say about it.'

'How about if I come over?'

A pause, neither pensive nor evasive. Call it provocative. 'That sounds nice,' she said. 'What time?'

'I don't know.'

'You won't be, uh—?'

'Drunk? I'm staying away from olive oil tonight.'

'I think you should stay away from Frankie while you're at it.'

'Sounds like a good idea. I don't know what time I'll be over because I don't know how much time everything else is going to take. Should I call first? Yeah, I'll call first. I lost the card with your number on it. Let me get a pen. Here we go. What's your number?'

'Rhinelander seven, eighteen oh two.'

'One year before the Louisiana Purchase. That's what I dialed but there was no answer. Oh, of course there wasn't, you were at the office. In fact you still are, aren't you?'

'Bernie—'

'I'm a little crazy but I'm told I have nerves of steel and that's something. It looks as though I'm going to need them, too. I'll call you.'

'Bernie? Be careful.'

14

'Jeez, if it ain't my old buddy,' Dennis said. 'Saturday night and look what a crowd fulla stiffs they get here, will ya? It's a great place during the week but on weekends everybody's home with their wife and kids. People don't have to work, they don't have to unwind after work, you know what I mean? But the parking garage business, that's no five-days-a-week operation. You run a garage and they keep you hopping around the clock, and who the hell wants to waste Saturday night on his wife and kids anyway? You're not in the garage business. You told me your line but it slipped my mind.'

What had I told him? I'd said I was a burglar, but what else? 'Investments,' I said.

'Right. Jeez, can you believe it, I can't remember your name? I got it on the tip of my tongue.'

'It's Ken. Ken Harris.'

'Of course it is. Just what I was gonna say. Dennis is mine, I'm in the garage business. One thing I don't forget, though, I'll bet I remember your drink. Hey, Knobby, get your ass over here, huh? Make it another of the same for me and bring my friend Kenny here a Cutty Sark on the rocks. Am I right or am I right, Ken?'

'You're right but you're wrong, Dennis.'

'How's that?'

To Knobby I said, 'Just make it black coffee for the time being. I got to get sober before I go and get drunk again.'

I didn't have to get sober. I'd had nothing alcoholic all day except for that solitary glass of beer on Spring Street, and a couple of hours had passed since then. But what I did have to do was stay sober because I am always sober when I work and I planned to work tonight. I was standing with my old buddy Dennis at the bar of Spyder's Parlor, and good old Knobby was building the drinks, and straight black coffee was just what the burglar ordered.

'I guess you been making the rounds, eh, Kenny?'

Who was Kenny? Oh, right. I was. 'I hit a few places, Dennis.'

'See Frankie anywhere?'

'No. Not tonight.'

244

'She was supposed to drop by here after dinner. Sometimes she'll put roots down in Joan's Joynt or one of those gin mills, but she's generally pretty dependable, you know what I mean? And she's not at home. I called her a few minutes ago and nobody answered.'

'She'll be around,' Knobby said. His head must have earned him his name. He was young, early thirties, but his bald dome made him look older at first glance. He had a fringe of dark brown hair around a prominent and shiny head of skin. His eyebrows were thick and bushy, his jaw under-slung, his nose a button and his eyes a warm liquid brown. He had a lean, wiry body and he looked good in the official Spyder's Parlor T-shirt, a bright-red affair with a design silk-screened in black, a spider's web, a leering macho spider in one corner, arms extended to welcome a hesitant girlish fly. 'Ol' Frances, she's got to make her rounds,' he said. 'Stick around and you'll see her before the night's over.'

He moved off down the bar. 'She'll show or she won't,' Dennis said. 'Least you're here, I got a buddy to drink with. I hate to drink alone. You drink alone and you're just a boozer, know what I mean? Me, I can take the alcohol or leave it alone. I'm here for the companionship.'

'I know what you mean,' I said. 'I guess Frankie's got things to drink about these days.'

'You mean What's-her-name? That got killed?'

'Right.'

'Yeah, hell of a thing. She sounded bad when I talked to her a couple hours ago.'

'Depressed?'

He thought it over. 'Disturbed,' he said. 'She was saying how they let the husband off, the veterinarian or whatever he is.'

'I think he's a dentist.'

'Well, same difference. She said she oughta do something. I dunno, maybe she had a few already. You know how she gets.'

'Sure.'

'Women don't hold it the way you and I do. It's a physical thing, Ken.'

Cue or not, I acted on it, waving to Knobby and springing for a drink for Dennis and coffee for myself. When the bartender moved away I said, 'Knobby here, a minute ago he called her Frances.'

'Well, that's her name, Ken. Frances Ackerman.'

'Everybody calls her Frankie.'

'So?'

'I was, you know, just thinking.' I moved my hand in a vague circle. 'What's Knobby's name, you happen to know?'

'Shit, lemme think. I used to know. I *think* I used to know.'

'Unless his parents named him Knobby, but what kind of name is that for a little baby?'

'Naw, they wouldn't give him a name like that. He musta had hair then. The day his mother dropped him he musta had more hair than he does today.'

'Here we've bought all these drinks from him and neither of us know's the bastard's name, Dennis.'

'It's funny when you put it that way, Ken.' He lifted his glass, drained it. 'What the hell,' he said, 'drink up and we'll buy another round off him and ask him who the hell he is. Or who the hell he thinks he is, right?'

It took more than one round. It took several, and I had a pretty fair case of coffee nerves building by the time we established that Knobby's first name was Thomas, that his last name was Corcoran, and that he lived nearby. On a trip to the men's room I stopped to look up Knobby in the phone book. There was a Thos Corcoran listed on East Twenty-eighth Street between First and Second. I tried the number and let it ring an even dozen times and nobody answered. I looked over my shoulder, saw no one paying attention to me, and tore the page out of the book for future reference.

Back at the bar Dennis said, 'She got a friend?'

'Huh?'

'I figured you were on the phone with a broad and I asked if she's got a friend.'

'Oh. Well, she hasn't got any enemies.'

'Hey, that's pretty good, Ken. I bet when he was a kid they called him Corky.'

'Who?'

'Knobby. Last name's Corcoran, it figures they'll call him Corky, right?'

'I guess so.'

'Shit,' Dennis said. 'Drink up and we'll ask the bum. Hey, Corky! Get over here, you bum!'

I put a hand on Dennis's shoulder. 'I'll pass for now,' I said, sliding a couple of bills across the bar for Knobby. 'I've got somebody to see.'

'Yeah, and she's got no enemies. Well, if she's got a friend, bring her around later, huh? I'll be here for a while. Maybe Frankie'll drop by and have a couple, but either way I'll be holding the fort.'

'So maybe I'll see you later, Dennis.'

'Oh, I'll be here,' he said. 'Where else am I gonna go?'

15

Knobby Corcoran's building was a twelve-story prewar job with an Art Deco lobby and a doorman who thought he was St. Peter. I lurked across the street watching him make sure every supplicant was both expected and desired by a bona fide tenant. I thought of passing myself off as a tenant unknown to him, but his manner suggested this wouldn't be a breeze and I wasn't sure I had self-confidence equal to the chore.

The building on the right was a five-story brownstone. The building on the left, however, was a fourteen-story building, which, given the curiosities of superstition in the New York real-estate trade, meant it was only one story taller than Knobby's building. It too had a doorman but he hadn't been through the same assertiveness-training course as Knobby's and I could have walked past him wearing convict's stripes without creating an incident.

First, though, I had to learn the number of Knobby's apartment, and I did that by presenting myself as his visitor and watching which buzzer the doorman rang for the intercom. When no one answered I knew two things for certain – Knobby lived in 8-H and nobody was home. I walked to the far corner, came partway back, and breezed past the doorman of the building next door with a nod and a smile and a 'Nice night, eh?' He agreed that it was without even looking up from his paper.

I took the elevator to the top floor and climbed a flight of stairs to the roof. Some Manhattan rooftops feature amateur astronomers and some sport courting couples and still others are given over to roof gardens. This roof, praise be to God, was empty. I walked to its edge and gazed down through the darkness for about twelve feet, which is a much greater distance to fall down than to walk across. It could have been worse – there might have been a gap between the buildings. But then I wouldn't have been there in the first place.

I must have wasted a few minutes getting my courage up. But this was nothing I hadn't done before, and if you can't contend with acrophobia when there's no way around it, well, burglary's not the right trade for you, my boy. I went over there and I jumped, and while I landed with a little pain I did so with my ankles unturned. I did a few shallow kneebends to make sure that my legs still worked, let out the breath I hadn't known I'd been holding, and made my way over to the door leading back into the building.

It was locked from the inside, but of course that was the least of my problems.

Knobby's lock was no problem, either. I got to his door just as a middle-aged man emerged from a door down the hall and began walking in my direction. I could have sworn I recognized him from one of those Haley's M-O commercials, asking his pharmacist for some commonsense advice about, uh, irregularity. I knocked on Knobby's door, frowned, said, 'Yeah, it's me, man. You gonna open the door or what?'

Silence from within, of course.

'Yeah, right,' I said. 'But hurry it up, huh?' I looked at the approaching gentleman, caught his eye, rolled my own eyes in exasperation. 'Taking a shower,' I confided. 'So I gotta stand here while he dries off and gets dressed and everything.'

He nodded sympathetically and hurried on by, hoping no doubt that I'd keep the rest of my sorrows to myself. When he turned the corner I hauled out my ring of tools and popped Knobby's lock in less time than it takes to announce the fact. He had one of those spring locks that engages automatically when you close the door, and he hadn't bothered to use the key to engage the deadbolt, so all I had to do was snick the thing back with a strip of spring steel and give the door a push.

I slipped inside, closed the door, locked it more thoroughly than Knobby had done, and groped around for a light switch. I didn't have rubber gloves with me and this time I didn't care, because I didn't expect to steal anything. All I really wanted was to find some evidence, and once I found it I could leave it there and quick go bring it to the attention of the police. There would probably be some subtle way to do this.

If I got really lucky, of course, I might just find the caseful of jewels. In which event I would liberate my attaché case with the greater portion of its contents intact, minus a few choice and eminently traceable items which I could hide here and there on the premises where Todras and Nyswander could uncover them at their leisure. But it seemed all too probable that, if Knobby was the killer and thief, the jewels were tucked away someplace where I wouldn't find them, not left in this apartment behind an imperfectly locked door.

While I thought all of these things I was already getting busy tossing the place. This was a relatively simple job because of its size. Knobby had a studio apartment not very much bigger than Jillian's place and a good deal more sparsely furnished. There was a captain's bed in unpainted birch, a mahogany set of drawers with mismatched drawer

248

pulls, clearly acquired secondhand, a comfortable chair and a pair of straightbacked side chairs. A stove and refrigerator and sink stood at the rear, ineffectively screened from the rest of the room by a beaded curtain.

The place was sloppy. Bartenders have to be very neat at their work and I'd spent enough hours watching them polish glasses and put things away in their proper places to assume they were just naturally precise individuals. Knobby's apartment disabused me of this notion. He had scattered dirty clothes here and there around the room, his bed was unmade, and one got the general impression that his cleaning woman had died months ago and had not yet been replaced.

I kept at it. I checked the kitchen area first. There was no cold cash in the fridge, no hot jewelry in the oven. There was, as a matter of fact, mold and dead food in the former and stale grease and crud in the latter, and I moved on to other areas as quickly as possible.

The drawers in the captain's bed contained a jumble of clothing, the wardrobe running mostly to jeans in various stages of disrepute and T-shirts, some of them red Spyder's Parlor numbers, others imprinted to promote other establishments, causes, or life styles. One drawer held a variety of contraceptive devices plus the sort of sex aids available at adult bookstores – vibrators, stimulators, and diverse rubber and leather objects the specific functions of which I could only guess at.

No jewels. No dental instruments from Celniker Dental and Optical Supply. No objects of enormous value. It had occurred to me earlier that even if Knobby had no connection with the killing, I could at least make expenses out of the visit. After all, the way things were going it looked as though I'd need money for a lawyer, or for a plane to Tierra del Fuego, or something, and when I open a door without a key I expect to get something tangible for my troubles. I'm no amateur, for God's sake. I don't do it for love.

Hopeless. He had a portable TV, a radio on the dresser top, an Instamatic camera, all items that might have gladdened the heart of a junkie who'd kicked the door in looking for the price of a bag of smack, but nothing I'd lower myself to take. There was a little cash in the top right-hand dresser drawer, accumulated tips I suppose, and I reimbursed myself for what I'd spent at the bar – and his tip was part of it, as far as that goes. Actually I did a little better than get even. There was somewhere between one and two hundred dollars in ones and fives and tens, and I scooped it all up and shook the bills down into a neat stack and found them a home on my hip. No big deal, certainly, but when I find cash around I make it mine. There was change, too, lots of it, but I left it right there and closed the drawer. You've got to have standards or where the hell are you?

Enough. I could inventory every piece of debris in the lad's apartment, but why bother? I opened his closet, I burrowed among his jackets and coats, and on the overhead shelf I saw something that made my heart turn over, or skip a beat, or stand still, or – you get the idea.

An attaché case.

Not mine. Not Ultrasuede but Naugahyde, black, shiny Naugahyde. The Nauga and the Ultra are two altogether different animals. My disappointment at this second discovery was greater than you can possibly imagine. For one moment I'd had the jewels at hand and the murder of Crystal Sheldrake all solved, and now that moment was over and I was back where I'd started.

Naturally I took the case down and opened it anyway.

Naturally I was somewhat surprised to find it absolutely jam-packed with money.

16

The bills were arranged in inch-thick stacks with buff-colored paper bands around their middles. The stacks rested on their edges so that I couldn't tell whether the bills were singles or hundreds. For a moment I just stared and wondered. Then I dug out one of the little stacks and riffled through it. The bills were twenties, and I had perhaps fifty of them in my hand. Say a thousand dollars in that stack alone.

I sampled a few other stacks. They also consisted of twenty-dollar bills, all fresh and crisp. I was looking at – what? A hundred thousand dollars? A quarter of a million?

Ransom money? A drug payoff? Transactions of that sort usually called for old bills. An under-the-table stock deal? A real-estate transaction, all cash and off the books?

And how did any of these notions mesh with Knobby Corcoran, a bartender who lived in one disorderly room, owned hardly any furniture, and couldn't be bothered to double-lock his door?

I gave the money itself some further study. Then I took ten fresh twenties from the stack and added them to the bills in my wallet. I tucked the rest back in place, closed the case, fastened the hasps.

I put his tip money back. I'd incorporated his funds with my own and hadn't kept a close count on what I'd taken, but I didn't figure he knew, either. I returned around a hundred dollars in assorted bills to his top left-hand dresser drawer, thought about it, and added one of the twenties to the collection. I dropped another bill behind the drawer so that it could only be found by someone who was searching for it. I placed a third bill out of sight at the rear of the closet shelf and wedged a fourth into one of a pair of worn cowboy boots that stood at the back of the closet.

Neat.

I turned out the light, let myself out, closed the door behind me. The elevator took me down to the lobby and the doorman wished me good evening. I gave him a curt nod; the soles of my feet still ached from that jump and I blamed him for it.

A cab came along the minute I got to the street. Sometimes things just work out that way.

They have these lockers all over New York, in subway stations, at railroad terminals. I used one at Port Authority Bus Terminal on Eighth Avenue; I opened the door, popped the attaché case inside, dropped a pair of quarters in the slot, closed the door, turned the key, took the key out and carried it off with me. It had felt very odd, carrying all that currency around with me, and it felt even odder abandoning it like that in a public place.

But it would have been stranger still running down to SoHo with it.

God knows I didn't want to go there. It hadn't been that long since I'd faked a heart attack to get away from Walter Ignatius Grabow, and here I was climbing right back onto the horse and sticking my head in the lion's mouth again.

But I told myself it wasn't all that dangerous. If he was home he'd buzz back when I rang his bell, and I'd just make an abrupt U-turn and take off. And he wouldn't be home anyway, because it was Saturday night and he was an artist and they all go out and drink on Saturday night. He'd be partying it up at somebody else's loft or knocking back boilermakers at the Broome Street Bar or sharing a jug of California Zinfandel with someone of the feminine persuasion.

Except that his girlfriend Crystal was dead, and maybe he'd be doing some solitary drinking to her memory, sitting in the dark in his loft, downing shots of cheap rye and not answering the bell when I rang, just moping in a corner until I popped his lock and sashayed flylike into his parlor—

Unpleasant thought.

The thought stayed with me after I rang his bell and got no answer. The lock on the downstairs door was a damned good one and the metal stripping where the door met the jamb kept me from prying the bolt back, but no lock is ever quite so good as the manufacturer would have you believe. I did a little of this and a little of that and the pins dropped and the tumblers tumbled.

I walked up two flights. The second-floor tenant, the one with all the plants, had soft rock playing on the stereo and enough guests to underlay the music with a steady murmur of conversation. As I passed his door I smelled the penetrating aroma of marijuana, its smoke an accompaniment to the music and the talk. I went up another flight and listened carefully at Grabow's door, but all I could hear was the music from the apartment below. I got down on hands and knees and saw that no light was visible beneath his door. Maybe he was downstairs, I thought, getting happily stoned and tapping his foot to the Eagles and telling everybody about the lunatic he'd cornered that afternoon in the lobby.

Meanwhile, the lunatic braced himself and opened the door. Grabow had a good thick slab of a door, and holding it in place was a Fox police lock, the kind that features a massive steel bar angled against the door and mounted in a plate bolted to the floor. You can't kick a door in when it has that kind of a lock, nor can you take a crowbar and pry it open. It's about the strongest protection there is.

Alas, no lock is stronger than its cylinder. Grabow's had a relatively common five-pin Rabson, mounted with a flange to discourage burglars from digging it out. Why should I dig it out? I probed it with picks and talked to it with my fingers, and while it played the maiden I played Don Juan, and who do you think won that round?

Grabow lived and worked in one enormous room, with oceans of absolutely empty space serving to divide the various areas of bedroom and kitchen and living room and work space from one another. The living-room area consisted of a dozen modular sofa units covered in a rich brown plush and a couple of low parson's tables in white Formica. The sleeping area held a king-size platform bed with a sheepskin throw on it. Individual sheepskin rugs covered the floor around the bed. The wall behind the bed was exposed brick painted a creamy buff a little richer than the paper wrapper on the twenty-dollar bills, and hanging on that wall were a shield, a pair of crossed spears, and several primitive masks. The pieces looked to be Oceanic, New Guinea or New Ireland, and I wouldn't have minded having them on my own wall. Nor would I have minded having what they'd be likely to bring at a Parke-Bernet auction.

The kitchen was a beauty – large stove, a fridge with an automatic ice-maker in the door, a separate freezer, a double stainless-steel sink, a dishwasher, a washer-drier. Copper and stainless-steel cookware hung from wrought-iron racks overhead.

The work area was just as good. Two long narrow tables, one chest height, the other standard. A couple of chairs and stools. Printmaking equipment. A ceramicist's kiln. Floor-to-ceiling steel shelving filled with neatly arranged rows of paints and chemicals and tools and gadgets. A hand-cranked printing press. A few boxes of 100-percent rag-content bond paper.

It must have been around 10:15 when I opened his door, and I suppose I spent twenty minutes giving the apartment a general search.

Here are some of the things I did not find: A human being, living or dead. An attaché case, Ultrasuede or Naugahyde or otherwise. Any jewelry beyond some mismatched cufflinks and a couple of tie clips. Any money beyond a handful of change which I found – and left – on a bedside table. Any paintings by Grabow or anyone else. Any artwork except for the Oceanic pieces over the bed.

Here's what I did find: Two pieces of meticulously engraved copper plate, roughly two and a half by six inches, mounted on blocks of three-quarter-inch pine. A key of the type likely to fit a safe-deposit box. A desk-top pencil holder, covered in richly embossed red leather, containing not pencils but various implements of the finest surgical steel, each fitted with a hexagonal handle.

When I left Walter Grabow's loft I took nothing with me that had not been on my person when I came. I did move one or two of his possessions from their accustomed places to other parts of the loft, and I did place several crisp new twenty-dollar bills here and there.

But I didn't steal anything. There was a moment, I'll admit, when I had the urge to fit one of those masks over my face, snatch the shield and a spear from the wall, and race through the streets of SoHo emitting wild Oceanic war whoops. The impulse was easily mastered, and I left masks and spears and shield where they hung. They were nice, and undeniably valuable, but when you've just stolen somewhere in the neighborhood of a quarter of a mill in cash, lesser larceny does seem anti-climactic.

Just as my cab pulled up in front of Jillian's building I spotted the blue-and-white cruiser next to the hydrant. 'Keep going,' I said. 'I'll take the corner.'

'I already threw the flag,' my driver complained. 'I'm risking a ticket.'

'What's life without taking chances?'

'Yeah, you can say that, friend. You're not the one who's taking 'em.'

Indeed. His tip was not all it might have been and I watched him drive off grumbling. I walked back to Jillian's, staying close to the buildings and keeping an eye open for other police vehicles, marked or unmarked. I didn't see any, nor did I notice any coplike creatures lurking in the shadows. I lurked in the shadows myself, and after a ten-minute lurk a pair of familiar shapes emerged from Jillian's doorway. They were Todras and Nyswander, not too surprisingly, and it was nice to see them still on the job after so many hours. I was happy to note that their schedule was as arduous as my own.

When they drove off I stayed right where I was for five full minutes in case they were going to be cute and circle the block. When this didn't happen I considered calling from the booth on the corner to make sure the coast was clear. I didn't feel like bothering. I buzzed Jillian from the vestibule.

All the distortion of the intercom couldn't hide the anxiety in her voice. She said, 'Yes? Who is it?'

'Bernie.'

'Oh. I don't—'

'Are you alone, Jillian?'

'The police were just here.'

'I know. I waited until they left.'

'They say you killed Crystal. They say you're dangerous. You never

254

went to the boxing matches. You were in her apartment, you killed her—'

All this over the intercom, yet. 'Can I come up, Jillian?'

'I don't know.'

I'll pick the fucking lock, I thought, *and I'll huff and I'll puff and I'll kick your door in.* But I said, 'I've made a lot of progress tonight, Jillian. I know who killed her. Let me up and I'll explain the whole business.'

She didn't say anything, and for a moment I wondered if she'd heard me. Perhaps she had closed the intercom switch. Perhaps at this very moment she was dialing 911, and in a scant hour the swift and efficient New York police would arrive with drawn guns. Perhaps—

The buzzer buzzed and I opened the door.

She wore a wool skirt, a plaid of muted greens and blues, and a navy sweater. Her tights were also navy, and on her little feet she wore deerskin slippers with pointed toes that suited her elfin quality. She poured me a cup of coffee and apologized for giving me a hard time over the intercom.

'I'm a nervous wreck,' she said. 'I've had a parade of visitors tonight.'

'The cops?'

'They came at the very end. Well, you know that, you saw them leave. First there was another policeman. He told me his name—'

'Ray Kirschmann?'

'That's right. He said he wanted me to give you a message. I said I wouldn't be hearing from you but he gave me a very knowing wink. I wouldn't be surprised if I blushed. It was that kind of a wink.'

'He's that kind of a cop. What was the message?'

'You're supposed to get in touch with him. He said you've really got the guts of a burglar and you proved it going back to the scene of the crime. He said something about he's sure you got what you went there for and he'll want to be on hand to check it out. When I told him I didn't really understand he said you would understand, and that the main thing was that you should get in touch with him.'

' "Back to the scene of the crime." What's that supposed to mean?'

'I think I know from something the other cops said. And other things. After Kirschmann left Craig came over.'

'I thought you told him not to.'

'I did, but he came anyway and it was easier to let him come up than make a fuss. I told him he couldn't stay.'

'What did he want?'

She made a face. 'He was horrid. He really thinks you killed Crystal. He said the police were sure of it and he blames himself for setting it up for you to steal the jewels. That was what he really wanted to tell me – to deny that you had any arrangement with him. He said you'd prob-ably blab if the police arrested you and that it would be his word against yours and naturally they'd take the word of a respectable dentist over that of a convicted burglar—'

'Naturally.'

'—but that I would have to swear that your story was a lot of nonsense or he might be in trouble. I said I didn't believe you would kill anybody and he got very mad and accused me of siding with you against him, and I got nasty myself, and I don't know what I ever saw in him, I swear I don't.'

'He's got nice teeth.'

'Then when he left, I was just getting interested in television when his lawyer came over.'

'Verrill?'

'Uh-huh. I think he came over mainly to back up Craig. Craig told him about the arrangement with you and naturally he wouldn't want that to come out, and he tried to let me know how important it was to keep it a secret. I think he was building up to offer me a bribe but he didn't come right out and say it.'

'Interesting.'

'He was really pretty slick, but in a very Establishment way. As if the kind of bribe I could expect wouldn't be an envelope full of cash but some sort of tax-free trust fund. Not really, but he had that kind of attitude. He said there was no question you murdered Crystal. He said the police had evidence.'

'What kind of evidence?'

'He didn't say.' She looked away, swallowed. 'You didn't kill her, did you, Bernie?'

'Of course not.'

'But you'd say that anyway, wouldn't you?'

'I don't know what I'd say if I killed her. I've never killed anybody so the question's never come up. Jillian, why on earth would I kill the woman? If she came in and caught me in the act, all I'd want to do would be to get away before the police came. Maybe I'd give her a shove to get out of there, if I had to—'

'Is that what happened?'

'No, because she didn't catch me. But if she did, and if I did shove her, and if she took a bad fall, well, I can see how a person could get hurt that way. It's never happened yet but I suppose it's possible. What's not possible is that I'd stab her in the heart with a dental scalpel I wouldn't have with me in the first place.'

'That's what I told myself.'

'Well, you were right.'

Her eyes widened, her lower lip trembled. She gnawed prettily at it. 'Those two policemen got here about three-quarters of an hour after Mr Verrill left. They said you broke into Crystal's apartment again last night. There were police seals on it and it was broken into. They say you did it.'

'Somebody hit Crystal's place again?' I frowned, trying to figure it. 'Why would I do that?'

'They said you must have left something behind. Or you wanted to destroy evidence.'

That was what Kirschmann had been talking about. He thought I'd make a second trip for the jewels. 'Anyway,' I said, 'I was here last night.'

'You could have stopped on the way here.'

'I couldn't have stopped anywhere last night. I couldn't see straight, if you'll remember.'

She avoided my eyes. 'And the night before that,' she said. 'They say they have a witness who spotted you leaving Crystal's building right around the time she was killed. And they have another woman who says she actually spoke to you in Gramercy Park earlier that night.'

'Shit. Henrietta Tyler.'

'What?'

'A sweet little old lady who hates dogs and strangers. I'm surprised she remembered me. And that she talked to the law. I figured no one who hates dogs and strangers can be all bad. What's the matter?'

'Then you were there!'

'I didn't kill anybody, Jillian. Burglary was the only felony I committed that night, and I was busy committing it while somebody else killed Crystal.'

'You were—'

'On the premises. In the apartment.'

'Then you saw—'

'I saw the closet door from the inside, that's what I saw.'

'I don't understand.'

'I don't blame you. I didn't *see* who killed her but I had a busy night tonight and now I *know* who killed her. It all fits, even the second breakin.' I leaned forward. 'Do you suppose you could put up a fresh pot of coffee? Because it's a long story.'

257

17

She listened with appropriately wide eyes while I recreated the circumstances of the burglary and the murder. When I moved along to the
story of my visit to Knobby Corcoran's humble digs, she stared in awe
and admiration. I may have improved on reality a bit, come to think of
it. I may have made the drop from one rooftop to the other greater than
it actually was, and I may have added a gap of a few yards between the
buildings. Poetic license, you understand.

When I got to the attaché case she made oohing sounds. When it was
Naugahyde instead of Ultrasuede she groaned, and when I opened it up
and found all the money she gasped. 'So much money,' she said. 'Where
is it? You don't have it with you, do you?'

'It's in a safe place. Or else I wasted fifty cents.'

'Huh?'

'Nothing important. I stashed the attaché case but I held onto a
few bills because I thought they might come in handy.' I took out my
wallet. 'I've got two left. See?'

'What about them?'

'Nice, aren't they?'

'They're twenty-dollar bills. What's so special about them?'

'Well, if you saw a whole suitcase full of them you'd be impressed,
wouldn't you?'

'I suppose, but—'

'Compare the serial numbers, Jillian.'

'What about them? They're in sequence. Wait a minute, they're not
in sequence, are they?'

'Nope.'

'They're . . . Bernie, both of these bills have the same serial number.'

'Really? Jesus, that's remarkable, isn't it?'

'Bernie—'

'A world where no two snowflakes are the same, where every human
being has a different set of fingerprints, and here I go and take two
twenties out of my wallet and I'll be damned if they don't both have the
same serial number. It makes you think, doesn't it?'

'Are they—?'

'Phony? Yeah, that's what it means, I'm afraid. Hell of a note, isn't it? All that money and all it is is green paper. Take a close look, Jillian, and you'll see it's a long way from perfect. The portrait of Andy Jackson is damn good compared to most counterfeits I've seen, but if you really look at the bill it doesn't look wonderful.'

'Around the seal here—'

'Yeah, the points aren't sharp. And if you turn the bill over you'll see some other faults. Of course these bills are new ones. If you age them and distress them a little, give 'em fold lines and take the newness out of the paper by cooking them with a little coffee – well, there are tricks in every trade and I don't pretend to know some of the ones counterfeiters have come up with lately. I have enough work staying ahead of the locksmiths. I'll tell you, though, those bills you've got in your hand would pass banks nineteen times out of twenty. The serial number's about the only obvious fault. Would you look twice at one of these if you got it in change?'

'No.'

'Neither would anybody else. As soon as I saw the money was counterfeit I went straight back to Grabow's place. One step inside the door and I knew I was on the right track. He was an unsuccessful artist who'd turned to printmaking and had made no big success of that, and here he was living in a loft most New Yorkers would kill for, tons of space, beautiful furniture, a few thousand dollars' worth of primitive artifacts on the wall. I poked around and found enough inks and paper to make better money than the Bureau of Engraving and Printing turns out, and if there was any doubt it vanished when I found the actual printing plates. He does beautiful line work. It's really high-quality engraving.'

'Grabow's a counterfeiter?'

'Uh-huh. I wondered why he was so suspicious when he had me trapped in the vestibule of his building. I did a pretty good job of looking like a dumb schmuck who was chasing the wrong Grabow, but he was full of questions. Who was I? How'd I get his address? How come I was working on a Saturday? He came up with questions faster than I could come up with answers, that's why I had to run out on him, but why would he have so many suspicions if he didn't have something to hide? Yes, he's a counterfeiter. I can't swear that he made the plates himself, but he's got them now. And he certainly did the printing.'

'And then he gave the money to Knobby Corcoran? I don't understand what happened next.'

'Neither do I, but I can make a few guesses. Suppose Crystal brought Knobby and Grabow together. Grabow was her boyfriend and maybe she took him around the bars a few times. That's what she did with the Legal Beagle, her other boyfriend, so why wouldn't she do the same thing with Grabow?

259

'Anyway, Grabow and Corcoran set something up. Maybe Grabow was going to produce the counterfeit twenties and Knobby was going to find a way to turn them into real money. There was some kind of a doublecross. Say Knobby wound up with the twenties and Grabow wound up talking to himself. Maybe Crystal crossed him one way or another, maybe *she* wound up with the money.'

'How?'

I shrugged. 'Beats me, but it could have happened. Or maybe the deal with the counterfeit went fine but Grabow found out she was just using him, two-timing him with other men and stringing him along for the sake of the counterfeiting deal. Maybe he learned she was sleeping with Knobby, maybe he found out about the other boyfriend. He got jealous and he got mad and he picked up a dental scalpel and went after her.'

'Where would he get a dental scalpel?'

'Celniker Dental and Optical, same as Craig.'

'But why would he—'

'He's got a whole collection of them. All sorts of picks and probes and scalpels, and it looks to me as though they're all made by Celniker unless other manufacturers also put hexagonal shafts on their instruments. I suppose they're handy for printing and printmaking, cutting linoleum blocks, making woodcuts, any of that sort of detail work. Either he took one along as a murder weapon or he just happened to have one in his pocket.'

'That seems strange, doesn't it?'

It did at that. 'Try it this way, then. He'd had Crystal up to his loft and she spotted the tools and mentioned that Craig had the same kind at his office. After all, she was his hygienist back before she married him. Matter of fact, that could explain the coincidence of Grabow having the same kind of tools as Craig. Maybe he was using something else, X-acto knives or God knows what, and Crystal told him he should get a set of dental instruments because the steel's high quality or whatever the hell she told him. Anyway, if he knew Craig used Celniker instruments, he could have taken the scalpel along to make it look as though Craig did the killing. He wouldn't have any reason to get rid of his own Celniker tools because there's nothing to connect him with Crystal in the first place, and once Craig's tagged with the crime the cops won't have any reason to look any further.'

'So he took the scalpel along with the intention of using it as a murder weapon?'

'He must have.'

'And he picked her up and went to bed with her first?'

'That would have been fiendish, wouldn't it? I just met him briefly but I didn't get the impression that he was that devious a person. He struck me as pretty direct, the strong and silent type. When she went out to the bar she probably met the Legal Beagle and brought him back. I don't remember their conversation very well because I was making such a determined effort to ignore it, but it certainly wasn't Grabow. At least I don't think it was.

'No, here's what I figure happened. Say Grabow was watching the house, or maybe he tracked her from the bar where she met the lawyer. Or whoever she met, it doesn't have to be the lawyer. In fact we can forget the lawyer because I don't think he really enters into it. The fact that Frankie Ackerman mentioned three men as friends of Crystal's doesn't mean all three of them are involved in her murder. It's remarkable enough that two of them are.'

'Anyway,' Jillian prompted, 'she brought home some man or other and Grabow was watching.'

'Right. Then the guy left. Grabow saw him leave. He gave him a minute or two to get lost, then came on over and leaned on the bell. When Crystal let him in, he did his strong and silent number and stuck the scalpel straight into her heart.'

Jillian clutched her own heart, her small hand pressing high on the left-hand side of the navy sweater. She was following the line as if it were a movie and she were seeing it on TV.

'Then he came on into the bedroom,' I went on. 'First thing he saw was my attaché case standing against the wall under the French woman's portrait. He went over and—'

'What French woman?'

'It's not important. A picture on Crystal's wall. But he didn't see the picture because he only had eyes for the attaché case. See, he figured an attaché case is an attaché case. He assumed it was full of the counterfeit money and this was his chance to swipe it back.'

'But the money was in a black vinyl case, wasn't it?'

'Black Naugahyde. Right. But how would Grabow know that?'

'Wouldn't he have packed it like that to begin with?'

'Maybe, but how do we know that? Maybe he gave Crystal the money in a Bloomingdale's shopping bag. That's what I usually use on burglaries. It looks like you belong, striding along with a Bloomie's bag full of somebody else's property. Suppose he just knew someone had transferred it to an attaché case, and here was an attaché case, the very item he was looking for. The natural thing would be for him to grab it and get the hell out and worry later what was in it.'

'And later, when he opened the case—'

'It probably confused the daylights out of him. For a minute he must have thought Crystal was some kind of medieval alchemist who managed to transmute paper into gold and diamonds. Then when he had it figured he had to go back for the money. That would explain the second break-in, the burglary after the police had already sealed the apartment. Grabow went back for the money, broke the seals, searched the place, and went home empty-handed. Because the counterfeit bills were all packed up at Knobby Corcoran's apartment, sitting on a shelf in the closet.'

Jillian nodded, then frowned. 'What happened to the jewels?'

'I suppose Grabow held onto them. People tend to retain jewelry rather than leave it for the garbage man. I didn't see them around his loft, but that doesn't necessarily mean anything. The jewels are evidence and he wouldn't leave them lying around because they'd lock him into the murder.'

'He kept the dental tools around.'

'That's different. There's no way to explain the jewelry and he'd have to realize that. He must have stashed it somewhere. It's possible he tucked it away right there on King Street. It wouldn't be terribly difficult to hide the jewels under the floorboards or inside the modular furniture where I wouldn't find them on a routine search. As far as that goes, I found a safe-deposit key among his other stuff. It's possible the jewels are already in the bank. He could have gone Friday before the banks closed and stashed them in his safe-deposit box. Or he might even have fenced them. That's not inconceivable. As a counterfeiter, the odds are he knows somebody who knows somebody who fences stolen gems. It's no harder to find a fence in this town than it is to place a football bet or buy a number or score drugs. But there's really no reason to speculate about the jewels. There's already enough evidence against Grabow to put him away for years.'

'You mean the dental tools?'

'That's a start,' I said. 'I moved things around at his place, just in case he decides to get rid of the evidence. I put some of the twenties where you'd have to search to find them. Same with a few dental instruments. If he panics and throws out the instruments, there'll be a few he won't find that the police would turn up easily on a search. And I hid the printing plates. That might make him panic if he goes looking for them, but the way I left things he'll never believe a burglar set foot in the place. I even picked the lock on my way out to relock it, and that's a service relatively few burglars perform for you. I left his loft empty-handed, you know. In fact I walked out of there with less than I brought, since I planted those fake twenties on him. If I did that all the time I'd have a problem coming up with the rent every month.'

She giggled. 'My mother used to say that if burglars came to our house they'd leave something. But you're the only one I ever heard of who actually did.'

'Well, I'm not going to make a habit of it.'

'Have you been a burglar all your life, Bernie?'

'Well, not all my life. I started out as a little kid, just like everybody else. I love the way you giggle, incidentally. It's very becoming. I guess I've been a burglar since I got done being a kid.'

'I don't think you ever did get done being a kid, Bernie.'

'I sometimes have that feeling myself, Jillian.'

And I got to talking about myself and my crazy criminous career, how I'd started out sneaking into other people's houses for the sheer thrill of it and learned before long that the thrill was all the keener if you stole something while you were at it. I talked and she listened, and somewhere in the course of things we finished the coffee and she broke out a perfectly respectable bottle of Soave. We drank the chilled white wine out of stemmed glasses and sat side-by-side on the couch, and I went on talking and wished the couch would do its trick of converting into a bed. She was lovely, Jillian was, and she was a most attentive listener, and her hair smelled of early spring flowers.

Around the time the bottle became empty she said, 'What are you going to do now, Bernie? Now that you know who the killer is.'

'Find a way to get information to the cops. I suppose I'll run the play through Ray Kirschmann. It's not his case but he smells money and that'll make him bend procedures like pretzels. I don't know how he's going to make a dollar out of this one. If the jewels turn up they'll be impounded as evidence. But if there's a buck in it he'll find it, and that'll be his problem not mine.'

'I know he wants you to call him.'

'Uh-huh. But not now, I'm afraid. It's the middle of the night.'

'What time is it? Oh, it really *is* the middle of the night. I didn't realize it was so late.'

'I'll have to find someplace to stay. I'm afraid my own apartment's no good for the time being. They probably don't have it staked out but I'm not going to risk it now, not if they've got a pickup order out on me. I can get a hotel room.'

'Don't be ridiculous.'

'You figure that might be ridiculous? I suppose you're right. Hotels don't get that many check-ins at this hour and it might look suspicious. Well, there's something else I could always try. Just scout an empty apartment, one where the tenants are gone for the weekend, and make myself right at home. That worked well enough for Goldilocks.'

'Don't be ridiculous. You stayed here last night and you can stay here again. I don't want you to take a chance of getting arrested.'

'Well, Craig might—'

'Don't be ridiculous. Craig won't be coming over and I wouldn't let him in if he did. I'm pretty angry with Craig, if you want to know. I think he behaved terribly and he may be a great dentist but I'm not sure he's a very wonderful human being.'

'Well, that's great of you,' I said. 'But this time I'll take the chair.'

'Don't be ridiculous.'

'Well, you're not going to sit up in that thing, for God's sake. I'm not going to let you give up your bed again.'

'Don't be ridiculous.'

'Huh? I don't—'

'Bernie?' She gazed up at me from beneath those long eyelashes. 'Bernie, don't be ridiculous.'

'Oh,' I said, and looked deeply into her eyes, and smelled her hair. '*Oh.*'

18

It must have been around ten when we woke up the next morning. There were a few churches on the block and it kept being some denomination's turn to ring bells. We lay in bed for the next two hours, sometimes listening to the church bells and sometimes ignoring them. There are worse ways to spend a Sunday morning.

Finally she got up and put on a robe and made coffee while I set about getting into the same clothes I seemed to have been wearing forever. Then I got on the phone.

Ray Kirschmann's wife said he was out. Working, she said. Did I want to leave a message? I didn't.

I tried him at the precinct. He had the day off, somebody told me. Probably at home with his feet up and a cold beer in his fist and a ball game on television. Was there anybody else I would talk to? There wasn't. Did I want to leave a message? I didn't.

Did I dare go home? I wanted a shower but there wasn't much point taking one if I had to put on the same clothes again. And it was Sunday, so I couldn't go out and buy a shirt and socks and underwear.

I picked up the phone again and dialed my own number.

The line was busy.

Well, that doesn't necessarily prove anything. Somebody else could have called me a few seconds before I did; he'd get an unanswered ring while I got a busy signal. So I hung up and gave him a minute to get tired of the game, and then I dialed my number again, and it was still busy.

Well, that didn't prove anything either. Perhaps I'd had a visitor who knocked the phone off the hook. Perhaps phone lines were down on the West Side. Perhaps—

'Bernie? Something wrong?'

'Yes,' I said. 'Where's the phone book?'

I looked up Mrs Hesch and dialed her number. When she answered I heard her television set in the background, then her dry cigarette-hardened voice. I said, 'Mrs Hesch, this is Bernard Rhodenbarr. Your neighbor? Across the hall?'

'The burglar.'

265

'Uh, yes. Mrs Hesch—'

'Also the celebrity. I seen you on television maybe an hour ago. Not you personally, just a picture they had of you. It must have been from prison, your hair was so short.'

I knew the picture she meant.

'Now we got cops all over the building. They was here asking about you. Do I know you're a burglar? they asked me. I said all I know is you're a good neighbor. I should tell them anything? You're a nice young man, clean cut, you dress decent, that's all I know. You work hard, right? You make a living, right?'

'Right.'

'Not a bum on welfare. If you take from those rich *momsers* on the East Side, do I care? Did they ever do anything for me? You're a good neighbor. You don't rob from this building, am I right?'

'Right.'

'But now there's cops in your apartment, cops in the halls. Taking pictures, ringing doorbells, this, that and the other thing.'

'Mrs Hesch, the cops. Was there—'

'Just a minute, I got to light a cigarette. There.'

'Was there a cop named Kirschmann?'

'Cherry.'

'Jerry?'

'No, Cherry. That's Kirsch in German. Kirschmann he told me, Cherry Man is what went through my mind. He could lose thirty pounds and he wouldn't miss it.'

'He's there?'

'First two of them came to my door, a million questions they had for me, and then this Kirschmann came with the same questions and a hundred others. Mr Rhodenbarr, you ain't a killer, are you?'

'Of course not.'

'That's what I told them and what I said to myself, that's what I always said about you. You didn't kill that *nafkeh* by Gramercy Park?'

'No, of course not.'

'Good. And you didn't—'

'What did you call her?'

'A *nafkeh*.'

'What does that mean?'

'A whore, you should pardon the expression. You didn't kill the man either, did you?'

What man? 'No, of course not,' I said. 'Mrs Hesch, could you do me a favor? Could you get Ray Kirschmann to come to the phone without letting anybody know that's what you want? You could say you have something you just remembered about me, find some way to get him into your apartment without letting the other policemen know what's happening.'

She could and did. It didn't take her very long, either, and all at once I heard a familiar voice, careful, cagey, say, 'Yeah?'

'Ray?'

'No names.'

'No names?'

'Where the hell are you?'

'On the phone.'

'You better tell me where. You and me, we better get together right away. You really stepped in it this time, Bernie.'

'I thought you said no names.'

'Forget what I said. You were pretty cute, hitting the dame's apartment a second time and coming up with the loot. But you shoulda connected with me right away, Bern. I don't know what I can do for you now.'

'You can lock up a killer, Ray.'

'That's what I can do, all right, but I never figured you for a killer, Bern. It's a surprise to me.'

'It would be a bigger surprise to me, Ray. As far as the jewels are concerned—'

'Yeah, well, we found 'em, Bern.'

'What?'

'Right where you left 'em. If it was just me it's a different story, but I had to break my ass to get here along with Todras and Nyswander, let alone gettin' here ahead of 'em, and it was Nyswander who found the stuff. A diamond bracelet and an emerald doodad and those pearls. Beautiful.'

'Just three pieces?'

'Yeah.' A pause, speculative in nature. 'There was more? You got the rest stashed somewhere else, right, Bern?'

'Somebody planted those pieces, Ray.'

'Sure. Somebody's givin' away jewelry. Christmas is comin' up in a few months and somebody's got the spirit ahead of schedule.'

I took a deep breath and plunged ahead. 'Ray, I never stole the jewels. They were planted on me. The man who stole them is the same man who killed Crystal, and he planted a handful of the jewels in my apartment, at least I guess that's where you found them—'

'I didn't find 'em. Nyswander found 'em and that tears it because the bastard's incorruptible. And you bet your ass they were in your apartment, Bern, 'cause that's where you left 'em.'

I let it pass. 'The man who did it, the theft and the murders, is somebody you probably never heard of.'

'Try me.'

'He's dangerous, Ray. He's a killer.'

'You were gonna tell me his name.'

'Grabow.'

267

'Somebody I never heard of, you said.'

'Walter I. Grabow. The I stands for Ignatius, if that matters. I don't suppose it does.'

'Funny.'

'It's complicated, Ray. The plot's pretty involved. I think we ought to meet somewhere, the two of us, and I could explain it to you.'

'I just bet you could.'

'Huh?'

'We better meet somewhere, that's the truth. Bernie, you know what happened to you? Somewhere along the line you went bananas. I think it was the second murder that unhinged you.'

'What are you talking about?'

'I never figured you for a killer,' he went on. 'But I suppose you could do it, as cool as you are. The second killing, in your apartment and all, I guess it unhinged you.'

'What are you talking about?'

'Sayin' I never heard of him. Grabow, for Christ's sake. Sayin' he's dangerous. Here's the poor sonofabitch lyin' dead on the floor of your apartment with one of them dentist things in his heart and you're tellin' me he's dangerous. Jesus, Bern. You're the one who's dangerous. Now how about if you tell me where you are and I'll bring you in nice and safe so you don't get shot by somebody who's gun-happy? It's the best way, believe me. You get yourself a good lawyer and you're on the street in seven years, maybe twelve or fifteen at the outside. Is that so bad?'

He was still talking, earnest, sincere, when I cradled the receiver.

19

'I've got him on the run now,' I said to Jillian. 'He's starting to panic. He knows I'm closing in on him and he's scared.'

'Who, Bernie?'

'Well, that's a good question. If I knew who he was I'd be in a lot better shape.'

'You said Grabow killed her.'

'I know.'

'But if Grabow killed her, who killed Grabow?'

'Grabow didn't kill her.'

'But it worked out so perfectly. The counterfeiting and the dental scalpels and everything.'

'I know.'

'So if Grabow *didn't* kill her—'

'Somebody else did. And killed Grabow so that I'd get blamed for it, although why I'd kill that gorilla in my own apartment is something else again. And whoever it was scattered some of Crystal's jewelry around so that I'd be locked into her murder, as if I wasn't already. That would be really intelligent of me, wouldn't it? Killing Grabow with another convenient dental scalpel and then tucking one of Crystal's bracelets under the corpse.'

'Is that where they found it?'

'How in hell do I know where they found it? Nyswander found it, whatever the hell it was. Diamonds, emeralds, I don't know. I haven't seen any of that garbage since I got it all packed up for someone else to steal. How the hell do I know where it was? I barely remember what it looked like.'

'You don't have to snap at me, Bernie.'

'I'm sorry,' I said. 'I've got my head in a frame and I can't think straight. It's all crazy, it's all circumstantial evidence and it doesn't make any sense, but I think they've got enough to nail me.'

'But you didn't do it,' she said, and then her gaze narrowed slightly. 'You *said* you didn't do it,' she said.

'I didn't. But if you put twelve jurors in a box and showed them all this evidence and I stood up there and said I didn't do it and they should believe me because it would have been stupid for me to do it that way – well, I know what my lawyer would say. He'd tell me to make a deal.'

'What do you mean?'

'He'd arrange for me to plead guilty to a reduced charge. And the District Attorney's office would be glad to get a sure conviction without the hazard of a trial, and I'd cop a plea to something like manslaughter or felony murder and I'd wind up with, I don't know, five-to-ten upstate. I could probably be back on the street in three years.' I frowned. 'Of course it may be different with Grabow dead, too. With two corpses in the picture they'd probably hold out for Murder Two and even with good behavior time and everything I'd be out of circulation for upward of five years.'

'But if you were innocent, how could your lawyer make you plead guilty?'

'He couldn't make me do anything. He could advise me.'

'That's why Craig switched lawyers. That man Blankenship just assumed he was guilty, and Mr Verrill knew he wasn't.'

'And now Craig's out on the street.'

'Uh-huh.'

'Even if I had a lawyer who believed in me, he'd have to be crazy to go to court with what they've got against me.'

She started to say something but I wasn't listening. I felt a thought slipping around somewhere in the back of my mind and I went after it like a dog trying to catch his tail.

I got the phone book. What was Frankie's last name? Ackerman, Frances Ackerman. Right. I found her listed as *Ackerman F* on East Twenty-seventh Street, just a few blocks from all her favorite bars. I dialed the number and listened to the telephone ring.

'Who are you calling, Bernie?'

I hung up, looked up Knobby Corcoran's number, dialed it. No answer.

I tried Frankie a second time. Nothing.

'Bernie?'

'I'm in a jam,' I said.

'I know.'

'I think I'm going to have to turn myself in.'

'But if you're innocent—'

'I'm wanted on murder charges, Jillian. Maybe I'll even wind up copping a plea. I hate the idea, but it looks as though I might not have any choice. Maybe I can get lucky and some new evidence will come to light while I'm awaiting trial. Maybe I can hire a private detective to investigate this thing professionally. I'm not having much luck as an amateur. But if I keep running around like this I'm taking the chance of getting shot by some trigger-happy cop. And the corpses are just piling

270

up around me and I'm scared. If I'd turned myself in a day ago nobody could have framed me for Grabow's murder.'

'What are you going to do? Go down to police headquarters?'

I shook my head. 'Kirschmann wanted me to surrender to him. He said I'd be safe that way. All he wanted was to be credited with the pinch. What I want is to have a lawyer present when I turn myself in. They can keep you incommunicado for seventy-two hours, just shuttling you around from one precinct to another without formally booking you. I don't know that they'd do that to me but I don't want to take any chances.'

'So do you want to call your lawyer?'

'I was just thinking about that. My lawyer's always been fine at representing me because I've always been guilty as charged. But what good would he be at representing an innocent man? It's exactly the same problem Craig had with Errol Blankenship.'

'So what do you want to do?'

'I want you to do me a favor,' I said. 'I want you to call Craig. I want him to get hold of his lawyer, What's-his-name, Verrill, and I want the two of them to meet me in his office.'

'Mr Verrill's office?'

'Let's make it Craig's office. That way we all know where it is. Central Park South, nice convenient location. It's twelve-thirty now so let's set the meeting for four o'clock because I've got a couple of things I have to do first.'

'You want Craig there too?'

I nodded. 'Definitely, and if he doesn't show up tell him I'm going to throw him to the wolves. He set me on the hunt for Crystal's jewelry. That fact is the only trump card I've got. The last thing he wants is for me to tell the police about our little arrangement, and there's a price for my silence. I want Verrill on my side. I want him to arrange the surrender to the police and I want the best defense money can buy. Maybe Verrill will wind up hiring a criminal lawyer to assist, maybe he'll bring in private eyes. I don't know how he'll do it and we can arrange that this afternoon, but if the two of them don't show up on schedule you can tell Craig I'll sing my little heart out.'

'Four o'clock at his office?'

'That's right.' I reached for my jacket. 'I've got some things to do,' I said. 'Some places to go. Make sure they get there on time, Jillian.' I went to the door, turned toward her. 'You come along, too,' I said. 'It might get interesting.'

'Are you serious, Bernie?'

I nodded. 'I'm a threat to Craig,' I told her. 'If that's my trump card, I don't want to throw it away. He and Verrill might agree to anything just to get me to turn myself in. Then they could forget all about it and leave me stranded after I told my story the way I promised. I want you around as a witness.'

I had a busy afternoon. I made some phone calls, I took some cabs, I talked to some people. All the while I kept looking over my shoulder for cops, and now and then I saw one. The city's overflowing with them, on foot and in cars, uniformed and otherwise. Fortunately none of the ones I saw were looking for me – or if they were I saw them first.

A few minutes after three I found the man I was looking for. He was in a Third Avenue saloon. He had his elbow on the bar and his foot on the brass rail, and when he saw me coming through the front door his eyes widened in recognition and his mouth curved in a smile.

'Cutty on the rocks,' he said. 'Get your ass over here and have a drink.'

'How's it going, Dennis?'

'It's going. That's all you can say for it. How's it with you, Ken?'

I extended my hand horizontally, palm down, and wagged it like an airplane tipping its wings. 'So-so,' I said.

'Ain't it the truth. Hey, Ace, bring Ken here a drink. Cutty on the rocks, right?'

Ace was wearing a sleeveless undershirt and an uncertain expression. He looked like a sailor who'd given up trying to find his way back to his ship and was making the best of a bad situation. He made me a drink and freshened Dennis's and went back to the television set. Dennis picked up his glass and said, 'You're a friend of Frankie's, right? Well, here's to Frankie, God love her.'

I took a sip. 'That's a coincidence,' I said, 'because I was trying to get hold of Frankie, Dennis.'

'You don't know?'

'Know what?'

He frowned. 'I saw you last night, didn't I? 'Course I did, you were drinking coffee. We were talking with Knobby. And I was waiting for Frankie to show up.'

'That's right.'

'She never showed. You didn't hear, Ken? I guess you didn't. She took her own life, Ken. Booze and pills. There was something bothering her about her friend, girl named Crystal. You know about Crystal, don't you?' I nodded. 'Well, she had some drinks and she took some Valium. Who's to say if she did it on purpose or if it was an accident, right? Who's to say?'

'Not us.'

'That's the truth. A hell of a nice woman and she took her life, accidentally or on purpose and who's to say, and God rest her is all *I* got to say.'

We drank to that. I'd been looking for Frankie, at her place, at some

272

of the bars in the neighborhood. I hadn't heard what happened to her but the news didn't surprise me. Maybe it was an accident. Maybe it was suicide. Or maybe it was neither and maybe she had help, the kind of help Crystal Sheldrake and Walter Grabow had had.

He said, 'I had a whatchacallit last night. A premonition. I sat there all night with Knobby, coasting on the drinks and trying her number from time to time. I was there waiting for her till Knobby closed the joint. Maybe I could of gone over there, done something.'

'When did Knobby close up, Dennis?'

'Who knows? Two, three o'clock. Who pays attention? Why?'

'He went back to his place but he didn't stay there. He packed a suitcase and left right away.'

'Yeah? So?'

'Maybe he got on a plane,' I said. 'Or maybe he met somebody and got into trouble.'

'I don't follow you, Ken. What's Knobby got to do with what happened to Frankie?'

I said, 'Well, I'll tell you, Dennis. It's sort of complicated.'

20

I was ten minutes early at the Central Park South office. I'd spoken to Jillian around two-thirty and she'd told me that the meeting with Craig and his lawyer was all set, but I wasn't surprised that they weren't there when I arrived and I had the feeling they wouldn't show at all. I planted myself in the hallway beside the frosted glass door, and at 3:58 on my watch the elevator doors opened and all three of them emerged, Craig and Jillian and a tall slender man in a vested black pinstripe suit. When he turned out to be Carson Verrill I was not wildly astonished.

Craig introduced us. The lawyer shook my hand harder than he had to and showed me a lot of his teeth. They were good teeth, but that didn't surprise me either, because it stood to reason that he patronized the World's Greatest Dentist. We stood there, Verrill and I shaking hands and Craig shifting his weight from foot to foot and clearing his throat a lot, while Jillian sifted through her purse until she found the key and unlocked the office door. She switched on the overhead light and a lamp on Marion the Receptionist's desk. Then she sat in Marion's chair and I motioned Craig and Verrill to the couch before turning to shut the outer door.

There was a little nervous chatter, Craig supplying something about the weather, Verrill saying he hoped I hadn't been waiting long. Just a few minutes, I said.

Then Verrill said, 'Well, perhaps we should come to the point, Mr Rhodenbarr. It's my understanding that you have something to trade. You've threatened to tell the police some story of my client's alleged involvement in a burglary of his ex-wife's apartment unless he underwrites the cost of your defense.'

'That's really something,' I said.

'I beg your pardon?'

'To be able to talk like that right off the bat. It's an amazing talent, but can't we put our cards on the table? Craig arranged for me to knock off Crystal's place. We're all friends here and we all know that, so what's with this alleged business?'

Craig said, 'Bernie, let's do this Carson's way, huh?'

Verrill glanced at Craig. I got the impression that he didn't appreciate

Craig's support quite so much as he'd have appreciated silence. He said, 'I'm not prepared to acknowledge anything of the sort, Mr Rhodenbarr. But I do want to get a firm understanding of your position. I've talked with Miss Paar and I've talked with Dr Sheldrake and I think I may be able to help you. I don't have a criminal practice and I don't see how I could undertake to prepare a defense per se, but if your interest lies in turning yourself in and arranging a guilty plea—'

'But I'm innocent, Mr Verrill.'

'It was my understanding—'

I smiled, showing some good teeth of my own. I said, 'I've been framed for a pair of murders, Mr Verrill. A very clever killer has been setting me up. He's not only clever. He's adaptable. He originally arranged things so that your client would wind up framed for murder. Then he found it would be more effective to shift the frame onto my shoulders. He's done a pretty good job, but I think you'll be able to see a way out for me if I explain what I think actually happened.'

'Miss Paar says you suspected this artist of murder. Then he was in turn murdered in your apartment.'

I nodded. 'I should have known he didn't kill Crystal. He might have strangled her or beaten her to death but stabbing wasn't Grabow's style. No, there was a third man, and he's the one who did both killings.'

'A third man?'

'There were three men in Crystal's life. Grabow, the artist. Knobby Corcoran, a bartender at a saloon in the neighborhood. And the Legal Beagle.'

'Who?'

'A colleague of yours. A lawyer named John who occasionally made the rounds of the neighborhood bars with Crystal. That's all anybody seems to know about him.'

'Then perhaps we ought to forget about him.'

'I don't think so. I think he killed her.'

'Oh?' Verrill's eyebrows climbed up his high forehead. 'Then perhaps it would help if we knew who he was.'

'It would,' I agreed, 'but it's going to be hard to find out. A woman named Frankie told me that he existed. She'd say "Heeeeeeeeere's Johnny!" just the way Ed McMahon does it. But sometime last night she drank a lot of gin and swallowed a whole bottle of Valium and died.'

Craig said, 'Then how are you going to find out who this Johnny is, Bernie?'

'It's a problem.'

'Maybe he doesn't even fit in. Maybe he was just another friend of Crystal's. She had a lot of friends.'

'And at least one enemy,' I said. 'But what you have to remember is that she was at the hub of something and somebody had to have a good reason to kill her. *You* had a reason, Craig, but you didn't kill her. You were framed.'

'Right.'

'And I had a reason – to avoid getting arrested for burglary. I didn't kill her either. But this Johnny had a real reason.'

'And what was that, Bern?'

'Grabow was a counterfeiter,' I explained. 'He started out as an artist, turned himself into a print-maker, and then decided to forget the artsy-fartsy stuff and go for the money. With his talents, he evidently figured that the easiest way to make money was to make money, and that's what he did.

'He was good at it. I saw samples of his work and they were just about as good as the stuff the government turns out. I also saw the place where he lived and worked, and for an unsuccessful artist he lived damn well. I can't prove it, but I've got a hunch he made those counterfeit plates a couple of years ago and passed bills himself, moving them one at a time across bars and cigarette counters. Remember, the man was an artist, not a professional criminal. He didn't have mob connections and didn't know anything about wholesaling big batches of schlock bills. He just ran off a few at a time on his hand-cranked printing press, then passed them one by one. When he had enough turned into real money he went and got himself some good furniture. It was a one-man cottage industry, and he could have gone on with it forever if he didn't get too greedy.'

'What does this have to do with—'

'With all of us? You'll see. I'd bet that Grabow covered a lot of ground, stopping in a bar long enough to cash a twenty, then moving on to another one. Somewhere along the way he ran into Crystal and they started keeping company. And maybe he wanted to show off or maybe she asked the right questions, but one way or another she learned he was a counterfeiter.

'She was already having a now-and-then affair with Knobby Corcoran. He was a bartender, but he was also a pretty savvy guy who probably knew how things could be bought and sold. Maybe it was her idea, maybe it was Knobby's, but I'd guess that the lawyer was the one who came up with it.'

'Came up with what?' Jillian wondered.

'The package. Grabow was printing the stuff up and unloading it a bill at a time. But why should he do that when he could wholesale a big batch of the stuff and coast on the proceeds for a year or two? The stuff he was turning out would change hands at a minimum of twenty cents on the dollar in large lots. If he could set up a deal for a quarter of a million dollars' worth, he could put fifty thousand dollars in his pocket and not wear out his liver buying drinks in bars all over town.

'So the lawyer set it up. He had Crystal show Knobby some sample twenties. Then Knobby could find somebody who was willing to pay fifty thou, say, for the counterfeit. Crystal would be in the middle. She'd get the real dough from Knobby and the schlock from Grabow, and she'd turn the dough over to Grabow and pass on the counterfeit to Knobby, and that way they wouldn't ever have to see each other. Grabow was crazy about his privacy. He didn't want anybody to know where he lived, so he'd be glad to work a deal that kept him out of the limelight.'

'And the lawyer set this up, Bern? This guy John?'

I nodded at Craig. 'Right.'

'What was in it for him?'

'Everything.'

'What do you mean?'

'Everything,' I said. 'Fifty thousand in cash, because he didn't intend for it to go to Grabow. And a quarter of a mill in counterfeit, because that wouldn't go to Knobby. He got each of them to deliver first. They were both sleeping with Crystal so each of them figured he could trust her. Maybe Crystal knew the lawyer was setting up a double cross. Maybe not. But when she got the money from Knobby she turned it over to the lawyer, and then Grabow delivered the counterfeit dough and she told him he'd get paid in a day or two, and then all the lawyer had to do was kill her and he was home free.'

'How do you figure that, Mr Rhodenbarr?'

'He already had the money from Knobby Corcoran, Mr Verrill. Now he kills Crystal and takes the counterfeit and that's the end of it. He'd have kept his own name out of it. As far as the others are concerned, Crystal's in the middle, setting up the exchange. When she's dead, what are they going to do? If anything, each one figures the other for a double cross. Maybe they kill each other. That's fine as far as the lawyer's concerned. He's home free. He's got the cash in hand and he can look around to make a deal on his own for the counterfeit. If he gets an average price that's another fifty thousand, so the whole deal's worth somewhere around a hundred thousand dollars to him, and there are people in this world who think that's enough to kill for. Even lawyers.'

Verrill smiled gently. 'There are members of the profession,' he said, 'who aren't as ethical as they might be.'

'Don't apologize,' I said. 'Nobody's perfect. You'll even run across an immoral burglar if you look long and hard enough.' I walked over to the window and looked down at the park and the horse-drawn hansom cabs queued up on Fifty-ninth Street. The sun was blocked by clouds now. It had been ducking in and out of them all afternoon. I said, 'Thursday's the night I went to Crystal's apartment looking for jewels. I wound up locked in the closet while she rolled around in the sack with a friend. Then the friend left. While I was picking my way out of the closet

Crystal was taking a shower. The doorbell interrupted her. She answered it and the lawyer came on in and stuck a dental scalpel in her heart.

'Then he walked past her to the bedroom. He hadn't just come to kill her. He was picking up the counterfeit money that she was holding, presumably for Knobby. She'd told him Grabow had delivered it previously in an attaché case, and he walked into the bedroom and saw an attaché case standing against the wall.

'Of course it was the wrong case. The case with the counterfeit was probably right there in the closet with me all along. I think that's probably where Crystal had stowed it, because why else would she automatically turn the key and lock me in the closet? She kept her jewelry where it was easy to get at. But there must have been something in that closet that she wasn't used to having around or she wouldn't have been such a fanatic on the subject of keeping the door locked.

'Well, the lawyer just grabbed that attaché case and took off. When he got home and opened it he found a ton of jewelry all rolled up in enough linen to keep it from rattling around. It wasn't what he'd wanted and it was too hot for him to unload it easily, but at least he had the fifty grand in cash free and clear and he could probably raise close to that much again on the jewelry when it was safe to show it around.

'Maybe he even planned to go back and take another shot at the counterfeit money. But Knobby Corcoran didn't give him the chance. Knobby switched shifts with the other bartender the day after Crystal was murdered, and he was the one who broke the police seals on her door and gave her apartment a second run-through. Maybe he knew where to look, maybe she'd said something like "Don't worry, it's all here on a shelf in my closet." Because he broke in and went home with the counterfeit money and tucked it away on the shelf in *his* closet.'

'How do you know that, Mr Rhodenbarr?'

'Simple. That's where I found it.'

'That's where you—'

'Found the case full of counterfeit twenties. How else would I know about them? I left them there to keep from rattling Knobby.'

Jillian knew better. I'd told her something about stowing the funny twenties in the bus locker and hoped she wouldn't pick this time to remember what I'd said. But she had something else on her mind.

'The scalpel,' she said. 'The lawyer killed Crystal with one of our dental scalpels.'

'Right.'

'Then he must have been a patient.'

'A lawyer named John,' Craig said. 'What lawyers do we have as patients?' He frowned and scratched his head. 'There's lots of lawyers,' he said, 'and John's not the scarcest name in the world, but—'

'It wouldn't have to be a patient,' I said. 'Try it this way. Crystal's been to Grabow's loft on King Street. She saw the dental instruments he used for his printmaking work and recognized them as the same line Craig stocks. That was a coincidence and she happened to mention it to the lawyer. And that made his choice of a murder weapon the simplest thing in the world. He'd use one of the dental implements. It would point to Craig, and if Craig somehow managed to get out from under, he could always find a way to steer the cops toward Grabow.'

I'd been pacing around. Now I went over and sat on the edge of Marion the Receptionist's desk. 'His plan was a pretty good one,' I said. 'There was just one thing to screw it up and that was me.'

'You, Bern?'

'Right,' I told Craig. 'Me. The cops had you in a cell and you were looking for a way out, and you decided to throw them your old buddy Bernie.'

'Bern, what choice did I have?' I looked at him. 'Besides,' he said, 'I knew *I* hadn't killed Crystal, and if you were in her apartment, and one of my scalpels, hell, it started looking as though you were trying to frame *me*, and—'

'Forget it,' I said. 'You were looking for a way out and you took it. And Knobby broke into the apartment and snatched the counterfeit money, and that break-in made it obvious there was more going on than a simple case of a man killing his ex-wife. The lawyer saw that he had to move quickly. There were loose threads around and he had to tie them off, because if the police ever really checked into Crystal's background his role in the whole affair might start to become evident.

'And he was worried about Grabow. Maybe the two of them had met. Maybe Grabow knew about the lawyer's relationship with Crystal, or maybe the lawyer didn't know for certain just how much talking Crystal might have done. For one reason or another, Grabow was a threat. And Grabow himself was nervous when I saw him. Maybe he got in touch with the lawyer. Anyway, he had to go, and the lawyer decided he might as well kill Grabow and tighten the frame around me at the same time. He managed somehow to get the artist over to my apartment, killed him with another of those goddamned dental scalpels, and planted a couple of pieces of Crystal's jewelry there to tie it all together for the police. Now why I would kill Grabow in the first place, and why I would kill him with a dental scalpel in my own apartment, and why I would then leave Crystal's jewels around, that was all beside the point. It might not make any absolute sense but it would certainly make the police put out a pick-up order on me, and of course that's what they did.' I drew a breath, looked at each of them in turn, Jillian and Craig and Carson Verrill. 'And that's where we are,' I said, 'and that's why we're here.'

The silence built up rather nicely. Finally Verrill broke it. He cleared his throat. 'You see the problem,' he said. 'You've developed a convincing case against this nameless attorney. But you don't know who he is and I gather it's not going to be terribly easy to track him down. You mentioned a woman, a friend of Crystal Sheldrake's?'

'Frankie Ackerman.'

'But did you say she killed herself?'

'She died mixing alcohol and Valium. It could have been an accident or it could have been suicide. She'd been brooding about Crystal and something was on her mind. It's not impossible that she got in touch with the lawyer directly. Maybe he fed her the booze and pills as part of his process of tying off loose ends.'

'That sounds a little farfetched, doesn't it?'

'A little,' I admitted. 'But either way she's dead.'

'Exactly. And a chance to identify this lawyer seems to have died with her. Now this bartender. Corcoran? Is that his name?'

'Knobby Corcoran.'

'And he has the counterfeit money?'

'He had it the last I saw of it, but that was yesterday evening. I'd guess he still has it and I'd guess he and the money are a long ways from here. After he closed the bar last night he went home and grabbed a suitcase and left town. I don't think he'll be back. Either all the killings scared him or he'd been planning all along to cross his mob associates. He was living on tips and leavings and maybe the sight of all that money was too much for him. Remember, it looked like a quarter of a million bucks, even if you could only get twenty cents on the dollar for it. I'll bet Knobby took a cab to Kennedy and a plane to someplace warm, and I wouldn't be surprised if a lot of counterfeit twenties turn up in the West Indies between now and next spring.'

Verrill nodded, frowning. 'Then you don't really have anything to work with,' he said slowly. 'You don't have any leads to the identity of this lawyer and you don't know who he is.'

'Well, that's not exactly true.'

'Oh?'

'I know who he is.'

'Really?'

'And I've even got some proof.'

'Indeed.'

I got up from the desk, opened the frosted glass door, motioned Dennis inside. 'This is Dennis,' I announced. 'He knew Crystal pretty well and he was a good friend of Frankie Ackerman.'

'She was a hell of a fine woman,' Dennis said.

'Dennis, that's Jillian Paar. And this is Dr Craig Sheldrake, and Mr Carson Verrill.'

'A pleasure,' he said to Jillian. 'Pleasure, Doc,' he said to Craig. And he smiled at Verrill.

To me – to all of us – he said, 'That's him.'

'Huh?'

'That's him,' he said again, pointing now at Carson Verrill. 'That's Crystal's boyfriend. That's the Legal Beagle. That's Johnny, all right.'

Verrill broke the silence. It took him a while to do it, and first he got up from the chair and extended himself to his full height, and when he spoke the words were on the anticlimactic side.

'This is ridiculous,' he said.

What I said wasn't much better. 'Murder,' I said, 'is always ridiculous.' I'm not proud of it but that's what I said.

'Ridiculous, Rhodenbarr. Who is this oaf and where did you find him?'

'His name's Dennis. He runs a parking garage.'

'I don't just run it. I happen to own it.'

'He happens to own it,' I said.

'I think he's been drinking. And I think you've taken leave of your senses, Rhodenbarr. First you try to manipulate me into defending you and now you accuse me of murder.'

'It does seem inconsistent,' I allowed. 'I guess I don't want you defending me after all. But I won't need anybody to defend me. You just have to confess to the two murders and the police'll probably drop their charges against me.'

'You must be out of your mind.'

'I should be, with the kind of week I've had. But I'm not.'

'Out of your mind. In the first place, my name's not John. Or hasn't that occurred to you?'

'It was a problem,' I admitted. 'When I first expected you I wondered if maybe your name was John Carson Verrill and you dropped the John. No such luck. Carson's your first name, all right, and your middle name is Woolford. Carson Woolford Verrill, the man with three last names. But you're the man Frankie Ackerman was talking about. It's pretty obvious, when you stop to think about it.'

'I don't follow you, Bernie.' Jillian did look puzzled, all right. 'If his name is Carson—'

I said, ' "And now, heeeeeeeere's Johnny." Johnny *Who*, Jillian?'

'Oh!'

'Right. There's millions of people named John, it's hardly a rare enough name to make Frankie go into Ed McMahon's routine every time she met somebody with the name. But Carson, that's something else again. That's not so common as a first name, and maybe it struck Frankie funny.'

'Ridiculous,' Verrill said. 'I'm a respectable married man. I love my wife and I've always been faithful to her. I was never involved with Crystal.'

'You're not that respectable,' Jillian said. 'You flirt.'

'Nonsense.'

'You'd have made a pass at me last night. You were sort of moving in that direction. But I wasn't interested and you backed off.'

'That's absurd.'

'You knew Crystal years ago,' I said. 'You knew her when she was married to Craig. That's right, isn't it?'

Craig confirmed that it was. 'Carson represented me in my divorce,' he said. 'Hey, maybe that's why I got such a reaming in the alimony. Maybe my trusted attorney was already hopping in the sack with my wife and the two of them teamed up to put me through the wringer.' The World's Greatest Dentist let that thought sink in, and his face took on a new set. Murder was one thing, he seemed to be thinking, but shafting a pal in the alimony department was really rotten. 'You sonofabitch,' he said.

'Craig, you can't believe—'

'I wish I had you in the chair right now. I'd grind your teeth clear to the gum line.'

'Craig—'

'You'll have free dental care for the next few years, Mr Verrill,' I said. 'Those penitentiary dentists are terrific. You're in for a treat.'

He turned on me, and if those weren't a killer's eyes then seeing's not believing. 'You're out of your mind,' he said. 'You have a lot of theories and nothing else. You don't have any proof.'

'That's what the bad guy always says in the movies,' I said. 'That's when you know he's really guilty, when he starts talking about the lack of proof.'

'You've got the prattling of a convicted burglar and a drunken car parker. That's all you've got.'

'What's this car-parker crap? I don't park the cars. I own the garage.'

'But as for hard evidence—'

'Well, it's a funny thing about evidence,' I said. 'You usually find it when you know what to look for. When the police start showing your photo around it's going to turn out that more people saw you with Crystal than you ever realized. You found a way to get past my doorman last night, and that couldn't have been the hardest thing in the world, but he or someone else in the building will probably remember you. And then there's the jewelry. You didn't plant all of Crystal's stuff at my place because you're too damned greedy for that. Where's the rest of it? Your apartment? A safe-deposit box?'

282

'They won't find any jewelry.'

'You sound pretty confident. I guess you found a safe place for it.'

'I never took any jewelry. I don't know what you're talking about.'

'Well, there's the counterfeit money. That ought to be enough to hang you.'

'What counterfeit money?'

'The twenties.'

'Ah, the elusive twenties.' He arched an eyebrow at me. 'I thought we were to understand that the equally elusive Knobby headed south with them.'

'That's what he must have done. But I've got a hunch there was a sample batch that Grabow ran off in advance, because I've got the damnedest feeling there's a couple thousand dollars' worth of those phony bills in your office.'

'In my office?'

'On Vesey Street. It's funny how deserted the downtown section is on a Sunday. It's as if a neutron bomb got rid of all the people and just left the buildings standing there. I've got a strong hunch there's a thick stack of twenties in the center drawer of your desk, and I'll bet they're a perfect match to the plates in Walter Grabow's loft.'

He took a step toward me, then drew back. 'My office,' he said.

'Uh-huh. Nice place you've got there, incidentally. No view of the park like Craig has, of course, but you can see a little of the harbor from the one window, and that's something.'

'You planted counterfeit money there?'

'Don't be silly. Knobby took the money south. How could I plant it?'

'I should have killed you, Rhodenbarr. If I'd known you were in the closet I could have set it all up right then and there. I'd have left it looking as though you and Crystal killed each other. You stabbed her and she shot you, something like that. I could have worked it out.'

'And then you could have taken the twenties from the closet while you were at it. It would have simplified things, all right.'

He wasn't even listening to me. 'I had to get rid of Grabow. I'd met him. And she might have talked to him. Knobby was just someone who took her home now and then after a hard night's drinking, but she had a real relationship with Grabow. He could have known my name, could have guessed I was involved.'

'So you got him to meet you at my apartment?'

'He thought he was meeting you. I had his phone number. It was unlisted but of course he'd given it to Crystal. I called him, told him to come up to your apartment. I told him I had his counterfeit bills and I'd give them back to him. It wasn't hard getting past your doorman.'

'It never is. How did you get into the apartment itself?'

'I kicked the door in. The way they do on television.'

So much for my pick-proof locks. One of these days I'll get one of

283

those Fox police numbers like Grabow had. Not that it had done Grabow much good—

'Then when Grabow got there the doorman buzzed upstairs and I told him to send the man up. Naturally the doorman assumed I was you.'

'Naturally.'

'Grabow said I didn't seem like a burglar. But he wasn't at all suspicious.' He considered for a moment. 'He was easier to kill than Crystal. He was big and strong, but it wasn't hard to kill him.'

'They say it gets easier as you go along.'

'I was hoping you'd come. I'd make it look as though you fought and killed each other. But you didn't come home.'

'No,' I said. I started to say I was at Jillian's, then remembered Craig was there. 'I was afraid the police would have the place staked out,' I said, 'so I got a hotel room.'

'I didn't wait that long anyway. I was uncomfortable staying there with his body in the middle of the room.'

'I can understand that.'

'So I left. The doorman didn't notice me coming or going. And I didn't leave any fingerprints there. I don't think it means that much, a little counterfeit money planted in my desk. I'm a respected attorney. When it comes down to my word against yours, who do you think the police will believe?'

'What about these people, Verrill?'

'What, this drunk from the garage?'

'I own the damn place,' Dennis said. 'It's not like it was a hot-dog wagon. You talk about a parking garage and you're talking about a piece of profitable real estate.'

'I don't think Craig will want to tell the police everything that's come to light,' Verrill went on. 'And I trust Miss Paar knows which side of her bread holds the butter.'

'It won't work, Verrill.'

'Of course it will.'

'It won't.' I raised my voice. 'Ray, that's enough, isn't it? Come on out and arrest this son of a bitch so we can all go home.'

The door to the inner office opened and Ray Kirschmann came through it. 'This is Ray Kirschmann,' I told them. 'He's a policeman. I let Ray in earlier before I went to pick up Dennis. I suppose that was forward of me, Craig, picking your lock and everything, but it's sort of a habit of mine. Ray, this is Craig Sheldrake. Jillian you've met. This is Carson Verrill, he's the murderer, and this fellow here is Dennis. Dennis, I don't believe I know your last name.'

'It's Hegarty, but don't apologize, for God's sake. Here I had your name all wrong myself. I was calling you Ken.'

'Mistakes happen.'

'Jesus,' Ray said to me. 'You're the coolest thing since dry ice.'

284

'I've got the guts of a burglar.'

'You said it, fella.'

'No, as a matter of fact *you* said it. Do you want to read Carson here his rights?'

'The guts of a burglar.'

I let him go on thinking so, but weren't we all pretty cool? Dennis was positively gelid, identifying Verrill so beautifully when he'd never seen the man before in his life. If I hadn't introduced him all around, he might just as easily have picked Craig as the elusive Legal Beagle.

And I'm not so sure I had the ice-cold nerves he'd credited me with, either. I have to admit I got pretty shaky when Verrill drew yet another dental scalpel from his jacket pocket while Ray droned on about his right to remain silent. Ray was reading from the Miranda card and didn't even see what was going on, and my jaw dropped and I froze, and then Carson Verrill gave out with a desperate little yelp and stuck the scalpel straight in his own heart. Then I went back to being cool again.

21

'The usual thing,' I told Jillian. 'He spent more than he earned, he dropped some money in the stock market, he got himself in debt up to his ears, and then he misappropriated funds from a couple of estates he was handling. He needed money, and you'd be surprised what people will do for money. He probably started the deal in motion with the idea of picking up a commission of a few grand. Then he saw a way to get the whole thing. Besides, by this time Crystal was probably more of a liability than an asset. The relationship had dragged on for years and here was a way for him to end it once and for all and pick up a hundred thousand dollars in the process.'

'He seemed so respectable.'

'I guess he didn't kill Frankie Ackerman. He didn't mention it and it's too late to ask him now. I thought she might have called him last night but I guess her death was either an accident or suicide. If he'd killed her he'd have done it with a dental scalpel.'

She shuddered. 'I was looking right at him when he did it.'

'So was I. So was everybody but Ray.'

'Every time I close my eyes I see him doing it, stabbing himself in the chest.'

It bothered me, too, but I had an image to maintain and wasn't about to show it. 'It was considerate of him,' I said breezily. 'He saved the state the cost of a trial, not to mention the expense of housing and feeding him for a few years. And he gave Craig an opportunity to keep out of the limelight and made Ray Kirschmann a few dollars richer.'

And that was neat, wasn't it? A few thousand dollars had changed ownership, moving from Craig to Ray, and as a result certain details of the crime would never find their way into the record books. There hadn't been any burglary, for example. I was never in the place on Gramercy Park. With the right murderer tagged for the murders and nobody in a position to complain, it was easy enough to sweep unpleasant details under the rug.

I leaned back, took a sip of wine. It was night-time and I was at Jillian's place and I didn't have to worry about the police dropping in. Sooner or later Todras and Nyswander would collect some kind of statement from me, but in the meantime I had other things on my mind.

I moved to put an arm around Jillian.

She drew away.

I stretched, forced a yawn. 'Well,' I said, 'I guess it might not be a bad idea to take a shower, huh? I haven't had a chance to change my clothes, and—'

'Bernie.'

'What?'

'I, uh, well, the thing is Craig's coming over soon.'

'Oh.'

'He said he'd be coming over around nine-thirty.'

'I see.'

She turned to look at me, her eyes round and sorrowful. 'Well, I have to be practical,' she said. 'Don't I?'

'Sure you do.'

'I was upset with him because of the way he acted, Bernie. Well, it's certainly true that some people are better under pressure than others. And different people work well under different kinds of pressure. Craig's a dentist.'

'The World's Greatest Dentist.'

'When he's doing some tricky work on a patient, he's got nerves of steel. But he wasn't prepared for being arrested and thrown in a jail cell.'

'Few people are.'

'Anyway, he's serious about me.'

'Right.'

'And he's a fine man who is well established in a decent profession. He's respectable.'

'Carson Verrill was respectable.'

'And he's got security, and that's important. Bernie, you're a burglar.'

'True.'

'You don't save money. You live from one job to the next. You could wind up in jail at any time.'

'No argument.'

'And you probably wouldn't want to get married anyway.'

'Nope,' I said, 'I wouldn't.'

'So I'd be crazy to throw away something solid with Craig for . . . for nothing. Wouldn't I?'

I nodded. 'No question about it, Jillian.'

Her lower lip trembled. 'Then how come I feel *rotten* about it? Bernie—'

It was time to reach out and take her in my arms and kiss her. It was definitely time to do just that, but instead I put my wineglass on the coffee table and got to my feet. 'Getting late,' I said. 'I'm tired, believe it

287

or not. Had a busy day, all that running around and everything. And you want to freshen up so you'll be at your best when Mr Thirsty drops in. Me, I want to get on home and hang a couple of new locks on my door and take a shower.'

'Bernie, we could still, uh, see each other. Couldn't we?'

'No,' I said. 'No, I don't think we could, Jillian.'

'Bernie, am I making a big mistake?'

I gave the question some real thought, and the answer I supplied was the honest one. 'No,' I said. 'You're not.'

In the cab heading through the park I had a moment or two where I felt like Sidney Carton. *A far, far better thing that I do, than I have ever done.* And all that crap about how noble it is to lay down one's life for a friend.

Except crap was what it was, all right. Because the World's Greatest Dentist wasn't all that much of a friend, and what was I giving up anyway? She was cute and cuddly and she made good coffee, but lots of women are cute and cuddly and into more interesting things than the polishing of teeth. And I've never met one yet who makes better coffee than I make for myself, with my filter pot and my custom-blended mixture of Colombian and Guatemalan beans.

The closest I came to Sidney Carton was that I was showing a little quiet class, which is about what Carson Verrill did when he died neatly instead of doing something gross like taking a header out the window. Because I could have complicated that young woman's life no end.

I could have told her, for example, who the ardent lover was who'd been with Crystal while I was cooped up in her closet. I could have said it was none other than Craig himself, and the What's-Her-Name he'd said he had to hurry back to was none other than Jillian herself, and I hadn't recognized his voice because the closet muffled it. I don't know if that's true or not. It would explain some of Craig's confused behavior, and I really tried not to hear the voice and might not have recognized it if it was Craig. But I never pursued the question, not then and not later on. To this day I don't know if it was him.

If I'd advanced the theory, though, it certainly could have screwed things up between the two of them.

But why play dog in the manger?

Or I could have told her that burglary wasn't quite the dead-end profession it might appear to be, and that this case, for all the mess it had been, was by no means leaving me destitute. I might have alluded to the quarter of a million dollars' worth of queer twenties which, but for a couple thousand planted in Verrill's desk, still reposed in a locker at Port Authority. They hadn't gone anywhere with Knobby, of course, all that double-talk notwithstanding. Knobby'd gotten his ass out of town the minute he saw they were gone, because he knew some mob heavies were going to expect him to turn up with either fifty grand in cash or five times that amount in counterfeit, and since he couldn't do either New York was a lousy place to be.

So I'd find somebody who knew somebody, and if I couldn't get twenty or thirty grand as my end of the transaction, well, I'd be surprised. Of course I could always decide to do it Grabow's way and pass the bills myself one at a time, but for that occupation you don't need the guts of a burglar. You have to have the gall of a con man and the patience of a saint, and that's a hell of a combination.

For that matter, I could have told her Crystal's jewels still existed somewhere, that Verrill couldn't have sold them yet and certainly hadn't stashed them where the police would trip over them. When things cooled down a little I might have a go at turning them up. So there might not be a future in burglary, and God knows there's no pension plan and no retirement benefits, but if there's no future there's a pretty good present with it, and I was coming out with fair compensation for what had been admittedly a pretty rough couple of days.

So I could have had a shot at changing her mind. But if I had to go through all that then she wasn't worth it, so the hell with her.

There's plenty of women in this world.

Like that one I talked to on the phone. Narrow-back Gallery. What the hell was her name? Denise. Denise Raphaelson. She'd been lots of fun over the phone, and fun was something Jillian was manifestly not. Cute and cuddly is nice, but after you've done the dirty deed a few times it's nice if you can also lie around and have a few laughs.

Of course she could turn out to be a beast. Or the chemistry in person could be far different from what it had been over the phone. But in a day or three I'd go look at some paintings, and if the signs were right I'd introduce myself, and if it worked that would be nice, and if it didn't that would be okay, too.

Plenty of women in this world.

But where was I going to find another dentist?

The Burglar Who
Liked to Quote Kipling

For Cheryl Morrison

When from 'ouse to 'ouse you're 'untin' you must always work in pairs—
    It 'alves the gain, but safer you will find—
For a single man gets bottled on them twisty-wisty stairs.
    An' a woman comes and clobs 'im from be'ind.
When you've turned 'em inside out, an' it seems beyond a doubt
    As if there weren't enough to dust a flute
      (*Cornet:* Toot! toot!)—
Before you sling your 'ook, at the 'ouse-tops take a look,
    For it's underneath the tiles they 'ide the loot.
      (*Chorus.*) 'Ow the loot!
          Bloomin' loot!
        That's the thing to make the boys git up an' shoot!
          It's the same with dogs an' men,
          If you'd make 'em come again
        Clap 'em forward with a Loo! loo! Lulu! Loot!
        Whoopee! Tear 'im, puppy! Loo! loo! Lulu!
          Loot! loot! Loot!

                    – Rudyard Kipling
                    'Loot'

1

I suppose he must have been in his early twenties. It was hard to be sure of his age because there was so little of his face available for study. His red-brown beard began just below his eyes, which in turn lurked behind thick-lensed horn-rims. He wore a khaki army shirt, unbuttoned, and beneath it his T-shirt advertised the year's fashionable beer, a South Dakota brand reputedly brewed with organic water. His pants were brown corduroy, his running shoes blue with a gold stripe. He was toting a Braniff Airlines flight bag in one ill-manicured hand and the Everyman's Library edition of *The Poems of William Cowper* in the other.

He set the book down next to the cash register, reached into a pocket, found two quarters, and placed them on the counter alongside the book.

'Ah, poor Cowper,' I said, picking up the book. Its binding was shaky, which was why it had found its way to my bargain table. 'My favorite's "The Retired Cat." I'm pretty sure it's in this edition.' He shifted his weight from foot to foot while I scanned the table of contents. 'Here it is. Page one-fifty. You know the poem?'

'I don't think so.'

'You'll love it. The bargain books are forty cents or three for a dollar, which is even more of a bargain. You just want the one?'

'That's right.' He pushed the two quarters an inch or so closer to me. 'Just the one.'

'Fine,' I said. I looked at his face. All I could really see was his brow, and it looked untroubled, and I would have to do something about that. 'Forty cents for the Cowper, and three cents for the Governor in Albany, mustn't forget him, and what does that come to?' I leaned over the counter and dazzled him with my pearly-whites. 'I make it thirty-two dollars and seventy cents,' I said.

'Huh?'

'That copy of Byron. Full morocco, marbled endpapers, and I believe it's marked fifteen dollars. The Wallace Stevens is a first edition and it's a bargain at twelve. The novel you took was only three dollars or so, and I suppose you just wanted to read it because you couldn't get anything much reselling it.'

'I don't know what you're talking about.'

I moved out from behind the counter, positioning myself between him and the door. He didn't look as though he intended to sprint but he was wearing running shoes and you never can tell. Thieves are an unpredictable lot.

'In the flight bag,' I said. 'I assume you'll want to pay for what you took.'

'This?' He looked down at the flight bag as if astonished to find it dangling from his fingers. 'This is just my gym stuff. You know – sweat socks, a towel, like that.'

'Suppose you open it.'

Perspiration was beading on his forehead but he was trying to tough it out. 'You can't make me,' he said. 'You've got no authority.'

'I can call a policeman. He can't make you open it, either, but he can walk you over to the station house and book you, and *then* he can open it, and do you really want that to happen? Open the bag.'

He opened the bag. It contained sweat socks, a towel, a pair of lemon-yellow gym shorts, and the three books I had mentioned along with a nice clean first edition of Steinbeck's *The Wayward Bus*, complete with dust wrapper. It was marked $17.50, which seemed a teensy bit high.

'I didn't get that here,' he said.

'You have a bill of sale for it?'

'No, but—'

I scribbled briefly, then gave him another smile. 'Let's call it fifty dollars even,' I said, 'and let's have it.'

'You're charging me for the Steinbeck?'

'Uh-huh.'

'But I had it with me when I came in.'

'Fifty dollars,' I said.

'Look, I don't want to *buy* these books.' He rolled his eyes at the ceiling. 'Oh God, why did I have to come in here in the first place? Look, I don't want any trouble.'

'Neither do I.'

'And the last thing I want is to buy anything. Look, keep the books, keep the Steinbeck too, the hell with it. Just let me get out of here, huh?'

'I think you should buy the books.'

'I don't have the money. I got fifty cents. Look, keep the fifty cents too, okay? Keep the shorts and the towel, keep the sweat socks, okay? Just let me get the hell out of here, okay?'

'You don't have any money?'

'No, nothing. Just the fifty cents. Look—'

'Let's see your wallet.'

'What are you – I don't have a wallet.'

'Right hip pocket. Take it out and hand it to me.'

'I don't believe this is happening.'

I snapped my fingers. 'The wallet.'

It was a nice enough black pinseal billfold, complete with the telltale outline of a rolled condom to recall my own lost adolescence. There was almost a hundred dollars in the currency compartment. I counted out fifty dollars in fives and tens, replaced the rest, and returned the wallet to its owner.

'That's my money,' he said.

'You just bought books with it,' I told him. 'Want a receipt?'

'I don't even want the books, dammit.' His eyes were watering behind the thick glasses. 'What am I going to do with them, anyway?'

'I suppose reading them is out. What did you plan to do with them originally?'

He stared at his track shoes. 'I was going to sell them.'

'To whom?'

'I don't know. Some store.'

'How much were you going to get for them?'

'I don't know. Fifteen, twenty dollars.'

'You'd wind up taking ten.'

'I suppose so.'

'Fine,' I said. I peeled off one of his tens and pressed it into his palm. 'Sell them to me.'

'Huh?'

'Saves running from store to store. I can use good books, they're the very sort of item I stock, so why not take the ten dollars from me?'

'This is crazy,' he said.

'Do you want the books or the money? It's up to you.'

'I don't want the books.'

'Do you want the money?'

'I guess so.'

I took the books from him and stacked them on the counter. 'Then put it in your wallet,' I said, 'before you lose it.'

'This is the craziest thing ever. You took fifty bucks from me for books I didn't want and now you're giving me ten back. I'm out forty dollars, for God's sake.'

'Well, you bought high and sold low. Most people try to work it the other way around.'

'*I* should call a cop. I'm the one getting robbed.'

I packed his gym gear into the Braniff bag, zipped it shut, handed it to him. Then I extended a forefinger and chucked him under his hairy chin.

'A tip,' I said.

'Huh?'

'Get out of the business.'

He looked at me.

'Find another line of work. Quit lifting things. You're not terribly good at it and I'm afraid you're temperamentally unsuited to the life that goes with it. Are you in college?'

'I dropped out.'

'Why?'

'It wasn't relevant.'

'Few things are, but why don't you see if you can't get back in? Pick up a diploma and find some sort of career that suits you. You're not cut out to be a professional thief.'

'A professional—' He rolled his eyes again. 'Jesus, I ripped off a couple of books. Don't make a life's work out of it, huh?'

'Anybody who steals things for resale is a professional criminal,' I told him. 'You just weren't doing it in a very professional manner, that's all. But I'm serious about this. Get out of the business.' I laid a hand lightly on his wrist. 'Don't take this the wrong way,' I said, 'but the thing is you're too dumb to steal.'

2

After he'd left I tucked his forty dollars into my wallet, where it promptly became *my* forty dollars. I marked the Steinbeck down to fifteen dollars before shelving it and its companions. While doing this I spotted a few errant volumes and put them back where they belonged.

Browsers came and went. I made a few sales from the bargain table, then moved a Heritage Club edition of Virgil's *Eclogues* (boxed, the box water-damaged, slight rubbing on spine, price $8.50). The woman who bought the Virgil was a little shopworn herself, with a blocky figure and a lot of curly orange hair. I'd seen her before but this was the first time she'd bought anything, so things were looking up.

I watched her carry Virgil home, then settled in behind the counter with a Grosset & Dunlap reprint of *Soldiers Three*. I'd been working my way through my limited stock of Kipling lately. Some of the books were ones I'd read years ago, but I was reading *Soldiers Three* for the first time and really enjoying my acquaintance with Ortheris and Learoyd and Mulvaney when the little bells above my door tinkled to announce a visitor.

I looked up to see a man in a blue uniform lumbering across the floor toward me. He had a broad, open, honest face, but in my new trade one learned quickly not to judge a book by its cover. My visitor was Ray Kirschmann, the best cop money could buy, and money could buy him seven days a week.

'Hey, Bern,' he said, and propped an elbow on the counter. 'Read any good books lately?'

'Hello, Ray.'

'Watcha readin'?' I showed him. 'Garbage,' he said. 'A whole store full of books, you oughta read somethin' decent.'

'What's decent?'

'Oh, Joseph Wambaugh, Ed McBain. Somebody who tells it straight.'

'I'll keep it in mind.'

'How's business?'

'Not too bad, Ray.'

'You just sit here, buy books, sell books, and you make a livin'. Right?'

'It's the American way.'

'Uh-huh. Quite a switch for you, isn't it?'

'Well, I like working days, Ray.'

'A whole career change, I mean. Burglar to bookseller. You know what that sounds like? A title. You could write a book about it. *From Burglar to Bookseller*. Mind a question, Bernie?'

And what if I did? 'No,' I said.

'What the hell do you know about books?'

'Well, I was always a big reader.'

'In the jug, you mean.'

'Even on the outside, all the way back to childhood. You know what Emily Dickinson said. "There is no frigate like a book." '

'Frig it is right. You didn't just run around buyin' books and then open up a store.'

'The store was already here. I was a customer over the years, and I knew the owner and he wanted to sell out and go to Florida.'

'And right now he's soakin' up the rays.'

'As a matter of fact, I heard he opened up another store in St Petersburg. Couldn't take the inactivity.'

'Well, good for him. How'd you happen to come up with the scratch to buy this place, Bernie?'

'I came into a few dollars.'

'Uh-huh. A relative died, somethin' like that.'

'Something like that.'

'Right. What I figure, you dropped out of sight for a month or so during the winter. January, wasn't it?'

'And part of February.'

'I figure you were down in Florida doin' what you do best, and you hit it pretty good and walked with a short ton of jewelry. I figure you wound up with a big piece of change and decided Mrs Rhodenbarr's boy Bernard oughta fix hisself up with a decent front.'

'That's what you figure, Ray?'

'Uh-huh.'

I thought for a minute. 'It wasn't Florida,' I said.

'Nassau, then. St Thomas. What the hell.'

'Actually, it was California. Orange County.'

'Same difference.'

'And it wasn't jewels. It was a coin collection.'

'You always went for them things.'

'Well, they're a terrific investment.'

'Not with you on the loose they aren't. You made out like a bandit on the coins, huh?'

'Let's say I came out ahead.'

'And bought this place.'

302

'That's right. Mr Litzauer didn't want a fortune for it. He set a fair price for the inventory and threw in the fixtures and the good will.'

'Barnegat Books. Where'd you get the name?'

'I kept it. I didn't want to have to spring for a new sign. Litzauer had a summer place at Barnegat Light on the Jersey shore. There's a light-house on the sign.'

'I didn't notice. You could call it Burglar Books. "These books are a steal" – there's your slogan. Get it?'

'I'm sure I will sooner or later.'

'Hey, are you gettin' steamed? I didn't mean nothin' by it. It's a nice front, Bern. It really is.'

'It's not a front. It's what I do.'

'Huh?'

'It's what I do for a living, Ray, and it's *all* I do for a living. I'm in the book business.'

'Sure you are.'

'I'm serious about this.'

'Serious. Right.'

'I am.'

'Uh-huh. Listen, the reason I dropped in, I was thinkin' about you just the other day. What it was, my wife was gettin' on my back. You ever been married?'

'No.'

'You're so busy gettin' settled, maybe marriage is the next step. Nothin' like it for settlin' a man. What she wanted, here it's October already and she's expectin' a long winter. You never met my wife, did you?'

'I talked to her on the phone once.'

'"The leaves are turnin' early, Ray. That means a cold winter." That's what she tells me. If the trees don't turn until late, then *that* means a cold winter.'

'She likes it cold?'

'What she likes is if it's cold and she's warm. What she's drivin' at is a fur coat.'

'Oh.'

'She goes about five-six, wears a size-sixteen dress. Sometimes she diets down to a twelve, sometimes she packs in the pasta and gets up to an eighteen. Fur coats, I don't figure they got to fit like gloves anyway, right?'

'I don't know much about them.'

'What she wants is mink. No wild furs or endangered species because she's a fanatic on the subject. Minks, see, they grow the little bastards on these ranches, so there's none of that sufferin' in traps, and the animal's not endangered or any of that stuff. All that they do is they gas 'em and skin 'em out.'

'How nice for the minks. It must be like going to the dentist.'

'Far as the color, I'd say she's not gonna be too fussy. Just so it's one of your up-to-date colors. Your platinum, your champagne. Not the old dark-brown shades.'

I nodded, conjuring up an image of Mrs Kirschmann draped in fur. I didn't know what she looked like, so I allowed myself to picture a sort of stout Edith Bunker.

'Oh,' I said suddenly. 'There's a reason you're telling me this.'

'Well, I was thinkin', Bern.'

'I'm out of the business, Ray.'

'What I was thinkin', you might run into a coat in the course of things, know what I mean? I was thinkin' that you and me, we go back a ways, we been through a lot, the two of us, and—'

'I'm not a burglar anymore, Ray.'

'I wasn't countin' on a freebie, Bernie. Just a bargain.'

'I don't steal anymore, Ray.'

'I hear you talkin', Bern.'

'I'm not as young as I used to be. Nobody ever is but these days I'm starting to feel it. When you're young nothing scares you. When you get older everything does. I don't ever want to go inside again, Ray. I don't like prisons.'

'These days they're country clubs.'

'Then they changed a whole hell of a lot in the past few years, because I swear I never cared for them myself. You meet a better class of people on the D train.'

'Guy like you, you could get a nice job in the prison library.'

'They still lock you in at night.'

'So you're straight, right?'

'That's right.'

'I been here how long? All that time you haven't had a single person walk in the store.'

'Maybe the uniform keeps 'em away, Ray.'

'Maybe business ain't what it might be. You been in the business how long, Bern? Six months?'

'Closer to seven.'

'Bet you don't even make the rent.'

'I do all right.' I marked my place in *Soldiers Three*, closed the book, put it on the shelf behind the counter. 'I made a forty-dollar profit from one customer earlier this afternoon and I swear it was easier than stealing.'

'Is that a fact. You're a guy made twenty grand in an hour and a half when things fell right.'

'And went to jail when they didn't.'

'Forty bucks. I can see where that'd really have you turning hand-springs.'

304

'There's a difference between honest money and the other kind.'

'Yeah, and the difference comes to somethin' like $19,960. This here, Bern, this is nickels and dimes. Let's be honest. You can't live on this.'

'I never stole that much, Ray. I never lived that high. I got a small apartment on the Upper West Side, I stay out of night clubs, I do my own wash in the machines in the basement. The store's steady. You want to give me a hand with this?'

He helped me drag the bargain table in from the sidewalk. He said, 'Look at this. A cop and a burglar both doin' physical work. Somebody should take a picture. What do you get for these? Forty cents, three for a buck? And that's keepin' you in shirts and socks, huh?'

'I'm a careful shopper.'

'Look, Bern, if there's some reason you don't wanna help me out on this coat thing—'

'Cops,' I said.

'What about cops?'

'A guy rehabilitates himself and you refuse to believe it. You talk yourselves hoarse telling me to go straight—'

'When the hell did I ever tell you to go straight? You're a first-class burglar. Why would I tell you to change?'

He let go of it while I filled a shopping bag with hardcover mysteries and began shutting down for the night. He told me about his partner, a clean-cut and soft-spoken young fellow with a fondness for horses and a wee amphetamine habit.

'All he does is lose and bitch about it,' Ray complained, 'until this past week when he starts pickin' the ponies with x-ray vision. Now all he does is win, and I swear I liked him better when he was losin'.'

'His luck can't last forever, Ray.'

'That's what I been tellin' myself. What's that, steel gates across the windows? You don't take chances, do you?'

I drew the gates shut, locked them. 'Well, they were already here,' I said stiffly. 'Seems silly not to use them.'

'No sense makin' it easy for another burglar, huh? No honor among thieves, isn't that what they say? What happens if you forget the key, huh, Bern?'

He didn't get an answer, nor do I suppose he expected one. He chuckled instead and laid a heavy hand on my shoulder. 'I guess you'd just call a locksmith,' he said. 'You couldn't pick the lock, not bein' a burglar anymore. All you are is a guy who sells books.'

Barnegat Books is on East Eleventh Street between Broadway and University Place. When I'd finished locking up I carried my shopping bag two doors east to a dog-grooming salon called the Poodle Factory. Carolyn Kaiser had a skittish Yorkie up on the grooming table and was buffing its little nails. She said, 'Hey, is it that time already? Just let me

305

finish with Prince Philip here and I'll be ready to go. If I don't get a drink in me soon I'll start yipping like a chihuahua.'

I got comfortable on the pillow sofa while Carolyn put the final touches on the terrier's pedicure and popped him back in his cage. During the course of this she complained at length about her lover's misbehavior. Randy had come home late the previous night, drunk and disheveled and marginally disorderly, and Carolyn was sick of it.

'I think it's time to end the relationship,' she told me, 'but the question is how do I *feel* about ending the relationship? And the answer is I don't *know* how I feel because I can't get in *touch* with my feelings, and I figure if I can't get in touch with them I might as well not feel them altogether, so let's go someplace with a liquor license, because all I want to feel right now is better. And how was *your* day, Bernie?'

'A little long.'

'Yeah, you do look faintly tuckered. Let's go, huh? I'm so sick of the smell of this place. I feel like I'm wearing Wet Dog perfume.'

We ducked around the corner to a rather tired saloon called the Bum Rap. The jukebox leaned toward country and western, and Barbara Mandrell was singing about adultery as we took stools at the long dark bar. Carolyn ordered a vodka martini on the rocks. I asked for club soda with lime and got a nod from the bartender and a puzzled stare from Carolyn.

'It's October,' she said.

'So?'

'Lent's in the spring.'

'Right.'

'Doctor's orders or something? Giving the old liver a rest?'

'Just don't feel like a drink tonight.'

'Fair enough. Well, here's to crime. Hey, did I just say something wrong?'

So that got me onto the subject of Ray Kirschmann and his mink-loving wife, and it became Carolyn's turn to make sympathetic noises. We've become good at playing that role for one another. She's crowding thirty, with Dutch-cut dark-brown hair and remarkably clear blue eyes. She stands five-one in high heels and never wears them, and she's built like a fire hydrant, which is dangerous in her line of work.

I met her around the time I took over the bookshop. I didn't know Randy as well because I didn't see as much of her; the Poodle Factory was a solo venture of Carolyn's. Randy's a stewardess, or was until she got grounded for biting a passenger. She's taller and thinner than Carolyn, and a year or two younger, and faintly flighty. Randy and I are friends, I suppose, but Carolyn and I are soulmates.

My soulmate clucked sympathetically. 'Cops are a pain,' she said. 'Randy had an affair with a cop once. I ever tell you?'

'I don't think so.'

'She had this phase she went through, three months or so of panic before she was ready to come out as a lesbian. I think it was some kind of denial mechanism. She slept with dozens of men. This one cop was impotent and she made fun of him and he held his gun to her head and she thought he was going to kill her. Which somebody ought to, and why the *hell* am I talking about her again, will you tell me that?'

'Beats me.'

'You got anything on tonight? You still seeing the woman from the art gallery?'

'We decided to go our separate ways.'

'What about the crazy poet?'

'We never really hit it off.'

'Then why don't you come by for dinner? I got something sensational working in the slow cooker. I put it in this morning before I remembered how mad I was. It's this Flemish beef stew with beer and shallots and mushrooms and all kinds of good things. I got plenty of Amstel for us to wash it down with, plus some Perrier if you're serious about this temperance bit.'

I sipped my club soda. 'I wish I could,' I said. 'But not tonight.'

'Something on?'

'Just that I'm beat. I'm going straight home, and the most active thing I intend to do is say a quick prayer to St John of God.'

'Is he somebody I should know about?'

'He's the patron saint of booksellers.'

'Yeah? Who's the patron saint of dog groomers?'

'Damned if I know.'

'I hope we've got one. I've been bitten and scratched and peed on and I ought to have someplace to turn. As far as that goes, I wonder if there's a patron saint of lesbians. All those cloistered nuns, there damn well ought to be. Seriously, do you suppose there is?'

I shrugged. 'I could probably find out. I only know about St John of God because Mr Litzauer had a framed picture of him in the back room of the shop. But there must be books with lists of the patron saints. I've probably got something in the store, as far as that goes.'

'It must be great, having that shop. Like living in a library.'

'Sort of.'

'The Poodle Factory's like living in a kennel. You going? Hey, have a nice night, Bern.'

'Thanks. And I'll check out St Sappho tomorrow.'

'If you get a chance. Hey, is there a patron saint of burglars?'

'I'll check that, too.'

I rode three different subway trains to Broadway and Eighty-sixth and walked a block to Murder Ink, where I sold my shopping bag full of books to Carol Bremer. She got all my vintage mysteries; I could do better wholesaling them to her than waiting for somebody to pick them off my shelves.

She said, 'Charlie Chan, Philo Vance – this is wonderful, Bernie. I've got want-list customers for all this stuff. Buy you a drink?'

For a change everybody wanted to buy me a drink. I told her I'd take a rain check, left her shop just in time to miss a bus on West End Avenue, and walked the sixteen blocks downtown to my apartment. It was a nice crisp fall afternoon and I figured I could use the walk. You don't get all that much fresh air and exercise in a bookstore.

There was mail in my box. I carried it upstairs and put it in the wastebasket. I was half-undressed when the phone rang. It was a woman I know who runs a day-care center in Chelsea, and the parent of one of her charges had just given her two tickets to the ballet, and wasn't that terrific? I agreed that it was but explained I couldn't make it. 'I'm bushed,' I said. 'I've ordered myself to go to bed without supper. I was just about to take the phone off the hook when it rang.'

'Well, drink some coffee instead. What's-his-name's dancing. You know, the Russian.'

'They're all Russians. I'd fall asleep in the middle. Sorry.'

She wished me pleasant dreams and broke the connection. I left the phone off the hook. I'd have enjoyed eating Carolyn's beef stew and I'd also have enjoyed watching the Russian hop around the stage, and I didn't want the phone to let me know what else I was missing. It made an eerie sound for a while, then fell into a sullen silence. I finished undressing and turned off the lights and got into bed, and I lay there on my back with my arms at my sides and my eyes closed, breathing slowly and rhythmically and letting my mind go here and there. I either dreamed or daydreamed, and I was in some sort of doze when the alarm went off at nine o'clock. I got up, took a quick shower and shave, put on some clean clothes, and made myself a nice cup of tea. At a quarter after nine I put the phone back on the hook. At precisely nine-twenty it rang.

I picked it up and said hello. My caller said, 'There's been no change.'

'Good.'

'Things are as planned at your end?'

'Yes.'

'Good,' he said, and rang off. No names, no pack drill. I looked at the telephone receiver for a moment, then hung it up, then thought better of it and took it off the hook once again. It whined for a while, but by the time I was done with my tea it was quiet.

I finished dressing. I was wearing a three-piece navy pinstripe suit, a Wedgwood-blue shirt, a tie with narrow green and gold diagonal stripes on a navy field. My shoes combined black calfskin moccasin-toe uppers and thick crepe soles. Wearing them, I made no sound as I scurried around the apartment, gathering up one thing and another, making my final preparations.

While my shoes were silent, my stomach was rumbling a bit. I hadn't eaten anything since lunch some nine hours earlier. But I didn't want to eat, and I knew better than to drink anything.

Not now.

I checked, made sure I had everything. I went out into the hall, double-locked my own door, then rode the elevator past the lobby to the basement, letting myself out via the service entrance to avoid passing my doorman.

The air had an edge to it. It wasn't cold enough for mink, but it was certainly topcoat weather. I had mine over my arm, and I took a moment to put it on.

Was there a patron saint of burglars? If so, I didn't know his name. I murmured a quick prayer, addressed it to whom it might concern, and set off to resume my life of crime.

3

Halfway across the Queensboro Bridge, I happened to glance at the fuel gauge. The needle was all the way over to the left, way past the big E, and I had what suddenly looked like a mile of bridge stretching out in front of me. I could see myself running out of gas smack in the middle of the East River. Horns would blare all around me, and when horns blare, can cops be far behind? They'd be understanding at first, because motorists do get stranded all the time, but their sympathy would fade when they learned I was driving a stolen car. And why, they might wonder, had I stolen a car without checking the gas?

I was wondering much the same thing myself. I stayed in lane and let my foot rest easy on the accelerator, trying to remember what the ecology commercials were always telling me about ways to conserve gasoline. No fast starts, no jamming on the brakes, and don't spend too much time warming up on cold mornings. Sound advice, all of it, but I couldn't see how it applied, and I clutched the steering wheel and waited for the engine to cut out and the world to cave in.

Neither of these things happened. I found a Chevron station a block from the bridge and told the attendant to fill the tank. The car was a sprawling old Pontiac with an engine that never heard about fuel crises, and I sat there and watched it drink twenty-two gallons of high-test. I wondered what the tank's capacity might be. Twenty gallons, I decided, figuring the pumps were crooked. It's a dog-eat-dog world out there.

The tab came to fifteen dollars and change. I gave the kid a twenty and he gave me a smile in return and pointed to a sign on a pillar between the two pumps. You had to have exact change or a credit card after 8 P.M. *Help us thwart crime*, the sign urged. I don't know that they were thwarting anything, but they were certainly taking the profit out of it.

I have a couple of credit cards. I've even opened doors with them, although it's not the cinch TV shows might lead you to believe. But I didn't want a record of my presence in Queens, nor did I want anyone copying down the Pontiac's license number. So I let the little snot keep

310

the change, which got me a mean grin, and I drove east on Queens Boulevard mumbling to myself.

It wasn't the money. What really troubled me was that I'd been driving around unwittingly with an empty tank. The thing is, I don't steal cars very often. I don't even drive them all that frequently, and when I do go and rent one for a weekend in the country, the Olins people give it to me with the tank full. I can be halfway to Vermont before I even have to think about gasoline.

I wasn't going to Vermont tonight, just to Forest Hills, and I could have gone there easily enough on the E train. That's how I'd made the trip a few days earlier when I did some basic reconnaissance. But I hadn't felt like coming home by subway, preferring as I do to avoid public transportation when my arms are full of somebody else's belongings.

And when I found the Pontiac on Seventy-fourth Street, I'd figured it for a sign from on high. GM cars are the easiest for me to get into and the simplest to start, and this one had Jersey plates, so no one would be surprised if I drove it eccentrically. Finally, the owner was unlikely to report it stolen. He'd parked it next to a fire hydrant, so he'd have to assume the cops had towed it away.

Jesse Arkwright lived in Forest Hills Gardens. Now Forest Hills itself is a nice solid middle-class neighborhood set south of Flushing Meadows in the very center of the Borough of Queens. Three out of four houses there contain at least one woman who plays mah-jongg when she's not at a Weight Watchers meeting. But Forest Hills Gardens is an enclave within an enclave, a little pocket of *haute bourgeoise* respectability. Every house is three stories tall, with gables and a tile roof. All of the lawns are manicured, all of the shrubbery under tight discipline. A neighborhood association owns the very streets themselves, keeping them in good repair and restricting on-street parking to neighborhood residents.

Cars from underprivileged neighborhoods make frequent forays into the quiet streets of Forest Hills Gardens, their occupants darting out to knock down matrons and make off with alligator handbags. And private police cruisers patrol those same streets twenty-four hours a day to keep that sort of thing to a minimum. It's not Beverly Hills, say, where every pedestrian is perforce a suspicious character, but the security's pretty tight.

It's even tighter on Copperwood Crescent, an elegant semicircle where massive piles of stone and brick sprawl on spacious wooded lots. The residents of Copperwood Crescent include a shipping-line heir, two upper-echelon mafiosi, the owner of a chain of budget funeral parlors, and two to three dozen similarly well-heeled citizens. One private cop car has as its sole responsibility the safeguarding of

311

Copperwood Crescent, along with four adjoining and similarly exclusive streets – Ironwood Place, Silverwood Place, Pewterwood Place, and Chancery Drive.

If Forest Hills Gardens is the soft underbelly of Queens, Copperwood Crescent is the ruby in its navel.

I didn't have any trouble finding the ruby. On my earlier trip I'd walked all around the neighborhood armed with pocket atlas and clipboard – a man with a clipboard never looks out of place. I'd found Copperwood Crescent then and I found it now, barely slowing the Pontiac as I rolled past Jesse Arkwright's house, an enormous beamed Tudor number. On each of the three floors a light burned in a mullioned window.

At the end of Copperwood Crescent I took a sharp left into Bellnap Court, a quiet block-long cul-de-sac that was out of bounds for the Copperwood-Ironwood-Silverwood-Pewterwood-Chancery patrol car. I parked at the curb between a couple of sizable oaks and cut the engine, removing my jumper wire from the ignition.

You need a sticker to park on the street, but that's to keep commuters from cluttering the area during daylight hours. Nobody gets towed at night. I left the car there and walked back to Copperwood Crescent. If the patrol car was on the job, I didn't see it, nor did I notice anyone else walking about.

The same three lights were lit in the Arkwright house. Without hesitation I walked the length of the driveway at the right of the house. I shined my pencil-beam flashlight through a garage window. A gleaming Jaguar sedan crouched on one side of the garage. The other stall was quite empty.

Good.

I went to the side door. Below the bell on the door-jamb was an inch-square metal plate slotted for a key. A red light glowed within, indicating that the burglar alarm was set. If I were Mr Arkwright, equipped with the proper key, I could insert it in the slot and turn off the alarm. If, on the other hand, I were to insert anything other than the proper key, sirens would commence to sound and some signal would go off in the nearest police station.

Fine.

I rang the doorbell. The car was gone and the alarm was set, but you just never know, and the burglar least likely to wind up in slam is the sort of chap who wears suspenders and a belt, just in case. I'd rung this bell before, when I'd come calling with my clipboard, asking meaningless questions in aid of a nonexistent sewer survey. As then, I listened to the four-note chime sound within the large old house. I pressed my ear to the heavy door and listened carefully, and when the chimes quit echoing I heard nothing at all. No footsteps, no sign of human life. I rang again, and again I heard nothing.

Good.

I walked around to the rear of the house again. For a moment I just stood there. It was pleasant enough, the air uncharacteristically clear and clean. The moon wasn't visible from where I stood but I could see a scattering of stars overhead. What really awed me was the silence. Queens Boulevard was only blocks away but I couldn't hear any of its traffic. I suppose the trees kept the noise at bay.

I felt hundreds of miles from New York. The Arkwright house belonged in a Gothic novel, brooding over windswept moors.

Myself, I had no time for brooding. I put on my rubber gloves – skintight, their palms cut out for comfort's sake – and went to have a look at the kitchen door.

Thank God for burglar alarms and pickproof locks and tight security systems. They all help discourage the amateurs even as they give the citizenry a nice sense of safety and well-being. Without them, everybody would stash all the good stuff in safe-deposit boxes. Beyond that, they help make burglary the challenging occupation I've always found it. If any splay-fingered oaf could do as well, what fun would it be?

The Arkwright home had a first-rate burglar alarm, Fischer Systems' model NCN-30. I could see for myself that it was wired to all the ground-floor doors and windows. It might or might not have been connected to higher windows – most people don't take the trouble – but I didn't want to walk up a wall to find out one way or the other. It was simpler to rewire the system.

There are a few ways to beat a burglar alarm. One brutally direct method calls for cutting the lines supplying power to the house. This does lack subtlety – all the lights go out, for openers – and it's counterproductive when you're dealing with a good system like the NCN-30, because they have fail-safe devices that trigger them under such circumstances. (This can have interesting ramifications during a power failure, incidentally.)

Ah, well. I used some wires of my own, splicing them neatly into the picture, wrapping their ends ever so neatly with electrical tape, and by the time I was done the alarm was working as well as it had ever worked, but for the fact that it no longer covered the kitchen door. A regiment of cavalry could parade through that door without NCN-30 kicking up a fuss. The whole operation was more than your average burglar could do, and isn't it lucky that I'm not your average burglar?

With the alarm *hors de combat*, I turned my attention to the thick oak door, an *hors* of another color. A skeleton key opened its original lock, but there were two others, a Segal and a Rabson. I held my little flashlight in one hand and my ring of picks and probes in the other and went to work, pausing now and again to press an ear against the thick wood. (It's like seashells; if you listen carefully you can hear the forest.)

313

When the last tumbler tumbled I turned the knob and tugged and shoved and nothing happened.

There was a manual bolt on the inside. I ran the flashlight beam down the edge of the door until I located it, then made use of a handy little tool I'd fashioned from a hacksaw blade, slipping it between door and jamb and working it to and fro until the bolt parted. I tried the door again, and wouldn't you know there was a chain lock that stopped it when it was three inches ajar? I could have sawed through that as well, but why? It was easier to slip my hand inside and unscrew the chain lock from its moorings.

I pushed the door all the way open and made an illegal entry a crooked accountant would have been proud of. For a moment I just stood there, glowing, radiant. Then I closed the door and locked the locks. I couldn't do anything about the bolt I'd sawed through, but I did take a moment to restore the chain bolt.

Then I set out to explore the house.

There's absolutely nothing like it.

Forget everything I said to Ray Kirschmann. True, I was getting older. True, I shrank from the prospect of getting chewed by attack dogs and shot by irate householders and locked by the authorities in some pick-proof penitentiary cell. True, true, all of it true, and so what? None of it mattered a whit when I was inside someone else's dwelling place with all his worldly goods spread out before me like food on a banquet table. By God, I wasn't *that* old! I wasn't *that* scared!

I'm not proud of this. I could spout a lot of bilge about the criminal being the true existential hero of our times, but what for? I don't buy it myself. I'm not nuts about criminals and one of the worst things about prison was having to associate with them. I'd prefer to live as an honest man among honest men, but I haven't yet found an honest pursuit that lets me feel this way. I wish there were a moral equivalent of larceny, but there isn't. I'm a born thief and I love it.

I made my way through a butler's pantry and an enormous brick-floored kitchen, crossing a hallway to the formal living room. The light I'd noted from the street cast a warm glow over the room. It was a noteworthy object in and of itself, a leaded-glass dragonfly lamp by Tiffany. I'd last seen one in an antique shop on upper Madison Avenue with a $1,500 tag on it, and that was a few years ago.

But I hadn't come all the way to Queens to steal furniture. I'd come with a very specific purpose, and I didn't really need to be in the living room at all. I didn't have to take inventory, but old habits die hard, and I could hardly avoid it.

The lamp made it easy, saving me the trouble of using my flashlight. There was a timer so that it would turn itself off during daylight hours and resume its vigil at dusk, burning bravely until dawn, announcing to passers-by that nobody was home.

Considerate of them, I thought, to leave a light for the burglar.

The lamp was perched on an ornamental French kneehole desk. Four of the desk's six drawers were fakes, but one of the others held a Patek Philippe pocket watch with a hunting scene engraved on its case.

I closed the drawer without disturbing the watch.

The dining room was worth a look. A sideboard absolutely loaded with silver, including two complete sets of sterling tableware and a ton of hallmarked Georgian serving pieces. No end of fine porcelain and crystal.

I left everything undisturbed.

The library, also on the ground floor, was a room I would have gladly called my own. It measured perhaps twelve by twenty feet, with a glorious Kerman carpet covering most of the buffed parquet floor. Custom-built bookshelves of limed English oak lined two walls. In the middle of the room, centered beneath a fruited Tiffany shade, stood a tournament-size pool table. At the room's far end, twin portraits of Arkwright ancestors in gilded oval frames looked down in solemn approbation.

A pair of wall racks, one holding cue sticks, the other a locked cabinet that displayed sporting rifles and shotguns. A couple of over-stuffed leather chairs. An elaborate bar, the crystal glassware etched with game birds in flight. Enough liquor in one form or another to float a fair-sized cabin cruiser, plus decanters of sherry and port and brandy placed at convenient intervals about the room. A smoker's stand, mahogany, with a few dozen briar pipes and two cased meerschaums. A cedar cabinet of Havanas. A whole room of brass and wood and leather, and I yearned to nail the door shut and pour myself a stiff Armagnac and stay there forever.

Instead I scanned the bookshelves. They were a jumble, but there was no shortage of dollar value. While they ran heavily to uncut sets of leather-bound memoirs of unremembered hangers-on at pre-Revolutionary Versailles, there were plenty of other items as well, many of which I'd never seen outside of the catalogs of the better book dealers and auction galleries. I happened on a pristine first of Smollet's rarest novel, *The Adventures of Sir Laurence Greaves*, and there were any number of fine bindings and important first editions and Limited Editions Club issues and private press productions, all arranged in no discernible order and according to no particular plan.

I took one book from the shelves. It was bound in green cloth and not much larger than an ordinary paperback. I opened it and read the flowing inscription on the flyleaf. I paged through it, closed it, and put it back on the shelf.

I left the library as I'd found it.

The stairs were dark. I used my flashlight, went up and down the staircase three times. There was one board that creaked and I made sure I knew which one it was. Fourth from the top.

The others were comfortingly silent.

Twin beds in the master bedroom, each with its own bedside table. His and hers closets. His ran to Brooks Brothers suits and cordovan shoes. I especially liked one navy suit with a muted stripe. It wasn't that different from the one I was wearing. Her closet was full of dresses and furs, including one Ray's wife would have salivated over. Good labels in everything. A drawer in the dressing table – French Provincial, white enamel, gold trim – held a lot of jewelry. A cocktail ring caught my eye, a stylish little item with a large marquise-cut ruby surrounded by seed pearls.

There was some cash in the top drawer of one of the bedside tables, a couple hundred dollars in tens and twenties. In the other table I found a bankbook – eighteen hundred dollars in a savings account in the name of Elfrida Grantham Arkwright.

I didn't take any of these things. I didn't take the Fabergé eggs from the top of the chest of drawers, or the platinum cuff links and tie bar, or any of the wrist-watches, or, indeed, anything at all.

In Jesse Arkwright's study, all the way at the rear of the house's second floor, I found a whole batch of bankbooks. Seven of them, secured by a robber band, shared the upper right drawer of his desk with postage stamps and account ledgers and miscellaneous debris. The savings accounts all had sizable balances and the quick mental total I ran came to a little better than sixty thousand dollars.

I'll tell you. It gave me pause.

I once knew a fellow who'd been tossing an apartment in Murray Hill, filling a pillowcase with jewelry and silver, when he came across a bankbook with a balance in five figures. Clever lad that he was, he promptly turned his pillowcase inside out and put everything back where he'd found it. He left the premises looking as though he'd never visited them in the first place, taking nothing but that precious bankbook. That way the residents wouldn't know they'd been burgled, and wouldn't miss the bankbook, and he could drain their account before they suspected a thing.

Ah, the best-laid plans. He presented himself at the teller's window the very next morning, withdrawal slip in hand and bankbook at the ready. It was a small withdrawal – he was merely testing the waters – but that particular teller happened to know that particular depositor by

316

sight, and the next thing the chap knew he was doing a medium-long bit in Dannemora, which is where I ran into him.

So much for bankbooks.

So much, too, for a double handful of Krugerrands, those large gold coins the South Africans stamp out for people who want to invest in the yellow metal. I like gold – what's not to like? – but they were in a drawer with a handgun, and I dislike guns at least as much as I like gold. The ones in the library were for show, at least. This one was here for shooting burglars.

So much for the Krugerrands. So much, too, for a shoulder-height set of glassed-in shelves full of Boehm birds and Art Nouveau vases and glass paperweights. I spotted a Lalique ashtray just like the one on my grandmother's coffee table, and a positive gem of a Daum Nancy vase, and Baccarat and Millefiori weights galore, and—

It was starting to get to me. I couldn't look anywhere without seeing ten things I wanted to steal. Every flat surface in that study held bronzes, all of them impressive. Besides the usual bulls and lions and horses, I noticed one of a camel kneeling alongside a Legionnaire. The latter wore a kepi on his head and a pained expression on his face, as if he were sick of jokes about Legionnaire's Disease.

A couple of stamp albums. One general worldwide collection that didn't look to be worth much, but the other was a Scott Specialty Album for the Benelux countries, and a quick thumbing didn't reveal too many blank spaces.

And a coin collection. Lord above, a coin collection! No albums, just a dozen black cardboard boxes two inches square and ten inches long. Each was crammed to capacity with two-by-two coin envelopes. I didn't have time to check them but I couldn't resist. I opened one box at random and found it was filled with Barber quarters and halves, all Proofs or Uncirculated specimens. Another box contained superb Large Cents catalogued by Sheldon numbers.

How could I possibly leave them?

I left them. I didn't take a thing.

I was in one of the guest bedrooms on the second floor, playing my penlight over the walls and admiring a very nice pencil-signed Rouault lithograph, when I heard a car in the driveway. I checked my watch. It was 11:23. I listened as the automatic garage door swung upward, listened as the car's engine cut out. As the garage door swung down again I quit listening and walked the length of the hall to the staircase leading to the third floor. I was up those stairs and crouching on the third-floor landing by the time Jesse Arkwright's key hit the slot at the side of the house. First he turned off the burglar alarm, then he opened the door, and I fancied I could hear him refastening half a dozen locks after he and Elfrida had made their entrance.

Muffled conversation, barely audible two floors below me. I moved a rubber-gloved forefinger and wiped perspiration from my forehead. I'd planned on this, of course. I'd even checked the attic stairs earlier to make sure there were no squeakers in the lot.

All the same, I didn't like it. Burglary's a tightly wired proposition at best, but I generally get to do my work in precious solitude. If house-holders come home while I'm on the job, my usual impulse is to depart abruptly.

This time I had to linger.

Two floors below, a teakettle whistled briefly, then sighed as some-one removed it from the flame. For an instant I'd mistaken its cry for a police siren. Nerves, I thought, taking deep breaths, beseeching the patron saint of burglars for a dose of serenity.

Maybe I'd been right when I talked to Kirschmann. Maybe I was getting too old for this. Maybe I didn't have the requisite sang-froid. Maybe—

Crouching was uncomfortable. I got stiffly to my feet. The attic was finished off, its central hallway covered with a length of faded maroon carpeting. I walked clear to the front of the house, where a brass floorlamp equipped with a timer sent out forty watts' worth of light through a curtained window. A maid's room, it looked to be, although the household no longer employed live-in servants.

A day bed stretched along one wall. I lay down on top of it, pulled a green and gold afghan coverlet over myself, and closed my eyes.

I couldn't really hear much from where I was. At one point I thought I heard footsteps on the stairs, and then a few moments later I fancied that I could hear the clatter of balls on the pool table in the library. This was probably a case of my imagination filling in the blanks. After an evening at the theater, the Arkwright routine was supposed to be quite predictable. Home around eleven-thirty, a spot of coffee and something sweet in the breakfast nook, and then Elfrida would pop upstairs with a book of crosswords while Jesse ran a rack or two at the pool table, nipped at one of the crystal decanters, read a few pages of one of his leather-bound classics, and then hied his own bulk up the stairs and joined his wife in their chamber.

Would he take a final tour of the downstairs, making sure all the doors were locked? Would he happen to check the sliding bolt on the kitchen door, and would he happen to notice that some clever chap had sawn through it? Was he, even as I thought these grim thoughts, lifting a receiver to summon the local constabulary?

I could have been at the ballet, watching a Russian imitate a gazelle. I could have gone home with Carolyn and eaten Flemish stew and drunk Dutch beer. Or I could have been home in my own little bed.

I stayed where I was and I waited.

*

At one-thirty I got to my feet. I hadn't heard a sound within the house for an entire half-hour. I padded silently to the stairs, crossing right over the master bedroom where I hoped my hosts were sleeping soundly. I went down the stairs, treading ever so gingerly on my crepe soles, and I crossed the second-floor hallway and went on down the other stairs to the ground floor. It was no great feat to remember to avoid the fourth step from the top; I'd obsessed on that very subject for the past twenty minutes.

The lights were out once again on the ground floor, except for the indomitable dragonfly lamp in the living room. I didn't have to use my penlight to find my way to the library, but once I was in that room I played its beam here and there.

Arkwright had paid the room his nightly visit. He'd left a pool cue on top of the table, along with the cue ball and one or two of its fellows. A small brandy snifter stood on a leather-topped table beside one of the big chairs. It was empty, but a quick sniff revealed it had recently held cognac – a very good cognac at that, judging from the bouquet.

There was a book next to the snifter, *Sheridan's Plays*, bound in red leather. Bedtime reading.

I went to the bookshelves. Had Arkwright inspected the little green clothbound volume as part of his nightly ritual? I couldn't tell, as it was right where I'd found it earlier in the evening. But it was his treasure. He'd probably had a look at it.

I took it from the shelf and just managed to fit it into my jacket pocket. Then I nudged the surrounding volumes so as to fill up the space where it had been.

And left the library.

He had turned off the alarm to enter the house, then reset it once he and Elfrida were inside. All the while, of course, the alarm system continued to guard all of the house but the kitchen door. I now left through that very portal, closing it after me and relocking its three locks by picking them in reverse. I had to leave the chain bolt dangling and I couldn't do anything about the bolt I'd hacksawed earlier. Nobody's perfect.

I was very damned close to perfection, though, in the way I restored the alarm system, rewiring it to render the kitchen door once more unbreachable. Every impulse urged me to quit Arkwright's property while I had the chance, but I spent a few extra minutes, and only an imperceptible scrap of electrical tape hinted that the wires had ever been tampered with.

Professionalism? I call it the relentless pursuit of excellence.

I had almost reached the end of Copperwood Crescent when the police car turned the corner. I managed to furnish a smile and a perfunctory nod without breaking stride. They went along their merry way, and why not? They'd seen only a well-dressed and self-possessed gentleman who looked as though he belonged.

They hadn't seen any palmless rubber gloves. Those wound up tucked in a pocket before I left the Arkwright driveway.

The Pontiac was where I'd left it. I hooked up my jumper wire and was on my way. In due course I was back on West Seventy-fourth Street. One nice thing about swiping a car from a hydrant is you can generally put it back where you found it. I did just that, pulling in next to the fireplug even as a brindle boxer was lifting a leg against it. I unhooked my jumper wire and got out of the car, careful to push down the lock buttons before I swung the door shut.

The boxer's equally brindle owner, leash in one hand and wad of paper towel in the other, admonished me that I was risking a ticket or a tow. I couldn't think of an answer so I walked off without giving him one.

'Crazy,' he told the dog. 'They're all crazy here, Max.'

I couldn't argue with that.

In my own apartment, nibbling cheese and crunching Triscuits and sipping the special-occasion Scotch, I let go and enjoyed the glow that comes afterward on those too-rare occasions where everything goes like clockwork. All the tension, all the discomfort, all the anxiety – it was all bought and paid for by moments like this.

Earlier, stretched out on that lumpy day bed, I'd been unable to stop thinking of all the treasures the Arkwright house contained. The cash, the jewels, the stamps, the coins, the *objets d'art*. I'd had fantasies of backing a moving van onto the lawn and just stealing every damned thing, from the oriental rugs on the floors to the cut-crystal chandeliers overhead. That, I'd decided, was really the only way to do it. A person who wanted to be selective would have his problems. He wouldn't know what to steal first.

And what did I have for my troubles?

I picked up the book, taking pains not to dribble Scotch on it, though someone had dribbled one thing or another on it over the years. It certainly didn't look like such a much, and the leisurely inspection I could give it now was disclosing flaws I hadn't spotted earlier. There was water damage on the front cover. Some of the pages had been foxed. The past half-century had not been gentle with the little volume, and no bookseller could conscientiously grade it higher than Very Good.

I flipped through it, read a stanza here and a stanza there. The author's meter was unmistakable and he had never lost his dexterity at rhyming, but what I was reading looked like doggerel to me.

For this I'd passed up Krugerrands and Barber Proofs, Fabergé and Baccarat and Daum Nancy. For this I'd returned the pearl-and-ruby ring to its little velvet case.

Mr Whelkin would be proud of me.

4

I met J. Rudyard Whelkin on a slow mid-week morning two weeks prior to my little venture in breaking and entering. The Yankees had just dropped the first two games of the Series, and the night before I'd watched a kid barely old enough to shave strike out Reggie Jackson with the bases loaded. This morning it was damp and drizzly, and it figured.

I hadn't had any customers yet and I didn't much care. I was settled in behind the counter with a paperback. I don't stock paperbacks, and the ones that come in I wholesale to a guy on Third and Sixteenth who deals in nothing else.

Sometimes, though, I read them first. The one I was reading was one of Richard Stark's books about Parker. Parker's a professional thief, and every book runs pretty much to form – Parker puts together a string of crooks, he goes someplace like Spartanburg, South Carolina, to buy guns and a truck, he gets a dentist in Yankton Falls to put up front money for the operation, he and his buddies pull the job, and then something goes horribly wrong. If nothing went horribly wrong, all of the books would end around page 70 and by now Parker would own his own island in the Caribbean.

Last time I was inside, everybody was a big fan of Parker's. My colleagues read everything they could get their hands on about him, even if they had to move their lips to get the job done. I swear there were grizzled cons in that joint who would walk around quoting passages at each other, especially parts where Parker maimed someone. One safecracker always quoted the part where Parker settled a score with an unworthy fellow laborer by breaking three important bones and leaving him in a swamp. It was the adjective that did it for him, the idea of deliberately breaking important bones.

I had just reached the part where Parker was putting in an urgent call to Handy McKay at his diner in Presque Isle, Maine, when the little bells above the door tinkled to announce I had company. I moved the paperback out of sight as my visitor approached the counter. After all, antiquarian booksellers have an image to protect. We're not supposed to read trash.

He was a stout man, florid of face, jowly as a bulldog, with thinning mahogany hair combed straight back over a glossy salmon scalp. He wore a charcoal-brown herringbone tweed jacket with suede elbow patches, a tobacco-brown sweater vest, a tan oxford-cloth shirt with a button-down collar, a chocolate-brown knit tie. His trousers were fawn cavalry twill, his shoes brown wing tips. He had a long narrow nose, a graying guardsman's mustache. His eyebrows were untamed tangles of briar; beneath them his eyes (brown, to match his outfit) were keen and cool and just a trifle bloodshot.

He asked if Mr Litzauer was expected, and I explained about the change in ownership. 'Ah,' he said. 'No wonder he hasn't been in touch. I'm a collector, you see, and he always lets me know when he runs across an item I might fancy.'

'What do you collect?'

'Victorian poets, for the most part, but I follow my taste, you know. I'm partial to artful rhymers. Thomas Hood. Algernon Charles Swinburne. William Mackworth Praed. Kipling, of course, is my keenest enthusiasm.'

I told him whatever I had was on the shelves. He went to look for himself and I got Parker out from beneath the counter and returned to vicarious crime. Two of Parker's henchpersons were just getting ready to set up a doublecross when my tweedy customer presented himself once again at the counter, a small cloth-bound volume in hand. It contained the collected lyric poems of Austin Dobson and I had it priced at six or seven dollars, something like that. He paid in cash and I wrapped it for him.

'If you happen on anything you think I might like,' he said, 'you might want to ring me up.'

He handed me his card. It bore his name, an address in the East Thirties, and a phone number with a MUrray Hill 8 exchange. The card conveyed no suggestion of what the man did for a living.

I looked from it to him. 'You collect Kipling,' I said.

'Among others, yes.'

'Is there a family connection?'

He smiled broadly. 'Because of the name, you mean? Natural guess, of course. But no, I'm no relative of Kipling's. Rudyard's not a family name, you see. It's the name of a lake.'

'Oh?'

'In Staffordshire. Kipling's parents first met on a picnic at Lake Rudyard. When in due course their son was born he was given the lake's name as a middle name. His first name was Joseph, actually, although he never did use it and was known as Ruddy from earliest childhood.'

'And your first name—'

'Is James, as it happens, and I don't use it either. James Rudyard

Whelkin. I was eight years old when Kipling died and I remember the day very well. That was in 1936, just two days after George V preceded him to the grave. A day of mourning in our household, as you can well imagine. My father admired Kipling enormously. He'd have to have done, to name his only son after him, wouldn't he? Because I was named for Kipling, of course, not for a lake in Staffordshire. "First the old king and now the Bard of Empire," my father said. "Mark my words, Ruddy. There'll be war in Europe within the next two years." He was off by a year of course, and I don't suppose Kipling's demise had much to do with Hitler's invading Poland, but it all linked up in the old fellow's mind, you see.' He smiled fiercely and his great eyebrows shook. 'Are you interested in Kipling, Mr Rhodenbarr?'

'I read him when I was a kid.'

'You might try him again. He's returning to fashion, you know, after altogether too many years of neglect. Have you had a look at *Kim* lately? Or *The Light That Failed?* Or – But reading must be a bit of a busman's holiday for you, eh? Must grow sick and tired of the printed word by the end of a long day.'

'Oh, I still enjoy reading. And maybe I will try Kipling again.'

'Do. There's books on your own shelves, for a starter.' An appraising glance from his alert brown eyes. 'I say, sir. Do you suppose you could possibly lunch with me this afternoon? I might have something to say that would interest you.'

'I'd like that.'

'My club, then. Do you know the Martingale? And how's half past twelve?'

I told him I knew where the club was, and that twelve-thirty was fine.

He'd already said something that interested me.

The Martingale Club was just right for him, a good match for his dress and his faintly pukka sahib manner. It stood at the corner of Madison Avenue and Thirtieth Street and was decorated largely with un-comfortable Jacobean oak furniture and the heads of innumerable dead animals.

We dined in a fair-sized room on the second floor under the glass-eyed stare of a bison allegedly shot by Theodore Roosevelt for reasons I could not begin to guess. Lunch was a leathery mixed grill with thawed green peas and spineless French fried potatoes. The waiter who brought this mess to the table was a rheumy-eyed chap who walked as though his feet were killing him. He looked almost as woebegone as the bison.

Whelkin and I talked books through the meal, then both turned down dessert. The sad waiter brought us a large silver coffeepot of the sort they used to serve you on trains. The coffee was even better than the old Pennsy dining car once supplied, rich and winy and aromatic.

Our table was next to a pair of casement windows. I sipped my coffee and looked out at Madison Avenue. The last of the Good Humor men was doing light business on the corner. In a matter of days he'd be gone, yielding place to a seller of hot pretzels and chestnuts as the seasons changed in their inexorable fashion. You couldn't watch the leaves turn, not from this window, but you could mark time's passage by keeping an eye on the street vendors.

Whelkin cleared his throat, interrupting this reverie. 'H. Rider Haggard,' he said. 'I told you I collect him as well?'

'I think you mentioned him.'

'Interesting man. Did for South Africa what Kipling did for India. *She, King Solomon's Mines* – but of course you know his work.'

'In a general way.'

'He and Kipling became great friends, you know. Both of them were on the outs with the Bloomsbury crowd. Both lived long enough to see their own literary reputations fade dismally. The public came to think of them in the same breath as apologists for a discredited imperialism. Do you know the J. K. Stephens poem?'

I didn't even know whom he was talking about, but he managed to quote the poem from memory:

> *'Will there never come a season*
> *Which shall rid us from the curse*
> *Of a prose which knows no reason*
> *And an unmelodious verse:*
> *When the world shall cease to wonder*
> *At the genius of an Ass,*
> *And a boy's eccentric blunder*
> *Shall not bring success to pass:*
> *When mankind shall be delivered*
> *From the clash of magazines,*
> *And the inkstand shall be shivered*
> *Into countless smithereens:*
> *When there stands a muzzled stripling,*
> *Mute, beside a muzzled bore:*
> *When the Rudyards cease from Kipling*
> *And the Haggards Ride no more.'*

He moved to refill our coffee cups. 'Nasty piece of billingsgate, eh? One of many such. Just drove the two of them closer together, however. Haggard spent as much time at Kipling's house in Surrey as he did at home. They'd actually work together in Kipling's study, sitting on opposite ends of the long desk, batting ideas back and forth, then scribbling away furiously at one thing or another.'

'Interesting,' I said.

'Isn't it? Not too long after the 1918 Armistice the two men set about organizing the liberty League, a sort of anti-Communist affair which never got terribly far off the ground. The bit of doggerel someone wrote gives a fair idea of the Liberty League's slant on current affairs. You know the poem?'

'I don't think so.'

'It's cleverly rhymed, and I think I mentioned my admiration for a facility at rhyming.

> " 'Every Bolsh is a blackguard,'
> Said Kipling to Haggard.
> 'And given to tippling,'
> Said Haggard to Kipling.
> 'And a blooming outsider,'
> Said Rudyard to Rider.
> 'Their domain is a bloodyard,'
> Said Rider to Rudyard."

'Neatly done, don't you think? I could quote others of a similar nature but I'll spare you that.'

I very nearly thanked him. I was beginning to think I'd been mistaken, that he'd just brought me here to quote verse at me. Well, at least the coffee was good.

Then he said, 'Liberty League. After it fell apart, Kipling went through a difficult time. His health was poor. Gastritis, which he thought might be symptomatic of cancer. Turned out he had duodenal ulcers. He was subject to depression and it may have affected his thinking.

'The man became briefly fixated on the curious notion that the British Empire was menaced by an unholy alliance of Jewish international financiers and Jewish Bolsheviks. These two unlikely forces were joining together to destroy Christianity by wresting the overseas empire from the British crown. Kipling wasn't the sort of moral degenerate to whom anti-Semitism comes naturally, and he didn't persist in it for any length of time, nor did it color his work to a considerable extent.

'But he did write one extremely bizarre piece of work on an anti-Semitic theme. It was a narrative poem in ballad meter, some three thousand two hundred lines called *The Deliverance of Fort Bucklow*. The plot line concerns the efforts of a gallant British regiment to save India from a revolution stirred up by Jewish agitators, and it's quite clear that the battle for Fort Bucklow is not merely the decisive battle of this war but Kipling's version of the Battle of Armageddon, with the forces of Good and Evil pitted against one another to decide the fate of humankind.

'Do you remember *Soldiers Three?* Learoyd, Ortheris and Mulvaney? Kipling brought them back to make them the heroes who deliver Fort Bucklow and save the day for God and King George. Oh, there are some stirring battle scenes, and there's a moment when "two brave men stand face to face" in a manner reminiscent of *The Ballad of East and West*, but poor Kipling was miles from the top of his form when he wrote it. The premise is absurd, the resolution is weak, and there are elements of frightful unwitting self-parody. He often skated rather close to the edge of self-parody, you know, and here he lost his footing.

'Perhaps he recognized this himself. Perhaps his vision of the Hebraic Conspiracy embraced the world of publishing. In any event, he didn't offer *The Deliverance of Fort Bucklow* to his London publishers. He may have planned to do so ultimately, but in the meantime he elected to safeguard the copyright by bringing out the poem in a small private edition.'

'Ah.'

'Ah indeed, sir. Kipling found a printer named Smithwick & Son in Tunbridge Wells. If Smithwick ever printed another book before or since, I've never heard of it. But he did print this one, and in an edition of only one hundred fifty copies. It's not fine printing by any means because Smithwick wasn't capable of it. But he got the job done, and the book's quite a rarity.'

'It must be. One hundred fifty copies . . .'

Whelkin smiled widely. 'That's how many were printed. How many do you suppose survive?'

'I have no idea. *The Deliverance of Fort Bucklow?* I've never heard the title.'

'I'm not surprised.'

'Fifty copies? Seventy-five? I have no idea what the survival rate would be.'

The coffeepot was empty. Whelkin frowned and rang a bell mounted on the wall. He didn't say anything until the waiter limped over with a fresh pot.

Then he said, 'Kipling wrote the poem in 1923. He'd hoped to give out copies to close friends for Christmas that year, but the holiday had come and gone before Smithwick was able to make delivery. So Kipling decided to hold them over for Christmas of '24, but sometime in the course of the year he seems to have come to his senses, recognizing the poem as a scurrilous piece of Jew-baiting tripe and bad verse in the bargain.

'As was his custom, Kipling had presented his wife, Carrie, with an inscribed copy. He asked for it back. He'd given another copy to a Surrey neighbor of his named Lonsdale as a birthday gift in early spring and he managed to get it back as well, giving the man several other books in exchange. These two books, as well as the other bound volumes, the printer's proofs, and the original holograph manuscript plus the typed manuscript from which Smithwick set type – all of this went up the chimney at Bateman's.'

'Bateman's?'

'Bateman's was the name of Kipling's house. There's an undated letter to a London acquaintance, evidently written in the late summer or early fall of '24, in which Kipling talks of having felt like an erring Israelite who had just sacrificed a child by fire to Moloch. "But this was a changeling, this bad child of mine, and it was with some satisfaction I committed it to the flames."' Whelkin sighed with contentment, sipped coffee, placed his cup in its saucer. 'And that,' he said, 'was the end of *The Deliverance of Fort Bucklow*.'

'Except that it wasn't.'

'Of course not, Mr Rhodenbarr. The Rider Haggard copy still existed. Kipling, of course, had given a copy to his closest friend almost as soon as he received the edition from Smithwick. Had it slipped his mind when he set about recalling the other copies? I don't think so.

'Haggard, you see, was in failing health. And Kipling had dedicated the book to Haggard, and had added a personal inscription to Haggard's own copy, a paragraph running to over a hundred words in which he hailed Haggard as a kindred spirit who shared the author's vision of the peril of Jewish-inspired holocaust, or words to that effect. I believe there's a letter of Rider Haggard's in the collection of the University of Texas acknowledging the gift and praising the poem. After all that, Kipling may have been understandably reluctant to disown the work and ask for the book's return. In any event, the copy was still in Haggard's possession upon his death the following year.'

'Then what happened to it?'

'It was sold along with the rest of Haggard's library, and no one seems to have paid any immediate attention to it. The world didn't know the book existed, and no doubt it was sold, in a lot with the other copies of Kipling's works, and for very little money, I'm sure. It came to light shortly after Kipling's death – not the copy, but the realization that Kipling had written an anti-Semitic poem. The British Union of Fascists wanted to disseminate it, and Unity Mitford was rumored to have been on the trail of the Haggard copy when war broke out between Britain and Germany.

'Nothing further was heard until after the war, when the Haggard copy turned up in the possession of a North Country baronet, who sold it privately. There were supposed to have been two or three additional private transactions before the volume was scheduled to appear in Trebizond & Partners auction of effects from the estate of the twelfth Lord Ponsonby.'

'You say scheduled to appear?'

He nodded shortly. 'Scheduled, catalogued and withdrawn. Six weeks ago I took one of Freddie Laker's no-frills flights to London with the sole purpose of bidding on that book. I calculated that the competition would be keen. There are some rabid Kipling collectors, you know, and his reputation's been making a comeback. The University of Texas has a well-endowed library and their Kipling collection is a sound one. I expected there would be buyers for other institutions as well.'

'Did you expect to outbid them?'

'I expected to try. I didn't know just how high I myself was prepared to go, and of course I had no way of knowing what levels the bidding might reach. Upon arriving in London, I learned there was a Saudi who wanted that particular lot, and rumor had it that an agent for some sort of Indian prince or Maharajah was paying extraordinary prices for top-level Kiplingana. Could I have outbid such persons? I don't know. *The Deliverance of Fort Bucklow* is interesting and unique, but it hasn't been publicized sufficiently to have become *important*, really, and the work itself is of low quality from a literary standpoint.' He frowned, and his eyebrows quivered. 'Still in all, I should have liked the chance to bid in open auction.'

'But the lot was withdrawn.'

'By the heirs prior to sale. The gentleman from Trebizond's was quite apologetic, and reasonably indignant himself. After all, his agreement with the heirs precluded their making private arrangements. But what could he possibly do about it? The buyer had the book and the heirs had the money and that was the end of it.'

'Why arrange a private sale?'

'Taxes, Mr Rhodenbarr. Taxes. Death duties, Inland Revenue enquiries – the tax laws make finaglers of us all, do they not? What voice on earth speaks with the volume of unrecorded cash? Money in hand, passed under the table, and the heirs can swear the book was set aside as an heirloom, or destroyed in a flash flood, or whatever they choose. They won't be believed, but what matter?'

'Who bought the book?'

'The good people at Trebizond's didn't know, of course. And the heirs weren't telling – their official line was that the book hadn't been sold at all.' He put his elbows on the table and placed his fingertips together. 'I did some investigatory work of my own. *The Deliverance of Fort Bucklow* was sold to Jesse Arkwright, an artful dabbler in international trade.'

'And a collector, I suppose?'

'An acquirer, sir. Not a collector. A gross ill-favored man who surrounds himself with exquisite objects in the hope that they will somehow cloak his own inner ugliness. He has a library, Mr Rhodenbarr, because to do so fits the image he would like to project. He has books, some of them noteworthy, because books are the *sine qua non* of a proper library. But he is hardly a collector, and he most certainly does not collect Kipling.'

'Then why—'

'Should he want this book? Because *I* wanted it, Mr Rhodenbarr. It's that simple.'

'Oh.'

'Do you remember the Spinning Jenny?'

'It was a dance craze, wasn't it?'

He looked at me oddly. 'It was a machine,' he said. 'The first machine capable of producing cotton thread. Sir Richard Arkwright patented it in 1769 and launched the modern British textile industry.'

'Oh, right,' I said. 'The Industrial Revolution and all that.'

'And all that,' he agreed. 'Jesse Arkwright claims descent from Sir Richard. I'm no more inclined to take his word on that point than any other. His surname means *builder of arks*, so perhaps he'll next hire a genealogist to trace his roots clear back to Noah.'

'And he bought the book to keep you from having it?'

'I once acquired something that he wanted. This seems to have been his way of paying me back.'

'And he won't sell it.'

'Certainly not.'

'And there's no other copy extant.'

'None has come to light in half a century.'

'And you still want this particular copy.'

'More than ever.'

'How fortunate that you happened to pop into Barnegat Books this morning.'

He stared.

'You called me by name before I had a chance to supply it. You came into the shop looking for me, not for Mr Litzauer. Not because I sell secondhand books but because I used to be a burglar. You figure I'm still a burglar.'

'I—'

'You don't believe people change. You're as bad as the police. "Once a burglar, always a burglar" – that's the way you figure it, isn't it?'

'I was wrong,' he said, and lowered his eyes.

'No,' I said. 'You were right.'

5

I don't know what time I got into bed, but by some miracle I got out of it in time to open the store by ten-thirty. At a quarter to eleven I called the number on J. Rudyard Whelkin's business card. I let it ring unheeded for a full minute, then dialed 411 for the number of the Martingale Club. They charge you for those calls, and I could have taken a minute to look it up in the White Pages, but I'd earned a fortune the night before and I felt like sharing the wealth.

The attendant at the Martingale Club said he didn't believe Mr Whelkin was on the premises but that he'd page him all the same. Time scuttled by. The attendant reported mournfully that Mr Whelkin had not responded to the page, and would I care to leave a message? I decided not to.

A couple of browsers filtered into the store. One of them looked potentially larcenous and I kept an eye on him as he worked his way through Biography and Belles-Lettres. He surprised me in the end by spending a few dollars on a volume of Macaulay's historical essays.

Carolyn popped in a few minutes after noon and deposited a paper bag on the counter. 'Felafel sandwiches on pita bread,' she announced. 'I decided I was in the mood for something different. You like felafel?'

'Sure.'

'I went to that place at the corner of Broadway and Twelfth. I can't figure out whether the owner's an Arab or an Israeli.'

'Does it matter?'

'Well, I'd hate to say the wrong thing. I was going to wish him a happy Rosh Hashanah, but suppose that's the last thing he wants to hear? So I just took my change and split.'

'That's always safe.'

'Uh-huh. You missed a terrific meal last night. I ate half the stew and froze the rest and started watching the new sitcom about the three cheerleaders. I turned the sound off and it wasn't half bad. But I got to bed early and I got a ton of sleep and I feel great.'

'You look it.'

'You, on the other hand, look terrible. Is that what a night on club soda does to a person?'

331

'Evidently.'

'Maybe you got too much sleep. That happens sometimes.'

'So they tell me.'

The phone rang. I went and took it in the little office in back, figuring it was Whelkin. Instead it was a slightly breathless woman who wanted to know if the new Rosemary Rogers book had come in yet. I told her I handled used books exclusively and suggested she call Brentano's. She asked what their number was and I was reaching for the phone book to look it up when I came to my senses and hung up on her.

I went back to my felafel. Carolyn said, 'Something wrong?'

'No. Why?'

'You jumped three feet when the phone rang. The coffee okay?'

'Fine.'

'The felafel?'

'Delicious.'

Mondays and Wednesdays I buy lunch and we eat at the Poodle Factory. Tuesdays and Thursdays Carolyn brings lunch to the book-shop. Fridays we go out somewhere and toss a coin for the check. All of this is subject to last-minute cancellation, of course, in the event of a business luncheon, such as my earlier date with Whelkin.

'Oh,' I said, and finished swallowing a mouthful of felafel. 'I haven't squandered the morning.'

'I never said you had.'

'I did some research. On patron saints.'

'Oh yeah? Who's my patron saint?'

'I don't think you've got one.'

'Why the hell not?'

'I don't know. I checked a lot of different books and kept finding partial lists. I don't know if there's an official all-inclusive list any-where.' I groped around, found the notepad I'd been scribbling on earlier. 'I told you about St John of God, didn't I?'

'Yeah, but I forget what. The store?'

'Patron saint of booksellers. He was born in Portugal in 1495. He worked as a shepherd, then became a drunkard and gambler.'

'Good for him. Then he switched to club soda and became a saint.'

'The books don't say anything about club soda. At forty he went through a mid-life crisis and moved to Granada. In 1538 he opened a shop—'

'To sell books?'

'I suppose so, but did they have bookstores then? They barely had movable type. Anyway, two years later he founded the Brothers Hospi-talers, and ten years later he died, and his picture's hanging over my desk, if you'd care to see it.'

'Not especially. That's all you found out?'

'Not at all.' I consulted my notes. 'You asked if there was a patron saint of burglars. Well, Dismas is the patron saint of thieves. He was the Good Thief.'

'Yeah, I remember him.'

'He's also one of the patron saints of prisoners, along with St Joseph Cafasso. Thieves and prisoners do overlap, although not as thoroughly as you might think.'

'And prisoners need an extra patron saint because they're in real trouble.'

'Makes sense. A burglar's a thief, when all is said and done, and there doesn't seem to be a special burglar's saint, but there's always St Dunstan.'

'Who he?'

'The patron saint of locksmiths. Burglars and locksmiths perform essentially the same task, so why shouldn't they both turn to Dunstan in time of stress? Of course, if the situation's really dire, a burglar could turn to St Jude Thaddeus or St Gregory of Neocaesarea.'

'Why would he want to do that?'

'Because those guys are the patron saints of persons in desperate situations. There were times in my burglar days when I could have used their help. For that matter, I didn't know about St Anthony of Padua, the patron saint of seekers of lost objects.'

'So if you couldn't find what you were looking for . . .'

'Precisely. You're laughing. That means I should give thanks to St Vitus.'

'The patron saint of dancers?'

'Comedians, actually. Dancers have somebody else, but don't ask me who.'

'What about dog groomers?'

'I'll have to consult more sources.'

'And lesbians. You honestly couldn't find anything about lesbians?'

'Well, there's somebody who comes to mind. But I don't know his name and I don't think he was a saint.'

'Lesbians have a male saint?'

'He's probably not a saint anyway.'

'Well, don't keep me in suspense. Who is he?'

'That little Dutch boy.'

'*What* little Dutch boy?'

'You know. The one who put his finger—'

'Nobody likes a smartass, Bernie. Not even St Vitus.'

The afternoon sped by without further reference to patron saints. I racked up a string of small sales and moved a nice set of Trollope to a fellow who'd been sniffing around it for weeks. He wrote out a check for sixty bucks and staggered off with the books in his arms.

Whenever I had a minute I called Whelkin without once reaching him. When he didn't answer the page at the Martingale Club, I left a message for him to call Mr Haggard. I figured that would be subtle enough,

The phone rang around four. I said, 'Barnegat Books?' and nobody said anything for a moment. I figured I had myself a heavy breather, but for the hell of it I said, 'Mr Haggard?'

'Sir?'

It was Whelkin, of course. And he hadn't gotten my message, having been away from home and club all day long. His speech was labored, with odd pauses between the sentences. An extra martini at lunch, I figured.

'Could you pop by this evening, Mr Rhodenbarr?'

'At your club?'

'No, that won't be convenient. Let me give you my address.'

'I already have it.'

'How's that?'

'You gave me your card,' I reminded him, and read off the address to him.

'Won't be there tonight,' he said shortly. He sounded as though someone had puffed up his tongue with a bicycle pump. He went on to give me an address on East Sixty-sixth between First and Second avenues. 'Apartment 3-D,' he said. 'Ring twice.'

'Like the postman.'

'Beg pardon?'

'What time should I come?'

He thought it over. 'Half past six, I should think.'

'That's fine.'

'And you'll bring the, uh, the item?'

'If you'll have the, uh, cash.'

'Everything will be taken care of.'

Odd, I thought, hanging up the phone. I was the one running on four hours' sleep. He was the one who sounded exhausted.

I don't know exactly when the Sikh appeared. He was just suddenly there, poking around among the shelves, a tall slender gentleman with a full black beard and a turban. I noticed him, of course, because one does notice that sort of thing, but I didn't stare or gawp. New York is New York, after all, and a Sikh is not a Martian.

Shortly before five the store emptied out. I stifled a yawn with the back of my hand and thought about closing early. Just then the Sikh emerged from the world of books and presented himself in front of the counter. I'd lost track of him and had assumed he'd left.

'This book,' he said. He held it up for my inspection, dwarfing it in his large brown hands. An inexpensive copy of *The Jungle Book*, by our boy Rudyard K.

'Ah, yes,' I said. 'Mowgli, raised by wolves.'

He was even taller than I'd realized. I looked at him and thought of What's-his-name in Little Orphan Annie. He wore a gray business suit, a white shirt, an unornamented maroon tie. The turban was white.

'You know this man?'

Punjab, I thought. That was the dude in Little Orphan Annie. And his sidekick was The Asp, and—

'Kipling?' I said.

'You know him?'

'Well, he's not living now,' I said. 'He died in 1936.' And thank you, J. R. Whelkin, for the history lesson.

The man smiled. His teeth were very large, quite even, and whiter than his shirtfront. His features were regular, and his large sorrowful eyes were the brown of old-fashioned mink coats, the kind Ray Kirschmann's wife didn't want for Christmas.

'You know his books?' he said.

'Yes.'

'You have other books, yes? Besides the ones on your shelves.'

An alarm bell sounded somewhere in the old cerebellum. 'My stock's all on display,' I said carefully.

'Another book. A private book, perhaps.'

'I'm afraid not.'

The smile faded until the mouth was a grim line hidden at its corners by the thick black beard. The Sikh dropped a hand into his jacket pocket. When he brought it out there was a pistol in it. He stood so that his body screened the pistol from the view of passers-by and held it so that it was pointed directly at my chest.

It was a very small gun, a nickel-plated automatic. They make fake guns about that size, novelty items, but somehow I knew that this one wouldn't turn out to be a cigarette lighter in disguise.

It should have looked ridiculous, such a little gun in such a large hand, but I'll tell you something. Guns, when they're pointed at me, never look ridiculous.

'Please,' he said patiently. 'Let us be reasonable. You know what I want.'

6

I wanted to look him in the eyes but I couldn't keep from staring at the gun.

'There is something,' I said.

'Yes.'

'I've got it behind the counter, see, because of a personal interest—'

'Yes.'

'But since you're a fan of Kipling's, and because your devotion is obvious—'

'The book, please.'

IBs free hand snatched it up the instant I laid it on the counter. The smile was back now, broader than ever. He tried the book in his jacket pocket but it didn't fit. He set it back on the counter for a moment while he drew an envelope from an inside pocket. He was still pointing the gun at me and I wished he'd stop.

'For your trouble,' he said, slapping the envelope smartly on the counter in front of me. 'Because you are a reasonable man.'

'Reasonable,' I said.

'No police, no troubles.' His smile spread. 'Reasonable.'

'Like Brutus.'

'I beg your pardon?'

'No, he was honorable, wasn't he? And I'm reasonable.' The book screamed at me from the counter top. 'This book,' I said, my hand pawing the air above it. 'You're a stranger in my country, and I can't let you—'

He scooped up the book and backed off, teeth flashing furiously. When he reached the door he pocketed the gun, stepped quickly outside, and hurried off westward on Eleventh Street.

Gone but not forgotten.

I stared after him for a moment or two. Then I suppose I sighed, and finally I picked up the envelope and weighed it in my hand as if trying to decide how many stamps to put on it. It was a perfectly ordinary envelope of the sort doctors mail their bills in, except that there was no return address in its upper left-hand corner. Just a simple blank envelope, dime-store stationery.

336

Rudyard Whelkin had agreed to pay me fifteen thousand dollars for the book he wanted. Somehow I couldn't make myself believe this little envelope contained fifteen thousand dollars.

I opened it. Fifty-dollar bills, old ones, out of sequence.

Ten of them.

Five hundred dollars.

Big hairy deal.

I dragged the bargain table in from the street. Somehow I wasn't eager to stay open a few extra minutes in order to peddle a few old books at three for a buck. I hung the *Closed* sign in the window and set about shutting things down, transferring some cash from the register to my wallet, filling out a deposit slip for the check I'd taken in on the Trollope set.

I folded the ten fifties and buttoned them into a hip pocket. And snatched up a brown-wrapped book from a drawer in the office desk, and let myself out of the store and went through my nightly lock-up routine with the steel gates.

For a few minutes I just walked, north on Broadway, then east on Thirteenth Street, then uptown on Third Avenue. The corner of Four-teenth and Third was aswarm with persons addicted to any of a variety of licit and illicit substances. Junkies scratched themselves, winos passed pints around, and a methadone enthusiast kept slamming the heel of his hand thoughtfully against a brick building. I straightened the knot in my tie – I'd put the tie on before leaving the store – and walked onward, resisting the temptation to give my hip pocket a reassuring pat.

Five hundred dollars.

There's a big difference between five hundred and fifteen thousand, and while the latter sum represents a very decent return on a night's labor, the former is small compensation for risking life and limb, not to mention liberty. So a five-hundred-dollar payment for *The Deliverance of Fort Bucklow* was like no money at all.

On the other hand, five hundred dollars was a princely sum for the Grosset & Dunlap reprint edition of *Soldiers Three*, which is what my turbaned and bearded visitor had taken from me at gunpoint. I rather doubt it was what he wanted, but you don't always get what you want, do you?

I'd had the book priced reasonably enough at $1.95. And I had the Haggard copy of *The Deliverance of Fort Bucklow* all nicely wrapped in brown kraft paper and tucked under my arm, and wouldn't Rudyard Whelkin be happy to see it?

It's funny how things work out.

7

I was early, of course. My appointment with Whelkin wasn't until six-thirty and I'd locked up the shop just a few minutes after five, not wanting to stick around in case the Sikh realized his mistake. I had a sign on the wall emphasizing that all sales were final, but I had a feeling he'd expect me to make an exception in his case. So I took my time walking uptown, and I was still twenty minutes early when I reached the corner of Sixty-sixth and Second. A bar on the corner looked inviting, and I accepted the invitation.

I don't drink when I'm working. But this wasn't exactly work, and I'd felt the need for something after staring into the barrel of the Sikh's automatic. As a matter of fact, I'd stopped for a quick bracer in a Third Avenue ginmill on my way uptown. Now I wanted something a little more civilized, a dry Rob Roy in a stemmed and frosted glass.

I sipped it and did a little thinking, ticking off points on my fingers.

Point One: Only J. Rudyard Whelkin had known I was going to steal the book from the Arkwright house in Forest Hills Gardens.

Point Two: It was four o'clock before Whelkin knew I had the book. He'd known I was going there, but there's many a slip between the cup and the whatsit, and it wasn't until he called me at the bookstore that he knew for certain my trip to Queens had paid off. In all likelihood, Arkwright himself didn't even know the book was missing yet.

Point Three: The Sikh had not been a bizarre coincidence, one of those phenomena that make life the ever-exciting proposition it indisputably is. No way. The Sikh had darkened my doorway because he knew I had stolen Arkwright's copy of *The Deliverance of Fort Bucklow.*

Hard work, thinking. I checked my watch, took another sip of my Rob Roy.

Assumption: The Sikh did not have mystical powers. He knew I had the book because the information had somehow reached him via Whelkin.

Hypothesis: J. Rudyard Whelkin was as reluctant as the next skinflint to part with fifteen grand. Once he'd established that I had the book in my possession, he simply dispatched his faithful native servant

338

to fetch it for him, instructing him to slip me the ten fifties to smooth my ruffled feathers.

The hypothesis had me clenching my teeth and making a fist at the very thought. I had a little more of my Rob Roy and did some deep breathing.

Rebuttal: The hypothesis didn't make sense. If Whelkin was going to rob me, why send someone to the store? He'd already taken pains to set up a meeting on East Sixty-sixth Street, where he could set up an elaborate ambush with ease.

Alternate Hypothesis: The Sikh was somebody else's faithful native servant. Hadn't Whelkin mentioned that several parties had intended to bid on the book at Trebizond's London auction? Was it not possible that one of them had followed the book to New York, scheming to wrest it away from Arkwright's possession, only to see it whisked out from under his nose by one B. G. Rhodenbarr?

That seemed to make more sense, but it still left a stone or two unturned. I found myself wondering what would happen when the Sikh's employer took a look at *Soldiers Three*. The sooner I turned the book over to Whelkin and collected my fifteen thousand dollars, the better I'd be able to cope with him. The best way to cope, I felt, would be to take a quick vacation somewhere, spending a portion of the boodle and giving him time to cool off or leave town or, ideally, both.

I stood up.

And sat down again.

Did I have anything to fear from Whelkin? I was pretty sure he hadn't sent the Sikh, but suppose I was wrong? Or suppose he had not sent the Sikh and indeed knew nothing about the Sikh, but suppose he had his own ideas about doing me out of my fee? Was it possible I'd let myself be snowed by the elegant manner and the Martingale Club membership? The rich, I've noted, are no more eager to part with a bundle than anyone else. And here I was, meeting him on his own turf, bringing him the book like a dutiful dog with the evening paper in his mouth. Lord, I couldn't even testify that Whelkin *had* fifteen thousand dollars, let alone that he was prepared to hand it over to me.

I went to the men's room, book in hand. When I returned I had both hands free. The book was wedged under my belt against the small of my back, out of sight beneath my suit jacket.

I finished the last of my drink. I'd have liked another, but that could wait until the completion of my business transaction.

First things first.

The house on Sixty-sixth Street was an elegant brown-stone with a plant-filled bay window on the parlor floor. Taller buildings stood on either side of it, but the old brownstone held its own. I walked up a half flight of stairs and studied a row of bells in the vestibule.

M. Porlock. 3-D.

I rang twice. Nothing happened for a moment and I checked my watch again. It said 6:29 and it is a watch that rarely lies. I placed my finger on the bell again, tentatively, and at that instant the answering buzzer sounded and I pushed the door open.

There were two apartments on the parlor floor, four each on the three floors above it. (The basement had its own entrance.) I mounted two flights of carpeted stairs with an increasing feeling of mingled anticipation and dread. The D apartments were at the rear of the building. The door of 3-D was slightly ajar. I gave it a rap with my knuckles and it was almost immediately drawn open by a square-shouldered woman wearing a muted-plaid skirt and a brass-buttoned navy blazer. Her dark-brown hair was very short and irregularly cut, as if the barber had been either a drunken friend or a very trendy beautician.

She said, 'Mr Rhodenbarr? Do come in.'

'I was supposed to meet—'

'Ruddy Whelkin, I know. He's expected at any moment. He rang up not ten minutes ago to say he'd been momentarily detained.' She smiled suddenly. 'I'm to make you comfortable, you see. I'm Madeleine Porlock.'

I took the hand she extended. 'Bernie Rhodenbarr,' I said. 'But you already know that.'

'Your reputation precedes you. Won't you have a seat? And may I get you a drink?'

'Not just now,' I said. To the drink, that is; I seated myself in a tub chair upholstered in glove-soft green Naugahyde. The living room was small but comfortable, with a Victorian rosewood love seat and a floral-slip-covered easy chair in addition to the tub chair. The bold abstract oil over the love seat somehow complemented the furnishings. It was a nice room, and I said as much.

'Thank you. You're sure you won't have a little sherry?'

'I'll pass for now.'

There was classical music playing on the radio, a woodwind ensemble that sounded like Vivaldi. Madeleine Porlock crossed the room, adjusted the volume. There was something familiar about her but I couldn't think what it was.

'Ruddy should be here any moment,' she said, again.

'Have you known him long?'

'Ruddy? Seems like ages.'

I tried picturing them as a couple. They didn't bear mentioning in the same breath with Steve and Eydie, or even Bob and Carol and Ted and Alice, but they weren't utterly inconceivable. He was a good deal older than she, certainly. She looked to be in her early thirties, although I'm terrible at judging people's ages.

Did I know her from somewhere?

I was on the verge of asking when she clapped her hands together as if she'd just hit on the principle of specific gravity. 'Coffee,' she said.

'I beg your pardon?'

'You'll have a cup of coffee. It's freshly made. You will have some, won't you?'

I'd turned down the drink because I wanted to remain alert. All the more reason to have the coffee. We agreed on cream and sugar and she went off to prepare it. I settled myself in the tub chair and listened to the music, thinking how nice it would be to be able to play the bassoon. I'd priced bassoons once and they cost a lot, and I understand the instrument's exceedingly difficult to learn, and I don't even remember how to read music, so I don't suppose I'll ever go so far as to acquire a bassoon and set about taking lessons, but whenever I hear the instrument in a concerto or a chamber work it occurs to me how nice it would be to go to sleep one night and wake up the following morning owning a bassoon and knowing how to play it.

Things go so much simpler in fantasy. You leave out all the scut work that way.

'Mr Rhodenbarr?'

I took the coffee from her. She'd served it in a chunky earthenware mug ornamented with a geometric design. I sniffed at the coffee and allowed that it smelled good.

'I hope you like it,' she said. 'It's a Louisiana blend I've been using lately. It has chicory in it.'

'I like chicory.'

'Oh, so do I,' she said. She made it sound as though our mutual enthusiasm could be the start of something big. The woodwind quintet ended – it *was* Vivaldi, according to the announcer – and a Haydn symphony replaced it.

I took a sip of my coffee. She asked if it was all right and I assured her that it was wonderful, although it really wasn't. There was a slight off-taste discernible beneath the cream and sugar, and I decided that chicory was one of those things I don't really like but just think I do.

'Ruddy said you were bringing him something, Mr Rhodenbarr.'

'Yes.'

'He seemed very anxious about it. You have it with you, of course?'

I drank more coffee and decided that it wasn't really all that bad. The Haydn symphony rolled in waves, echoing within the little room.

'Mr Rhodenbarr.'

'Nice music,' I said.

'Do you have the book, Mr Rhodenbarr?'

I was smiling. I had the feeling it was a sort of dopey smile but I couldn't seem to do anything about it.

'Mr Rhodenbarr?'

'You're very pretty.'

'The book, Mr Rhodenbarr.'

'I know you from somewhere. You look familiar.' I was spilling coffee on myself, for some reason, and I felt deeply embarrassed. I shouldn't have had that Rob Roy, I decided, and then Madeleine Porlock was taking the cup away from me and placing it carefully on the glass-topped coffee table.

'I always walk into those things,' I confided. 'Glass tables. Don't see them. Walk right into them. You have orange hair.'

'Close your eyes, Mr Rhodenbarr.'

My eyes slammed shut. I pried them open and looked at her. She had a mop of curly orange hair, and as I stared at her it disappeared and her hair was short and dark again. I blinked, trying to make it orange, but it stayed as it was.

'The coffee,' I said, brilliantly. 'Something in the coffee.'

'Sit back and relax, Mr Rhodenbarr.'

'You drugged me.' I braced my hands on the arms of the chair and tried to stand. I couldn't even get my behind off the chair. My arms had no strength in them and my legs didn't even appear to exist anymore.

'Orange hair,' I said.

'Close your eyes, Mr Rhodenbarr.'

'Have to get up—'

'Sit back and rest. You're very tired.'

God, that was the truth. I gulped air, shook my head furiously in an attempt to shake some of the cobwebs loose. That was a mistake – the motion set off a string of tiny firecrackers somewhere in the back of my skull. Haydn dipped and soared. My eyes closed again, and I strained to get them open and saw her leaning over me, telling me how sleepy I was.

I kept my eyes open. Even so, my field of vision began to darken along its edges. Then patches of black appeared here and there, and they grew together until it was all black, everywhere, and I gave up and let go and fell all the way down to the bottom.

I was dreaming something about an earthquake in Turkey, houses crumbling around me, boulders rolling down the sides of mountains. I fought my way out of the dream like an underwater swimmer struggling to reach the water's surface. The Turkish earthquake was part of the hourly newscast on the radio. The Social Democrats had scored substantial gains in parliamentary elections in Belgium. A Hollywood actor had died of an overdose of sleeping pills. The President was expected to veto something or other.

A buzzer was sounding nearby, interrupting the monotony of the newscast. I managed to open my eyes. My head ached and my mouth tasted as though I'd fallen asleep sucking the wad of cotton from the vitamin jar. The buzzer buzzed again and I wondered why nobody was answering it.

I opened my eyes again. Evidently they had closed without my knowing it. The radio announcer was inviting me to subscribe to *Backpacker Magazine*. I didn't want to but wasn't sure I had the strength to refuse. The buzzer was still buzzing. I wished Madeleine Porlock would get up from the Victorian love seat and answer it, or make them stop buzzing, or something.

The radio switched to music. Something with violins. Soothing. I opened my eyes again. The buzzing had stopped and there was the sound of heavy footsteps on the stairs.

I was still in the tub chair. My left hand lay in my lap like a small dead animal. My right arm was draped over the side of the chair, and there was something in my right hand.

I opened my eyes again, gave my head a shake. Something loose rattled around inside it. Someone was knocking on the door. I wished the Porlock woman would answer it, but she was in no better shape than I was.

They banged harder on the door and I opened my eyes again, and this time I managed to straighten up in the chair and kick through to something resembling actual consciousness. I gulped air and blinked rapidly and remembered where I was and what I was doing there.

I moved my left hand, reached around and felt the small of my back. *The Deliverance of Fort Bucklow* was gone.

Well, that figured.

'Open up in there!'

Knock, knock, knock, and I felt like the drunken porter in *Macbeth*. I called out for them to wait a minute and reached to check my hip pocket for the Sikh's five hundred dollars. I couldn't reach that pocket with my left hand. And why was I using my left, anyway? Oh, sure. Because there was something heavy in my right hand.

'Police! Open up in there!'

More furious pounding on the door. I raised my right hand. There was a gun in it. I stared stupidly at it, then raised it to my face and sniffed its muzzle. I smelled that particular mix of gun oil and gunpowder and burnt odor characteristic of a recently fired weapon.

I looked at the love seat again, hoping to find it empty, wishing what I'd seen earlier had been a mirage. But Madeleine Porlock was still there, and she hadn't moved, and I could see now that she wasn't likely to, not without more help than I could give her.

She'd been shot in the middle of the forehead, right where the horrid little girl had a little curl, and I had a fairly good idea what gun had done the deed.

8

I got up quickly – too quickly – the blood rushed to my feet, or wherever it goes under such circumstances, and I very nearly fell back down again. But I stayed on my feet and fought to clear my head a little.

The radio was still playing. I wanted to turn it off but left it alone. The cops had left off knocking on the door and were slamming into it every few seconds. Any moment now the door would give and they'd come stumbling into the room.

I decided I didn't want to be there when that happened.

I was still holding the damned gun. I dropped it, and then I picked it up and wiped my prints off it, and then I dropped it again and made my way past the radio and through a short hallway with a bathroom and closet on one side and a pullman kitchen on the other. At the end of the hallway a door opened into a fair-sized bedroom furnished with a four-poster spool bed and a Pennsylvania Dutch blanket chest. There was a window on the far wall over the bed, and *it* opened onto a fire escape, and I damn well opened it.

Fresh air, cold fresh air. I filled both lungs and felt some of the cobwebs leave my brain. I climbed out onto the fire escape and closed the window after me. With it shut I could just barely hear the sounds of police officers caroming off the apartment door.

Now what?

I looked down and a wave of vertigo hit me. I thought of all the drug labels with their warnings about driving or operating machinery. *If drowsiness occurs, stay off rickety fire escapes.*

I took another look. Below me, the fire escape terminated in a court-yard walled off on all three sides. I might get into the basement, but there was sure to be a cop posted downstairs, most likely a fat one who hadn't wanted to climb up two flights in the first place.

So I started up the fire escape, up past the fourth floor and on to the roof. Someone had built a redwood sundeck up there, and there were trees and shrubs in large redwood planters. It was all very lovely, but there was one trouble with it – I couldn't get off it. The adjoining buildings were both a hundred or more feet taller than the one I was standing on, and the heavy fire door leading back into the building couldn't be opened without a key. This wouldn't have been a problem if I'd had my tools along, but who figured I'd need them?

Back down the fire escape. I paused at the fourth-floor landing, trying to decide if I wanted to take my chances with whoever was posted at ground level. I could always break into the basement and just hide there in the boiler room until the heat died down, but did I really want to do that? For that matter, did I want to scurry past the bedroom window of the Porlock apartment when the police were most likely already in there?

I took a moment to check the two fourth-floor apartments. The one on the right – 4-D, I suppose, directly above the Porlock place – had its shade drawn. I pressed my ear to the windowpane and caught *Brady Bunch* reruns on the television set. The shade was drawn a few yards to the left at 4-C, but I couldn't hear anything inside, nor could I see any light around the edges of the window shade.

Of course the window was locked.

If I'd had a glass cutter I could have drawn a neat freehand circle on the appropriate pane of glass, reached in and turned the window lock. If I'd had some tape I could have broken any pane I wanted with no more noise than you'd make snapping a dry twig. If I'd had . . .

If wishes were horses, burglars would ride. I kicked in a pane of glass and closed my eyes until the tinkling stopped. I put my ear to the opening I'd created and listened for a moment or two, then unlocked the window, raised it, and stepped through it.

A few minutes later I left that apartment in a more conventional manner than I'd entered it, departing through the door and walking briskly down a flight of stairs. I encountered a couple of uniformed patrolmen on the third floor. The door to 3-D was open now, with other cops making themselves busy inside the apartment, while these two stood in the hall with nothing to do.

I asked one what the trouble was. He jutted out his chin at me and told me it was just routine. I nodded, reassured, and went down the other two flights and out.

I wanted to go home. It may or may not be where the heart is but it's where the burglar's tools are, and a burglar, like a workman, is only as good as his tools, and I felt naked without mine. I wasn't sure if the cops had a make on me yet. They'd get one before long, I was fairly sure of that, but I didn't doubt my ability to get in and out of my apartment before they set about looking for me. I had my tools there, I had cash there, and I would have liked to make a quick pit stop and equip myself for whatever lay ahead.

Because what lay ahead didn't look too good from where I sat. Madeleine Porlock had been left with more than the traditional number of holes in her head, and my fingerprints were undoubtedly plastered all over that apartment – on the cup I'd been drinking from, on the glass-topped table, and God knows where else. The same criminal genius that had wrapped my inert fingers around the murder gun would have seen to that.

The police would have a lot of questions for me, and they wouldn't even pay attention to my answers. I, on the other hand, had some hard questions of my own.

Who was Madeleine Porlock? How did she fit into the whole business? Why had she drugged me, and where had her killer come from, and why had he murdered her?

Whatever had become of Rudyard Whelkin?

And, finally, how did the Sikh fit into all of this?

The last question was no more easily answered than the others, but it made me realize I couldn't go home. By now the Sikh and whoever had sent him would know they'd been hoodwinked, which meant I had to avoid whatever places they might logically expect to find me. The store was out, obviously, and so was the apartment, since anyone with access to a Manhattan phone book can ferret out my address.

I flagged a cab heading downtown on Second Avenue. The driver was young and Hispanic, with alert eyes. Were those eyes registering me even as he asked my destination?

'The Village,' I said.

'What part of it?'

'Sheridan Square.'

He nodded shortly and away we went.

Carolyn Kaiser's apartment was on Arbor Court, one of those side-goggled Village lanes I can only find if I start out from the right place. Sheridan Square was the wrong place, so I had to walk up to Greenwich Avenue and then west and south until I hit it. I didn't remember which building was hers, so I went into the vestibules of several until I found her name on a mailbox and rang her bell.

Nobody home. I'd have called first but I didn't have her number with me and it was unlisted, and it's easier to pass a needle through the eye of a camel than to get an unlisted number out of an Information operator. It's hard enough to get listed numbers. I rang a couple of top-floor bells until someone buzzed me into the building. Carolyn lived on the first floor. I took one look at the locks on her door and turned around and left.

I checked a couple of hardware stores on Hudson. All closed. There was a locksmith, but could I really ask him to sell me burglar's tools? I didn't even try. I went to a drugstore and bought masking tape and paper clips and hairpins and a couple of nail files. At the tobacco counter I added a pipesmoker's gizmo equipped with different

346

doohickeys for tamping, reaming, probing, and otherwise mistreating a pipe. It looked to be made of pretty decent steel.

I went back to Carolyn's building and annoyed the top-floor tenants again and got buzzed in a second time. I went to her door and got busy.

With my ring of picks and probes, the operation wouldn't have taken five minutes. With makeshift tools from the drugstore it took closer to ten, during which time two persons entered the building and one left it. If any of them took any notice of me they were too polite to make a scene, and I finished the task at hand and let myself into her place.

Cozy. Very Village, really. One room about fifteen feet square with a teensy lavatory added on in back, so small that your knees nudged the door when you sat on the potty. The bathtub, a large claw-footed relic, was over in the kitchen area with the sink and stove and fridge; Carolyn had had a plywood cover cut to fit it so that she could use it for chopping up vegetables. The walls were painted blue, a deep rich tone, and the window frames and exposed plumbing were a bright yellow.

I used the loo, lit a fire under the leftover coffee (with a match, the pilot didn't work), and let one of the cats check me out. He was a Burmese and nothing intimidated him. His buddy, a wary-eyed Russian Blue, reposed on the double bed, where he tried to blend with the patchwork quilt. I scratched the Burmese behind the ear and he made that bizarre sound they make and rubbed his head against my ankle. I guess I passed inspection.

The coffee boiled. I poured a cup, took a taste, and got flashes of the mug of doctored coffee Madeleine Porlock had given me. I poured it out, heated some water and made some tea, and fortified the brew with an authoritative slug of California brandy from a bottle I found on the shelf over the sink.

It was six-thirty when I kept my appointment at Chez Porlock, and I'd bolted from the place during the seven o'clock newscast. I didn't look at my watch again until I was sitting in Carolyn's wicker chair with my feet up, the second cup of brandied tea half gone and the Russian Blue purring insanely in my lap. It was then just eighteen minutes after nine.

I moved the cat long enough to turn Carolyn's radio to one of the all-news stations, then settled back on the chair again. The cat reclaimed his place and helped me listen to a report on the Turkish earthquake and the presidential veto. There was a disgruntled Albanian holding a couple of people hostage up in Washington Heights, and a reporter on the scene did more than was necessary to put me right in the picture. I stroked the Russian Blue patiently while his Burmese buddy sat on top of a bookcase and made yowling noises.

It was coming up on eleven o'clock when I heard Carolyn's key in the lock. By then I'd switched to an FM jazz station and I had both cats on my lap. I stayed where I was while she unlocked the door, and as she opened it I said, 'It's me, Carolyn. Don't panic.'

'Why should I panic?' She came in, closed the door, locked up. 'Been here long? I was over at the Dutchess and you know what that's like. Except you probably don't, because they don't allow men in there.' She slipped off her jacket, hung it on a doorknob, walked toward the coffee-pot, then spun around suddenly and stared at me. 'Hey,' she said. 'Did we make a date that I forgot?'

'No,'

'Randy let you in? I thought she was visiting her goddam aunt in Bath Beach. What was she doing here? Did she go out to Brooklyn afterward or what?'

'I haven't seen Randy.'

'Then how'd you get in, Bernie?'

'I sort of let myself in.'

'Yeah, but where'd you get a key?' She frowned at me. Then light dawned. 'Oh,' she said, '*I* get it. Other people need keys. You're like Casper the Ghost. You walk through walls.'

'Not exactly.'

The cats had deserted my lap and were brushing themselves passion-ately against her ankles, desperate to be fed. She ignored them.

She said, 'Bernie?'

'The radio.'

'Huh?'

'It'll answer part of your question.'

She listened, cocked her head. 'Sounds like Monk,' she said. 'But I don't know, it's not as choppy as Monk and he's doing a lot of things with his left hand.'

'It's Jimmy Rowles, but that's not what I meant. After the record ends, Carolyn.'

After the record ended we got a quickie commercial for a jazz cruise to the Bahamas, and I had to explain that that wasn't it either. Then they gave us the eleven o'clock news, and high time, too. The Turkish earthquake, the flaky Albanian, the probable presidential veto, and then the extraordinary news that a convicted burglar, Bernard Rhoden-barr by name, was sought in connection with the murder of one Madeleine Porlock, who had been shot to death in her own apartment on East Sixty-sixth Street.

The announcer moved on to other matters. Carolyn cut him off in the middle of a sentence, looked at me for a moment, then went over to the kitchen area and fed the cats. 'Chicken and kidneys tonight,' she told them. 'One of your all-time favorites, guys.'

She stood for a moment with her back to me, her little hands on her hips, watching the wee rascals eat. Then she came over and sat on the edge of the bed.

'I should have known it was Jimmy Rowles,' she said. 'I used to catch him at Bradley's all the time. I haven't been going there lately because Randy hates jazz, but if we break up, which I think we're in the process of doing, the hell, I'll get to the jazz clubs more, so it's an ill wind, right?'

'Right.'

'Madeleine Doorlock? Funny name.'

'Porlock.'

'Still unusual. Who was she, Bern?'

'Beats me. We were strangers until this afternoon.'

'You kill her?'

'No.'

She crossed her legs at the knee, planted an elbow on the upper knee, cupped her hand, rested her chin in it. 'All set,' she announced. 'You talk and I'll listen.'

'Well,' I said, 'it's a long story.'

9

It *was* a long story, and she listened patiently through the whole thing, leaving the bed only to fetch the brandy bottle. When I finished she cracked the seal on a fresh bottle and poured us each a generous measure. I'd given up diluting mine with tea and she'd never started.

'Well, here's to crime,' she said, holding her glass on high. 'No wonder you almost spilled your club soda last time I said that. You were all set to go out and commit one. That's why you weren't drinking, huh?'

'I never drink when I work.'

'I never work when I drink. Same principle. This is all taking me a little time to get used to, Bernie. I really believed you were a guy who used to be a burglar, but now you'd put all of that behind you and you were selling used books. Everything you told that policeman—'

'It was all true up to a point. I don't make a profit on the store, or maybe I do. I'm not much of an accountant. I buy and I sell, and I probably come out ahead, even allowing for rent and light bills and the phone and all. If I worked harder at it I could probably make enough to live on that way. If I hustled, and if I shelved paperbacks instead of wholesaling them, and if I read the want ads in *AB* every week and sent out price quotes all over the place.'

'Instead you go out and knock off houses.'

'Just once in a while.'

'Special occasions.'

'That's right.'

'To make ends meet.'

'Uh-huh.'

She frowned in thought, scratched her head, sipped a little brandy. 'Let's see,' she said. 'You came here because it's a safe place for you to be, right?'

'Right.'

'Well, that's cool. We're friends, aren't we? I know it means I'm harboring a fugitive, and I don't particularly give a shit. What are friends for?'

'You're one in a million, Carolyn.'

350

'You bet your ass. Listen, you can stay as long as you like and no questions asked, but the thing is I do have some questions, but I won't ask them if you don't want.'

'Ask me anything.'

'What's the capital of South Dakota? No, seriously, folks. Why'd you wait until the Arkwrights came home? Why not just duck in and out quick like a bunny? I always thought burglars preferred to avoid human contact.'

I nodded. 'It was Whelkin's idea. He wanted the book to be stolen without Arkwright even realizing it was gone. If I didn't take anything else and didn't disturb the house, and if the book was still there when Jesse Arkwright played his bedtime game of pocket billiards, it would be at least a day before he missed it. Whelkin was certain he'd be the prime suspect, because he wants the book so badly and he's had this feud with Arkwright, and an alibi wouldn't really help because Arkwright would just figure he hired someone to do it.'

'Which he did do.'

'Which he did do,' I agreed. 'But the longer it takes for Arkwright to know the book's missing, and the harder it is for him to dope out how or when it disappeared, and the more time Whelkin has to tuck it away where it will never be found—'

'And that's why you just took the book and left everything else.'

'Right.'

'Okay. That part makes sense now, I guess. But what happened to Whelkin?'

'I don't know.'

'You figure he killed her?'

'I don't think so.'

'Why not? He set up the meeting. He got her to drug you, and then when you were unconscious he killed her.'

'Why?'

'To frame you, I suppose. To get you out of the picture.'

'Why not just kill me?'

'I don't know.' She gnawed at a knuckle. 'She can't just come out of the air, this Porlock babe. Whelkin sent you to her, she doped your coffee, and she must have been after the book because she was asking you for it before you had a chance to nod out. Then she frisked you and took it herself.'

'Or the killer did.'

'You never heard a gunshot?'

'I was really out cold. And maybe he used a silencer, but if he did he took it along with him. He also took the book, plus the five hundred dollars the Sikh gave me.' I shrugged. 'I figured all along that was too much to charge for a reprint copy of *Soldiers Three*. Well, easy come, easy go.'

351

'That's what they say. Maybe the Sikh killed her.'

'How do you figure that?'

'Maybe they were working together and he double-crossed her at the end.' She shrugged elaborately. 'I don't know, Bern. I'm just spinning my wheels a little. She must have been connected with Whelkin, though, don't you think?'

'I suppose so. He did lead me straight to her apartment. But—'

'But what?'

'But why wouldn't he just *buy* the book?'

'Maybe he couldn't afford it. But you're right, that would have been the easiest thing for him to do. He already paid you some of it in advance, didn't he? How much did he still owe you?'

I didn't say anything.

'Bernie?'

I sighed. 'Just yesterday,' I said, 'I told a shoplifter he was too dumb to steal. He's not the only one.'

'You didn't—'

'I didn't get *any* of the money in advance.'

'Oh.'

I shrugged, sighed, drank. 'He was a member of the Martingale Club,' I said, 'Had a sort of English accent. Dressed very tweedy.'

'So?'

'So his front snowed me, that's all. He finessed the whole topic of advance payment. I don't know how, but I walked into that house with nothing in my pocket but my hands. Jesus, Carolyn, I even dipped into my own funds for gasoline and bridge tolls. I'm beginning to feel really stupid.'

'Whelkin conned you. He set you up and she polished you off, and then he shot her and left you in the frame.'

I thought it over. 'No,' I said.

'No?'

'I don't think so. Why use her at all? He could slip me a mickey as easily as she could. And there's something else. That last telephone conversation I had with him, when he set up the meeting at her apartment. He sounded out of synch. I thought at the time he'd been drinking.'

'So?'

'I bet they drugged him.'

'The way they drugged you?'

'Not quite. Not the same drug, or the poor bastard wouldn't have been able to talk at all. I wonder what she gave me. It must have been powerful stuff. It had me hallucinating.'

'Like acid?'

'I never had any acid.'

'Neither did I.'

352

'And this wasn't that kind of hallucination, with animals materializing on the walls and things like that. My perceptions just got distorted there before I blacked out. The music was getting loud and soft alternately, for example. And her face seemed to melt when I stared at it, but that was just before I went under.'

'And you said something about her hair.'

'Right, it kept turning orange. She had really short hair, dark brown, and I kept flashing that she had a head full of bright orange curls. Then I would blink and she'd have short dark hair again. Oh, for Christ's sake.'

'What is it, Bernie?'

'I know where I saw her before. And she *did* have curly orange hair. It must have been a wig.'

'The dark hair?'

'The orange hair. She came to the shop and she must have been wearing an orange wig. I'm positive it was the same woman. Squared shoulders, blocky figure, a kind of a stern square-jawed face – I'm positive it was her. She must have come to the shop three or four times.'

'With Rudyard Whelkin?'

'No. He only came there once. Then we had lunch in the Martingale Club that same day, and I met him once more at the club for drinks and we talked several times over the phone. She came to the shop – well, I don't know when I first noticed her, but it must have been within the past week. Then yesterday she bought a book from me. Virgil's *Eclogues*, the Heritage Club edition. It was her. No question about it.'

'What was she doing?'

'Looking things over, I suppose. Same reason I went out to Forest Hills with a clipboard. Reconnaissance. Say, can I put the radio on?'

'What for?'

'Midnight news.'

'It's that time already? Sure, put it on.'

I moved a cat and switched on the radio. I sat down and the cat returned to my lap and resumed purring. The news broadcast was a repeat of the eleven o'clock summary, except that the Albanian had surrendered without harming any of his hostages. He'd evidently gone bananas when he learned that his common-law wife had another common-law husband, which made them common-law husbands-in-law, or something. Madeleine Porlock was still dead and the police were still looking for one Bernard Rhodenbarr.

I moved the cat again, switched off the news, and sat down again. Carolyn asked me how it felt to be wanted by the police. I told her it felt terrible.

'How'd they know it was you, Bernie? Fingerprints?'

'Or the wallet.'

'What wallet?'

353

'My wallet. Whoever frisked me got it – Madeleine Porlock or her killer. The book, the five hundred bucks, and the wallet. Maybe somebody stashed it where the cops would be sure to find it.'

'Weren't you supposed to be unconscious when they arrived?'

'Maybe the wallet was a form of insurance. Or maybe the killer took the wallet on the chance I had something incriminating in it, like the card Whelkin gave me or some notes to myself.' I shrugged. 'I suppose the wallet could be anywhere right now. I suppose I should be all worked up about stopping my Master Charge card before someone charges a ton of airline tickets to my account. Somehow that's way down on my list of priorities.'

'I can understand that.' She put her chin in her hand again and leaned forward to fasten her blue eyes on me. 'What's at the top of the list, Bernie?'

'Huh?'

'The priority list. What are you going to do?'

'Beats me.'

'How about another drink while you think about it?'

I shook my head. 'I think I've had enough.'

'I had enough two or three drinks ago but I'm not going to let a little thing like that stop me.' She got the bottle and helped herself. 'You can just know when you've had enough and then stop?'

'Sure.'

'That's remarkable,' she said. She sipped her brandy, looked at me over the brim of the glass. 'Did you know there was anybody else in the apartment? Besides the Porlock woman?'

'No. But I never got past the living room until she was dead. I thought it was just the two of us and we were waiting for Whelkin.'

'The killer could have been in the other room.'

'It's possible.'

'Or she was alone, and she drugged you and took the book and the money and the wallet, and then she was on her way out the door and in came a man with a gun.'

'Right.'

'Who? The Sikh? Whelkin?'

'I dunno, Carolyn.'

'Why on earth would she wear a wig? I mean, she wasn't anybody you knew to begin with, right? So why would she want to disguise herself?'

'Beats me.'

'How about the Sikh? Was that a disguise? Maybe the Sikh was Rudyard Whelkin.'

'He had a beard and a turban.'

'The beard could have been a fake. And a turban is something you can put on and then take off.'

'The Sikh was enormous. Six-four easy, maybe more.'

'You never heard of elevator shoes?'

'Whelkin wasn't the Sikh,' I said. 'Trust me.'

'All I do is trust you. But back to the other question. How do you get out of the mess you're in? Can you go to the cops?'

'That's the one thing I *can't* do. They'll book me for Murder One. I could try pleading to a lesser charge, or gamble that my lawyer could find a way to addle the jury, but the odds are I'd spend the next ten or twenty years with free room and board. I don't really want to do that.'

'I can understand that. Jesus. Can't you—'

'Can't I what?'

'Tell them what you told me? Scratch that question, huh? Just blame it on the brandy. Because why on earth would they believe you? Nobody'd believe a story like yours except a dyke who shaves dogs. Bernie, there's got to be a way out, but what the hell is it?'

'Find the real killer.'

'Oh, sure,' she said. She clapped a hand to her forehead. 'Now why didn't I think of that? Just find the real killer, solve the crime, get the stolen book back, and everything's copasetic. Just like TV, right? With everything wrapped up in time for the final commercial.'

'And some scenes from next week's show,' I said. 'Don't forget that.'

We talked for a while longer. Then Carolyn started yawning inter-mittently and I caught it from her. We agreed that we ought to get some sleep. We weren't accomplishing anything now and our minds were too tired to work properly.

'You'll stay here,' she said. 'You take the bed.'

'Don't be silly. I'll take the couch.'

'Don't *you* be silly. You're six feet long and so's the bed. I'm five feet long and so's the couch. It's good the Sikh didn't drop in because there's no place to put him.'

'I just thought—'

'Uh-huh. The couch is perfectly comfortable and I sleep on it a lot. I wind up there whenever Randy and I have a medium-level fight.'

'What's a medium-level fight?'

'The kind where she doesn't go home to her own apartment.'

'I didn't know she had one. I thought the two of you lived together.'

'We do, but she's got a place on Morton Street. Smaller than this, if you can believe it. Thank God she's got a place of her own, so that she can move right back into it when we split up.'

'Maybe you should stay there tonight, Carolyn.' She started to say something but I pressed onward. 'If you're at her place, then you're not an accessory after the fact. But if you're here, then there's no question but that you're harboring a fugitive, and—'

'I'll take my chances, Bernie.'

'Well—'

'Besides, it's possible Randy didn't go to Bath Beach. It's possible she's home.'

'Couldn't you stay with her, anyway?'

'Not if someone else is staying with her at the same time.'

'Oh.'

'Uh-huh. We live in a world of infinite possibilities. You get the bed and I get the couch. Okay?'

'Okay.'

I helped her make up the couch. She went into the lavatory and emerged wearing Dr Denton's and scowling as if daring me to laugh. I did not laugh.

I washed up at the kitchen sink, turned off the light, stripped down to my underwear and got into bed. For a while nobody said anything.

Then she said, 'Bern?'

'Yes?'

'I don't know how much you know about gay women, but you probably know that some of us are bisexual. Primarily gay but occasionally interested in going to bed with a man.'

'Uh, I know.'

'I'm not like that.'

'I didn't think you were, Carolyn.'

'I'm exclusively gay.'

'That's what I figured.'

'*I* figured it went without saying, but it's been my experience that a lot of things that go without saying, that you're better off if you say them.'

'I understand.'

More silence.

'Bernie? She took the five hundred dollars and the wallet, right?'

'I had about two hundred dollars in my wallet, too. That was an expensive cup of coffee she gave me, let me tell you.'

'How'd you pay for the cab?'

'Huh?'

'The cab downtown. And how did you buy that stuff at the drugstore so you could pick my lock? What did you use for money?'

'Oh,' I said.

'Do you keep a few extra dollars in your shoe for emergencies?'

'Well, no,' I said. 'Not that it doesn't sound like a good idea, but no, Carolyn.'

'Well?'

'I told you about the fire escape, didn't I? How I tried the roof and that was no good, so I went down and broke into an apartment on the fourth floor?'

'You told me.'

'Well, uh, since I was there and all. I, uh, took a few minutes to look around. Opened a few drawers.'

'In the fourth-floor apartment?'

'That's right. There was just small change in a dresser drawer, but one of the kitchen canisters had money in it. You'd be surprised how many people keep cash in the kitchen.'

'And you took it?'

'Sure. I got a little over sixty dollars. Not enough to retire on, but it covered the cab and what I spent at the drugstore.'

'Sixty dollars.'

'More like sixty-five. Plus the bracelet.'

'The bracelet?'

'Couldn't resist it,' I said. 'There was other jewelry that didn't tempt me at all, but this one bracelet – well, I'll show you in the morning.'

'You'll show me in the morning.'

'Sure. Don't let me forget.'

'Jesus!'

'What's the matter?'

'You actually committed a burglary.'

'Well, I'm a burglar, Carolyn.'

'That's what I have to get used to. You're a burglar. You steal things out of people's homes. That's what burglars do. They steal things.'

'As a general rule.'

'You took the money because you needed it. Your own money was gone and you had to get away from the police and the money was there, so you took it.'

'Right.'

'And you took the bracelet because – Why'd you take the bracelet, Bernie?'

'Well—'

'Because it was there. Like Mt Everest. But it was a bracelet instead of a mountain, and instead of climbing it you stole it.'

'Carolyn—'

'It's all right, Bernie. Honest it is. I'll get used to it. You'll show me the bracelet in the morning?'

'I'll show you right now if you want.'

'No, the morning's soon enough, Bernie. Bernie?'

'What?'

'Goodnight, Bernie.'

'Goodnight, Carolyn.'

10

It was one of those chatty morning programs that tells you more about weather and traffic than anyone could possibly care to know. There was a massive tie-up on the Major Deegan Expressway, I learned, and a thirty-percent chance of rain.

'Something ominous has happened to weather reports,' I told Carolyn. 'Have you noticed how they never tell you what it's going to do anymore? They just quote you the odds.'

'I know.'

'That way they're never wrong because they've never gone out on a limb. If they say there's a five-percent chance of snow and we wind up hip-deep in it, all that means is a long shot came in. They've transformed the weather into some sort of celestial crap game.'

'There's another muffin, Bernie.'

'Thanks.' I took it, buttered it. 'It's all tied into the moral decline of the nation,' I said. 'Lottery tickets. Off-track betting. Gambling casinos in Atlantic City. Can you tell me what in the hell a thirty-percent chance of rain means? What do I do, carry a third of an umbrella?'

'Here comes the news, Bernie.'

I ate my muffin and sipped my coffee and listened to the news. My reaction to the weather report notwithstanding, I felt pretty good. My sleep had been deep and uninterrupted, and Carolyn's morning coffee, unadulterated with chicory or knockout drops, had my eyes all the way open.

So I sat wide-eyed and heard how I'd gained access to the house on Sixty-sixth Street via the fire escape, first visiting the fourth-floor apartment of Mr and Mrs Arthur Blinn, where I'd stolen an undisclosed sum of money, a diamond bracelet, a Piaget wristwatch, several miscellaneous pieces of jewelry, and a full-length Russian sable coat. I'd descended a flight to 3-D, where Madeleine Porlock had interrupted my larcenous labors, only to be shot dead with a .32-caliber automatic for her troubles. I'd left the gun behind, escaping with my loot, scampering down the fire escape moments before the police arrived on the scene.

When the announcer moved on to other topics I switched him off. Carolyn had a funny expression on her face. I reached into my pants

358

pocket and came up with the bracelet, plopping it down on the table in front of her. She turned it in her hand so that light glinted off the stones.

'Pretty,' she said. 'What's it worth?'

'I could probably get a few hundred for it. Art Deco's the rage these days. But I just took it because I liked the looks of it.'

'Uh-huh. What did the coat look like?'

'I never even looked in the closets. Oh, you thought—' I shook my head. 'More evidence of the moral decline of the nation,' I said. 'All I took was the cash and the bracelet, Carolyn. The rest was a little insurance scam the Blinns decided to work.'

'You mean—'

'I mean they decided they've been paying premiums all these years, so why not take advantage of the burglary they've been waiting for? A coat, a watch, some miscellaneous jewelry, and of course they'll report a higher cash loss than they actually sustained, and even if the insurance company chisels a little, they'll wind up four or five grand to the good.'

'Jesus,' she said. 'Everybody's a crook.'

'Not quite,' I said. 'But sometimes it seems that way.'

I made up the bed while she did up the breakfast dishes. Then we sat down with the last of the coffee and tried to figure out where to start. There seemed to be two loose ends we could pick at, Madeleine Porlock and J. Rudyard Whelkin.

'If we knew where he was,' I said, 'we might be able to get somewhere.'

'We already know where *she* is.'

'But we don't know who she is. Or was. I wish I had my wallet. I had his card. His address was somewhere in the East Thirties but I don't remember the street or the number.'

'That makes it tough.'

'You'd think I'd remember the phone number. I dialed it enough yesterday.' I picked up the phone, dialed the first three numbers hoping the rest would come to me, then gave up and cradled the phone. The phone book didn't have him and neither did the Information operator. There was an M. Porlock in the book, though, and for no particular reason I dialed the listed number. It rang a few times and I hung up.

'Maybe we should start with the Sikh,' Carolyn suggested.

'We don't even know his name.'

'That's a point.'

'There ought to be something about her in the paper. The radio just gives you the surface stuff, but there ought to be something beyond that in the *Times*. Where she worked and if she was married, that kind of thing.'

'And Whelkin belonged to the Martingale Club.'

'True.'

'So we've each got a place to start, Bernie. I'll be back in a minute.' It was closer to ten minutes when she returned with both papers. She read the *News* while I read the *Times*. Then we switched.

'Not a whole lot,' I said.

'Something, though. Who do you want, Whelkin or Porlock?'

'Don't you have to trim a poodle or something?'

'I'm taking Whelkin. You've got Porlock, Bernie. Okay?'

'Okay.'

'I guess I'll go over to his club. Maybe I can learn something that way.'

'Maybe.'

'How about you? You won't leave the apartment, will you?'

I shook my head. 'I'll see what I can find out over the phone.'

'That sounds like a good idea.'

'And maybe I'll pray a little.'

'To whom? St Dismas?'

'Wouldn't hurt.'

'Or the lost-objects guy, because we ought to see about getting that book back.'

'Anthony of Padua.'

'Right.'

'Actually,' I said, 'I was thinking more of St Raymond Nonnatus. Patron saint of the falsely accused.'

She looked at me. 'You're making this up.'

'That's a false accusation, Carolyn.'

'You're not making it up?'

'Nope.'

'There's really a—'

'Yep.'

'Well, by all means,' she said. 'Pray.'

The phone started ringing minutes after she left the apartment. It rang five times and stopped. I picked up the *Times* and it started ringing again and rang twelve times before it quit. I read somewhere that it only takes a minute for a telephone to ring twelve times. I'll tell you, it certainly seemed longer than that.

I went back to the *Times*. The back-page story gave Madeleine Porlock's age as forty-two and described her as a psychotherapist. The *Daily News* had given her age but didn't tell what she did for a living. I tried to imagine her with a note pad and a faint Viennese accent, asking me about my dreams. Had she had an office elsewhere? The Victorian love seat was a far cry from the traditional analyst's couch.

Maybe Whelkin was her patient. He told her all about his scheme to gain possession of *The Deliverance of Fort Bucklow*, and then she hypnotized him and got him to make the call to me, and then he got unhypnotized and killed her and took the book back, and . . .

I called the *Times*, got through to someone in the city room. I explained I was Art Matlovich of the Cleveland *Plain Dealer*. We thought the Porlock woman might be a former resident of Cleveland, and did they have anything on her besides what they'd run in the paper?

What they had was mostly negative. No information about next of kin. No clue as to where she'd lived before taking the Sixty-sixth Street apartment fourteen months ago. If she'd ever been in Cleveland, or even flown over the State of Ohio, they didn't know anything about it.

The same call to the *News* was about as unproductive. The man I talked to said he didn't know where the *Times* got off calling Porlock a psychotherapist, that he had the impression she was somebody's mistress, but that they weren't really digging into it because all she was was the victim of an open-and-shut burglary turned homicide. 'It's not much of a story for us,' he said. 'Only reason we played it at all is it's the Upper East Side. See, that's a posh neighborhood and all. I don't know what the equivalent would be in Cleveland.'

Neither did I, so I let it pass.

'This Rhodenbarr,' the *News* man went on. 'They'll pick him up tomorrow or the next day and that's the end of the story. No sex angle, nothing colorful like that. He's just a burglar.'

'Just a burglar,' I echoed.

'Only this time he killed somebody. They'll throw the key away on him this time. He's a guy had his name in the papers before. In connection with homicide committed during a job he was pulling. Up to now he always managed to weasel out of it, but this time he's got his dick in the wringer.'

'Don't be too sure of that,' I said.

'Huh?'

'I mean you never know,' I said quickly. 'The way criminals manage to slip through cracks in the criminal-justice apparatus these days.'

'Jesus,' he said. 'You sound like you been writin' our editorials.'

I no sooner hung up the phone than it started ringing. I put up a fresh pot of coffee. The phone stopped ringing. I went over to it, about to make a call, and it rang again. I waited it out, then used it to call the police. This time I said I was Phil Urbanik of the Minneapolis *Tribune*. I was tired of Cleveland for the time being. I got bounced from one cop to another, spending a lot of time on Hold in the process, before I managed to establish that nobody around the squad-room knew more

361

about Madeleine Porlock than that she was dead. The last cop I spoke with was sure of one other thing, too.

'No question,' he said. 'Rhodenbarr killed her. One bullet, close range, smack in the forehead. M.E.'s report says death was instantaneous, which you don't have to be a doctor to tell. He left prints in both apartments.'

'He must have been careless,' I suggested.

'Getting old and sloppy. Losing his touch. Here's a guy, his usual MO's to wear rubber gloves with the palms cut out so he don't leave a print anywhere.'

'You know him?'

'No, but I seen his sheet. You'd figure him to be pretty slick, plus he always stayed away from violence, and here he's sloppy enough to leave prints and he went and killed a woman. You know what I figure? What I figure is drugs.'

'He's involved with drugs?'

'I think he musta been high on them. You get hopped up and you're capable of anything.'

'How about the gun? Was it his?'

'Maybe he found it there. We didn't trace it yet. Could be the Porlock woman had it for protection. It wasn't registered, but what does that mean? Maybe he stole it upstairs. The couple up there said no, but if it was an unregistered weapon they'd deny it. What's your interest in the gun, anyway?'

'Just making conversation.'

'Minneapolis, you said?'

'That's right,' I said smoothly. 'Well, I guess that gives us a good hometown angle on the story. All right to say you're close to an arrest?'

'Oh, we'll get him,' he assured me. 'A crook like Rhodenbarr's a creature of habit. He'll be what they call frequenting his old haunts and we'll pick him up. Just a question of time.'

I was standing behind the door when she opened it. She moved into the room saying my name.

'Behind you,' I said, as gently as possible. She clapped her hand to her chest as if to keep her heart where it belonged.

'Jesus,' she said. 'Don't *do* that.'

'Sorry. I wasn't sure it was you.'

'Who else would it be?'

'It could have been Randy.'

'Randy,' she said heavily. Cats appeared and threaded figure eights around her ankles. 'Randy. I don't suppose she called, did she?'

'She might have. It rang a lot but I wasn't answering it.'

'I know you weren't. I called twice myself, and when you didn't answer I figured you weren't picking up the phone, but I also figured maybe you got cabin fever and went out, and then I came home and you weren't here and all of a sudden you were behind me. Don't do that again, huh?'

'I won't.'

'I had a busy day. What time is it? Almost two? I've been running all over the place. I found out some stuff. What's this?'

'I want you to make a phone call for me.'

She took the sheet of paper I handed her but looked at me instead. 'Don't you want to hear what I found out?'

'In a minute. I want you to call the *Times* and insert the ad before they close.'

'What ad?'

'The one I just handed you. In the Personal column.'

'You got some handwriting. You should have been a doctor, did anyone ever tell you that? "Space available on Kipling Society charter excursion to Fort Bucklow. Interested parties call 989–5440.' That's my number.'

'No kidding.'

'You're going to put my number in the paper?'

'Why not?'

'Somebody'll read it and come here.'

'How? By crawling through the wires? The phone's unlisted.'

'No, it's not. This place is a sublet, Bernie, so I kept the phone listed under Nathan Aranow. He's the guy I sublet from. It's like having an unlisted number except there's no extra charge for the privilege, and whenever I get a call for a Nathan Aranow I know it's some pest trying to sell me a subscription to something I don't want. But it's a listed number.'

'So?'

'So the address is in the book. Nathan Aranow, 64 Arbor Court, and the telephone number.'

'So somebody could read the ad and then just go all the way through the phone book reading numbers until they came to this one, right, Carolyn?'

'Oh. You can't get the address from the number?'

'No.'

'Oh. I hope nobody does go through the book, because Aranow's right in the front.'

'Maybe they'll start in the back.'

'I hope so. This ad—'

'A lot of people seem to be anxious to get their hands on this book,' I explained. 'All different people, the way it looks to me. And only one of them knows I don't have it. So if I give the impression that I do have it, maybe one or more of them will get in touch and I'll be able to figure out what's going on.'

363

'Makes sense. Why didn't you just place the ad yourself? Afraid somebody in the *Times* classified department would recognize your voice?'

'No.'

'And they'd say, "Aha, it's Bernard G. Rhodenbarr the burglar, and let's go through the telephone wires and take him into custody.' My God, Bernie, you thought I was being paranoid about the number, and you're afraid to make a phone call.'

'They call back,' I said.

'Huh?'

'When you place an ad with a phone number. To make sure it's not a practical joke. And the phone was ringing constantly, and I wasn't answering it, and I figured the *Times* would call to confirm the ad and how would I know it was them? Paranoia, I suppose, but it seemed easier to wait and let *you* make the call, although I'm beginning to wonder. You'll place the ad for me, won't you?'

'Sure,' she said, and the phone rang as she was reaching for it.

She picked it up, said, 'Hello?' Then she said, 'Listen, I can't talk to you right now. Where are you and I'll call you back.' Pause. 'Company? No, of course not.' Pause. 'I was at the shop. Oh. Well, I was in and out all day. One thing after another.' Pause. 'Dammit, I *can't* talk now, and—' She took the receiver from her ear and looked beseechingly at me. 'She hung up,' she said.

'Randy?'

'Who else? She thought I had company.'

'You do.'

'Yeah, but she thought you were a woman.'

'Must be my high-pitched voice.'

'What do you mean? You didn't say anything. Oh, I see. It's a joke.'

'It was trying to be one.'

'Yeah, right.' She looked at the telephone receiver, shook her head at it, hung it up. 'She called here all morning,' she said. 'And called the store, too, and I was out, obviously, and now she thinks—' The corners of her mouth curled slowly into a wide grin. 'How about that?' she said. 'The bitch is jealous.'

'Is that good?'

'It's terrific.' The phone rang again, and it was Randy. I tried not to pay too much attention to the conversation. It ended with Carolyn saying, 'Oh, you demand to know who I've got over here? All right, I'll tell you who I've got over here. I've got my aunt from Bath Beach over here. You think you're the only woman in Manhattan with a mythical aunt in Bath Beach?'

She hung up, positively radiant. 'Gimme the ad,' she said. 'Quick, before she calls back. You wouldn't believe how jealous she is.'

She got the ad in, then answered the phone when they called back to confirm it. Then she was getting lunch on the table, setting out bread and cheese and opening a couple bottles of Amstel, when the phone rang again. 'Randy,' she said. 'I'm not getting it.'

'Fine.'

'You had this all morning, huh? The phone ringing like that?'

'Maybe eight, ten times. That's all.'

'You find out anything about Madeleine Porlock?'

I told her about the calls I'd made.

'Not much,' she said.

'Next to nothing.'

'I learned a little about your friend Whelkin, but I don't know what good it does. He's not a member of the Martingale Club.'

'Don't be silly. I ate there with him.'

'Uh-huh. The Martingale Club of New York maintains what they call reciprocity with a London club called Poindexter's. Ever hear of it?'

'No.'

'Me neither. The dude at the Martingale said it as though it was a household word. The Martingale has reciprocity with three London clubs, he told me. White's, Poindexter's, and the Dolphin. I never heard of any of them.'

'I think I heard of White's.'

'Anyhow, that's how Whelkin got guest privileges. But I thought he was an American.'

'I think he is. He has an accent that could be English, but I figured it was an affectation. Something he picked up at prep school, maybe.' I thought back to conversations we'd had. 'No,' I said, 'he's American. He talked about making a trip to London to attend that auction, and he referred to the English once as "our cousins across the pond."'

'Honestly?'

'Honestly. I suppose he could be an American and belong to a London club, and use that London membership to claim guest privileges at the Martingale. I suppose it's possible.'

'Lots of things are possible.'

'Uh-huh. You know what I think?'

'He's a phony.'

'He's a phony who faked me out of my socks, that's what he is. God, the more I think about it the phonier he sounds, and I let him con me into stealing the book with no money in front. All of a sudden his whole story is starting to come apart in my hands. All that happy horseshit about Haggard and Kipling, all that verse he quoted at me.'

'You think he just made it all up?'

'No, but—'

'Leave me alone, Ubi. You don't even like Jarlsberg.' Ubi was short for Ubiquitous, which was the Russian Blue's name. Jarlsberg was the cheese we were munching. (Not the Burmese, in case you were wondering. The Burmese was named Archie.)

To me she said, 'Maybe the book doesn't exist, Bernie.'

'I had it in my hands, Carolyn.'

'Oh, right.'

'I was thinking that myself earlier, just spinning all sorts of mental wheels. Like it wasn't a real book, it was hollowed out and all full of heroin or something like that.'

'Yeah, that's an idea.'

'Except it's a dumb idea, because I actually flipped through that book and read bits and pieces of it, and it's real. It's a genuine old printed book in less than sensational condition. I was even wondering if it could be a fake.'

'A fake?'

'Sure. Suppose Kipling destroyed every last copy of *The Deliverance of Fort Bucklow*. Suppose there never was such a thing as a Rider Haggard copy to survive, or suppose there was but it disappeared forever.' She was nodding encouragingly. 'Well,' I went on, 'suppose someone sat down and faked a text. It'd be a job, writing that long a ballad, but Kipling's not the hardest writer in the world to imitate. Some poet could knock it out between greeting-card assignments.'

'Then what?'

'Well, you couldn't sell it as an original manuscript because it would be too easily discredited. But if you had a printer set type—' I shook my head. 'That's where it breaks down. You could set type and run off one copy, and you could bind it and then distress it one way or another to give it some age, and you could even fake the inscription to H. Rider Haggard in a way that might pass inspection. But do you see the problem?'

'It sounds complicated.'

'Right. It's too damned complicated and far too expensive. It's like those caper movies where the crooks would have had to spend a million dollars to steal a hundred thousand, with all the elaborate preparations they go through and the equipment they use. Any crook who went through everything I described in order to produce a book you could sell for fifteen thousand dollars would have to be crazy.'

'Maybe it's worth a lot more than that. Fifteen thousand is just the price you and Whelkin worked out.'

'That's true. The fifteen-thousand figure doesn't really mean anything, since I didn't even get a smell of it, did I?' I sighed. Wistfully, I imagine. 'No,' I said. 'I know an old book when I look at it. I look at a few thousand of them every day, and old books are different from new ones, dammit. Paper's different when it's been around for fifty years. Sure, they could have used old paper, but it keeps not being worth the trouble. It's a real book, Carolyn. I'm sure of it.'

'Speaking of the old books you look at every day.'

'What about them?'

'Somebody's watching your store. I was at my shop part of the time, I had to wash a dog and I couldn't reach the owner to cancel. And there was somebody in a car across the street from your shop, and he was still there when I walked past a second time.'

'Did you get a good look at him?'

'No. I didn't get the license number, either. I suppose I should have, huh?'

'What for?'

'I don't know.'

'It was probably the police,' I said. 'A stake-out.'

'Oh.'

'They've probably got my apartment staked out, too.'

'Oh. That's how they do it, huh?'

'That's how they do it on television. This cop I talked to earlier said they'd get me when I returned to my old haunts. I wanted to tell him I didn't have any old haunts, but I suppose he meant the store and the apartment.'

'Or this place.'

'Huh?'

'Well, we're friends. You come over here a lot. If they talk to enough people they'll learn that, won't they?'

'I hope not,' I said, and the phone rang. We looked at each other, not very happily, and didn't say a word until it stopped ringing.

11

At six-fifteen I was sitting at the counter of the Red Flame at the corner
of Seventieth and West End. I had a cup of coffee and a wedge of prune
Danish in front of me and I wasn't particularly interested in either. The
other two customers, a teenaged couple in a back booth, were interested only in each other. The counterman wasn't interested in anything; he stood beside the coffee urns chewing a mint-flavored
toothpick and staring at the opposite wall, where a bas-relief showed a
couple of olive-skinned youths chasing sheep over a Greek hillside. He
shook his head from time to time, evidently wondering what the hell
he was doing here.

I kept glancing out the window and wondering much the same thing.
From where I sat I could almost see my building a block uptown. I'd
had a closer look earlier from the sidewalk, but I hadn't been close
enough then to tell if there were cops staked out in or around the place.
Theoretically it shouldn't matter, but theoretically bumblebees can't
fly, so how much faith can you place in theory?

One of the teenagers giggled. The counterman yawned and scratched
himself. I looked out the window for perhaps the forty-first time and
saw Carolyn half a block away, heading south on West End with my
small suitcase in one hand. I put some money on the counter and went
out to meet her.

She was radiant. 'Piece of cake,' she said. 'Nothing to it, Bern. This
burglary number's a cinch.'

'Well, you had my keys, Carolyn.'

'They helped, no question about it. Of course, I had to get the right
key in the right lock.'

'You didn't have any trouble getting into the building?'

She shook her head. 'Mrs Hesch was terrific. The doorman called her
on the intercom and she said to send me right up, and then she met me
at the elevator.'

I'd called Mrs Hesch earlier to arrange all this. She was a widow who
had the apartment across the hall from me, and she seemed to think
burglary was the sort of character defect that could be overlooked in a
friend and neighbor.

'She didn't have to meet you,' I said.

'Well, she wanted to make sure I found the right apartment. What she really wanted was a good look at me. She's a little worried about you, Bern.'

'Hell, I'm a little worried about me myself.'

'She thought you were all respectable now, what with the bookstore and all. Then she heard about the Porlock murder on the news last night and she started to worry. But she's positive you didn't kill anybody.'

'Good for her.'

'I think she liked me. She wanted me to come in for coffee but I told her there wasn't time.'

'She makes good coffee.'

'That's what she said. She said you like her coffee a lot, and she sort of implied that what you need is somebody to make coffee for you on a full-time basis. The message I got is that living on the West Side and burgling on the East Side is a sort of Robin Hood thing, but there's a time in life when a young man should think about getting married and settling down.'

'It's nice the two of you hit it off.'

'Well, we only talked for a couple of minutes. Then I went and burgled your apartment.' She hefted the suitcase. 'I think I got everything. Burglar tools, pocket flashlight, all the things you mentioned. And shirts and socks and underwear. There was some cash in your shirt drawer.'

'There was? I guess there was. I usually keep a few dollars there.'

'Thirty-eight dollars.'

'If you say so.'

'I took it.'

'Oh,' I said. 'Well, I don't suppose thirty-eight dollars one way or the other is going to make a difference. But it can't hurt to have it along.'

She shrugged. 'You said you always take cash,' she said. 'So I took it.'

'It's a good principle. You know something? We're never going to get a cab.'

'Not when it's raining. Can we get a subway? No, not across town. Isn't there a bus that goes over Seventy-ninth Street?'

'It's not a good idea to take buses when you're wanted for homicide. It's awfully public.'

'I suppose we'll get a cab sooner or later.'

I took the suitcase in one hand and her arm in the other. 'The hell with that,' I said. 'We'll take a car.'

The Pontiac was right where I'd left it. Sometimes the tow-truck division lets things slide for a while, and this time the Pontiac's owner was the beneficiary of their lapse. I popped the door on the passenger's side, let Carolyn in, and took a ticket from underneath the windshield wiper while she leaned across the seat to unlatch the door for me.

'See?' someone said. 'You got a ticket. Did I tell you you'd get a ticket?'

I didn't recognize the man at first. Then I saw the brindle boxer at the end of the leash he was holding.

'Sooner or later,' he told me, 'they'll tow you away. Then what will you do?'

'Get another car,' I said.

He shook his head, tugged impatiently at the dog's leash. 'Come on, Max,' he said. 'Some people, you can't tell them a thing.'

I got into the car, set about jumping the ignition. Carolyn watched the process fascinated, and it wasn't until we pulled away from the curb that she asked who the man was and what he had wanted.

'He wanted to be helpful,' I said, 'but all in all he's a pest. The dog's all right, though. His name is Max. The dog, I mean.'

'He looks okay,' she said, 'but he'd probably be murder to wash.'

I left the Pontiac in a bus stop around the corner from where we were going. Carolyn said it might get towed and I said I didn't care if it did. I got tools and accessories from the suitcase, then left the case and the clothes it contained on the back seat of the Pontiac.

'Suppose they tow the car,' she said, 'and suppose they identify the clothing from laundry marks. Then they'll know you were here, and—'

'You've been watching too much television,' I said. 'When they tow cars they take them over to that pier on the Hudson and wait for the owner to turn up. They don't check the contents. You could have a dead body in the trunk and they'd never know.'

'I wish you hadn't said that,' she said.

'There's nothing in the trunk.'

'How do you know for sure?'

We went around the corner. No one seemed to be keeping an eye on the elegant little brownstone. A woman stood in the bay window on the parlor floor, watering the plants with a long-spouted watering can. The can was gleaming copper, the plants were all a lush green, and the whole scene was one of upper-middle-class domestic tranquillity. Outside, watching this and getting rained on, I felt like a street urchin in a Victorian novel.

I looked up. There were lighted windows on the third and fourth floors, but they didn't tell me anything. The apartments that interested me were at the rear of the building.

We entered the vestibule. 'You don't have to come,' I said.

'Ring the bell, Bern.'

'I'm serious. You could wait in the car.'

'Wonderful. I can play it safe by sitting in a stolen car parked at a bus stop. Why don't I just wait in the subway? I could cling to the third rail for security.'

'What you could do is spend the next half-hour in the bar on the corner. Suppose we walk into an apartment full of cops?'

'Ring the bell, Bernie.'

'It's just that I hate to see you walk into trouble.'

'So do I, but let's play the hand out as dealt, huh? I'll be with the two of them so they can't get cute while you're downstairs. We worked it out before, Bern, and it made sense then and it still makes sense now. You want to know something? It's probably dangerous for us to spend the next six hours arguing in the vestibule, if you're so concerned with what's dangerous and what's not, so why don't you ring their bell and get it over with?'

First, though, I rang the bell marked *Porlock*. I poked it three times, waited half a minute, then gave it another healthy tickle. I didn't really expect a response and I was happy not to get one. My finger moved from the *Porlock* bell to the one marked *Blinn*. I gave it a long and two shorts, and the answering buzzer sounded almost at once. I pushed the door and it opened.

'Darn,' Carolyn said. I looked at her. 'Well, I thought I'd get to watch you pick it,' she said. 'That's all.'

We went up the stairs and stopped at the third floor long enough to peek at the door of 3-D. As I'd figured it, the cops had sealed it, and the door was really plastered with official-looking material. I could have opened it with a scout knife, but I couldn't have done so without destroying the seals and making it obvious that I'd been there.

Instead, we went up another flight. The door of 4-C was closed. Carolyn and I looked at each other. Then I reached out a hand and knocked.

The door opened. Arthur Blinn stood with one hand on its knob and the other motioning us in. 'Come on, come on,' he said urgently. 'Don't stand out there all night.' In his hurry to close the door he almost hit Carolyn with it, but he got it shut and fussed with the locks and bolts. 'You can relax now, Gert,' he called out. 'It's only the burglar.'

They made a cute couple. They were both about five-six, both as roly-poly as panda bears. Both had curly dark-brown hair, although he'd lost most of his in the front. She was wearing a forest-green pants suit in basic polyester. He wore the trousers and vest of a gray glen-plaid business suit. His white shirt was unbuttoned at the neck and his tie was loosened for comfort. She poured coffee and pushed Scottish short-bread at us. He told us, over and over again, what a relief it was to see us.

'Because I told Gert, suppose it's a setup? Suppose it's the insurance company running a bluff? Because honestly, Mr Rhodenbarr, who ever heard of such a thing? A burglar calls up, says hello, I'm you're friendly neighborhood burglar, and if you cooperate with me a little I won't rat to the insurance people and tell them your claim is lousy. I figured a burglar with troubles like you got, wanted for killing a woman and God knows what else, I figure you're not going to knock yourself out shouting you never stole a coat or a watch.'

'And what *I* figured,' Gert said, 'is why would you be coming here, anyway? "He wants to get rid of witnesses," I told Artie. "Remember, he already killed once."'

'What I said is what did we ever witness? I told her, I said forget all that. Just hope it's the burglar, I told her. All we need is some insurance snoop. You don't care for the shortbread, young lady?'

'It's delicious,' Carolyn said. 'And Bernie never killed anybody, Mrs Blinn.'

'Call me Gert, honey.'

'He never killed anyone, Gert.'

'I'm sure of it, honey. Meeting him, seeing the two of you, my mind's a hundred percent at ease.'

'He was framed, Gert. That's why we're here. To find out who really killed Madeleine Porlock.'

'If we knew,' Arthur Blinn said, 'believe me, we'd tell you. But what do we know?'

'You lived in the same building with her. You must have known something about her.'

The Blinns looked at each other and gave simultaneous little shrugs. 'She wasn't directly under us,' Gert explained. 'So we wouldn't know if she had loud parties or played music all night or anything like that.'

'Like Mr Mboka,' Artie said.

'In 3-C,' Gert said. 'He's African, you see, and he works at the UN. Somebody said he was a translator.'

'Plays the drums,' Artie said.

'We don't know that, Artie. He either plays the drums or he plays recordings of drums.'

'Same difference.'

'But we haven't spoken to him about it because we thought it might be religious and we didn't want to interfere.'

'Plus Gert here thinks he's a cannibal and she's *afraid* to speak to him.'

'I don't think he's a cannibal,' Gert protested. 'Who ever said I thought he was a cannibal?'

I cleared my throat. 'Maybe the two of you could talk to Carolyn about Miss Porlock,' I suggested. 'And if I could, uh, be excused for a few moments.'

'You want to use the bathroom?'

'The fire escape.'

Blinn furrowed his brow at me, then relaxed his features and nodded energetically. 'Oh, right,' he said. 'For a minute there. I thought – But to hell with what I thought. The fire escape. Sure. Right through to the bedroom. But you know the way, don't you? You were here yesterday. It's spooky, you know? The idea of someone else being in your apartment. Of course, it's not so spooky now that we know you, you and Carolyn here. But when we first found out about it, well, you can imagine.'

'It must have been upsetting.'

'That's exactly what it was. Upsetting. Gert called the super about the pane of glass, but it's like pulling teeth to get him to do anything around here. Generally he gets more responsive right before Christmas, so maybe we'll get some action soon. Meanwhile I taped up a shirt cardboard so the wind and rain won't come in.'

'I'm sorry I had to break the window.'

'Listen, these things happen.'

I unlocked the window, raised it, stepped out onto the fire escape. The rain had stepped up a little and it was cold and windy out there. Behind me, Blinn drew the window shut again. He was reaching to lock it when I extended a finger and tapped on the glass. He caught himself, left the window unlocked, and smiled and shook his head at his absent-mindedness. He went off chuckling to himself while I headed down a flight of steel steps.

This time I was properly equipped. I had my glass cutter and a roll of adhesive tape, and I used them to remove a pane from the Porlock window swiftly and silently. I turned the catch, raised the window, and let myself in.

'That's what I was talking about before,' Gert said. 'Listen. Can you hear it?'

'The drumming.'

She nodded. 'That's Mboka. Now, is that him drumming or is it a record? Because I can't tell.'

'He was doing it while you were downstairs,' Carolyn said. 'Personally I think it's him drumming.'

I said I couldn't tell, and that I'd been unable to hear him from the Porlock apartment.

'You never hear anything through the walls,' Artie said. 'Just through the floors and ceilings. It's a solid building as far as the walls are concerned.'

'I don't mind the drumming most of the time,' Gert said. 'I'll play music and the drumming sort of fits in with it. It's in the middle of the night that it gets me, but I don't like to complain.'

'She figures it's the middle of the afternoon in Africa.'

We had a hard time getting out of there. They kept giving us shortbread and coffee and asking sincere little questions about the ins and outs of burglary. Finally we managed to fight our way to the door. We said our goodbyes all around, and then Gert hung back a little while Artie caught at my sleeve in the doorway.

'Say, Bernie,' he said, 'we all squared away now?'

'Sure thing, Artie.'

'As far as the insurance company's concerned . . .'

'Don't worry about a thing. The coat, the watch, the other stuff. I'll back your claim.'

'That's a relief,' he said. 'I must have been crazy, putting in that claim, but I'd look like a horse's ass changing it now, and why did we pay premiums all those years anyway, right?'

'Right, Artie.'

'The thing is, I hate to mention this, but while you were downstairs Gert was wondering about the bracelet.'

'How's that, Artie?'

'The bracelet you took. It was Gert's. I don't think it's worth much.'

'A couple of hundred.'

'That much? I would have said less. It belonged to her mother. The thing is, I wondered what's the chance of getting it back?'

'Oh,' I said. 'I see what you mean. Well, Artie, I'm kind of pressed right now.'

'I can imagine.'

'But when things are back to normal, I'm sure we can work something out.'

He clapped me on the shoulder. 'That's terrific,' he said. 'Listen, take all the time you need. There's no rush.'

12

The Pontiac, untowed and unticketed, waited for us at the bus stop. The suitcase huddled undisturbed on the floor in back. All of this surprised Carolyn, but I'd expected nothing less. There was something about that car that inspired confidence.

On the way downtown I learned what Gert Blinn had told her. While I was a floor below in Madeleine Porlock's apartment, Gert had maneuvered Carolyn into the kitchen, presumably to copy down a recipe but actually to dish a little dirt. The late Madeleine Porlock, she'd confided, was no better than she should be.

'Gert was vague,' Carolyn said. 'I don't know that Porlock was a hooker exactly, but I got the impression that her life tended to revolve around men. Whenever Gert met her on the stairs she was with some man or other, and I gather that's how her rent got paid.'

'Doesn't surprise me.'

'Well, it surprises me,' she said. 'I never saw Porlock, but the way you described her she was the furthest thing from slinky. The woman you were talking about sounded like she could play the mean matron in all the old prison movies.'

'That's on a bad day. On a good day she could have played the nurse in *Cuckoo's Nest*.'

'Uh-huh. Bern, I admit I don't know what men go for, because it's never been a burning issue with me, but she doesn't sound the type to get her rent paid.'

'You didn't go through her drawers and closets.'

'Oh?'

A cab stopped abruptly in front of us. I swung the wheel to the right and slipped neatly around it. No question, I thought. The Pontiac and I were made for each other.

'Lots of sexy underwear,' I said.

'Oh?'

'Wispy things. Scarlet gauze and black lace. Peekaboo bras.'

'Men really go for that crap, huh?'

'So it would seem. Then there were a few garter belts, and a couple of tight corsets that you'd have to be a graduate engineer to figure out.'

375

'Tight corsets?'

'A couple of pairs of boots with six-inch stiletto heels. Lots of leather stuff, including those cunning wrist and ankle bracelets decorated with metal studs.'

'A subtle pattern begins to emerge.'

'Doesn't it? And I haven't even mentioned the small but tasteful wardrobe in skintight black latex or the nifty collection of whips and chains. Or the whole dresser drawer full of gadgets which we might euphemistically designate as marital aids.'

She twirled an imaginary mustache. 'This Porlock creature,' she said, 'was into kink.'

'A veritable mistress of kink,' I said. 'It was beginning to get to me, prowling around in all that weirdness.'

'I'm surprised it didn't make the papers. *"Dominatrix Slain in East Side Pleasure Pad"* – that should be good for page three in the *Daily News* any day of the week.'

'I thought of that. But nothing was out in plain sight, Carolyn, and when I was up there the first time, all I saw was a tastefully decorated apartment. Remember, the cops had an open-and-shut case, a woman shot in her own apartment by a burglar she'd evidently caught in the act. They didn't have any reason to toss her apartment. And she really lived there, it wasn't just her office. She had street clothes there, too, and there were dishes in the kitchen cupboards and Q-tips and dental floss in the medicine cabinet.'

'Find any cash? Any jewelry?'

'There's a jar in the kitchen where she used to throw her pennies. And there was some loose jewelry in one of the bedroom drawers, but none of it looked like much. I didn't steal anything, if that's what you were getting at.'

'I just wondered.'

A siren opened up behind us. I edged over to the right to give them room. A blue-and-white police cruiser sailed past us, wailing madly, barreling on through a red light. I braked for the same light, and as we waited for it to turn green a pair of foot patrolmen crossed the street in front of us. The one with the mustache was doing baton-twirler tricks with his nightstick. At one point he swung around so that he was looking directly at us, and Carolyn gripped my arm and didn't let go until he and his companion had continued on across the street.

'Jesus,' she said.

'Not to worry.'

'I could just picture a lightbulb forming over his head. Like in the comic strips. Are you sure he didn't recognize you?'

'Positive. Otherwise he'd have come over to the car for a closer look.'

'And what would you have done?'

'I don't know. Run the light, probably.'

'Jesus.'

I felt the subject deserved changing. 'I thought of bringing you a present,' I said. 'A fur jacket, really smart-looking.'

'I don't like fur.'

'This was a good one. It had an Arvin Tannenbaum label in it.'

'Is that good?'

'He's as good as furriers get. I don't know much about furs but I know labels. This was pretty. I think it was Canada lynx. What's the matter?'

'That's a kind of a cat, Bernie. Don't tell me how pretty it was. A lynx is like a bobcat. Wearing a lynx coat would be like having lampshades made of human skin. Whether or not they're attractive is beside the point.'

Another siren oogah-oogahed in the distance. An ambulance, from the sound of it. They've got ambulances these days that sound like Gestapo cars in war movies.

That last thought blended with Carolyn's lampshade image and made me ready for another change of subject. 'The wig was there,' I said hurriedly. 'The orange one that she wore to the bookstore. So it wasn't just that my brain was addled from the drug. That was her buying Virgil's *Eclogues*.'

'She must have been afraid someone would recognize her.'

I nodded. 'She could have worn the wig so I wouldn't recognize her at a later meeting, but that doesn't really make much sense. I suppose she was afraid Whelkin would spot her. They must have known each other because he sent me over to her apartment, but I wish I had something more concrete to tie them together.'

'Like what?'

'Pictures, for instance. I was hoping for a batch of telltale snapshots. People with a closetful of whips and chains tend to be keen Polaroid photographers. I didn't turn up a one.'

'If there were any pictures, the killer could have taken them.'

'Possible.'

'Or maybe there weren't any to begin with. If she was only with one person at a time there wouldn't be anybody to take the pictures. Did you find a camera?'

'Nary a camera.'

'Then there probably weren't any pictures.'

'Probably not.'

I turned into Fourteenth Street, headed west. Carolyn was looking at me oddly. I braked for a red light and turned to see her studying me, a thoughtful expression on her face.

'You know something I don't,' she said.

'I know how to pick locks. That's all.'

'Something else.'

'It's just your imagination.'

377

'I don't think so. You were uptight before and now you're all loose and breezy.'

'It's just self-confidence and a feeling of well-being,' I told her. 'Don't worry. It'll pass.'

There was a legal parking place around the corner from her apartment, legal until 7 A.M., at any rate. I stuck the Pontiac into it and grabbed up the suitcase.

The cats met us at the door. 'Good boys,' Carolyn said, reaching down to pat heads. 'Anybody call? Did you take messages like I taught you? Bernie, if it's not time for a drink, then the liquor ads have been misleading us for years. You game?'

'Sure.'

'Scotch? Rocks? Soda?'

'Yes, yes, and no.'

I unpacked my suitcase while she made the drinks, then made myself sit down and relax long enough to swallow a couple of ounces of Scotch. I waited for it to loosen some of my coiled springs, but before that could happen I was on my feet again.

Carolyn raised her eyebrows at me.

'The car,' I said.

'What about it?'

'I want to put it back where I found it.'

'You're kidding.'

'That car's been very useful to me, Carolyn. I want to return the favor.'

I paused at the door, reached back under my jacket. There was a book wedged beneath the waistband of my slacks. I drew it free and set it on a table. Carolyn looked at it and at me again.

'Something to read while I'm gone,' I said.

'What is it?'

'Well,' I said, 'it's not Virgil's *Eclogues*.'

13

I felt good about taking the car back. You don't spit on your luck, I told myself. I thought of stories of ballplayers refusing to change their socks while the team was on a winning streak. It was high time, I mused, to change my own socks, winning streak or no. A shower would be in order, and a change of garb.

I headed uptown on Tenth Avenue, left hand on the wheel, right hand on the seat beside me, fingers drumming idly. Somewhere in the Forties I snuck a peek at the gas gauge. I had a little less than half a tank left and I felt a need to do something nice for the car's owner, so I cut over to Eleventh Avenue and found an open station at the corner of Fifty-first Street. I had them fill the tank and check the oil while they were at it. The oil was down a quart and I had them take care of that, too.

My parking space was waiting for me on Seventy-fourth Street, but Max and his owner were nowhere to be seen. I uncoupled my jumper wire, locked up the car, and trotted back to West End Avenue to catch a southbound cab. It was still drizzling lightly but I didn't have to wait long before a cab pulled up. And it was a Checker, with room for me to stretch my legs and relax.

Things were starting to go right. I could feel it.

Out of habit, I left the cab a few blocks from Arbor Court and walked the rest of the way. I rang, and Carolyn buzzed me through the front door and met me at the door to her apartment. She put her hands on her hips and looked up at me. 'You're full of surprises,' she said.

'It's part of my charm.'

'Uh-huh. To tell you the truth, poetry never did too much for me. I had a lover early on who thought she was Edna St Vincent Millay and that sort of cooled me on the whole subject. Where'd you find the book?'

'The Porlock apartment.'

'No shit Bern. Here I thought you checked it out of the Jefferson Market library. Where in the apartment? Out in plain sight?'

'Uh-uh. In a shoe box on a shelf in the closet.'

'It must have come as a surprise.'

'I'll say. I was expecting a pair of Capezios, and look what I found.'

'*The Deliverance of Fort Bucklow*. I didn't really read much of it. I skimmed the first three or four pages and I didn't figure it was going to get better.'

'You were right.'

'How'd you know it would be there, Bern?'

I went over to the kitchen area and made us a couple of drinks. I gave one to Carolyn and accompanied it with the admission that I hadn't known the book would be there, that I hadn't even had any particular hope of finding it. 'When you don't know what you're looking for,' I said, 'you have a great advantage, because you don't know what you'll find.'

'Just so you know it when you see it. I'm beginning to believe you lead a charmed life. First you run an ad claiming you've got the book, and then you open a shoe box and there's the book. Why did the killer stash it there?'

'He didn't. He'd have taken it with him.'

'Porlock stashed it?'

'Must have. She drugged me, frisked me, grabbed the book, tucked it away in the closet, and got it hidden just in time to let her killer in the front door. She must have been alone in the apartment with me or he'd have seen her hide the book. She let him in and he killed her and left the gun in my hand and went out.'

'Without the book.'

'Right.'

'Why would he kill her without getting the book?'

'Maybe he didn't have anything to do with the book. Maybe he had some other reason to want her dead.'

'And he just happened to walk in at that particular time, and he decided to frame you because you happened to be there.'

'I haven't got it all worked out yet, Carolyn.'

'I can see that.'

'Maybe he killed her first and started looking for the book and came up empty. Except the apartment didn't look as though it had been searched. It looked as neat as ever, except for the body on the love seat. When I came to, I mean. There was no body there tonight.'

'How about the trunk of the Pontiac?'

I gave her a look. 'They did leave chalkmarks, though. On the love seat and the floor, to outline where the body was. It was sort of spooky.' I picked up the book and took it and my drink to the chair. Archie was curled up in it. I put down the book and the drink and moved him and sat down, and he hopped onto my lap and looked on with interest as I picked up the book again and leafed through it.

'I swear he can read,' Carolyn said. 'Ubi's not much on books but

Archie loves to read over my shoulder. Or *under* my shoulder, come to think of it.'

'A cat ought to like Kipling,' I said. 'Remember the *Just So Stories*? "I am the cat who walks by himself, and all places are alike to me." '

Archie purred like a bandsaw.

'When I met you,' I said, 'I figured you'd have dogs.'

'I'd rather go to them than have them. What made you think I was a dog person?'

'Well, the shop.'

'The Poodle Factory?'

'Yeah.'

'Well, what choice did I have, Bernie? I couldn't open a cat-grooming salon, for Christ's sake. Cats groom themselves.'

'That's a point.'

I read a little more of the book. Something bothered me. I flipped back to the flyleaf and read the handwritten inscription to H. Rider Haggard. I pictured Kipling at his desk in Surrey, dipping his pen, leaning over the book, inscribing it to his closest friend. I closed the book, turned it over and over in my hands.

'Something wrong?'

I shook my head, set the book aside, dispossessed Archie, stood up. 'I'm like the cats,' I announced, 'and it's time I set about grooming myself. I'm going to take a shower.'

A while later I was sitting in the chair again. I was wearing clean clothes and I'd had a nice close shave with my own razor.

'I could get a paper,' Carolyn offered. 'It's after eleven. The *Times* must be out by now. The first edition.'

We'd just heard the news and there wasn't anything about the Porlock murder. I pointed out that there wouldn't very likely be anything in the paper, either.

'Our ad'll be in, Bern. In the Personals.'

'Where's the nearest newsstand open at this hour?'

'There's one on Greenwich Avenue but they don't get the early *Times* because they close around one or two. There's an all-night stand at the subway entrance at Fourteenth and Eighth.'

'That's too far.'

'I don't mind a walk.'

'It's still raining and it's too far anyway, and why do we have to look at the ad?'

'To make sure it's there, I suppose.'

'No point. Either somebody'll see it or they won't, and either the phone'll ring or it won't, and all we can do is wait and see what happens.'

'I suppose so.' She sounded wistful. 'It just seems as though there ought to be something active we can do.'

'The night's been active enough for me already.'

'I guess you're right.'

'I feel like a little blissful inactivity, to tell you the truth. I feel like sitting here feeling clean. I feel like having maybe one more drink in a few minutes and then getting ready for bed. I don't even know if people really read Personal ads in the *Times*, but I'm fairly sure they don't race for the bulldog edition so they can read about missing heirs and volunteers wanted for medical experiments.'

'True.'

'I'm afraid so. The phone's not going to ring for a while, Carolyn.'

So of course it picked that minute to ring.

We looked at each other. Nobody moved and it went on ringing. 'You get it,' she said.

'Why me?'

'Because it's about the ad.'

'It's not about the ad.'

'Of course it's about the ad. What else would it be?'

'Maybe it's a wrong number.'

'Bernie, for God's sake . . .'

I got up and answered the phone. I didn't say anything for a second, and then I said, 'Hello.'

No answer.

I said hello a few more times, giving the word the same flat reading each time, and I'd have gotten more of a response from Archie. I stared at the receiver for a moment, said 'Hello' one final time, then said 'Goodbye' and hung up.

'Interesting conversation,' Carolyn said.

'It's good I answered it. It really made a difference.'

'Someone wanted to find out who placed the ad. Now they've heard your voice and they know it's you.'

'You're reading a lot into a moment of silence.'

'Maybe I should have picked it up after all.'

'And maybe what we just had was a wrong number. Or a telephone pervert. I didn't hear any heavy breathing, but maybe he's new at it.'

She started to say something, then got to her feet, popping up like a toaster. 'I'm gonna have one more drink,' she said. 'How about you?'

'A short one.'

'They know it's you, Bernie. Now if they can get the address from the number—'

'They can't.'

'Suppose they're the police. The police could get the phone company to cooperate, couldn't they?'

'Maybe. But what do the police know about the Kipling book?'

'I don't know.'

'Well, neither do they.' She handed me a drink. It was a little heftier than I'd had in mind but I didn't raise any objections. Her nervousness was contagious and I'd managed to pick up a light dose of it. I prescribed Scotch, to be followed by bed rest.

'It was probably what I said it would be when I answered it,' I suggested. 'A wrong number.'

'You're right.'

'For all we know, the ad didn't even make the early edition.'

'I could take a quick run over to Fourteenth Street and check—'

'Don't be ridiculous.' I picked up the book again and found myself flipping through its pages, remembering how I'd done so on an earlier occasion, sitting in my own apartment with a similar drink at hand and flushed with the triumph of a successful burglary. Well, I'd stolen the thing again, but somehow I didn't feel the same heady rush.

Something nagged at me. Some little thought out there on the edge of consciousness . . .

I finished my drink and tuned it out.

Half an hour after the phone call we were bedded down for the night. *I* was bedded down, anyway; Carolyn was couched. The clock radio was supplying an undercurrent of mood music, all set to turn itself off thirty minutes into the Mantovani.

I was teetering on the edge of sleep when I half heard footsteps approaching the door of the apartment. I didn't really register them; Carolyn's was a first-floor apartment, after all, and various feet had been approaching it all night long, only to pass it and continue on up the stairs. This time the steps stopped outside the door, and just as that fact was beginning to penetrate I heard a key in the lock.

I sat up in bed. The key turned in the lock. Beside me, a cat sat quivering with excitement. As another key slipped into another of the locks, Carolyn stirred on the couch and whispered my name urgently.

We were both on our feet by the time the door opened. A hand reached in to switch on the overhead light. We stood there blinking.

'I'm dreaming,' Randy said. 'None of this is really happening.'

Shoulder-length chestnut hair. A high broad forehead, a long oval face. Large eyes, larger now than I'd ever seen them, and a mouth in the shape of the letter O.

'Jesus,' Carolyn said. 'Randy, it's not what you think.'

'Of course not. The two of you were playing canasta. You had the lights out so you wouldn't disturb the cats. Why else would you be wearing your Dr Denton's, Carolyn? And does Bernie like the handy drop seat?'

'You've got it all wrong.'

'I know. It's terrible the way I jump to conclusions. At least you're

383

dressed warmly. Bernie, poor thing, you're shivering in your under-shorts. Why don't the two of you huddle together for warmth, Carolyn? It wouldn't bother me a bit.'

'Randy, you just don't understand.'

'You're dead right about that. I figured you knew what you were by now. Aren't you a little old for a sexual-identity crisis?'

'Dammit, Randy—'

'Dammit is right. Dammit is definitely right. I *thought* I recognized Bernie's voice on the telephone. And I was struck tongue-tied. After I hung up I told myself it was probably innocent, the two of you are friends, and I asked myself why I reacted with such paranoia. But you know what they say, Carolyn. Just because you're paranoid doesn't mean real little people aren't following you.'

'Will you please listen to me?'

'No, *you* listen to *me*, you little shit. What I said was, well, screw it, Miranda, you've got a key, so go over and join the two of them and see how silly you're being, or maybe you'll get lucky and Carolyn'll be alone and you can have some laughs and patch things up, and – God *damn* you, Carolyn. Here's your set of keys, bitch. I won't walk in on you two again. Count on it.'

'Randy, I—'

'I said here's your keys. And I think you have *my* keys, Carolyn, and I'd like them back. Now, if you don't mind.'

We tried to say something but it was pointless. There was nothing she wanted to hear. She gave back Carolyn's keys and pocketed her own and stormed out, slamming the door hard enough to rattle the dishes on the kitchen table, stamping her way down the hall, slamming the vestibule door on her way out of the building.

Carolyn and I just stood there looking at each other. Ubi had gone to hide under the bed. Archie stood up on the chair and let out a tentative yowl. After a couple of minutes Carolyn went over to the door and set about locking the locks.

14

The Personal ads were on the penultimate page of the second section of the *Times*, along with the shipping news and a few other high-priority items. Ours was the third listing, following a plea for information from the parents of a fourteen-year-old runaway.

I read our ad three or four times and decided that it did its job efficiently enough. It hadn't brought any response yet, but it was still early; Carolyn had awakened at dawn and gone for the paper as soon as she'd fed the cats. At this hour our presumably interested parties might well be snug in their beds. If, like me and Carolyn, they were already warming themselves over morning coffee, they'd still have the whole paper to wade through before they got to the Personals. True, it was a Saturday. The daily *Times* has added on feature sections in recent years, padding itself like a bear preparing to hibernate, but the Saturday paper remains fashionably slender. On the other hand, a good many people take a break from the *Times* on Saturdays, readying themselves for the onslaught of the enormous Sunday paper, so it was possible our prospective customers would never pick up the paper at all. The ad was set to run for a week, but now that I looked at it, a few lines of type on a remote back page, I wasn't too cocky about the whole thing. We couldn't really count on it, I decided, and it would be advisable to draft a backup plan as soon as possible.

'Oh, wow. I'm glad I went out for the paper, Bernie.'

'So am I,' I said. 'I just hope you're not the only person who took the trouble.'

She had the first section and she was pointing to something. 'You'd better read this,' she said.

I took it and read it. A few inches of copy on one of the back pages, out of place among the scraps of international news but for its faintly international flavor. Bernard Rhodenbarr, I read, the convicted burglar currently sought by police investigating the slaying Thursday of Madeleine Porlock in her East Side apartment, had narrowly escaped apprehension the previous night. Surprised by an alert police officer while attempting to break into Barnegat Books on East Eleventh Street, Rhodenbarr whipped out a pistol and exchanged shots with the policeman. The officer, I read, suffered a flesh wound in the foot and was treated at St Vincent's Hospital and released. The burglar-turned-gunman, owner of the store in question, had escaped on foot, apparently uninjured.

As an afterthought, the last paragraph mentioned that Rhodenbarr had disguised himself for the occasion by donning a turban and false beard. 'But he didn't fool me,' Patrolman Francis Rockland was quoted as saying. 'We're trained to see past obvious disguises. I recognized him right away from his photograph.'

'The Sikh,' I told Carolyn. 'Well, that's one person who hasn't got the book, or he wouldn't have been trying to break into the store to search for it. I wonder if it was him you spotted watching the store yesterday.'

'Maybe.'

'The tabloids'll probably give this more of a play. They like irony, and what's more ironic than a burglar caught breaking into his own place? They should only know how ironic it is.'

'What do you mean?'

'Well, the cop could have arrested the Sikh. That wouldn't have cleared me on the murder rap but at least they wouldn't be after me for this, too. Or the Sikh could have been a worse shot, so I wouldn't be charged with shooting a cop. Wounding a police officer is a more serious crime than murdering a civilian, at least as far as the cops are concerned. Or, if he had to shoot him, the Sikh could have *killed* young Mr Rockland, Then he wouldn't have been able to tell them I was the one who did it.'

'You wouldn't really want the policeman dead, Bernie.'

'No. With my luck he'd live long enough to tell a brother officer who shot him. Then I'd be a cop killer. What if Randy sees this? She must have missed the first story, or at least she never connected it with me, because she didn't seem concerned last night about your harboring a fugitive. She was too busy feeling betrayed.'

'She never looks at the *Times*.'

'It'll be in the other papers, too.'

'She probably won't read them, either. I don't even know if she knows your last name.'

'She must.'

'Maybe.'

'Would she call the cops?'

'She's a good person, Bernie. She's not a fink.'

'She's also jealous. She thinks—'

'I know what she thinks. She must be a lunatic to think it, but I know what she thinks.'

'She could decide to give the cops an anonymous tip. She could tell herself it was for your own good, Carolyn.'

'Shit.' She gnawed a thumbnail. 'You figure it's not safe here any-more?'

'I don't know.'

'But the phone's here. And the number's in the paper, and how are we going to answer it from a distance?'

'Who's going to call, anyway?'

'Rudyard Whelkin.'

'He killed Madeleine Porlock Thursday night. I'll bet he took a cab straight to Kennedy and was out of the country by midnight.'

'Without the book?'

I shrugged.

'And the Sikh might call. What happened to his five hundred dollars?'

'You figure he'll call so he can ask me that question?'

'No, I'm asking it, Bern. You had the money on you when Madeleine Porlock drugged you, right?'

'Right.'

'And it was gone when you came to.'

'Right again.'

'So what happened to it?'

'She took it. *Oh*. What happened to it *after* she took it?'

'Yeah. Where did it go? You went through her things last night. It wasn't stashed with the book, was it?'

'It wasn't stashed anywhere. Nowhere that I looked, that is. I suppose the killer took it along with him.'

'Wouldn't he leave it?'

'Why leave money? Money's money, Carolyn.'

'There's always stories about killings in the paper, and they say the police ruled out robbery as a motive because the victim had a large sum of cash on his person.'

'That's organized crime. They want people to know why they killed somebody. They'll even plant money on a person so the police will rule out robbery. Either the killer took the money this time or Porlock found a hiding place that didn't occur to me. Or some cop picked it up when no one was looking. That's been known to happen.'

'Really?'

'Oh, sure. I could tell you no end of stories. But what's the point? I'd be interrupted by the insistent ringing of the telephone.'

And I turned to the instrument, figuring it would recognize a cue when it heard one. It stayed silent, though, for upwards of half an hour.

But once it started ringing, I didn't think it was ever going to stop.

Rrrring!

'Hello?'

387

'Ah, hello. I've just read your notice in the *Times*. I'm only wondering if I'm interpreting it correctly.'

'How are you interpreting it?'

'You would appear to have something to sell.'

'That's correct.'

'Passage to, ah, Fort Bucklow.'

'Yes.'

'Would it be possible for me to know to whom I am speaking?'

'I was going to ask you that very question.'

'Ah. An impasse. Let me consider this.'

An English inflection, an undertone of Asia or Africa. A slightly sibilant *s*. Educated, soft-spoken. A pleasant voice, all in all.

'Very well, sir. I believe you may already have encountered an emissary of mine. If my guess is right, you overcharged him in a transaction recently. He paid five hundred dollars for a book priced at a dollar ninety-five.'

'Not my fault. He ran off without his change.'

An appreciative chuckle. 'Then you are the man I assumed you to be. Very good. You have pluck, sir. The police seek you in connection with a woman's death and you persist in your efforts to sell a book. Business as usual, eh?'

'I need money right now.'

'To quit the country, I would suppose. You have the book at hand? It is actually in your possession as we talk?'

'Yes. I don't believe I caught your name.'

'I don't believe I've given it. Before we go farther, sir, perhaps you could prove to me that you have the volume.'

'I suppose I could hold it to the phone, but unless you have extraordinary powers . . .'

'Open it to page forty-two, sir, and read the first stanza on the page.'

'Oh. Hold on a minute. 'Now if you should go to Fort Bucklow / When the moon is on the wane, / And the jackal growls while the monkey howls / Like a woman struck insane . . . Is that the one you mean?'

A pause. 'I want that volume, sir. I want to buy it.'

'Good. I want to sell it.'

'And your price?'

'I haven't set it yet.'

'If you will do so . . .'

'This is tricky business. I have to protect myself. I'm a fugitive, as you said, and that makes me vulnerable. I don't even know whom I'm dealing with.'

'A visitor in your land, sir. A passionate devotee of Mr Kipling. My name is of little importance.'

'How can I get in touch with you?'

'It's of less importance than my name. I can get in touch with *you*, sir, by calling this number.'

'No. I won't be here. It's not safe. Give me a number where I can reach you at five o'clock this afternoon.'

'A telephone number?'

'Yes.'

'I can't do that.'

'It can be any telephone at all. Just so you'll be at it at five o'clock.'

'Ah. I will call you back, sir, in ten minutes.'

Rrrring!

'Hello?'

'Sir, you have pencil and paper?'

'Go ahead.'

'I will be at this number at five o'clock this afternoon. RH4–5198.'

'RH4–5198. At five o'clock.'

Rrrring! Rrrring!

'Hello?'

'Hello?'

'Hello.'

'Ah. If you could say something more elaborate than a simple *hello . . .*'

'What do you want me to say?'

'Very good. I'd hoped it was you. I won't use your name aloud, and I trust you won't use mine.'

'Only if I want to call your club and have you paged.'

'Don't do that.'

'They said you weren't a member. Extraordinary, isn't it?'

'Perhaps I haven't been altogether straightforward with you, my boy. I can explain everything.'

'I'm sure you can.'

'The elusive item. Can I assume from your advertisement that it hasn't slipped out of your hands?'

'It's in front of me even as we speak.'

'Excellent.'

' "Now if you should go to Fort Bucklow / When the moon is on the wane, / And the jackal growls while the monkey howls . . ." '

'For heaven's sake, don't *read* it to me. Or have you committed great stretches of it to memory?'

'No, I was reading.'

'Oh, to prove possession? Hardly necessary, my boy. You'd scarcely have shot the woman and then left the book behind, would you? Now how are we going to manage this transaction?'

'We could meet someplace.'

'We could. Of course neither of us would welcome the attention of the police. I wonder . . .'

'Give me a number where I can reach you at six o'clock.'

'Why don't I simply call you?'

'Because I don't know where I'll be.'

'I see. Well, my boy, at the risk of appearing to play them close to the vest, I'm not sure I'd care to give out this number.'

'Any number, then.'

'How's that?'

'Pick a pay phone. Give me the number and be there to answer it at six.'

'Ah. I'll get back to you.'

Rrrring!
  'Hello?'
  'CHelsea 2–9419.'
  'Good.'
  'At six o'clock.'
  'Good.'

Rrrring!
  'Hello?'
  'Hello. I believe you advertised—'
  'Passage to Fort Bucklow. That's correct.'

'May I speak frankly? We're talking about a book, are we not?'

'Yes.'

'And you wish to purchase it?'

'I have it for sale.'

A pause. 'I see. You actually own a copy. You have it in your possession.'

'". . . The jackal growls while the monkey howls / Like a woman struck insane . . ." '

'What did you say?'

'I'm reading from the top of page forty-two.'

'That would hardly seem necessary.' Another pause. 'This is confusing. Perhaps I should give you my name.'

'That'd be nice.'

'It's Demarest. Prescott Demarest, and I don't suppose it will mean anything to you. I'm acting as agent for a wealthy collector whose name would mean something to you, but I haven't the authority to mention it. He was recently offered a copy of this book. The offer was suddenly withdrawn. I wonder if it's the same copy?'

'I couldn't say.'

'The copy he was offered was represented as unique. It was our understanding that only one copy of the book exists.'

'Then it must be the same copy.'

'So it would seem. I don't think you gave your name.'

'I'm careful about my privacy, Mr Demarest. Like your employer.'

'I see. I'd have to consult him, of course, but if you could let me know your price?'

'It hasn't been set yet.'

'There are other potential buyers?'

'Several.'

'I'd like to see the book. Before you offer it to anyone else. If we could arrange to meet—'

'I can't talk right now, Mr Demarest. Where can I reach you this afternoon at, say, four o'clock? Will you be near a telephone?'

'I can arrange to be.'

'Could I have the number?'

'I don't see why not. Take this down. WOrth 4–1114. You did say four o'clock? I'll expect to hear from you then.'

'I think that's it,' I told Carolyn, after I'd summarized the Demarest conversation for her. 'I don't think there are going to be any more calls.'

'How can you tell?'

'I can't, but it's one of my stronger hunches. The first caller was foreign and he's the one who sicked the Sikh on me. The Sikh came around Thursday afternoon, so he's known at least that long that I had the book, but he made me read it to him over the phone.'

'What does that prove?'

'Beats me. Right now I'm just piling up data. Interpreting it will have to wait. The second call was from Whelkin and he wasn't terribly interested in howling jackals or growling monkeys.'

'I think it's the other way around.'

'Monkeys and jackals aren't terribly interested in Whelkin?'

'The jackal was growling and the monkey was howling. Not that it makes a hell of a lot of difference. What are you getting at, Bernie?'

'Good question. Whelkin seemed to take it for granted that I killed Madeleine Porlock. That's why he wasn't surprised I had the book. Which means he didn't kill her. Unless, of course, he was pretending to believe I killed her, in which case . . .'

'In which case what?'

'Damned if I know. That leaves Demarest, and there's something refreshing about him. He was very open about his name and he didn't have to be coaxed into supplying his phone number. What do you suppose that means?'

'I don't know.'

'Neither do I.' I helped myself to more coffee. 'The murder's what screws things up. If somebody hadn't killed Madeleine Porlock I wouldn't have a problem. Or if the police weren't looking to hang the killing on me. I'd just sell the book to the highest bidder and spend the next two weeks in the Bahamas. One of those three killed her, Carolyn.'

'One of the ones who just called?'

'Uh-huh.' I looked at my watch. 'We don't have a hell of a lot of time,' I said. 'I'm supposed to call them at hourly intervals, starting with Demarest at four. That gives us a couple of hours to set things up.'

'To set what up?'

'A trap. It's going to be tricky, though, because I don't know who to set it for or what to use for bait. There's only one thing to do.'

'What's that?'

'What I always do in time of stress,' I said. 'Bribe a cop.'

15

When he came to the phone I apologized for the intrusion. 'Your wife didn't want to disturb you,' I said, 'but I told her it was important.'

'Well, I got Wake Forest and ten points,' he said. 'So all I been doin' is watch twenty bucks go down the chute.'

'Who are they playing?'

'University of Georgia. The Bulldogs got what they call the Junkyard Dog defense. All it means is they're chewin' the ass offa poor Wake Forest.' There was a long and thoughtful pause. 'Who the hell,' he said, '*is* this?'

'Just an old friend and enemy who needs a favor.'

'Jesus, it's you. Kid, I seen you step in it before, but I swear this time you got both feet smack in the middle of God's birthday cake. Where are you callin' from, anyway?'

'The Slough of Despond. I need a favor, Ray.'

'Jesus, that's the truth. Well, you came to the right place. You want me to set up a surrender, right? First smart move you made since you iced the Porlock dame. You stay out there and it's just a question of time before somebody tags you, and what do you want to get shot for? And the word is shoot first on you, Bern.' He clucked at me. 'That wasn't too brilliant, you know. Shootin' a cop. The department takes a dim view.'

'I never shot him.'

'C'mon, kid. He was there, right? He saw you.'

'He saw a clown with a beard and a turban. I never shot him and I never shot her either.'

'And all you do is sell books. You told me the whole story, remember? How you're straight as a javelin and all? Listen, you'll be okay now. I'll set up a surrender, and don't think I don't appreciate it. Makes me look good, no question about it, and it saves your ass. You get yourself a decent lawyer and who knows, you might even beat the whole thing in court. Worst comes to worst, so you do a couple of years upstate. You done that before.'

'Ray, I never—'

'One thing that's not so good, this Rockland kid's young and feisty,

393

you know? If it was an old-timer you shot, he'd probably take a couple of kay to roll over in court and fudge the testimony. 'Course, if it was an old-timer, he probably woulda shot you instead of waitin' to get hisself shot in the foot. So I guess you break even on that one, Bern.'

We went a few more rounds, me proclaiming my innocence while he told me how I could cop a plea and probably get off with writing 'I won't steal no more' one hundred times on the blackboard after school. Eventually I shifted gears and told him there was something specific I wanted from him.

'Oh?'

'I have three phone numbers. I want you to run them down for me.'

'You nuts, Bernie? You know what's involved in tracin' a call? You gotta set up in advance, you gotta be able to reach somebody at the phone company on another line, and then you gotta keep the mark on the phone for a couple of minutes and even then they sometimes can't make the trace work. And then if you—'

'I already know the three numbers, Ray.'

'Huh?'

'I know the numbers, I want to know the locations of the phones. As if I already traced the calls successfully and I want to know where I traced them to.'

'Oh.'

'You could do that couldn't you?'

He thought it over. 'Sure,' he said, 'but why should I?'

I gave him a very good reason.

'I don't know,' he said, after we'd discussed my very good reason for a few minutes. 'Seems to me I'm takin' a hell of a chance.'

'What chance? You'll make a phone call, that's all.'

'Meanwhile I'm cooperatin' with a fugitive from justice. That's not gonna go down too good if anybody ever hears about it.'

'Who's going to hear?'

'You never know. Another thing, how in the hell are you ever gonna deliver? You make it sound good, but how can you deliver? If some rookie with high marks on the pistol range whacks you out, Bern, where does that leave me?'

'It leaves you alive. Think where it leaves me.'

'That's why I'm sayin' you oughta surrender.'

'Nobody's going to shoot me,' I said, with perhaps a shade more confidence than I possessed. 'And I'll deliver what I promised. When did I ever let you down?'

'Well . . .'

'Ray, all you have to do is make a phone call or two. Isn't it worth a shot? For Christ's sake, if Wake Forest is worth a twenty-dollar investment—'

'Don't remind me. My money's gurglin' down the drain and I'm not even watchin' it go.'

'Look at the odds I'm giving you. All you got with Wake Forest is ten points.'

'Yeah.' I listened while his mental wheels spun. 'You ever tell anybody we had this conversation—'

'You know me better than that, Ray.'

'Yeah, you're all right. Okay, gimme the numbers.'

I gave them to him and he repeated them in turn.

'All right,' he said. 'Now gimme the number where you're at and I'll get back to you soon as I can.'

'Sure,' I said. 'The number here.' I was about to read it off the little disc on the telephone when Carolyn grabbed my arm and showed me a face overflowing with alarm. 'Uh, I don't think so,' I told Ray. 'If it's that easy for you to find out where a phone's located—'

'Bern, what kind of a guy do you think I am?'

I let that one glide by. 'Besides,' I said, 'I'm on my way out the door, anyway. Best thing is if I call you back. How much time do you need?'

'Depends what kind of cooperation I get from the phone company.'

'Say half an hour?'

'Yeah,' he said. 'Sounds good. Try me in half an hour, Bernie.'

I cradled the receiver. Carolyn and both cats were looking at me expectantly. 'A camera,' I said.

'Huh?'

'We've got half an hour to get a camera. A Polaroid, actually, unless you know somebody with a darkroom, and who wants to screw around developing film? We need a Polaroid. I don't suppose you've got one?'

'No.'

'Is there one you could borrow? I hate the idea of running out and buying one. The midtown stores are likely to be crowded and I don't even know if there's a camera place in the Village. There's stores on Fourteenth Street but the stuff they sell tends to fall apart on the way home. And there's pawnshops on Third Avenue but I hate to make the rounds over there with a price on my head. Of course you could go over there and buy one.'

'If I knew what to buy. I'd hate to get it home and find out it doesn't work. What do we need a camera for, anyway?'

'To take some pictures.'

'I never would have thought of that. It's a shame Randy walked in when she did. She's got one of those new Polaroids, you take the picture and it's developed before you can let go of the shutter.'

'Randy's got a Polaroid?'

'That's what I just said. Didn't I show you pictures of the cats last week?'

'Probably.'

'Well, she took them. But I can't ask her to borrow it, because she's convinced we're having an affair and she'd probably think I wanted us to take obscene pictures of each other or something. And she's probably not home, anyway.'

'Call her and see.'

'Are you kidding? I don't want to talk to her.'

'Hang up if she answers.'

'Then why call in the first place?'

'Because if she's *not* home,' I said, 'we can go pick up the camera.'

'Beautiful.' She reached for the phone, then sighed and let her hand drop. 'You're forgetting something. Remember last night? I gave her keys back.'

'So?'

'Huh?'

'Who needs keys?'

She looked at me, laughed, shook her head. 'Far out,' she said, and reached for the phone.

Randy lived in a tiny studio on the fifth floor of a squat brick apartment house on Morton Street between Seventh Avenue and Hudson. There's an article in the New York building code requiring an elevator in every structure of seven or more stories. This one was six stories tall, and up the stairs we went.

The locks were candy. They wouldn't have been much trouble if I'd been limited to my drugstore tools. Now that I had my pro gear, I went through them like the Wehrmacht through Luxemburg. When the penny dropped and the final lock snicked open, I looked up at Carolyn. Her mouth was wide open and her blue eyes were larger than I'd ever seen them.

'God,' she said. 'It takes me longer than that when I've got the keys.'

'Well, they're cheap locks. And I was showing off a little. Trying to impress you.'

'It worked. I'm impressed.'

We were in and out quicker than Speedy Gonzales. The camera was where Carolyn thought it would be, in the bottom drawer of Randy's dresser. It nestled in a carrying case with a shoulder strap, and an ample supply of film reposed in the case's zippered film compartment. Carolyn slung the thing over her shoulder, I locked the locks, and we were on our way home.

I'd told Ray I would call him in half an hour and I didn't miss by more than a few minutes. He answered the phone himself this time. 'Your friend moves around,' he said.

'Huh?'

'The guy with the three phone numbers. He covers a lot of ground. The Rhinelander number's a sidewalk pay phone on the corner of Seventy-fifth and Madison. The Chelsea number's also a pay phone. It's located in the lobby of the Gresham Hotel. That's on Twenty-third between Fifth and Sixth.'

'Hold on,' I said, scribbling furiously. 'All right. How about the Worth number?'

'Downtown. I mean way downtown, in the Wall Street area. Twelve Pine Street.'

'Another lobby phone?'

'Nope. An office on the fourteenth floor. A firm called Tontine Trading Corp. Bern, let's get back to the coat, huh? You said ranch mink, didn't you?'

'That's right.'

'What did you say the color was?'

'Silver-blue.'

'And it's full-fashioned? You're sure of that?'

'Positive. You can't go wrong with this one, Ray. It's carrying an Arvin Tannenbaum label, and that's strictly carriage trade.'

'When can I have it?'

'In plenty of time for Christmas, Ray. No problem.'

'You son of a bitch. What are you givin' me? You haven't got the coat.'

'Of course not. I retired, Ray. I gave up burglary. What would I be doing with a hot coat?'

'Then where'd the coat come from?'

'I'm going to get it for you, Ray. After I get myself out of the jam I'm in.'

'Suppose you don't get out of it, Bern? Then what?'

'Well, you better hope I do,' I said, 'or else the coat's down the same chute as your twenty-buck bet on Wake Forest.'

16

I cabbed uptown for the Pontiac. By the time I brought it downtown again Carolyn had familiarized herself with the intricacies of the Polaroid camera. She proved this by clicking the shutter at me as I came through the door. The picture popped out and commenced developing before my eyes. I looked startled, and guilty of something or other. I told Carolyn I wasn't going to order any enlargements.

'You're a better model than the cats,' she said. 'Ubi wouldn't sit still and Archie kept crossing his eyes.'

'Archie always keeps crossing his eyes.'

'It's part of being Burmese. Wanna take my picture?'

'Sure.'

She was wearing a charcoal-gray turtleneck and slate-blue corduroy jeans. For the photo she slipped on a brass-buttoned blazer and topped things off with a rakish beret. So attired, she sat on the edge of a table, crossed her legs, and grinned at the camera like an endearing waif.

Randy's Polaroid captured all of this remarkably well. We studied the result together. 'What's missing,' Carolyn said, 'is a cigar.'

'You don't smoke cigars.'

'To pose with. It'd make me look very *Bonnie and Clyde*.'

'Which of them do you figure you'd look like?'

'Oh, very funny. Nothing like a little sexist humor to lighten the mood. Are we ready to go?'

'I think so. You've got the Blinns' bracelet?'

'In my pocket.'

'And you're comfortable with the camera?'

'It's about as tricky to operate as a self-service elevator.'

'Then let's go.'

And on the sidewalk I said, 'Uh, Carolyn, you may not remind anybody of Faye Dunaway, but you look terrific today.'

'What's all this about?'

'And you're not bad to have around, either.'

'What *is* this? A speech to the troops before going into battle?'

'Something like that, I guess.'

'Well, watch it, will you? I could get misty-eyed and run my mascara. It's a good thing I don't wear any. Can't you drive this crate, Bern?'

On weekends, New York's financial district looks as though someone zapped it with one of those considerate bombs that kills people without damaging property. Narrow streets, tall buildings, and no discernible human activity whatsoever. All the shops were closed, all the people home watching football games.

I left the Pontiac in an unattended parking lot on Nassau and we walked down to Pine. Number 12 was an office building that towered above those on either side of it. A guard sat at a desk in the lobby, logging the handful of workers who refused to let the weekend qualify their devotion to the pursuit of profit.

We stood on the far side of Pine for eight or ten minutes, during which time the attendant had nothing whatever to do. No one signed in or out. I looked up and counted nine lighted windows on the front of the building. I tried to determine if one of these might be on the fourteenth floor, a process made somewhat more difficult by the angle at which I had to gaze and the impossibility of determining which was the fourteenth floor, since I had no way of knowing if the building had a thirteenth floor.

I couldn't find a pay phone in line of sight of the building. I went around the corner and walked a block up William Street. At two minutes past four I dialed the number Prescott Demarest had given me. He picked it up after it had rung twice but didn't say anything until I'd said hello myself. If I'd shown similar restraint the night before we could have had Randy's Polaroid without breaking and entering to get it.

'I have the book,' I told him. 'And I need cash. I have to leave town. If you're ready to deal, I can offer you a bargain.'

'I'll pay a fair price. If I'm convinced the item is genuine.'

'Suppose I show it to you tonight? If you decide you want it, then we can work out a price.'

'Tonight?'

'At Barnegat Books. That's a store on East Eleventh Street.'

'I know where it is. There was a story in this morning's paper—'

'I know.'

'You feel it's entirely safe? Meeting at this store?'

'I think so. There's no police surveillance, if that's worrying you. I checked earlier this afternoon.' And so I had, driving past slowly in the Pontiac. 'Eleven o'clock,' I said. 'I'll see you then.'

I hung up and walked back to the corner of William and Pine. I could see the entrance of Number 12 from there, though not terribly well. I'd left Carolyn directly across the street in the doorway of a shop that offered old prints and custom framing. I couldn't tell if she was still there or not.

I stayed put for maybe five minutes. Then someone emerged from the building, walking off immediately toward Nassau Street. He'd no sooner disappeared from view than Carolyn stepped out from the printshop's doorway and gave me a wave.

I sprinted back to the telephone, dialed WOrth 4–1114. I let it ring a full dozen times, hung up, retrieved my dime, and raced back to where Carolyn was waiting. 'No answer,' I told her. 'He's left the office.'

'Then we've got his picture.'

'There was just the one man?'

'Uh-huh. Somebody else left earlier, but you hadn't even gotten to the phone by then, so I didn't bother taking his picture. Then one man came out, and I waved to you after I snapped him, and there hasn't been anybody since then. Here's somebody now. It's a woman. Should I take her picture?'

'Don't bother.'

'She's signing out. Demarest didn't bother. He just waved to the guard and walked on by.'

'Doesn't mean anything. I've done that myself, hitting doormen with the old nonchalance. If you act like they know you, they figure they must.'

'Here's his picture. What we really need is one of those zoom lenses or whatever you call them. At least this is a narrow street or you wouldn't be able to see much.'

I studied the picture. It didn't have the clarity of a Bachrach portrait but the lighting was good and Demarest's face showed up clearly. He was a big man, middle-aged, with the close-cropped gray hair of a retired Marine colonel.

The face was vaguely familiar but I couldn't think why. He was no one I'd ever seen before.

On the way uptown Carolyn used the rear-view mirror to check the angle of her beret. It took a few minutes before she was satisfied with it.

'That was really funny,' she said.

'Taking Demarest's picture?'

'What's funny about taking somebody's picture? It wasn't even scary. I had visions of him coming straight across the street and braining me with the camera, but he never even noticed. Just a quiet little click from the shadows. No, I was talking about last night.'

'Oh.'

'When Randy turned up. The ultimate bedroom farce. I swear, if jumping weren't allowed she'd never get to a conclusion.'

'Well, from her point of view—'

'Oh, the whole thing's ridiculous from anybody's point of view. But there's one thing you've got to admit.'

'What's that?'

'She's really cute when she's mad.'

By a quarter to five we were in a cocktail lounge called Sangfroid. It was as elegant as the surrounding neighborhood, its floor deeply carpeted, its décor running to black wood and chrome. Our table was a black disc eighteen inches in diameter. Our chairs were black vinyl hemispheres with chrome bases. My drink was Perrier water with ice and lime. Carolyn's was a martini.

'I know you don't drink when you work,' she said. 'But this isn't drinking.'

'What is it?'

'Therapy. And not a moment too soon, because I think I'm hallucinating. Do you see what I see?'

'I see a very tall gentleman with a beard and a turban walking south on Madison Avenue.'

'Does that mean we're both hallucinating?'

I shook my head. 'The chap's a Sikh,' I said. 'Unless he's a notorious homicidal burglar wearing a fiendishly clever disguise.'

'What's he doing?'

He had entered the telephone booth. It was on our corner, a matter of yards from where we sat, and we could see him quite clearly through the window. I couldn't swear he was the same Sikh who'd held a gun on me, but the possibility certainly did suggest itself.

'Is he the man who called you?'

'I don't think so.'

'Then why's he in the booth? He's ten minutes early, anyway.'

'Maybe his watch is fast.'

'Is he just going to sit there? Wait a minute. Who's he calling?'

'I don't know. If it's Dial-A-Prayer, you might get the number from him.'

'It's not Dial-A-Prayer. He's saying something.'

'Maybe it's Dial-A-Mantra and he's chanting along with the recording.'

'He's hanging up.'

'So he is,' I said.

'And going away.'

But not far. He crossed the street and took a position in the doorway of a boutique. He was about as inconspicuous as the World Trade Center.

'He's standing guard,' I said. 'I think he just checked to make sure the coast was clear. Then he called the man I spoke with earlier and told

401

him as much. Those may have been his very words – *The coast is clear* – but somehow I doubt it. Here comes our man now, I think.'

'Where did he come from?'

'The Carlyle, probably. It's just a block away, and where else would you stay if you were the sort to employ turbaned Sikhs? The Waldorf, perhaps, if you had a sense of history. The Sherry-Netherlands, possibly, if you were a film producer and the Sikh was Yul Brynner in drag. The Pierre maybe, just maybe, if—'

'It's definitely him. He's in the booth.'

'So he is.'

'Now what?'

I stood up, found a dime in my pocket, checked my watch. 'It's about that time,' I said. 'You'll excuse me, won't you? I have a call to make.'

It was a longish call. A couple of times the operator cut in to ask for nickels, and it wasn't the sort of conversation where one welcomed the intrusion. I thought of setting the receiver down, walking a few dozen yards, tapping on the phone-booth door and hanging onto my nickels. I decided that would be pound foolish.

I hung up, finally, and the operator rang back almost immediately to ask for a final dime. I dropped it in, then stood there fingering my ring of picks and probes and having fantasies of opening the coin box and retrieving what I'd spent. I'd never tried to pick a telephone, the game clearly not being worth the candle, but how hard could it be? I studied the key slot for perhaps a full minute before coming sharply to my senses.

Carolyn would love that one, I thought, and hurried back to the table to fill her in. She wasn't there. I sat for a moment. The ice had melted in my Perrier and the natural carbonation, while remarkably persistent, was clearly flagging. I gazed out the window. The phone booth on the corner was empty, and I couldn't spot the Sikh in the doorway across the street.

Had she responded to a call of nature? If so, she'd toted the camera along with her. I gave her an extra minute to return from the ladies' room, then laid a five-dollar bill atop the little table, weighted it down with my glass, and got out of there.

I took another look for the Sikh and still couldn't find him. I crossed the street and walked north on Madison in the direction of the Carlyle. Bobby Short was back from his summer break, I seemed to recall reading, and Tommie Flanagan, Ella Fitzgerald's accompanist for years, was doing a solo act in the Bemelmans Lounge. It struck me that I couldn't think of a nicer way to spend a New York evening, and that I hadn't been getting out much of late, and once this mess was cleared up I'd have to pay another visit to this glittering neighborhood.

402

Unless, of course, this mess didn't get cleared up. In which case I wouldn't be getting out much for years on end.

I was entertaining this grim thought when a voice came at me from a doorway on my left. 'Pssssst,' I heard. 'Hey, Mac, wanna buy a hot camera?'

And there she was, a cocky grin on her face. 'You found me,' she said. 'I'm keen and resourceful.'

'And harder to shake than a summer cold.'

'That too. I figured you were in the john. When you failed to return, I took action.'

'So did I. I tried taking his picture while you were talking to him. From our table. All I got was reflections. You couldn't even tell if there was anyone inside the telephone booth.'

'So you went out and waylaid him.'

'Yeah. I figured when he was done he'd probably go back where he came from, so I found this spot and waited for him. Either he made more calls or you were talking a long time.'

'We were talking a long time.'

'Then he showed up, finally, and he never even noticed me. He passed close by, too. Look at this.'

'A stunning likeness.'

'That's nothing. The film popped out the way it does, and I watched it develop, and it's really amazing the way it does that, and then I tore it off and put it in my pocket, and I popped out of the doorway, ready to go back and look for you, and who do you think I bumped into?'

'Rudyard Whelkin.'

'Is he around here? Did you see him?'

'No.'

'Then why did you say that?'

'Just a guess. Let's see. Prescott Demarest?'

'No. What's the matter with you, Bern? It was the Sikh.'

'That would have been my third guess.'

'Well, you would have been right. I popped out with my camera in my hot little hands and I almost smacked right into him. He looked down at me and I looked up at him, and I'll tell you, Bernie, I could have used a stepstool.'

'What happened?'

'What happened is I was incredibly brilliant. A mind like quicksilver. I went all saucer-eyed and I said, "Oh, wow, a turban! Are you from India, sir? Are you with the United Nations? Gosh, will you pose for me so I can take your picture?" '

'How did this go over?'

'Smashingly. Look for yourself.'

'You're getting pretty handy with that camera.'

'You're no more impressed than he was. He's going to buy himself a

Polaroid first thing Monday morning. I had to take two pictures, incidentally, because he wanted one for a souvenir. Turn it over, Bernie. Read the back.'

An elegant inscription, with lots of curlicues and nonfunctional loops and whorls. *To my tiny princess / With devotion and esteem / Your loyal servant / Atman Singh.*

'That's his name,' she explained. 'Atman Singh.'

'I figured that.'

'Clever of you. The guy you were on the phone with is Atman Singh's boss, which you also probably figured. The boss's name is – Well, come to think of it, I don't know his name, but his title is the Maharajah of Ranchipur. But I suppose you knew that too, huh?'

'No,' I said softly. 'I didn't know that.'

'They're at the Carlyle, you were right about that. The Maharajah likes to take people with him when he travels. Especially women. I had the feeling I could have joined the party if I played my cards right.'

'I wonder how you'd look with a ruby in your navel.'

'A little too femme, don't you think? Anyway, Atman Singh likes me just the way I am.'

'So do I.' I put a hand on her shoulder. 'You did beautifully, Carolyn. I'm impressed.'

'So am I,' she said, 'if I say so myself. But it wasn't just me alone. I could never have done it without the martini.'

Driving south and east, she said, 'It was exciting, doing that number with Atman Singh. At first I was scared and then I didn't even notice I was scared because I was so completely into it. Do you know what I mean?'

'Of course I know what you mean. I get the same feeling in other people's houses.'

'Yeah, that was a kick. In Randy's place. I never realized burglary could be thrilling like that. Now I can see how people might do it primarily for the kick, with the money secondary.'

'When you're a pro,' I said, 'the money's never secondary.'

'I guess not. She was really jealous, wasn't she?'

'Randy?'

'Yeah. Hey, when this is all over, maybe you could teach me a few things.'

'Like what?'

'Like opening locks without keys. If you think I could learn.'

'Well, there's a certain amount a person can learn. I think there's a knack for lockpick work that you either have or you don't, but beyond that there are things I could teach you.'

'How about starting a car without a key?'

'Jumping the ignition? That's a cinch. You could learn that in ten minutes.'

'I don't drive, though.'

'That does make it a pointless skill to acquire.'

'Yeah, but I'd sort of like to be able to do it. Just for the hell of it. Hey, Bern?'

'What?'

She made a fist, punched me lightly on the upper arm. 'I know this is like life and death,' she said, 'but I'm having a good time. I just wanted to tell you that.'

By five-fifty we were parked – legally, for a change – about half a block from the Gresham Hotel on West Twenty-third Street. The daylight was fading fast now. Carolyn rolled down her window and snapped a quick picture of a passing stranger. The result wasn't too bad from an aesthetic standpoint, but the dim light resulted in a loss of detail.

'I was afraid of that,' I told her. 'I booked the Maharajah at five and Whelkin at six, and then when I spoke to Demarest, I was going to set up the call for seven. I made it four instead when I remembered we'd need light.'

'There's flashcubes in the carrying case.'

'They're a little obvious, don't you think? Anyway, I'm glad we caught Demarest when it was still light enough out to see him. With Whelkin it may not matter. We may not be able to coax him out of the hotel.'

'You think he's staying there?'

'It's certainly possible. I'd have called, but what name would I ask for?'

'You don't think he's staying there under his own name?'

'In the first place, no. In the second place, I have no idea what his right name might be. I'm sure it's not Rudyard Whelkin. That was a cute story, being named for Kipling and growing up to collect him, but I have the feeling I'm the only person he told it to.'

'His name's not Rudyard Whelkin?'

'No. And he doesn't collect books.'

'What does he do with them?'

'I think he sells them. I think' – I looked at my watch – 'I think he's sitting in a booth in the lobby of the Gresham,' I went on, 'waiting for my call. I think I better call him.'

'And I think I better take his picture.'

'Be subtle about it, huh?'

'That's my trademark.'

The first phone I tried was out of order. There was another one diagonally across the street but someone was using it. I wound up at a phone on the rear wall of a Blarney Rose bar that had less in common with Sangfroid than the Hotel Gresham did with the Carlyle. Hand-lettered signs over the back bar offered double shots of various brands of blended whiskey at resistibly low prices.

I dialed the number Whelkin had given me. He must have had his hand on the receiver because he had it off the hook the instant it started to ring.

The conversation was briefer than the one I'd had with the Maharajah. It took longer than it had to because I had trouble hearing at one point; the television announcer was delivering football scores and something he said touched off a loud argument that had something to do with Notre Dame. But the shouting subsided and Whelkin and I resumed our chat.

I apologized for the interference.

'It's nothing, my boy,' he assured me. 'Things are every bit as confused where I am. A Eurasian chap's sprawled on a bench in what looks to be a drug-induced coma, a wildeyed old woman's pawing through a shopping bag and nattering to herself, and another much younger woman's flitting about taking everyone's picture. Oh, dear. She's headed this way.'

'She sounds harmless,' I said.

'One can only hope so. I shall give her a dazzling smile and let it go at that.'

A few minutes later I was back in the Pontiac studying a close-up of Rudyard Whelkin. He was showing all his teeth and they fairly gleamed.

'Subtle,' I told Carolyn.

'There's a time for subtlety,' she said, 'and there's a time for derring-do. There is a time for the rapier and a time for the bludgeon. There is a time for the end-around play and a time to plunge right up the middle.'

'There's a Notre Dame fan in the Blarney Rose who would argue that last point with you. I wanted a drink by the time I got out of there. But I had the feeling they were out of Perrier.'

'You want to stop someplace now?'

'No time.'

'What did Whelkin say?'

I gave her the *Reader's Digest* version of our conversation as I headed uptown and east again. When I finished she frowned at me and scratched her head. 'It's too damned confusing,' she complained. 'I can't tell who's lying and who's telling the truth.'

'Just assume everybody's lying. That way the occasional surprises will be pleasant ones. I'll drop you at the Blinns' place. You know what to do?'

'Sure, but aren't you coming in?'

'No need, and too many other things to do. You know what to do after you're through with the Blinns?'

'Have a big drink.'

'And after that?'

'I think so. Want to run through it all for me one more time?'

I ran through it, and we discussed a couple of points, and by then I was double-parked on East Sixty-sixth next to a Jaguar sedan with DPL plates and a shamefully dented right front fender. The Jag was parked next to a hydrant, and its owner, safe beneath the umbrella of diplomatic immunity, didn't have to worry about either ticket or tow.

'Here we are,' I said. 'You've got the pictures?'

'All of them. Even Atman Singh.'

'You might as well take the camera, too. No sense leaving it in the car. How about the Blinns' bracelet? Got that with you?'

She took it from her pocket, slipped it around her wrist. 'I'm not nuts about jewelry,' she said. 'But it's pretty, isn't it? Bern, you're forgetting something. You have to come in with me now if you want to get to the Porlock apartment.'

'Why would I want to get to the Porlock apartment?'

'To steal the lynx jacket.'

'Why would I want to steal the lynx jacket? I'm starting to feel like half of a vaudeville act. Why would I—'

'Didn't you promise it to the cop?'

'Oh. I was wondering where all of that was coming from. No, what Ray wants for his wife is a full-length mink, and what's hanging in Madeleine Porlock's closet is a waist-length lynx jacket. Mrs Kirschmann doesn't want to have any part of wild furs.'

'Good for her. I wasn't listening too closely to your conversation, I guess. You're going to steal the mink somewhere else.'

'In due time.'

'I see. I heard you mention the furrier's name and that's what got me confused.'

'Arvin Tannenbaum,' I said.

'Right, that's it.'

'Arvin Tannenbaum.'

'You just said that a minute ago.'

'Arvin Tannenbaum.'

'Bernie? Are you all right?'

'God,' I said, looking at my watch. 'As if I didn't have enough things to do and enough stops to make. There's never enough time, Carolyn. Have you noticed that? There's never enough time.'

'Bernie . . .'

I leaned across, opened the door on her side. 'Go make nice to the Blinns,' I said, 'and I'll catch you later.'

17

I called Ray Kirschmann from a sidewalk phone booth on Second Avenue. The Bulldogs had more than doubled the point spread, he informed me dolefully. 'Look at the bright side,' I said. 'You'll get even tomorrow.'

'Tomorrow I got the Giants. They never got anybody even unless he started out ahead.'

'I'd love to chat,' I said, 'but I'm rushed. There's some things I'd like you to find out for me.'

'What am I, the Answer Man? You want a lot for a coat.'

'It's mink, Ray. Think what some women have to do to get one.'

'Funny.'

'And it's not just a coat we're talking about. You could get a nice collar to go with it.'

'Think so?'

'Stranger things have happened. Got a pencil?' He went and fetched one and I told him the things I wanted him to find out. 'Don't stray too far from the phone, huh, Ray? I'll get back to you.'

'Great,' he said. 'I can hardly wait.'

I got back into the car. I'd left the motor running, and now I popped the transmission in gear and continued downtown on Second Avenue. At Twenty-third Street I turned right, favored the Hotel Gresham with no more than a passing glance, turned right again at Sixth Avenue and left at Twenty-ninth Street, parking at a meter on Seventh Avenue. This time I cut the engine and retrieved my jump wire.

I was in the heart of the fur market, a few square blocks that added up to an ecologist's nightmare. Several hundred small businesses were all clustered together, sellers of hides and pelts, manufacturers of coats and jackets and bags and accessories, wholesalers and retailers and somewhere-in-betweeners, dealers in trimming and by-products and fastenings and buttons and bows. The particular place I was looking for was on the far side of the avenue a couple doors west on Twenty-ninth Street. There Arvin Tannenbaum occupied the entire third floor of a four-story loft building.

A coffee shop, closed for the weekend, took up the ground floor. To its right was a door opening onto a small hallway which led to an elevator and the fire stairs. The door was locked. The lock did not look terribly formidable.

The dog, on the other hand, did. He was a Doberman, bred to kill and trained to be good at it, and he paced the hallway like an institutionalized leopard. When I approached the door he interrupted his exercise and gave me all his attention. I put a hand on the door, just out of curiosity, and he crouched, ready to spring. I withdrew my hand, but this did not mollify him much.

I wished Carolyn were with me. She could have given the bastard a bath. Clipped his nails, too, while she was at it. Filed his teeth down a bit.

I don't screw around with guard dogs. The only way I could think to get past this particular son of a bitch was to spray poison on my arm and let him bite me. I gave him a parting smile, and he growled low in his throat, and I went over and broke into the coffee shop.

That wasn't the easiest thing in the world – they had iron gates, like the ones at Barnegat Books – but it was more in my line of work than doing a wild-animal act. The gate had a padlock, which I picked, and the door had a Yale lock, which I also picked. No alarms went off. I drew the gate shut before closing the door. Anyone who took a close look would see it was unfastened, but it looked good from a distance.

There was a door at the side of the restaurant that led to the elevator, but it unfortunately also led to the dog, which lessened its usefulness. I went back through the kitchen, opening a door at the rear which led into an airless little airshaft. By standing on a garbage can, I could just reach the bottom rung of the fire escape. I pulled myself up and started climbing.

I would have gone right up to the third floor if I hadn't noticed an unlocked window on the second floor. It was too appealing an invitation to resist. I let myself in, walked through a maze of baled hides, climbed a flight of stairs, and emerged in the establishment of Arvin Tannenbaum and Sons.

Not too many minutes later I left the way I'd come, walking down a flight, threading my way between the bales of tanned hides, clambering down the fire escape and bopping nimbly to earth from my perch on the garbage can. I stopped in the coffee-shop kitchen to help myself to a Hostess Twinkie. I can't say it was just what I wanted, but I was starving and it was better than nothing.

I didn't bother picking the lock shut after me. The springlock would have to do. But I did draw the gates shut and fasten the padlock.

Before returning to the Pontiac, I walked over to say goodbye to the dog. I waved at him and he glowered at me. From the look he gave me I could have sworn he knew what I was up to.

*

It was Mrs Kirschmann who answered the phone. When I asked to speak to her husband she said 'Just a minute,' then yelled out his name without bothering to cover the mouthpiece. When Ray came on the line I told him my ear was ringing.

'So?'

'Your wife yelled in it.'

'I can't help that, Bernie,' he said. 'You all right otherwise?'

'I guess so. What did you find out?'

'I got a make on the murder weapon. Porlock was shot with a Devil Dog.'

'I just ate one of those.'

'Huh?'

'Actually, what I ate was a Twinkie, but isn't a Devil Dog about the same thing?'

He sighed. 'A Devil Dog's an automatic pistol made by Marley. Their whole line's dogs of one kind or another. The Devil Dog's a .32 automatic. The Whippet's a .25 automatic, the Mastiffs a .38 revolver, and they make a .44 Magnum that I can't remember what it's called. It oughta be something like an Irish Wolfhound or a Great Dane because of the size, but that's no kind of name for a gun.'

'There's a hell of a lot of dogs in this,' I said. 'Did you happen to notice? Between the Junkyard Dog defense and the Marley Devil Dog and the Doberman in the hallway—'

'What Doberman in the hallway? What hallway?'

'Forget it. It's a .32 automatic?'

'Right. Registration check went nowhere. Coulda been Porlock's gun, could be the killer brought it with him.'

'What did it look like?'

'The gun? I didn't see it, Bern. I made a call, I didn't go down to the property office and start eyeballin' the exhibits. I seen Devil Dogs before. It's an automatic, so it's a flat gun, not too large, takes a five-shot clip. The ones I've seen were blued steel, though you could probably get it in any kind of finish, nickel-plated or pearl grips, anything you wanted to pay for.'

I closed my eyes, trying to picture the gun I'd found in my hand. Blued steel, yes. That sounded right.

'Not a big gun, Bern. Two-inch barrel. Not much of a kick when you fire it.'

'Unless that's how you get your kicks.'

'Huh?'

'Nothing.' I frowned. It had seemed big, compared to the little nickel-plated item I'd seen in the Sikh's enormous hand.

Which reminded me.

'Francis Rockland,' I said. 'The cop who was wounded outside my bookshop. What gun was he shot with? Did you find that out?'

'You still say you weren't there, huh?'

'Dammit, Ray—'

'Okay, okay. Well, he wasn't shot with the Marley Devil Dog, Bern, because the killer left it on the floor of the Porlock apartment. Is that what you were gettin' at?'

'Of course not.'

'Oh. You had me goin' for a minute there. Rockland was shot – well, it's hard to say what he was shot with.'

'No slug recovered?'

'Right. The bullet fragmented.'

'There must have been fragments to recover.'

He cleared his throat. 'Now I'll deny I said this,' he said, 'but from what I heard, and nobody exactly spelled it out for me, but puttin' two and two together—'

'Rockland shot himself.'

'That's how it shapes up to me, Bern. He's a young fellow, you know, and bein' nervous and all . . .'

'How bad were his injuries?'

'Well, it seems he lost a toe. Not one of the important ones.'

I thought of Parker, going around breaking important bones. Which toes, I wondered, were the important ones?

'What did you find out about Rockland?'

'Well, I asked around, Bern. The word I get is he's young all right, which we already knew, but he's also the kind of guy who can listen to reason.'

'How do you translate that?'

'I translate it Money Talks.'

'There's not enough money in this one to make much noise,' I said. 'Unless he'll operate on credit.'

'You're askin' a lot, Bern. The poor kid lost a toe.'

'He shot it off himself, Ray.'

'A toe's a toe.'

'You just said it wasn't an important one.'

'Even so—'

'Would he settle for future payment if he got a piece of the bust? If he's the ambitious kid you say he is, he'd be crazy not to.'

'You got a point.'

I had more than a point I had a whole bunch of things to tell him, some of which provoked argument, some of which did not. At the end I told him to take it easy and he told me to take care.

It sounded like good advice for both of us.

The owner of Milo Arms, Inc., had a commendable sense of humor. His Yellow Pages ad showed the company trademark, the Venus de Milo's limbless torso with a holster on her hip. Who could resist?

411

I make it a point to stay out of gun shops, but one thing I've noticed is that I don't generally notice them. They're almost invariably located one flight above street level. I guess they're not that keen on the drop-in trade and the impulse shoppers.

Milo Arms didn't break the rule. They had the second floor of a weary red brick building on Canal between Greene and Mercer. The shop on the ground floor sold plumbing supplies and the upper floors had been carved into residential units. I was loitering in the vestibule, reading names on doorbells, when a young couple left the building, the smell of an illicit herb trailing after them. The girl giggled infectiously while her escort held the door for me.

The gun-shop door was a solid wooden one with the torso-cum-holster motif repeated, along with an extensive list of the death-dealing items on sale within. There was the usual run of locks, plus a padlock on the outside.

I gave a knock and was reassured to hear neither a human response nor the guttural greeting of an attack dog. Just blessed silence. I got right to work.

The locks weren't much trouble. The padlock had a combination dial that looked like an interesting challenge, and if I hadn't been out in public view and urgently pressed for time, I might have sandpapered my fingertips and tried out my Jimmy Valentine impression. Instead I tried my hacksaw blade on the thing, and when that didn't work – it was a damned good lock, made of damned good steel – I took the easy way out and unscrewed the hasp from its mounting on the jamb. There's tricks to every trade, and if you just live long enough you get to use 'em all.

God, what a grim place! I was only inside for five minutes or so, but what an uncomfortable five minutes they were. All those guns, all close together like that, reeking of oil and powder and whatever else it is that makes them smell the way they do. Infernal machines, engines of death and destruction, killers' tools.

Ugh.

I locked up carefully on my way out. The last thing I wanted to do was make it easy for some maniac to rip off a wholesale lot of guns and ammo. I even took the time to remount the padlock, leaving the hasp more tightly bolted to the jamb than I'd found it.

Guns!

Busy, busy, busy.

I found Carolyn at the Poodle Factory, where she was catching up on her bookkeeping and not enjoying it much. 'This is such an *unpleasant* business,' she said, 'that you'd think there'd be money in it, wouldn't you? You'd be wrong. Well, at least there's a big show coming up at the Armory.'

412

'Does that mean business for you?'

'Sure, You can't win ribbons with a dirty dog.'

'That sounds like a proverb. How were the Blinns?'

'Their usual charming selves. I pigged out on shortbread.'

'Beats Twinkles and Devil Dogs. Was Gert happy to see her bracelet back?'

'Oh,' she said. 'Yeah, I guess so.'

'You guess so?'

'We mainly concentrated on the photographs,' she said, all crisp efficiency now. She spread out the four snapshots on the mottled formica counter. 'Gert never saw this guy before in her life,' she said, pointing. 'She's sure about that. She doesn't think she saw this one, either, but she can't swear to it.'

'But she recognized the other two?'

Her forefinger hovered above one of the snaps. She'd been nibbling the nail again, I noticed. 'This dude,' she said, 'has been around a lot. No idea when she first saw him but it was a while ago. He's been there with Madeleine and he's also been there alone, entering or leaving the building by himself.'

'Fascinating. What about our other friend?'

'Artie thinks he saw them together once. And Gert says he's got a familiar look about him.'

'I'll borrow this one,' I said, picking one up. 'See you when I see you.'

The Gresham's lobby had changed some since Rudyard Whelkin had described it to me over the phone. Carolyn was gone and so was the shopping-bag lady. There was a junkie nodding on a bench, but he didn't look Eurasian to me. Perhaps he'd taken over when the Eurasian went off duty.

The phone Whelkin had used was in use now. An immense woman was talking on it. Too large for the booth, she was standing outside it and bellowing into the mouthpiece, telling someone that she had paid back the money, that she didn't owe nothing to nobody. Her presumptive creditor was evidently hard to convince.

The little man behind the desk possessed a skin the sun had never seen. He had tiny blue eyes and a small and virtually lipless mouth. I showed him the picture I'd taken from Carolyn. He gave it a long and thoughtful look, and then he gave that same long and thoughtful look to me.

'So?' he said.

'Is he in?'

'No.'

'When did he leave?'

'Who remembers?'

'I'd like to leave him a message.'

He handed me a pad. I had my own pen. I wrote *Please call as soon as possible* and signed it *R. Whelkin,* not to be cute but because it was the only name I could think of other than my own. A cinch he wasn't using it here, anyway.

I folded the slip; passed it to the clerk. He took it and gazed blankly at me. Neither of us moved. Behind me, the immense woman was announcing that she didn't have to take that kind of language from nobody.

'You'll want to put the message in his box,' I said.

'In a while.'

Now, I thought. So I can see what room he's in.

'I better do it soon,' he went on, 'before I forget who the message is for. You didn't put his name on it, did you?'

'No,'

'Come to think of it, who *is* it for?'

'You got no call to call me that,' the large woman said firmly. 'A name like that, I wouldn't call a dog by a name like that. You watch what you call me.'

The desk clerk had wispy eyebrows. I don't suppose they'd have been equal to their God-given task of keeping perspiration from dripping into his eyes, but it probably didn't matter because he probably avoided ever working up a sweat. He had enough eyebrows to raise, though, and he raised them now. Eloquently.

I put a twenty-dollar bill on the counter. He gave me a key to Room 311. Fifteen minutes later, on my way out, I gave it back to him.

The large woman was still on the phone. 'Talk about a snotass,' she was saying, 'I'll tell you who's a snotass. You're a snotass, if you want my opinion.'

Back in the Pontiac, back downtown again. God, was there no end to this? Back and forth, to and fro, hither and yon, pillar to post. Interminable.

The lot on Nassau Street was still unattended. A sign informed me it was illegal to leave a car there under such circumstances. It was not an illegality I could take too seriously at the moment. Violators, the sign assured me, would be towed at the owner's expense. It was a risk I was prepared to run.

I found a phone, dialed WOrth 4–1114. I didn't expect anyone to answer and nobody did.

I walked down to Pine Street and east to the building Prescott Demarest had emerged from hours earlier. (Hours? Weeks of subjective time.) Now only half as many windows showed lights as had done so earlier. I wished for a clipboard or a briefcase, something to make me look as though I belonged.

The lobby attendant was dozing over a newspaper but he snapped into consciousness as I entered the building. He was an older man with a tired face, probably eking out a pension. I walked toward him, then halted in mid-stride and let myself be overcome by a coughing fit. While it subsided I checked the building directory on the wall and picked out a likely firm for myself.

'Bless you,' the old man said.

'Thanks.'

'You want to watch that cough.'

'It's the weather. Nice one day and nasty the next.'

He gave me a knowing nod. 'It didn't used to be like this,' he said. 'Weather was always something you could count on, and now everything's changed.'

I signed in. *Name – Peter Johnson. Firm – Wickwire and McNally. Floor – 17.* At least I wasn't calling myself Whelkin for lack of imagination. And Peter Johnson was nicely anonymous. If Wickwire and McNally was a sizable firm, they very likely had a Peter Johnson in their employ. Or a John Peterson, or something close.

I rode the elevator to the seventeenth floor. Not that he would have been likely to check the indicator, but why be sloppy? I scooted down three flights of stairs and searched the corridors until I found a door with Tontine Trading Corp. painted on its frosted glass. The office within was completely dark, as were all the other offices I'd passed. Saturday night is the loneliest night in the week, let me tell you.

It's also the longest and I had places to go and people to see. I put my ear to the glass, rapped smartly on the wooden part of the door, listened carefully, then popped the lock with a strip of flexible steel in not much more time than it takes to tell about it.

Office locks are often like that, and why shouldn't they be? There's not much point in hanging a pick-proof whizbang of a lock on a door with a window in it. All you get for your trouble is a lot of broken glass.

Besides, there was a man downstairs to keep people like me from walking off with the IBM Selectrics, and what else was there to steal? I certainly didn't find anything. When I left the Tontine office – and walked up to 17 and rode down from there – I didn't have anything with me that I hadn't carried into the building.

The old man looked up from his paper. 'Now that was quick,' he said.

'Like a bunny,' I agreed, and signed myself out.

18

'I suppose you're wondering why I summoned you all here.'

Well, how often do you get to use a line like that? Here they all were, gathered together at Barnegat Books. When I bought the store from old Litzauer I'd had visions of little informal assemblies like this one. Sunday-afternoon poetry readings, say, with little glasses of medium-dry sherry and a tray of cucumber sandwiches handed round. Literary kaffee klatsches, with everybody smoking European cigarettes and arguing about what Ionesco really meant. I figured it would bring people around and garner the shop some useful word-of-mouth publicity. More to the point, it sounded like a great way to meet girls.

This evening's convocation was not quite what I'd had in mind. No one was snarling in iambs or trochees. Kafka's name had not come up. The store had already had more publicity than it needed. And I didn't expect to meet any girls.

The only one on hand, Carolyn, was perched on the high stool I used for fetching the loftier volumes from the loftier shelves. She sat off to one side, while the rest of my guests were strung out in an irregular half-circle facing the sales counter. I myself was standing behind the counter; I didn't have a chair to sit on because the one I usually kept behind the counter was occupied at the moment by Prescott Demarest.

See, my place was a bookstore, not a library. There weren't enough chairs to go around. The Maharajah of Ranchipur had the best seat in the house, a swivel-based oak armchair from my office in back. Atman Singh, his spine like a ramrod, sat upon an upended wooden packing case that had held Rome Beauty apples sometime in the dim past before Mr Litzauer used it to store surplus stock. Rudyard Whelkin had a folding chair Carolyn had brought over from the Poodle Factory.

I hadn't introduced anyone to anyone else, nor had any of them seen fit to offer small talk about football or the weather or crime in the streets. They'd arrived not in a body but all within a fairly brief span of time, and they'd remained remarkably silent until I did my suppose-you're-wondering number. Even then, all I got was a bunch of sharp stares.

'Actually,' I went on, 'you all know why I summoned you here.

Otherwise you wouldn't have come. We're here to discuss a book and a murder.'

A hush didn't fall over the room. You can't have everything.

'The murder,' I went on, 'was that of Madeleine Porlock. She was shot the day before yesterday in her apartment on East Sixty-sixth Street. The killer shot her once in the forehead, using a .32-caliber automatic pistol. The gun was a Marley Devil Dog, and the killer left it at the scene of the crime. He also left me at the scene of the crime, unconscious, with the murder gun in my hand.'

The Maharajah frowned in thought. 'You are saying you did not kill the woman.'

'I am indeed. I was there to deliver a book. I was supposed to get paid for the book. Instead I got drugged and framed, drugged by Miss Porlock and framed by the man who killed her. But' – I smiled brightly – 'I still have the book.'

I also had their attention. While they watched, silent as stones, I reached under the counter and came up with *The Deliverance of Fort Bucklow*. I flipped it open at random and read:

> 'Old Eisenberg was a crafty cod
> With the cunning of his breed,
> And he ate a piece of honey cake
> And he drank a glass of mead,
> And he wiped his lips and his fingertips
> While he swore a solemn oath
> That if they should go by Fort Bucklow
> They'd perish – not one but both.'

I closed the book. 'Horrid last line,' I said. 'Bad verse is when you can tell which line is there to rhyme with the other, and the whole book's like that. But it didn't become the object of our attention because of its literary merits. It's unique, you see. One of a kind. A pearl beyond price, a published work of Kipling's of which only one copy exists. And this is it, right here.'

I set the book on the counter. 'At the time I agreed to steal this book,' I went on, 'it was in the personal library of a gentleman named Jesse Arkwright. I was reliably informed that he had acquired it by private negotiation with the heirs of Lord Ponsonby, who withdrew it from a scheduled auction and sold it to him.' I fixed my gaze on Rudyard Whelkin. 'There may have been a Lord Ponsonby,' I said. 'There may still be a Lord Ponsonby. But that is not how Jesse Arkwright got his copy of *The Deliverance of Fort Bucklow*.'

Demarest asked how he'd got it.

'He bought it,' I said, 'from the very man who engaged me to steal it back. The arrangements for the original sale were worked out by

417

Madeleine Porlock.' The Maharajah wanted to know how she came into it.

'She was Arkwright's mistress,' I told him. 'She was also a lifelong acquaintance of my client, who told her that he'd come into possession of an exceedingly desirable book. She in turn remarked that a friend of hers – one might almost say *client* – was a passionate collector with an enthusiasm for books. It only remained to bring buyer and seller together.'

'And the sale went through?' Demarest seemed puzzled. 'Then why would the seller want to steal the book back? Just because of its value?'

'No,' I said. 'Because of its lack of value.'

'Then it is counterfeit,' said the Maharajah.

'No. It's quite genuine.'

'Then . . .'

'I wondered about that,' I said. 'I tried to figure out a way that the book could be a phony. It could be done, of course. First you'd have to find someone to write thirty-two hundred lines of doggerel in a fair approximation of Kipling's style. Then you'd have to find a printer to hand-set the thing, and he'd need a stock of fifty-year-old paper to run it off on. Maybe you could use fresh stock and fake it, but' – I tapped the book – 'that wasn't done here. I handle books every day and I know old paper. It looks and feels and smells different.

'But even if you had the paper, and if you could print the thing and have it bound and then distress it in a subtle fashion so that it looked well-preserved, how could you come out ahead on the deal? Maybe, if you found the absolutely right buyer, you could get a five-figure price for it. But you'd have about that much invested in the book by then, so where's your profit?'

'If the book is genuine,' the Maharajah said, 'how can it be worthless?'

'It's not literally worthless. The day after I stole it, a gentleman tried to take it from me at gunpoint. As luck would have it' – I smiled benignly at Atman Singh – 'he selected the wrong book by mistake. But he tried to placate me by giving me five hundred dollars, and coincidentally enough, that's a fair approximation of the book's true value. It might even be worth a thousand to the right buyer and after the right sort of build-up, but it's certainly not worth more than that.'

'Hey, c'mon, Bern.' It was Carolyn piping up from the crow's nest. 'I feel like I missed a few frames, and I was around for most of it. If it's supposed to be worth a fortune, and it's not a phony, why's it only worth five hundred or a thousand?'

'Because it's genuine,' I said. 'But it's not unique. Kipling had the book privately printed in 1923 in a small edition. That much was true. What wasn't true was the appealing story about his incinerating every copy but one. There are quite a few copies in existence.'

418

'Interesting thought,' Prescott Demarest said. He was dressed as he'd been when Carolyn took his picture, but then I'd simply been able to see that he was wearing a dark suit. Now I could see that it was navy blue, with a muted stripe that had been invisible in the photograph. He straightened in my chair now. 'So the book's one of many,' he said. 'How do you know that, Rhodenbarr?'

'How did I find it out?' It wasn't quite the question he'd asked but it was one I felt like answering. 'I stole a copy from Jesse Arkwright's house Wednesday night. Thursday I delivered that copy to Madeleine Pollock's apartment. I was drugged and the book was gone when I came to. Then last night I returned to the Porlock apartment' – gratifying, the way their eyes widened – 'and found *The Deliverance of Fort Bucklow* in a shoe box in the closet.

'But it wasn't the same copy. I figured it was possible that she could have stowed the book in the closet before admitting her killer to the apartment. But wouldn't he look for the book before he left? Wouldn't he have held the gun on her and made her deliver it before shooting her? He'd taken the trouble to scoop up five hundred dollars of my money before he left. Either he or Porlock took the money out of my back pocket, and if she took it, then he must have taken it from her himself, because it wasn't there to be found.' The cops could have taken it, I thought, but why muddy the waters by suggesting that possibility?

'My copy was all neatly wrapped in brown paper,' I went on. 'Now Madeleine Porlock might have unwrapped it before she hid it, just to make sure it wasn't a reprint copy of *Soldiers Three* or something equally tacky.' I avoided Atman Singh's eyes. 'If so, what happened to the brown paper? I didn't see it on the floor when I came to. Granted, I might not have noticed it or much else under the circumstances, but I looked carefully for that paper when I tossed the apartment last night, and it just plain wasn't there. The killer wouldn't have taken it and the police would have had no reason to disturb it, so what happened to it? Well, the answer's clear enough now. It was still fastened around the book when the killer walked off with it. Madeleine Porlock most likely had the wrapped book in her hands when he shot her, and he took it as is.'

'That's quite a conclusion,' Rudyard Whelkin said. 'My boy, it would seem that your only clues were clues of omission. Rather like the dog that didn't bark, eh? Five hundred missing dollars, a missing piece of brown paper. Rather thin ice, wouldn't you say?'

'There's something else.'

'Oh?'

I nodded. 'It's nothing you could call evidence. Pure subjective judgment. I sat up reading that book Wednesday night. I held it in my hands, I turned the pages. Last night I had my hands on it again and it

419

wasn't the same book. It was inscribed to H. Rider Haggard, same as the copy I stole from Arkwright, but there was something different about it. I once knew a man with a yard full of laying hens. He swore he could tell those birds apart. Well, I can tell books apart. Maybe one had some pages dog-eared or a differently shaped water stain – God knows what. They were different books. And, once I realized that, I had a chance to make sense of the whole business.'

'How?'

'Let's say, just hypothetically, that someone turned up a carton of four or five dozen books in the storage room of a shuttered printshop in Tunbridge Wells.' I glanced at Whelkin. 'Does that sound like a reasonable estimate?'

'It's your hypothesis, my boy.'

'Call it fifty copies. The entire edition, or all that remains of it, outside of the legendary long-lost copy the author was supposed to have presented to H. Rider Haggard. Now what would those books bring on the market? A few hundred dollars apiece. They'd be legitimate rarities, and Kipling's becoming something of a hot ticket again, but this particular work is not only a minor effort but distinctly inferior in the bargain. It has curiosity value rather than literary value. The books would still be worth hauling home from the printshop, but suppose they could be hawked one at a time as unique specimens? Suppose each one were furnished with a forged inscription in a fair approximation of Kipling's handwriting? It's hard to produce a new book and make it look old, but it's not too tricky to scribble a new inscription in an old book. I'm sure there are ways to treat ink so that it looks fifty years old, with that iridescence some old inscriptions have.

'So my client did this. He autographed the books or had some artful forger do it for him, and then he began testing the waters, contacting important collectors, perhaps representing the book as stolen merchandise so the purchaser would keep his acquisition to himself. Because the minute anyone called a press conference or presented the book to a university library, the game was up. All the collectors he'd stung along the way would be screaming for their money back.'

'They couldn't do anything about it, could they?' Carolyn wanted to know. 'If he was a shady operator, they couldn't exactly sue him.'

'True, but there's more than one way to skin a cat.' She made a face and I regretted the choice of words. 'At any rate,' I went on, 'the inflated market for the remaining books would collapse in a flash. Instead of realizing several thousand dollars a copy, he'd have a trunkful of books he couldn't give away. The high price absolutely depended on the books being one of a kind. When they were no longer unique, and when the holograph inscriptions proved to be forgeries, my client would have to find a new way to make a dishonest living.'

'He could always become a burglar,' the Maharajah suggested, smiling gently.

I shook my head. 'No. That's the one thing he damn well knew he couldn't do, because when he needed a burglar he came to this very shop and hired one. He found out, undoubtedly through Madeleine Porlock, that Arkwright was planning to go public with his copy of *Fort Bucklow*. Maybe public's the wrong word. Arkwright wasn't about to ring up the *Times* and tell them what he had. But Arkwright was a businessman at least as much as he was a collector, and there was someone he was trying to do business with who had more of a genuine interest in Fort Bucklow than Arkwright himself, who had no special interest in Kipling or India or anti-Semitic literature or whatever this particular book might represent.'

Whelkin asked if I had someone specific in mind.

'A foreigner,' I said. 'Because Arkwright was engaged in international commerce. A man with the wealth and power of an Indian prince.'

The Maharajah's jaw stiffened. Atman Singh inclined his body a few degrees forward, prepared to leap to his master's defense.

'Or an Arab oil sheikh,' I continued. 'There's a man named Najd al-Ouhaddar who comes to mind. He lives in one of the Trucial States, I forget which one, and he pretty much owns the place. There was a piece about him not long ago in *Contemporary Bibliophile*. He's supposed to have the best personal library east of Suez.'

'I know him,' the Maharajah said. 'Perhaps the best library in the Middle East, although there is a gentleman in Alexandria who would almost certainly wish to dispute that assertion.' He smiled politely. 'But surely not the best library east of Suez. There is at least one library on the Indian subcontinent which puts the Sheikh's holdings to shame.'

Mother taught me never to argue with Maharajahs, so I nodded politely and went on. 'Arkwright had a brilliant idea,' I told them. 'He was trying to rig a deal with the Sheikh. Work up some sort of trade agreements, something like that. *The Deliverance of Fort Bucklow* would be a perfect sweetener. Najd al-Quahaddar is a heavy supporter of the Palestinian terrorist organizations, a position that's not exactly unheard of among the oil sheikhs, and here's a unique specimen of anti-Semitic literature with a whole legend to go with it, establishing a great English writer as an enemy of world Jewry.'

'There was only one problem. My client had already sold a book to the Sheikh.'

I looked at Whelkin. His expression was hard to read.

'I didn't read this in *Contemporary Bibliophile*,' I went on. 'The Sheikh was told when he bought the book that he had to keep it to himself, that it was stolen goods with no legitimate provenance. That was fine with him. There are collectors who find hot merchandise

421

especially desirable. They get a kick out of the cloak-and-dagger aspects – and of course they figure they're getting a bargain.

'If Arkwright showed his copy to Najd, the game was up and the fat was in the fire. First off, Arkwright would know he'd been screwed. More important, Najd would know – and Arab oil sheikhs can get all sorts of revenge without troubling to call an attorney. In some of those countries they still chop hands off pickpockets. Imagine what they'd come up with if they had a personal grudge against you.'

I stopped for breath, 'My client had another reason to keep Arkwright from adding to the Sheikh's library. He was negotiating another sale to Najd, and it was designed to net him a fortune. The last thing he wanted was for Arkwright to queer it.'

Carolyn said, 'I'm lost, Bern. What was he going to sell him?'

'*The Deliverance of Fort Bucklow.*'

'I thought he already did.'

'He sold him the Rider Haggard copy. Now he was going to sell him something a little special.' I tapped the book on the counter. 'He was going to offer him this copy,' I said.

'Wait one moment,' Prescott Demarest said. 'You have me utterly confused. That copy in front of you – it's not the one you took from this man Arkwright's home?'

'No. That copy left Madeleine Porlock's apartment in the possession of the man who killed her.'

'Then the book in front of you is another copy which you found in her closet?'

I shook my head. 'I'm afraid not,' I said ruefully. 'You see, the copy from the shoe box in the closet was a second Rider Haggard copy, and how could my client possibly sell it to the Sheikh? He'd already done that once. No, this is a third copy, curiously enough, and I have to apologize for lying earlier when I told you this was the Porlock copy. Well, see, maybe I can just clear up the confusion by reading you the inscription on the flyleaf.'

I opened the book, cleared my throat. God knows I had their attention now.

' "For Herr Adolf Hitler," ' I read, ' "whose recognition of the twin Damocletian swords of Mosaic Bolshevism and Hebraic International Finance have ignited a new torch in Germany which, with the Grace of God, will one day brighten all the globe. May your present trials prove no more than the anvil upon which the blade of Deliverance may be forged. With abiding good wishes and respect, Rudyard Kipling, Bateman's, Burwash, Sussex, U.K., 1 April 1924." '

I closed the book. 'The date's significant,' I said. 'I was looking at John Toland's biography of Hitler before you gentlemen arrived. One of the fringe benefits of owning a bookstore. The date Kipling supposedly inscribed this book was the very day Hitler was sentenced to five years in Landsberg Prison for his role in the Munich Beer Hall Putsch. A matter of hours after the sentence was announced he was in his cell writing the title page of *Mein Kampf*. Meanwhile, Rudyard Kipling, moved by the future Führer's plight, was inscribing a book to him. There's some rubber stamping in ink on the inside front cover, too. It's in German, but it seems to indicate that the book was admitted to Landsberg Prison in May of 1924. Then there are some marginal notes here and there, presumably in Hitler's hand, and some underlining, and some German phrases scribbled on the inside back cover and the blank pages at the back of the book.'

'Hitler might have had it in his cell with him,' Rudyard Whelkin said dreamily. 'Took inspiration from it. Tried out ideas for *Mein Kampf* – that's what those scribbles could indicate.'

'And then what happened to the book?'

'Why, that's still a bit vague. Perhaps the Führer presented it to Unity Mitford and it found its way back to Britain with her. That's not an unappealing little story. But all the details have yet to be worked out.'

'And the price?'

Whelkin raised his imposing eyebrows. 'For Adolf Hitler's personal copy of a work of which only one other copy exists? For a source book for *Mein Kampf*? Inscribed to Hitler and chock-full of his own invaluable notes and comments?'

'How much money?'

'Money,' Whelkin said. 'What is money to someone like Najd al-Quhaddar? It flows in as fast as the oil flows out, more money than one knows what to do with. Fifty thousand dollars? One hundred thousand? A quarter of a million? I was just beginning to dangle the bait, you see. Just letting that Arab get the merest idea of what I had to offer. The ultimate negotiations would have to be positively Byzantine in their subtlety. How much would I have demanded? How much would he have paid? At what point would the bargain be struck?' He spread his hands. 'Impossible to say, my boy. What is that phrase of Dr Johnson's? "Wealth beyond the dreams of avarice." Avarice is quite a dreamer, you know, so his words might be the slightest bit hyperbolic, but suffice it to say that the book would have brought a nice price. A very nice price.'

'But not if Arkwright ruined the deal.'

'No,' Whelkin said. 'Not if Mr Arkwright ruined the deal.'

'How much did he pay you for his copy?'

'Five thousand dollars.'

'And the Sheikh? He'd already bought a copy with the Haggard inscription.'

He nodded. 'For a few thousand. I don't remember the figure. Is it of great importance?'

'Not really. How many other copies did you sell?'

Whelkin sighed. 'Three,' he said. 'One to a gentleman in Fort Worth who is under the impression that it was surreptitiously removed from the Ashmolean at Oxford by a greedy sub-curator with gambling debts. He'll never show it around. Another to a retired planter who lives in the West Indies now after making a packet in Malayan rubber. The third to a Rhodesian diehard who seemed more excited by the poem's political stance than its collector value. The Texan paid the highest price – eighty-five hundred dollars, I believe. I was selling off the books one by one, you see, but it was a laborious proposition. One couldn't advertise. Each sale called for extensive research and elaborate ground-work. My travel expenses were substantial. I was living reasonably well and covering my costs, but I wasn't getting ahead of the game.'

'The last copy you sold was to Arkwright?'

'Yes.'

'How did you know Madeleine Porlock?'

'We were friends of long standing. We'd worked together now and again, over the years.'

'Setting up swindles, do you mean?'

'Commercial enterprises is a less loaded term, wouldn't you say?'

'How did a copy of *Fort Bucklow* get in her closet?'

'It was her commission for placing a copy with Arkwright,' he said. 'I needed cash. Normally I'd have given her a thousand dollars or so for arranging the sale. She was just as pleased to have the book. She expected to sell it eventually for a good sum. She knew, of course, not to do anything with it until I'd had my shot at the big money with Najd al-Quhaddar.'

'Meanwhile, you needed Arkwright's copy back.'

'Yes.'

'And offered me fifteen thou to fetch it for you.'

'Yes.'

'Where was the fifteen thousand going to come from?'

He avoided my eyes. 'You'd have received it eventually, my boy. I simply didn't have it at the moment, but once I was able to place the Hitler copy with the Sheikh I'd be in a position to afford generosity.'

'You might have told me that in advance.'

'And where would that have gotten me?'

'Nowhere,' I said. 'I'd have turned you down flat.'

'And there you have it.' He sighed, folded his hands over his abdo-men. 'There you have it. Ethics are so often a function of circumstance. But I'd have settled with you in due course. You have my word on that.'

Well, that was comforting. I exchanged glances with Carolyn, came out from behind the counter. 'The situation became complicated,' I said, 'because a gentleman from India happened to be in New York at the same time as all of this was going on. Some months ago he had heard rumors about the Kipling property recently acquired by a particular Arab Sheikh. Now he was contacted by a woman who told him that such a book existed, that it was presently in the possession of a man named Arkwright, that it would soon be in her possession and that she could be induced to part with it for the right price.

'The woman, of course, was Madeleine Porlock. She learned somehow that the Maharajah was in town and evidently knew of his interest in Rudyard Kipling and his works. She had a copy of *The Deliverance of Fort Bucklow*, her commission for pushing a copy to Arkwright, and here was a chance to dispose of it. She offered the book to the Maharajah for – how much?'

'Ten thousand,' said the Maharajah.

'A healthy price, but she was dealing with a resourceful man in more ways than one. He had her tracked down and followed. She wore a wig to disguise herself when she came down for a close look at me. Maybe that was so I wouldn't recognize her when she slipped me the doped coffee. Maybe it was because she knew she was being checked out herself. Whatever she had in mind, it didn't work. The Maharajah's man tagged her to this shop, and a little research turned up the fact that the new owner of Barnegat Books had a master's degree in breaking and entering.'

I grinned. 'Are you people following all this? There are wheels within wheels. The Maharajah wasn't going to shell out ten grand for *Fort Bucklow*, not because he'd miss the money but for a very good reason. He knew for a fact that the book was a fake. For one thing, he'd heard about Najd's copy. And you had another reason, didn't you?'

'Yes.'

'Would you care to share it?'

'I own the original.' He smiled, glowing with the pride of ownership that they used to talk about in Cadillac ads. '*The* genuine copy of *The Deliverance of Fort Bucklow*, legitimately inscribed to Mr H. Rider Haggard and removed from his library after his death. The copy which passed through the hands of Miss Unity Mitford and which may indeed have been in the possession of the Duke of Windsor. A copy, I must emphasize, which was delivered into my hands six years ago, long before this gentleman' – a brief nod at Whelkin – 'happened on some undestroyed printer's overstock, or whatever one wishes to call the cache of books from the Tunbridge Wells printshop.'

'So you wanted the phony copy?'

'I wanted to discredit it. I knew it was a counterfeit but I could not be certain in what way it had been fabricated. Was it a pure invention? Had someone happened on a manuscript and caused a spurious edition to be printed? Or was it what I now realize it to be, a genuine book with a faked inscription? I wished to determine just what it was and establish that Najd al-Quhaddar had a similarly bogus article, but I did not want to pay ten thousand dollars for the privilege, or I would be making myself the victim of a swindle.'

'So you tried to eliminate the middleman. You sent your friend here' – I smiled at Atman Singh, who did not smile back – 'to collect the book from me as soon as I had it. And you instructed him to give me five hundred dollars. Why?'

'To compensate you. It seemed a fair return on your labor, considering that the book itself was of no value.'

'If you think that's a fair price for what I went through, you've obviously never been a burglar. How did you know I had the book?'

'Miss Porlock informed me she would have it that evening. That indicated to me that you'd already retrieved it from its owner.'

Rudyard Whelkin shook his head. 'Poor Maddy,' he said sadly. 'I told her to hold onto the book. She'd have spiked an enormous sale of mine by what she did, but I guess she was restless. Wanted to pick up a bundle and get out of town.' He frowned. 'But who killed her?'

'A man with a reason,' I said. 'A man she double-crossed.'

'For God's sake,' Whelkin said. 'I wouldn't kill anyone. And I certainly wouldn't kill Madeleine.'

'Maybe not. But you're not the only man she crossed. She did a job on everybody, when you stop to think about it. She drugged me and stole a book from me, but I certainly didn't kill her. She was fixing to swindle the Maharajah, and he might well have felt a certain resentment when his agent came back from my shop with a worthless copy of *Soldiers Three*. But this wouldn't leave him feeling betrayed because he didn't expect anything more from the woman. Neither did I. We never had any reason to trust her in the first place, so how could we feel betrayed? There's only one man she really betrayed.'

'And who might that be?'

'Him,' I said, and leveled a finger at Prescott Demarest.

Demarest looked bewildered. 'This is insane,' he said levelly. 'Utterly insane.'

'Why do you say that?'

'Because I've been wondering what I'm doing in this madhouse and now I find myself accused of murdering a woman I never even heard of before tonight. I came here to buy a book, Mr Rhodenbarr. I read a newspaper advertisement and made a telephone call and came here prepared to spend substantial money to acquire an outstanding rarity. I've since heard some fascinating if hard-to-grasp story about genuine books with fake inscriptions, and some gory tales of double-crosses and swindles and murders, and now I find myself accused of homicide. I don't want to buy your book, Mr Rhodenbarr, whether it's inscribed to Hitler or Haggard or Christ's vicar on earth. Nor do I want to listen to any further rubbish of the sort I've heard here tonight. If you'll excuse me . . .'

426

He started to rise from his chair. I held up a hand, not very threateningly, but it stopped him. I told him to sit down. Oddly enough, he sat.

'You're Prescott Demarest,' I said.

'I thought we weren't using names here tonight. Yes, I am Prescott Demarest, but—'

'Wrong,' I said. 'You're Jesse Arkwright. And you're a murderer.'

19

'I watched you this afternoon,' I told him. 'I saw you leave an office building on Pine Street. I'd never seen you before in my life but I knew there was something familiar about you. And then it came to me. Family resemblance.'

'I don't know what you're talking about.'

'I'm talking about the portraits in your library in Forest Hills. The two ancestors in the oval frames whose job it is to bless the pool table. I don't know if you're really a descendant of the guy who put the Spinning Jenny together, but I'm willing to believe the codgers on the wall are legitimate forebears of yours. You look just like them, especially around the jaw-line.'

I glanced at Whelkin. 'You sold him a book,' I said. 'Didn't you ever meet him?'

'Maddy handled everything. She was the middleman.'

'Middleperson, I think you mean. I suppose you spoke to him on the telephone?'

'Briefly. I don't recognize the voice.'

'And you?' I asked the Maharajah. 'You phoned Mr Arkwright this morning, didn't you?'

'This could be the man whose voice I heard. I am unable to say one way or the other.'

'This is absurd,' Demarest said. Hell, let's call him Arkwright. 'A presumed resemblance to a pair of portraits, an uncertain identification of a voice supposedly heard over a telephone—'

'You forget. I saw you leave an office building on Pine Street. I called you there at a certain number, and the phone you answered was in the office of Tontine Trading Corp., and the owner of Tontine is a man named Jesse Arkwright. I don't think you're going to get very far insisting the whole thing's a case of mistaken identity.'

He didn't take much time to think it over. 'All right,' he said. 'I'm Arkwright. There's no reason to continue the earlier charade. I received a call earlier today, apparently from this gentleman whom you call the Maharajah. He wanted to know if I still possessed a copy of *Fort Bucklow*.'

'I had seen the advertisement,' the Maharajah put in, 'and I wondered at its legitimacy. When I was unable to obtain the book either from this store or from Miss Porlock, I thought it might remain in Mr Arkwright's possession. I called him before responding to the advertisement.'

'And he referred to the ad,' Arkwright went on. 'I looked for myself. I called you on the spur of the moment. I thought I could poke around and find out what was going on. A book disappeared from my house in the middle of the night. I wanted to see if I could get it back. I also wanted to determine whether it was indeed the rarity I'd been led to believe it was. So I called you, and came here tonight to bid on the book if it came to that. But none of that makes me a killer.'

'You were keeping Madeleine Porlock.'

'Nonsense. I'd met her twice, perhaps three times. She knew of my interest in rare books and approached me out of the blue to offer me the Kipling volume.'

'She was your mistress. You had a kinky sex scene going in the apartment on East Sixty-sixth Street.'

'I've never even been there.'

'There are neighbors who saw you there. They recognized your photograph.'

'What photograph?'

I took it out and showed it to him. 'They've identified you,' I said. 'You were seen in Porlock's company and on your own. Apparently you had a set of keys because some of the neighbors saw you coming and going, letting yourself in downstairs.'

'That's circumstantial evidence, isn't it? Perhaps they saw me when I collected the book from her. Perhaps she let me in with the buzzer and they thought they saw me using a key. Memories are unreliable, aren't they?'

I let that pass. 'Maybe you thought she loved you,' I said. 'In any event, you felt personally betrayed. I'd robbed you, but that didn't make you want to kill me. It was enough for you to get my prints on everything and leave me with a gun in my hand. But you wanted Madeleine Porlock dead. You'd trusted her and she'd cheated you.'

'This is all speculation. Sheer speculation.'

'How about the gun? A Marley Devil Dog, a .32 automatic.'

'I understood it was unregistered.'

'How did you come to understand that? It wasn't in the papers.'

'Perhaps I heard it over the air.'

'I don't think so. I don't think the information was released. Anyway, sometimes an unregistered gun can be traced more readily then you might think.'

'Even if you could trace it to me,' he said carefully, 'that wouldn't prove anything. Just that you'd stolen it when you burglarized my house.'

'But it wasn't in your house. You kept it in the lower left drawer of your desk in the Tontine office downtown.'

'That's absolutely untrue.'

The righteous indignation was fetching. I'd seen that blued-steel automatic in the study on Copperwood Crescent. And now I was telling him it had been at his office, and it hadn't, and he was steamed.

'Of course it's true,' I said. 'Anybody would keep the gun and the bullets in the same place. And I have the damnedest feeling that you've got an almost full box of .32 shells in that drawer, along with a cleaning cloth and a pair of spare clips for a Marley Devil Dog.'

He stared at me. 'You were in my office!'

'Don't be ridiculous.'

'You – you *planted* those items. You're framing me.'

'And you're grabbing at straws,' I sailed on. 'Do you still claim you weren't keeping Madeleine Porlock? If that's so, why did you buy her a lynx jacket? It's not hard to guess why she'd want one. It's a stunning garment.' *Pace*, Carolyn. 'But why would you buy it for her if you were just casual acquaintances?'

'I didn't.'

'I looked in your closets when I was checking out a book from your library, Mr Arkwright. Your wife had a couple of pretty impressive furs there. They all had the same label in them. Arvin Tannenbaum.'

'What does that prove?'

'There's a lynx jacket in the Porlock apartment with the same label in it.'

'I repeat, what does that prove? Tannenbaum's a top furrier. Any number of persons patronize him.'

'You bought that jacket for Madeleine last month. There's a record of the sale in their files with your name on it and a full description of the jacket.'

'That's impossible. I never – I didn't—' He paused and regrouped, choosing his words more carefully this time around. 'If I were keeping this woman, as you put it, and if I did purchase a jacket for her, I would certainly have paid cash. There would surely be no record of the transaction.'

'You'd think that, wouldn't you? But I guess they know you up there, Mr Arkwright. You must be a treasured customer or something. I could be mistaken, but I have a hunch if the police looked through Tannenbaum's files, they'd find the sales record I described. They might even find the actual bill of sale in your desk at Tontine, with your name and the notation that you'd paid cash.'

'My God,' he said, ashen-faced. 'How did you—'

'Of course I'm just guessing.'

'You framed me.'

'That's not a very nice thing to say, Mr Arkwright.'

He put his hand to his chest as if in anticipation of a coronary. 'All of these lies and half-truths,' he said. 'What do they amount to? Circumstantial evidence at best.'

'Circumstantial evidence is sometimes all it takes. You were keeping Porlock and your gun killed her, and you had the strongest possible motive for her murder. What was the Watergate expression? The smoking pistol? Well, they didn't catch you with the smoking pistol in your hand because you were considerate enough to leave it in my hand, but I think the DA'll have enough to make your life difficult.'

'I should have killed you while I was at it,' he said. Positively venomous, his voice was. He was still holding onto his chest. 'I should have tacked your finger around the trigger and put the gun in your mouth and let you blow your little brains out.'

'That would have been cute,' I agreed. 'I killed her while commiting a burglary, then took my own life in a fit of remorse. I haven't had a remorse attack since the fifth grade, but who could possibly know that? How come you didn't do it that way?'

'I don't know.' He looked thoughtful. 'I . . . never killed anyone before. After I shot her I just wanted to get away from there. I never even thought of killing you. I simply put the gun in your hand and left.'

Beautiful. A full admission, and as much as anyone was likely to get without reading him his rights and letting him call his lawyer. It was about time for the Cavalry to make its appearance. I started to turn toward the rear of the store, where Ray Kirschmann and Francis Rockland were presumably taking in all of this, when the hand Arkwright had been clutching to his breast snaked inside his jacket and back out again, and when it reappeared there was a gun in it.

He pushed his chair back as he drew the gun, moving briskly backward so that he could cover the four of us at once – Whelkin and Atman Singh and the Maharajah. And me, at whom the gun was pointed. It was a larger gun than the one I'd come to clutching, far too large to be a Whippet or a Devil Dog. And a revolver, I noted. Perhaps, if he was partial to the Marley line, it was a Mastiff. Or a Rhodesian Ridgeback, or whatever.

'Let's hold it right there,' he said, waving the gun around. 'I'll shoot the first person who moves a hair. You're a clever man, Rhodenbarr, but it won't do you any good this time. I don't suppose the world will miss a burglar. They ought to gas people like you in the first place, loathsome vermin with no respect for property rights. As for you' – this to Whelkin – 'you cheated me. You employed Madeleine to swindle me out of some money. You made a fool of me. I won't mind killing you. You other gentlemen have the misfortune of being present at an awkward time. I regret the necessity of doing this—'

Killing women's bad policy. Ignoring them can be worse. He'd forgotten all about Carolyn, and he was still running his mouth when she brained him with a bronze bust of Immanuel Kant. I'd been using it as a bookend, in the Philosophy and Religion section.

20

At a quarter to twelve Monday morning I hung the *Out to Lunch* sign in the window and locked up. I didn't bother with the iron gates, not at that hour. I went to the place Carolyn had patronized Thursday and bought felafel sandwiches and a container of hummus and some flat crackers to scoop it up with. They were oddly shaped and reminded me of drawings of amoebae in my high-school biology textbook. I started to order coffee too but they had mint tea and that sounded interesting so I picked up two containers. The counterman put everything in a bag for me. I still didn't know if he was an Arab or an Israeli, so instead of chancing a *shalom* or a *salaam* I just told him to have a nice day and let it go at that.

Carolyn was hard at work combing out a Lhasa Apso. 'Thank God,' she said when she saw me, and popped the fluffy little dog into a cage. 'Lunchtime, Dolly Lama. I'll deal with you later. Whatcha got, Bern?'

'Felafel.'

'Sensational. Grab a chair.'

I did and we dug in. Between bites I told her that everything looked good. Francis Rockland wouldn't be hassling either me or the Sikh, having accepted three thousand of the Maharajah's American dollars as compensation for his erstwhile toe. It struck me as a generous settlement, especially so when you recalled that he'd shot the toe off all by his lonesome. And I gather a few more rupees found their way into Ray Kirschmann's pocket. Money generally does.

Rudyard Whelkin, who incredibly enough proved to have a walletful of identification in that unlikely name, was booked as a material witness and released in his own recognizance. 'I'm pretty sure he's out of the country,' I told Carolyn. 'Or at least out of town. He called me last night and tried to talk me into parting with the Hitler copy of *The Deliverance of Fort Bucklow*.'

'Don't tell me he wants to sell it to the Sheikh.'

'I think he knows what that would get him. Flayed alive, for instance. But there are enough other weirdos who'd pay a bundle for an item like that, and Whelkin's just the man to find one of them. He may never make the big score he's trying for but he hasn't missed many meals so far in life and I don't figure he'll start now.'

'Did you give him the book?'

'No way. Oh, he's got a satchel full of copies. I only took the Hitler specimen from his room at the Gresham. I left him some Haggard copies and a few that hadn't been tampered with, so he can cook up another Hitler copy if he's got the time and patience. If he forged all of that once, he can do it again. But I'm holding onto the copy I swiped from him.'

'You're not going to sell it?'

I may have managed to look hurt. 'Of course not,' I said. 'I may be a crook in my off-hours, but I'm a perfectly honest bookseller. I don't misrepresent my stock. Anyway, the book's not for sale. It's for my personal library. I don't figure to read it very often but I like the idea of having it around.'

The Maharajah, I told her, was on his way to Monaco to unwind with a flutter at roulette or baccarat or whatever moved him. The whole experience, he told me, had been invigorating. I was glad he thought so.

And Jesse Arkwright, I added, was in jail. Jugged, by George, and locked up tighter than the Crown jewels. They'd booked the bastard for Murder One and you can't get bailed out of that charge. Doesn't matter how rich you are.

'Not that he'll be imprisoned on that charge,' I explained. 'To tell you the truth, I'll be surprised if the case ever comes to trial. The evidence is sketchy. It might be enough to convict a poor man but he's got the bread for a good enough lawyer to worm his way out. He'll probably plead to a reduced charge. Manslaughter, say, or overtime parking. He'll pull a sentence of a year or two and I'll bet you even money he won't serve a day. Suspended sentence. Wait and see.'

'But he killed that woman.'

'No question.'

'It doesn't seem fair.'

'Few things do,' I said philosophically. Move over, Immanuel Kant. 'At least he's not getting off scot-free. He's behind bars even as we speak, and his reputation is getting dragged through the mud, and he'll pay a lot emotionally and financially even if he doesn't wind up serving any prison time for what he did. He's lucky, no question, but he's not as he thought he'd be before you nailed him with the bookend.'

'It was a lucky shot.'

'It was a perfect strike from where I stood.'

She grinned and scooped up some hummus. 'Maybe I'm what the Mets could use,' she said.

'What the Mets could use,' I said, 'is divine intercession. Anyway, lots of things aren't fair. The Blinns are getting away with their insurance claim, for example. I'm off the hook for burglarizing their

434

apartment. The police agreed not to. press charges in return for my cooperation in collaring Arkwright for murder, which is pretty decent of them, but the Blinns still get to collect for all the stuff I stole, which I didn't steal to begin with, and if that's fair you'll have to explain it to me.'

'It may not be fair,' she said, 'but I'm glad anyway. I like Gert and Artie.'

'So do I. They're good people. And that reminds me.'

'Oh?'

'I had a call from Artie Blinn last night.'

'Did you? This mint tea's terrific, incidentally. Sweet, though. Couldn't you get it without sugar?'

'That's how it comes.'

'It's probably going to rot my teeth and my insides and everything. But I don't care. Do you care?'

'I can't get all worked up about it. There was something Artie wanted to know, to get back to Artie.'

'There are things *I've* been wanting to know,' she said. 'Things I've been meaning to ask you.'

'Oh?'

'About Rudyard Whelkin.'

'What about him?'

'Was he really drugged when he set up the appointment with you? Or did he just sound that way?'

'He just sounded that way.'

'Why? And why didn't he show up at Porlock's place?'

'Well, it was her idea. Her reason was that she was going to sandwich in a meeting with the Maharajah so she could sell him the odd copy of the book. She certainly didn't want Whelkin around while all that was going on. The way she sold it to him was to leave things open so that I wouldn't know he was involved in double-crossing me. He could always get in touch with me later on and explain that he'd been doped, too, and that was why he missed the appointment. Of course, all of that went sour when Arkwright gave her a hole in the head. But that's why he sounded groggy when I spoke to him – he was putting on an act in advance.'

She nodded thoughtfully. '*I* see,' she said. 'A subtle pattern begins to emerge.'

'Now if we can get back to Artie Blinn—'

'What happened to your wallet?'

'Arkwright took it and stuck it under a cushion where the cops would be sure to find it. I told you, didn't I? That's how they knew to suspect me.'

'But what happened to it since then?'

'Oh,' I said. I patted my pocket. 'I got it back. They had it impounded as evidence, but no one could say exactly what it was evidence of, and Ray talked to somebody and I got it back.'

'What about the five hundred dollars?'

'It was either gone before the cops got it, or some cop made a profit on the day. But it's gone now.' I shrugged. 'Easy come, easy go.'

'That's a healthy attitude.'

'Uh-huh. Speaking of Artie—'

'Who was speaking of Artie?'

'Nobody was, but we're going to. Artie wanted to know what happened to the bracelet.'

'Shit.'

'He said he asked you about it when you were over there with the photographs, but you said you'd forgotten to bring it along.'

'Double shit.'

'But I seem to remember that I asked you about it just before you got out of the car, and you said you had it right there in your pocket.'

'Yeah,' she said. She drank some more of the mint tea. 'Well, I lied, Bernie.'

'Uh-huh.'

'Not to you. To Artie and Gert. It was in my pocket but I told him it wasn't.'

'I'll bet you had a super reason.'

'As a matter of fact I had a shitty reason. I kept thinking how nice it would look on a certain person's arm.'

'The certain person wouldn't be Miranda Messinger, I don't suppose.'

'It's your intuitive brilliance that makes me love you, Bernie.'

'Here I thought it was my engaging smile. Does she like the bracelet?'

'Loves it.' She grinned up at me. 'I went over there last night to return the Polaroid. She never even noticed it was missing. I gave her the bracelet as a peace offering, and I told her everything, and—'

'And you're back together again.'

'Well, last night we were. I wouldn't want to make any long-range projections. I'll tell you, the way to that woman's heart is through her wrist.'

'Whatever works.'

'Yeah. "You wouldn't want to go and wear it on the East Side," I told her. "Because it's just the least bit hot." '

'Did you talk like that when you told her? Out of the side of your mouth?'

'Yeah. It really got to her. I swear the next time I buy her something I'm gonna tell her I stole it.' She sighed. 'Okay, Bern. What do we do about the Blinns?'

'I'll think of something.'

'I was gonna tell you, but—'

436

'I could tell you were eager to discuss it. The way you were so anxious to talk about the Blinns and all.'

'Well, I—'

'It's cool,' I said. 'Relax and eat your hummus.'

A little later she said, 'Listen, Randy's got a dance class tonight. You want to come by after work? We can have dinner in or out and then catch a movie or something.'

'I'd love to,' I said, 'but tonight's out.'

'Heavy date?'

'Not exactly.' I hesitated, then figured what the hell. 'When we meet for drinks tonight,' I said, 'I'll make mine Perrier.'

She sat forward, eyes wide. 'No shit. You're going on a caper?'

'That's not the word I'd use, but yeah, that's about it.'

'Where?'

'Forest Hills Gardens.'

'The same neighborhood as the last time?'

'The same house. The coat I described to Ray Kirschmann wasn't a fantasy. I saw it Wednesday night in Elfrida Arkwright's closet. And I promised it to Ray, and when I make promises to cops I like to keep them. So I'm going back there tonight to get it.'

'Won't Elfrida object?'

'Elfrida's not home. She visited her hubby in jail yesterday, and then she went home and thought things through, and then she packed a bag and took off for parts unknown. Home to Mama, maybe. Or home to Palm Beach. I guess she didn't want to stick around for the notoriety.'

'I can dig that.' She cocked her head and there was a faraway look in her eye. 'He's got it coming,' she said. 'The bastard killed his mistress and he's not going to serve time for it. I remember when you were describing the house to me, Bern. You said you wanted to back up a truck onto the front lawn and steal everything from the chandeliers down to the rugs.'

'I had the impulse.'

'Is that what you're gonna do?'

'No.'

'You're just taking the coat?'

'Well . . .'

'You said there was jewelry, didn't you? Maybe you can find something to replace Gert Blinn's bracelet.'

'The thought had crossed my mind.'

'And there's a coin collection.'

'I remember the coin collection, Carolyn.'

'I remember the other things you mentioned. Are you going to take the Pontiac?'

'I think that might be pushing my luck.'

'You'll steal some other car, then.'

'I suppose so.'

'Take me with you.'

'Huh?'

'Why not?' She leaned forward, laid a hand on my arm. 'Why the hell not, Bern? I can help. I didn't get in the way when we stole Randy's Polaroid, did I?'

'We *borrowed* Randy's Polaroid.'

'Bullshit. We stole it. Then we happened to give it back when we were done with it. If you look at it that way, I'm an old hand at this breaking-and-entering business. Take me along, Bern. Please? I'll get rubber gloves and cut the palms out, I'll pass up my afterwork drink, I'll do anything you say. *Please?*'

'Jesus,' I said. 'You're . . . you're an honest citizen, Carolyn. No record. A respectable position in the community.'

'I wash dogs, Bern. Big hairy deal.'

'There's a risk.'

'Screw the risk.'

'And I always work alone, see. I never use a partner.'

'Oh.' Her face felt. 'Well, that's it, then. I didn't think of it that way. I'd probably be a drag anyway, wouldn't I? It's okay, Bern. I don't mind.'

'No drink after work.'

'Not a drop. I can come?'

'And you can't ever tell a soul. Not Randy, not some future lover. Nobody.'

'My lips are sealed. Are you serious? I can come?'

I shrugged. 'What the hell,' I said. 'You were handy the other night. You might be useful to have around.'

The Burglar Who Studied Spinoza

For Caryl Carnow

1

Around five-thirty I put down the book I'd been reading and started shooing customers out of the store. The book was by Robert B. Parker, and its hero was a private detective named Spenser who compensated for his lack of a first name by being terribly physical. Every couple of chapters would find him jogging around Boston or lifting weights or finding some other way to court a heart attack or a hernia. I was getting exhausted just reading about him.

My customers shooed easily enough, one pausing to buy the volume of poetry he'd been browsing, the rest melting off like a light frost on a sunny morning. I shlepped my bargain table inside ('All books 40¢ / 3 for $1'), flicked off the lights, let myself out, closed the door, locked it, drew the steel gates across the door and windows, locked them, and Barnegat Books was bedded down for the night.

My shop was closed. It was time to get down to business.

The store is on East Eleventh Street between University Place and Broadway. Two doors east is the Poodle Factory. I let myself in, heralded by the tinkling of the door chimes, and Carolyn Kaiser's head emerged from the curtain at the back. 'Hi, Bern,' she said. 'Get comfy. I'll be right out.'

I arranged myself on a pillow sofa and started leafing through a copy of a trade journal called *The Pet Dealer*, which was about what you'd expect. I thought maybe I'd see a picture of a Bouvier des Flandres, but no such luck. I was still trying when Carolyn came in carrying a very small dog the color of Old Crow and soda.

'That's not a Bouvier des Flandres,' I said.

'No kidding,' said Carolyn. She stood the little thing up on a table and commenced fluffing him. He looked fluffy enough to start with. 'This is Prince Valiant, Bernie. He's a poodle.'

'I didn't know poodles came that small.'

'They keep making them smaller. He's a miniature, but he's actually smaller than the usual run of minis. I think the Japanese are getting into the field. I think they're doing something cunning with transistors.'

Carolyn doesn't normally do short jokes for fear of casting the first stone. If she wore high heels she might hit five-one, but she doesn't. She has Dutch-cut dark-brown hair and Delft-blue eyes, and she's built along the lines of a fire hydrant, no mean asset in the dog-grooming trade.

'Poor Prince,' she said. 'The breeders keep picking out runts and cross-breeding them until they come up with something like this. And of course they breed for color, too. Prince Val's not just a mini poodle. He's an apricot mini poodle. Where the hell's his owner, anyway? What time is it?'

'Quarter to six.'

'She's fifteen minutes late. Another fifteen and I'm locking up.'

'What'll you do with Prince Valiant? Bring him home with you?'

'Are you kidding? The cats would eat him for breakfast. Ubi might coexist with him but Archie'd disembowel him just to keep in practice. No, if she doesn't show by six it's Doggie Dannemora for the Prince. He can spend the night in a cage.'

That should have been Val's cue to give a cute little yap of protest, but he just stood there like a dummy. I suggested his color was less like an apricot than a glass of bourbon and soda, and Carolyn said, 'Jesus, don't remind me, I'll start drooling like one of Pavlov's finest.' Then the door chimes sounded and a woman with blue-rinsed gray hair came strutting in to collect her pet.

I went back to *The Pet Dealer* while they settled Val's tab. Then his owner clipped one end of a rhinestone-studded leash to the beast's collar. They walked off together, turning fast when they hit the pavement and probably bound for Stewart House, a large co-op apartment building that runs heavily to blue-rinsed gray hair, with or without an apricot poodle on the side.

'Poodles,' Carolyn said. 'I wouldn't have a dog because of the cats, and if I didn't have the cats I still wouldn't have a dog, but if I did it wouldn't be a poodle.'

'What's wrong with poodles?'

'I don't know. Actually there's nothing wrong with standard poodles. Big black unclipped standard poodles are fine. Of course if everybody had a big black unclipped poodle I could hang up my shears and go out of business, and that might not be the worst thing in the world, anyway, come to think of it. Would you live with one of those, Bernie? A miniature poodle?'

'Well, I don't—'

'Of course you wouldn't,' she said. 'You wouldn't and neither would I. There are only two kinds of people who'd have a dog like that, and they're the two classes of human beings I've never been able to understand.'

'How's that?'

'Gay men and straight women. Can we get out of here? I suppose I could have an apricot brandy sour. I had a lover once who used to drink them. Or I could have that bourbon and soda you mentioned. But I think what I really want is a martini.'

What she had was Perrier with lime.

But not without protest. Most of the protest was vented on the open air, and by the time we were at our usual table around the corner at the Bum Rap, Carolyn was agreeable if not happy about it. The waitress asked if we wanted the usual, whereupon Carolyn made a face and ordered French seltzer water, which was not her usual by any stretch of the imagination. Neither was it mine at the end of the day's work, but the day's work was not yet over. I, too, ordered Perrier, and the waitress went off scratching her head.

'See, Bern? Uncharacteristic behavior. Arouses suspicion.'

'I wouldn't worry about it.'

'I don't see why I can't have a real drink. The thing tonight is hours in the future. If I had a drink it would wear off in plenty of time.'

'You know the rules.'

'Rules.'

'Without them, society would crumble. We'd have anarchy. Crime in the streets.'

'Bernie—'

'Of course,' I said, 'I could always do a single-o tonight.'

'The hell you could.'

'The job wouldn't be that much harder with one than with two. I could handle it.'

'Who found it in the first place?'

'You did,' I said, 'and you're in for fifty percent whatever happens, but you could stay home tonight and still collect it. Why run extra risks? And this way you can have your martini, or even three or four of them, and—'

'You made your point.'

'I just thought—'

'I said you made your point, Bern.'

We stopped talking while the waitress brought two glasses of Perrier to the table. On the jukebox, Loretta Lynn and Conway Twitty were singing a duet about a Mississippi woman and a Louisiana man. Perhaps it was the other way around. No matter.

Carolyn wrapped one hand around her glass and glowered at me. 'I'm coming,' she said.

'If you say so.'

'Damn right I say so. We're partners, remember? I'm in all the way. You think because I'm a goddamn woman I should sit home keeping the goddamn home fires burning.'

'I never said—'

'I don't *need* a goddamn martini.' She lifted her glass. 'Here's to crime, dammit.' She drank it like gin.

The whole project had gotten underway at the Bum Rap, and at that very table. Carolyn and I generally get together for a drink after work, unless one or the other of us has something on, and a couple of weeks earlier we'd been raising a couple of glasses, neither of them containing Perrier water.

'It's funny how people pick dogs,' Carolyn had said. 'I have this one customer, her name's Wanda Colcannon, and she's got this Bouvier.'

'That's funny, all right.'

She looked at me. 'Don't you want to hear this, Bern?'

'Sorry.'

'The thing is, when she came in with the dog I figured they were a natural combination. She's a tall stern blonde out of a masochist's dream. Wears designer dresses. Cheekbones straight out of the Social Register. Yards of class, you know?'

'Uh-huh.'

'And the Bouvier's a very classy dog. Very trendy these days. It's only been an AKC recognized breed for a couple of years now. They're expensive dogs, and they look pretty classy even if you don't happen to know how much they cost, and here's this leggy blonde in a leather coat with this jet-black Bouvier at her side, and they looked right for each other.'

'So?'

'She picked the dog because of its name.'

'What was his name?'

'Her name, not his name. The dog's a bitch.'

'That's pretty trendy, too. Being a bitch.'

'Oh, it never goes out of style. No, the dog's name is Astrid, as a matter of fact, but that's the name Wanda gave her. What made her pick the dog was the name of the breed.'

'Why?'

'Because Wanda's maiden name is Flanders.'

'Jackie Kennedy's maiden name is Bouvier,' I said, 'and I don't know what kind of a dog she has, and I'm not sure I care. You lost me somewhere. What does Flanders have to do with Bouvier?'

'Oh, I thought you knew. The Bouvier originated in Belgium. The full name of the breed is Bouvier des Flandres.'

'Oh.'

'So that's what got her interested in the breed, and she wound up buying a puppy a couple of years ago, and it turned out to be the perfect choice. She's crazy about Astrid, and the dog's incredibly devoted to

446

her, and in addition to being a classy animal Astrid's also extremely intelligent and a great watchdog.'

'I'm really happy for them,' I said.

'I think you should be. I've been grooming her dog for about a year now. She'll bring her in for routine bathing and grooming every couple of months, and then she'll get the full treatment before shows. They don't show Astrid all that often but now and then they'll hit a show, and she's picked up a couple of ribbons along the way, including a blue or two.'

'That's nice for her.'

'For Wanda and Herb, too. Wanda loves to walk the dog. She feels safe in the streets when she's got Astrid with her. And she and her husband both feel safe with the dog guarding the house. They don't worry about burglars.'

'I can understand that.'

'Uh-huh. Astrid's their burglar insurance. She's due to go into heat in a couple of weeks and this time they're going to breed her. Wanda's concerned that the experience of motherhood might undercut her abilities as an attack dog, but she's going ahead with it anyway. The stud dog is a famous champion. He lives out in the country in Berks County, Pennsylvania. I think that's around Reading. They ship bitches to him from all over the country and he gets paid for it. The dog's owner gets paid, I mean.'

'It's still a pretty good life for the dog.'

'Isn't it? Wanda's not shipping Astrid. She and her husband are taking her out there. When you breed dogs you put the animals together two days in a row, to make sure you hit the peak ovulation period. So they'll drive out to Berks County with Astrid and stay overnight and have the second breeding the next day and drive back.'

'Should make a nice trip for all three of them.'

'Especially if the weather's nice.'

'That's always a factor,' I said. 'I just know there's a reason you're telling me all this.'

'Sharp of you. They'll be gone overnight, and so will Astrid, and Astrid's their burglar protection. They're rich enough to afford designer dresses and trendy purebred dogs. And for him to indulge his little hobby.'

'What little hobby?'

'He collects coins.'

'Oh,' I said, and frowned. 'You told me his name. Not Flanders, that was her maiden name, like the dog. Colcannon. But you didn't say his first name. Wait a minute. Yes, you did. His first name's Herb.'

'You've got a great mind for details, Bern.'

'Herb Colcannon. Herbert Colcannon. Herbert *Franklin* Colcannon. Is he *that* Herbert Colcannon?'

447

'How many do you figure there are?'

'He was buying proof pattern gold at a Bowers and Ruddy auction last fall and he picked up something a few months ago at a sale at Stack's. I forget what. I read something about it in *Coin World*. But the odds are he keeps the stuff in the bank.'

'They've got a wall safe. What does that do to the odds?'

'Shaves them a little. How do you happen to know that?'

'She mentioned it once. How she'd wanted to wear a piece of jewelry one night and couldn't because it was locked up and she'd forgotten the combination and he was out of town. I almost told her I had a friend who could have helped her, but I decided it might be better if she didn't know about you.'

'Wise decision. Maybe he doesn't keep everything in the bank. Maybe some of his coins keep her jewelry company.' My mind was starting to race. Where did they live? What was the security like? How could I crack it? What was I likely to walk out with, and through whose good offices could I most expediently turn it into clean anonymous cash?

'They're in Chelsea,' Carolyn went on. 'Tucked away off the street in a carriage house. Not in the phone book, but I have the address. And the phone number.'

'Good to have.'

'Uh-huh. They have the whole house to themselves. No children. No servants living in.'

'Interesting.'

'I thought so. What I thought is this sounds like a job for the Dynamic Duo.'

'Good thinking,' I said. 'I'll buy you a drink on the strength of that.'

'It's about time.'

2

Illegal entry is a good deal less suspicious beneath the warm benevolent gaze of the sun. Nosy neighbors who'd dial 911 if they spotted you after dark will simply assume you've showed up at last to tend to the leaky faucet. Give me a clipboard or a toolbox and an hour between noon and four and the staunchest citizen crime-fighter on the block will hold the door for me and tell me to have a nice day. All things being equal, the best time for a residential burglary is the middle of the afternoon.

But when are all things ever equal? The cloak of darkness is comforting garb to the burglar, if not to the householder, and when one operates a legitimate business one hesitates to close it abruptly in the middle of the day for no good reason. The Colcannons' schedule, too, favored a nocturnal visit. We knew they would be away overnight, and knew too that the premises would be unencumbered by handymen or cleaning women (handy persons? cleaning persons?) once the sun was over the yardarm.

The sun had long since crossed the yardarm and disappeared somewhere in New Jersey by the time we ventured forth. From the Bum Rap we'd taken a couple of subway trains and walked a block to my building at Seventy-first and West End, where I shucked the jeans and sweater I'd worn at the store and put on flannel slacks and a tie and jacket. I filled my pockets with useful odds and ends, packed another couple of articles into my Ultrasuede attaché case, and took a moment and manicure scissors to snip the palms out of a fresh pair of rubber gloves. With rubber gloves one leaves no tattletale fingerprints behind, and with the palms out one is less likely to feel that one has abandoned one's hands in a sauna. Sweaty palms are bad enough in Lover's Lane; one tries to avoid them when burgling. Of course there's always the chance of leaving a tattletale palm print, but it wouldn't be burglary without the occasional risk, would it now?

We were almost on our way again before I remembered to change my shoes. I'd been wearing Weejun penny loafers at the store, for both nostalgia and comfort, and I switched to a pair of capable-looking Puma running shoes. I certainly had no intention of moving faster than a brisk walk, but you never know what life has in store for you, and the

Pumas with their rubber soles and springy insoles let me move as soundlessly as, well, as a panther, I suppose.

Carolyn lives on Arbor Court, one of those oblique little streets in a part of the West Village that must have been laid out by someone on something stronger than Perrier. Until a couple of months ago she had been sort of living with another woman named Randy Messinger, but they'd had the last of a series of notable battles in early February and Randy had moved everything to her own place on Morton Street. It was May now, late May, and every evening the sun took a little longer to get over the yardarm, and the breach showed no signs of healing. Every now and then Carolyn would meet somebody terrific at Paula's or the Duchess, but true love had not yet bloomed, and she didn't seem to mind.

She put some coffee up, tossed a salad, warmed up a couple wedges of leftover quiche. We both ate sparingly and drank a lot of the coffee. The cats polished off their own food and rubbed against our ankles until they got the unfinished quiche, which they promptly finished. Ubi, the Russian Blue, settled in my lap and got into some serious purring. Archie, his Burmese buddy, stalked around and did some basic stretching to show off his muscles.

Around eight the phone rang. Carolyn answered it and settled into a long gossipy conversation. I got a paperback and turned its pages, but the words didn't really register. I might as well have been reading the phone book.

When Carolyn hung up I did read the phone book, long enough to look up a number, anyway. I dialed, and Abel Crowe picked up midway through the fourth ring. 'Bernie,' I said. 'I turned up a book I think you might like. Wondered if you'd be home tonight.'

'I have no plans.'

'I thought I might stop by around eleven, twelve o'clock.'

'Excellent. I keep late hours these days.' You could hear the Mittel Europa accent over the phone. Face to face, it was barely detectable. 'Will your charming friend be with you?'

'Probably.'

'I'll provide accordingly. Be well, Bernard.'

I hung up. Carolyn was sitting on the bed, one foot tucked beneath her, dutifully cutting the palms out of her own pair of rubber gloves. 'Abel's expecting us,' I told her.

'He knows I'm coming?'

'He asked specifically. I told him you'd probably show up.'

'What's this probably? I love Abel.'

She got up from the bed, stuffed the gloves in a back pocket. She was wearing slate-gray brushed-denim jeans and a green velour top, and now she added her navy blazer. She looked terrific, and I told her as much.

She thanked me, then turned to the cats. 'Hang in there, guys,' she told them. 'Just write down the names if anybody calls. Tell 'em I'll get back to 'em.'

Herbert and Wanda Colcannon lived on West Eighteenth Street between Ninth and Tenth Avenues. Until fairly recently that was a great neighborhood to visit if you were looking to get mugged, but somewhere along the line Chelsea became a desirable neighborhood. People commenced buying the old brownstones and sprucing them up, converting rooming houses into floor-through apartment buildings and apartment buildings into single-family houses. The streets were lined with newly planted ginkgo and oak and sycamore, and it was getting so that you couldn't see the muggers for the trees.

No. 442 West Eighteenth was an attractive four-story brownstone house with a mansard roof and a bay window on the parlor floor. No. 444, immediately to its left, was the same thing all over again, distinguishable only by a few minor architectural details and the pair of brass carriage lamps that flanked the entrance. But between the two houses there was an archway and a heavy iron gate, and above the gate was the number 442½. There was a bell alongside, and a blue plastic strip with the name Colcannon embossed on it beneath the bell.

I'd called the Colcannon house earlier from a pay phone on Ninth Avenue. An answering machine had invited me to leave my name and number, an invitation I'd failed to accept. Now I rang the doorbell, giving it a good long poke and waiting a full minute for a response. Beside me, Carolyn stood with her hands in her pockets and her shoulders drawn inward, shifting her weight from foot to foot.

I could imagine how she felt. This was only her third time. She'd been with me once in Forest Hills Gardens, a ritzy enclave in darkest Queens, and more recently when we hit an apartment in the East Seventies. I was an old hand at this sort of thing, I'd grown up letting myself into other people's houses, but even so the edgy anxious thrill had not worn off. I have a hunch it never will.

I shifted the attaché case to my left hand and dug out a ring of keys with my right. The iron gate was a formidable affair. It could be opened electrically by someone in the carriage house pushing a button, or it would yield to a key. And it was the type of old-fashioned lock that accepted a skeleton-type key, and there are only so many types, and I had a ringful of them. I'd looked the lock over some days ago and it had looked easy enough at the time, and easy it was; the third key I tried was a near miss, and the fourth one turned in the lock as if it had been placed on earth to do precisely that.

I wiped my prints off the lock and the surrounding metal, shouldered the gate open. Carolyn followed me into the covered passageway and drew the gate shut behind her. We were in a long narrow tunnel, all brick-lined and with a damp feel to it, but there was a light at the end of it and we homed in on it like moths. We came out into a garden that nestled between the brownstone in front and the Colcannons' carriage house. The light that had drawn us did a fair job of showing off the garden, with its flower beds bordering a central flagstone patio. Late daffodils and early tulips put on a good show, and I suppose when the roses bloomed the place might look fairly spectacular.

There was a semicircular bench next to what looked to be a fish pond fed by a little fountain. I wondered how they could keep fish there without their being wiped out by the local cats, and I would have enjoyed passing a few minutes on the bench, peering into the pond for signs of fish while listening to the tranquil gurgle of the fountain. But the setting was a trifle exposed for that sort of behavior.

Besides, time was a-wasting. It was twenty to ten – I'd checked my watch before unlocking the iron gate. In a sense we had all night, but the less of it we used the happier I'd be, and the sooner we'd be out of there and on our way to Abel Crowe's.

'Lit up like a Christmas tree,' Carolyn said.

I looked. I hadn't paid much attention to the carriage house, intent as I was on checking out flowers and fish, and if it didn't look like a Christmas tree neither did it look like your standard empty house. It stood three stories tall, and I suppose it had once had horses on the ground floor and servants overhead before someone converted it for human occupancy throughout. Now there were lights burning on all three floors. They weren't the only source of illumination in the garden – there was also an electrified lantern mounted a few steps from the fountain – but they were probably responsible for most of the light that had reached us in the passageway.

Most people leave a light or two for the burglar, that brave little beacon that shines away at four in the morning, announcing to all the world that nobody's home. Some people improve on this with cunning little timing devices that turn the lights on and off. But Herbert and Wanda seemed to me to have gone overboard. Maybe they had overreacted to the notion of leaving the place unprotected by the noble Astrid. Maybe Herb had a ton of Con Ed stock and Wanda had overdosed on those five-year light bulbs blind people sell you over the telephone.

Maybe they were home.

I mounted the stoop and put my ear to the door. There was noise inside, radio or television, but nothing that sounded like live conversation. I rang the doorbell and listened carefully, and there was no change in the sounds within the house. I set down my attaché case and pulled on my rubber gloves while Carolyn put hers on. I said a silent prayer that the house wasn't hooked into a burglar alarm that I didn't know about, addressing the prayer to Saint Dismas. He's the patron saint of thieves, and he must get to hear a lot of prayers these days.

Let there not be a burglar alarm, I urged the good Dismas. Let the dog really be in Pennsylvania. Let what lies within be a burglar's fondest dream, and in return I'll – I'll what?

I took out my ring of picks and probes and went to work.

The locks were pretty good. There were three of them on that door, two Segals and a Rabson. I left the Rabson for last because I knew it would be the toughest, then surprised myself by knocking it off in no more than a minute. I heard Carolyn's intake of breath when the bolt turned. She knows a little about locks now, and has been known to open her own without a key, and she's driven herself half mad practicing with a Rabson I gave her, and she sounded impressed.

I turned the knob, opened the door a crack, stood aside for Carolyn. She shook her head and motioned for me to go first. Age before beauty? Pearls before swine? Death before dishonor? I opened the door and committed illegal entry.

Lord, what a feeling!

I'm grateful there isn't something even more despicable than burglary that gives me that feeling, because if there were I probably wouldn't be able to resist it. Oh, I'm a pro, all right, and I do it for the money, but let's not kid ourselves. I draw such an intense charge out of it it's a wonder lamps don't dim all over the city every time I let myself into somebody else's abode.

God knows I'm not proud of it. I'd think far more highly of myself if I eked out a living at Barnegat Books. I never quite cover expenses at the store, but maybe I could if I took the trouble to learn to be a better businessman. The shop supported old Mr Litzauer for years before he sold it to me and retired to St Petersburg. It ought to be able to support me. I don't live all that high. I don't shoot crap or snort coke or zoom around with the Beautiful People. Nor do I consort with known criminals, as the parole board so charmingly phrases it. I don't like criminals. I don't like being one myself.

But I love to steal. Go figure.

The radio program was one of those talk-show things with listeners calling in to share their views on fluoridation and child labor and other burning issues. I stood there and resented its blaring away at me. The lights were a nice touch – we wouldn't have to turn on lights ourselves, which might draw attention, nor would we have to curse the darkness. But I stood there in the entrance foyer and resolved to turn off the damned radio. It was a distraction. You have to think straight to burgle efficiently, and who could do so with all that noise?

'Jesus, Bern.'

'What?'

'She always dresses so nice. Who figured she'd be such a slob around the house?'

I followed her into the living room to see what she was talking about. It looked as though an out-of-season tropical storm had wandered far off course, only to sneak down through the chimney and kick the crap out of everything. The pillows were off the couch. Desk drawers had been pulled out and upended, their contents strewn all over the Aubusson carpet. Pictures had been taken down from the walls, books tossed from their shelves.

'Burglars,' I said.

Carolyn stared.

'They beat us to the punch.'

'Are they still around, Bern? We better get out of here.'

I went back to the front door and checked it. I'd re-locked the locks when we were inside, fastening an additional chain lock for good measure. The three locks had been locked when I found them, the chain bolt unengaged.

Strange.

If burglars had come through that door, and if they'd locked themselves in as I had done, wouldn't they put the chain bolt on as well? And if they'd already left, would they bother locking up from outside? I generally do that sort of thing as a matter of course, but then I'm not apt to leave a room looking as though it had been visited by the Gadarene swine, either. Whoever tossed that room was the type who kicked doors in, not the type who took extra time to lock up afterward.

Unless—

Lots of possibilities. I eased past Carolyn and began tracking the radio to its source. I passed through the dining room, where a mahogany breakfront and buffet had been rifled in fashion similar to the living-room desk, and entered a kitchen that had received a dose of the same treatment. A Panasonic stood on the butcher-block counter beside the refrigerator, blaring its transistorized heart out. I turned to Carolyn, raised a finger to my lips for silence, and switched off the radio in the middle of a rant about the latest increase in the price of oil.

I closed my eyes and listened very carefully to the ensuing silence. You could have heard a pin drop, and I was certain no one had dropped one.

'They're gone,' I said.

'How can you be sure?'

'If they were here we'd hear them. They're not the silent type, whoever they are.'

'We better get out.'

'Not yet.'

'Are you crazy, Bern? If they're gone, that just means the cops are on their way, and even if they're not, what are we gonna find to steal? Whoever did this already took everything.'

'Not necessarily.'

'Well, they took the sterling. What are we gonna do, swipe the stainless?' She followed me out of the kitchen and up a flight of stairs. 'What do you expect to find, Bern?'

'A coin collection. Maybe some jewelry.'

'Where?'

'Good question. What room is the wall safe in?'

'I don't know.'

'Then we'll have to look for it, won't we?'

We didn't have to look very hard because our predecessors in crime had taken all the pictures off the walls. We checked the library and guest bedroom on the second floor, then climbed another flight of stairs and found the wall safe in the master bedroom. The dreamy pastoral landscape which had screened it from view was on the floor now, along with the contents of both dressers and some broken glass from the overhead skylight. That, no doubt, was how they'd entered. And how they'd exited as well, I felt certain, lugging their loot across the rooftops and into the night. These clowns hadn't locked up downstairs because they'd never opened the locks in the first place. They couldn't have dealt with that Rabson in a year and a day.

Nor had they been able to deal with the wall safe. I'm not sure how hard they tried. There were marks around the combination dial to show that someone had worked on it with a punch, hoping to knock the lock out and get into the safe that way. I didn't see any evidence that they'd had an acetylene torch along, nor would one very likely have worked anyway. The safe was a sound one and the lock was a beauty.

I commenced fiddling with the dial. Carolyn stood beside me, watching with more than idle curiosity, but before long we started to fidget and we were getting on each other's nerves. Before I could suggest it she said something about having a look around. I promised to call her when I got the thing open.

It took a little doing. I stripped off my rubber gloves – that Jimmy Valentine number of sanding one's fingertips for increased sensitivity is nonsense, but there's no point in making things more difficult than they have to be. I did a little of this and a little of that, using the combination of knowledge and intuition that you have to have if you're going to be good with locks, and I got the last number first, as one always does with combination locks, and one at a time I got the other three numbers, and then I put my gloves on again and wiped the surfaces I'd touched and took a deep breath and whistled for Carolyn.

She came in carrying a framed print. 'It's a Chagall lithograph,' she said. 'Pencil-signed and numbered. I guess it's worth a few hundred, anyway. Is it worth stealing?'

'If you want to take it out of the frame.'

She held it up. 'I think it'll fit in the attaché case. Are you getting anywhere with that mother?'

'I'm just going to try a couple numbers at random,' I said. I dialed the four numbers in their proper sequence, felt a little click in my own head if not in the locking mechanism as the tumblers lined up, then swung the handle around to the left and opened the safe.

We left the house as we'd entered it. I suppose we could have gone over the rooftops ourselves, but why? I paused in the kitchen to turn the radio on again. A commercial was offering a three-LP set of the hundred greatest rumba and samba hits. There was a toll-free number to call, but I neglected to jot it down. I unhooked the chain bolt and unlocked three locks, and out we went, and I let Carolyn hold the attaché case while I used my ring of picks and probes to manipulate all three locks shut again. In school they taught me that neatness counts, and the lessons you learn early in life stay with you.

The fountain was still gurgling and the little garden was still being charming. I stripped off my rubber gloves, tucked them into a back pocket. Carolyn did the same with hers. I retrieved the attaché case and we made our way through the dark tunnel to the heavy iron gate. You didn't need a key to let yourself out – there was a knob to turn, unreachable from the street side. I turned it and let us out, and the gate swung shut and locked after us.

On the other side of the street, a slender young man with a wad of paper towel in his hand was bending over to clean up after his Airedale. He took no notice of us and we headed off in the opposite direction.

At the corner of Ninth Avenue Carolyn said, 'Somebody else must have known about their trip. That they were taking the dog and all. Unless someone was just going over the roofs and got lucky.'

'Not very likely.'

'No. Wanda must have told someone else. Nobody heard it from me, Bernie.'

'People talk,' I said, 'and a good burglar learns how to listen. If we'd gotten there first we'd have scored a lot bigger, but this way we can travel light. And we're free and clear, look at it that way. Those clowns went through that poor house like Cromwell's men at Drogheda, and it shouldn't take the cops too long to catch up with them. And we didn't leave a trace, so they'll hang the whole thing on them.'

'I thought of that. What did you think of the Chagall?'

'I hardly looked at it.'

'I was wondering how it would look in my apartment.'

'Where?'

'I was thinking maybe over the wicker chair.'

'Where you've got the Air India poster now?'

456

'Yeah. I was thinking maybe it's time I outgrew my travel poster phase. I might want to have the litho re-matted, but that's no big deal.'

'We'll see how it looks.'

'Yeah.' Three cabs sailed by, all with their off-duty signs lit. 'I just took it because I wanted to take something, you know? I didn't want to leave empty-handed.'

'I know.'

'I had figured you'd be cracking the safe while I went through the drawers, but some bastards already went through the drawers and there was nothing for me to do. I felt sort of out of it.'

'I can imagine.'

'So I stole the Chagall.'

'It'll probably look terrific over the chair, Carolyn.'

'Well, we'll see.'

3

Abel Crowe lived in one of those towering prewar apartment buildings on Riverside Drive. Our taxi let us out in front and we walked around the corner to the entrance on Eighty-ninth Street. The doorman was planted in the entranceway, holding his post like Horatius at the bridge. His face was a glossy black, his uniform a rich cranberry shade. It sported more gold braid than your average rear admiral and he wore it with at least as much pride of place.

He gave Carolyn a quick look-see, then checked me out from haircut to Pumas. He did not appear impressed. He was no more moved by my name, and while Abel Crowe's name didn't quite strike him with awe, either, at least it took the edge off his hostility. He rang upstairs on the intercom, spoke briefly into the mouthpiece, then informed us we were expected.

'Apartment 11-D,' he said, and waved us on to the elevator.

A lot of those buildings have converted to self-service elevators as a means of cutting overhead in the name of modernization, but Abel's building had gone co-op a few years ago and the tenants were big on keeping up the old standards. The elevator attendant wore a uniform like the doorman's but didn't fill it nearly so well. He was a runty wheyfaced youth with a face that had never seen the sun, and about him there hung an aroma that gave the lie to the advertiser's assurance that vodka leaves you breathless. He did his job, though, wafting us ten flights above sea level and waiting to see that we went to the designated apartment, and that the tenant was happy to see us.

There was no question about that last point.

'My dear Bernard!' Abel cried out, gripping me urgently by the shoulders. 'And the beloved Carolyn!' He let go of me and embraced my partner in crime. 'I'm so glad you could come,' he said, ushering us inside. 'It is half past eleven. I was beginning to worry.'

'I said between eleven and twelve, Abel.'

'I know, Bernard, I know, and all the same I began at half past ten to check my watch, and I seemed to be doing so every three minutes. But come in, come in, let us make ourselves comfortable. I have a house full of wonderful things to eat. And of course you'll want something to drink.'

'Of course we will,' Carolyn agreed.

He took a moment to lock up, sliding the massive bolt of the Fox lock into its mount on the jamb. Fox makes a couple of police locks. The kind I have features a five-foot steel bar fixed at a forty-five-degree angle between a plate set into the floor and a catch on the door. Abel's was a simpler mechanism but almost as good insurance against some-body's knocking the door down with anything lighter than a medieval battering ram. It featured a bolt two feet long and a good inch wide, made of tempered steel and mounted securely on the door and sliding sideways to engage an equally solid catch on the doorjamb. I'd learned on a previous visit that an identical lock secured the apartment's other door, the one leading to the service area and freight elevator.

I don't suppose most of the tenants bothered with such heavy-duty locks, not in a building so well protected by the staff. But Abel had his reasons.

His occupation, for one. Abel was a fence, and probably the best in the New York area when it came to top-quality collections of rare stamps and coins. He would take other things as well – jewelry, objets d'art – but stamps and coins were the sort of stolen goods he was hap-piest to receive.

Fences are natural targets for thieves. You'd think they'd be off-limits, that criminals would forbear to bite the hands that feed them, but it doesn't work that way. A fence generally has something on hand worth stealing – either goods he's lately purchased or the cold cash with which he conducts all his business. Perhaps as important, he can't complain to the police. As a result, most of the fences I know live in fully serviced buildings, double-lock their doors, and tend to have a gun or two within easy reach.

On the other hand, Abel might have been almost as security-conscious however he earned his living. He had spent the Second World War in Dachau, and not as a guard. I can understand how the experience might leave one with a slight streak of healthy paranoia.

Abel's living room, richly paneled in dark woods and lined with book-shelves, looks westward over Riverside Park and the Hudson River to New Jersey. Almost a year earlier, on the Fourth of July, the three of us had watched the Macy's fireworks display from Abel's windows, listen-ing to a radio broadcast of classical music with which the fireworks were presumably coordinated and putting away vast quantities of pastry.

We were seated in the same fashion now, Carolyn and I with glasses of Scotch, Abel with a mug of espresso topped with fresh whipped cream. WNCN was playing a Haydn string quartet for us, and outside there was nothing more spectacular to watch than the cars on the West Side Highway and the joggers circumvolving the park. No doubt some of the latter had shoes just like mine.

When Haydn gave way to Vivaldi, Abel set his empty mug aside and leaned back in his chair with his pink hands folded over his ample abdomen. Only his midsection was fat; his hands and arms were lean, and there was not much spare flesh on his face. But he had a Santa Claus belly and upper thighs that bulged in his blue gabardine trousers, attributes quite consistent with his boundless enthusiasm for rich desserts.

According to him, he had never been fat until after the war. 'When I was in the camps,' he had told me once, 'I thought constantly of meat and potatoes. I dreamed of fat sausages and great barons of beef. Crown roasts of pork. Kids roasted whole on a spit. Meanwhile I grew gaunt and my skin shrank on my bones like leather left to dry in the sun. When the American forces liberated the camps they weighed us. God knows why. Most fat men claim to be large-boned. Doubtless some of them are. I have small bones, Bernard. I tipped the scales, as they say, at ninety-two pounds.

'I left Dachau clinging to one certainty. I was going to eat and grow fat. And then I discovered, to my considerable astonishment, that I had no interest in the meat and potatoes I had grown up on. That SS rifle butts had relieved me of my own teeth was only a partial explanation, for I had for meat itself a positive aversion – I could not eat a sausage without feeling I was biting into a plump Teutonic finger. And yet I had an appetite, a bottomless one, but it was a most selective and specific appetite. I wanted sugar. I craved sweetness. Is there anything half so satisfying as knowing precisely what one wishes and being able to obtain it? If I could afford it, Bernard, I would engage a live-in pastry cook and keep him occupied around the clock.'

He'd had a piece of Linzer torte with his coffee and had offered us a choice of half a dozen decadently rich pastries, all of which we'd passed for the time being while we tended to our drinks.

'Ah, Bernard,' he said now. 'And the lovely Carolyn. It is so very good to see you both. But the night is growing old, isn't it? You have brought me something, Bernard?'

My attaché case was close at hand. I opened it and drew out a compact volume of Spinoza's *Ethics*, an English edition printed in London in 1707 and bound in blue calf. I passed it to Abel and he turned it over and over in his hands, stroking the smooth old leather with his long and slender fingers, studying the title page at some length, flipping through the pages.

He said, 'Regard this, if you will. "It is the part of the wise man to feed himself with moderate pleasant food and drink, and to take pleasure with perfumes, with the beauty of living plants, dress, music, sport

460

and theaters, and other places of this sort which man may use without any injury to his fellows." If Baruch Spinoza were in this room I'd cut him a generous piece of Linzer torte, and I don't doubt he'd relish it.' He returned to the title page. 'This is quite nice,' he allowed. '1707. I have an early edition in Latin, printed in Amsterdam. The first edition was when, 1675?'

'1677.'

'My own copy is dated 1683, I believe. The only copy I own in English is the Everyman's Library edition with the Boyle translation.' He moistened a finger, turned some more pages. 'Quite nice. A little water damage, a few pages foxed, but quite nice for all that.' He read to himself for a moment, then closed the book with a snap. 'I might find a spot for this on my shelves,' he said carelessly. 'Your price, Bernard?'

'It's a gift.'

'For me?'

'If you can find a spot for it. On your shelves.'

He colored. 'But I expected no such thing! And here am I, mean-spirited enough to point out water damage and the odd foxed page as if to lay the groundwork for some hard bargaining. Your generosity shames me, Bernard. It's a splendid little volume, the binding's really quite gorgeous, and I'm thrilled to have it. You're quite certain you don't want any money for it?'

I shook my head. 'It came into the store with a load of fine bindings, decorator specials with nothing substantial between the covers. You wouldn't believe what people have seen fit to wrap in leather down through the years. And I can sell anything with a decent binding. Interior decorators buy them by the yard. I was sorting this lot and I spotted the Spinoza and thought of you.'

'You are kind and thoughtful,' he said, 'and I thank you.' He drew a breath, let it out, turned to place the book on the table beside his empty mug. 'But Spinoza alone did not bring you out at this hour. You have brought me something else, have you not?'

'Three things, actually.'

'And they will not be gifts.'

'Not quite.'

I took a small velvet bag from the attaché case, handed it to him. He weighed it in his hand, then spilled its contents into his palm. A pair of teardrop earrings, emeralds, quite simple and elegant. Abel drew a jeweler's loupe from his breast pocket and fixed it in his eye. While he was squinting through it at the stones, Carolyn crossed to the sideboard where the liquor and pastries were laid out. She freshened her drink. She was back in her chair and her glass was a third empty by the time Abel was through examining the emerald earrings.

'Good color,' he said. 'Slight flaws. Not garbage, Bernard, but nothing extraordinary, either. Did you have a figure in mind?'

'I never have a figure in mind.'

'You should keep these. Carolyn should wear them. Model them for us, *liebchen*.'

'I don't have pierced ears.'

'You should. Every woman should have pierced lobes, and emerald teardrops to wear in them. Bernard, I wouldn't care to pay more than a thousand for these. I think that's high. I'm basing that figure on a retail estimate of five thousand, and the true price might be closer to four. I will pay a thousand, Bernard. No more than that.'

'Then a thousand is the price.'

'Done,' he said, and returned the earrings to their velvet bag and placed the bag on top of Spinoza's *Ethics*. 'You have something else?'

I nodded and took a second velvet bag from the attaché case. It was blue – the one with the earrings had been the color of the doorman's uniform – and it was larger, and equipped with a drawstring. Abel undrew the string and took out a woman's wristwatch with a rectangular case, a round dial, and a gold mesh band. I don't know that he needed the loupe, but he fixed it in his eye all the same and took a close look.

'Piaget,' he said. 'What time do you have, Bernard?'

'Twelve oh seven.'

'Mr Piaget agrees with you to the minute.' I wasn't surprised; I'd wound and set the watch when I took it from the safe. 'You'll excuse me for a moment? I just want to look at a recent catalog. And won't you help yourselves to some of those pastries? I have eclairs, I have Sacher torte, I have Schwarzwälder kuchen. Have something sweet, both of you. I'll be with you in a moment.'

I broke down and took an eclair. Carolyn selected a wedge of seven-layer cake with enough chocolate between the layers to make an entire high school class break out. I filled two mugs with coffee and two small snifters with tawny Armagnac that was older than we were. Abel came back, visibly pleased to see us eating, and announced that the retail price of the watch was $4,950. That was a little higher than I'd thought.

'I can pay fifteen hundred,' he said. 'Because I can turn it over so quickly and easily. Satisfactory?'

'Satisfactory.'

'That's twenty-five hundred so far. You said three items, Bernard? The first two are nice merchandise, but I hope they don't represent too great an investment of time and effort on your part. Are you sure you wouldn't prefer to keep them? Ears can be pierced readily enough, and painlessly, I'm told. And wouldn't the watch grace your wrist, Carolyn?'

'I'd have to keep taking it off every time I washed a dog.'

'I hadn't thought of that.' He grinned widely. 'What I should do,' he

462

said, 'is put aside both of these articles and make you a present of them when the two of you get married. I'd have to find something suitable for you as well, Bernard, though wedding presents are really for the bride, don't you think? What about it, Carolyn? Shall I put these away?'

'You'd have a long wait, Abel. We're just good friends.'

'And business associates, eh?'

'That too.'

He chuckled heartily and sat back and folded his hands once again on his belly, an expectant look on his face. I let him wait. Then he said, 'You said you had three items.'

'Two earrings and a watch.'

'Ah, my mistake. I thought the earrings counted as a single unit. Then the total sum is twenty-five hundred dollars.'

'Well, there is something else you might want to look at,' I said carelessly, and from the attaché case I produced a brown kraft envelope two inches square. Abel shot me a look, then took the envelope from me. Inside it was a hinged Plexiglas box just small enough to fit into the envelope, and inside that was a wad of tissue paper. Abel opened the tissue paper very deliberately, his fingers moving with the precision of one accustomed to handling rare coins. When a nick or a scratch can reduce a coin's value substantially, when a finger mark can begin the hateful process of corrosion, one learns to grasp coins by their edges and to hold them gently but securely.

The object Abel Crowe held gently but securely between the thumb and index finger of his left hand was a metallic disc just under seven-eighths of an inch in diameter – or just over two centimeters, if you're into metrics. It was, in short, the size and shape of a nickel, the sort of nickel that's the price of the good cigar this country is purported to need. It was the color of a nickel, too, although its frosted features and mirrorlike field were a ways removed from anything you'd be likely to have in your pocket.

By and large, though, it looked like a nickel. And well it might, for that was precisely what it was.

All it lacked was Thomas Jefferson's head on the one side and his house on the other. The side Abel looked at first showed a large V within a wreath open at the top, the word *Cents* inscribed directly beneath the V. Circling the wreath were the issuing nation's name and motto – *United States of America* above, *E Pluribus Unum* below.

Abel flicked me a glance from beneath upraised eyebrows, then deftly turned the coin in his fingers. Its obverse depicted a woman's head facing left, her coronet inscribed *Liberty*. Thirteen stars circled Miss Liberty, and beneath her head was the date.

'*Gross Gott!*' said Abel Crowe. And then he closed his eyes and said another long sentence that I didn't understand, possibly in German, possibly in some other language.

Carolyn looked at me, her expression quizzical. 'Is that good or bad?' she wanted to know.

I told her I wasn't sure.

4

He didn't say anything else until he'd looked long and hard at both sides of the coin through his jeweler's loupe. Then he wrapped the coin in tissue paper, returned it to the Plexiglas box and tucked the box into the kraft envelope, which he placed on the table beside him. With an effort he heaved himself out of his chair to fetch another slab of nutritionist's nightmare and a fresh cup of coffee *mil schlag*. He sat down, ate for a while, set his plate down half finished, sipped the coffee through the thick whipped cream, and glared at me.

'Well?' he demanded. 'Is it genuine?'

'I just steal them,' I said. 'I don't authenticate them. I suppose I could have dropped in on Walter Breen or Don Taxay for a professional opinion, but I figured it was late.'

His glance moved to Carolyn. 'You know about this coin?'

'He never tells me anything.'

'A Liberty Head Nickel,' he said. 'Nickel five-cent pieces were first issued in this country in 1866. The original design showed a shield. In 1883 the government switched to this design, although the initial run of coins lacked the word *cents* on the reverse. There was thus some confusion as to the coin's denomination, and it was cleverly compounded by those who filed the edge of the coin to simulate the milling on a gold coin, then plated it lightly with gold and passed it as a five-dollar gold piece.'

He paused and had himself a sip of coffee, used a napkin to blot a thin line of whipped cream from his upper lip. 'The coin was issued without interruption through 1912,' he continued. 'In 1913 it was replaced by the Buffalo Nickel. The Mint had problems with that issue, too, in the first year. Originally the mound on which the bison stands was in excessive relief and the coins would not stack properly. This was corrected, but the dates of these coins tended to wear off prematurely. It was a poor design.

'But I am telling you more than you would care to know. The last Liberty Head Nickels, or V-Nickels, as they are sometimes called, were struck in Philadelphia and Denver and San Francisco in 1912.' He paused again, breathed in, breathed out. 'The specimen you were so kind as to bring me tonight,' he said, 'is dated 1913.'

'That must make it special,' Carolyn said.

'You might say that. Five specimens of the 1913 V-Nickel are known to exist. They are clearly a product of the US Mint, although the Mint has always denied having produced them.

'It is fairly clear what must have happened. Dies for a 1913 V-Nickel must have been prepared before the decision to switch to the buffalo design was finalized. Possibly a few pieces were struck as the trials; alternately, an enterprising employee may have produced these trial pieces on his own initiative. In any event, five specimens left the Mint by the back door.'

He sighed, removed one of his slippers, massaged his arch. 'I carry too much weight,' he said. 'It is alleged to endanger the heart. My heart makes no objection but my feet protest incessantly.

'But no matter. Let us return to the year 1913. At the time, a gentleman named Samuel Brown worked at the Mint in Philadelphia. He left shortly thereafter and next emerged in North Tonawanda, a suburb of Buffalo, where he placed advertisements seeking to buy 1913 Liberty Head Nickels – which of course no one had heard of at the time. He subsequently announced that he had managed to purchase five such nickels, and those are the only five which were ever to see the light of day. Perhaps you can guess how he happened to get them.'

'He walked out of the Mint with them,' I said, 'and the ads were his way of explaining his ownership of the coins.'

Abel nodded. 'And his way of publicizing them in the bargain. You are familiar with the name of E. H. R. Green? Colonel Edward Green? His mother was Hetty Green, the notorious witch of Wall Street, and when her son came into his money he was able to indulge his eccentricities, one of which was numismatics. He did not wish merely one specimen of a rarity; he wanted as many as he could lay hands on. Accordingly, he bought all five of Samuel Brown's 1913 V-Nickels.

'They remained in his possession until his death, and I trust he enjoyed owning them. When he died his holdings were dispersed, and a dealer named Johnson wound up with all five of the nickels. I believe he lived in the Midwest, St Louis or perhaps Kansas City.'

'It doesn't matter,' I said.

'Probably not,' he agreed. 'In any event, Mr Johnson sold them off one at a time to individual collectors. While he was doing this, a dealer in Fort Worth by the name of B. Max Mehl was busy making the 1913 V-Nickel the most famous rare coin of the century simply by offering to buy it. He placed advertisements everywhere offering fifty dollars for the coin, with the implication that one might come across it in one's pocket change. He did so in order to attract customers for a rare coin catalog he was peddling, and I don't doubt he sold a great many catalogs, but in the course of it he assured the future of the 1913 nickel. No American coin ever received so much publicity. Americans who knew nothing else about coins knew a 1913 V-Nickel was valuable. Virtually everyone knew this.'

I did. I remembered the ads he was talking about. They were still running when I was a boy, and I was one of the guppies who sent for the book. None of us found 1913 V-Nickels in our pockets, since they weren't there to be found, but many of us began collecting coins and grew up to swell the ranks of the numismatic fraternity. Others of us grew up to be thieves, seeking our fortunes in other men's pocket change, as it were.

'There's no logical explanation for the coin's value,' Abel went on. 'At best it's a trial piece, at worst an unauthorized fantasy item. As such it should be worth a few thousand dollars at most. The Mint struck pattern nickels in 1881 and 1882 in a variety of metals and with a variety of designs. Some are as rare or rarer than the 1913 nickel, yet you can buy them for a few hundred dollars. In 1882 a pattern coin was struck identical in design to the V-Nickel, and in the same metal, but with that year's date. It's quite rare, and if anything it ought to be more desirable than the 1913 coin, if only because its existence is legitimate. Yet a couple of thousand dollars will buy it, assuming you can locate an example for sale.'

Carolyn's face was showing a lot of excitement about now, and I could understand why. If another coin was worth a couple of thousand, and that made it strictly minor-league compared to what we'd come up with, then we were in good shape. But she still didn't know just how good that shape was. She was waiting for him to tell her.

He made her wait. He reached for his plate, finished his pastry, switched plate for cup, drank coffee. Carolyn got herself more Armagnac, drank some of it, watched him sip his coffee, drank the rest of the Armagnac, made her hands into fists, planted them on her hips, and said, 'Aw, come on, Abel. What's it worth?'

'I don't know.'

'Huh?'

'No one knows. Maybe you should put it in a parking meter. Bernard, why did you bring me this?'

'Well, it seemed like a good idea at the time, Abel. If you want I'll take it home with me.'

'And do what with it?'

'I don't have a car so I won't put it in a parking meter. Maybe I'll punch a hole in it and Carolyn can wear it around her neck.'

'I almost wish you would do that.'

'Or maybe somebody else'll buy it.'

'Who? To whom would you offer it? No one will deal more equitably with you than I, Bernard.'

'That's why I brought it to you in the first place, Abel.'

'Yes, yes, of course.' He sighed, fished out a handkerchief, wiped his high forehead. 'The *verdammte* coin has agitated me. What is it worth? Who *knows* what the thing is worth? Five specimens exist. As I recall, four are in museum collections, only one in private hands. I remember seeing a 1913 V-Nickel just once in my life. It was perhaps fifteen years ago. A gentleman named J. V. McDermott owned it and he liked to exhibit his treasure. He put it on display at coin shows whenever asked, and the rest of the time he was apt to carry it around in his pocket and show it to people. Few collectors get the pleasure out of their possession that Mr McDermott derived from his nickel.

'When the coin passed into another pair of hands it brought fifty thousand dollars, as I recall. There have been sales since. In 1976, I believe it was, a 1913 nickel changed hands for a hundred and thirty thousand. I don't remember if it was the McDermott coin or not. It might have been. More recently there was a private sale reported with an announced figure of two hundred thousand.'

Carolyn put her glass to her lips, tipped it up. She didn't seem to notice that there was nothing in it. Her eyes were on Abel, and they were as wide as I had ever seen them.

He sighed. 'What do you want for this coin, Bernard?'

'Wealth beyond the dreams of avarice.'

'A felicitous phrase. Your own?'

'Samuel Johnson said it first.'

'I thought it had a classic ring to it. Spinoza called avarice "nothing but a species of madness, although not enumerated among diseases." Are you mad enough yourself to have a price in mind?'

'No.'

'It's so difficult to put a value on the damned thing. When they sold the John Work Garrett collection, a Brasher doubloon brought seven hundred twenty-five thousand. What might this coin bring at auction? Half a million? It's possible. It's not sane, not by any means, but it's possible nevertheless.'

Carolyn, glassy-eyed, went for more Armagnac. 'But you can't consign this piece for auction sale,' he continued, 'and neither can I. Where did it come from?'

I hesitated, but only for a moment 'A man named Colcannon owned it,' I said, 'until a couple of hours ago.'

'H. R. Colcannon? I know of him, of course, but I didn't know he bought the 1913 nickel. When did he acquire it?'

'No idea.'

'What else did you get from him?'

'Two earrings and a watch. There was nothing else in his safe except legal papers and stock certificates, and I left them as I found them.'

'There were no other coins?'

'None.'

'But—' He frowned. 'The V-Nickel,' he said. 'Didn't he have it in a frame or a custom lucite holder or something of the sort?'

'It was just as I gave it to you. Tissue paper and a hinged box in a two-by-two coinvelope.'

'Remarkable.'

'I thought so.'

'Simply remarkable. He must have just purchased it. You found it in a safe in his home? He must keep his holdings in a bank vault. Is this the McDermott coin, do you know? Or did one of the museums sell it? Museums don't hold on to things forever, you know. They don't just buy. They sell things off now and then, although they prefer to call it deaccessioning, which is a particularly choice example of newspeak, don't you think? Where did Herbert Colcannon get this coin?'

'Abel, I didn't even know he had it until I found it in his safe.'

'Yes, of course.' He reached for the coin, opened the envelope, unwrapped a half million dollars' worth of nickel. With the loupe in one eye and the other squeezed shut in a squint, he said, 'I don't think it's counterfeit. Counterfeits exist, you know. One takes a nickel from 1903, say, or 1910 or '11 or '12, grinds off the inappropriate digit and solders on a replacement removed from another coin. But there would be visible evidence of such tampering on a coin in proof condition, and I see no such evidence here. Besides, it would cost you several hundred dollars for a proof common-date V-Nickel to practice on. I'm almost certain it's genuine. An X-ray would help, or the counsel of an expert numismatist.'

He sighed gently. 'At a more favorable hour I could establish the coin's bona fides without leaving this building. But at this time of night let us merely assume the coin is genuine. To whom could I sell it? And for what price? It would have to go to a collector who would be willing to own it anonymously, one who could accept the fact that open resale would be forever impossible. Art collectors of this stripe abound; the pleasure they take in their paintings seems to be heightened by their illegitimate provenance. But coin collectors respond less to the aesthetic beauty of an object and more to the prestige and profit that accompany it. Who would buy this piece? Oh, there are collectors who'd be glad to have it, but which of them might I approach and what might I ask?'

I got some more coffee. I started to pour a little Armagnac into it to give it a bit more authority, then told myself the Armagnac was entirely too good to be so dealt with. And then I reminded myself that I had just lifted a half-million-dollar coin, so why was I holding back on some thirty-bucks-a-bottle French brandy? I laced my coffee with it and took a sip, and it warmed me clear down to my toes.

'You have three choices,' Abel said.

'Oh?'

'One: You can take the coin home with you and enjoy the secret ownership of an object more valuable than you are ever likely to own again. This coin is worth at least a quarter of a million, perhaps twice that, possibly even more. And I have been holding it in my hand. Extraordinary, is it not? For a few hours' work, you can have the pleasure of holding it in your own hands whenever you want.'

'What are my other choices?'

'Two: You can sell it to me tonight. I'll give you cash, unrecorded fifties and hundreds. You'll leave here with the money in your pocket.'

'How much, Abel?'

'Fifteen thousand dollars.'

'For a coin worth half a million.'

He let that pass. 'Three: You can leave the coin with me. I will sell it for what I can and I will give you half of whatever I receive. I'll take my time, but I'll certainly endeavor to move the coin as quickly as possible. Perhaps I'll find a customer. Perhaps the *verdammte* thing's insured by a carrier with a policy of repurchasing stolen goods. It's a delicate business, dealing with those companies. You can't always trust them. If it was a recent acquisition, Colcannon may not even have insured it yet. Perhaps he never insures his coins, perhaps he regards his safe-deposit box as insurance enough, and intended placing this coin there after he'd had an appropriate case made for it.'

He spread his hands, sighed heavily. 'Perhaps, perhaps, perhaps. Dozens of perhapses. I'm an old man, Bernard. Take the coin with you tonight and save me a headache. What do I need with the aggravation? I have enough money.'

'What will you try to sell it for?'

'I already told you I don't know. You want a rough estimate? I shall pluck a figure out of the air, then, and say a hundred thousand dollars. A nice round number. The final price might be a great deal more or a great deal less, depending on circumstances, but you ask me to come up with a figure and that is the figure that comes to mind.'

'A hundred thousand.'

'Perhaps.'

'And our half would be fifty thousand.'

'And to think you made the calculation without pencil and paper, Bernard.'

'And if we take the cash tonight?'

'What sum did I offer? Fifteen thousand. Plus the twenty-five hundred I owe you for the earrings and the watch. That would total seventeen-five.' No pencil and paper for him, either. We were a couple of mathematical wizards. 'I'll tell you what. Let's deal in round numbers tonight. Twenty thousand dollars for everything.'

'Or twenty-five hundred now plus half of what you get for the coin.'

470

'If I get anything for it. If it proves to be genuine, and if I find someone who wants it.'

'You wouldn't care to make it three thousand for the watch and earrings plus a split on the coin?'

He thought a moment. 'No,' he said, 'I wouldn't want to do that, Bernard.'

I looked at Carolyn. We could walk away with ten thou apiece for the night's work or settle for a little over a tenth of that plus a shot at wealth beyond the etc. I asked her what she thought.

'Up to you, Bern.'

'I just wondered what—'

'Uh-uh. Up to you.'

Take the money and run, a voice whispered in my head. Take the cash and let the credit go. A bird in the hand is worth two in the bush. The voice that whispers in my head isn't terribly original, but it does tend to cut to the heart of the matter.

But did I want to be known as the man who got a hot ten grand for the Colcannon V-Nickel? And how happy would I be with my ten thousand dollars when I thought of Abel Crowe getting a six-figure price for it?

I could have topped his Spinoza quote. *'Pride, Envy and Avarice are the three sparks that have set the hearts of all on fire.'* From the Sixth Canto of Dante's *Inferno*.

My heart burned from all three, not to mention the eclair and the Armagnac. 'We'll take the twenty-five hundred,' I told him.

'If you want more time to think about it—'

'The last thing I want is more time to think about it.'

He smiled. He looked like a benevolent grandfather again, honest as any man living. 'I'll be just a moment,' he said, getting to his feet. 'There's more food, more coffee, plenty to drink. Help yourselves.'

While he was in the other room Carolyn and I had one short drink apiece to toast the night's work. Then Abel returned and counted out a stack of twenty-five bills. He said he hoped we didn't mind hundreds. Not at all, I assured him; I wished I had a million of them. He chuckled politely.

'Take care of our nickel,' I urged. 'There's thieves everywhere.'

'They could never get in here.'

'Gordius thought nobody could untie that knot, remember? And the Trojans were suckers for a horse.'

'And pride goeth before a fall, eh?' He laid a reassuring hand on my shoulder. 'The doormen are very security-conscious here. The elevator is always attended. And you have seen the police locks on my doors.'

'What about the fire escape?'

'It is on the front of the building, where anyone using it could be seen

471

from the street. The window that opens onto it is secured by steel gates. I can assure you no one could get in that way. I only hope I could get out if there were ever a fire.' He smiled. 'In any event, Bernard, I shall conceal the nickel where no one will think to look for it. And no one will know I have it in the first place.'

5

I'm not entirely sure why I wound up spending what was left of the night at Carolyn's. All that sugar and caffeine and alcohol, plus enough tension and excitement for your average month, had left us a little wired and a little drunk. It's as well neither of us had any life-or-death decisions to make just then. I wanted her to come up to my place so we could split the money, but she wanted to be downtown because she had a customer coming by early with a Giant Schnauzer, whatever the hell that is. We couldn't get a cab on West End Avenue, walked to Broadway, and ultimately kept the cab clear to the Village, where the driver was unable either to find Arbor Court on his own or to follow Carolyn's directions. We gave up finally and walked a couple of blocks. I hope he didn't squander his tip. Seventy years from now it might be valuable.

In Carolyn's apartment we got the Chagall litho out of my attaché case and held it up to the wall above the wicker chair. (That was another reason I'd accompanied her downtown, come to think of it. So that the picture could travel south in my case.) It looked good but the mat was the wrong color, so she decided to take it to a framer before hanging it. She poured herself a nightcap while I divvied up the cash. I gave her her share and she fanned the bills and whistled soundlessly at them. She said, 'Not bad for a night's work, huh? I know it's not much for burglary, but it's different when your frame of reference is dog-grooming. You got any idea how many mutts I'd have to wash for this?'

'Lots.'

'Bet your ass. Hey, I think you owe me a couple of bucks. Or are you charging me for the Chagall?'

'Of course not.'

'Well, you gave me twelve hundred, and that's fifty dollars short of half. Not to be chintzy, but—'

'You're forgetting our expenses.'

'What, cabfare? You paid one way and I paid coming back. What expenses?'

'Spinoza's *Ethics*.'

'I thought it came in with a load of books you bought by the yard. Or

473

are you figuring on the basis of value instead of cost? That's fair, I don't care one way or the other, but—'

'I bought the book at Bartfield's on Fifty-seventh Street. It was a hundred dollars even. I didn't have to pay sales tax because I have a re-sale number.'

She stared at me. 'You paid a hundred dollars for that book?'

'Sure. Why? The price wasn't out of line.'

'But you told Abel—'

'That I got it for next to nothing. I think he believed me, too. I also think it got us an extra five hundred bucks for the watch and the earrings. It put him in a generous frame of mind.'

'Jesus,' she said. 'There's a lot I don't understand about this business.'

'There's a lot nobody understands.'

'Whoever heard of buying presents for a fence?'

'Whoever heard of a fence who quotes Spinoza?'

'That's a point. You sure you don't want a nightcap?'

'Positive.'

'Did you know the nickel was worth that much?'

'I had a pretty good idea.'

'You were so cool about it on the way up there. I had no idea it was worth a fortune.'

'I just seemed cool.'

'Yeah?' She cocked her head, studied me. 'I'm glad we didn't take the ten grand apiece and say the hell with it. Why not take a gamble? It's not like I needed ten thousand dollars to get my kid brother an operation. How long do you think it'll take him to sell it?'

'There's no telling. He could move it tomorrow or sit on it for six months.'

'But sooner or later the phone'll ring and we'll find out we just hit the Irish Sweepstakes.'

'Something like that.'

She stifled a yawn. 'I thought I'd feel like celebrating tonight. But it's not really over yet, is it? It's probably a good thing. I don't think I've got the strength for a celebration. Besides, I'm sure to have a bitch of a sugar hangover in the morning.'

'A sugar hangover?'

'All that pastry.'

'You think it's the sugar that's going to give you a hangover?'

'What else?' She picked a cat off the couch, set him on the floor. 'Sorry, fellow,' she told him, 'but it's bedtime for Mama.'

'You sure you don't want the bed, Carolyn?'

'How are you supposed to fit on the couch? We'd have to fold you in half.'

'It's just that I hate to chase you out of your own bed.'

474

'Bern, we have this same argument every time you stay over. One of these days I'll actually let you have the couch and you'll never make the offer again.'

So I took the bed and she took the couch, as usual and I slept in my underwear and she in her Dr Denton's. Ubi joined her on the couch. Archie, the Burmese, was restless at first, pacing the perimeters of the dark apartment like a rancher checking his fences. After a few circuits he threw himself onto the bed, flopped against me, and got the purring machine going. He was great at it, but then he's had all his life to practice.

Carolyn had had about three drinks to each of mine and they kept her from spending much time tossing and turning. In minutes her breathing announced that she was asleep, and in not too many more minutes she began emitting a ladylike snore.

I lay on my back, hands behind neck, eyes open, running the night's events through my mind. However long it took Abel to sell the nickel and whatever price we ultimately received for it, the Colcannon burglary was over and we were clear of it. As unpromising as it had been at first glance, when I'd seen we were not the first burglars to pay a call, things had worked out rather well. The loot was out of our hands, all but a rather anonymous minor Chagall litho which, given the chaos in the Colcannon carriage house, might never even get reported. And if it did, so what? It was one of a series of 250, and who'd come looking for it on Carolyn's wall anyway?

All the same, I put it in her closet when I awoke the next morning. It was around nine-thirty and she'd already fed herself and the cats and left for her Schnauzer appointment. I had a cup of coffee and a roll, tucked the litho away, let my attaché case keep it company rather than carry my burglar tools to work with me. The sun was shining, the air fresh and clean, and instead of contending with the subway I could walk to work. I could have run, for that matter – I had the shoes for it – but why spoil a beautiful morning? I strode along briskly, inhaling great lungfuls of air, swinging my arms at my sides. There was even a point when I caught myself whistling. I don't remember the tune.

I opened up around ten-fifteen and had my first customer twenty minutes later, a bearded pipe smoker who chose a couple volumes of English history. Then I sold a few things from the bargain table, and then trade slowed down enough for me to get back to the book I'd been reading yesterday. Old Spenser was still knocking himself out. This time he was doing bench presses, whatever they are, on a Universal machine. Whatever that is.

Two men in their forties walked in a little before eleven. They both wore dark suits and heavy shoes. One of them could have trimmed his sideburns a little higher. He was the one who walked to the back of the store while the other took an immediate and unconvincing interest in the poetry section.

I had Abel's thirteen hundred dollars in my wallet, plus the thousand dollars I always carry on a job in case I have to bribe somebody. I hoped they would settle for the money in the register. I hoped the bulge under the jacket of the sideburned chap wasn't really a gun, and that if it was he wouldn't decide to shoot me with it. I sent up an urgent brief prayer to Saint John of God, the patron saint of book-sellers, a framed picture of whom old Mr Litzauer had left hanging in the office. No point praying to Dismas now. I was bookselling, not burgling.

There was nothing I could do but wait for them to make a move, and I didn't have to do that for very long. They approached the counter, the one with the sideburns returning from the rear of the store, the other still clutching a volume of Robert W. Service's verses. I had a flash vision of one of them shooting me while the other recited 'The Cremation of Sam McGee.'

They reached the counter together. The Service fan said, 'Rhodenbarr? Bernard Rhodenbarr?'

I didn't deny it.

'Better get your coat. Want to talk to you downtown.'

'Thank God,' I said.

Because, as you must have guessed and as I should have guessed, they weren't robbers after all. They were cops. And while cops may indeed rob you now and then, it's uncommon for them to do so at gunpoint. And gunpoint is something I prefer not to be at.

'He's glad to see us,' said the sideburned chap.

The other nodded. 'Probably a load off his mind.'

'Sure. Probably up all night with guilt, aching to confess.'

'I think you're right, Phil. Here's a guy, small-time burglar, he's in over his head. You look at his sheet, you can patch it together pretty good. He teamed up with somebody violent.'

'I'm right with you, Dan. Bad companions.'

'Do it every time. Now he's probably up to his kidneys in guilt and remorse. He can hand us the partner, make him the heavy, turn state's evidence and cop to a lesser charge. Good lawyer and the right attitude and what do you bet he's on the street in three years?'

'No bet, Phil. Three years, four at the outside. You want to close the store, Bernie? We'll just take a little ride downtown.'

The fog lifted slowly. I'd been so relieved at not being robbed that it took a minute or two to realize I was being arrested, which is no pleasure in and of itself. They were talking to each other as if I weren't even in the room, but it was easy to see that I was the intended object of this merry little Phil-and-Dan patter. (Phil was the one with the sideburns, Dan the poetry lover.) According to their private script, I was supposed to be shaking in my Pumas even as they spoke.

476

Well, it was working.

'What's it all about?' I managed to ask.

'Some people would like to talk to you,' Dan said.

'About what?'

'A little visit you paid last night to a house on Eighteenth Street,' Phil said. 'A little unannounced call.'

Shit, I thought. How had they tagged us for Colcannon? My stomach turned with the beginnings of despair. It's particularly disheartening to be charged with a crime, I've found, when it's one you've committed. There's rather less opportunity for righteous indignation.

'So let's get going,' Dan said. He set the book of poems on the counter. I found myself hoping his last name was McGrew, and that Phil would shoot him.

I'd just opened the store and now I had to close it. 'Am I under arrest?' I asked.

'Do you want to be?'

'Not especially.'

'Well, if you come with us voluntarily we won't have to arrest you.'

That seemed fair enough. Phil helped me drag the bargain table inside, so I guessed that Dan ranked him. I locked the door and closed the gates, and while I was doing this they made the predictable jokes about a burglar locking up his own place, and how I didn't have to worry about forgetting my keys. Real side-splitters, let me tell you.

Their car was a blue-and-white police cruiser. Phil drove while I sat in back with Dan. A couple blocks from the store I said, 'What am I supposed to have done, anyway?'

'As if you didn't know.'

'Right, as if I didn't. It happens I don't, so humor me. What's the charge?'

'He's cool now,' Dan said to Phil. 'Notice how the professional attitude comes into play? He was nervous before, but now he's cool as a pickle.' He turned to me and said, 'There's no charge. How can there be a charge? We didn't arrest you.'

'If you arrested me, what would the charge have been?'

'Just hypothetically?'

'Okay.'

'Burglary, first degree. And homicide, first degree.' He shook his head. 'You poor bastard,' he said. 'You never killed anybody before, did you?'

6

Herbert and Wanda Colcannon had not stayed in Pennsylvania overnight after all. They had indeed driven out to Berks County, where
they'd bred their beloved Bouvier to the chosen champion. Then they'd
boarded Astrid overnight with the stud's owner, evidently a recom-
mended procedure, and drove back to New York for dinner with business associates of Herbert's and an evening at the theater. After-theater
drinks kept them out late, and they'd arrived home after midnight,
intending to get a night's sleep and drive back to Pennsylvania first
thing in the morning.

Instead, they had walked in on a burglary in progress. The burglars
relieved Herbert of his cash and Wanda of the jewels she was wearing,
then attempted to tie them up. When Herb protested, he got a punch in
the mouth for his troubles. This provoked a voluble protest from
Wanda, which earned her a couple of whacks on the head. Herb saw
her fall and lie there motionless, and that was the last thing he saw,
because that was when he got hit on the head himself.

When he came to he was tied up, and it took him a while to work his
way loose. Wanda was also tied up, and she couldn't work her way
loose because she was dead. She'd been hit on the head with something
harder than her skull, and the fracture she'd sustained had proved fatal.

'That was your partner's doing,' Sam Richler told me. He was the
detective who seemed to be in charge of the case, and it was to him that
Phil and Dan had turned me over upon arrival at police headquarters.
'We know you're not violent by nature or habit, Rhodenbarr. You always
used to work alone. What made you decide you needed a partner?'

'I don't have a partner,' I said. 'I don't even work alone anymore. I'm
a legitimate businessman, I have a store, I sell books.'

'Who was your partner? For Christ's sake, you don't want to protect
him. He's the one put you in the soup. Look, I can see how it shapes.
You retired, tried to make a go of it selling books' – he didn't believe
this but was humoring me – 'and this hard case talks you into trying
one more job. Maybe he's got the place set up and he needs somebody
with your talents to get around the locks. You figure you'll take one
last job to keep you going while the store gets off its feet, and all of a

sudden a woman's dead and your partner's off spending his money and you've got your head in the toilet. You know what you wanna do? You wanna pick your head up outta the bowl before somebody pulls the chain.'

'That's a horrible image.'

'You want a horrible image, I'll give you a horrible image.' He opened a desk drawer, shuffled papers, came up with an eight-by-ten glossy. A woman, blond, wearing an evening gown, half sat against a wall in what looked to be the Colcannon living room. Her shoes were off, her ankles tied together, and her hands looked to be tied behind her back. The photo wasn't in color – which was just as well, thank you – but even in black and white one could see the discoloration right below the hairline where someone had struck her with something heavy. She looked horrible, all right; I had Carolyn's word that Wanda Colcannon was a beauty, but you couldn't prove it by this photograph.

'You didn't do that,' Richler said. 'Did you?'

'Do it? I can't even look at it.'

'So give us the man who did. You'll get off light, Rhodenbarr. You might even walk with the right lawyer.' Sure. 'Thing is, we're certain to nail your partner anyway, with your help or without it. He'll run his mouth in a saloon and the right ear'll pick it up and we'll have him in a cell before it gets dark out. Or Colcannon'll find his mug shot in one of the books. Either way we get him. Only difference is if you help us you do your own self some good.'

'It makes sense.'

'That's just what it makes. Damn good sense. Plus you don't owe him a thing. Who got you in this mess, anyway?'

'That's a good question.'

'So?'

'There's only one thing,' I said.

'Oh?'

'I wasn't there. I never heard of anybody named Colcannon. I was nowhere near West Eighteenth Street. I gave up burglary when I bought the store.'

'You're going to stick with that story?'

'I'm stuck with it. It happens to be the truth.'

'We've got hard evidence that puts you right in that house.'

'What evidence?'

'I'm not revealing that now. You'll find out when the time comes. And we've got Colcannon. I guess you didn't realize the woman was dead or you wouldn't have left him alive. Your accomplice wouldn't, anyway. We know he's the violent one. Maybe she was still alive when you left her. She could have died while he was unconscious. We don't have the medical examiner's report on that yet. But the thing is, see, we've got Colcannon and he can identify both you and your partner. So what's the point of sticking with your story?'

'It's the only story I've got.'

'I suppose you've got an alibi to go with it?'

It would have been nice, but you can't have everything. 'I sat home and watched television,' I said. 'Had a few beers, put my feet up.'

'Just spent the whole night at home, huh?'

A little alarm went off. 'The whole evening,' I corrected. 'After the eleven o'clock newscast I went out.'

'And knocked over the Colcannon place.'

'No. I had a late date.'

'With anyone in particular?'

'With a woman.'

'The kind of woman you can drop in on at eleven o'clock.'

'It was more like midnight by the time I met her.'

'She got a name?'

'Uh-huh. But I'm not going to give it unless I have to. She's my alibi for the whole night, because I was with her from around midnight through breakfast this morning, and I'll use her if I don't have any choice, but not otherwise. She's separated from her husband and she's got a couple of young children and she doesn't need her name dragged into this. But that's where I was.'

He frowned in thought 'You didn't get home last night,' he said. 'We know that much.'

'I just told you.'

'Yeah. We checked your apartment around four-thirty and left it staked out and you never showed up. But that's not enough to make me believe in your secret divorced lady.'

'Not divorced. Separated.'

'Uh-huh.'

'And you don't have to believe in her. Just put me in the lineup and let Colcannon fail to identify me. Then I can go home.'

'Who said anything about a lineup?'

'Nobody had to. You brought me here instead of the precinct because this is where the mug shots are and you've got Colcannon looking through them. You haven't arrested me yet because he took a look at my picture and shook his head. Well, who knows, maybe I'm not photogenic, and it's worth letting him have a look at me in person, so that's why I'm here. Now you'll put me in a lineup and he'll say the same thing and I'll go back to my store and try to sell some books. It's hard to do much business when the store's closed.'

'You really don't think he'll identify you.'

'That's right.'

'I don't get it,' he said. He got to his feet. 'Come on along,' he said. 'Let's take a walk.'

480

We took a walk down the corridor and came to a door with frosted glass in the window and nothing written on it. 'I'm not sure whether we want to bother with a lineup or not,' he said, holding the door for me. 'Whyntcha have a seat in here while I talk to some people and find out how they want to proceed?'

I went in and he closed the door. There was one chair in the room and it faced a large mirror, and Mrs Rhodenbarr didn't raise no fools, so I knew right away why I was supposed to cool my heels in this particular little cubicle. What we were going to have was a one-man lineup, an unofficial lineup, and if it came out negative there wouldn't be a record of it to prejudice any case the State might decide to bring against one Bernard Grimes Rhodenbarr.

The mirror, I was bright enough to figure out, was of the one-way-glass variety. Herbert Franklin Colcannon would be positioned on the other side of it, where he could see me while I could not see him.

Fine with me.

In fact, I decided after a moment's reflection, it was more than fine with me, and the one thing I wanted to make sure of was that he got a good look at me, a good enough one to convince him once and for all that he had never seen me before. So I walked right up to the mirror, approaching it as if I thought it were indeed a mirror and nothing more. It was hard to repress the urge to make a face, but I squelched the impulse and adjusted the knot in my tie instead.

A funny thing about one-way glass. When you get close enough to it you can see through it. The vision you get is imperfect, because there's still a mirror effect and you get a sort of double image like a piece of twice-exposed photographic film, seeing what's in front of you and what's behind you at the same time. What I saw for a while was an empty room, and then I saw Richler bring in a man in a gray suit with a bandage on his head and a lot of swelling and discoloration around it.

He approached the mirror and stared at me, and I stared right back at him. It took an enormous effort of will to avoid winking or extending my tongue or rolling my eyes or doing something similarly hare-brained. Instead I took my time looking him over.

He wasn't terribly impressive. He was an inch or two below medium height and he looked to be about fifty-five. An oval face, slate-gray hair, a small clipped mustache with some white in with the gray. A snub nose, a small mouth. Eyes an indeterminate color somewhere between brown and green. If you saw him you'd guess banker first, tax lawyer second. He didn't particularly look like a man who'd just lost a glamorous wife and a $500,000 coin, but then he didn't look like a man who'd had either of them in the first place.

He looked at me and I looked at him, and he shook his head from side to side, solemn as an owl.

I don't think I smiled, not just then, but when he turned at Richler's

481

touch and followed the detective out of the room I grinned like a Hallowe'en pumpkin. When Richler walked in a few minutes later I was sitting in the chair cleaning my fingernails with the blunt end of a toothpick. I looked up brightly and asked him if they were going to put me in a lineup.

'You're cute as a button,' he said.

'Pardon me?'

'Straightening your goddamn tie. No, there's not going to be a lineup, Rhodenbarr. You can go home now.'

'The police realize their mistake?'

'I don't think we made one. I think you pulled that burglary last night. I think you were upstairs goosing the wall safe while your partners were roughing up the Colcannons. That way he never got a look at you, and you think that's gonna save your neck. It's not. We'll still get your pals, and we've still got evidence against you, and you'll wind up taking twice the fall you'd take if you cooperated. But you're a wiseass and it's your funeral.'

'I'm just a used-book dealer.'

'Sure you are. What you can do right now is get the hell out of here. You're not bright enough to recognize it when someone's trying to give you a break. If you wake up in a couple of hours, give me a call. But you don't want to wait too long. If we get one of your partners first, he'll be the one turning state's evidence and what'll we need with you? You'll be the one doing the long time, and you weren't even there when the woman got killed, and what sense does that make? You sure you still don't want to come clean?'

'I already came clean.'

'Yeah, sure. Get out, Rhodenbarr.'

I was on my way out of the building when I heard a familiar voice speak my name. 'If it ain't Bernie Rhodenbarr. Hang around No. 1 Police Plaza and you never know who you'll run into.'

'Hello, Ray.'

'Hello yourself, Bernie.' Ray Kirschmann gave me a lopsided grin. His suit didn't fit him very well, but then his suits never do. You'd think with all the shakedown money he takes he could afford to dress better. 'Beautiful mornin', huh, Bern?'

'Beautiful.'

'Except it's past noon now. An' I see I won a little bet I made with myself. They're lettin' you go home.'

'You know about it?'

'Sure. The Colcannon thing. I knew you didn't do it. When did you ever work with a partner? And when did you ever pull anything violent. Except' – and he looked reproachful – 'for the time you hit me and knocked me down. You remember that, Bern?'

482

'I panicked, Ray.'

'I remember it well.'

'And I wasn't trying to hurt you. I was just trying to get away.'

'Uh-huh. They still figure you're it, you know. Richler's got enough to hold you on. He thinks he'll have a stronger case in the long run if he doesn't slap you in a cell just yet.'

We were standing on the pavement outside the redbrick structure, looking across the plaza at the central arch of the Municipal Building. Ray cupped his hands to light a cigarette, inhaled, coughed, took another drag. 'Beautiful day,' he said. 'Just gorgeous.'

'Why do they think I was involved in the Colcannon burglary?'

'Your MO, Bern.'

'You've got to be kidding. When did I ever turn a place upside down and leave a mess? When did I ever hurt anybody, or do anything but run like a thief if the owners came home while I was working? When did I ever get into a place by smashing a skylight? How does all that add up to my *modus operandi*?'

'They figure your partners were sloppy and violent. But they've got evidence that fits you like a glove.'

'What do you mean?'

'Here's what I mean.' He reached into his jacket pocket and came up with something that he dangled from thumb and forefinger. It was a Playtex Living Glove, but he held it as if it had died.

The palm had been cut out of it.

'That's your evidence?'

'Their evidence, not mine. It's on the sheet, Bern. "Wears rubber gloves with palms excised." I like that word, excised. That means you cut the palms out but they can't come right out and say so, you know?'

'For God's sake,' I said. 'Where did they find this?'

'Right outside of Colcannon's house. There's a garden there and that's where it was.'

'Can I see it?'

'It's evidence.'

'So was the glass slipper,' I said, taking the glove from him, trying to force my hand into it. 'And I must be one of Cinderella's ugly sisters because this thing doesn't fit. It doesn't even come close to fitting. They make these things in sizes, Ray, and this one's just not my size.'

He took a close look. 'You know somethin'? I think you're right.'

I gave the glove back to him. 'Take care of this. You might even tell them the glove's the wrong size. They can start looking around for a klutzy burglar with very small hands.'

'I'll spread the word. You headin' back to the store now? I'll give you a ride.'

'All part of the service?'

'Just that it's on my way. What the hell.'

This time I got a ride in an unmarked car. We made small talk about the Mets' new third baseman, a possible garbage strike, and a shakeup in the Queens District Attorney's office. Crooks and cops always have plenty of things to talk about once they can get past the basic adversary nature of their relationship. The two classes actually have more in common than either of us would like to admit. Phil and Dan, who couldn't have looked more like cops unless they'd been in uniform, had looked like robbers to me when they came into my store.

Ray dropped me right in front of Barnegat Books, told me to take care, gave me a slow wink, and drove off. I started to open up, looked to see if he was gone, then said to hell with it and refastened the locks I'd opened. I had to do a few things that were more important than selling books.

I hadn't been part of the gang of burglars who'd killed Wanda Colcannon. Her husband hadn't merely failed to identify me. He'd given them a firm negative identification. And if the rubber glove was all they had, their evidence was a joke.

But Richler still thought I was involved.

And something funny, something I'd realized at the very end of the ride back to the store. Ray Kirschmann thought so, too.

7

Carolyn and I usually have lunch together. Mondays and Wednesdays I pick up something and we eat at the Poodle Factory. Tuesdays and Thursdays she brings our lunch to the bookstore. Fridays we generally go someplace ethnic and inexpensive and toss a coin for the check. All of this, of course, is subject to change if anything comes up, and Carolyn must have gathered that something had. It was a Wednesday, so when I'd failed to turn up around noon she'd evidently gone somewhere herself. The Poodle Factory was closed, with a cardboard sign hanging on the back of the door. BACK AT, the sign said, and beneath it the movable clock hands pointed to one-thirty.

I looked in at the coffee shop on the corner of Broadway but didn't see her. There was a pay phone on the wall at the back but it looked a little too exposed. I walked north a block and checked the felafel place. She wasn't there, either, but their pay phone was a little more private. I ordered a cup of coffee and a hummus sandwich. I wasn't especially hungry but I hadn't had anything since my roll for breakfast and figured I probably ought to eat. I ate most of my sandwich, drank all of my coffee, and made sure I got some dimes in my change.

The first call I made was to Abel Crowe. The *Post* was on the street by now, and I didn't have to look at it to know that Wanda Colcannon would be spread all over page three. Her murder might even get the front page, unless something more urgent displaced it, like a projected invasion of killer bees from South America. (Once, during the Son of Sam foofaraw, they'd given the entire front page to a photo of David Berkowitz asleep in his cell. SAM SLEEPS! the headline shrieked.)

At any rate, the murder was general knowledge by now and one medium or another was sure to call it to Abel's attention. Any stolen object with a six-figure price tag is hot enough to blister the skin, but homicide always turns up the heat, and Abel would not be happy. Nor could I make him happy, but I could at least assure him that we were burglars, not murderers.

I let the phone ring an even dozen times. When my dime came back I stood there for a minute, then tried the number again. One sometimes misdials, and telephone-company equipment sometimes misbehaves.

485

No answer. I'd dialed his number from memory and there was no directory handy to confirm my recollection, so I let Information check it for me. I'd remembered correctly, but to be on the safe side I dialed it yet again, and when there was still no answer I gave up. Maybe he was already out selling the coin. Maybe he was at his favorite bakery on West Seventy-second Street, buying up everything in sight. Maybe he was napping with the phone's bell muffled, or soaking in the tub, or tempting muggers in Riverside Park.

I dialed 411 again and let them look up another number for me. Narrowback Gallery, on West Broadway in SoHo. The phone rang four times, just long enough for me to decide I wasn't destined to reach anybody this afternoon, and then Denise Raphaelson answered, her voice scratchy from the cigarettes she chain-smoked.

'Hi,' I said. 'Are we set for dinner tonight?'

'Bernie?'

'Uh-huh.'

There was a pause. 'I'm a little confused,' she said finally. 'I've been painting my brains out and I think the fumes are starting to get to me. Did we have a dinner date for tonight?'

'Well, yeah. It was sort of mentioned casually. Too casually, I guess, if it slipped your mind.'

'I should write these things down,' she said, 'but I never do. I'm sorry, Bernie.'

'You made other plans.'

'I did? I don't think I did. Of course if I could forget a dinner date with you, I could forget other things at least as easily. For all I know I'm throwing a party tonight. Truman and Gore are coming, and Hilton wanted a quick look at my latest work before he does his piece for the Sunday *Times*, and Andy said he'd bring Marlene if she's in town. What do you suppose it's like being one of those people that people know who you are without hearing your last name? I bet if I was Jackie I'd still have to show ID to cash a check at D'Agostino's.'

Telephonic whimsy is her specialty. We'd first met over the phone when I was trying to find an artist without knowing anything about him but his last name. She'd told me how to manage that, and one thing had led to another, as it so often does. We have since seen each other now and again, and if it's all remained very casual and on the surface, that's not the worst thing that can be said of what one has learned to call interpersonal relationships.

'What I should have done,' she said now, 'is fake it. When you asked if we were set for dinner tonight I should have said yes and let it go at that. It's a shame I don't take drugs. Then I could blame this mental sluggishness on the joint I'd just smoked. Would you believe paint fumes?'

'Sure.'

'Because I *am* free for dinner, and just because I don't seem to recall our date shouldn't prevent me from keeping it. Did we make plans to meet someplace?'

'Not yet.'

'Should we?'

'Why don't I drop by your place around seven-thirty?'

'Why don't you?'

'I think I will.'

'I think you should. Shall I cook something?'

'We'll go out.'

'This is sounding better and better. Maybe I'll have this painting finished and you can look at it. Maybe I won't and you can't. "Bernie at 7:30." I've written it down. I can't possibly forget now.'

'I have faith in you, Denise.'

'Shall I wear anything in particular?'

'Just a smock and a smile.'

'Ta.'

I tried Abel again, twelve rings and out. By then it was one-thirty. I hiked back to the Poodle Factory and caught Carolyn between appointments. 'There you are,' she said. 'When you didn't show I went looking for you, and when I saw your store was closed I figured you'd just ducked out to pick up lunch, so I came back here and waited, and when you still didn't show I said the hell with it and went out and ate.'

'Not at the coffee shop,' I said, 'and not at Mamoun's.'

'I went and had some curry. I figured some really hot food would counteract the sugar from last night. God, what a morning!'

'Bad?'

'My head felt like the soccer ball from Pélé's last game. You have any idea what it's like to face a Giant Schnauzer on top of a sugar hangover?'

'No.'

'Count your lucky stars. The coffee shop and Mamoun's – what did you do, go out looking for me?'

'Sort of.'

'Any particular reason?'

I hated to ruin her day, but what else could I do? 'Just wanted to tell you you were missing a glove,' I said. 'Of the rubber variety, and with the palm cut out.'

'Son of a bitch.'

'You weren't going to say that, remember? You were going to switch to "child of a dog" because "son of a bitch" is sexist.'

'Shit. I saw the glove was missing last night when I checked my pockets. I threw away the one but the other was gone. I thought it over

487

and decided not to tell you. How'd you find out? What did you do, go through my garbage?'

'I always go through your garbage. It started out as a perversion and now it's a hobby.'

'That's the way it always works.'

'I didn't go through your garbage. You dropped it in the garden, in case you were wondering.'

'I did? Jesus, they ought to put me away. How do you know this? You didn't go back there, did you? No, of course you didn't.'

'No. Somebody showed me the glove.'

'Who would—' Light dawned and her face fell. 'Oh, no,' she said. 'Cops.'

'Right.'

'You got arrested.'

'Not officially.'

'What happened?'

'They let me go. My hands are bigger than yours. The glove didn't fit. And Herbert Colcannon didn't recognize me.'

'Why would he recognize you? He never met you.'

'Right. I'll bet you didn't read the paper at lunch.'

'I read the *Times* this morning. Why?'

'It's complicated,' I said, 'but it's important. You'd better hear the whole thing.'

Her phone rang a couple of times while I was going through it. She switched on the answering machine and let her callers leave messages if they wanted. We were interrupted once by a sad-eyed man wearing an obvious toupee who wanted to inquire about services and rates. If his pet resembled him, he probably had a basset hound.

When I was finished Carolyn just sat there shaking her head. 'I don't know what to say,' she said. 'I'm sorry about the glove, Bern. I feel rotten about it.'

'These things happen.'

'I thought I'd be a help and look what I did. I might as well have left a trail of bread crumbs.'

'The birds would have eaten them.'

'Yeah. I can't believe she's dead. Wanda Flanders Colcannon. I can't believe it.'

'You'd believe it if you saw the picture.'

She shuddered, made a face. 'Burglary's fun,' she said. 'But murder—'

'I know.'

'I don't understand how it happened. The other burglars, the slobs, got there *before* we did.'

'Right.'

'And turned the place upside down and stole God knows what and left.'

'Right.'

'And then came back? Why? Don't tell me it's true about criminals returning to the scene of the crime?'

'Only to commit another crime. Remember, we didn't know the Colcannons were planning to leave Astrid. We thought they were staying overnight.'

'I'm sorry about that, too.'

'Don't be. You couldn't know otherwise. The point is, the other burglars probably made the same assumption. Suppose they grabbed up everything they could, took off over the rooftops, then decided they'd like to have another shot at the wall safe. They had time to pick up a torch or a drill. They might not have brought the right equipment the first time because they might not even have known about the safe, but if they had time to pick up a torch and all night to work on the safe, why not give it the old college try?'

'And then the Colcannons came home right in the middle of it?'

'Evidently.'

'If they did, wouldn't the burglars make them give them the combination of the safe?'

'Probably. Unless they'd already opened it.'

'If they had, why would they still be hanging around?'

'They wouldn't. But the Colcannons could have walked in the door just as the burglars were on their way out.'

'Wouldn't they leave the way they came? Through the skylight?'

'You're right,' I said. I frowned. 'Anyway, there's a third possibility. There could have been a third set of burglars.'

'A third set? How many people knew that damned dog was going to Pennsylvania to get laid?'

'Maybe these last burglars weren't real burglars,' I suggested. 'Maybe they were kids or junkies on the prowl, just roaming across the rooftops to see what they turned up. They'd notice the broken skylight and drop in for a look around. There were still plenty of things there to steal if you were an amateur on the prowl. Remember the radio? That would bring the price of a bag of heroin.'

'There was at least one television set. Plus some stereo components on the second floor.'

'See what I mean? Loads of goodies for a thief with low standards. But there wasn't a lot of money, and sometimes amateur thieves take that sort of thing personally. You know how muggers sometimes beat up people who don't have any cash on them?'

'I've heard of that.'

'Well, there's a class of burglars who get the same sort of resentment. I can imagine a couple of punks dropping in through the broken skylight, picking up a radio and a portable TV, then deciding to hang around until the householders come home so they can rob them of their cash.' I followed that train of thought for a minute, then dropped it and shrugged. 'It doesn't really matter. I may have to spend the next week looking over my shoulder for cops, but basically we're in the clear. The thing is, they're going to find the guys who did it. There'll be a lot of heat with her murdered, and Richler was right. He said somebody would blab at a bar and somebody else would overhear him. That's what usually happens and it's how most crimes get solved.'

'And you think we're all right?'

'Sure. Colcannon can identify the men who killed his wife. We've already established that he can't identify me. All they've got that leads to me is a rubber glove, and if the glove doesn't fit, how can I wear it? If one of us had to drop a glove, I'm damned glad it was you.'

'I wish that made me feel better.'

'You've got to look on the bright side. Another thing to be glad of is that Colcannon wasn't killed. If they had known Wanda was dead they probably would have killed him, too, and then he wouldn't have been around to get me off the hook.'

'I didn't think of that.'

'I did.' I lifted the phone from her desk. 'Anyway, I'd better call Abel.'

'Why?'

'To tell him we didn't kill anybody.'

'He already knows that, doesn't he? It's a shame neither of us bothered to read the *Post*, but won't it tell what time she was killed?'

'Probably.'

'Well, it was around 11:30 when we got to Abel's. I remember it was 12:07 when he checked the Piaget watch against yours. And it was after midnight when the Colcannons walked in on the burglars, so how could Abel think we did it?'

'My God,' I said. 'He's our alibi.'

'Sure.'

'I hope to God we never have to use him. Imagine trying to beat a burglary charge by insisting you were spending the time with a fence, trying to sell the things you'd already lifted from the burglary victim.'

'When you put it that way, it does sound bizarre.'

'I know.' I began dialing. 'I'll call him anyway and put him in the picture. He may not have noticed the timing and assume we killed that woman, and I wouldn't want that.'

'Would he refuse to handle the coin?'

'Why?'

'If we were killers—'

The phone was ringing. I let it ring. 'Abel's a fence,' I said. 'Not a judge. Anyway, we didn't do it and I can make him believe it. If he'd ever answer his goddamned phone.'

I hung up. Carolyn frowned to herself for a moment, then said, 'It's just business as usual, isn't it? Wanda's dead but nothing's changed. Abel will sell the coin in a few days or a few months and we'll get our share, same as if nothing ever happened to her.'

'That's right.'

'It seems wrong. I don't know why.'

'We didn't kill her, Carolyn.'

'I know that.'

'We didn't do anything to cause her death.'

'I know that, too. It was some other guys and they had no connection with us. I understand all that, Bern. I just feel funny, that's all. What do you think we'll get?'

'Huh?'

'For the coin.'

'Oh. I don't know.'

'How will we know what price he sells it for?'

'He'll tell us.'

'What I mean is he won't cheat us, will he?'

'Abel? He might.'

'Really?'

'Well, the man's a receiver of stolen goods,' I said. 'I imagine he's told a lie or two in the course of a long life. I don't suppose he'd draw the line at telling another. And it's the easiest sort of a lie because there's no way for us to know about it.'

'Then how can we trust him?'

'In a sense I don't suppose we can. Not to be perfectly honest, anyway. If he got lucky and peddled the V-Nickel for half a million dollars, say, I'd guess he might tell us he got two hundred thousand dollars for it. We'd get half of that, and I suppose he'd have cheated us out of a bundle if that happened, but would we really have a complaint? It would be hard for me to work up much indignation if my end of a night's work came to fifty thousand dollars.'

'Suppose he tells us he sold it for fifty thousand? Then what?'

'Then he'll probably be telling the truth. My guess is that he'd be most likely to cheat us if the coin sells high and most likely to be completely honest if the selling price is low. And we can be sure that our end won't drop below seventeen thousand five hundred, because he offered us that much for cash on delivery, so he'll make sure we get more than that if we have to wait for our money. Unless the coin turns out to be a counterfeit, in which case all bets are off.'

'Is that a possibility?'

'No. It's a genuine coin. My prediction is that you and I will wind up dividing fifty thousand dollars.'

'Jesus. And all we have to do is sit around and wait for it?'

'Right. What was it the German officer used to say to POWs in the war movies? "My friend, for you ze var is over." I think I'll celebrate the end of the war by opening the store for a couple of hours. You doing anything special tonight?'

'I'll probably bounce around the bars eventually. Why? Want to have dinner?'

'Can't. I've got a date.'

'Anybody I know?'

'Denise.'

'The painter? The one who doesn't shut up?'

'She has a ready wit and a self-deprecatory sense of humor.'

'If you say so, Bern.'

'Do I criticize your taste in women?'

'Sometimes.'

'Hardly ever,' I said. I got up. 'I'm going to sell some books. I'll call you later if I hear anything. Have a good time at the dyke bars.'

'I intend to,' she said. 'Give my love to Denise.'

8

Denise Raphaelson is long-legged and slender, although Carolyn insists on describing her as gawky and bony. Her hair is dark brown and curly and worn medium-long, her complexion fair with a dusting of unobtrusive freckles. Her blue-gray eyes are artist's eyes, always measuring and assessing and seeing the world as a series of framed rectangles.

There was no end of rectangles, albeit unframed, on the walls of Narrowback Gallery, where she lived and worked. It's on the third floor of a loft building on West Broadway between Grand and Broome, and its name derived from the loft's unusual shape, narrow at the back and wider at the front. Denise subsequently discovered that *narrowback* is a term of contempt applied by native Irish to those kinsmen of theirs who have emigrated to America. No one has yet satisfactorily explained the term to her, although speculation on the subject has sparked any number of drunken conversations at the Broome Street Bar.

I looked at a couple of paintings she'd done since I was last at the loft, including the one she'd been working on that day. I exchanged a few sentences with Jared, her twelve-year-old genius son, and gave him the stack of paperback science fiction I'd been setting aside for him. (I don't handle paperbacks in the store, wholesaling the ones that come in to a store that sells nothing else.) He seemed happy with what I'd brought, especially an early Chip Delaney novel that he'd been wanting to read, and we had the sort of stilted conversation one has with the precocious and overly hip child of a woman with whom one occasionally beds down.

I'd gone home to shave and change clothes before trekking down to SoHo. I had my Weejuns on my feet again and was comfortably casual in Levi's and a flannel shirt. Denise was wearing a lime turtleneck and a pair of those forty-dollar jeans with an over-the-hill debutante's autograph on a rear pocket. Remember when clothes had their labels on the inside?

We had a glass of wine each at the gallery, then moved on to an Ethiopian place in Tribeca where you bring your own wine and eat unpronounceable dishes at your peril. We brought a rosé to see if it really does go with anything, and it did, but not terribly well. Our dishes, hers made with chicken and mine with lamb, were identically sauced and hot enough to blister paint. They came with a disc of spongy bread the size of a small pizza, and we tore off hunks of this gooey muck and used it to scoop up mouthfuls of the hot stuff. In the name of ethnic authenticity, a whole lot of New Yorkers are relearning the table manners of messy children.

When we got out of there – and not a moment too soon – we walked around for a while and wound up listening to a jazz trio on Wooster Street. We had a couple of Scotches there and Denise worked her way through a pack of Virginia Slims. I tried Abel once or twice, and then we walked north a ways and caught Lance Hayward's ten o'clock set at the Village Corner. Denise knows him, so we chatted with him after the set and it turned out there was another pianist we simply had to hear at a new club in my neighborhood. I dialed Abel's number again and we had a quick drink with Lance – we were drinking stingers by this time – before grabbing a cab uptown.

The new club was on Columbus Avenue in the low eighties and the piano player was a young black kid who kept reminding me of a Lenni Tristano record I hadn't listened to in years. We got out of there when the set ended and cabbed to my place, where I dug out the record in question and put it on. We had a nightcap and threw our clothes on the floor and dived into bed.

I did not find her to be gawky and bony. I found her to be warm and soft and quick and eager, and the music's eccentric harmonies and offbeat rhythm didn't interfere with the pleasure we took with one another. If anything, it gave a nice brittly atonal edge to our lovemaking.

The tone arm had just dropped to begin replaying the record for the third time when she yawned and stretched and reached for the inevitable cigarette. She got it lit and said something about going home.

'Stay over,' I suggested.

'I didn't say anything to Jared. I figured we'd wind up at my place.'

'And if you're not there when he wakes up?'

'He'll figure I'm here, which is cool, but if I'd known I would have called him earlier. I'd call now but I don't want to wake him.'

I thought of trying Abel again but it would have involved moving.

'I think I *will* stay,' she said, after a moment's reflection. 'Mind if I change the record?'

'Not at all. Put on a stack.'

She crouched at the record rack, her bare behind tilted charmingly in my direction. Bony? Gawky? Pfui.

When she came back to bed I slipped an arm around her and told her I was glad she was staying.

'Me too,' she said.

'You said earlier that you went to the movies last night.'

'Right. I took the kid and we saw the new Woody Allen picture.'

'And you loved it but he thought it was superficial.'

'Yeah, the little wiseass.'

'Do anything afterwards?'

She shifted around, glanced up at me. 'A little dancing,' she said, 'but no fooling around. What do you mean?'

'You went to the movies and then you and Jared went home and you stayed there?'

'Right. Except that we stopped on the way home for frozen yogurt. Why?'

'When did he go to sleep?'

'Around eleven, maybe a little later.'

'It won't come up,' I said, 'but if it does, I was over at your place last night. I got there around midnight after the kid went to bed and left first thing in the morning.'

'I see.'

'What do you see?'

She sat up, lit another Virginia Slim. 'I see why you called me this afternoon.'

'You do like hell.'

'Oh? You burgled somebody last night and you need an alibi, so Denise is elected. I thought you gave up stealing, you swore you gave up stealing, but what does it mean when a thief takes an oath? Good old Denise. Take her out for a meal, pour a few drinks into her, hit a few jazz clubs, then throw her a friendly fuck—'

'Cut it out.'

'Why should I? Isn't that about how it goes?'

Jesus, why had I brought it up? Well enough seems to be the one thing I'm incapable of leaving alone.

I said, 'You're wrong, but maybe you're too mad to listen to an explanation. I called you because we had a date for tonight.' The best defense is a good offense, isn't it? 'Don't blame me for your bad memory. I can't help that.'

'I didn't—'

'I *did* give up burglary, and I'm not exactly in trouble, but someone committed a crime last night and used the type of gloves I used to use, and the police found one on the scene and think I'm involved. And I don't happen to have an alibi because I happened to spend the night alone, because who knew I was going to *need* an alibi? When you don't do anything criminal you don't bother to arrange an alibi in advance.'

'And you just sat home in front of the television set?'

'As a matter of fact I was reading Spinoza.'

'I don't suppose anyone would make that up. Except you might.' She fixed those artist's eyes on me. 'I don't know how much of your word to take. Where was the burglary? Oh, wait a minute. It wasn't the one I read about in the paper? That poor woman in Chelsea?'

'That's the one.'

'You didn't do that, did you, Bernie?' Her eyes probed mine for a long moment. Then she took one of my hands in both of hers and looked at my fingers. 'No,' she said, more to herself than to me. 'You're very gentle. You couldn't kill someone.'

'Of course I couldn't.'

'I believe you. You said they found a glove? Does that mean you're in trouble?'

'Probably not. They'll probably catch the guys who did it within a couple of days. But in the meantime I figured it wouldn't hurt to have someone back up my story, in case anybody ever leans on it.'

She asked what story I'd told them and I repeated my conversation with Richler.

'You didn't tell them my name,' she said. 'That's good. So I won't come into it unless they give you more trouble and you need a backup.'

'That's right.'

'Why didn't you just tell them the truth? That you were home watching TV?'

'I tend to lie to cops.'

'Oh?'

'Old habits die hard.'

'I guess.' She leaned over to stub out her cigarette in the ashtray on the bedside table. In that position the curve of her pendant breast was particularly appealing, and I reached out a hand and stroked her. Bony? Gawky?

'I feel manipulated,' she said lazily. 'And as though I've been lied to a little.'

'Maybe a very little,' I conceded.

'Well, nobody's perfect.'

'That's the prevailing opinion, anyway.'

'And I'm a little sleepy and the least bit horny, and isn't Duke Ellington divine? Thief that you are, why don't you steal a little kiss?'

'God knows where that might lead.'

'He's not the only one.'

9

I woke up around seven to let her out. I have several locks on the door in addition to the police lock, and she was having a hell of a time getting them all lined up. I unlocked everything and told her I'd call her, and she said that would be nice, and we gave each other one of those near-miss kisses you exchange when one or more of you has not recently employed a toothbrush.

I locked up after her and went to the bathroom, where I employed a toothbrush and swallowed a couple of aspirin. I thought about breakfast, thought better of it, and decided to lie down for a minute to give the aspirins a chance to work.

Next thing I knew, someone was pummeling my door. I thought first that it was Denise, come to retrieve something. But it didn't sound like her. Nor did it sound like little Mrs Hesch, my one friend in that soulless building. Mrs Hesch drops by now and again to pour me a cup of great coffee and bitch about the building management's failure to keep the washers and dryers in good repair. But Mrs Hesch is a little bird of a woman, not much given to pounding on one's door.

More knocking. I had my feet on the floor now and some of the fog was starting to lift from my brain. It was cops, of course, as I realized as soon as I was awake enough to be capable of things like realization. Nobody else knocks like that, as if you should have been expecting them and ought to have met them at the door.

I went to the door and asked who it was. 'Well, it ain't Santy Claus,' said a recognizable voice. 'Open up, Bern.'

'Oh, hell.'

'What kind of attitude is that?'

'You picked a bad time,' I said. 'Why don't I meet you in the lobby in say five minutes?'

'Why don't you open the door in say ten seconds?'

'The thing is,' I said, 'I'm not dressed.'

'So?'

'Give me a minute.'

What time was it, anyway? I found my watch and learned it was a few minutes past nine, which meant I was going to be late opening up the store. I might miss selling a few three-for-a-buck books as a result, and while that's hard to take seriously when you've just stolen something with a six-figure price tag, standards must be maintained.

I got into some clothes, splashed a handful of cold water on my face, and opened a window to air the place out a little. Then I unlocked all my locks for the second time that morning, and Ray Kirschmann shook his head at them as he lumbered across my threshold.

'Look at that,' he said. 'Figure you got enough security devices there, Bern?'

Security devices, yet. Anybody but a cop would have called the damn things locks. 'They say you can't be too careful,' I said.

'That's what they say, all right. Police lock's new, isn't it? You gettin' paranoid in your old age?'

'Well, we've had a rash of burglaries in the neighborhood. Four or five right in this building.'

'Even with the doorman on the job?'

'He's not exactly the Secret Service,' I said. 'Incidentally, I must not have heard him ring to announce you.'

'I sort of told him not to take the trouble, Bern. I said I'd just make things easy and go straight up.'

'Did you tell him you were Santa Claus?'

'Why would I do that?'

'Because that's who's going to have to take care of him at Christmas. I'm not even putting coal in his stocking.'

'Funny. What did you have, company last night?'

'You didn't get that from the doorman.'

He looked pleased. 'I'm a detective,' he said. 'What I did, I detected it. Well, look around, Bern. Ashtray full of cigarette butts and you don't smoke. Two glasses, one on each of the bedside tables. If she's hidin' in the bathroom, tell her to come join the party.'

'She already went home, but I'm sure she'd appreciate the invitation.'

'She's not here?'

'No. You missed her by a couple hours.'

'Well, thank God for small favors.'

'Huh?'

'Now I can use your bathroom.'

When he emerged from it I was sipping a glass of orange juice and feeling more alert, if not altogether on top of things. 'You just dropped in to use the John,' I said. 'Right?'

'You kiddin', Bern? I came by to see you. We don't see each other that often.'

'I know. It's been ages.'

'It seems I only see you when somebody gets killed. You had overnight company, huh? That's not bad, two nights in a row.'

'The other night I was at her place.'

'Same lady, huh?'

'That's right.'

'Handy.'

'Ray, it's always wonderful to see you,' I said, 'but I overslept and I'm late getting to the store as it is, and—'

'Business comes first, right?'

'Something like that.'

'Sure, I know how it is, Bern. I wouldn't be here myself if it wasn't business. Who's got the time for social calls, right?'

'Right.'

'So I guess you got yourself an alibi for last night. The little lady who smoked all the cigarettes.'

'She's not so little. There are those who would call her gawky. And I already told Richler all that. I'll give her name if I absolutely have to, if I'm charged and booked, but until then—'

'That's the night before last, Bern. The Colcannon job, I'm talkin' about last night.'

'What about last night?'

'Tell me about it. Matter of fact, take it from when I dropped you off at the store yesterday around noon. Run it down for me.'

'What's last night got to do with anything?'

'You first, Bern.'

He listened attentively, and I could almost see wheels turning behind his forehead. Just because his integrity's for sale doesn't change the fact that Ray Kirschmann's a pretty good cop. It is not for nothing that he is known as the best cop money can buy.

When I was finished he frowned, sucked at his teeth, clucked his tongue, yawned, and allowed as to how my alibi sounded pretty good.

'It's not an alibi,' I said. 'It's what I did yesterday. An alibi's when something happened and you have to prove you didn't do it.'

'Right.'

'What happened?'

'Friend of yours got hisself killed. Least he used to be a friend of yours. Before you went straight and gave up burgling for books.'

I felt a chill. He could have meant anyone but I knew without a moment's doubt just who it was that he was talking about.

'A top fence. What the papers'll call a notorious receiver of stolen goods, except they better say *alleged* because he never took a fall for it. Somebody got into his apartment yesterday and beat him to death.'

10

'You're not a suspect,' Ray assured me. 'Nobody on the case even gave a thought to you. Then I went in this morning and I got the word on Crowe and the first person I thought of was you. "Here I just saw my old friend Bernie Rhodenbarr yesterday," I said to myself, "and here's an old friend of his that turns up murdered, and one thing Crowe and the Colcannon woman got in common is they both died from a beatin'." So what I thought is you might know somethin'. What do you know, Bern?'

'Nothing.'

'Yeah. But what do you know besides that?'

We were in the same car we'd ridden in a day ago, and once again he was driving me to my store. I told him I hadn't seen Abel Crowe since a friend and I had watched the fireworks from his living-room window almost a year ago.

'Yeah, that's some view,' he said. 'I dropped by on my way to your place just to see what I could see. What I could see was half of Jersey from the living-room window. That's where they found the body, over by the window, all crumpled in a heap. You never saw him since the Fourth of July?'

'We may have talked a few times on the phone, but not recently. And I haven't seen him since last July.'

'Yeah. What happened yesterday, a neighbor rang his bell around six, six-thirty in the afternoon. When he didn't answer she got concerned and checked with the doorman, and he didn't remember Crowe leavin' the buildin'. An old man like that, you worry about his heart or maybe he had a fall, things like that. The guy was seventy-one.'

'I didn't realize he was that old.'

'Yeah, seventy-one. So the doorman went upstairs, or more likely he sent somebody, the elevator operator or a porter or somebody, and they tried the door. But that didn't do 'em any good because he had police locks like you got on your door. A different model, the kind with the bolt that slides across.'

'I know.'

'Oh, yeah? You remember his locks clear from last July?'

500

'Now that you mention it I do. The business I was in, you tend to pay attention to locks.'

'I'll bet you do. What they did, they banged on the door and tried to get an answer, and then they called the precinct and a patrolman was sent up, and what could he do? He tried to force the door and you can't with a lock like that, and finally someone got the bright idea to call a locksmith, and by the time they found someone who would come and he finally got there and managed to open the lock it must have been close to ten o'clock.'

Indeed it must have. It wasn't too much earlier than that when I last tried Abel's number, and if they'd gotten in earlier some cop would have answered Abel's telephone.

'They almost expected to find the old man lyin' dead there,' he went on. 'What they didn't expect was to find him murdered.'

'There's no question it was murder?'

'No question at all. The Medical Examiner on the scene said so, although you didn't have to be a doctor to see it. It wasn't one blow. Somebody hit him a lot of times in the face and over the head.'

'God.'

'Time of death's a guess at this stage, but the ballpark figure is early afternoon yesterday. So you could have raced up there after I dropped you at the store, killed the old man, then raced back down to open up for business. Just a little lunch-hour homicide. Except that's not your style an' we both know it, plus I got a look at your face when I told you about Crowe bein' dead, Bern, and you were learnin' it for the first time.'

We caught a light at Thirty-seventh Street and he braked the car. 'The thing is,' he said, 'it's a coincidence, isn't it? Colcannon and now this, both hit on the head and both dead and not twenty-four hours apart. More like twelve hours.'

'Was Crowe's apartment robbed?'

'It wasn't taken apart. If anybody stole anything it didn't show. I got there long after the lab crew came and went, but even so there wasn't much of a mess. But maybe the killer knew where to look. Did Crowe keep large sums of cash around the apartment?'

'I wouldn't know.'

'Sure you would, but we'll let it pass. Maybe it was straight robbery and murder, with the killer forcing the old man to fork over the money, then killing him. Or maybe it was somebody with a reason to kill him, a motive. He have any enemies?'

'Not that I know of.'

'Maybe he cheated somebody and yesterday it caught up with him. He had a long life. You can make a lot of enemies in seventy-one years.'

'He was a nice man. He ate pastries and quoted Spinoza.'

'And bought things from people who didn't own them.'

I shrugged.

'Who did the Colcannon job?'

'How would I know?'

'You had some connection there, Bern. And one way or another Colcannon ties into Abel Crowe.'

'How?'

'Maybe the old man set it up. Fences do that all the time, set up a place and get a burglar to knock it off. Maybe he did that and then there was an argument over the payoff. When Wanda Colcannon got killed maybe he decided there was more heat than he wanted to handle and he refused to buy whatever they stole, or wouldn't pay the price that was set in advance. Something like that.'

'I suppose it's possible.'

We batted it around until we were at the curb in front of Barnegat Books. I'd glanced at the Poodle Factory as we drove by and Carolyn was open for business. I started to thank Ray for the ride but he interrupted me with a heavy hand on my shoulder.

'You know more than you're lettin' on, Bern.'

'I know it's hard enough to make a living selling used books. It's impossible if you never open the store.'

'There's a killer out there,' he said. 'Maybe that's somethin' you oughta remember. He killed the Colcannon woman and he killed Crowe, and I'd say that's beginnin' to make him look like one dangerous son of a bitch.'

'So?'

'So we'll pick him up before too long. Meanwhile, there's that Colcannon loot floatin' around, and who knows what else is up for grabs? And you always did have itchy fingers, Bern.'

'I don't know what you're getting at.'

' 'Course you don't. Just a couple of suggestions. If you know who did the killin', or if you happen to get wind of it, I'm the person you tell. Got that?'

'Fair enough.'

'I'd like to bag whoever did it. Crowe was a nice old gentleman. The two times I met him, we never had anythin' we could make stick, nothin' that even came close, but he was a gentleman all the same. What he was, he was generous.' Free with a bribe, in other words. 'And there's another thing.'

'Oh?'

'There's money in this, Bern. I keep gettin' this sense of money, you know what I mean? I'd say I smell it, but that's not it because it ain't a smell, it's a feel in the air. You know what I mean?'

'I know what you mean.'

'Like the feel right before it rains. So the thing is, Bern, if you're out there and it starts rainin' money, don't forget you got a partner.'

11

Carolyn came over around twelve-fifteen with a sack of carry-out from Mamoun's. We had a felafel sandwich apiece and split a side order of roasted peppers. They made a nice mint tea there and we each drank a container of it. The stuff comes with the sugar already in it, and that reminded Carolyn of the sugar hangover she'd had the day before, and that reminded her of Abel, and she wondered aloud what he was having for lunch, what sort of yummy good he was ingesting even as we spoke.

'He's not,' I said.

'How do you know?'

'He's dead,' I said, and while she sat staring at me I told her what I had learned from Ray Kirschmann. He had told me to remember I had a partner, and I had indeed remembered, but somehow I hadn't had the heart to go straight to the Poodle Factory and ruin Carolyn's day. So I'd opened the store instead, and dawdled in it, figuring it would be time enough when I saw her. Then she'd appeared with lunch and I had postponed the revelation so as to avoid ruining our appetites, and then, once the subject had come up, I'd blurted.

She listened all the way through, her frown deepening all the while. When I'd finished, and after we had spent a few minutes telling each other what a fine man Abel was and how obscene it was that he'd been murdered, she asked me who did it.

'No idea.'

'You think it was the same ones who murdered Wanda Colcannon?'

'I don't see how. The police don't suspect a link between the Colcannon burglary and Abel's death. Ray does. He's positive there's a connection. But the only thing that connects Colcannon and Abel is us, and we're not connected with either one of the murders. So there's no real link between the house on West Eighteenth Street and the apartment on Riverside Drive, except that we took something from one place and left it at the other.'

'Maybe that's the link.'

'The coin?'

She nodded. 'Twelve hours after we left it with him he was dead. Maybe someone killed him for it.'

'Who?'

'I don't know.'

'Who would even know he had it?'

'Somebody he was trying to sell it to.'

I thought it over. 'Maybe. Say he got up yesterday morning and called somebody to come over and have a look at the coin. Guy comes over, has a look, likes what he sees. More than that – one look and he knows he has to own the coin.'

'But he can't afford it.'

'Right. He can't afford it but he has to have it, and he gets carried away and picks up something heavy. Like what?'

'Who knows? A bookend, maybe.'

A natural object for her to think of, given our surroundings. And, in those very surroundings, she had once picked up a bronze bust of Immanuel Kant which I'd been using as a bookend in the philosophy and religion section, only to bounce it off the skull of a murderer who'd been holding a gun on me at the time.

'Maybe a bookend,' I agreed. 'He gets carried away, brains Abel with the bookend, puts the 1913 V-Nickel in his pocket, and away he goes. And on his way he locks up after himself.'

'Huh?'

'The doors were locked. Remember the police locks with the sliding bolts? The killer locked up after. Now I tend to do that after a burglary, picking the locks all over again, but who else do you know who does? And what passionate numismatist would think to do it, let alone have the ability?'

'Why wouldn't he just lock the door with Abel's keys?'

'Oh,' I said.

'Did I say something wrong, Bern?'

'I would have thought of it myself sooner or later,' I said sullenly. 'In another minute I would have thought of it.'

'It's just that you're not used to the idea of locking and unlocking doors with a key.'

'Maybe.'

'Anyway, it's interesting he thought of it. Most people would just get out of there and be satisfied with the lock that locks when you close the door.'

'The spring lock.'

'Right, the spring lock. But he must have wanted to keep the body from being discovered for as long as possible, and that mattered enough to him to make him take the trouble to find Abel's keys.'

'Maybe he didn't have to look for them.'

'Maybe. Even so—'

'Right,' I said. 'But so what? We still don't know anything much about him that we didn't know before we went through all this, except that he's reasonably clever and that he doesn't let a little thing like murder throw him off-stride. I can't see any reason to suspect either set of Colcannon burglars. The ones that got there before we did were slobs. They would never know about Abel and they never would have been capable of getting into his apartment. They evidently stole a ton of stuff from the Colcannon house and they'll have to fence it some-where or other, but I can't believe they tried to use Abel. Even if burglars like that knew him, he'd be all wrong for what they stole. They must have loaded up on silver and furs, all the things Colcannon didn't keep in the safe, and Abel pretty much limited himself to stamps and coins and jewelry.'

'And the ones who got there after we did?'

'The ones who killed Wanda Colcannon? We have to assume they just dropped in because the broken skylight looked like an engraved invitation. What quirk of fate do you figure got them all the way to Riverside Drive?'

'I guess they're out.'

'I guess so. And I guess the cops'll have to work this one out for themselves, because I'm stumped. The best thing we've come up with so far is a homicidal numismatist who locks up after himself, and how many of those have you known in your life? I figure they're in the same category as hen's teeth and 1913 V-Nickels. I'm sorry he's dead, dammit. I liked him.'

'So did I.'

'And I'm sorry Wanda Colcannon's dead, even though I never met her. I'm sorry we got involved in this mess in the first place, and if I'm glad of anything it's that we're out of it. I think it's time I unlocked my own door again and tried selling a few books.'

'I better get back myself. I got a dog to wash.'

'Catch you later?'

'Sure.'

Five hours later we were continuing our conversation at the Bum Rap, she with a martini, I with Scotch and water. I'd had a long slow afternoon, the store full of customers who browsed endlessly without buying anything. On days like that it's murder trying to keep up with the shoplifters, and I'm pretty sure a studious lank-haired young woman got away with a copy of Sartre's *Being and Nothingness*. If she reads it, I figure that's punishment enough.

'I just hope the police wrap up both killers in a hurry,' I told Carolyn. 'We're out of it for the moment, and if they close both cases we'll stay out of it, and that would be fine with me.'

'And if they don't?'

'Well, we *were* at Abel's place the night before last, and if they really dig they might try showing my picture to the doorman, and he might remember me. I told Ray I haven't been over there since July. There's no law against telling a lie to a policeman, but it doesn't make them look on you with favor. I've got an alibi, but I don't know how well it'll hold up.'

'What alibi?'

'Denise.'

'That's for last night, Bern. We were at Abel's the night before.'

'Denise is my alibi for both nights.'

'I hope she knows it.'

'We talked about it.'

'She knows about the Colcannon job?'

'She knows they suspected me. I told her I had nothing to do with the murder. I didn't mention that I happened to burgle the place earlier.'

'Because she thinks you're retired.'

'Something like that. At least she tells herself she thinks I'm retired. God knows what women think.'

'So the bony blabbermouth is your alibi. I wondered why you were seeing her last night.'

'That's not why.'

'It's not?'

'It's not the only reason. I don't know what you've got against Denise. She always speaks well of you.'

'The hell she does. She can't stand me.'

'Well—'

'I don't know what kind of an alibi she'll make. She doesn't strike me as the type to lie convincingly. I hope you won't need her.'

'So do I.'

She signaled for another round of drinks. The waitress brought them to our table, and Carolyn's eyes followed her as she walked away. 'She's new,' she said. 'What's her name, did you happen to notice?'

'I think someone called her Angela.'

'Pretty name.'

'I suppose.'

'She's pretty, too. Don't you think?'

'She's all right.'

'Probably straight.' She drank some of her martini. 'What do you think?'

'About the waitress?'

'Yeah. Angela.'

'What about her? Whether she's straight or gay?'

'Yeah.'

'How should I know?'

'Well, you could have an impression.'

'I don't,' I said. 'All I've noticed is what she plays on the jukebox. Fall in love with her and you'll spend the rest of your life listening to

506

country and western. You'll have Barbara Mandrell coming out of your ears. Could we forget about Angela for a minute?'

'You could. I'm not sure I can. Yeah, sure, Bern. What is it?'

'Well, I was thinking about Abel. About the murderous coin collector who did him in.'

'And?'

'And I don't believe it,' I said. 'The timing's no good. Say he goes to sleep right after we leave, gets up first thing in the morning and calls a collector. The guy comes over almost immediately, kills Abel and leaves. That's about how it would have had to happen, and Abel wouldn't work it that way. He'd have wanted to turn it over quickly, but not that quickly. First he'd want to convince himself the coin was genuine, and didn't he say something about X-raying it? He'd have done that first, and he'd have waited to see what kind of heat the Colcannon job generated, and if the theft of the V-Nickel was reported in the press. That would help determine the price he could charge for it, so he wouldn't sell it until he had the information. I don't think his murder had a damned thing to do with that coin, because I don't think anyone in the world outside of you and me had the slightest idea that he had it. Nobody followed us there. Nobody saw us walk in. And we didn't tell anybody anything. At least I didn't.'

'Who would I tell? You're the only person who knows I ever do anything besides groom dogs.'

'Then someone had another reason for killing Abel. Maybe it was a straight and simple robbery. Maybe somebody else tried to sell him something and they argued. Or maybe it was someone from his past.'

'You mean Dachau? Someone he knew in the concentration camp?'

'It's possible, or maybe someone from his more recent past. I don't know much about him. I know Crowe's not the name he was born with. He told me once that his name was originally Amsel, which means blackbird in German. From blackbird to crow is a simple leap. But another time he told me the same story except the name wasn't Amsel, it was Schwarzvogel. That means blackbird, too, but you'd think he'd remember which one of the words was his original name. Unless neither was.'

'He was Jewish, wasn't he?'

'I don't think so.'

'Then what was he doing in Dachau?'

'You know the rye-bread ads? "You don't have to be Jewish to love Levy's." Well, you didn't have to be Jewish to go to Dachau. Abel told me he was a political prisoner, a Social Democrat. That may have been the truth, or he could have landed there for some ordinary crime – receiving stolen goods, for instance. Or maybe he was gay. That was another good way to get to Dachau.'

She shuddered.

'The thing is,' I went on, 'I don't know a hell of a lot about Abel's past. It's possible nobody does. But he could have made an enemy along the way. Or it could have been a robbery or a disagreement or any damned thing. If he *was* gay, for example, maybe he brought a hustler home and got killed out of simple meanness, or for the money in his wallet.'

'It happens all the time. Do you really think he could have been gay, Bern? He kept trying to marry the two of us off. If he was gay himself, wouldn't he have been quicker to pick up on the fact that I'm not your standard marriage material?' She finished her drink. 'And isn't the whole thing too much of a coincidence? His death and Wanda's death, one right after the other?'

'Only because we're the link between them. But we're not connected with their deaths, and we're the only link between them otherwise, you and I and the nickel. And that's no link at all.'

'I guess not.'

I made interlocking rings on the tabletop with the wet bottom of my Scotch glass. 'Maybe I'm just telling myself this because it's what I want to believe,' I said. 'Except that I'm not altogether sure I want to believe it anyway, because of where it leads.'

'You just lost me.'

'The nickel,' I said. 'The 1913 V-Nickel, the Colcannon nickel, the one we could have taken $17,500 for if we hadn't picked pie in the sky instead.'

'Don't remind me.'

'If he wasn't killed for the nickel,' I said, 'and if he was murdered by some clown who didn't even *know* about the nickel, don't you see what that means?'

'Oh.'

'Right. The nickel's still there.'

I spent the evening at home. Dinner was a can of chili with some extra cumin and cayenne stirred in to pep it up. I ate it in front of the television set and kept it company with a bottle of Carta Blanca. I caught the tail end of the local news while the chili was heating. There was a brief and uninformative item about Abel, nothing about the Colcannon burglary. I watched John Chancellor while I ate, and I sat through half of *Family Feud* before I overcame inertia sufficiently to get up and turn it off.

I tidied up, stacked a mix of jazz and classical music on the record player, settled in with the latest *Antiquarian Bookman*, a magazine consisting almost exclusively of dealers' lists of books they wish to acquire for resale. I scanned the ads lazily, making a mark now and then when I found something I remembered having in stock. Several of the marks I made were for books presently reposing on my bargain table, and if I could sell them to someone who was actively seeking them I could certainly get more than forty cents apiece for them.

If I took the trouble to write to the advertisers and wait for their orders and wrap the books and ship them. That was the trouble with the used-book business. There were so many niggling things you had to attend to, so much watching the pence in hope that the pounds would take care of themselves. I didn't make a decent living from Barnegat Books, didn't even make a profit at it, but I probably could have if I'd had that infinite capacity for taking pains that success seems to demand.

The thing is, I love the book business. But I like to do it my way, which is to say in a distinctly casual fashion. Burglary spoils one. When you've grown accustomed to turning a big dollar in a few hours by means of illegal entry, it's hard to work up much enthusiasm for a lot of routine work that won't yield more than the price of a movie ticket.

Still, it was fun reading through the ads and checking off titles. Even if I'd probably never follow it up.

I called Denise around nine. Jared answered, told me *Babel-17* was all he'd hoped it would be, then summoned his mother to the phone. We talked for a few minutes about nothing in particular. Carolyn's name came up, I don't remember how, and Denise referred to her as 'that lesbian dwarf, the fat little one who always smells of Wet Dog.'

'Funny,' I said, 'she always speaks well of you.'

Carolyn called a little later. 'I was thinking about what we were talking about,' she said. 'You're not going to do anything about it, are you?'

'I guess not.'

'Because it's impossible, Bern. Remember the conversation we had with Abel? The fire escape's on the front of the building and he's got gates on the window anyway. And the doorman takes his job twice as seriously as Saint Peter, and there are those police locks on the doors—'

'There used to be,' I said, 'but the cops got a locksmith to open one of them.'

'What's the difference? You still can't get into the building.'

'I know.'

'And it's driving you crazy, isn't it?'

'How'd you guess?'

'Because it's driving me crazy, too. Bernie, if we hadn't already stolen the damned coin once, and all you knew about it was that it was probably somewhere in that apartment, an apartment the police have probably sealed off because someone was killed in it yesterday, and you knew what kind of security they have in the building and all, and you knew that the coin was probably hidden somewhere in the apartment and that you wouldn't even know where to start looking for it,

509

assuming it was there in the first place, which you can't be positive of—'

'I get the picture, Carolyn.'

'Well, assuming all that, would you even think twice about stealing the coin?'

'Of course not.'

'That's what I mean.'

'But we already stole it once.'

'I know.'

'And that makes me tend to think of it as my coin,' I explained. 'They say thieves don't respect private property. Well, I have a very strongly developed sense of private property, as long as it's my property we're talking about. And it's not just the money, either. I had a great rarity in my hands and now I've got nothing. Think what a blow that is to the old self-esteem.'

'So what are you going to do about it?'

'Nothing.'

'That's good.'

'Because there's nothing I *can* do.'

'Right. That's what I wanted to check, Bern. I'm on my way over to the Duchess. Maybe I'll get lucky and meet somebody sensational.'

'Good luck.'

'I'm so goddamn restless lately. Must be a full moon. Maybe I'll run into Angela. She'll be feeding the jukebox and playing all the Anne Murray records. I guess she must be straight, huh?'

'Anne Murray?'

'Angela. Figure she's straight?'

'Probably.'

'If she's straight and Abel was gay they could have raised poodles together.'

'And you could have clipped them.'

'I could have clipped the poodles, too. Jesus, how do I get out of this conversation?'

'I don't know. Which way did you get in?'

'Bye, Bern.'

The eleven o'clock news brought no fresh revelations, and who wants a stale one? I turned the set off as soon as they'd announced who Johnny's guests were, grabbed a jacket and went out. I hiked up West End Avenue, took a left at Eighty-sixth, walked the rest of the way on Riverside Drive.

The air was cooler now, and heavy with impending rain. You couldn't see any stars but you hardly ever can in New York, even on cloudless nights. The pollution's always thick enough to obscure them. I did see a moon, about half full with a haze around it. That means something, either that it's going to rain or it isn't, but I can never remember which.

There were a surprising number of people on the street – joggers plodding around Riverside Park, dog owners walking their pets, other people bringing home a quart of milk and the early edition of the *Times*. I crossed the street for a better view and looked up at Abel's building, counting floors to find his window. It was dark, naturally enough. I let my eyes travel around the corner and noted the fire escape on the Eighty-ninth Street side. It looked substantial enough, but it was right out there in plain view and you couldn't reach the bottom rungs from the sidewalk unless you had a long ladder.

Pointless anyway. As Carolyn had made quite clear.

I walked toward Ninetieth Street. The building immediately adjacent to Abel's stood three stories taller, which meant I couldn't get from its roof to Abel's unless I was prepared to lower myself on a rope. I wasn't, nor did I have any reason to assume security there would be any less rigid than at its neighbor. I returned to Eighty-ninth Street and walked a few doors past Abel's building. It was bounded on that side by a long row of late-nineteenth-century brownstones, all of them four stories tall. The windows in Abel's building that looked out over the brownstones were too high to be readily accessible from the rooftop, and there were steel guards over them anyway.

I started walking toward West End Avenue again, then doubled back for another look, feeling like an addled criminal drawn irresistibly back to the scene of someone else's crime. The doorman was the same stiff-spined black man who'd been on duty during our previous visit, and he looked as formidable as ever. I watched him from across the street. Waste of time, I told myself. I wasn't accomplishing anything. I was as restless as Carolyn and instead of going to the Duchess I was going through the motions.

I crossed the street, approached the entrance. The building was a massive old pile of brick, safe as a fortress and solid as the Bank of England. Engaged columns of a dull red marble flanked the double entrance doors. Bronze plaques on either side announced the professional tenants within. I noted three shrinks, a dentist, an ophthalmologist, a podiatrist and a pediatrician, a fairly representative Upper West Side mix.

I saw no plaque for Abel Crowe, Receiver of Stolen Goods, and I shook my head at the thought. Give me half a chance and I can become disgustingly maudlin.

The doorman approached, asked if he could help me. I got the feeling he'd lately graduated with honors from an assertiveness-training workshop.

'No,' I said sadly. 'Too late for that.' And I turned away and went home.

The phone rang while I unlocked all of my locks and gave up in mid-ring as I was shoving the door open. If it's important, I told myself, they'll call back.

I took a shower which no one could have called premature, got into bed, dozed off. I was dreaming about a perilous descent – a fire escape, a catwalk, something vague – when the phone rang. I sat up, blinked a few times, answered it.

'I want the coin,' a male voice said.

'Huh?'

'The nickel. I want it.'

'Who is this?'

'Not important. You have the coin and I want it. Don't dispose of it. I'll contact you.'

'But—'

The phone clicked in my ear. I fumbled it back onto the receiver. The bedside clock said it was a quarter to two. I hadn't been sleeping long, just long enough to get into the swing of it. I lay down and reviewed the phone call and tried to decide whether to get up and do something about it.

While I was thinking it over I fell back asleep.

12

Murray Feinsinger's goatee had just a touch of gray in it a little to the right of center. He looked to be around forty, with a round face, a receding hairline, and massive horn-rimmed glasses that had the effect of magnifying his brown eyes. He was kneeling now and looking up at me, with my shoe in one hand and my bare foot in the other. My sock lay on the floor beside him like a dead laboratory rat.

'Narrow feet,' he said. 'Long, narrow feet.'

'Is that bad?'

'Only if it's extreme, and yours aren't. Just a little narrower than average, but you're wearing Pumas, which are a little wider than average. Not as much so as the wide versions of shoes that come in widths, but what do you need with extra width when you've got a narrow foot to begin with? Your feet wind up with too much room and that increases the tendency of the ankle to pronate. That means it turns in, like this' – he positioned my foot for demonstration – 'and that's the source of all your problems.'

'I see.'

'New Balance makes variable widths. You could try a pair on for size. Or there's Brooks – they make a good shoe and they're a little on the narrow side, and they ought to fit you fine.'

'That's great,' I said, and would have gotten up from the chair, except it's tricky when somebody's holding one of your feet. 'I'll just get a new pair of shoes,' I said, 'and then I'll be all set.'

'Not so fast, my friend. How long have you been running?'

'Not very long.'

'Matter of fact you just started. Am I right?'

As a matter of fact, I hadn't even started, and didn't intend to. But I told him he was right. And then I emitted a foolish little giggle, not because anything struck me funny but because the good Dr Feinsinger was tickling my foot.

'That tickle?'

'A little.'

'Inhibition,' he said. 'That's what makes tickling. I tickle people day in and day out. No avoiding it when you've got your hands full of other

513

people's feet for six or eight hours at a stretch. Ever tickle your own feet?'

'I never gave it a thought.'

'Well, trust me – you couldn't do it if you tried. It wouldn't work. The ticklishness is a response to being touched in a certain way by another person. Inhibition. That's what it's all about.'

'That's very interesting,' I said. Untruthfully.

'I tickle a patient less over a period of time. Not that I touch him differently. But he gets used to my touch. Less inhibited. That's what tickling's all about. And what your feet are all about, my friend, is something else again. Know what you've got?'

Five toes on each of them, I thought, and a loquacious podiatrist for company. But evidently it was something more serious than that. I hadn't expected this.

'You've got Morton's Foot,' he said.

'I do?'

'No question about it.' He curled his index finger and flicked it sharply against my index toe. 'Morton's Foot. Know what that means?'

Death, I thought. Or amputation, or thirty years in a wheelchair, and at the least I'd never play the piano again. 'I really don't know,' I admitted. 'I suppose it has something to do with salt.'

'Salt?' He looked confused, but only for a moment. 'Morton's Foot,' he said, and flicked my toe again. It didn't tickle, so maybe I was overcoming my inhibitions. 'Sounds ominous, doesn't it? All it means is that this toe here' – another flick – 'is longer than your big toe. Morton's the doctor who first described the syndrome, and what it amounts to is a structural weakness of the foot. I have a hunch it's a throwback to the time when we all lived in trees and used our big toes as thumbs and wrapped our second toes around vines and branches for leverage. Next time you get to the Bronx Zoo, make sure you go to the monkey house and look at the little buggers' feet.'

'I'll do that.'

'Not that Morton's Foot is like being born with a tail, for God's sake. In fact, it's more common to have Morton's Foot than not to have it, which is bad news for runners but good news for podiatrists. So you've not only got a nasty-sounding complaint, my friend, but you've got a very *ordinary* nasty-sounding complaint.'

All my life the only trouble I'd had with my feet was when some klutz stepped on them on the subway. Of course I'd never tried wrapping my toes around vines. I asked Feinsinger if what I had was serious.

'Not if you live a normal life. But runners' – and he chuckled with real pleasure here – 'runners give up normal life the day they buy their first pair of waffle trainers. That's when Morton's Foot starts causing problems. Pain in the ball of the foot, for example. Heel spurs, for instance. Shin splints. Achilles tendinitis. Excessive pronation –

remember our old friend pronation?' And he refreshed my memory by yanking my ankle inward. 'And then,' he said darkly, 'there's always chondromalacia.'

'There is?'

He nodded with grim satisfaction. 'Chondromalacia. The dreaded Runner's Knee, every bit as fearful as Tennis Elbow.'

'It sounds terrible.'

'Potentially terrible. But never fear,' he added brightly, 'for Feinsinger's here, and relief is right around the corner. All you need is the right pair of custom orthotics and you can run until your heart gives out. And for that I'll refer you to my brother-in-law Ralph. He's the cardiologist in the family.' He patted my foot. 'Just my little joke. Stay with running and the chances are you won't *need* a cardiologist. It's the best thing you can do for yourself. All we have to do is make sure your feet are up to it, and that's where I come in.'

Orthotics, it turned out, were little inserts for me to wear in my shoes. They would be custom-made for me out of layers of leather and cork after the good Dr Feinsinger took impressions of my feet, which he did right there and then before I had much of a chance to think about what I was getting into. He took my bare feet one at a time and pressed them into a box containing something like styrofoam, except softer.

'You've made a good first impression,' he assured me. 'Now come into the other room for a moment, my friend. I want to have a look at your bones.'

I followed him, walking springily on the balls of my feet, while he told me how my personal pair of orthotics would not only enable me to run without pain but were virtually certain to change my whole life, improve my posture and penmanship, and very likely elevate my character in the bargain. He led me into a cubicle down the hall where a menacing contraption with a faintly dental air about it was mounted on the wall. He had me sit in a chair and swung the gadget out from the wall so that a cone-shaped protuberance was centered over my right foot.

'I don't know about this,' I said.

'Guaranteed painless. Trust me, friend.'

'You hear a lot of things about X-rays, don't you? Sterility, things like that.'

'All I take is a one-second exposure and nothing goes higher than the ankle. Sterility? There's such a thing as the ball of the foot, my friend, but unless you've actually got your balls in your feet I assure you you've got nothing to worry about.'

In a matter of minutes the machine had done its nasty work and I was back in the other room pulling up my socks and lacing up my Pumas. They had never felt wide before, but they certainly felt wide now. With every step I took I imagined my Mortonic feet slipping dangerously from side to side. Heel spurs, shin splints, the dreaded Runner's Knee—

And then we were back in the reception room where I let a redhead with a Bronx accent book an appointment three weeks hence for me to pick up my orthotics. 'The full price is three hundred dollars,' she told me, 'and that includes the lab charges and this visit and all subsequent visits, in case you need any adjustments. It's a one-time charge and there's nothing additional, and of course it's fully deductible for taxes.'

'Three hundred dollars,' I said.

'No cost compared to other sports,' Feinsinger said. 'Look what you'd spend on a single ski weekend, let alone buying your equipment. Look at the hourly rates they're getting for tennis courts. All you have to do to get the full benefits of running is get out there and run, and isn't it worth it to spend a few dollars on the only feet God gave you?'

'And running's good for me, I guess.'

'Best thing in the world for you. Improves your cardiovascular system, tones your muscles, keeps you trim and fit. But your feet take a pounding, and if they're not set up to handle the task—'

Three hundred dollars still seemed pretty pricey for a custom version of the little arch supports they sell for $1.59 at the corner drugstore. But it dawned on me that I didn't have to pay it now, that a thirty-dollar deposit would keep everybody happy, and in three weeks' time they could sit around wondering why I hadn't shown up. I handed over three tens and pocketed the receipt the redhead handed me.

'Running must be great for podiatrists,' I ventured.

Feinsinger beamed. 'Nothing like it,' he said. 'Nothing in the world. You know what this business was a few years ago? Old ladies with feet that hurt. Of course they hurt, they weighed three hundred pounds and bought shoes that were too small. I removed corns, I wrapped bunions, I did a little of this and a little of that and I told myself I was a professional person and success wasn't all that important to me.

'Now it's a whole new world. Sports podiatry is my entire practice. Feinsinger orthotics were on the road in Boston last month. Feinsinger orthotics carried dozens upon dozens of runners to the finish line of the New York Marathon last October. I have patients who love me. They know I'm helping them and they love me. And I'm a success. You're lucky I had a cancellation this morning or I'd never have been able to fit you in. I'm booked way in advance. And you want to know something? I like success. I like getting ahead in the world. You get a taste of it, my friend, and you develop an appetite for it.'

He dropped an arm around my shoulders, led me through a waiting room where several slender gentlemen sat reading back copies of *Runner's World* and *Running Times*. 'I'll see you in three weeks,' he said. 'Meanwhile you can run in the shoes you're wearing. Don't buy new shoes because you'll want to have the orthotics when you try 'em on. Just go nice and easy for the time being. Not too far and not too fast, and I'll see you in three weeks.'

Out in the hallway, the Pumas felt incredibly clumsy. Odd I'd never noticed their ungainly width in the past. I walked on down the carpeted hall to the elevator, glanced over my shoulder, looked around furtively, and went on past the elevator to open the door to the stairwell.

I wasn't sure what effect Morton's Foot might have on stairclimbing. Was I running a heavy risk of the dreaded Climber's Fetlock?

I went ahead and took my chances. Murray Feinsinger's office was on the fourth floor, which left me with seven flights to ascend. I was panting long before I reached my destination, either because my feet lacked the benefit of orthotics or because my cardiovascular system had not yet been improved by long-distance running. Or both of the above.

Whatever the cause, a minute or two was time enough for me to catch my breath. Then I eased the door open, looked both ways much like a tractable child about to cross a street, and walked past the elevator and down another carpeted hallway to the door of Abel Crowe's apartment.

Well, why else would I be getting my feet tickled? I had awakened a few hours earlier, had a shower and a shave, and while I sat spreading gooseberry preserves on an English muffin and waiting for my coffee to drip through, I recalled my reconnaissance mission to Riverside Drive and the telephone call that had interrupted my sleep.

Someone wanted the coin.

That wasn't news. When an object originally valued at five cents has increased over the years by a factor of approximately ten million, the world is full of people who wouldn't be averse to calling it their own. Who wouldn't want a 1913 Liberty Head Nickel?

But my caller not only wanted the coin. He wanted it from me. Which meant he knew the coin had been liberated from Colcannon's safe, and he knew furthermore just who had been the instrument of its delivery.

Who was he? And how might he know a little thing or two like that?

I poured my coffee, munched my muffin, and sat a while in uffish thought. I found myself thinking of that impregnable fortress where my friend Abel had lived and died, and where the coin – my coin! – survived him. I pictured that doorman, a gold-braided Cerberus at the gate of hell, a three-headed Bouvier des Flandres in burgundy livery. (The old mind's not at its best first thing in the morning, but the imagination is capable of great flights of fancy.) I visualized that entrance, those dull rosy marble columns, the bronze plaques. Three shrinks, a dentist, a pediatrician, a podiatrist, an ophthalmologist—

Whereupon dawn broke.

517

I finished breakfast and became very busy. I hadn't remembered the names on those plaques, or bothered noticing them in the first place, so for openers I cabbed up to Eighty-ninth and Riverside, where I sauntered nonchalantly past the entrance and quickly memorized the seven names in question. A few doors down the street I took a moment to jot them all down before they fled my memory, and then I continued east to Broadway, where I had a cup of coffee at the counter of a Cuban Chinese luncheonette. Perhaps the Cuban food's good there, or the Chinese food. The coffee tasted as though each roasted bean had been tossed lightly in rancid butter before grinding.

I turned a dollar into dimes and made phone calls. I tried the psychiatrists first and found them all booked up through the following week. I made an appointment with the last of them for a week from Monday, figuring I could always show up for it if nothing else materialized by then, by which time a shrink's services might be just what I needed.

Then I looked at the four remaining names. The pediatrician would be tricky, I decided, unless I wanted to borrow Jared Raphaelson for the occasion, and I wasn't sure that I did. The dentist might be able to fit me in, especially if I pleaded an emergency, but did I want some unknown quantity belaboring my mouth? As things stand, I get free life-time dental care from Craig Sheldrake, the World's Greatest Dentist, and I'd last seen Craig just a couple of weeks ago when I'd dropped by for a cleaning. My mouth was in no need of a dentist's attention, and I didn't feel much like saying Ah.

The ophthalmologist looked like the best choice, better even than the shrinks. An eye exam doesn't take long, either. I'd have to make sure he didn't put drops in my eyes, since that could make lockpicking a far cry from child's play. And wasn't I about due to get my eyes looked at? I had never needed glasses, and I hadn't yet noticed myself holding books at arm's length, but neither was I getting younger with each passing day, and they say it's a good idea to get your eyes checked annually so that you can nip glaucoma in the bud, or the pupil or iris, or wherever one nips it, and—

And I made the call and the guy was in the Bahamas until a week from Monday.

So I called Murray Feinsinger's office, wondering upon what pretext a podiatric appointment might be booked, and a young woman with a Bronx accent (and, I was to learn, with red hair as well) asked me the nature of my problem.

'It's my feet,' I said.

'You a runner or a dancer?'

Dancers look like dancers. Anybody can look like a runner. All you have to do is sweat and wear funny shoes.

'A runner,' I said, and she gave me an appointment.

Whereupon I went home and changed my Weejuns for my Pumas, all in the interest of verisimilitude, and then I called Carolyn and begged out of our standing lunch date, pleading a doctor's appointment. She wanted to know what kind of doctor, and I said an ophthalmologist instead of a podiatrist because I'd have been stuck for an answer if she asked what was the matter with my feet. I didn't yet know I had Morton's foot with chondromalacia just a hop, skip and a jump away. When she asked what was the matter with my eyes, I muttered something about getting headaches when I did a lot of reading, and that seemed to satisfy her.

I didn't mention the middle-of-the-night phone call.

At one-fifteen I showed for my appointment with Feinsinger. The doorman called upstairs to make sure I was expected and the elevator operator lingered to check that I entered the right door. Now I was out thirty bucks and my feet felt too narrow while my shoes felt impossibly wide. Maybe I should have gone to the pediatrician instead. I could have lied about my age.

I put my ear to Abel's door, listened carefully, heard nothing. There was a button recessed in the doorjamb and I gave it a poke, and a muted bong sounded within the apartment. I heard no other sound in response to the bong, nor did a brisk knock provoke any reaction, so I took a deep breath, drew the tools of my trade from my pocket, and opened the door.

It was at least as easy as it sounds. The police had slapped a sticker on the door forbidding entry to anyone other than authorized police personnel, which I emphatically was not but, they hadn't taken the trouble to seal the apartment in any meaningful fashion, perhaps because the building's security was so forbidding. The locksmith who'd knocked off Abel's police lock (by drilling the cylinder rather than picking it, I noted with some professional disapproval) had left only the door's original lock as a deterrent to entry. It was a Segal, with both an automatic spring lock that engaged when you closed the door and a deadbolt that you had to turn with a key. The cops had probably had keys – they could have obtained one from the doorman or the super – but the last man out hadn't bothered to use one, because only the spring lock secured the door, and it was no harder to open than those childproof bottles of aspirin. It would have been faster if I'd had the key, but just barely.

I stepped inside, drew the door shut, turned the little knob to engage the deadbolt. I hesitated in the foyer, trying to figure out what was wrong. Something was bothering me and I couldn't pin it down.

The hell with it. I moved from the dimness of the foyer into the living room, where light streamed in through the windows. Near the window on the left I saw an outline in chalk, half on the burnished

519

parquet floor and half on the oriental rug. The rug was a Sarouk and it was a nice one and the chalk marks didn't do anything for it.

Looking at the outline, I could picture his body lying there, one arm outstretched, one leg pointing directly at the chair where I'd been sitting Tuesday night. I didn't want to look at the chalk marks and I didn't seem able to keep my eyes away from them. I felt funny. I turned away from them and turned back again, and then I skirted the chalk marks and walked to the window and looked out over the park, out across the river.

And then I realized what had been bothering me in the foyer. It was an absence that I had been faintly aware of, as Sherlock Holmes had remarked on the dog's not barking in the night.

The thrill was gone. That little boost I always get when I cross a threshold without an invitation, that little up feeling that comes on like coffee in a vein, simply wasn't there. I had come as a burglar, had managed entry by means of my cleverness and my skills, yet I felt neither triumph nor anticipation.

Because it was my old friend's place and he had lately died in it, and that took the joy out of the occupation.

I gazed at New Jersey in the distance – which is where it belongs. The sky had darkened in the few minutes since I'd entered the apartment. It looked like rain, which would mean either that the haze around last night's moon had been an accurate forecaster or that it had not, depending on what it's supposed to herald.

I felt a little better once I knew what was bothering me. Now I could forget about it and get on with the business of robbing the dead.

Of course that's not what I was doing. I was merely bent on recovering what was rightfully mine – or wrongfully mine, if you want to be technical about it. By no stretch of the imagination could the coin be considered Abel's property; he'd had it strictly on consignment, having neither bought nor stolen it from me.

So all I had to do was find it.

I suppose I could have aped the method of the clods who'd preceded us to the Colcannon house. The fastest way to search a place is to let the chips fall where they may, along with everything else. But that would have made it quite obvious that someone had come a-hunting, and what was the point of that? And, even if I hadn't cared about that, I'm neat by inclination, and particularly indisposed to desecrate the home of a departed friend.

Abel too had been neat. There was a place for everything and everything was already in it, and I took care to put it all back where I'd found it.

This made the process difficult beyond description. The proverbial needle in the proverbial haystack would have been a piece of cake in comparison. I started off looking in the obvious places because that's where people hide things, even the people you'd think would know better. But I found nothing but water and Ty-D-Bol in his toilet tank and nothing but flour in the flour canister and nothing but air in the hollow towel bars I unbolted from the bathroom wall. I pulled out drawers to see what was taped to their backs or bottoms. I went through the closets and checked suit pockets, thrust my hands inside shoes and boots, looked under rugs.

I could go step by step and fill a dozen pages with an explanation of the search I gave those rooms, but what's the point? Three things I didn't find were the philosopher's stone, the Holy Grail, and the golden fleece. A fourth was the Colcannon V-Nickel.

I did find any number of other interesting articles. I found books in several languages ranging in value to over a thousand dollars. It was no great accomplishment finding them; they constituted Abel Crowe's personal library and were out in the open on his shelves.

I looked behind each book, and I flipped the pages of each book, and I found nineteenth-century postage stamps from Malta and Cyprus in the pages of Hobbes's *Leviathan* and five hundred pounds in British currency tucked into a copy of *Sartor Resartus* by Thomas Carlyle. On a high shelf I found what were probably Sassanian coins tucked behind three leather-bound volumes of the poetry of Byron and Shelley and Keats.

There were two telephones in the bedroom, one on the bedside table, the other across the room on a dresser. That seemed excessive. I checked, and both of them were hooked up to wall plugs, but the one on the dresser didn't seem to be in working order. So I unscrewed the base plate and discovered that the thing had been gutted, its working parts replaced with a wad of fifties and hundreds. I counted up to $20,000, which brought me close enough to the end of the stock to estimate that it totaled perhaps $23,000 in all. I put the phone back together again, with the money back inside where I'd found it.

That's enough to give you the idea. I found no end of valuable booty, which is just what you'd expect to find in the home of a civilized and prosperous fence. I found more cash, more stamps, more coins, and a fair amount of jewelry, including the watch and earrings from the Colcannon burglary. (They were in a humidor beneath a layer of cigars. I got excited when I came upon them, thinking the nickel might be nearby, but it wasn't. I'd never known Abel to smoke a cigar.)

In his kitchen, I helped myself to a piece of dense chocolatey layer cake. I think it was of the sort he called Schwarzwälder kuchen. Black Forest cake. Except for that and the glass of milk I drank along with it, I took nothing whatsoever from Abel Crowe's apartment.

I thought of it. Every time I hit something really tempting I tried to talk myself into it, and I just couldn't manage it. You'd think it would have been easy to rationalize. As far as I knew, Abel had no heirs. If an heir did turn up, he'd probably never see half the swag stashed in that apartment. The library would be sold *en bloc* to a book dealer, who in turn would profit handsomely enough reselling the volumes individually without ever discovering the bonuses that some of them contained. The watch and earrings would wind up the property of the first cigar smoker to wander in, while the $23,000 would stay in the telephone forever. What happens to telephones when somebody dies? Do they go back to the phone company? If they don't work, does somebody repair them? Whoever repaired this particular one was in for the surprise of his life.

So why didn't I help myself?

I guess I just plain found out that robbing the dead was not something I was prepared to do. Not the newly dead, anyway. Not a dead friend. All things considered, I'll be damned if I can think of a single logical argument against robbing the dead. One would think they'd mind it a good deal less than the living. If they can't take it with them, why should they care where it goes?

And God knows the dead do get robbed. Cops do it all the time. When a derelict dies in a Bowery flophouse, the first thing the officers on the scene do is divvy up whatever cash they find. Admittedly I've always set higher standards for myself than those of a policeman, but my standards weren't all that lofty, were they?

It was hard leaving the cash. When I've broken into a home or place of business I invariably take whatever cash presents itself. Even if I've entered the place for some other purpose, I still pocket cash automatically, reflexively. I don't have to think about it. I just do it.

This time I didn't. Oddly enough, I came close to taking the Piaget watch and the emerald earrings. Not that I found them tempting, but because I thought I might take them with something approaching legitimacy. After all, Carolyn and I had stolen them to begin with.

But we had been paid for them, hadn't we? So they weren't ours any longer. They were Abel's, and they would remain in his apartment.

One of the books I paged through was the copy of Spinoza's *Ethics* we'd brought him, and when I'd run out of places to search I took it down from its shelf and flipped idly through it. Abel had made shelf space for it on the last night of his life. Perhaps he'd paused first to thumb through it, reading a sentence here, a paragraph there.

'It may easily come to pass,' I read, 'that a vain man may become proud and imagine himself pleasing to all when he is in reality a universal nuisance.'

I took the book with me when I left. I don't know why. It was Abel's property – a gift is a gift, after all – but I somehow felt entitled to reclaim it.

I guess I just hate to leave a place empty-handed.

13

I would have taken the stairs as far as Murray Feinsinger's floor, on the chance that the same elevator operator was on the job and that his memory was working overtime. But as I neared the elevator an elderly woman slowed me with a nod and a smile. She was wearing a black Persian lamb jacket and held a very small dog in her arms. It might have been a Maltese. Carolyn would have known at a glance.

'You'll be caught in the rain,' she told me. 'Go back and get your raincoat.'

'I'm running late as it is.'

'I have a plastic raincoat,' she said. 'Folded, and in my purse at all times.' She patted her shoulder bag. 'You're the Stettiner boy, aren't you? How's your mother?'

'Oh, she's fine.'

'The sore throat's better?'

'Much better.'

'That's good to hear,' she said, and scratched the little dog behind the ear. 'It must be doing her a world of good to have you home for a few days. You'll be here how long? The weekend or a little longer?'

'Well, as long as I can.'

'Wonderful,' she said. The elevator arrived, the door opened. I followed her onto it. The same operator was indeed running the car, but there was no recognition in his eyes. 'You wouldn't remember me,' the woman said. 'I'm Mrs Pomerance in 11-J.'

'Of course I remember you, Mrs Pomerance.'

'And your mother's feeling better? I'm trying to remember the last time I talked with her. I was so sorry to hear about her brother. Your uncle.'

What about him? 'Well,' I said, tightening my grip on Spinoza, 'these things happen.'

'His heart, wasn't it?'

'That's right.'

'Listen, it's not the worst way. You must have heard about our neighbor? Mr Crowe in 11-D?'

'Yes, I heard. Just the other day, wasn't it?'

'The day before yesterday, they say. You've heard what they're saying about him? That he bought from thieves? It was in the papers. Imagine in this building, after the co-op conversion and everything, and one of the residents is a man who buys from thieves. And then to be struck down and killed in his own apartment.'

'Terrible.'

We had reached the ground floor and walked together through the lobby. Just inside the entrance she stopped to clip a leash to the little dog's collar, then extracted a folded plastic raincoat from her bag. 'I'll just carry this over my arm,' she said, 'so that when it starts raining I won't have to go looking for it. That Mr Crowe – it makes a person think. He was always a nice man, he always had time for a kind word on the elevator. If he was a criminal, you would still have to say he was a good neighbor.'

We strolled past the doorman, hesitated beneath the canopy. The little dog was pulling at his leash, anxious to head west toward River-side Park. I was at least as anxious to head east.

'Well,' I said, 'he was a fence.'

'That's the word. A fence.'

'And you know what they say. Good fences make good neighbors.'

There was no point going downtown. It was already past closing time when I left Abel's apartment. I got a bus on Broadway, not wanting to get caught in the rain with Spinoza under my arm. The rain was still holding off when I got off at Seventy-second Street and walked home.

Nothing but bills and circulars in my mailbox. I carried them up-stairs, threw away the offers from those who wanted to sell me some-thing, filed the demands from those who wished to be paid. Getting and spending we lay waste our powers, I thought, and put Spinoza up there on the shelf alongside of Wordsworth.

I called Carolyn's apartment. She didn't answer. I called Narrowback Gallery and Jared answered and told me his mother was out. I called the Poodle Factory and got Carolyn's machine. I didn't leave a message.

I hung up the phone and it rang before I could get three steps away from it. I picked it up and said hello. I was about to say hello a second time when it clicked in my ear.

A wrong number. Or my caller of the night before. Or some friend who'd decided at the last moment that she didn't really want to talk to me tonight after all. Or someone, anyone, who'd merely wanted to establish that I was at home.

Or none of the above.

I got an umbrella, started for the door. The phone rang again. I let myself out, locked up after me. The ringing followed me down the hall.

*

A block away on Broadway I had a big plate of spaghetti and a large green salad with oil and vinegar. I hadn't had anything since breakfast aside from the cake and milk at Abel's apartment, and I was hungry and angry and lonely and tired, and the first of the four seemed the only one I could do anything about for the moment. Afterward I had a small portion of tortoni, which never turns out to be as interesting a dessert as one would hope, and with it I drank four tiny cups of inky espresso in quick succession, each flavored with just a drop of anisette. By the time I got out of there caffeine was perking through my veins. I was neither hungry nor tired now, and it was hard to remember what I'd been angry about. I was still lonely but I figured I could live with it.

I walked home through the rain, and I couldn't see the moon to check whether it had a haze around it. When I got back to my building, the usually stolid Armand greeted me by name. He had managed to ignore me when I'd come in earlier, and when I'd left for the restaurant. He and Felix are quite a pair, one more lethargic than the other, while the third doorman, the guy who works midnight to eight, makes it a rule never to appear sober in public. Somebody ought to send the three of them up to Eighty-ninth and Riverside for six weeks of basic training.

As I crossed the lobby, a woman got up from the floral-pattern wing chair. She looked to be around twenty-eight. A mane of loose black curls fell a few inches past her shoulders. Her face was an inverted triangle, tapering past a small mouth to a sharp chin. Her mouth was glossy with scarlet lipstick, her eyes deeply shadowed, and if her lashes were natural she must have stimulated their growth with heavy doses of chemical fertilizers.

She said, 'Mr Rhodenbarr? I got to see you.'

Well, that explained Armand's greeting. It was his subtle way of fingering me. I hoped he'd been richly rewarded for this service, because he'd just managed to work his way off my Christmas list.

'Well,' I said.

'It's kind of important. Would it be okay if we went upstairs? Like to your place?'

She batted her improbable lashes at me. Above them, two narrow curved lines replaced the brows God had given her. If thine eyebrow offend thee, pluck it out.

She looked like a masochist's dream as interpreted by the fevered pen of an adolescent cartoonist. Spike-heeled black shoes with ankle straps. Black wet-look vinyl pants that fitted like paint. A blood-red blouse of some shiny synthetic fabric, tight and clingy enough to prevent one's forgetting even momentarily that human beings are mammals.

A rolled red-and-black umbrella. A black wet-look vinyl purse, a perfect match for the pants. Gold teardrop earrings. The emeralds we'd taken from Colcannon and sold to Abel might look splendid dangling from those little lobes, I thought, and wondered if she'd like me to go back and fetch them for her.

'My place,' I said.

'Could we?'

'Why not?'

We ascended in the elevator, and in its confined space I got a full dose of her perfume. There was a lot of musk in it and some patchouli, and the effect was at once erotic and cheap. I couldn't dismiss the notion that she wasn't really wearing perfume, that she had been born smelling like that.

The elevator reached my floor. The door opened. We walked down the narrow hallway and I imagined that all my neighbors were at their doors, eyes pressed to their peepholes, for a glimpse of what the resident burglar had brought home for the night. As we passed Mrs Hesch's door, I fancied I could hear her going *tssst-tssst* in reproach.

We hadn't talked in the elevator and we didn't talk in the hallway. I felt like showing off by opening my door without a key. I restrained myself and unlocked my several locks in the conventional fashion. Inside, I bustled around switching on lamps and wishing I'd changed the sheets since Denise's visit. Not that my guest looked likely to object to rolling around in a bed where another woman had lately lain, but—

'How about a drink?' I suggested. 'What can I fix you?'

'Nothing.'

'Cup of coffee? Tea, either herb tea or tea tea?'

She shook her head.

'Well, have a seat. Might as well make yourself comfortable. And I don't think I know your name.'

I don't think I've ever felt less suave but there didn't seem to be anything I could do about it. She was tacky and obvious and completely irresistible, and I couldn't recall ever having been so thoroughly turned on in my life. I had to fight the urge to get down on my hands and knees and chew the carpet.

She didn't sit down, nor did she tell me her name. Her face clouded for an instant, and she lowered her eyes and reached into her purse.

Her hand came out with a gun in it.

'You son of a bitch,' she said. 'Stay right where you are, you son of a bitch, or I'll blow your fucking head off.'

14

I stayed right where I was, and she stayed right where she was, and the gun stayed right where it was. In her hand, wobbling a little but not a lot, and pointed straight at me.

It didn't look like a cannon. The guns that get pointed at fictional detectives always look like cannons, and the holes in their muzzles are said to resemble caverns. This gun was undeniably small, just the right size proportionally for her small hand. The latter, I noted now, was a well-shaped hand, its fingernails painted the exact shade of her blouse and her lipstick. And the gun, of course, was black, a flat black automatic pistol with no more than a two-inch barrel. Everything about this lady was red or black. Her favorite birds, I felt certain, were the red-winged blackbird and the scarlet tanager. Her favorite author would have to be Stendhal.

The phone rang. Her eyes flicked toward it, then returned to me. 'I'd better answer that,' I said.

'You move and I shoot.'

'It might be someone important. Suppose it's *Dialing for Dollars*?'

Was it my imagination or had her finger tightened on the trigger? The phone went on ringing. She was done looking at it, though, and I was incapable of looking at anything but the gun.

I don't like guns. They are cunning little machines crafted exclusively for the purpose of killing people, and it is a purpose I deplore. Guns make me nervous and I do what I can to avoid them, and consequently I don't know a great deal about them. I did know that revolvers have cylinders, which makes them suitable for Russian roulette, whereas automatics, of which my guest's was an example, are generally fitted with safety catches. When engaged, such a device prevents one from depressing the trigger sufficiently to fire the gun.

I could see what might have been a safety catch toward the rear of the gun's muzzle. And I had read enough to know that persons unfamiliar with guns sometimes forget to disengage the safety catch. If I could tell whether the safety was on or off, then perhaps—

'It's loaded,' she said. 'In case that's what you're wondering.'

'I wasn't.'

'You're wondering something,' she said. Then she said, 'Oh,' and flicked the safety catch with her thumb. 'There. Now don't you try anything, you understand?'

'Sure. If you could just point that thing somewhere else—'

'I don't want to shoot somewhere else. I want to be able to shoot you.'

'I wish you wouldn't say that.' The phone had stopped ringing. 'I don't even know you. I don't even know your name.'

'What difference does it make?'

'I just—'

'It's Marilyn.'

'That's a step.' I tried my winningest smile. 'I'm Bernie.'

'I know who you are. You still don't know who I am, do you?'

'You're Marilyn.'

'I'm Marilyn Margate.'

'Not the actress?'

'What actress?'

I shrugged. 'I don't know. The way you said your name I thought you expected me to recognize it. I don't. Do you suppose it's possible you've got the wrong Bernard Rhodenbarr? I know it's not a very common name but there might be more than one of us. My name is Bernard *Grimes* Rhodenbarr, Grimes was my mother's maiden name, like Bouvier or Flanders, so—'

'You son of a bitch.'

'Did I say something wrong?'

'You bastard. Bouvier. Flanders. You killed Wanda.' This time it wasn't my imagination; her finger definitely tightened on the trigger. And the thing was finally beginning to look like a cannon, and its mouth like the black hole of Calcutta.

'Look,' I said, 'you're making a terrible mistake. I've never killed anybody in my life. It bothers me to step on a cockroach. I'm the guy who taught Gandhi how to be nonviolent. Compared to me, Albert Schweitzer was a mad-dog killer. I—'

'Shut up.'

I shut up.

She said, 'You don't know who I am, do you? I thought my last name would tip you off. Rabbit Margate is my brother.'

'Rabbit Margate.'

'Right.'

'I don't know who that is.'

'George Edward Margate, but everybody called him Rabbit. They arrested him this afternoon and charged him with burglary and murder. They say he killed Wanda Tuesday night. My brother never killed anybody.'

'Neither did I. Look—'

'Shut up. Either you killed her or you know who did. And you're gonna cop to it. You think I'm letting my kid brother go up for a murder he didn't commit? The hell I am. Either you're gonna confess or I'm gonna shoot you dead.'

The phone rang again. She didn't pay any attention to it, and I didn't pay it much mind myself beyond idly wondering who it might be. Was it my caller of a few minutes ago? Was it the person whose call I'd failed to answer when I went out to dinner? Was it the one who'd hung up on me, or the one of the night before who wanted to buy the V-Nickel? Or all of the above, or none of the above?

I decided it didn't matter much, and the ringing stopped, and I said, 'George Edward Margate. Rabbit Margate. So you're Rabbit's sister Marilyn.'

'Then you *do* know him!'

'Nope. Never heard the name until tonight. But now I know who he is. He's the one who hit the Colcannon place Tuesday and left the radio on.'

'You were there. You just admitted it.'

'And Rabbit was there. Wasn't he?'

Her expression was wary. 'Where do you get off asking the questions? You're not the cops.'

'No, I'm not. I'm not the killer, either. I didn't kill anyone Tuesday night. And neither did your brother.'

'You're saying he didn't do it.'

'That's right. He didn't. He burgled the place though, didn't he? He went in through the skylight in the bedroom. Was he all by himself?'

'No. Wait a minute. You don't get to ask me questions, for chrissake. I don't have to say he was there and I don't have to say he was with somebody.'

'You don't have to say anything. It's all right, Marilyn. Rabbit didn't kill anybody.' I took a breath. It seemed like a good time for disarming candor. '*I* was there,' I said, 'after Rabbit and his partner had come and gone. The Colcannons weren't home when they burgled the place, and they weren't back yet when I was there, either.'

'You can't prove that.'

'Nobody can prove I was there in the first place, either. And I *can* prove I didn't meet the Colcannons, because Herbert Colcannon had a nice long look at me through a one-way mirror the other morning and he couldn't identify me.'

She nodded slowly. 'That's what they said, that there was another suspect named Rhodenbarr but he was cleared because Colcannon hadn't seen him before. But he identified Rabbit and I know he never saw Rabbit, so I thought maybe it was a mistake or you paid somebody off or something. I don't even *know* what I thought. All I knew was my brother was in trouble for something he didn't do, and I figured if I got the person who really did it—'

'But I'm not that person, Marilyn.'

'Then who is?'

'I don't know.'

'Neither do I, and—' She broke off abruptly and looked at the gun in her hand as if wondering how it had gotten there. 'It's loaded,' she said.

'I figured it was.'

'I almost shot you. I wanted to. As if shooting you would solve everything for Rabbit.'

'It would have solved everything for me. But not in a positive way.'

'Yeah. Look, I—'

Knock knock knock!

No question who was knocking this time. I cautioned Marilyn with a finger to my lips, then approached her and put those same lips inches from her gold teardrop earring. 'Cops,' I whispered. I pointed to the bathroom door and she didn't waste time asking questions. She scooted for the bathroom, gun in hand, and she was just closing the door as my latest unannounced guest repeated his knocking.

I asked who it was. 'It's who you thought it was, Bern. Open the door, huh?'

I unlocked my locks and admitted Ray Kirschmann. He was wearing the same suit he'd worn yesterday and now it was wet, which didn't improve the fit any. 'Rain,' he said heavily, and removed his hat, holding it so that all the water which had collected in the brim could spill onto my floor.

'Thanks,' I said.

'Huh?'

'I've had this problem with the floorboards drying out. I was hoping somebody'd come along and water them. What you could do sometime, Ray, is you could call first.'

'I did. Line was busy.'

'Funny. I wasn't on the phone.' Maybe he'd tried while someone else was ringing. 'What brings you?'

'The goodness of my heart,' he said. 'These days I been doin' you nothin' but favors. Drivin' you to your store twice. And stoppin' in tonight to let you know you're in the clear on the Colcannon job. They already got one of the guys who did it.'

'Oh?'

He nodded. 'Guy named George Margate. Young guy, but he's got a pretty good sheet on him already. Two, three busts for B and E. Never roughed anybody up before, but you know the young ones. They're not what you'd call stable. Maybe his partner was a rough piece of work, or maybe they had drugs in 'em. We found a Baggie full of marijuana in his refrigerator.'

'The killer weed.'

'Yeah. The marijuana's not what hangs him. It's what else we found at his place. He's been livin' in two rooms on Tenth Avenue in the Forties, maybe a block and a half from the tenement he grew up in. Hell's Kitchen, except you're supposed to call it Clinton now so's people'll forget it's a slum. We tossed his two rooms and he's got half of Colcannon's house packed away there. Silver, Jesus, he had a whole service for twelve in sterling plus all of these bowls and platters. Worth a fortune.'

'I remember when it was hardly worth stealing,' I said nostalgically. 'Then it went from a dollar twenty-nine an ounce to forty dollars an ounce. I remember when *gold* was less than that.'

'Yeah. Found some furs, too. Floor-length ranch mink, marten jacket, something else I don't remember. Straight off the list we had from Colcannon, right down to the furriers' labels. All told, we found better'n half of what Colcannon reported as missin', plus some stuff he never listed, because who's got a complete inventory of everythin' right at his fingertips? We figure they split the loot down the middle and the other half's at the partner's place, unless they fenced it already.'

'Who's the partner?'

'We don't know yet. He'll tell us when he dopes out that it's the only way he's gonna pull short time, but right now he's James Cagney in every prison movie you ever saw.'

'How did you get on to him, Ray?'

'Usual way. Somebody snitched. Maybe he was braggin' in the bars, or just lookin' good and showin' a lot of money, and somebody took two an' two an' put 'em together. Neighborhood he lives in, every third person on the street is a snitch, and the Colcannon job was close to home. What was it, a mile away? Mile and a half?'

I nodded. 'Well,' I said, 'thanks for dropping by to tell me, Ray. I appreciate it.'

'Actually,' he said, 'it's like the other day. I mostly came by to use your bathroom.'

'It's out of order.'

'Oh yeah?' He went on walking toward the door. 'Sometimes these things fix themselves, you know? Or maybe I can fix it for you. I had an uncle was a plumber, showed me a thing or two some years back.'

Had she locked the door? I held my breath and he tried the knob and it was locked.

'Door's stuck,' he said.

'Must be the weather.'

'Yeah, there's a lot of that goin' around. Old retired burglar like yourself, Bern, you oughta be able to get the door open for me.'

'A man loses his touch.'

'Isn't that just the truth.' He walked from the bathroom door to my

531

window and gazed out through the gloom. 'I bet you could see the Trade Center,' he said, 'if the weather was half decent.'

'You could.'

'And old Abel Crowe got to look over at Jersey all the time. I swear the crooks all get picture-book views. What I get from my window is a close-up of Mrs Houlihan's washline. You know what I keep wantin' to do, Bern, is tie up Colcannon and Crowe. We got no leads on Crowe, see. Nobody knows nothin'.'

'What does Rabbit know about Abel?' Oh God, why was I calling him that?

'Rabbit?' He frowned, blinked. 'I told you, he's Cagney playin' tough. I don't think he ever heard the name, but he's got a partner, right? Even if we don't know who it is.'

'So?'

'What you could tell me, Bern, is would anybody try to peddle jewels and silver to Abel Crowe?'

I thought about it, or tried to look as though that was what I was doing. 'Abel never took furs,' I said. 'Stamps, coins, jewelry – that was his field. Silver? Oh, if I found myself with a Revere tankard on my hands, Abel was one of several men I might have offered it to. But garden-variety silver? He'd have had no interest in it. Of course it might be different since silver shot up in price, but who in his right mind would need a fence for it now? You just take it to any of those places where they buy silver by weight for the melting pot. Or you let somebody with a legitimate front do it for you, if you're afraid you'll have trouble cashing a check. You don't need a fence. No, I can't see anybody taking bulk silver to Abel.'

'Yeah, that's about what I figured. Who's in your bathroom, Bern?'

'Greta Garbo.'

'She wanted to be alone, huh?'

'That's what she told me.'

'Well, I don't figure she'd lie about somethin' like that. Anymore'n you'd lie about it. I know she's not the same woman who was here the other night. No cigarettes in the ashtrays. And this is a different perfume. I didn't smell it here before tonight.'

'It's, uh, getting late, Ray.'

'Uh-huh. It never does get earlier, does it? What did you get out of Colcannon's safe, Bern?'

'I never got into it.'

'He listed a couple of things that were in the safe. A watch and some jewelry. Earrings, I think it was. They didn't turn up at Margate's. Be funny if we found them up on Riverside Drive, wouldn't it?'

'I don't know what you're getting at.'

'I'll tell you, Bern, half the time I don't know myself. All I do is poke around and see where it gets me. Like doin' a jigsaw puzzle by trial and error, pickin' up different pieces and tryin' 'em this way an' that an' seein' what works an' what doesn't.'

'It must be fascinating.'

'Uh-huh. How'd you come to know Margate?'

'I didn't. Those two puzzle pieces don't fit.'

'No? I coulda sworn they did. Then how'd you happen to know they call him Rabbit?'

'That's what you called him, Ray.'

'I don't think so. I think I called him George.'

'Right, the first time you referred to him. Then there was another time when you called him Rabbit.'

He shook his head. 'I still don't think so. I think I made a point of it not to call him Rabbit just to see if you would.'

'Your tongue must have slipped.'

'Somebody's did.' He took his hat off, adjusted the brim, put it back on his head. 'Well, time I got myself home. You can let the little lady out of the bathroom, Bern. This day an' age, it makes you wonder what she's got to be shy about. But that's just a cop talkin'. This line of work, you're suspicious all the time.' He sighed. 'Burglars and fences, they got the beautiful views and all. And the women. The only woman you'll find in my bathroom is my wife, and when I look out the window if I don't see Mrs Houlihan's wash then what I see is Mrs Houlihan, and between the two I'd as soon look at the laundry. It's no bargain, let me tell you.'

'I can imagine.'

'I figured you could. What I'd hate to see, Bern, is for you to take a fall for Colcannon. If they already got Rabbit, why should you do time for it? Know what I mean?'

I didn't say anything.

'An' if I can come out with something for my troubles, maybe I can forget some of the things I happened to pick up on. Know what I mean, Bern?'

I knew what he meant.

I locked up after Ray left. Then I stood at the door for a long moment, unlocked the locks, and opened the door far enough to afford me a view of the hallway clear to the elevators. Unless he'd gotten cute enough to duck around a corner, he was gone.

So I locked up again and went over to the bathroom door and told Marilyn the coast was clear.

She had heard most of it. We talked, and by the time we were done she seemed to believe that I'd had nothing to do with the murder of Wanda Colcannon. But she knew Rabbit was equally innocent of murder and she wanted to get him off the hook.

I said, 'What about the partner? How many guys did Rabbit work with?'

'Just one.'

'Do you know who he was?'

'I don't know if I should say.'

'Well, I'm not going to tell anybody. And the police probably already know who he is, if they don't have him in custody by now.'

'Rabbit wouldn't fink.'

'He might,' I said. 'Mostly people will, sooner or later. But even if Rabbit's the toughest nut since G. Gordon Liddy, the cops'll probably get the partner the same way they got Rabbit. Some neighborhood snitch'll add two and two and call the cops.'

'Why do you want to know who it was?'

'Because maybe he split with Rabbit and went back alone for another try at the safe. Or with a third person.'

'Oh.' She put a finger to her pointed chin. Her eyes, I noted, didn't need all that makeup. They were large enough without it. 'I don't think Harlan would do that,' she said.

'Harlan?'

'Harlan Reese. They pulled it off together. If Harlan went back – no, I don't think he would do that, not without telling Rabbit.'

'Maybe they both went back.'

'You still think Rabbit killed her.'

'I didn't say that. But how do you know what Harlan might have done?'

'Rabbit didn't go back a second time. I'm positive of that.'

I let it go. We talked about the Third Burglars Carolyn and I had hypothesized, and as I explained the theory it seemed as difficult to pin down as the elusive Third Murderer in *Macbeth*. A couple of roaming vandals, skipping idly over the rooftops in search of loot, happening by chance on a smashed skylight, dropping in for criminous purposes, and committing a slight case of homicide on their way out.

Earlier, I had believed all that. Now it struck me as occupying a rung on the plausibility ladder somewhere between the Great Pumpkin and the Tooth Fairy.

Because Ray was right, albeit for all the wrong reasons. Somehow the two murders, Crowe and Colcannon, were connected. And the only way Rabbit Margate was going to beat a murder rap was by someone's coming up with the real killer, and the police couldn't possibly do that because they already figured they had the real killer, so why look elsewhere?

And if Rabbit didn't wind up in the clear, I was in trouble. Because Rabbit's sister knew I'd been at the Colcannon place after her brother left it, and Ray knew I had heard of Rabbit before he'd mentioned him, and Ray figured there was a connection between me and Colcannon and me and Crowe, and sooner or later he'd do something with his suspicions.

For one thing, he might give Abel's place a really thorough toss of the sort I'd given it, and while I didn't think he'd find the money in the telephone or the rare stamps in the books, neither did I think he'd miss the watch and earrings that were hidden beneath the cigars. Once he found them he'd almost certainly order the place swept for prints again.

And then I'd be in trouble. They had already dusted for prints after Abel's body was found, which was why I hadn't encumbered myself with gloves on my recent visit, that and the fact that I, uh, hadn't thought to bring a pair with me. So my prints were now all over the damned apartment, and while that might not be evidence of homicide (since the prints hadn't been there for the first inspection), it would be very powerful evidence indeed that I'd paid Abel a visit *after* his death, and how was I going to explain that one?

I picked up the phone and called Carolyn. No answer. I called Denise and learned from Jared that she had not come home yet. There was something seriously wrong with telephones, I decided, because I kept calling people and people kept calling me and nobody ever got to talk with anyone else. My life was turning into a clumsy metaphor for the failure of communications in the Age of Alienation.

I dialed 246–4200. It rang and was answered, and for a minute or so I listened without saying a word. Then I replaced the receiver and turned to Marilyn, who was looking at me oddly.

'You didn't say anything,' she said.

'That's true. I'm going to help you.'

'How?'

'By getting them to release Rabbit.'

'How can you do that?'

'By finding out who the Third Burglar was. By learning who really killed Wanda Colcannon.'

I was afraid she'd ask how I was going to bring that off, and I would have been stuck for an answer. Instead she asked why.

'That last call I made,' I said. 'It was Dial-a-Prayer.'

'Very funny.'

'I'm serious. The prayer today was something like, "Oh Lord, let me do something today I have never done before. Show me a new way in which I can be of service to a fellow human being." There was more to it than that, but that's the gist of it.'

She raised her penciled eyebrows. 'Dial-a-Prayer,' she said.

'Call it yourself if you don't believe me.'

'And that's why you're going to help Rabbit.'

'It's a reason. Won't it do?'

'Yeah,' she said. 'I guess it will. I guess it'll have to.'

15

Marilyn wanted to leave right away. She had to see a lawyer about getting Rabbit out on bail, which might or might not be possible, and she said something about getting in touch with Harlan Reese. Then, when I warned her that Ray Kirschmann might be lurking in the lobby or laying doggo across the street, she reversed direction completely.

'Oh, God,' she said. 'Maybe what I oughta do is stay right here.'

I looked at her, a veritable vision in *rouge et noir*, and I inhaled her scent, and I listened with amazement to my very own voice telling her I didn't think that was a good idea. 'You have things to do,' I said, 'and *I* have things to do, and we'd better go do them. Besides, Ray could turn ornery and come back with a warrant and a crowbar, and then the bathroom wouldn't be sacrosanct anymore. One thing, though. Maybe you should leave the gun here.'

She shook her head. 'It doesn't belong to me. My boss keeps it in case we get held up. I think she just likes having it, you know? I mean who's gonna hold up a beauty parlor?'

'Is that where you work?'

She nodded. 'Hair Apparent. There's four operators plus Magda, she's the owner. I'm working tomorrow. I'll put the gun back then.'

'Good. Because if the police found it in your purse—'

'I know.'

We were in the hallway and I was locking the last of the locks when the phone started ringing. I gritted my teeth. If I unlocked everything and raced I still wouldn't get to the phone on time, and if I did it would just be somebody offering me free home delivery of the Newark *Star-Ledger*. The hell with it.

The elevator took us down past the lobby to the basement. We went through the laundry room and down a dimly lit corridor to the service entrance. I held the door for her and she climbed a short flight of stairs, opened her red-and-black umbrella, and disappeared into the night.

Back in my apartment, I stood for a moment glaring at my phone and wondering how many times it had rung while I was letting Marilyn out. It wasn't ringing now, and it was getting late enough to discourage

536

me from placing many calls of my own. I tried one, dialing Carolyn's number, and wasn't surprised when nobody answered.

The four little cups of espresso were starring to wear off and I poured myself a healthy hooker of straight Scotch to speed them on their way. I drank it down, then got a taller glass from the cupboard and stirred an ounce or two of Scotch into four or five ounces of milk. The perfect nightcap – the milk coats your stomach while the Scotch rots your liver.

The phone rang.

I leaped for it, then made myself draw a calming breath before lifting the receiver to my ear. A male voice, one I'd last heard almost twenty-two hours ago, said, 'Rhodenbarr? I want the nickel.'

'Who doesn't?'

'What do you mean?'

'Everybody wants it. I wouldn't mind getting my own hands on it.'

'Don't joke with me. I know you have the coin.'

'I had it. I don't have it anymore.'

There was a pause, and for a moment I thought I'd lost him. Then he said, 'You're lying.'

'No. Do you think I'm crazy enough to pop it in the same pocket as the keys and the Saint Christopher medal? I wouldn't do that, and I wouldn't keep it around the house, either. Not with all the burglaries you hear about in this town.'

This last didn't win a chuckle. 'You have access to the coin?'

'It's where I can get it.'

'Get it now,' he urged. 'And name your price and we will arrange a meeting. I have the rest of the night at my disposal, and—'

'I'm afraid I can't say the same,' I said. 'If I don't get enough sleep I'm a terrible grouch the next day. Anyway, I couldn't get hold of the coin at this hour even if I wanted to, which I don't. I'm afraid it'll have to be tomorrow.'

'What time tomorrow?'

'That's hard to say. Give me a number where I can reach you.'

This time I got the chuckle. 'I think not, Rhodenbarr. It will be better if I continue to call you. Estimate how much time you'll need to gain possession of the coin, then return to your apartment at an appointed hour and I'll telephone you. Merely tell me the hour.'

In other words, be at a specific place at a specific time with the coin in my hand. 'Inconvenient,' I said. 'Tell you what. There's another number where I'll be tomorrow afternoon at two.'

'And the number?'

I gave him Carolyn's. She sublets her rent-controlled apartment from a man named Nathan Aranow, and as he remains the tenant of record her phone is listed in his name. (Half the people in New York operate this way. The other half pay $500 a month for a studio apartment.) I didn't think he could get the name and address from the number, and if he did how was he going to find Nathan Aranow? Carolyn simply mailed a money order in that name to her landlord every month. For all any of us knew, Nathan Aranow had been wiped out years ago in a flash flood.

He repeated the number. 'And the coin,' he said. 'Who else knows you have it?'

'Nobody.'

'You had no accomplice?'

'I always work alone.'

'And you haven't spoken to anyone?'

'I've spoken to plenty of people, but not about the coin.'

'So no one else knows you have it.'

'As far as I know,' I said, 'nobody else even knows it's missing. Just you and I and Herbert Franklin Colcannon, unless he's told somebody, and I don't think he has.' Or else Ray Kirschmann would have been sniffing after half a million dollars, and if that had been the case he'd have been drooling all over my rug. 'He might not report it, not if it wasn't insured. And if he had reasons.'

'I'm sure he didn't report it.'

'Of course Rabbit might talk.'

'Rabbit?'

'George Edward Margate. Isn't that why you fingered the Colcannon place for him? You should have picked someone who knew how to punch a safe. I guess the nickel was supposed to be your finder's fee for setting up the job.'

A long low chuckle. 'Clever,' he said. 'I should have made my arrangements with you in the first place.'

'You certainly should have. It might help if I knew your name.'

'It might,' he said. 'I'll call you tomorrow at two o'clock. That number's in the Village, isn't it?'

'I own a bookstore on East Eleventh Street. There's two phones, one listed and one unlisted. I gave you the number of the unlisted one.'

'Shall I simply meet you at your store, then?'

'No,' I said. 'Call the number at two.'

I hung up and returned to my Scotch and milk. The milk was warmish, but that's supposed to be an advantage when you're trying to go to sleep. I sat down and sipped and thought that I'd done rather a lot of lying. Well, Dial-a-Prayer hadn't said anything provocative about honesty. Just being of service to one's fellow man, and if I wasn't that, then what was I?

The phone rang. I picked it up and it was Carolyn. 'Been calling you all night,' she said. 'What the hell happened to you, Bernie? Either nobody answered or the line was busy, or once in a while I would get a wrong number. What's been happening?'

'Everything.'

'Are you gonna have to get glasses?'

'Glasses?'

'Didn't you say you were going to the eye doctor?'

'Oh. Yeah, right.'

'You have to get glasses?'

'No, but he said I should stop reading in the dark.'

'I could have told you that. You okay? You sound a little funny.'

She sounded about half lit, but I didn't bother to mention it. 'I'm fine,' I said. 'Just exhausted. A lot of things have happened but I can't really talk now.'

'Company?'

'Yes,' I said, and then it struck me that I'd better stop this lying before my nose started to grow. 'No,' I said.

'I knew it was one or the other. But which?'

'I'm alone,' I said, 'but evidently can't think straight. Are you at home?'

'No, I'm bopping around the bars. Why?'

'Going back to your place later?'

'Unless I get lucky, which it doesn't look like I'm gonna. Why?'

'You'll be home in the morning? Or will you be at the Poodle Factory?'

'I don't work Saturdays anymore, Bernie. I don't have to, not since I started doing a little burglary to make ends meet. Remember?'

'Maybe you could go over to the store when you wake up,' I said, 'and pick up your telephone answering machine, and take it back to your apartment.'

'Why would I want to do that?'

'I'll be over around ten or so and tell you all about it.'

'Jesus, I certainly hope so.'

I hung up and it rang again and it was Denise, home at last and returning my call. I asked her how she would like company around one-thirty.

'It's almost that now,' she said.

'I mean tomorrow afternoon. All right if I drop in for a few minutes?'

'Sure. Just for a few minutes?'

'Maybe an hour at the outside.'

'Sure, I guess. Does this mark a new development in our ever-evolving relationship, Bernie? Are you advance-booking a quickie or something?'

'No,' I said. 'I'll be over around one-thirty, maybe a quarter of two, and I'll explain everything.'

'I can hardly wait.'

I hung up and got undressed. When I took my socks off I sat for a moment on the edge of my bed and examined my feet. I had never really studied them before, and it had certainly never occurred to me that they were narrow. They definitely looked narrow now, long and skinny and foolish. And there was no question about it, my second toes extended beyond my big toes. I tried to retract the offending second toes, tried to extend the big toes, but this didn't work, and I must have been damned tired to think it might.

Morton's Foot. I had it, all right, and while it wasn't as dismaying as a positive Wassermann, I can't say I felt happy about it.

So the phone rang.

I picked it up. A woman with an English accent said, 'I beg your pardon?'

'Huh?'

'Is this Bernard Rhodenbarr?'

'Yes.'

'I thought I might have dialed the weather report by mistake. You said "It never rains but it pours." '

'I didn't realize I'd said that aloud.'

'You did, actually, and it *is* raining, and – I'm sorry to be calling you so late. I couldn't reach you earlier. My name is Jessica Garland. I don't know if that means anything to you.'

'Not offhand, but I don't think my mind's at its sharpest. Not if I'm capable of answering the phone with a code phrase from a spy movie.'

'You know, it did rather sound like that. I thought my grandfather might have mentioned me, Mr Rhodenbarr.'

'Your grandfather?'

'Abel Crowe.'

My jaw may have hung loose for a moment. Then I said, 'I never knew Abel had a grandchild. I never even knew he'd been married.'

'I don't know that he was. He was certainly never married to my grandmother. She was from Budapest originally, and the two of them were lovers in Vienna before the war. When the Nazis annexed Austria in '38 she got out with my mother in her arms and the clothes she was wearing and nothing else. Grandfather's parting gift to her was a small fortune in rare stamps which she concealed in the lining of her coat. She went from Vienna to Antwerp, where she sold the stamps, and from there to London, where she died in the Blitz. Grandfather wound up in a concentration camp and survived.'

'And your mother—?'

'Mother was five or six years old when Grandmother was killed. She was taken in by a neighbor family and grew up as an English girl. She married young, had me early on, and assumed her own father was dead, that he'd died in a concentration camp or in the war. It must have been about six years ago that she learned otherwise. I say, I'm doing a great lot of talking, aren't I? Do you mind terribly?'

'I find it rather soothing.'

'Do you? Well, Grandfather literally turned up on our doorstep in Croydon. It seems he'd hired agents and finally succeeded in tracing Mother. There was a joyful reunion, but before very long they found themselves with precious little to say to each other. She'd grown up to be a rather ordinary English suburban housewife, while Grandfather – well, you know the sort of life he led.'

'Yes.'

'He returned to the States. He wrote letters, but they were more to me and my brother than to Mum. I've a younger brother, you see. Two years ago Grandfather wrote suggesting I might care to try living in America, and the suggestion came at just the right time. I quit my hateful job, said goodbye to my dreary young man, and boarded one of Freddie Laker's DC-10s. And to make a long story short – do you know, when people say "To make a long story short," it's already too late. In any event, I've been here ever since.'

'In New York?'

'In Brooklyn, actually. Do you know Cobble Hill?'

'Sort of.'

'I lived at first in a women's residential hotel in Gramercy Park. Then I moved here. The job at which I work is not hateful, and the young man with whom I live is not at all dreary, and I'm hardly ever homesick, actually. I'm rambling all over the lot, aren't I? Chalk it up to exhaustion, physical and emotional. And there's a point to all this, actually.'

'I felt sure there would be.'

'How very trusting of you. The point is that Grandfather spoke of you, and not only as, oh, shall we say a business associate?'

'I guess we shall.'

'But also as a friend, don't you see. And now he's dead, as of course you know, and I shall miss him, and I think it's quite horrid how he died and I hope they catch the person responsible, but in the meantime it rather falls to me to get everything in order. I don't know what he would have wanted in the line of funeral arrangements because he never talked about the possibility of his own death, unless he left a letter of some sort, and if so it hasn't come to light yet. And of course the police have the body at the morgue and I don't know when they're likely to release it. When they do I suspect I'll manage some sort of private funeral without any ceremony, but in the meantime I think it would be fitting to have some sort of memorial service, don't you?'

'I guess that would be nice.'

'I've arranged something, actually. There'll be a service at the

Church of the Redeemer on Henry Street between Congress and Amity Streets. That's here in Cobble Hill. Do you know where it is?'

'I'll be able to find it.'

'It's the only church I could find that would allow a memorial service on a Sunday. We'll be meeting there that afternoon at two-thirty. The service won't be religious because Grandfather wasn't a religious man. He did have a spiritual side, however. I don't know if he ever showed that side to you.'

'I know the sort of reading he did.'

'Yes, all the great moral philosophers. I told them at the church that we'd conduct our own service. Clay, the chap I live with, is going to read something. He was quite fond of Grandfather. And I'll probably read something myself, and I thought you might be able to take part in the service, Mr Rhodenbarr.'

'Call me Bernie. Yes, I could probably find something to read. I'd like to do that.'

'Or just say a few words, or both. As you choose.' She hesitated. 'There's another thing, actually. I saw Grandfather every few weeks and we were close in certain ways, but he didn't mention many of his . . . business friends. I know you were a friend of his, and I know of one or two others in that category, but perhaps you'll be able to think of some other persons who might properly come to the service.'

'It's possible.'

'Would you just go ahead and invite anyone you think ought to be invited? May I just leave that up to you?'

'All right.'

'I've already spoken to several of the people in his building, and one woman's going to post a notice in the lobby. I suppose I should have made arrangements with a church in that neighborhood. Some of those people find it difficult to get around easily. But I'd already made plans with the Church of the Redeemer before I thought of it. I hope they won't mind coming all the way out to Brooklyn.'

'Perhaps it'll be an adventure for them.'

'I just hope the weather's decent. The rain's expected to have left off by then, but the weatherman doesn't give guarantees, does he?'

'Not as a general rule.'

'No, more's the pity. I'm sorry to have gone on so, Mr Rhodenbarr, but—'

'Bernie.'

'Bernie. It's late and I'm tired, perhaps more so than I'd realized. You will try to come? Sunday at two-thirty? And you'll invite anyone you think of?'

'Definitely,' I said. 'And I'll bring along something to read.'

*

I wrote down the time and the address and the name of the church. Carolyn would want to come, of course. Anybody else?

I got in bed and tried to think if I knew anyone who'd want to attend a memorial service for Abel. I wasn't acquainted with many other burglars, having a longstanding preference for the company of law-abiding citizens, and I didn't know who Abel's friends were. Would Ray Kirschmann want to make the trip? I thought about it and decided that he might.

My mind drifted around. So Abel had a granddaughter. How old was Jessica Garland likely to be? Her mum must have been born in 1936 or thereabouts, and if she had indeed married young and had Jessica early on, then twenty-four or twenty-five sounded like a reasonable ballpark figure. I didn't have any trouble picturing Abel playing host to a young woman about that age, telling her charming lies about the old days in the Viennese coffeehouses, plying her with strudel and eclairs.

And he'd never once mentioned her, the old fox.

I was almost asleep when a thought nudged me back awake again. I got out of bed, looked up a number, made a phone call. It rang four times before a man answered it.

I stayed as silent as if I'd called Dial-a-Prayer. I listened, and the man who'd answered said '*Hello?*' several times, querulously, while in the background music played and a dog interposed an occasional bark. Then he hung up – the man, I trust, rather than the dog – and I went back to bed.

16

One of the things I'd found time to do between late phone calls was set my alarm clock, and come morning it rang its fool head off. I got up and groped my way through a shower and a shave and the first cup of coffee, then turned on the radio and toasted a couple slices of whole-grain bread, buttered them, jammed them, ate them, drank some more coffee, drew the drapes and cocked an eye at the dawn.

It looked promising, even to a cocked eye. To the east, dark clouds still obscured the newly risen sun. But the sky was clear in the west, and the winds generally blow from that direction, sweeping yesterday's weather out over the Atlantic – which, in this case, was right where it belonged. The sky over the Hudson had a distinctly blue cast to it.

I poured myself one more cup of coffee, settled in my most nearly comfortable chair with the phone and the phone book, glanced ruefully at Morton's feet, and let my fingers do the walking.

My first call was to the American Numismatic Society, located some four miles north of me at Broadway and 156th Street. I introduced myself as James Klavin of the New York *Times* and explained I was doing a piece on the 1913 V-Nickel. Could he tell me a few things about the coin? Was it true, for example, that only five specimens were known to exist? And did he happen to know where those specimens were located at the present time? Could he say when a specimen had last changed hands? And for what price?

Almost everyone likes to cooperate with the press. Describe yourself as a reporter and you can ask no end of time-consuming and impertinent questions, and all people ask of you in return is that you spell their names right. The man I spoke with, a Mr Skeffington, said he might be a moment and offered to ring me back. I said I'd hold, and I held for ten minutes, sipping coffee and wiggling my toes, while he scurried around doing my legwork for me.

He came back in due course and told me more than I really needed to know, repeating a lot of what Abel had told us Tuesday night. There were indeed five specimens, four of them in public collections, one in private hands, and he was able to furnish me with the names of the four institutions and the private collector.

He was less helpful on the subject of value. The ANS is a high-minded outfit, more interested in scholarly matters like the varieties and the historical context of numismatics than such crass considerations as price. The most recent cash transaction of which Mr Skeffington had a record was a sale Abel had mentioned – in 1976, for $130,000. According to Abel there'd been a sale since then for a substantially higher price.

I called the four museums in turn. At the Smithsonian in Washington, the curator of coins and medals was a gentleman with a dry voice and a hyphenated surname. He confirmed that a 1913 V-Nickel was a part of the Smithsonian's numismatic holdings, having been acquired as a gift of Mrs R. Henry Norweb in 1978.

'It's on permanent display,' he informed me, 'and it's terribly popular. Tourists gawk at it and tell each other how beautiful it is. Now our coin is a frosty proof, but aside from that it looks like any Liberty Head Nickel, hardly an extraordinary item from the standpoint of numismatic design. You might care to argue that the Standing Liberty Quarter is beautiful, or the Saint-Gaudens high-relief twenty-dollar gold piece, but the Liberty Head Nickel? What makes this example beautiful? The date? Why, it's the value, of course. The rarity, the legends. People *ooh* and *ahh* at diamonds, too, and couldn't tell them from cut glass, not by looking at them. What exactly did you want to know about our coin?'

'I just wanted to make sure it was still there.'

A dry chuckle. 'Oh, it's still here. We haven't had to spend it yet. Not much you can buy with a nickel nowadays, anyway, so I guess we'll hang onto it for the present.'

A woman at the Boston Museum of Fine Arts confirmed that a 1913 V-Nickel was one of the stars of the museum's coin display and had been since its acquisition by bequest shortly after the Second World War. 'It's an extremely important numismatic item,' she said, sounding like catalog copy, 'and we're gratified to have it here in Boston.'

An assistant curator at the Museum of Science and Industry was similarly gratified to have Nickel No. 3 in Cincinnati, where it had reposed since the mid-thirties: 'We've deaccessioned a substantial portion of our coin holdings in the past few years,' he told me. 'We've had budget problems, and the coins have increased so dramatically in value that they seemed to represent a disproportionate amount of our capital in relation to their display value. There's been some pressure on us to eliminate coins altogether, as we did with our stamps, but then our philatelic collection was never more than third-rate. The 1913 Nickel's the star of our show. We've no plans to let it go, not that they've told me about. It's popular, you see, especially with the children. I wouldn't be surprised if someone's looking at it right now.'

Nickel No. 4 had belonged to the Museum of the Baltimore

Historical Society until a little over a year ago, I learned from a woman whose speech indicated an origin rather farther south than Baltimore. 'It was our only important coin,' she said. 'We're really only interested in articles relating to the history of the city of Baltimore, but people tend to will their prize possessions to museums, and we in turn tend to accept what's left to us. We had the nickel for years and years, and of course its value increased, and from time to time there was talk of consigning it to an auction or selling it privately to a fellow institution. Then a foundation in Philadelphia devoted exclusively to numismatics came to us offering to exchange the Copley portrait of Charles Carroll of Carrollton.' She went on to explain that Charles Carroll, born in Annapolis, had been a member of the Continental Congress, a signer of the Declaration of Independence, and a United States senator. I already knew who Copley was.

'It was an offah we couldn't refuse,' she said solemnly, and I pictured Marlon Brando as Don Corleone, holding a pistol to this Southern belle's head, urging her to swap the nickel for the portrait.

The place in Philadelphia called itself the Gallery of American and International Numismatics, and the man I spoke to gave his name as Milo Hracec, and spelled it for me. He was second in command, he explained; his boss was Howard Pitterman, which name he also spelled, and Pitterman had Saturdays off.

Hracec confirmed that the gallery did indeed own a 1913 Nickel. 'It is a part of our type set of United States coinage,' he said. 'You know what a type set is? One example of each design. Type collecting has become popular as fewer hobbyists can afford to collect complete sets by date and mint mark. Of course that is not the foremost consideration here, because Mr Ruslander has placed generous funds at the gallery's disposal.'

'Mr Ruslander?'

'Gordon Ruslander of the Liberty Bell Mint. You're probably familiar with their sets of medals for collectors.'

I was indeed. Like the Franklin Mint, also in Philadelphia, Liberty Bell specialized in series of contemporary medals which they peddled to collectors by subscription with the intimation that the little silver discs would someday increase in value. They'd always been a drug on the resale market, and on more than one occasion I'd left sets of the medals in their owners' desks, writing them off as not worth stealing. Now, with the surge in the price of silver, the damned things had soared to more than triple their issue price in bullion value.

Ruslander, I was told, had established the Gallery of American and International Numismatics three years previously, donating his own personal collection along with a hefty chunk of cash. And the US type set, in which the 1913 V-Nickel reposed, was the gallery's star attraction.

'In a type set,' Hracec explained, 'any coin of the type will do. But in the gallery's collection, we strive for the rarest date and mint variety attainable for that type, instead of settling for a common and readily affordable example. In 1873–4, for instance, Liberty Seated Dimes were struck with arrows flanking the date. Uncirculated specimens of the Philadelphia and San Francisco issues range from six or seven hundred to perhaps a thousand or twelve hundred dollars. Our coin is one struck at Carson City, the 1873-CC, and our specimen is superior in quality to the one which sold at a Kagin auction seven years ago for twenty-seven thousand dollars.

'Originally our V-Nickel slot was filled by a proof example of the 1885, the rarest date of the regular series. It's worth perhaps a thousand dollars, a little more than twice the price of common proofs. There was some question as to whether we would even want to have the 1913, since it was not a regularly issued coin, but when we learned the Baltimore Historical Society might let theirs go, Mr Ruslander wouldn't rest until we had it. He happened to own a portrait by Copley that he knew they would want—'

And I got to hear about Charles Carroll of Carrollton all over again. On and on it went, and when I was done with Mr Hracec I had to call Stillwater, Oklahoma, where I spoke with a man named Dale Arnott. Mr Arnott evidently owned a fair portion of Payne County and ran beef cattle on his land, moving them out of the way now and then to make room for an oil well. He had indeed owned the 1913 V-Nickel, having bought it in '76 for $130,000, and his had been the one resold a year or two ago for $200,000.

'I had my fun with it,' he said, 'and I got a kick at coin conventions, hauling it out of a pocketful of change and tossing it to match folks for drinks. You'd like to die from the look on their faces. Way I looked at it, a nickel's a nickel, so why not toss it heads or tails?'

'Weren't you worried you'd lower its value?'

'Nope. It wasn't in the best condition to start with, you see. Oh, it's better than extra fine, but the proof surface isn't what it was when they minted it. I guess the other four are in better shape. I saw the one in the Smithsonian Institution once and it was a perfect frosty proof with a mirrorlike field, and mine was nothing like that. So I had my pleasure owning it, and then a fellow offered me a handsome profit on it, and I told him if he'd up his price to an even two hundred thousand he could own himself a five-cent piece. I could give you his name but I don't know as he'd want me doing that.'

I asked if the buyer still had the coin.

'Less he sold it,' Arnott said. 'You in the market yourself? I could call the gentleman and find out if he wants to sell.'

'I'm just a reporter, Mr Arnott.'

'Well, I was thinking that it's easy to be a reporter over the phone.

I've been that in my time, and a Baptist minister and any number of lawyers. Now don't let me offend you, sir. If you want to be a reporter that's just what you are, and if you want to find out if the coin's for sale—'

'I just want to find out if he still owns it. I don't care if it's for sale or not.'

'Then you give me a telephone number where you'll be for an hour or so, and I'll see what I can find out.'

I gave him Carolyn's.

I made four more calls, to Washington, Boston, Cincinnati and Philadelphia. Then I called the ANS again, and I called *Coin World*, the weekly newspaper in Sidney, Ohio. By the time I was finished my fingers had done so much walking I was beginning to worry about them. After all, my hands were unquestionably narrow – odd I hadn't ever noticed this before. And there was no denying that my index fingers were substantially longer than my thumbs.

The implications were clear enough. I had Morton's Hand, and I knew only too well where that could lead. Pain in the palm. Wrist spurs. Forearm tendinitis. And, sooner or later, the dreaded Dialer's Shoulder.

I hung up and got the hell out of there.

17

I got to Carolyn's house around noon. I sat there with a cat on my lap and a cup of coffee at my elbow and did what I could to bring my hostess up to date.

I had my work cut out for me. There was a lot of water over the dam or under the bridge or wherever it goes these days, and my task wasn't rendered easier by Carolyn's headache. Another of those dreaded sugar hangovers, no doubt. Maybe the right pair of orthotics would solve everything.

'What I can't get over,' she said, 'is that you went to Abel's without me.'

'We couldn't have both gotten in. And it was risky, and there was nothing two people could do better than one.'

'And then you got home from Abel's and didn't say anything.'

'I tried, dammit. I kept calling you.'

'Bern, I kept calling *you*. Either you were out or the line was busy.'

'I know. I kept calling everybody and everybody kept calling me. These things happen. It doesn't matter. We finally reached each other, didn't we?'

'Yeah, last night. And you didn't tell me zip until just now.'

'It was too late last night.'

'Yeah.'

'And there wasn't that much to tell.'

'No, not much at all. Just that you got into Abel's apartment and came home and some beautician held a gun on you and accused you of framing her brother for murder.'

'That's not exactly what she said.'

'I don't really care what she said exactly.'

'You're pissed.'

'Kind of, yeah.'

'Would it help if I apologized?'

'Try it and let's see.'

'Well,' I said, 'I'm sorry, Carolyn. We're partners, and I certainly meant to keep you in the picture, but things got out of control for a little while there. I didn't know if I'd be able to get into Abel's apartment and I just went ahead and did things on my own, figuring I'd catch up with you later. And I'm sorry.'

She sat in silence for a moment. Then she said, 'Quit it, Ubi,' to the Russian Blue, who was scratching the side of the couch. From my lap, Archie purred with unmistakable moral superiority.

'Nope,' Carolyn said. 'It doesn't help.'

'My apology, you mean?'

'Uh-huh. Doesn't do a thing for me. I'm still pissed. But I'll get over it. Who killed Wanda?'

'I'm not sure.'

'How about Abel?'

'I'm not sure of that, either.'

'Well—'

The phone rang. I moved Archie and answered it, and it was Mr Arnott calling from Stillwater, Oklahoma. He hadn't reversed the charges, either. I guess people who can pay $130,000 for a nickel don't worry about their phone bills.

'The fellow who bought my nickel wants to remain anonymous,' he said. 'I couldn't say whether it's burglars or the tax collector he's scared of. Coin's not for sale, though. He's still got it, and he figures to keep it.'

'The hell with him,' I said. 'I think I'd rather buy a painting anyway.'

'That way you'll have something you can hang on the wall.'

'That's what I decided.'

I reported the conversation to Carolyn. 'Arnott's coin is still with the mysterious purchaser,' I explained. 'Anyway, it was a lightly circulated specimen, so it couldn't have been the one we carried from Eighteenth Street to Riverside Drive.'

She frowned. 'There were five of the nickels altogether.'

'Right.'

'Now there's one in Washington, one in Boston, one in Cincinnati, one in – Philadelphia?'

'Right.'

'And one that your friend in Oklahoma sold to some mystery man. So the mystery man is Colcannon. Except he can't be, because that coin's circulated and Colcannon's was a perfect proof.'

'Right.'

'So there are five nickels *plus* the Colcannon nickel.'

'Right.'

'Which Colcannon doesn't have anymore, and which wasn't at Abel's, so we don't know where it is.'

'Right.'

'Which means the nickel we stole was a counterfeit.'

'It's possible.'

'But you don't think so?'

'No. I'm positive it's genuine.'

'Then there are actually six nickels.'

'No. Only five.'

She sat for a moment, puzzling, then threw her hands in the air. 'Bern,' she said, 'would you for chrissake quit cocking around? My whole head hurts except for the part I normally think with, which is numb. Just explain, will you? Simply, so I can understand it.'

I explained. Simply. So she could understand it.

'Oh,' she said.

'Does it make sense? Stand up? Hold water?'

'I think so. What about the questions I asked you earlier? There was a Third Burglar who killed Wanda. Do you know who he was?'

'I have an idea.'

'And do you have an idea who killed Abel?'

'Sort of. But I can't be sure of it, and I certainly can't prove it, and—'

'Tell me anyway, Bernie.'

'I sort of hate to say anything at this stage.'

'Why? Because you don't want to spoil the surprise? Bern, if you were really sincere with that apology you gave me a few minutes ago, why don't you prove it?'

I shifted a little on the chair. There are those who might have said I squirmed. 'We've got to get out of here,' I said. 'It may have been a mistake giving out your number. If the man who wants to buy the coin could find out my name and how to reach me, he might have a connection in the Police Department or access to one of the phone company's reverse directories. I don't want us to be where he can get at us. He knows I'm going to be at this phone at two, so—'

'There's time, Bern. You can tell me your theories and we'll still have plenty of time.'

Archie extended his forepaws and stretched. 'Archie's no name for a cat,' I said. 'The cat's Mehitabel, remember?'

'He's a boy cat, dum-dum. He's Rex Stout's Archie, not Don Marquis's Archy.'

'Oh.'

'I could always get a pet cockroach and name her Mehitabel. If I knew it was a girl cockroach. Why am I sitting here talking about cockroaches? You changed the subject, dammit.'

'I guess I did.'

'Well, change it back again. Who killed Wanda and Abel?'

I gave up and told her.

Afterward we set up the answering machine with a simple message that I recorded, telling whoever called to ring me at Denise's number. I got my attaché case from Carolyn's closet, where it was still keeping the Chagall company. We got out of there and took a cab to the Poodle

Factory. We went inside, and when we emerged a couple of minutes later my attaché case was the slightest bit heavier. Carolyn locked up and we caught another cab to the Narrowback Gallery.

On the way there she wanted to know why we had to go to Denise's place. I said I'd already told her, and expressed the wish that the two of them got along better.

'You might as well wish for wings,' she said. 'Oh, she's all right for a scarecrow, but don't you have better taste than that? There must be an attractive straight woman somewhere in New York. How about Angela?'

'Who?'

'The waitress at the Bum Rap.'

'I thought you decided she was gay.'

'I decided the question calls for research. Monday I'm gonna ask her a question that'll let me know if she's gay without tipping her off if she isn't.'

'What's the question?'

'Something like, "Angela, how about you and me getting married?"'

'You don't think that's overly subtle?'

'Well, I might work on the phrasing a little.'

Any pleasure Denise might have felt at seeing me was completely obliterated by her reaction to the sight of Carolyn. The dismay showed clearly on her face. 'Oh, the dog lady,' she said, 'I don't seem to remember your name.'

'It's Carolyn,' I was saying, even as Carolyn was saying, 'You can call me Ms Kaiser.' It was going to be a long afternoon, I realized, and I was glad I wasn't going to be on hand for very much more of it.

'I didn't recognize you at first,' Denise said. 'I didn't remember you as being quite so short as you are, and at first glance I thought you were a child.'

'It's my air of innocence that does it,' Carolyn said. She stationed herself in front of one of the more striking paintings on display, tilting her head to one side and planting herself with her hands on her hips. 'Painting must really be fun when you don't have to make it look like anything,' she said. 'You can just sort of smear the paint on any old way, can't you?'

'I'll make some coffee,' Denise said. 'And I'm sure Ms Kaiser must want something to eat.'

'No, I don't think so,' Carolyn said. 'I haven't had much of an appetite lately. Maybe I'm getting anorexia. I understand it strikes some women late in life.'

It went on like this, and I might have been able to sit back and enjoy it if they hadn't both been favorite people of mine. God knows there was nothing else for me to do. They didn't need a referee; they were

552

doing fine all by themselves, and nobody was bothering to keep score. Jared, I learned, was out for the afternoon. I thought that showed sound judgment on his part.

The phone rang at two o'clock. I picked it up, held the receiver to my ear, and waited until I heard a familiar voice. Then I nodded shortly and passed the receiver to Carolyn.

'The gentleman you're calling hasn't arrived yet,' she said. 'Please call again in precisely fifteen minutes.'

She hung up, looked at me. I grabbed up my attaché case and got to my feet. 'I'm on my way,' I said. 'You know what you're supposed to tell him when he calls?'

'Uh-huh. He should go to the Squires coffee shop at the corner of Madison and Seventy-ninth. He should sit at the table farthest from the door and wait, and you'll either join him at his table or have him paged under the name of Madison, as in Avenue.'

'And if he asks about the coin—'

'You've got it.'

'Right.'

'You've got me involved in something,' Denise said. 'You're still a burglar, aren't you, Bernie? Of course you are. The leopard doesn't change his spots. Or the convict his stripes, apparently.'

'They don't wear stripes in prison anymore.'

'Oh, but they should. They're so slimming. But you'd know what they wear and don't wear, wouldn't you? You've been there. And you're still a burglar. Are you a killer, too?' She looked at Carolyn. 'And what are *you*, exactly? His henchperson?'

'Carolyn will explain everything,' I said. And I didn't envy her a bit.

All of a sudden I was taking cabs a lot. I took the third of the day to the corner of Eighteenth Street and Ninth Avenue. We made good time, and by two-fifteen I was staked out across the street from the heavy iron gate marked 442½. At that very moment he was supposed to be on the phone, and perhaps he was, because ten minutes later the gate swung open and Herbert Franklin Colcannon emerged from it. I was in a shadowy doorway where he couldn't have seen me, but he didn't even look in my direction, turning to his left and striding purposefully toward Tenth Avenue, either to catch a cab or because he had a car parked there.

I didn't care which it was. I let him reach the corner, then jogged across the street – I was wearing my Pumas, their excessive width notwithstanding. It was a bright sunny afternoon and there were people on the street, but that didn't bother me this time. I knew which of my skeleton keys would do for the lock on the iron gate, since I'd already determined that Tuesday night, so I had the key in hand as I crossed the street and I was through the gate and had it locked behind me in a matter of seconds.

I wasn't wearing rubber gloves, either. This time around I didn't care about prints. If things went wrong they'd go wrong dramatically, and fingerprints would be the least of my worries. If things went right, nobody would give a damn where my fingers had been.

Once I was through the gate and into the tunnel I unsnapped the locks on my attaché case and took the gun from it.

Nasty things, guns. This one looked to have been made of blued steel, but its surface was warmer to the touch. The material was some sort of high-impact phenolic resin. I suppose I could have carried it onto an airplane. I let my hand accustom itself to the feel of the weapon, checked its load, and made my way through the tunnel.

I wanted that gun in my hand in case Astrid was spending the afternoon in the garden. I didn't expect that would be the case, but the bitch was attack-trained and I wasn't, and I didn't want to be unprepared for an encounter with her. At the mouth of the tunnel I paused with the gun at my side and scanned the garden carefully.

No Astrid. No people, either. I slipped the gun beneath the waistband of my trousers where my jacket would screen it from view and then walked quickly across the flagstone patio with scarcely a glance at the tulips and daffodils, the little fishpond, the semicircular bench.

With a garden like that, why would a man go chasing phantom coins all over the place? Of course it might not be his garden, it might indeed belong to the front house, but surely he could sit in it, couldn't he?

I mounted the stoop and rang the bell. I'd seen him leave, but how did I know he'd been alone there? I put my ear to the door and listened, and I heard some barking that I could have heard without putting my ear to the door, and then a rumbling sound as if something bulky had just fallen down a flight of stairs. A chest of drawers, say, or an excitable Bouvier des Flandres. The barking was repeated and got louder, and all I had between me and Astrid was a wooden door about two inches thick.

Which I promptly set about opening.

The locks had been easy the first time, and they're always easier the second time around. My fingers remembered their inner workings, and I knocked them off one-two-three in not many more seconds than it takes to tell about it. If anyone had watched from a rear window of the front house, say, I don't think he'd have had cause for suspicion.

I turned the knob, opened the door the merest fraction of an inch. The barking increased in volume and climbed in pitch. There was a manic intensity in it now – or perhaps it just sounded that way to me.

I drew the gun, checked the load once more.

Was there any way I could avoid doing this? Couldn't I just close the door and lock up after myself and get the hell out? Maybe I could rush up to Madison and Seventy-ninth, maybe Colcannon and I could work something out, maybe—

Quit stalling, Rhodenbarr.

I leveled the gun in my right hand, held the door-knob in my left. In one motion I threw the door violently inward. The dog – a huge black beast, and utterly ferocious to look upon – recoiled reflexively, then gathered herself to spring at my throat.

I pointed the gun and fired.

18

The dart went right where I'd aimed it, taking Astrid in the left shoulder. Bouviers have a dense curly coat and there was no way to be sure the dart wouldn't get deflected en route, and for a moment I thought it had because she seemed unaffected by it.

Then the tranquilizer hit. Astrid was about halfway into her spring, forepaws off the ground, when all at once her eyes glazed over and her jaw went slack. Her paws worked in the air like the feet of the coyote in the Roadrunner cartoons when he runs off a cliff and tries to keep going. Astrid couldn't keep going. She settled back down again, her spring unsprung, and then she wobbled like a child in high heels, and finally she uttered a sort of whimpery sound and pitched over onto her side.

How do you check a dog's pulse? I actually tried, fumbling around with what I don't suppose you call a wrist when you're dealing with a dog, but I gave that up because I didn't know what I was doing, and what difference did it make, anyway? If she was alive all I could do was let her sleep it off, and if she was dead there was nothing anybody could do for her, and my own course of action was the same in either case.

And I didn't have all the time in the world, either.

I raced up the stairs. The bedroom was in good order now, I saw. Sheets of plywood had been secured over the broken skylight, and the pastoral landscape once again hung on the wall, hiding the safe. I took it from its hook, fluffy sheep and rose-cheeked shepherdess and all, and placed it on the bed.

I wasn't sure if I'd remember the safe's combination or not. I'd thought about it in the cab on the way over, trying to put all the numbers together in the proper sequence, but once I was up there with my fingers on the dial I took the problem away from my mind and entrusted it to my hands, and they remembered. I opened the safe as if its combination were written out for me.

Five minutes later – well, no more than ten, anyway – I was hanging Little Bo Peep back where she belonged. I did a couple of other things, and in the second-floor library I sat at a leather-topped kneehole desk and used a modern reproduction of an old brass telephone to call

Narrowback Gallery. I gave a progress report and established that Colcannon had not called since Carolyn sent him to Madison and Seventy-ninth.

I asked how long Astrid was likely to remain unconscious. 'I don't know,' Carolyn admitted. 'I bought the dart gun because it's supposed to be a good thing to have around, but I never used the thing. I didn't think you would need it, to tell you the truth. She's always a perfect lady when I give her a bath. She never even growls.'

'Well, she was ready to kill a few minutes ago.'

'It's a territorial thing, I guess. If she hadn't been on her own turf she'd have been gentle.'

'If she hadn't been on her own turf,' I said, 'we wouldn't have met. I just wish I knew how much time I've got.'

'Maybe you'd better not take any longer than you have to. That stuff works longer on a small dog than a large one, and Astrid's no Yorkie.'

'No kidding. She's the Hound of the goddamn Baskervilles, is what she is.'

'Well, get done as quickly as you can, Bern. If you have to use a second dart it might kill her. Or it might not work at all, or I don't know what.'

I hung up and made another phone call, this one to the pay phone at Squires coffee shop at Madison and Seventy-ninth. I asked the woman who answered if she would summon Mr Madison to the phone, and explained she'd be likely to find him at one of the rear booths. A moment later he said, 'Well? Where are you?'

'I'm at a pay phone in a coffee shop, same as you. Let's not use names, shall we? I don't like to talk over an open line.'

'Then why didn't you come here in person?'

'Because I'm afraid of you,' I said. 'I don't know who you are and you seem to know a lot about me. For all I know you're a violent person. I don't want to take the chance.'

'Do you have the coin?'

'I picked it up this morning. I don't have it with me now because I'm not willing to run the risk. It's in a safe place and I can pick it up on short notice. I'm calling you now because I think we should set a price.'

'Name your price.'

'What's it worth to you?'

'No, that's not how we'll work it, sir.' He seemed quite confident now, as if bargaining was something with which he had some reassuring familiarity. 'Set your price, and make it your best price, and I shall say yes or no to it.'

'Fifty thousand dollars.'

'No.'

'No?'

'According to the newspapers, a woman was killed when the coin was taken.'

'Ah, but nobody knows that the coin was connected with her death. Except you and me, that is. And her husband, of course.'

'Quite. I can pay you ten thousand dollars. I never argue price, sir.'

'Neither do I. I'll take twenty.'

'Impossible.'

Twelve thousand was the price we settled on. He probably would have gone higher, but my skill in negotiation was diminished by my knowledge that I didn't have a coin to sell, so why knock myself out? We agreed on the price, and he agreed to bring the money in old out-of-sequence bills, nothing larger than a hundred. I don't know where he was going to find the money, since the banks were closed and there was no cash in the safe, but maybe he had a friend he could go to or had cash stashed around the house. I hadn't searched the place in the fine-comb style I'd employed at Abel's apartment, nor did I intend to, not with the formidable Astrid stretched out downstairs in uncertain sleep.

'We can make the exchange tomorrow,' I said. 'A friend of mine died this past week and there's going to be a memorial service for him over in Brooklyn. Nobody knows me there and I don't suppose anybody'll know you either, though I can't say that for sure because I don't know you myself. Do you have a big following in Cobble Hill?'

'I'm afraid not.'

'Then we're in good shape. The service is at the Church of the Redeemer at two-thirty tomorrow afternoon. That's on Henry Street between Congress and Amity, and now you know as much about getting there as I do. I'll have the coin in an envelope, and if you could have the money the same way, we could make the exchange. I suppose there must be a bathroom, churches generally have bathrooms, and we can go there together and make sure it's the right coin and the money's all present and accounted for.'

'I don't see why we have to meet in Brooklyn.'

'Because I have to be there anyway, and because I won't pick up the coin until I'm on my way to the service, and because I want to make the swap in a public place, but not so public that there are likely to be police looking on. If you don't want to do it, I'm inclined to say the hell with it and put the coin in a gum machine, because this million-dollar coin has dropped in value to twelve grand and that's not all the money in the world to me, to be frank about it. So we'll do it my way or we won't do it at all, and maybe that's a better idea anyway, come to think of it.'

I let him cajole me out of my snit. I didn't require too much in the way of cajolery. It wasn't that deep a snit. Then I said, 'Wait a minute, how will we recognize each other? We've never met.'

'I'll know you. I've seen your picture.'

He'd done better than that. He'd seen me face to face, through a pane of presumably one-way glass. And I'd seen him the same way, although he didn't know it. I went along with the charade, saying I didn't look all that much like my picture and I wanted to be able to recognize him, too, so why didn't we both wear red carnations? He agreed, and I advised him to pick up his flower that evening, because it might be difficult finding a florist open on Sunday.

And through all this chatter I kept listening for Astrid's footfall on the stairs. At any moment she might come awake, anxious to demonstrate how attack dogs got their name.

'Tomorrow, then,' he said. 'At two-thirty. I'll be glad when this is over, Mr – I almost said your name.'

'Don't worry about it.'

'As I said, I'll be glad when this is over.'

He wasn't the only one.

I made sure the gun was armed with a little plastic dart, hurried downstairs with it and had a quick look at Astrid. She lay as I'd left her, sprawled on her side, and now I could see her chest heave with heavy breathing. While I stood there she made a small mewling sound and her forepaws twitched. The dart that had done the job lay alongside her. I retrieved it, dropped it into my attaché case.

I went upstairs and used the phone again. I had a lot of people I wanted to call, but I limited myself to dialing three numbers, all of them long distance. None of the calls lasted very long. After the third one I went back downstairs to find the big black dog almost awake but not quite able to get up on her feet. She turned woebegone ill-focused eyes on me, and it was difficult to regard her as a threat. She looked incapable of a hostile thought, let alone of tearing one's throat out. But I forced myself to remember her bark, and the way she'd coiled herself to spring.

I hoped she'd be her old alert self by the time her master returned.

I let myself out, locked up after myself. If anyone watched me I was unaware of it. I walked through the garden, still wondering if there were fish in the pond, and I searched the flower beds in vain for carnations, red or otherwise. I could have suggested that he wear a tulip.

Why, I wondered, had I bothered with that carnation business? All in the interest of verisimilitude, I suppose, but it could add an unnecessary complication, because now I had to remember to pick one up before the stores closed. Which ordinarily wouldn't have been such a chore, but it was one of a long list of things to do, and I had less than twenty-four hours to get them all done.

Which left me no time to squander in gardens. I hurried through the tunnel, looked left and right and straight ahead, opened the gate and let myself out.

So many things to do . . .

19

'I dunno, Bern. What it sounds like to me is you're settin' up somethin' complicated.'

'Isn't that what you wanted? You know I didn't have anything to do with either the Colcannon burglary or the murder of Abel Crowe, but you kept sniffing around, trying to stir something up.'

'You're in both of those things up to your eyes, Bern. I just don't know about this, that's all.'

It was Ray Kirschmann's day off and he was wearing brown gabardine slacks and a print sport shirt. The pants were baggy in the seat and too tight at the waist, and the shirt was one of those Korean imports in light green with dark-green stitching on the collar and pockets. I really wish he'd take his wife along when he buys clothes.

I said, 'What's to know, Ray? I'm giving you a chance to be a hero, make a couple of good busts, clear a few old cases and put a few dollars in your pocket. What else do you expect to do? Slay the dragon and screw the king's daughter?'

'I don't care about dragons, Bern.'

'You wouldn't like a princess much. One pea under the mattress keeps them bitching all night.'

'Yeah, I remember the story. Tell me again about the dollars I'm gonna put in my pocket.'

'There's a man who's willing to pay a reward for the recovery of his property.'

'What man?'

'You'll meet him tomorrow.'

'What property?'

'You'll find that out tomorrow, too.'

'How am I gonna recover it? That's somethin' else I'll find out tomorrow. This is soundin' like those old radio programs. "Tune in tomorrow an' see what happens to Jack Armstrong, the all-American boy." Remember Jack Armstrong, Bern? Whatever did happen to him?'

'He's doing short time at Attica.'

'Jesus, what a thought. How much of a reward are we talkin' about?'

'Ten grand.'

He nodded, sucked his teeth. 'But it's not offered officially,' he said. 'The guy could welsh.'

'If it's not official it doesn't have to be reported, either. No taxes to pay. No splits with anybody higher up in the department.'

His face took on a crafty look, and greed sparkled in his eyes. Spinoza may not have had a good word to say for avarice, but how would the wheels turn without it?

'The hell,' he said. 'We'll see how it goes.'

'Have you got that list?'

He nodded, drew a folded sheet of paper from the pocket of the green sport shirt. 'These here are burglaries committed in the past two years with an MO like the Colcannon job – forced entry and the place left like the burglars brought a cyclone with 'em. And it's the area you said – Manhattan south of Forty-second Street, west of Fifth Avenue and north of Fourteenth Street. Computers are wonderful. You just say what you want and you got it.'

'You wouldn't believe how comforting it is to know the police have these tools at their command.'

'I can imagine. You're not the first person to figure Rabbit Margate might have done this kinda thing before, you know. They been questionin' him left and right. Not goin' back two years, and not just the neighborhood you picked, but they been askin' him a question or two.'

'Are they getting anywhere?'

'He still bein' Humphrey Bogart.'

'Yesterday you said he was Jimmy Cagney.'

'Same difference.'

'You'll bring him tomorrow?'

'It's irregular. If he got loose and took a powder I'd have a little trouble explainin' it. I guess I could take a chance.'

'And you don't know who was working with him?'

'Not yet. He'll talk sooner or later.'

'Then I'll see you tomorrow,' I said, and went over the time and place with him again.

'Anythin' I should bring? Besides Rabbit?'

'Your gun.'

'I'm never without it.'

'Not even in the shower? Let me think. Handcuffs, Ray. Bring plenty of handcuffs.'

'Like I'm gonna arrest the whole Jesse James gang or somethin'. Well, you generally delivered in the past, Bern, so I'll play along. Anythin' else I can do for you in the meantime? Want a lift anywhere? Anythin' I can do to grease the skids for you a little?'

I thought it over, then resisted temptation. 'No,' I said. 'I can manage.'

*

I found Marilyn Margate at Hair Apparent. She was combing out a hard-faced woman with a headful of unconvincing auburn hair. 'He admits he sleeps with his wife,' the woman was saying, 'but he insists he never enjoys it, that it's just a sense of duty. But my experience is they always tell you that, so how do you know what to believe?'

'I know just where you're coming from,' Marilyn said. 'Believe me, I know.'

When she had a minute I drew her aside and gave her a slip of paper with the time and place of Abel's service. 'It's important for you to show up,' I said. 'And bring Harlan Reese.'

'Harlan? You think he went back and killed Wanda? That doesn't sound like Harlan.'

'Just bring him.'

'I don't know. He's not even leaving his room. And he was talking about splitting for the coast or something before the cops get onto him. I don't think he's gonna want to chase out to Brooklyn for some old guy's funeral.'

'Get him to come anyway. Your brother'll be there.'

'Rabbit's gonna be there? You mean they let him out?'

'They'll release him for the service. I arranged it.'

'You—' Her eyes were wide, her expression respectful. 'That's some kind of arranging,' she said. 'That's more than the lawyer could do. They wouldn't set bail for him. Wait'll I tell his lawyer.'

'Don't tell his lawyer anything.'

'Oh. All right.'

'Just show up tomorrow with Harlan.'

'If Rabbit's gonna be there, I'll get there. And I'll bring Harlan.'

I called Narrowback Gallery and Denise answered. 'I hope you're free tomorrow,' I said. 'I'd like you to come to a funeral in Brooklyn.'

'I'll wear a smock and a smile. You want to talk to your partner in crime?'

'Please.'

She put Carolyn on and I said things were going well, albeit hectically. 'I have to get into Abel's building,' I said, 'and I decided not to ask Ray for help because I didn't want him to know what I was up to. Any bright ideas?'

'I guess it's a little late for another doctor's appointment.'

'It's Saturday and it's close to dinnertime. That does make it tricky.'

'If there's anything I can do—'

'I can't think of anything. I'll probably be tied up most of the night, assuming I find a way in. I thought maybe I'd drop over to your place after I'm done.'

'Well, I sort of have a date, Bern.'

'Oh. Well, I'll see you tomorrow at Abel's service. You'd better take

562

down the address, or did I give it to you earlier?' I gave it to her again and she wrote it down. Then I asked her to put Denise on.

'Carolyn has the address for the service tomorrow. That's assuming that the two of you are speaking.'

'You assume a lot.'

'Uh-huh. What I wanted to say is I've got a batch of things to do tonight but I'll be done sooner or later, and I thought maybe I could drop over.'

'Oh.'

'Because I'd like to see you.'

'Tonight's a bad night, Bernie.'

'Oh. Well, I guess I'll see you tomorrow in Brooklyn.'

'I guess so. Okay to bring Gore and Truman?'

'They're already on my list.'

A machine answered Murray Feinsinger's telephone, inviting me to leave my name and number or call back at nine Monday morning if I wanted to speak to the doctor. I hung up without leaving a message and read through the listing of Feinsingers in the Manhattan directory until I found a listing for one Dorothy Feinsinger at the same address and dialed the number. Murray himself answered it.

I said, 'Dr Feinsinger? My name's Bernard Rhodenbarr, I was in to see you yesterday afternoon. About my feet.'

'That's why most people come to see me, Mr Rhodenbarr. My office is closed for the day, and—'

'I don't know if you remember me. I had Morton's Foot, and you're going to be making orthotics for me.'

'They're not ready yet, of course. It takes a couple of weeks.'

'Yes, I understand that. But I gave you a deposit, just a small deposit really, and—'

'I'm afraid I've already sent the order in, Mr Rhodenbarr. Is there a problem?'

'No problem at all,' I said, 'but I had a sudden cash windfall this afternoon, as a matter of fact I had a good day at the track, see, and I wanted to pay you the balance due before I blow it on necessities. And I'm in the neighborhood, so I thought maybe I could come up and pay you what I owe you, I guess it comes to two hundred and seventy dollars because I paid a thirty-dollar deposit, and—'

'That's very considerate of you, Mr Rhodenbarr. Why don't you stop in Monday?'

'Well, Monday's a hard day for me, and for all I know the money might be gone by then. It wouldn't take a minute if I could just come up and pay you and—'

'I can't really take money outside of business hours,' he said. 'I'm at my apartment. My office is across the hall and it's closed, and I'd have to open up and make out a receipt for you and enter the cash in my books, and I'd rather not do all that.'

'A receipt's not important to me. I could just pop up, pay you the cash, and off I'd go.'

There was a pause. By now he must have been certain he was dealing with a lunatic, and why should he want to invite a lunatic upstairs? There should have been a way to get to see him, but I had evidently blown it, and everything I said now was only going to make it worse.

'Well, I'll see you Monday,' I said. 'I hope I still have the money by then. Maybe I'll put it in my shoe in the meantime.'

Brooklyn Information had a listing for a J. L. Garland on Cheever Place. The operator had no better idea than I if that was in Cobble Hill, but she said the exchange sounded about right, so I dialed it and got a chap with a sort of reedy voice. I asked to speak to Jessica and she came to the phone.

'This is Bernie Rhodenbarr,' I told her. 'I'll be there tomorrow, and I just wanted to confirm the time and place. Two-thirty at the Church of the Redeemer, is that right?'

'That's correct.'

'Good. There are a couple of people I'd like you to call, if you would. To ask them to come. Neighbors of your grandfather's.'

'I already posted a notice in the lobby. But you can call anyone yourself if you think it's advisable.'

'I've already invited several people, as a matter of fact. I'd appreciate it if you'd make these particular calls, though. Could you write this down?'

She said she could and I gave her names and numbers and told her what to say. While I was doing this it occurred to me that she might have access to Abel's apartment. I wasn't quite sure I wanted to visit the place in her company, but it looked to be better than not going at all.

So I asked her if she'd been up to the place since the murder, and she hadn't. 'I don't have keys,' she said, 'and the doorman said the police had left strict instructions not to admit anyone. I don't know that they'd let me up anyway. Why?'

'No reason,' I said. 'I just wondered. You'll make those calls?'

'Right away.'

A few minutes after eight I presented myself at Abel Crowe's building. The doorman was a stranger to me, even as I presume I was to him. He looked as assertive as Astrid the Bouvier and I hoped I wouldn't have to take him out with a tranquilizer dart in the shoulder.

I had the dart pistol along, albeit not at hand. It was in my attaché case, along with burglar's tools, a fresh pair of palmless rubber gloves, and my wide-track Pumas. I was wearing black wingtips for a change, heavy and leather-soled and not particularly comfortable, but a better match than Weejuns or Pumas for my funereal three-button suit and the somber tie with the muted stripe.

'Reverend Rhodenbarr for Mrs Pomerance in 11-J,' I said. 'She's expecting me.'

20

'He had European manners,' Mrs Pomerance said. 'Always a smile and a kind word. The heat of summer bothered him, and sometimes you could tell his feet hurt by the way he walked, but you would never hear a complaint out of him. Not like some others I could mention.'

I wrote 'real gent' and 'never complained' in my little notebook and glanced up to catch Mrs Pomerance sneaking a peek at me. She didn't know how she knew me and it was driving her crazy. Since I was clearly the sincere Brooklyn clergyman Jessica Garland had called her about, the obliging chap gathering material for Abel Crowe's eulogy, it hadn't occurred to her that I might also be the Stettiner boy who'd shared an elevator with her a day earlier. But if I was Reverend Rhodenbarr of Cobble Hill, why did I look familiar?

We sat on plump upholstered chairs in her over-furnished little apartment, surrounded by bright-eyed photographs of her grandchildren and a positive glut of bisque figurines, and for twenty minutes or so she alternately spoke well of the dead and ill of the living, doing a good job of dishing the building's other inhabitants. She lived alone, did Mrs Pomerance; her beloved Moe was cutting velvet in that great sweat-shop in the sky.

It was about eight-thirty when I turned down a second cup of coffee and got up from my chair. 'You've been very helpful,' I told her, truthfully enough. 'I'll look forward to seeing you at the service to-morrow.'

She walked me to the door, assuring me she wouldn't miss it. 'I'll be interested to see if you use anything I told you,' she said. 'No, you have to turn the top lock, too. That's right. You want to know something? You remind me of somebody.'

'The Stettiner boy?'

'You know him?'

I shook my head. 'But I'm told there's a resemblance.'

She closed the door after me and locked up. I walked down the hall, picked Abel's spring lock and let myself into his apartment. It was as

566

I'd left it, but darker, of course, since no daylight was streaming through his windows.

I turned some lights on. I wouldn't have done this ordinarily, not without drawing drapes first, but the closest buildings across the way were also across the river, so who was going to see me?

I did a little basic snooping, but nothing like the full-scale search I'd given the place the day before. I went through the bedroom closet, looking at this and at that, and I paid a second visit to the cigar humidor. Then I browsed the bookshelves, looking not for stashed loot but simply for something to read.

What I would have liked was my Robert B. Parker novel. I would have enjoyed finding out what was going on with old Spenser, who was evidently capable of jogging without orthotics and lifting weights without acquiring a hernia. But light fiction was harder to find in that place than a 1913 V-Nickel, and any number of books which might have been interesting were less so because of my inability to read German, French or Latin.

I wound up reading Schopenhauer's *Studies in Pessimism*, which was not at all what I'd had in mind. The book itself was a cheap reading copy, a well-thumbed Modern Library edition, and either Abel himself or a previous owner had done a fair amount of underlining, along with the odd exclamation point in the margin when something struck his fancy.

'*If a man sets out to hate all the miserable creatures he meets,*' I read, '*he will not have much energy left for anything else; whereas he can despise them, one and all, with the greatest ease.*'

I rather liked that, but a little Schopenhauer does go a long way. I thought about playing a little music, decided that having turned on some lights was as dangerously as I cared to live for the time being.

Some of that ancient Armagnac would have gone nicely. I had a little milk instead, and somewhere between ten and eleven I turned off the lights in the living room and went into the bedroom and got undressed.

His bed was neatly made. I suppose he must have made it up himself upon arising on the last morning of his life. I set the bedside alarm for two-thirty, crawled under the covers, switched off the lamp and went to sleep.

The alarm cut right into a dream. I don't recall what the dream was about, but it very likely concerned illegal entry of one sort or another because my mind promptly incorporated the wail of the clock into the dream, where it became a burglar alarm. I did a lot of fumbling for the off-switch in the dream before I tore myself free of it and fumbled for the actual clock, which had just about ran down of its own accord by the time I got my hands on it.

Terrific. I sat for a few minutes in the dark, listening carefully, hoping no one would take undue note of the alarm. I don't suppose anybody even heard it. Those old buildings are pretty well sound-proofed. I certainly didn't hear anything, and after a bit I switched on the lamp and got up and dressed.

This time, though, I put on the Pumas instead of the black wingtips. And I put my gloves on.

I let myself out of Abel's apartment, pushing the latch button so that the spring lock wouldn't engage when I closed the door. I walked down the hallway past the elevator to the stairwell, and I walked down seven flights of stairs and made my way to 4-B.

No light showed beneath the door. No sound was audible within. There was only one lock on the door, and you could have taken it to the circus and sold it as cotton candy. I let myself in.

Ten minutes later I let myself out and locked the door behind me. I climbed up seven flights of stairs, let myself back into Abel's apartment by the simple expedient of turning the knob, closed and locked the door, took off my trusty Pumas and everything else, set the bedside alarm for seven, and got back into bed.

And couldn't sleep at first. I got up, found a robe in the closet, put it on. It dawned on me that I hadn't eaten enough all day to sustain a canary, so I went into the kitchen and knocked off the rest of the Black Forest cake and finished the quart of milk. Then I went back to bed and slept.

I was up before the alarm. I had a quick shower, found a safety razor and shaved with it. It was strange, living in his apartment, as if I'd slipped into the very life my old friend had lately given up, but I didn't let myself dwell on it. I made a cup of instant coffee, drank it, and got dressed. I put on the dress shoes again and packed the Pumas in the attaché case, along with another of the books I'd been browsing earlier.

Neither the elevator operator nor the doorman gave me a second glance. They had never seen me before, but I was leaving at a civilized hour of the morning, and even in a stuffy old co-op on Riverside Drive there are surely some tenants of either gender who are apt to have the occasional stranger spending the occasional night, and leaving under his or her own power by light of dawn.

Hair Apparent was on Ninth Avenue a few doors north of Twenty-fourth Street, next to a restaurant called Chelsea Commons. It was closed, of course, with a folding steel gate similar to the one I had at Barnegat Books. A padlock secured the gate across the doorway. I stood there in full view of passers-by and used a piece of spring steel to tease the lock until it opened.

Nobody paid any attention. It was broad daylight – and shaping up to be a beautiful day in the bargain. And I was well-dressed and obviously respectable, and to anyone watching I'd have looked as though I were using not a lock-pick but a perfectly legitimate key. Nothing to it, really.

Not much more to the business of unlocking the door. It took a little longer but it wasn't terribly tricky.

Then I opened the door and the burglar alarm went off.

Well, these things happen, in life as in dreams. I'd noted the alarm when I'd dropped in on Marilyn Margate the previous afternoon, and I'd looked around long enough to spot the cut-out switch on the wall near the first chair. I walked into the shop, proceeded directly to the cut-out switch, and silenced the shrill wailing.

No harm done. The neighbors were very likely used to that sort of thing. Business proprietors set off their own alarms all the time when they open up. It's when an alarm goes off in the middle of the night, or sounds for a long time unattended, that people reach for the phone and dial 911. Otherwise they assume it's all business as usual.

Anyway, what sort of idiot would burglarize a beauty shop?

I spent better than half an hour burglarizing this one. When I left, everything was as I had found it, with the sole exception of the burglar alarm, which I didn't reset for fear of setting it off again on my way out. I left the money in the register – just a few rolls of change and a dozen singles. And I left the gun Marilyn had pointed at me; she'd returned it to her employer's drawer, and that's where I let it remain.

I wiped the surfaces I was likely to have touched – rubber gloves didn't go well with my outfit. And I locked up after myself, and drew the window gates shut, and fastened the padlock.

Carolyn's number didn't answer. I started to call Denise, then changed my mind. I walked east on Twenty-third Street and read the plaques on the Chelsea Hotel, which boasted not of pediatricians and podiatrists in residence but writers who'd lived there in the past – Thomas Wolfe, Dylan Thomas. At Seventh Avenue I turned right and walked on downtown. Now and then I would pass a church, the worshipers all fresh-faced and spruced up as if in celebration of the season. A beautiful morning, I told myself. You couldn't ask for a finer day to bury Abel Crowe.

Of course, I reminded myself, we wouldn't actually bury him today. That would have to wait. But, if the service went as I hoped it would, perhaps we could lay my old friend to rest – his spirit if not his body. I had spent a night in his apartment, the apartment in which he'd been struck down and killed, and I couldn't say that I felt the presence of a restless spirit, an unquiet ghost. Then again, I'm not much at feeling presences. Someone who's more sensitive to that sort of thing might have felt Abel's shade close at hand in that living room, pacing the oriental carpet, crying out for vengeance. Just because I'm not aware of those things doesn't mean they don't exist.

I walked down below Fourteenth Street and had a big breakfast at a coffee shop in the Village – eggs, bacon, orange juice, toasted bran muffin, plenty of coffee. I picked up the Sunday *Times*, threw away all those sections nobody reads, and took the rest to Washington Square. There I sat on a bench, ignored all the obliging young men who offered to sell me every mood-altering chemical known to modern man, and read the paper while watching people and pigeons and the occasional ditsy gray squirrel. Kids climbed on the monkey bars. Young mothers pushed prams. Youths flung frisbees to and fro. Bums panhandled. Drunks staggered. Chess players advanced pawns while kibitzers shook their heads and clucked their tongues. People walked dogs, who ignored the signs and fouled the footpath. Drug dealers hawked their wares, as did the sellers of hot dogs, ice cream, Italian ices, helium-filled balloons, and organic snacks. I spotted my favorite vendor, a black man who sells large fuzzy yellow ducks with bright orange bills. They are the silliest damned things I have ever seen, and people evidently buy them, and I have never been able to figure out why.

I walked from the park to the subway, and by one-thirty I was in Cobble Hill and twenty minutes later I was at the Church of the Redeemer. I met Jessica Garland and the young man she lived with. His name was Clay Merriman, and he turned out to be a lanky fellow, all knees and elbows and a toothy smile. I told them both what I had in mind. He had a little trouble following me, but Jessica grasped it right away. Well, why not? She was Abel's granddaughter, wasn't she?

We looked over the room where the service was to take place. I told her where to seat people, assuming they didn't grab seats on their own. Then I left her and Clay to greet the guests as they arrived, biding my time in a room down the hall that looked to be the minister's study. The door was locked, but you can imagine the kind of lock they put on a minister's study.

At two-thirty the canned organ music started. By now the guests should have arrived, but stragglers will straggle, so the service itself was not going to start for another ten minutes. I waited out those ten minutes in the minister's study, doing a little pacing of the sort one probably does when rehearsing a sermon.

Then it was time. I took two books from my attaché case, refastened its clasps and left it in a corner of the room. I made my way down the corridor and entered the larger room where a fair crowd of people had assembled. I walked down the side aisle, mounted a two-foot platform, and took my place at the lectern.

I looked at all those people and took a deep breath.

21

'Good afternoon,' I said. 'My name is Bernard Rhodenbarr. I'm here, as we all are, because of my friendship for Abel Crowe. Our friend and neighbor was struck down in his own home this past week, and we have assembled here to pay final tribute to his memory.'

I looked over my audience. There were a great many unfamiliar faces in the crowd, and I guessed the older ones belonged to Abel's neighbors from Riverside Drive while the younger ones were Cobble Hill friends of Jessica's. Among them were quite a few people I recognized. I spotted Mrs Pomerance in the second row, and my hearty podiatrist was one row behind her. Over to the left Ray Kirschmann sat beside a skinny young man with a lot of forehead and not much chin, and it didn't take a great leap of logic to guess I was looking at George Edward Margate. His ears were no longer than anybody else's, and his nose didn't exactly twitch, but it wasn't hard to see why they called him Rabbit.

His sister Marilyn was in the first row all the way over on the right. She was dressed quite sedately in a black skirt and dark-gray sweater, but all the same she looked like a whore in church. The man sitting beside her, a round-faced lumpish lout, had to be Harlan Reese.

Denise and Carolyn were sitting together all the way at the back. Carolyn was wearing her blazer. Denise had a sweater on, but I couldn't see whether she was wearing pants or a skirt. No smock, though, and no smile.

As chief mourner, Jessica Garland sat front row center, with Clay Merriman on her left. A pity we hadn't all met before this unhappy occasion, I thought. Abel could have had us all over of an evening, Clay and Jessica and Carolyn and I, and we could have fattened up on pastry while he regaled us with stories of Europe between the wars. But, oddly, he'd never mentioned a granddaughter.

Three men in dark suits sat together at the right of the third row. The one closest to the center was tall and balding, with a long nose and very thin lips. Beside him sat the oldest of the trio, a gentleman about sixty with wide shoulders, snow-white hair and a white mustache. The third man, seated on the aisle, was a small and slightly built fellow with a button nose and thick eyeglasses.

571

I had never seen them before but I was fairly certain I knew who they were. I paused long enough to meet the eyes of the white-haired man in the middle, and while his face did not change its stern expression he gave a short but distinct nod.

At the opposite end of the second row sat another man I recognized. Oval face, clipped mustache, slate-gray hair, little mouth and nose – I'd seen him before, of course, but Jessica had known where to put him because Herbert Franklin Colcannon had obligingly worn a carnation in his lapel.

I winced when I saw it. Somehow with all the running around I'd done I hadn't remembered to get to a florist before they closed. I suppose I could have let myself into a shuttered flower shop that very morning, but the act seemed disproportionately risky.

Anyway, I'd just introduced myself to the company. So Colcannon knew who I was.

'We're told our good friend made his living as a receiver of stolen property,' I began. 'I, however, knew him in another capacity – as a student of philosophy. The writings of Spinoza were particularly precious to Abel Crowe, and I would like to read a brief passage or two as a memorial to him.'

I read from the leatherbound copy we'd given to Abel, the copy I'd retrieved Friday and had subsequently packed in my attaché case the following night. I read a couple short selections from the section entitled 'On the Origin and Nature of the Emotions.' It was dry stuff, and my audience did not look terribly attentive.

I closed Spinoza, placed the book on the lectern, and opened the other volume I'd brought along, one I'd selected last night from Abel's shelves.

'This is a book of Abel's,' I said. 'Selections from the writing of Thomas Hobbes. Here's a passage he underlined from *Philosophical Rudiments concerning Government and Society:* "The cause of mutual fear consists partly in the natural equality of men, partly in their mutual will of hurting; whence it comes to pass that we can neither expect from others nor promise to ourselves the least security. For if we look on men full-grown, and consider how brittle the frame of our human body is, which perishing, all its strength, vigor and wisdom itself perisheth with it; and how easy a matter it is even for the weakest man to kill the strongest; there is no reason why any man trusting to his own strength should conceive himself made by nature above others. They are equals who can do equal things one against the other; but they who can do the greatest thing, namely kill, can do equal things."'

I skipped to another marked passage. 'This is from *Leviathan,*' I said. ' "In the nature of man, we find three principal causes of quarrels. First, competition; second, diffidence; thirdly, glory. The first maketh man invade for gain, the second for safety, and the third for reputation." '

I placed Hobbes with Spinoza. 'Abel Crowe was killed for gain,' I announced. 'The person who killed him is right here. In this room.'

It was not without effect. The whole crowd seemed to draw breath at once. I fixed my eyes for the moment on Carolyn and Denise. They'd known what was coming but my announcement had gotten to them just the same, and they'd drawn a little closer together as if the drama of the moment had obscured their loathing for one another.

'Abel was murdered for a nickel,' I went on. 'People are killed every day for trifling sums, but this particular nickel was no trifle. It was worth something like a quarter of a million dollars.' Another collective gasp from the crowd. 'Tuesday night Abel came into possession of that coin. Twelve hours later he was dead.'

I went on to tell them a little about the history of the five legendary 1913 V-Nickels. 'One of these nickels wound up in the safe of a man who lived in a carriage house in Chelsea. The man and his wife had left town and weren't expected back until the following day. Tuesday evening, while they were gone, a pair of burglars broke through the skylight and ransacked the carriage house.'

'We didn't take no nickel!' Heads swiveled and eyes stared at Rabbit Margate. 'We never took no nickel,' he said again, 'and we never opened no safe. We found the safe, sure, but we couldn't punch it or peel it or nothing. I don't know shit about no nickel.'

'No.'

'And we didn't kill nobody. We didn't hurt nothing. Wasn't nobody home when we went in, and we went out again before nobody came home. I don't know shit about no murders and no nickels.'

He slumped in his seat. Ray Kirschmann turned to whisper something to him, and Rabbit's shoulders sagged in dejection. I don't know what Ray said, probably pointed out Rabbit had just admitted the burglary in front of God and everybody.

'That's true,' I said. 'The first burglars. Rabbit Margate and Harlan Reese' – and didn't Harlan look startled to hear his name spoken aloud – 'contented themselves with burglary and vandalism. Not long after they left, a second burglary took place. This burglar, a considerably more sophisticated and accomplished individual than Margate and Reese, went directly to the wall safe, opened it, and removed a pair of earrings, a valuable wristwatch, and the 1913 nickel. He took them directly to Abel's apartment, where he left them on consignment.'

No point, really, in mentioning we'd obtained some cash for the watch and earrings. No need to tell these people every last detail.

'While the second burglar was delivering the safe's contents to Abel Crowe, the nickel's owner and his wife were returning to their home. They'd had a change of plans that none of the burglars had any reason to be aware of, and so they walked in on a house that looked like Rome after the Goths sacked it. They also walked in on another burglary in progress, and this third burglary was the charm. The man and woman were knocked out and tied up, and when the man regained consciousness and worked free of his bonds he discovered that his wife was dead.'

I looked at Colcannon. He returned my glance, his face quite expressionless. I had the feeling he'd have preferred to be almost anywhere else, and I don't suppose he figured he was going to have the chance to buy his coin back, not this afternoon. He looked like a man who wanted to walk out of a bad movie but had to stay to find out what happened next.

'The nickel's owner called the police, of course. He was given the opportunity to look at the perpetrator of the second burglary but couldn't identify him. Subsequently he did make a positive identification of one of the participants in the first burglary.'

'That was a frame,' Rabbit Margate called out. 'He never saw me. That was a setup.'

'Let's just call it a mistake,' I suggested. 'The gentleman was under a lot of stress. He'd lost his wife, his house had been cruelly looted, and a coin worth a fortune was missing.

'And here's something interesting,' I said, glancing again at Colcannon. 'He never mentioned the coin to the police. He never said a word about it. You have to report losses to the police in order to make an insurance claim, but that didn't mean anything in this instance because the coin wasn't insured. And it wasn't insured for a very good reason. The gentleman didn't have title to it.'

'This has gone far enough.' It was Colcannon who spoke, and he managed to surprise me, not to mention the rest of the crowd. He got to his feet and glared at me. 'I don't know how I let myself be gulled into coming here. I never knew the late Mr Crowe. I was brought here on a false pretext. I never reported the loss of a 1913 V-Nickel and never carried insurance coverage on such a coin for a much better reason than the one you've advanced. I never had such a coin in my possession.'

'I almost believed that for a while myself,' I admitted. 'Oh, I knew you had one, but I thought it might be a counterfeit. I ran a check on the five V-Nickels to find out which one you bought, and it turned out that they were all accounted for. Four were in museum collections and the fifth was privately owned, and the private specimen was lightly circulated and easily distinguishable from the others, and certainly not the specimen I took from your safe.'

Another collective gasp – I'd gone and blown my anonymity, and now all and sundry knew who the perpetrator of the Second Burglary was. Ah, well. These things happen.

'But I had a good close look at that coin,' I went on, 'and I couldn't

574

believe it was a counterfeit. So I did a little more checking and I invited some museum people to take a close look at their coins, and three of the four told me their coins looked just fine, thank you.

'The fourth museum had a counterfeit in the case.'

I looked at the three men in dark suits. The one seated on the aisle, the little button-nosed guy with the thick glasses, was Milo Hracec, and he recognized his cue. 'It was not a bad counterfeit,' he said. 'It was made from a proof 1903 nickel. The zero was removed and a one soldered in place. It was good work, and no one glancing into our display case would be likely to think twice about it, but you could never sell it to anyone as genuine.'

The white-haired man cleared his throat. 'I'm Gordon Ruslander,' he announced. 'When Mr Hracec reported his discovery to me I went immediately to see for myself. He's right – the coin's not a bad counterfeit, but neither is it terribly deceptive at close glance. It's certainly not the coin I received when I traded a painting to the Baltimore Historical Society. That was a genuine specimen. I knew they wouldn't palm off a counterfeit on me, but as a matter of course I had it x-rayed anyway, and it was authentic. The coin that had been substituted for it didn't have to be x-rayed. It was visibly fraudulent.'

'What did you do after you'd seen the coin?'

'I went to my curator's home and confronted him,' he said. The man on Ruslander's other side, the balding chap with the long nose, seemed to shrink in his seat. 'I knew Howard Pitterman had been having his troubles,' Ruslander went on. 'He went through a difficult divorce and had some investment reverses. I didn't realize just how hard his circumstances had been or I would certainly have offered help.' He frowned. 'Instead he took matters into his own hands a couple of months ago. He substituted a counterfeit for the 1913 nickel, then sold off our most important rarity for a fraction of its value.'

'I got twenty thousand dollars for it,' Howard Pitterman said, his voice trembling. 'I must have been insane.'

'I don't know who that man is,' Colcannon said, 'but I've never seen him before in my life.'

'If that's the man who bought the coin,' Pitterman said, 'he didn't buy it from me. I sold it to a dealer in Philadelphia, a man with a shady reputation. Maybe he sold it to this Mr Colcannon, or maybe it went through another pair of hands first. I wouldn't know. I could give you the name of that dealer, although I'd rather not, but I don't think he'd admit to anything, and I can't prove he bought the coin from me.' His voice broke. 'I'd like to help,' he said, 'but I don't see that there's anything I can do.'

'I'll say it again,' Colcannon said. 'I don't know any disreputable coin dealers in Philadelphia. I scarcely know any reputable ones. I know Mr Ruslander by reputation, of course, as the founder of the Gallery of

American and International Numismatics as well as proprietor of the Liberty Bell Mint, but I've never met him or his employees.'

'Then why did you call Samuel Wilkes yesterday?'

'I never heard of Samuel Wilkes.'

'He has an office near Rittenhouse Square,' I said, 'and he deals in coins and medals, and shady's the word for him. You called him yesterday at his home and left your name, and you called his office, and you also put in a call to the Gallery of American and International Numismatics. You made those calls from your home telephone, and since they're long distance there'll be a record of them.'

There would be a record, all right. Colcannon was staring at me, trying to figure out how there would be a record of calls he had never made. Any minute now he'd recall that he'd been lured away from his house and hustled off to Madison and Seventy-ninth, and he might even figure out that he'd had company in his absence, but right now he seemed content to deny the whole thing.

'I never heard of this Wilkes,' he said, 'and I never called him, and I certainly didn't call the gallery.'

'What's it matter anyway, Bern?' It was Ray Kirschmann, and I wasn't sure how much of this he was following. 'If Crowe got killed for this nickel, all right, that makes sense, but who cares how the nickel got into the safe? Crowe got killed after it got outta the safe.'

'Ah,' I said. 'What's significant is that nobody knew it was in the safe in the first place. Except for the Third Burglar.'

'The *who?*'

'Rabbit Margate and Harlan Reese didn't know about the nickel,' I went on. 'All they knew was that the Colcannons were going to be out of town overnight. They knew that because Wanda Colcannon got her hair done at a beauty shop called Hair Apparent, where Rabbit's sister Marilyn was one of the operators. And she was quite an operator. Among her customers in the past year and a half, eight of them got burglarized while they were out of town on vacation. All eight of those burglaries had the same modus operandi. A crude break-in, a completely messy burglary, and a pattern of vandalism that was almost deliberate in nature. Marilyn just kept her ears open when her customers talked about going out of town, and she passed on the information to her brother, and that was all it took. What good does it do to stop the milk and mail and leave the lights on a timer if the sweet young thing who does your hair has a burglar for a brother?'

I avoided looking in Marilyn's direction while I said all this. Now I caught Carolyn's eye. 'Wanda used to stop in my bookstore when she brought her dog for grooming at a place down the street.' Might as well keep Carolyn out of it. 'The last time I saw her, she happened to mention she was taking the animal out of town to be bred. So, like

Rabbit and Harlan, I had inside information. I knew the Colcannons would be away overnight, and they knew the same thing.

'But the Third Burglar knew no such thing. The Third Burglar was waiting for the Colcannons to come home. Ever since I realized there was a third burglar involved, I've tended to think of him in capital letters, like the Third Murderer in *Macbeth*. Shakespearean scholars have a lot of fun with the Third Murderer, you know. Shakespeare didn't give him all that much to say, so the evidence is pretty sketchy, but one school of thought holds that the Third Murderer was actually Macbeth himself.'

A hush went over the room. It was, all things considered, one of your better hushes.

'That was a clue from my subconscious,' I said, 'but it took me a while to put it together. No one with inside information could have been the Third Burglar, because then he'd have known not to expect the Colcannons that night. And for someone to have dropped in through the skylight just by chance and then hanging around to commit homicide – well, it seemed to be stretching coincidence pretty thin. But my subconscious was trying to tell me something, and ultimately I managed to piece it together. Whether or not Shakespeare meant the Third Murderer to be Macbeth, the Third Burglar was Herbert Franklin Colcannon.'

He was on his feet. 'You're crazy,' he said. 'You're a raving maniac. Are you trying to say I staged a burglary of my own house? That I stole this nonexistent coin from myself?'

'No.'

'Then—'

'There was no third burglary,' I said. 'Rabbit and Harlan stole everything they could find, and I took the three items from your safe, and that's as much burglary as you had that night. There was no third burglary and there was no Third Burglar, and there was nobody hanging around to hit you over the head and tie you up. You killed your own wife.'

22

For a moment no one said anything. Then Colcannon told them that I was out of my mind. 'Why are we listening to him?' he demanded. 'This man is a self-confessed burglar and we're sitting here while he hands around accusations of larceny and homicide. I don't know about the rest of you, but I've had enough of this. I'm leaving.'

'You'll miss the refreshments if you leave now.'

His nostrils flared and he stepped away from his seat. Then a hand took him by the elbow and he spun around to meet the eyes of Ray Kirschmann.

'Easy,' Ray told him. 'Whyn't we have a listen to what Bern there has to say? Maybe he'll come up with somethin' interestin'.'

'Take your hand off me,' Colcannon barked. His bark was less reminiscent of a Bouvier than, say, a mini-poodle. 'Who do you think you are?'

'I think I'm a cop,' Ray said agreeably, 'and Bern thinks you're a murderer, and when he has thoughts along those lines they tend to pan out. Long as he's got the ball, let's just see where he runs with it.'

And where would that be? 'Mr Colcannon's right about one thing,' I said. 'I'm a burglar. More accurately, I'm a bookseller who's trying to break himself of the habit of burglary. But one thing I'm not is a policeman, and it's going to be the job of the police to put together a case against Colcannon for murdering his wife.

'But maybe I can tell them where to look. His finances wouldn't be a bad place to start. The Colcannons lived well and they owned a lot of valuable things, but the rich get into financial difficulties the same as the rest of us.

'One thing that made me suspicious was the emptiness of that wall safe when I opened it. One watch, one pair of earrings, one rare coin, plus a handful of papers – people who own wall safes generally utilize them more, especially people with attack dogs who believe their premises are impregnable. I made a few telephone calls yesterday, and I learned that Mr Colcannon has been selling off some of the coins he's bought in recent years.'

578

'That proves nothing,' Colcannon said. 'One's interest changes. One sells one article to buy another.'

'Maybe, but I don't think so. I think you took a couple of major gambles recently – your safe contains some stock certificates that represent securities you've taken a heavy loss on. And I think you paid a damn sight more for the 1913 V-Nickel than the twenty grand Mr Pitterman received for it. You probably couldn't afford that nickel when it came available, but you had to have it because you're an avaricious man, and unless Spinoza was off base, avarice is a species of madness, and not an endangered one, either.

'You bought the nickel, shelled out for it at a time when you were trying to raise cash to meet your other obligations. Then you took your dog to be bred – another damned expense, although it would pay off when Astrid had her pups – and you rushed back to New York rather than stay overnight in Pennsylvania, and maybe you and your wife had an argument at the theater or during dinner afterward. That's something the police can find out if they do a little legwork.

'It hardly matters. The two of you walked into your house to find the unmistakable evidence of a burglary. Maybe you'd been planning on selling various valuables that they'd walked off with. Maybe you were underinsured. You probably didn't ever think to raise the insurance coverage on your silver, hardly anybody does, and now the nice windfall you'd had during the sharp rise in silver was wiped out by thieves in the night.

'And maybe your wife made some smartass remark right about then, and maybe it was the last straw. Or did it just remind you that one of the few things remaining in your wall safe was an insurance policy on both your lives? If either of you died, the other collected half a million dollars. And there's a double indemnity clause for accidental death, and the companies consider murder an accident, although it's generally undertaken on purpose, which is a contradiction, don't you think? Maybe the first time you hit her was out of rage, and then the possibility of gain suggested itself to you. Maybe you took one look at the looted rooms of your house and saw instantly that the burglary would make a good smoke screen for murder. We probably won't know the answer to that one until you confess, and you probably *will* confess, Mr Colcannon, because amateurs generally do. And you're an amateur. You're an absolute pro at avarice, sir, but you're an amateur at homicide.'

I meant he'd most likely confess at the police station, not in front of the lot of us. But a shadow passed over his face right about then and I decided to shut up for a minute and give him room. Or rope, if you like.

His lip quivered. Then a muscle worked in his temple. 'I didn't mean to kill her,' he said.

I looked at Ray and Ray looked at me, and a smile blossomed on Ray's lips.

'I hit her once. It was an accident, really. She was railing at me, nagging me. She could be such a shrew. She'd married me for my money, of course. That was no secret. But now that money was tight—' He sighed. 'I swung at her. I could never have done that if the dog had been around. The bitch would have taken my arm off. I swung and she fell and she must have hit her head on something when she reached the floor.'

It was nice embroidery. I'd seen those pictures, and the woman had been systematically beaten to death, but let Colcannon put the best face on it for the time being. This was the opening wedge. Later on they'd crack him like a coconut.

'Then I tried to find her pulse and she was dead,' he went on, 'and I thought that my life was over, too, and then I thought, well, let the burglars take the blame for this one. So I tied her up and I struck myself over the head, it was hard to make myself do that hard enough to inflict damage but I steeled myself, and then after I'd set the stage I called the police. I thought they'd question me and break me down, but they took one look around and knew the house had been looted by burglars, and that evidently satisfied them.'

Ray rolled his eyes at the ceiling. Some members of the department, I suspected, were going to hear about this one.

'But I never killed Abel Crowe!' Colcannon was bristling suddenly with righteous indignation. 'That's what all this was supposed to be about, isn't it? The murder of a receiver of stolen goods? I never met Abel Crowe, I never even *heard* of Abel Crowe, and I certainly didn't kill him.'

'No,' I agreed. 'You didn't.'

'I didn't know he had my coin. I thought *you* had my coin.'

'So you did.'

'I thought you still had it. That's why I came here today in the first place, God damn it to hell. So how can you accuse me of killing Crowe?'

'I can't.'

'But—'

I sent my eyes on a tour of my audience. I had their attention, all right. I looked straight at the murderer and saw nothing there but the same rapt interest that was evident on all their faces.

'I think you would have killed Abel,' I told Colcannon, 'if you had thought it would get you the coin back. For all I know you were planning to kill me this afternoon rather than pay me the twelve thousand dollars for the coin. But you didn't know he had the coin, and there was no way you could know.'

'Unless Abel told him,' Carolyn piped up. 'Maybe Abel tried to sell the coin back to him.'

I shook my head. 'Not at that stage,' I said 'He might have tried to work a deal with the insurance company, after the loss was reported. But it was too early for Abel to know that the loss wasn't covered by insurance, and far too early for him to think about selling the coin back to its presumptive owner.

'My first thought was that Abel had invited a prospective buyer to view the coin, and that he'd sufficiently misjudged the man's character to get murdered for his troubles. But was that the first thing Abel would do?'

I shook my head. 'It wasn't,' I answered myself. 'Abel had just received a coin with a six-figure price tag. It had come from the hands of a thief who in turn had taken it from the house of a man who was not known to have possession of it. Before Abel did anything with the coin he had to determine whether or not it was genuine. Even though he could approach certainty by examining it closely, one doesn't take chances. Mr Ruslander obtained the coin from a reputable museum, but even so he took the normal precaution of having it X-rayed to determine its authenticity, and Abel would do no less when dealing with a coin of doubtful provenance.

'Abel said at the time that such a determination was his first order of business. "At a more favorable hour," he said, he could verify the coin's legitimacy without leaving the building. I took this to mean that he could have an expert numismatist drop by to look at the coin and authenticate it, but experts of that sort don't habitually make house calls in the middle of the night.

'But that wasn't what he meant at all.

'He meant that there was someone in his building who could provide verification of the coin's bona fides. I thought there might be a numismatic expert in residence, and then I stopped to think about it and realized that Abel wouldn't want an expert to know that he had the coin. The 1913 V-Nickel's too rare and too celebrated, and the real experts in the coin field are highly ethical men who would balk at authenticating a stolen coin and being expected to keep quiet about it.

'No, what Abel required was not an opinion. He wanted an X-ray.'

I scanned my audience. The murderer remained quite expressionless, so much so that I almost doubted my conclusion. But not really. I glanced at Carolyn and saw her nodding intently. She had it figured now.

'Where do you go for an X-ray? A lab? A hospital emergency room? A radiologist? You couldn't manage that without leaving Abel's building. A dentist? There's a dentist in the building, a Dr Grieg. I believe he specializes in root canal work.'

581

'He does,' Mrs Pomerance confirmed. 'He doesn't hurt you, either, but he charges a fortune.'

'They all charge a fortune,' someone else said. 'Grieg's no worse than the rest of them.'

'Abel had false teeth,' I said, 'so I doubt he'd have needed Dr Grieg's services, reasonable or otherwise. He might have become friendly with the man regardless and have used his X-ray equipment for examining rare coins and jewelry, but he wasn't a patient, and Abel doesn't seem to have developed intimate relationships with his neighbors.

'Anyway, Abel had a professional relationship with someone in the building who also had X-ray equipment. You see, Abel had trouble with his feet. I don't know if he had Morton's Foot or not, let alone chondromalacia, but he had bad feet and the weight he carried put an extra load on them. The shoes in his closet are all prescription items, with built-up arches and various oddities you can't buy in your friendly neighborhood Florsheims.'

I looked at the murderer. His face was no longer expressionless. I saw something in his eyes that looked like alarm. The goatee and mustache kept me from seeing if he was keeping a stiff upper lip, but I tended to doubt it.

'Abel was a frequent patient of Murray Feinsinger's,' I went on. 'He must have been quite a contrast to all those runners and dancers, but his chart shows that he turned up in that office a great deal. He had an appointment the morning of the day he was killed.'

'That's crazy!' Feinsinger was outraged. 'He had no such appointment. He was my patient, it's true, and he was also my friend. That is why I am here at what I was told was to be a service for him, not an inquisition. He had no appointment with me on the day of his death.'

'Funny. It's listed in your appointment book and on his chart.' It hadn't been until early that morning, but why stress the point? 'It wasn't the first time he used your X-ray equipment for nonpodiatric purposes, was it?'

Feinsinger shrugged. 'Perhaps not. He would drop in occasionally and ask if he could use the machine. What did I care? He was a friend and a patient, so I let him use it. But he didn't come in that morning, or if he did I paid no attention. I certainly didn't kill him.'

'Not then, no. You waited until your waiting room was clear during your lunch break. Then you went upstairs, and of course he let you in without a second thought. You asked for a look at the coin, and he showed it to you, and you killed him and took it.'

'Why would I do that? I don't need money. My practice is better than it's ever been. I'm no coin collector, either. Why would I kill the man?'

'Avarice,' I said. 'No more and no less. You're no coin collector but you don't have to be one to know about the 1913 V-Nickel. Everybody knows about it. And the improvement in your practice just served to give you a taste for the good life – you told me that much yourself when you measured me for orthotics.' And what would become of those orthotics now, I wondered. They'd already been ordered from the lab, but how could they find their way to me if my podiatrist was booked for homicide and jugged like a hare?

Never mind. 'Spinoza had the answer,' I said, opening the book to a place I'd marked. ' "From the mere fact of our conceiving that another person takes delight in a thing, we shall ourselves love that thing and desire to take delight therein. But we assumed that the pleasure in question would be prevented by another's delight in its object; we shall, therefore, endeavor to prevent his possession thereof." ' I closed the book. 'In other words, you saw how much Abel appreciated the coin and that made you hot for it yourself. You killed him and you took it, which is endeavoring to prevent his possession thereof if I ever heard of it.'

'You can't prove this,' he said. 'You can't prove a thing.'

'It's up to the police to prove things. But I don't think they'll have much trouble in this instance. You didn't just take the nickel. You also took the other articles I stole from Colcannon's safe – the emerald earrings and the Piaget watch. I wouldn't be surprised if they turn up somewhere in your office. In the locked center drawer of your desk, for instance.'

He stared. 'You put them there.'

'How could I do a thing like that? That's not all you took from Abel. You also took his keys so that you could lock up after you left. That delayed the discovery of the body and helped you cover your tracks. I would have thought you'd have the sense to get rid of the keys.'

'I did,' he said, then caught himself and shook his head violently. 'I did not take any keys,' he said, trying to cover. 'I did not kill him, I did not take the coin, I did not take any jewelry, and I most certainly did not take any keys.'

'You certainly didn't get rid of them. They're in the drawer with the earrings and the watch.' And they were, too. Not the set he'd taken with him, but who was to know that?

Well, *he* knew it. 'You've framed me,' he said. 'You planted those things.'

'Did I plant the nickel, too?'

'You won't find the nickel in my possession.'

'Are you sure of that? When the police search the place thoroughly? When they turn it upside down and know what they're looking for? Are you absolutely certain they won't find it? Think it over.'

He thought about it, and I guess I was convincing and evidently he had a higher opinion of the cops' ability to find a needle in a haystack than I did, because before anybody knew what was happening he pushed his chair back and shoved past the woman seated beside him and was on his way to the door.

Ray had his gun out almost immediately, but he was in the wrong position and there were too many people between him and Feinsinger, all of them on their feet and making noise. I could have let him go – how far was he going to run, orthotics or no?

Instead I reached under my jacket and got my gun, yelled for him to stop, and when he didn't I tranquilized the son of a bitch.

23

'What we want is Irish coffee,' Carolyn said, 'and where we want to go for it is McBell's.' McBell's is in the Village, on Sixth Avenue a couple of blocks below Eighth Street, and we went there by cab. It's not terribly hard to find a Brooklyn cabbie willing to go to Manhattan, although it can be quite a trick convincing a Manhattan cabbie to go to Brooklyn, which just proves once again that we live in an inequitable universe, and when was that ever news?

By this time the tumult and the shouting had died and the captives and the kings had departed, the kings in this case being Ray Kirschmann and a couple of stalwarts from the local precinct whom he'd called to help him with the captives. There were enough of the latter to go around – Murray Feinsinger, Herbert Franklin Colcannon, George Edward 'Rabbit' Margate, and, lest we forget, Marilyn Margate and Harlan Reese.

Jessica and Clay invited us back to their place, along with most of the crowd from the service, but I said we'd take a rain check. Nor did we spend much time talking with the three-man delegation from Philadelphia. It looked as though no charges would be pressed against Howard Pitterman, who was evidently a good curator when he wasn't rustling his employer's cattle. I had the feeling Milo Hracec was in for a bonus, and arrangements had already been made for Ray Kirschmann to put a ten-thousand-dollar reward in his pocket the day the coin found its way back to its rightful owner. Normal procedure would call for the nickel to be impounded as evidence, but normal procedure can sometimes be short-circuited when the right cop is properly motivated, and Gordon Ruslander had agreed to provide the proper motivation.

The cabbie took us over the Brooklyn Bridge, and it was a glorious view on a glorious Sunday. I sat in the middle, Denise on my right and Carolyn on my left and thought how fortunate a man I was. I'd solved two murders, one of them a friend's. I'd admitted to burglary in front of a roomful of people and didn't have to worry about being charged with it. And I was riding into Manhattan with my girlfriend on one side of me and my best buddy on the other, and they'd even left off sniping at each other, and who could ask for anything more?

Carolyn was right about the Irish coffee. It was what we wanted, all right, and it was as it ought to be, the coffee rich and dark and sweet with brown sugar, the Irish whiskey generously supplied, and the whole topped not with some glop out of a shaving-cream dispenser but real handwhipped heavy cream. We had one round, and then we had a second round, and I started making noises about eventually rounding off the day with a celebratory dinner, all three of us, unless of course somebody had other plans, in which case—

'Shit,' Denise said. We were sitting, all three of us, around a tiny table that had room for our three stemmed glasses and one big ashtray, and she'd almost filled the ashtray already, smoking one Virginia Slim after another. She ground one out now and pushed her chair back. 'I can't take any more of this,' she said.

'What's the matter?'

'I'm coming unglued, that's all. You two talk, huh? I'm going home so my kid doesn't forget what I look like. The two of you can kick it around, and then you'll come over to my place later, all right?'

'I guess so,' I said.

But she wasn't talking to me. She was talking to Carolyn, who hesitated, then gave a quick nod.

'Well,' Denise said. She grabbed up her purse, drew a breath, then put a palm on the table for support and leaned over to kiss Carolyn lightly on the mouth. Then, cheeks scarlet, she turned and strode out of the place.

For a few minutes nobody said anything. Then Carolyn managed to catch the waiter's eye and ordered a martini. I thought about having one myself but didn't really feel like it. I still had half of my second Irish coffee in front of me and I didn't much feel like finishing that, either.

Carolyn said, 'Couple of things, Bern. How'd you know Marilyn Margate set up all those burglaries?'

'I figured she knew Mrs Colcannon. When she turned up with a gun in her purse and accused me of murder, she called the woman Wanda. I figured they were friends, but what kind of friend gets her brother to knock off a friend's house? And it couldn't have been coincidence that Rabbit and Harlan found their way to Eighteenth Street, any more than it was coincidence they picked a time when nobody was home.

'Then when I dropped in at Hair Apparent I overheard a woman talking about something personal, and I realized women tell their hairdressers everything, and I got a list of similar burglaries committed in the immediate area of the beauty parlor.'

'And you found some of the names in their appointment book when you went there this morning. Bern? Wasn't that doing it the hard way?

586

Couldn't you have just called the burglary victims and asked where they got their hair done?'

'I thought of that. But that wouldn't prove Wanda got her hair done at Hair Apparent. Besides, if I couldn't find any of the other names in the appointment book, I could always write them in myself.'

'Falsify evidence, you mean.'

'I think of it more as supplying evidence than falsifying it. For another thing, I could have wound up spending hours on the phone without reaching anybody. People tend to go out on Saturday night. But maybe the most important reason, aside from the fact that I'm a burglar and it's natural for a burglar to take a burglaristic approach to problems, is that I wanted to see about the gun.'

'The gun?'

'The one Marilyn brought to my apartment. I was relieved to find it in a drawer. She'd said she had put it back, but if I didn't find it I was going to assume it was still in her purse, and that would have meant tipping off Ray so that she didn't get a chance to pull it when I exposed her role in the burglaries.'

'I see.'

'Uh, Carolyn—'

'Shit. You probably want to talk about Denise.'

'I don't know what I *want* to. But I think we have to. Don't we?'

'Double shit. Yeah, I guess we probably do.' She finished her martini, looked around in vain for the waiter, then gave up and put her glass down. 'Well, I'll be damned if I know how it happened, Bern. God knows I didn't plan it.'

'You didn't even like her.'

'Like her? I couldn't stand her.'

'And she wasn't crazy about you.'

'She despised me. Detested me. Thought of me as a dwarf who smelled like a wet dog.'

'And you thought she was bony and gawky.'

'Well, I was wrong, wasn't I?'

'How did it—'

'I don't *know*, Bern.' The waiter sailed by and she caught him by the hem of his jacket and pressed her empty glass into his hand. 'It's an emergency,' she told him, and to me she said, 'I swear I don't know how it happened. I guess there must have been an attraction all along and our hostility was a cover-up for it.'

'Best cover-up since Watergate.'

'Just about. The thing is I feel awful about it and so does Denise. We started off yesterday forcing ourselves to tolerate each other, and there was something in the air, and we both sensed it, and I decided to deny it, because I knew I didn't want to make a pass. In the first place she was your girlfriend and in the second place she wasn't gay.'

'So?'

'So she kept getting flirtier and flirtier, and you know me, Bern, I can resist anything but temptation. She wound up making the pass, and—'

'Denise made the pass?'

'Yeah.'

'I never suspected she was gay.'

'I don't think she is. I think she's straight enough to own a goddamn poodle, if you want to know, but right now she wants to go on going to bed with me, and I figure what I'll do is take it a day at a time and see where it goes. I don't think it's the love affair of the century, and if it's going to fuck up our relationship, Bern, then what I figure is the hell with her. There's women all over the place, but where am I gonna find another best friend?'

'It's okay, Carolyn.'

'It's not okay. It's crazy.'

'Don't worry about it. Denise and I weren't the love affair of the century, either. I called her the other day primarily because I figured I might need an alibi. You don't have to tell her that, but it's true.'

'She already knows. She said so herself as a way of justifying our going to bed together.'

'Well, what the hell.'

'You're not upset?'

'I don't know what I am exactly. Confused, mainly. You know the story about the guy whose wife dies and he's all broken up at the funeral, and his best friend takes him aside and tells him how he'll get over it?'

'It sounds familiar. Keep going.'

'Well, the best friend says that he'll get over it, the pain and loss will fade, and after a few months he'll actually start dating again, and he'll find a woman he responds to, and he'll fall in love and go to bed with her and start building a new life. And the bereaved widower says, "Yeah, sure, I know all that, but what am I going to do tonight?"'

'Oh.'

'Somehow I think Marilyn Margate is out. Even if somebody posts bail for her, I have a feeling she wouldn't welcome me with open arms.'

'Not now. How come you threw her to the wolves? You didn't have to, did you?'

'Well, it didn't hurt. Improved the case against Colcannon, tied up a few loose ends.'

'I thought, you know, honor among thieves and all. She and Harlan and Rabbit are fellow burglars or something, so I didn't think you'd tip them to the cops.'

'Fellow burglars? You saw what they did on Eighteenth Street.'

'Yeah.'

'They weren't burglars. They were barbarians. The best thing I could do for the profession of burglary was get them the hell out of it.'

'I suppose.' She sipped at her new martini. 'She was pretty cheap-looking, anyway.'

'True.'

'She must have been really sluttish in that red and black outfit.'

'You might say so.'

'Still,' she said thoughtfully, 'I can see how she'd be very attractive to someone who liked the type.'

'Uh-huh.'

'I like the type, myself.'

'So do I.'

'Of course it's not the only type I like.'

'Same here.'

'Bernie? You're not mad at me? You don't hate me?'

'Of course not.'

'We're still buddies?'

'You bet.'

'We're still partners in crime? I'm still your henchperson?'

'Count on it.'

'Then everything's okay.'

'Yeah, everything's okay. "But what am I gonna do tonight?"'

'Good question.' She stood up. 'Well, I know what I'm gonna do tonight.'

'Yeah, I'll bet you do. Give my love to Denise.'

After she left I thought about having another Irish coffee, or a martini, or any of a number of other things, but I didn't really want anything to drink. Some of Abel's ancient Armagnac might have tempted me but I didn't figure they'd have it in stock. I settled our tab, added a tip, and went for a walk.

I didn't consciously aim my feet at Washington Square but that's where they took me all the same. I bought a Good Humor, the special flavor of the month, something with a lot of goo on the outside and a fudgy chocolate core inside the ice cream. I decided it might give me one of Carolyn's sugar hangovers and I decided I didn't give a damn.

For one reason or another I kept bench-hopping, sitting in one place for a few minutes and then turning restless and scouting out another perch. I watched the dealers and the drunks and the junkies and the young mothers and the courting couples and the drug dealers and the three-card-monte con artists and the purveyors of one thing or another, and I watched the joggers relentlessly threading their way through the walkers as they made their endless counterclockwise circuits of the park, and I watched the children and wondered, not for the first time, where the hell they got their energy.

I was still restless. For a change I had more energy than the children

589

and no place to direct it. I got up after a while and walked past the chess players to the corner of Fourth and MacDougal. I was wearing a suit and carrying an attaché case and my shoes were too wide and I had Morton's Foot, but what the hell.

I tucked the case under my arm and started jogging. And that would be as good a place as any to leave it, except that Jessica Garland turned up at my store a few days later with the two books I'd read from at the service. She said she wasn't a student of moral philosophy herself, and would I like to have Spinoza and Hobbes in remembrance of Abel?

'I just hope I'll get something of his myself sooner or later,' she said. 'He doesn't seem to have left a will, and there's some question as to my ability to prove I'm his granddaughter. I have letters from him, or Mum has them back in England, but I don't know if they'll constitute proof, and meanwhile I expect the estate will be tied up for a long time. Until then there's no way for me to get into his apartment.'

'Even if you inherit,' I said, 'it'll have been searched by professionals first. I don't suppose Abel had clear title to most of the things he owned. Your best hope is that they won't find everything. Between the cops and the IRS people they'll find a lot, but there are things they'll miss. I'd be surprised if they get the money in the telephone.' She looked puzzled and I explained, and told her something about the other treasures tucked away here and there.

'They'll likely disappear before I see them,' she said. 'Stolen or not, I suspect they'll walk out of there, wouldn't you say?'

'Probably. Even if Abel bought them legitimately.' Not everyone, after all, shared my reluctance to rob the dead. 'Maybe the door-man would let you in. You could at least get the money out of the telephone.'

'I tried to get in. It's a very strictly run building from a security standpoint.' She frowned, and then her face turned thoughtful. 'I wonder.'

'You wonder what?'

'Do you suppose *you* could get in? I mean it is rather your line of country, isn't it? And I'd be more than willing to give you half of whatever you managed to salvage from the apartment. I've a feeling I'll never see any of it otherwise, between the police and the inland revenue and whatever bite the death duties take, or do you call them inheritance taxes over here? Half of something is considerably more than a hundred percent of nothing. Could you do it, do you suppose? It's not really stealing, is it?'

'It's an impossible building to get into,' I said.

'I know.'

'And I've already found two different ways in and used them both up. And that was before half the tenants knew me by face and name, not to mention occupation.'

590

'I know,' she said, looking downcast. 'I don't suppose you'd want to have a go at it, then.'

'I didn't say that.'

'But if there's no way for you to get in—'

'There's always a way in,' I said. 'Always. There's always a way to pick a lock, and to get past a doorman, and to open a safe. If you're resourceful and determined, there's always a way.'

Her eyes were huge. 'You sound in the grip of passion,' she said.

'Well, I, uh—'

'You're going to do it, aren't you?'

I tried to look as though I was thinking it over, but who was I kidding? 'Yes,' I said, 'I guess I am.'

The Burglar Who Painted Like Mondrian

This is for
LYNNE WOOD
with special thanks to
MICHAEL TROSSMAN
who taught me how to prepare the canvas
and
LAURENCE ANNE COE
who helped me assemble the frame

1

It was a slow day at Barnegat Books, but then most of them are. Antiquarian booksellers, after all, do not dream of retiring to the slow and simple life. They are already leading it.

This particular day had two high points, and as luck would have it they both came at once. A woman read me a poem and a man tried to sell me a book. The poem was 'Smith, of the Third Oregon, Dies,' by Mary Carolyn Davies, and the woman who read it was a slender and freshfaced creature with large long-lashed brown eyes and a way of cocking her head that she must have learned from a feathered friend. Her hands – small and well formed, unringed fingers, unpolished nails – held a copy of Ms Davies' first book, *Drums in Our Street*, which the Macmillan Company had seen fit to publish in 1918. And she read to me.

> 'Autumn in Oregon – I'll never see
> Those hills again, a blur of blue and rain
> Across the old Willamette. I'll not stir
> A pheasant as I walk, and hear it whirr
> Above my head, an indolent, trusting thing . . .'

I'm rather an indolent, trusting thing myself, but all the same I cast a cold eye on the Philosophy & Religion section, where my most recent visitor had stationed himself. He was a hulking sort, late twenties or early thirties, wearing low Frye boots and button-fly Levi's and a brown wide-wale corduroy jacket over a darker brown flannel shirt. Horn-rimmed glasses. Leather elbow patches on the jacket. A beard that had been carefully trimmed. A headful of lank brown hair that had not.

> When all this silly dream is finished here,
> The fellows will go home to where there fall
> Rose petals over every street, and all
> The year is like a friendly festival . . .

Something made me keep my eyes on him. Perhaps it was an air about him, a sense that he might at any moment commence slouching toward Bethlehem. Maybe it was just his attaché case. At Brentano's and the Strand you have to check bags and briefcases, but my customers are allowed to keep them at hand, and sometimes their carryalls are heavier upon departure than arrival. The secondhand book trade is precarious at best and one hates to see one's stock walk out the door like that.

> But I shall never watch those hedges drip
> Color, not see the tall spar of a ship
> In our old harbor. – They say that I am dying,
> Perhaps that's why it all comes back again:
> Autumn in Oregon and pheasants flying—

She let out a small appreciative sigh and closed the little book with a snap, then passed it to me and asked its price. I consulted the penciled notation on its flyleaf and the tax table that's taped to my counter. The last hike boosted the sales tax to 8 ¼%, and there are people who can figure out that sort of thing in their heads, but they probably can't pick locks. God gives us all different talents and we do what we can with them.

'Twelve dollars,' I announced, 'plus ninety-nine cents tax.' She put a ten and three singles on the counter, and I put her book in a paper bag, fastened it with a bit of Scotch tape, and gave her a penny. Our hands touched for an instant when she took the coin from me, and there was a bit of a charge in the contact. Nothing overpowering, nothing to knock one off one's feet, but it was there, and she cocked, her head and our eyes met for an instant. The author of a Regency romance would note that a silent understanding passed between us, but that's nonsense. All that passed between us was a penny.

My other customer was examining a buckram-bound quarto volume by Matthew Gilligan, S. J. *The Catogrammatic vs. the Syncogrammatic*, it was called, or was it the other way around? I'd had the book ever since old Mr Litzauer sold me the store, and if I'd never dusted the shelves it would never have been picked up at all. If this chap was going to steal something, I thought, let him hook that one.

But he returned Father Gilligan to his shelf even as Mary Carolyn Davies went out the door with my demure little poetry lover. I watched her until she crossed my threshold – she was wearing a suit and matching beret in plum or cranberry or whatever they're calling it this year, and it was a good color for her – and then I watched him as he approached my counter and rested one hand on it.

His expression, insofar as the beard showed it, was guarded. He asked me if I bought books, and his voice sounded rusty, as if he didn't get too many chances to use it.

I allowed that I did, if they were books I thought I could sell. He propped his attaché case on the counter, worked its clasps, and opened it to reveal a single large volume, which he took up and presented to me. *Lepidopterae* was its title, François Duchardin was its author, and Old World butterflies and moths were its subject matter, discussed exhaustively (I can only presume) in its French text and illustrated spectacularly upon its color plates.

'The frontispiece is missing,' he told me, as I paged through the book. 'The other fifty-three plates are intact.'

I nodded, my eyes on a page of swallowtail butterflies. When I was a boy I used to pursue such creatures with a homemade net, killing them in a mason jar, then spreading their wings and pinning them in cigar boxes. I must have had a reason for such curious behavior, but I can't begin to imagine what it might have been.

'Print dealers break these up,' he said, 'but this is such a desirable volume and in such good condition I thought it really ought to go to an antiquarian book dealer.'

I nodded again, this time looking at moths. One was a cecropia. That and the luna are the only moths I know by name. I used to know others.

I closed the book, asked him what he wanted for it.

'A hundred dollars,' he said. 'That's less than two dollars a plate. A print dealer would charge five or ten a plate, and he'd get that easily from decorators.'

'Could be,' I said. I ran my finger over the book's top edge, where a rectangle enclosed the stamped words *New York Public Library*. I opened the book again, looking for a *Withdrawn* stamp. Libraries do divest themselves of books, just as museums deaccession some of their holdings, though Duchardin's *Lepidopterae* hardly seemed a candidate for such treatment.

'Those overdue charges can mount up,' I said sympathetically, 'but they have these amnesty days now and then when you can return overdue books with no penalty. It seems unfair to those of us who pay our fines without protest, but I suppose it does get books back in circulation, and that's the important thing, isn't it?' I closed the book again, set it deliberately into his open attaché case. 'I don't buy library books,' I said.

'Somebody else will.'

'I don't doubt it.'

'I know one dealer who has his own *Withdrawn* stamp.'

'I know a carpenter who drives screws with a hammer,' I said. 'There are tricks to every trade.'

'This book didn't even circulate. It sat in a locked case in the reference section, available by special request only, and because of its value they found ways to avoid letting people have access to it. The

599

library's supposed to serve the public, but they think they're a museum; they keep their best books *away* from people.'

'It doesn't seem to have worked.'

'How's that?'

'They couldn't keep this one away from you.'

He grinned suddenly, showing clean if misaligned teeth. 'I can get anything out of there,' he said. 'Anything.'

'Really.'

'You name a book and I'll lift it. I'll tell you, I could bring you one of the stone lions if the price was right.'

'We're a little crowded around here just now.'

He tapped *Lepidopterae*. 'Sure you can't use this? I could probably ease up a little on the price.'

'I don't do much volume in natural history. But that's beside the point. I honestly don't buy library books.'

'That's a shame. It's the only kind I deal in.'

'A specialist.'

He nodded. 'I'd never take anything from a dealer, an independent businessman struggling to make ends meet. And I'd never steal from a collector. But libraries—' He set his shoulders, and a muscle worked in his chest. 'I was a graduate student for a long time,' he said. 'When I wasn't asleep I was in a library. Public libraries, university libraries. I spent ten months in London and never got out of the British Museum. I have a special relationship with libraries. A love-hate relationship, I guess you'd call it.'

'I see.'

He closed his attaché case, fastened its clasps. 'They've got two Gutenberg Bibles in the library of the British Museum. If you ever read that one of them disappeared, you'll know who got it.'

'Well,' I said, 'whatever you do, don't bring it here.'

A couple of hours later I was sipping Perrier at the Bum Rap and telling Carolyn Kaiser all about it. 'All I could think of,' I said, 'was that it looked like a job for Hal Johnson.'

'Who?'

'Hal Johnson. An ex-cop now employed by the library to chase down overdue books.'

'They've got an ex-cop doing that?'

'Not in real life,' I said. 'Hal Johnson's a character in a series of short stories by James Holding. He goes off on the trail of an overdue book and winds up involved in a more serious crime.'

'Which I suppose he solves.'

'Well, sure. He's no dope. I'll tell you, that book brought back memories. I used to collect butterflies when I was a kid.'

'You told me.'

'And sometimes we would find cocoons. I saw a picture of a cecropia moth and it reminded me. There were pussy willow bushes near the school I went to, and cecropia moths used to attach their cocoons to the branches. We would find the cocoons and put them in jars and try to let them hatch out.'

'What happened?'

'Generally nothing. I don't think any of my cocoons ever hatched. Not every caterpillar gets to be a moth.'

'Not every frog gets to be a prince, either.'

'Isn't that the truth.'

Carolyn finished her martini and caught the waitress's eye for a refill. I still had plenty of Perrier. We were in the Bum Rap, a comfortably tacky gin joint at the corner of East Eleventh Street and Broadway, which made it just half a block from both Barnegat Books and the Poodle Factory, where Carolyn earns her living washing dogs. While her trade provides relatively little in the way of ego gratification, it's more socially useful than looting libraries.

'Perrier,' Carolyn said.

'I like Perrier.'

'All it is, Bernie, is designer water. That's all.'

'I guess.'

'Got a busy night planned?'

'I'll go out for a run,' I said, 'and then I may bounce around a bit.'

She started to say something but checked herself when the waitress approached with the fresh martini. The waitress was a dark-roots blonde in tight jeans and a hot-pink blouse, and Carolyn's eyes followed her back to the bar. 'Not bad,' she said.

'I thought you were in love.'

'With the waitress?'

'With the tax planner.'

'Oh, Alison.'

'The last I heard,' I said, 'you were planning a tax together.'

'I'm planning attacks and she's planning defenses. I went out with her last night. We went over to Jan Wallman's on Cornelia Street and ate some kind of fish with some kind of sauce on it.'

'It must have been a memorable meal.'

'Well, I've got a rotten mind for details. We drank a lot of white wine and listened to Stephen Pender sing one romantic ballad after another, and then we went back to my place and settled in with some Drambuie and WNCN on the radio. She admired my Chagall and petted my cats. One of them, anyway. Archie sat on her lap and purred. Ubi wasn't having any.'

'What went wrong?'

'Well, see, she's a political and economic lesbian.'

'What's that?'

601

'She believes it's politically essential to avoid sexual relations with men as part of her commitment to feminism, and all her career interaction is with women, but she doesn't sleep with women because she's not physically ready for that yet.'

'What does that leave? Chickens?'

'What it leaves is me climbing the walls. I kept plying her with booze and putting the moves on her, and all I got for my trouble was nowhere fast.'

'It's good she doesn't go out with men. They'd probably try to exploit her sexually.'

'Yeah, men are rotten that way. She had a bad marriage and she's pretty steamed at men because of it. And she's stuck with her ex-husband's name because she's established professionally under it, and it's an easy name, too, Warren. Her own name is Armenian, which would be more useful if she were selling rugs instead of planning taxes. She doesn't exactly plan taxes, Congress plans taxes. I guess she plans avoiding them.'

'I plan to avoid them myself.'

'Me too. If she weren't so great looking I'd avoid her and say the hell with it, but I think I'll give it one more try. *Then* I'll say the hell with it.'

'You're seeing her tonight?'

She shook her head. 'Tonight I'll hit the bars. A couple of drinks, a couple of laughs, and maybe I'll get lucky. It's been known to happen.'

'Be careful.'

She looked at me. '*You* be careful,' she said.

A couple of subway trains whisked me home, where I changed to nylon shorts and running shoes and ducked out for a quick half hour in Riverside Park. It was mid-September, with the New York Marathon a little over a month away, and the park was thick with runners. Some of them were of my stripe, the casual sort who knocked off three or four sluggish miles three or four times a week. Others were in marathon training, grinding out fifty or sixty or seventy miles a week, and for them it was Serious Business.

It was thus for Wally Hemphill, but he was following a program of alternate short and long runs, and the night's agenda called for four miles so we wound up keeping each other company. Wallace Riley Hemphill was a recently divorced lawyer in his early thirties who didn't look old enough to have been married in the first place. He'd grown up somewhere in eastern Long Island and was now living on Columbus Avenue and dating models and actresses and (*puff puff*) training for the Marathon. He had his own one-man practice with an office in the West Thirties, and as we ran he talked about a woman who'd asked him to represent her in a divorce action.

602

'And I went ahead and drew up papers,' he told me, 'and it developed that this dizzy bitch wasn't married in the first place. She wasn't even living with anybody, didn't even have a boyfriend. But she has a history of this. Every once in a while something snaps inside her and she finds an attorney and institutes divorce proceedings.'

I told him about my book thief who specialized in libraries. He was shocked. 'Stealing from libraries? You mean there are people who would do that?'

'There are people to steal anything,' I said. 'From anyplace.'

'Some world,' he said.

I finished my run, stretched some, walked on home to my apartment building at the corner of Seventy-first and West End. I stripped and showered and did a little more stretching, and then I stretched out and closed my eyes for a while.

And got up and looked up two telephone numbers and dialed them in turn. No one answered my first call. My second was answered after two or three rings, and I chatted briefly with the person who answered it. Then I tried the first number again and let it ring an even dozen times. A dozen rings comes to one minute, but when you're calling it seems longer than that, and when someone else is calling and you let the phone go unanswered, it seems like an hour and a half.

So far so good.

I had to decide between the brown suit and the blue suit, and I wound up choosing the blue. I almost always do, and at this rate the brown'll still be in good shape when its lapels come back into style again. I wore a blue oxford button-down shirt and selected a striped tie which would probably have indicated to an Englishman that I'd been cashiered from a good regiment. To an American it would be no more than a mark of sincerity and fiscal integrity. I got the knot right on the first try and chose to regard that as a favorable omen.

Navy socks. Scotch-grained black loafers, less comfortable than running shoes but rather more conventional. And comfy enough once I'd slipped in my custom-made orthotic arch supports.

I took up my attaché case, a slimmer and more stylish affair than my book thief's, covered with beige Ultrasuede and glowing with burnished brass fittings. I filled its several compartments with the tools of my trade – a pair of rubber gloves with their palms cut out, a ring of cunning steel implements, a roll of adhesive tape, a pencil-beam flashlight, a glass cutter, a flat strip of celluloid and another of spring steel, and, oh, a bit of this and a little of that. Were I to be lawfully seized and searched, the contents of that case would earn me an upstate vacation as a guest of the governor.

My stomach did a little buck-and-wing at the thought, and I was glad I'd skipped dinner. And yet, even as I was recoiling at the idea of stone walls and iron bars, there was a familiar tingle in my fingertips and a racy edge to the blood in my veins. Lord, let me outgrow such childish responses – but, uh, not yet, if you please.

I added a lined yellow legal pad to the attaché case and outfitted my inside breast pocket with a couple of pens and pencils and a slim leather-bound notebook. My outside breast pocket already held a hankie, which I took out, refolded, and tucked back into place.

A phone rang as I walked down the hall to the elevator. It may have been mine. I let it ring. Downstairs, my doorman eyed me with grudging respect. A cab pulled up even as I was lifting a hand to summon it.

I gave the balding driver an address on Fifth Avenue between Seventy-sixth and Seventy-seventh. He took the Sixty-fifth Street transverse across Central Park, and while he talked about baseball and Arab terrorists I watched other runners stepping out the miles. They were at play while I was on my way to work, and how frivolous their pastime seemed to me now.

I stopped the cab a half block from my destination, paid and tipped and got out and walked. I crossed Fifth Avenue and mingled with the crowd at the bus stop, letting myself have a good look at the Impregnable Fortress.

Because that's what it was. It was a massive, brawny apartment house, built between the wars and looming some twenty-two stories over the park. The Charlemagne, its builder had dubbed it, and its apartments turned up in the Real Estate section of the Sunday *Times* every once in a while. It had gone co-op some years back, and when its apartments changed hands now they did so for six-figure sums. *High* six-figure sums.

From time to time I would read or hear of someone, a coin collector, let us say, and I would file his name away for future reference. And then I would learn that he lived at the Charlemagne and I would drop him from my files, because it was akin to learning that he kept all his holdings in a bank vault. The Charlemagne had a doorman and a concierge and attended elevators with closed-circuit television cameras in them. Other closed-circuit devices monitored the service entrance and the fire escapes and God knows what else, and the concierge had a console at his desk where he could (and did) watch six or eight screens at once. The Charlemagne made a positive fetish of security, and while I could readily understand their attitude, you could hardly expect me to approve.

A bus came and went, taking with it most of my companions. The light changed from red to green. I hoisted my case full of burglar's tools and crossed the street.

The doorman at the Charlemagne made mine look like an usher in a

Times Square peep show. He had more gold braid than an Ecuadorian admiral and at least as much self-assurance. He took me in from nose to toes and remained serenely unimpressed.

'Bernard Rhodenbarr,' I told him. 'Mr Onderdonk is expecting me.'

2

Of course he didn't take my word for it. He passed me on to the concierge and stood by in case I should give that gentleman any trouble. The concierge rang Onderdonk on the intercom, confirmed that I was indeed expected, and turned me over to the elevator operator, who piloted me some fifty yards closer to heaven. There was indeed a camera in the elevator, and I tried not to look at it while trying not to look as though I was avoiding it, and I felt about as nonchalant as a girl on her first night as a topless waitress. The elevator was a plush affair, paneled in rosewood and fitted with polished brass, with burgundy carpeting underfoot. Whole families have lived in less comfortable quarters, but all the same I was glad to leave it.

Which I did on the sixteenth floor, where the operator pointed to a door and hung around until it opened to admit me. It opened just a couple of inches until the chainlock stopped it, but that was far enough for Onderdonk to get a look at me and smile in recognition. 'Ah, Mr Rhodenbarr,' he said, fumbling with the lock. 'Good of you to come.' Then he said, 'Thank you, Eduardo,' and only then did the elevator door close and the cage descend.

'I'm clumsy tonight,' Onderdonk said. 'There.' And he unhooked the chainlock and drew the door open. 'Come right in, Mr Rhodenbarr. Right this way. Is it as pleasant outside as it was earlier? And tell me what you'll have to drink. Or I've a pot of coffee made, if you'd prefer that.'

'Coffee would be fine.'

'Cream and sugar?'

'Black, no sugar.'

'Commendable.'

He was a man in his sixties, with iron gray hair parted carefully on the side and a weathered complexion. He was on the short side and slightly built, and perhaps his military bearing was an attempt to compensate for this. Alternatively, perhaps he'd been in the military. I somehow didn't think he'd ever served as a doorman, or an Ecuadorian admiral.

We had our coffee at a marble-topped table in his living room. The carpet was an Aubusson and the furniture was mostly Louis Quinze. The several paintings, all twentieth-century abstracts in uncomplicated aluminum frames, were an effective contrast to the period furnishings. One of them, showing blue and beige amoeboid shapes on a cream field, looked like the work of Hans Arp, while the canvas mounted over the Adam fireplace was unmistakably a Mondrian. I don't have all that good an eye for paintings, and I can't always tell Rembrandt from Hals or Picasso from Braque, but Mondrian is Mondrian. A black grid, a white field, a couple of squares of primary colors – the man had a style, all right.

Bookshelves ran from floor to ceiling on either side of the fireplace, and they accounted for my presence. A couple of days ago, Gordon Kyle Onderdonk had walked in off the street, dropping in at Barnegat Books as casually as someone looking to buy *Drums in Our Street* or sell *Lepidopterae*. He'd browsed for a spell, asked two or three reasonable questions, bought a Louis Auchincloss novel, and paused on his way to the door to ask me if I ever appraised libraries.

'I'm not interested in selling my books,' he said. 'At least I don't think I am, although I'm considering a move to the West Coast and I suppose I'd dispose of them rather than ship them. But I have things that have accumulated over the years, and perhaps I ought to have a floater policy to cover them in case of fire, and if I ever do want to sell, why, I ought to know whether my library's worth a few hundred or a few thousand, oughtn't I?'

I haven't done many appraisals, but it's work I enjoy. You can't charge all that much, but the hourly return is greater than I get sitting behind the counter at the store, and sometimes the chance to appraise a library turns into the opportunity to purchase it. 'Well, if it's worth a thousand dollars,' a client may say, 'what'll you pay for it?' 'I won't pay a thousand,' I may counter, 'so tell me what you'll take for it.' Ah, the happy game of haggling.

I spent the next hour and a half with my legal pad and a pen, jotting numbers down and totting them up. I looked at all of the books on the open walnut shelves that flanked the fireplace, and in another room, a sort of study, I examined the contents of a bank of glassed-in mahogany shelves.

The library was an interesting one. Onderdonk had never specifically collected anything, simply allowing books to accumulate over the years, culling much of the chaff from time to time. There were some sets in leather – a nice Hawthorne, a Defoe, the inevitable Dickens. There were perhaps a dozen Limited Editions Club volumes, which command a nice price, and several dozen Heritage Press books, which retail for only eight or ten dollars but are very easy to turn over. He had some favorite authors in first editions – Evelyn Waugh, J. P. Marquand, John O'Hara, Wallace Stevens. Some Faulkner, some Hemingway, some early Sherwood Anderson. Fair history, including a nice set of Guizot's *France* and Oman's seven-volume history of the Peninsular War. Not much science. No *Lepidopterae*.

He had cost himself money. Like so many noncollectors, he'd disposed of the dust jackets of most of his books, unwittingly chucking out the greater portion of their value in the process. There are any number of modern firsts worth, say, a hundred dollars with a dust jacket and ten or fifteen dollars without it. Onderdonk was astonished to learn this. Most people are.

He brought more coffee as I sat adding up a column of figures, and this time he'd brought along a bottle of Irish Mist. 'I like a drop in my coffee,' he said. 'Can I offer you some?'

It sounded yummy, but where would we be without standards? I sipped my coffee black and went on adding numbers. The figure I came up with was somewhere in excess of $5,400, and I read it off to him. 'I was probably conservative,' I added. 'I'm doing this on the spot, without consulting references, and I shaded things on the low side. You'd be safe rounding that figure off at six thousand.'

'And what would that figure represent?'

'Retail prices. Fair market value.'

'And if you were buying the books as a dealer, presuming of course that this type of material was something you were interested in—'

'I would be interested,' I allowed. 'For this sort of material I could work on fifty percent.'

'So you could pay three thousand dollars?'

I shook my head. 'I'd be going with the first figure I quoted you,' I said. 'I could pay twenty-seven hundred. And that would include removal of the books at my expense, of course.'

'I see.' He sipped his own coffee, crossed one slim leg over the other. He was wearing well-cut gray flannel slacks and a houndstooth smoking jacket with leather buttons. His shoes might have been of sharkskin. They were certainly elegant, and showed off his small feet. 'I wouldn't care to sell now,' he said, 'but if I do move, and it's a possibility if not a probability, I'll certainly give your offer consideration.'

'Books go up and down in value. The price might be higher or lower in a few months or a year.'

'I understand that. If I decide to dispose of the books the primary consideration would be convenience, not price. I suspect I'd find it simpler to accept your offer than to shop around.'

I looked over his shoulder at the Mondrian and wondered what it was worth. Ten or twenty or thirty times the fair market value of his library, at a guess. And his apartment was probably worth three or four times as much as the Mondrian, so a thousand dollars more or less for some old books probably wouldn't weigh too heavily on his mind.

'I want to thank you,' he said, getting to his feet. 'You told me your fee. Did you say two hundred dollars?'

'That's right.'

He drew out a wallet, paused. 'I hope you don't object to cash,' he said.

'I never object to cash.'

'Some people don't like to carry cash. I can understand that; these are perilous times.' He counted out four fifties, handed them to me. I took out my own wallet and gave them a home.

'If I could use your phone—'

'Certainly,' he said, and pointed me to the study. I dialed a number I'd dialed earlier, and once again I let it ring a dozen times, but somewhere around the fourth ring I chatted into the mouthpiece, as if someone were on the other end. I don't know that Onderdonk was even within earshot of me, but if you're going to do something you might as well do it right, and why call attention to myself by holding a ringing phone to my ear for an unusually long time?

Caught up in my performance, I suppose I let the phone ring more than a dozen times, but what matter? No one answered it, and I hung up and returned to the living room. 'Well, thanks again for the business,' I told him, returning my legal pad to my attaché case. 'If you do decide to add a floater to your insurance coverage, I can give you my appraisal in writing if they require it. And I can adjust the figure higher or lower for that purpose, as you prefer.'

'I'll remember that.'

'And do let me know if you ever decide to get rid of the books.'

'I certainly will.'

He led me to the door, opened it for me, walked into the hall with me. The indicator showed the elevator to be on the ground floor. I let my finger hover over the button but avoided pressing it.

'I don't want to keep you,' I said to Onderdonk.

'It's no trouble,' he said. 'But wait, is that my phone? I think it is. I'll just say goodbye now, Mr Rhodenbarr.'

We shook hands quickly and he hurried back inside his apartment. The door drew shut. I counted to ten, darted across the hall, yanked open the fire door and scampered down four flights of stairs.

At the eleventh-floor landing, I paused long enough to catch my breath. This didn't take long, perhaps because of all those half-hour romps in Riverside Park. Had I known running would be such a help in my career I might have taken it up years ago.

(How did four flights of stairs get me from Sixteen to Eleven? No thirteenth floor. But *you* knew that, didn't you? Of course you did.)

The fire door was locked from the stairs side. Another security precaution; tenants (and anyone else) could go down and out in case of fire or elevator failure, but they could only leave the stairs at the lobby. They couldn't get off at another floor.

Well, that was nice enough in theory, but an inch-wide strip of flexible steel did its work in nothing flat, and then I was easing the door open, making sure that the coast (or at least the hallway) was clear.

I traversed the hallway to 11-B. No light showed under the door, and when I pressed my ear against it I couldn't hear a thing, not even the roar of the surf. I didn't expect to hear anything since I'd just let the phone in 11-B ring twelve or twenty times, but burglary is chancy enough even when you don't take chances. There was a bell, a flat mother-of-pearl button set flush against the doorjamb, and I rang it and heard it sound within. There was a knocker, an art nouveau affair in the shape of a coiled cobra, but I didn't want to make noise in the hallway. I didn't, indeed, want to spend an unnecessary extra second in that hallway, and with that in mind I bent to my task.

First the burglar alarm. You wouldn't think one was necessary at the Charlemagne, but then you probably don't have a houseful of objets d'art and a stamp collection on a par with King Farouk's, do you? If burglars don't take unnecessary chances, why should their victims?

You could tell there was a burglar alarm because there was a keyhole for it, set in the door at about shoulder height, a nickel-plated cylinder perhaps five-eighths of an inch in diameter. What man can lock, man can unlock, and that's just what I did. There was a handy little home-made key on my ring that fits most locks of that ilk, and with just the littlest bit of filing and fiddling it can make the tumblers tumble, and –

oh, but you don't want to know all this technical stuff, do you? I thought not.

I turned the key in the lock and hoped that was all you had to do. Alarm systems are cunning devices with no end of fail-safe features built in. Some go off, for example, if you cut the household current. Others get twitchy if you turn the key in other than the prescribed fashion. This one seemed docile, but what if it was one of those silent alarms, ringing nastily away downstairs or in the offices of some home-protection agency?

Ah, well. The other lock, the one that was keeping the door shut, was a Poulard. According to the manufacturer's advertisements, no one has ever successfully picked the Poulard lock. I'd walk into his offices and dispute that claim, but where would it get me? The lock mechanism's a good one, I'll grant them that, and the key's complicated and impossible to duplicate, but I have more trouble on average with your basic Rabson. Either I picked the Poulard or I made myself very long and narrow and slithered in through the keyhole, because within three minutes I was inside that apartment.

I closed the door and played my pencil-beam flashlight over it. If I'd made some grave error knocking off the burglar alarm, and if it was the sort that was ringing in some agency's office, then I had plenty of time to get away before they came calling. So I examined the cylinder to see how it was wired in and if anything seemed to have gone awry, and after a moment or two of frowning and head-scratching I started to giggle.

Because there was no alarm system. All there was was a nickel-plated cylinder, attached to nothing at all, mounted in the door like a talisman. You've seen those decals on car windows warning of an alarm system? People buy the decals for a dollar, hoping they'll keep car thieves at bay, and perhaps they do. You've seen those signs on houses, *Beware of the Dog*, and they haven't got a dog? A sign's cheaper than rabies shots and Alpo, and you don't have to walk it twice a day.

Why install a burglar alarm at a cost of a thousand dollars or more when you could mount a cylinder for a couple of bucks and get the same protection? Why have a system you'd forget to set half the time, and forget to turn off the other half of the time, when the illusion of a system was every bit as effective?

My heart filled with admiration for John Charles Appling. It was going to be a pleasure to do business with him.

I'd been reasonably certain he wasn't home. He was at the Greenbrier in White Sulphur Springs, West-by-God-Virginia, playing golf and taking the sun and attending a tax-deductible convention of the Friends of the American Wild Turkey, a band of conservationists dedicated to improving wilderness conditions to create a more favorable habitat for the birds in question, thereby to increase their numbers to the point where the Friends can hie themselves off to the woods in autumn with shotgun and turkey lure in tow, there to slay the object of their affections. After all, what are friends for?

I locked the door now, just in case, and I drew my rubber gloves from my attaché case and pulled them on, then took a moment to wipe the surfaces I might have touched while checking the fake alarm cylinder. There still remained the outside of the door, but I'd smudge those prints on the way out. Then I took another moment to lean against the door and let my eyes accustom themselves to the darkness. And – let's admit it – to Enjoy the Feeling.

And what a feeling it was! I read once of a woman who spent every free moment at Coney Island, riding the big roller coaster over and over and over. Evidently she got the thrill from that curious pastime that I get whenever I let myself into another person's place of residence. That charged-up sensation, that fire-in-the-blood, every-cell-alive feeling. I've had it ever since I first broke into a neighbor's house in my early teens, and all the intervening years, all the crimes and all the punishments, have not dulled or dimmed it in the slightest. It's as much of a thrill as ever.

I'm not boasting. I take a workman's pride in my skills but no pride at all in the forces that drive me. God help me, I'm a born thief, the urge to burgle bred in my bones. How could they ever rehabilitate me? Can you teach a fish to leave off swimming, a bird to renounce flight?

By the time my eyes had grown accustomed to the darkness, the thrill of illegal entry had subsided to a less acute sense of profound well-being. Flashlight in hand, I took a quick tour of the apartment. Even if Appling and his wife were sequestered with the rest of the turkeys, there was always the chance that one of the rooms held some relative or friend or servant, sleeping peacefully or cowering in terror or putting in a quiet call to the local precinct. I went quickly in and out of each room and encountered nothing living but the houseplants. Then I returned to the living room and switched on a lamp.

I had plenty to choose from. The cobra door knocker was the first but hardly the last piece of art nouveau I encountered, and the living room was festooned with enough Tiffany lamps to cause a power failure. Large lamps, small lamps, table lamps, floor lamps – no one could want that much light. But then the collecting mania is by definition irrational and excessive. Appling had thousands upon thousands of postage stamps, and how many letters do you suppose he sent out?

Tiffany lamps are worth a fortune these days. I recognized some of them – the Dragonfly lamp, the Wisteria lamp – and you can pick up a nice suburban house for what a couple of those would bring at Parke-Bernet. You could also earn a very quick trip to Dannemora trying to walk out of the Charlemagne weighted down with leaded-glass lamps. I went around examining them – the place was as good as a museum – but I left them as I found them, along with any number of other gewgaws and pretties.

The Applings seemed to have separate bedrooms, and I found jewelry in hers, in a stunning tortoiseshell jewelry box in her top dresser drawer. The box was locked and the key was right there next to it in the drawer. Go figure some people. I unlocked the box with its little key – I could have opened it almost as quickly without the key, but why show off when there's no one around to ooh and ahh? I was going to leave the jewelry, although it did look awfully nice, but a pair of ruby earrings proved irresistible, and into my pocket they went. Would she miss one pair of earrings out of a whole box full of jewelry? And, if she did, wouldn't she think she'd misplaced them? What kind of burglar, after all, would take a couple of earrings and leave everything else?

A cagey one. A burglar whose presence in the Charlemagne that night was a matter of record, and who thus had to avoid stealing anything that would be conspicuous by its absence. I did take the ruby earrings – my profession, after all, can never be 100% risk-free – but when I came upon a sheaf of fifty- and hundred-dollar bills in J. C. Appling's dresser drawer, I left them there.

Not without effort, let me admit. There wasn't a fortune there, $2,800 at a rough count, but money is money and you just can't beat cash. When you steal things you have to fence them, but with cash you just keep it and spend the stuff at leisure.

But he might notice that it was gone. It might in fact be the first thing he checked upon returning to the apartment, and if it was missing he'd know immediately that he hadn't misplaced it, that it hadn't walked off of its own accord.

I thought of taking a couple of bills, figuring they wouldn't be missed, but how much is too much? It's more trouble making such nice distinctions than the cash warranted. Easier to leave the money where it was.

I hit paydirt in the den.

There was a bookcase there, but nothing like Onderdonk's library. Some reference works, a shelf full of stamp catalogs, a few books on guns, and a cheap set of reprint editions of the novels of Zane Grey. Bargain-table stuff at Barnegat Books, forty cents each, three for a buck.

A glassed-in wall case held two shotguns and a rifle, their stocks elaborately tooled, their barrels agleam with menace. I suppose they were for shooting turkeys but they'd do in a pinch for shooting burglars and I didn't like the looks of them.

Over the desk, an Audubon print of an American wild turkey hung in an antiqued frame. The real thing, stuffed and mounted and looking only a little forlorn, stood guard atop the bookcase. I suppose its friend

J.C. shot it. First he'd have honked with one of the odd-looking wooden turkey lures he had on display, and then he'd have triggered the shotgun, and now the creature had achieved a sort of taxidermal immortality. Oh, well. People who break into houses, glass or otherwise, probably shouldn't cast stones. Or aspersions, or whatever.

In any event, the turkeys and the guns and the books were beside the point. Along the back of the large desk, below the Audubon turkey, ranged a dozen dark green volumes a bit over a foot high and a couple of inches wide. They were Scott Specialty Stamp Albums, and they were just what the burglar ordered. British Asia, British Africa, British Europe, British America, British Oceania. France and French Colonies. Germany, German States and German Colonies. Benelux. South and Central America. Scandinavia. And, in an album which did not match its fellows, the United States.

I went through one album after another. Appling's stamps were not affixed to the page with hinges but were encased individually in little plastic mounts designed for the purpose. (Hinging a mint stamp is as economically unsound as discarding a book's dust jacket.) I could have removed the plastic mounts, and thought about it, but it was faster and simpler and subtler to tear whole pages from the loose-leaf binders, and that's what I did.

I know a little about stamps. There's a lot I don't know, but I can skim through an album and make good spot decisions as to what to take and what to leave. In the Benelux album, for example – that's Belgium, the Netherlands and Luxembourg, along with Belgian and Dutch colonies – I cleaned out all of the semi-postal issues (all complete, all mint, all readily salable) and most of the good nineteenth-century classics. I left the more highly specialized stuff, parcel post and postage due and such. In the British Empire albums I loaded up on the Victoria, Edward VII and George V issues. I didn't take very many pages from the Latin American albums, having less knowledge of the material.

By the time I was done my attaché case was packed solid with album pages and the albums they'd come from were all back in order on the desk top, their bulk not visibly reduced. I don't suppose I took one page in twenty, but the pages I took were the ones worth taking. I'm sure I missed the odd priceless rarity, and I'm sure I took the bad with the good, even as I do in life itself, but on balance I felt I'd done a first-rate job of winnowing.

I hadn't a clue what the lot was worth. One of the US pages included the twenty-four-cent inverted airmail, a bicolor with the plane appearing upside-down, and I forget the most recent auction record for that issue but I know it ran well into five figures. On the other hand, it would have to be fenced, sold to someone who'd be aware he was buying stolen goods and who'd accordingly expect a bargain. Most of the other material was quite anonymous in comparison, and would bring a much higher proportion of its fair market value.

So what did I have in my attaché case? A hundred thousand? It wasn't impossible. And what could I net for it? Thirty, thirty-five thousand?

A fair ball-park figure. But it was no more than a guess and I might be miles off in either direction. In twenty-four hours' time I'd know a good deal more. By then all of the stamps would be off their pages and out of their mounts, sorted by sets and tucked into little glassine envelopes, their prices checked in last year's Scott catalog, which was the most recent copy to have turned up at the store. (I could buy the book new, but somehow it goes against the grain.) Then Appling's pages and mounts would go down the incinerator, along with any stamps that might have markings rendering them specifically identifiable. In a day's time, a box of stamps in glassine envelopes, all quite anonymous, would be my only link with the John Charles Appling collection. An indeterminate time after that, but surely not much more than a week, the stamps would have new owners and I'd have money in their stead.

And it might be months before Appling ever knew they were gone. It was likely that he'd detect their absence the first time he pulled out an album and paged through it, but it was by no means a sure thing. I'd left twenty times as much as I'd taken, in volume if not in value, and he might open a book, turn to a specific page, add a stamp, and never notice that other pages were missing.

It didn't really matter. He wouldn't notice the minute he walked into the house, and when he did notice he couldn't say when the theft had taken place – it might have occurred before or after his Greenbrier jaunt. His insurance company would pay, or it wouldn't, and he'd come out ahead or behind or dead even, and who cared? Not I. A batch of pieces of colored paper would have changed ownership, and so would a batch of pieces of green paper, and no one on God's earth was going to miss a meal as a result of my night's activities.

I'm not offering a moral defense of myself, you understand. Burglary is morally reprehensible and I'm aware of the fact. But I wasn't stealing the pennies off a dead man's eyes, or the bread from a child's mouth, or objects of deep sentimental value. I'll tell you, I love collectors. I can ransack their holdings with such little guilt.

The state, however, takes a sterner view of things. They draw no distinction between swiping a philatelist's stamps and lifting a widow's rent money. However good I get at rationalizing my pursuit, I still have to do what I can to stay out of jail.

Which meant getting the hell out of there. I turned off lights – there was a Tiffany lamp in the study, too, wouldn't you know – and I made my way to the apartment's front door. My stomach growled en route and I thought of checking the fridge and building myself a sandwich, figuring they'd no more miss a little food than a fortune in rare stamps. But Sing Sing and Attica are overflowing with chaps who stopped for a sandwich, and if I just got out of there I could buy myself a whole restaurant.

I squinted through the peephole, saw no one in the hallway, and put my ear to the door and heard no one in the hallway, either. I unlocked the door, eased it open, *saw* no one in the hallway, and let myself out. I picked the Poulard lock again, locking it this time so as to spare the manufacturer's feelings. I did not reset the spurious burglar alarm cylinder, just gave it a wink and went on my way, pausing only to smudge whatever prints I might have left on the outside of the door. Then, attaché case in hand, I crossed to the fire door, opened it, passed through it, and let out a long breath as it swung quietly shut behind me.

I climbed one flight, stopped long enough to strip off my rubber gloves and stuff them into my jacket pocket. (I didn't want to open the attaché case and chance spilling stamps all over the goddamn place.) I climbed three more flights of stairs, slipped the lock on the fire door, emerged in the hallway, and rang for the elevator. While it ascended from the lobby I checked my watch.

Twenty-five minutes to one. It had been close to eleven-thirty when I said good night to Onderdonk, so I'd spent just about an hour in the Appling apartment. It seemed to me that I should have been able to get in and out in half an hour, but I couldn't have shaved too many minutes off the time I spent going through the albums. I could have stayed out of the bedrooms, perhaps, and I didn't have to give as much attention as I did to the Tiffany lamps, but what is it they say about all work and no play? I was out of there safely and that was what counted.

A shame, though, that I couldn't have made my exit before midnight, when service shifts commonly change at apartment buildings. I'd be seen now by a second elevator operator, a second concierge, a second doorman. Otherwise I'd have been seen by the same set a second time, and which was riskier? Not that it mattered, since I'd already given my name, and—

The elevator arrived. As I stepped into the car I turned toward Onderdonk's closed door. ''Night now,' I said. 'I'll have those figures for you as soon as I can.'

The door closed, the car descended. I leaned back against its wood paneling and crossed my legs at the ankle. 'Long day,' I said.

'Just starting for me,' the operator said.

I tried to forget about the camera overhead. It was like trying to forget that you've got your left foot in a bucket of ice water. I couldn't look at it and I couldn't suppress the urge to look at it, and I did a lot of elaborate yawning. It was, actually, a rather quick ride, but it certainly didn't seem that way.

A brisk nod to the concierge. The doorman held the door for me, then hurried past me to the curb to summon a taxi. One turned up almost immediately. I gave the doorman a buck and told the driver to drop me at Madison and Seventy-second. I paid him, walked a block west to Fifth, and caught another cab back to my place. On the way I balanced the attaché case on my knees and relived some of the hour I'd spent in apartment 11-B. The moment when the Poulard lock, teased and tickled beyond endurance, threw up its tumblers and surrendered. The sight of that inverted airmail stamp, alone on a page, as if it had been waiting for me since the day they misprinted it.

I tipped the cabby a buck. My own doorman, a glassy-eyed young fellow who worked the midnight-to-eight shift in a permanent muscatel haze, did not rush to open the door of the taxi. I suppose he'd have held the lobby door for me but he didn't have to. It was propped open. He stayed on his stool, greeting me with a sly conspiratorial smile. I wonder what secret he thought we shared.

Upstairs I fumbled my own key into my own lock, for a change, and opened the door. The light was on. Considerate of them, I thought, to leave a light for the burglar. Wait a minute, I thought. What was this *them* stuff? I was the one who'd left the light on, except I hadn't, I never did.

What was going on?

I put a foot inside, then drew it warily back, as if trying to get the hang of a new dance step. I went on in and turned toward the couch and blinked, and there, blinking back at me like a slightly cockeyed owl, was Carolyn Kaiser.

'Well, Jesus,' she said, 'it's about time. Where the hell have you been, Bern?'

I pulled the door shut, turned the bolt. 'You picked your way through my Rabson lock,' I said. 'I didn't think you knew how to do that.'

'I don't.'

'Don't tell me the doorman let you in. He's not supposed to, and anyway he doesn't have a key.'

'*I* have a key, Bern. You gave me keys to your place. Remember?'

'Oh, right.'

'So I stuck the key in the lock and turned it, and damned if the thing didn't pop open. You ought to try it yourself sometime. Works like a charm.'

'Carolyn—'

'Have you got anything to drink? I know you're supposed to wait until it's offered, but who's got the patience?'

'There's two bottles of beer in the fridge,' I said. 'One's going to wash

617

down the sandwich I'm about to make, but you're welcome to the other one.'

'Dark Mexican beer, right? Dos Equis?'

'Right.'

'They're gone. What else have you got?'

I thought for a moment. 'There's a little Scotch left.'

'A single malt? Glen Islay, something like that?'

'You found it and it's gone, too.'

' 'Fraid so, Bern.'

'Then we're fresh out,' I said, 'unless you want to knock off the Lavoris. I think it's about sixty proof.'

'Child of a dog.'

'Carolyn—'

'You know something? I think I'm gonna go back to saying "son of a bitch." It may be sexist but it's a lot more satisfying than "child of a dog." You go around saying "child of a dog" and people don't even know you're cursing.'

'Carolyn, what are you doing here?'

'I'm dying of thirst, that's what I'm doing.'

'You're drunk.'

'No shit, Bernie.'

'You are. You drank two beers and a pint of Scotch and you're shitfaced.'

She braced an elbow on her knee, rested her head in the palm of her hand and gave me a look. 'In the first place,' she said, 'it wasn't a pint, it was maybe six ounces, which isn't even half a pint. We're talking about three drinks in a good bar or two drinks in a terrific bar. In the second place, it's not nice to tell your best friend that she's shitfaced. Pie-eyed, maybe. Half in the bag, three sheets to the wind, a little under the weather, all acceptable. But shitfaced, that's not a nice thing to say to someone you love. And in the third place—'

'In the third place, you're still drunk.'

'In the third place, I was drunk *before* I drank your booze in the first place.' She beamed triumphantly, then frowned. 'Or should that be the fourth place, Bernie? I don't know. It's hell keeping track of all these places. In the fifth place I was drunk when I got back to my place, and then I had a drink before I came up to your place, so that makes me—'

'Out of place,' I suggested.

'I don't know what it makes me.' She waved an impatient hand. 'That's not the important thing.'

'It's not?'

'No.'

'What is?'

She looked furtively around. 'I'm not supposed to tell anybody,' she said.

'To tell anybody what?'

'There aren't any bugs in this place, are there, Bern?'

'Just the usual roaches and silverfish. What's the problem, Carolyn?'

'The problem is my pussy's been snatched.'

'Huh?'

'Oh, God,' she said. 'My kid's been catnapped.'

'Your kid's been – Carolyn, you don't have any kids. How much did you have to drink, anyway? Before you got here?'

'Shit on toast,' she said, loud. 'Will you just listen to me? Please? It's Archie.'

'Archie?'

She nodded. 'Archie,' she said. 'They've kidnapped Archie Goodwin.'

4

'The cat,' I said.

'Right.'

'Archie the cat. Your Burmese cat. *That* Archie.'

'Of course, Bern. Who else?'

'You said Archie Goodwin, and the first thing I thought—'

'That's his full name, Bern.'

'I know that.'

'I didn't mean Archie Goodwin the person, Bern, because he's a character in the Nero Wolfe stories, and the only way he could have been kidnapped would be in a book, and if that happened I wouldn't run up here in the middle of the night and carry on about it. You want to know the truth, Bern, I think you need a drink more than I do, which is saying something.'

'I think you're right,' I said. 'I'll be back in a minute.'

It was more like five. I walked down the hall past my friend Mrs Hesch's apartment to Mrs Seidel's. Mrs Seidel was visiting family in Shaker Heights, according to Mrs Hesch. I rang her bell for safety's sake, then let myself into her apartment. (She'd gone off without double-locking her door, so all I had to do was loid the springlock with a strip of plastic. Someone, I thought, would have to talk to Mrs Seidel about that.)

I came back from there with a mostly full bottle of Canadian Club. I poured drinks for both of us. Carolyn had hers swallowed before I had the cap back on the bottle.

'That's better,' she said.

I took a drink myself, and as it hit bottom I remembered that I was pouring it into a very empty stomach. It would be a lot easier to get me drunk than to get Carolyn sober, but I wasn't sure it was a good idea. I opened the fridge and built a sandwich of thin-sliced Polish ham and Monterey jack cheese on one of those dark musky rye breads that comes in little square loaves. I took a big bite and chewed thoughtfully and could have killed for a bottle of Dos Equis.

'What about Archie?' I said.

'He doesn't drink.'

'Carolyn—'

'Sorry. I don't mean to be drunk, Bern.' She tilted the bottle and helped herself to a few more cc's of the CC, as it were. 'I went home and fed the cats and had something to eat, and then I got restless and went out. I kept bopping around. I think I had a touch of moon madness. Did you happen to notice the moon?'

'No.'

'Neither did I, but I'll bet it's full or close to it. I kept feeling as though the problem was that I just wasn't in the right place. So I'd go somewhere else and I'd feel the same way. I went to Paula's and the Duchess and Kelly's West and a couple of straight bars on Bleecker Street, and then I went back to Paula's and played a little pool, and then I hit this pigpen on Nineteenth Street, I forget the name, and then I hit the Duchess again—'

'I get the picture.'

'I was bouncing is what I was doing, and of course you have to have a drink when you go to a place, and I went to a lot of places.'

'And had a lot of drinks.'

'What else? But I wasn't looking to get drunk, see. I was looking to get lucky. Will true love ever come to Carolyn Kaiser? And, failing that, how about true lust?'

'Not tonight, I gather.'

'I'll tell you, I couldn't get arrested. I called Alison a couple of times, which I swore I wasn't gonna do, but it's all right because she didn't answer. Then I went home. I figured I'd make it a reasonably early night, maybe have a brandy before I turned in, and I opened the door and the cat was missing. Archie, I mean. Ubi was fine.'

Archie, full name Archie Goodwin, was a sleek Burmese given to eloquent yowling. Ubi, full name Ubiquity or Ubiquitous, I forget which, was a plump Russian Blue, more affectionate and a good deal less assertive than his Burmese buddy. Both had started life as males, and each had received at a tender age the sort of surgical attention which leaves one purring in soprano.

'He was hiding somewhere,' I suggested.

'No way. I looked in all his hiding places. In things, under things, behind things. Besides, I ran the electric can opener. That's like a fire alarm to a dalmatian.'

'Maybe he snuck out.'

'How? The window was shut and the door was locked. John Dickson Carr couldn't have slipped him out of there.'

'The door was locked?'

'Locked up tight. I always double-lock my dead bolt locks when I go out. You made me a believer in that department. And I locked the Fox police lock. I know I locked all those locks because I had to unlock them to get in.'

'So he went out when you left. Or maybe he snuck out while you were letting yourself in.'

'I would have noticed.'

'Well, you said yourself that you'd had a few drinks more than usual to celebrate the full moon. Maybe—'

'I wasn't that bad, Bern.'

'Okay.'

'And he never does that anyway. Neither of the cats ever tries to get out. Look, you could say this and I could say that and we'd be going around Robin Hood's barn because I know for a fact the cat was snatched. I got a phone call.'

'When?'

'I don't know. I don't know what time I got home and I don't know how much time I spent looking for the cat and running the electric can opener. There was a little brandy and I finally poured some for myself and sat down with it and the phone rang.'

'And?'

She poured another drink, a short one, and paused with the glass halfway to her lips. She said, 'Bern? It wasn't you, was it?'

'Huh?'

'I mean I could see how it could be a joke that got out of hand, but if it was, tell me now, huh? If you tell me now there won't be any hard feelings, but if you don't tell me now all bets are off.'

'You think I took your cat.'

'No I don't. I don't think you've got that kind of an asshole sense of humor. But people do wacky things, and who else could unlock all those locks and lock 'em up again on the way out? So all I want you to do is say, "Yes, Carolyn, I took your cat," or "No, you little idiot, I didn't take your cat," and then we can get on with it.'

'No, you little idiot, I didn't take your cat.'

'Thank God. Except if you had I'd know the cat was safe.' She looked at the glass in her hand as if seeing it for the first time. 'Did I just pour this?'

'Uh-hun.'

'Well, I must have known what I was doing,' she said, and drank it. 'The phone call.'

'Right. Tell me about it.'

'I'm not sure if it was a man or a woman. It was either a man making his voice high or a woman making her voice husky, and I couldn't tell you which. Whoever it was had an accent like Peter Lorre except really phony. "Ve haff ze poosycat." That kind of accent.'

'Is that what he said? "Ve haff ze poosycat"?'

'Or words to that effect. If I want to see him again, di dah di dah di dah di dah.'

'What are all the di dahs about?'

'You're not gonna believe this, Bern.'

'He asked for money?'

'A quarter of a million dollars or I'll never see my cat again.'

'A quarter of a—'

'Million dollars. Right.'

'Two hundred and fifty thousand.'

'Dollars. Right.'

'For—'

'A cat. Right.'

'I'll be a—'

'Child of a dog. Right. So will I.'

'Well, it's nuts,' I said. 'In the first place the cat's not worth any real money. Is he show quality?'

'Probably, but so what? You can't breed him.'

'And he's not a television star like Morris. He's just a cat.'

'Just my cat,' she said. 'Just an animal I happen to love.'

'You want a hankie?'

'What I want is to stop being an idiot. Shit, I can't help it. Gimme the hankie. Where am I gonna get a quarter of a million bucks, Bern?'

'You could start by taking all your old deposit bottles back to the deli.'

'They add up, huh?'

'Little grains of water, little drops of sand. That's another thing that's crazy. Who would figure you could come up with that kind of money? Your apartment's cozy, but Twenty-two Arbor Court isn't the Charlemagne. Anyone bright enough to get in and out and lock up after himself – he really locked up after himself?'

'Swear to God.'

'Who has keys to your place?'

'Just you.'

'What about Randy Messinger?'

'She wouldn't pull this kind of shit. And anyway the Fox lock is new since she and I were lovers. Remember when you installed it for me?'

'And you locked it when you left, and unlocked it when you came back.'

'Definitely.'

'You didn't just turn the cylinder. The bar moved and everything.'

'Bernie, trust me. It was locked and I had to unlock it.'

'That rules out Randy.'

'She wouldn't have done it.'

'No, but somebody could have copied her keys. Do I still have my set?' I went and checked, and I still had them. I turned, saw my attaché case propped up against the sofa. If I sold its contents for their full market value, I might have two-fifths of the price of a secondhand Burmese cat.

Oh, I thought.

'Take a couple of aspirin,' I said. 'And if you want another drink, have it with hot water and sugar. You'll sleep better.'

'Sleep?'

'Uh-huh, and the sooner the better. You take the bed, I'll take the couch.'

'Don't be ridiculous,' she said. 'I'll take the couch. Except I won't because I don't want to go to sleep and I can't stay here anyway. They said they would call me in the morning.'

'That's why I want you to get to sleep. So you'll be clearheaded when they call.'

'Bernie, I got news for you. I'm not gonna be clearheaded in the morning. I'm gonna have a head like a soccer ball that Pelé got pissed at.'

'Well, I'll be clearheaded,' I said, 'and one head is better than none. The aspirin's in the medicine cabinet.'

'What a clever place for it. I bet you're the kind of guy who keeps milk in the fridge and soap in the soap dish.'

'I'll fix you a hot toddy.'

'Didn't you hear what I said? I have to be at my place for when they call.'

'They'll call here.'

'Why would they do that?'

'Because you don't have a quarter of a million dollars,' I said, 'and who could mistake you for David Rockefeller? So if they want a hefty ransom for Archie they must expect you to steal it, and that means they must know you've got a friend in the stealing business, and that means they'll call here. Drink this and take your aspirin and get ready for bed.'

'I didn't bring pajamas. Have you got a shirt or something that I can sleep in?'

'Sure.'

'And I'm not sleepy. I'll just toss and turn, but I guess that's all right.'

Five minutes later she was snoring.

5

A sign on the counter said the suggested contribution was $2.50. 'Contribute more or less if you prefer,' it counseled, 'but you must contribute *something*.' The chap immediately in front of us plunked down a dime. The attendant started to tell him about the suggested contribution, but our lad wasn't open to suggestion.

'Read your own sign, sonny,' he said sourly. 'How many times do I have to go through this with you vermin? You'd think it was coming out of your own pockets. They haven't got you on commission, have they?'

'Not yet.'

'Well, I'm an artist. The dime's my widow's mite. Take it in good grace or in the future I'll reduce my contribution to a penny.'

'Oh, you can't do that, Mr Turnquist,' the attendant said archly. 'It would throw our whole budget out of whack.'

'You know me, eh?'

'Everybody knows you, Mr Turnquist.' A heavy sigh. 'Everybody.'

He took Turnquist's dime and gave him a little yellow lapel pin for it. Turnquist faced us as he fastened the pin to the breast pocket of his thrift shop suit jacket. It was a sort of gray, and came reasonably close to matching his thrift shop trousers. He smiled, showing misaligned tobacco-stained teeth. He had a beard, a ragged goatee a little redder than his rusty brown hair and a little more infiltrated with gray, and the rest of his face was two or three days away from a shave.

'Little tin gods on wheels,' he advised us. 'That's all these people are. Don't take any crap from them. If Art can be intimidated, it ain't Art.'

He moved on and I laid a five-dollar bill on the counter and accepted two lapel pins in return. 'An artist,' the attendant said meaningfully. He tapped another sign, which announced that children under the age of sixteen were not admitted, whether or not accompanied by an adult. 'We ought to amend our policy,' he said. 'No children, no dogs, and no artists.'

I'd awakened before Carolyn and went directly to a liquor store on West Seventy-second, where I bought a replacement bottle of Canadian

Club. I took it home and knocked on Mrs Seidel's door, and when my knock went unanswered I let myself in and cracked the seal on the bottle, poured an ounce or so down the sink drain, capped the bottle and put it back where I'd found its fellow the night before. I let myself out and met Mrs Hesch in the hallway, the inevitable cigarette burning unattended in the corner of her mouth. I stopped at her apartment for a cup of coffee – she makes terrific coffee – and we talked, not for the first time, about the coin-operated laundry in the basement. She was exercised about the driers, which, their dials notwithstanding, had two temperatures – On and Off. I was vexed with the washers, which were as voracious as Pac-Man when it came to socks. Neither of us said anything about the fact that I'd just let myself out of Mrs Seidel's place.

I went back to my apartment and listened to Carolyn being sick in the bathroom while I put a pot of coffee on. She came out looking a little green and sat in the corner of the couch holding her head. I showered and shaved and came back to find her staring unhappily at a cup of coffee. I asked her if she wanted aspirin. She said she wouldn't mind some Extra-Strength Tylenol, but I didn't have any. I ate and she didn't and we both drank coffee and the phone rang.

A woman's voice, unaccented, said, 'Mr Rhodenbarr? Have you spoken to your friend?'

I thought of pointing out that the question was implicitly insulting, presuming that I only had one friend, that I was the sort of person who couldn't possibly have more than a single friend, that I was lucky to have one and could probably expect to be deserted by her when she wised up.

I said, 'Yes.'

'Are you prepared to pay the ransom? A quarter of a million dollars?'

'Doesn't that strike you as a shade high? I know inflation's murder these days, and I understand it's a seller's market for Burmese cats, but—'

'Do you have the money?'

'I try not to keep that much cash around the house.'

'You can raise it?'

Carolyn had come over to my side when the phone rang. I laid a reassuring hand on her arm. To my caller I said, 'Let's cut the comedy, huh? Bring the cat back and we'll forget the whole thing. Otherwise—'

Otherwise what? I'm damned if I know what kind of a threat I was prepared to make. But Carolyn didn't give me the chance. She clutched my arm. She said, 'Bernie—'

''Ve vill kill ze cat,' the woman said, her voice much louder and suddenly accented. The effect was somewhere between an ad for Viennese pastry *mit schlag* and that guy in the World War II movies who reminds you that you've got relatives in Chermany.

626

'Now let's be calm,' I said, to both of them. 'No need to talk about violence.'

'If you do not pay ze ransom—'

'Neither of us has that kind of money. You must know that. Now why don't you tell me what you want?'

There was a pause. 'Tell your vriend to go home.'

'I beg your pardon?'

'Zere is somesing in her mailbox.'

'All right. I'll go with her, and—'

'No.'

'No?'

'Stay vere you are. You vill get a phone call.'

'But—'

There was a click. I sat looking at the receiver for a few seconds before I hung it up. I asked Carolyn if she'd heard any of it.

'I caught a few words here and there,' she said. 'It was the same person I talked to last night. At least I think it was. Same accent, anyway.'

'She switched it on in midstream. I guess she forgot it at the beginning, and then she remembered she was supposed to sound threatening. Or else she slips into it when she gets excited. I don't like the idea of splitting up. She wants you to go to your apartment and me to stay here and I don't like it.'

'Why?'

'Well, who knows what she's going to try to pull?'

'I have to go downtown anyway. Somebody's bringing me a schnauzer at eleven. Shit, I don't have much time, do I? I can't face a schnauzer with a head like I've got. Thank God it's a miniature schnauzer. I don't know what I'd do if I had to wash a giant schnauzer on a day like this.'

'Stop at your apartment on the way. If you've got time.'

'I'll make time. I have to feed Ubi, anyway. You don't think—'

'What?'

'That they took him too? Maybe that's why they want me to go to my apartment.'

'They said to check your mailbox.'

'Oh, God,' she said.

When she left I went to work on Appling's stamp collection. I suppose it was a cold-blooded thing to do, what with Archie's life hanging in the balance, but that still left him with eight and I wanted to render the Appling stamps unidentifiable as soon as possible. I sat under a good light at my kitchen table with a pair of stamp tongs and a box of glassine envelopes and a Scott catalog, and I transferred the stamps a set at a time from their mounts to the envelopes, making the appropriate notation on each envelope. I didn't bother figuring out the value. That would be another operation, and it could wait.

I was laboring over George V high values from Trinidad & Tobago when the phone rang. 'What's this crap about my mailbox?' Carolyn demanded. 'There's nothing in it but the Con Ed bill.'

'How's Ubi?'

'Ubi's fine. He looks lost and lonely and his heart is probably breaking, but aside from that he's fine. Did that Nazi call back?'

'Not yet. Maybe she meant the mailbox at your shop.'

'There's no box there. There's just a slot in the door.'

'Well, maybe she got a wire crossed. Go wash the saluki anyway and see what happens.'

'It's not a saluki, it's a schnauzer, and I know what'll happen. I'll wind up smelling of wet dog for a change. Call me when you hear from them, okay?'

'Okay,' I said, and fifteen minutes later the phone rang again and it was the mystery woman. No accent this time, and no elaborate run-around, either. She talked and I listened, and when she was done I sat for a minute and thought and scratched my head and thought some more. Then I put Appling's stamps away and called Carolyn.

And now we were in a small room on the second floor of the gallery. We'd followed my caller's directions to the letter, and we were accordingly standing in front of a painting that looked remarkably familiar.

A small bronze rectangle affixed to the wall beside it bore the following information: *Piet Mondrian. 1872–1944. Composition With Color, 1942. Oil on canvas, 86 x 94 cm. Gift of Mr & Mrs J. McLendon Barlow.*

I wrote the dimensions in my pocket notebook. In case you haven't caved in and learned to think metric, they worked out in real measurement to something like 35 by 39 inches, with the height greater than the width. The background color was white, tinted a little toward gray by either time or the artist. Black lines crisscrossed the canvas, dividing it into squares and rectangles, several of which were painted in primary colors. There were two red areas, two blue ones, and a long narrow section of yellow.

I stepped closer and Carolyn laid a hand on my arm. 'Don't straighten it,' she urged. 'It's fine the way it is.'

'I was just having a closer look.'

'Well, there's a guard by the door,' she said, 'and he's having a closer look at us. There's guards all over the place. This is crazy, Bern.'

'We're just looking at pictures.'

'And that's all we're gonna do, because this is impossible. You could no more get a painting out of this place than you could get a child into it.'

628

'Relax,' I said. 'All we're doing is looking.'

The building where we stood, like the painting in front of us, had once been in private hands. Years ago it had served as the Manhattan residence of Jacob Hewlett, a mining and transport baron who'd ground the faces of the poor with inordinate success around the turn of the century. He'd left his Murray Hill townhouse at the corner of Madison and Thirty-eighth to the city, with the stipulation that it be maintained as an art museum under the direction and control of a foundation established by Hewlett for that purpose. While his own holdings had served as the core of the collections, paintings had been bought and sold over the years, and the foundation's tax-exempt status had encouraged occasional gifts and bequests, such as the donation of the Mondrian oil by someone named Barlow.

'I checked the hours when we came in,' Carolyn was saying. 'They're open from nine-thirty to five-thirty during the week and on Saturdays. On Sunday they open at noon and close at five.'

'And they're closed Monday?'

'Closed all day Monday and open until nine on Tuesdays.'

'Most museums keep hours about like that. I always know when it's Monday because the impulse comes on me to go to a museum, and they're all closed.'

'Uh-huh. If we're planning to break in, we could do it either after hours or on Monday.'

'Either way's impossible. They'll have guards posted around the clock. And the alarm system's a beaut. You can't just cross a couple of wires and pat it on the head.'

'So what do we do? Snatch it off the wall and make a break for it?'

'Wouldn't work. They'd bag us before we got to the first floor.'

'What does that leave?'

'Prayer and fasting.'

'Terrific. Who's this guy? What's it say, van Doesburg? He and Mondrian must have gone to two different schools together.'

We had sidled around to our left and were standing in front of a canvas by Theo van Doesburg. Like Mondrian's work, his was all right angles and primary colors, but there was no mistaking one artist for the other. The van Doesburg canvas lacked the sense of space and balance that Mondrian had. How curious, I thought, that a man could go for months without standing in front of a single Mondrian canvas, and then he'd stand before two of them on successive days. All the more remarkable, it seemed to me, was the similarity of the Hewlett's Mondrian to the one I'd seen hanging over Gordon Onderdonk's fireplace. If memory served, they were about the same size and proportion, and must have been painted at about the same stage in the artist's career. I was willing to believe that they'd look very different if one saw them side by side, but such a simultaneous viewing didn't appear to be an option, and if someone had told me that the Onderdonk painting had been hustled downtown and stuck up on the Hewlett's wall, I couldn't have sworn he was wrong. Onderdonk's painting was framed, of course, while this canvas was left unframed so as to show how the artist had continued his geometric design around the sides of the canvas. For all I knew Onderdonk's painting had twice as many colored areas. It might be taller or shorter, wider or narrower. But—

But it still seemed oddly coincidental. Coincidences don't have to be significant, of course. I'd picked up Carolyn at the Poodle Factory and we'd shared a cab to the Hewlett, and I hadn't bothered reading our driver's name on the posted hack license, but suppose I had and suppose it had been Turnquist? Then, when the attendant had greeted the ill-clad artist by name, we might have remarked on the coincidence of having met two Turnquists in half an hour. But so what?

Still—

We circled the room, pausing now and then in front of a painting, including several that left me cold and a Kandinsky I liked a lot. There was an Arp. Onderdonk had an Arp, too, but since we hadn't been ordered to steal an Arp there was nothing particularly coincidental about it, or nothing remarkable about the coincidence, or—

'Bern? Should I just plain forget about the cat?'

'How would you go about doing that?'

'Beats me. Do you really think they'll do anything to Archie if we don't steal the painting?'

'Why should they?'

'To prove they mean business. Isn't that what kidnappers do?'

'I don't know what kidnappers do. I think they kill the victim to prevent being identified, but how's a Burmese cat going to identify them? But—'

'But who knows with crazy people? The thing is, they're expecting us to do the impossible.'

'It's not necessarily impossible,' I said. 'Paintings walk out of museums all the time. In Italy museum theft is a whole industry, and even here you see something in the papers every couple of months. The Museum of Natural History seems to get hit every once in a while.'

'Then you think we can take it?'

'I didn't say that.'

'Then—'

'Beautiful, isn't it?'

I turned at the voice, and there was our artist friend, his ten cent lapel badge fastened to his thrift shop jacket, his yellow teeth bared in a fierce grin. We were once again standing in front of *Composition With Color*, and Turnquist's eyes gleamed as he looked at the painting. 'You can't beat old Piet,' he said. 'Sonofabitch could paint. Something, huh?'

'Something,' I agreed.

'Most of this is crap. Detritus, refuse. In a word, you should pardon the expression, shit. My apologies, madam.'

'It's all right,' Carolyn assured him.

'The museum is the dustbin of the history of Art. Sounds like a quotation, doesn't it? I made it up myself.'

'It has a ring to it.'

'Dustbin's English for garbage can. English English, I mean to say. But the rest of this stuff, this is worse than garbage. *Dreck*, as some of my best friends would say.'

'Er.'

'Just a handful of good painters this century. Mondrian, of course. Picasso, maybe five percent of the time, when he wasn't cocking around. But five percent of Picasso is plenty, huh?'

'Er.'

'Who else? Pollack. Frank Roth. Trossman. Clyfford Still. Darragh Park. Rothko, before he got so far down he forgot to use color. And others, a handful of others. But most of this—'

'Well,' I said.

'I know what you want to say. Who's this old fart running off at the mouth? His jacket don't even match his pants and he's making judge-ments left and right, telling what's Art and what's garbage. That's what you're thinking, ain't it?'

'I wouldn't say that.'

'Of course you wouldn't say it, you or this young lady. She's a lady and you're a gentleman and you wouldn't say such a thing. Me, I'm an artist. An artist can say anything. It's an edge the artist has over the gentleman. I know what you're thinking.'

'Uh.'

'And you're right to think it. I'm nobody, that's who I am. Just a painter nobody ever heard of. All the same, I saw you looking at a real painter's work, I saw you keep coming back to this painting, and right off I knew you could tell the difference between chicken salad and chicken shit, if you'll pardon me once again, madam.'

'It's all right,' Carolyn said.

'But it puts my back up to see people give serious attention to most of this crap. You know how you'll read in the paper that a man takes a knife or a bottle of acid and attacks some famous painting? And you probably say to yourself what everybody else says. "How could any-body do such a thing? He'd have to be a madman." The person who does it is always an artist, and in the papers they call him a "self-styled" artist. Meaning *he* says he's an artist but you know and I know the poor fellow's got shit for brains. Once again, dear madam—'

'It's okay.'

'I'll say this,' he said, 'and then I'll leave you good people alone. It is a mark not of madness but of sanity to destroy bad art when it is placed

631

on display in the nation's temples. I'll say more than that. The destruction of bad art is in itself a work of art. Bakunin said the urge to destroy is a creative urge. To slash some of these canvases—' He took a deep breath, expelled it all in a sigh. 'But I'm a talker, not a destroyer. I'm an artist, I paint my paintings and I live my life. I saw the interest you were taking in my favorite painting and it provoked this outburst. Am I forgiven?'

'There's nothing to forgive,' Carolyn told him.

'You're kind people, gracious people. And if I've given you something to think about, why, then you haven't wasted the day and neither have I.'

6

'There's the answer,' Carolyn said. 'We'll destroy the painting. Then they couldn't expect us to steal it.'

'And they'll destroy the cat.'

'Don't even say that. Can we get out of here?'

'Good idea.'

Outside, a young man in buckskin and a young woman in denim were sprawled on the Hewlett's steps, passing an herbal cigarette back and forth. A pair of uniformed guards at the top of the stairs ignored them, perhaps because they were over sixteen. Carolyn wrinkled her nose as she passed the two.

'Sick,' she said. 'Why can't they get drunk like civilized human beings?'

'You could try asking them.'

'They'd say, "Like, man, wow." That's what they always say. Where are we going?'

'Your place.'

'Okay. Any particular reason?'

'Somebody took a cat out of a locked apartment,' I said, 'and I'd like to try to figure out how.'

We walked west, subwayed downtown, and walked from Sheridan Square to Carolyn's place on Arbor Court, one of those wobbly Village streets that slants off at an angle, bridging the gap between hither and yon. Most people couldn't find it, but then most people wouldn't have occasion to look for it in the first place. We walked through a lazy overcast September afternoon that made me want to dash uptown and lace up my running shoes. I told Carolyn it was a great day for running, and she told me there was no such thing.

When we got to her building I examined the lock out in front. It didn't look too challenging. Anyway, it's no mean trick to get in the front door of an unattended building. You ring the other tenants' bells until one of them irresponsibly buzzes you in, or you loiter outside and time your approach so that you reach the doorway just as someone else

633

is going in or out. It's a rare tenant who'll challenge you if you have the right air of arrogant nonchalance.

I didn't have to do all that, however, because Carolyn had her key. She let us in and we went down the hall to her apartment, which is on the ground floor in the back. I knelt and studied keyholes.

'If you see an eye staring back at you,' Carolyn said, 'I don't want to know about it. What are you looking for?'

'A sign that somebody tampered with the locks. I don't see any fresh scratches. Have you got a match?'

'I don't smoke. Neither do you, remember?'

'I wanted better light. My penlight's home. It doesn't matter.' I got to my feet. 'Let me have your keys.'

I unlocked all the locks, and when we were inside I examined them, especially the Fox lock. While I was doing this, Carolyn walked around calling for Ubi. Her voice got increasingly panicky until the cat appeared in response to the whirr of the electric can opener. 'Oh, Ubi,' she said, and scooped him up and plopped herself down in a chair with him. 'Poor baby, you miss your buddy, don't you?'

I went over to the little window and opened it. Cylindrical iron bars an inch thick extended the length of the window, anchored in the brick below and the concrete lintel above. All the window needed was a few similar bars running horizontally and a few squares of color and it could be a Mondrian. I took hold of a couple of bars and tugged them to and fro. They didn't budge.

Carolyn asked me what the hell I was doing. 'Someone could have hacksawed the bars,' I said, 'and fitted them back into place afterward.' I tugged on a couple more. They made the Rock of Gibraltar seem like a shaky proposition in comparison. 'These aren't going anyplace,' I said. 'They're illegal, you know. If there's ever a fire inspection they'll make you take them out.'

'I know.'

'Because if there's ever a fire, that's the only window and you'd never get out it.'

'I know. I also know I'm in a ground floor apartment facing out on an airshaft and the burglars would trip over each other if I didn't have bars on the window. I could get those window gates that you can unlock in case of fire but I know I'd never find the key if I had to, and I'm sure burglars can get through those gates. So I think I'll just leave well enough alone.'

'I don't blame you. Nobody got in this way unless he's awfully goddamn skinny. People can get through narrower spaces than you'd think. When I was a kid I could crawl through a milk chute, and I could probably still crawl through a milk chute, come to think of it, because I'm about the same size I was then. And it looked impossible. It was about ten inches wide by maybe fourteen inches high, but I made it. If you can get your head through an opening, the rest of the body will follow.'

'Really?'

'Ask any obstetrician. Oh, I don't suppose it works with really fat people.'

'Or with pinheads.'

'Well, yeah, right. But it's a good general rule. Nobody got in this window, though, because the bars are what? Three, four inches apart?'

'You can leave the window open, Bern. It's stuffy in here. They didn't get in through the window and they didn't pick the locks, so what does that leave? Black magic?'

'I don't suppose we can rule it out.'

'The flue's blocked on my fireplace, in case you figured Santa Claus pulled the job. How else could they get in? Up from the basement through the floor? Down through the ceiling?'

'It doesn't seem likely. Carolyn, what did the place look like when you came in?'

'Same as it always looks.'

'They didn't go through the drawers or anything?'

'They could have opened drawers and closed them again and I wouldn't have noticed. They didn't mess anything up, if that's what you mean. I didn't even know I'd had anybody here until I couldn't find the cat. I *still* didn't know somebody'd been in here, not until I got the phone call and realized somebody stole the cat. He didn't just disappear on his own, Bernie. What difference does it make?'

'I don't know.'

'Maybe somebody hooked my keys out of my purse. It wouldn't be that hard to do. Somebody could have come in while I was at the Poodle Factory, got ahold of my key ring, had a locksmith copy everything, then dropped the keys back in my bag.'

'All without your noticing?'

'Why not? Say they swipe the keys while they're inquiring about getting a dog groomed, and then they come back to make an appointment and return the keys. It's possible, isn't it?'

'You leave your bag where anybody can get at it?'

'Not as a general rule, but who knows? Anyway, what the hell difference does it make? We're not just locking the barn after the horse has been stolen. We're checking the locks and dusting the bolt for fingerprints.' She frowned. 'Maybe we should have done that.'

'Dusted for prints? Even if there'd been any, what good would they have done us? We're not the cops, Carolyn.'

'Couldn't you get Ray Kirschmann to run a check on a set of finger-prints?'

'Not out of the goodness of his heart, and you can't really run a check on a single print unless you've already got a suspect in hand. You need a whole set of prints, which we wouldn't have even if whoever it was left prints, which they probably didn't. And they'd have to have been fingerprinted anyway for a check to reveal them, and—'

'Forget I mentioned it, okay?'

'Forget you mentioned what?'

'Can't remember. Well, let's just – *shit*,' she said, and moved to answer the phone. 'Hello? Huh? Hold on, I just – shit, they hung up.'

'Who?'

'The Nazi. I'm supposed to look in the mailbox. I looked, remember? All I got was my Con Ed bill and that was enough bad news for one day. And there was nothing in the slot at the Poodle Factory except a catalog of grooming supplies and a flier from one of the animal cruelty organizations. There won't be another delivery today, will there?'

'Maybe they put something in the box without sending it through the mail, Carolyn. I know it's a federal offense but I think we're dealing with people who'll stop at nothing.'

She gave me a look, then went out to the hall. She came back with a small envelope. It had been folded lengthwise for insertion through the small slot in the mailbox. She unfolded it.

'No name,' she said. 'And no stamp.'

'And no return address either, and isn't that a surprise? Why don't you open it?'

She held it to the light, squinted at it. 'Empty,' she said.

'Open it and make sure.'

'Okay, but what's the point? For that matter, what's the point of stuffing an empty envelope into somebody's mailbox? Is it really a federal offense?'

'Yeah, but they'll be tough to prosecute. What's the matter?'

'Look!'

'Hairs,' I said, picking one up. 'Now why in—'

'Oh, God, Bernie. Don't you see what they are?' She gripped my elbows in her hands, stared up at me. 'They're the cat's whiskers,' she said.

'And you're the cat's pajamas. I'm sorry. That just came out. Are they really? Why would anybody do that?'

'To convince us that they mean business.'

'Well, I'm convinced. I was convinced earlier when they managed to get the cat out of a locked room. They've got to be crazy, cutting off a cat's whiskers.'

'That way they can prove they've actually got him.'

I shrugged. 'I don't know. One set of whiskers looks a lot like another one. I figure you've seen one set, you've seen 'em all. Jesus Christ.'

'What's the matter?'

'We can't get the Mondrian out of the Hewlett.'

'I know that.'

'But I know where there's a Mondrian that I *could* steal.'

'Where, the Museum of Modern Art? They've got a couple. And there are a few in the Guggenheim too, aren't there?'

'I know one in a private collection.'

'The Hewlett's was in private hands, too. Now it's in public hands, and unless it gets to be in our hands soon—'

'Forget that one. The one I'm talking about is still in a private collection, because I saw it last night.'

She looked at me. 'I know you went out last night.'

'Right.'

'But you didn't tell me what you did.'

'Well, you can probably guess. But what I did first, what got me into the building, is I appraised a man's library. A nice fellow named Onderdonk, he paid me two hundred dollars to tell him what his books were worth.'

'Were they worth much?'

'Not compared to what he had hanging on his wall. He had a Mondrian, among other things.'

'Like the one in the Hewlett?'

'Well, who knows? It was about the same size and shape and I think the colors were the same, but maybe they'd look completely different to an expert. The thing is, if I could get in there and steal his Mondrian—'

'They'll know it's not the right one because it'll still be on the wall at the Hewlett.'

'Yeah, but will they want to argue the point? If we can hand them a genuine Mondrian worth whatever it is, a quarter of a million is the figure they came up with—'

'Is it really worth that much?'

'I have no idea. The art market's down these days but that's about as much as I know. If we can give them a Mondrian in exchange for a stolen cat, don't you think they'd go for it? They'd have to be crazy to turn it down.'

'We already know they're crazy.'

'Well, they'd also have to be stupid, and they couldn't be too stupid if they managed to swipe the cat.' I grabbed her phone book, looked up Onderdonk's number, dialed it. I let it ring a dozen times and nobody answered it. 'He's out,' I said. 'Now let's just hope he stays out for a while.'

'What are you gonna do, Bern?'

'I'm going home,' I said, 'and I'm going to change my clothes and put some handy gadgets into my pockets—'

'Burglar's tools.'

'And then I'm going to the Charlemagne, and I'd better get there before four or someone'll recognize me, the doorman or the concierge or the elevator operator. But maybe they won't. I was wearing a suit last night and I'll dress down this time around, but even so I'd rather get there before four.'

'How are you going to get in, Bern? Isn't that one of those places that's tighter than Fort Knox?'

'Well, look,' I said, 'I never told you it was going to be easy.'

I hurried uptown and changed into chinos and a short-sleeved shirt that would have been an Alligator except that the embroidered device on the breast was not that reptile but a bird in flight. I guess it was supposed to be a swallow, either winging its way back to Capistrano or not quite making a summer, because the brand name was Swallowtail. It had never quite caught on and I can understand why.

I added a pair of rundown running shoes, filled my pockets with burglar's tools – an attaché case wouldn't fit the image I was trying to project. I got out a clipboard and mounted a yellow pad on it, then set it aside.

I dialed Onderdonk's number again and let it ring. Nobody answered. I looked up another number and no one answered it, either. I tried a third number and a woman answered midway through the fourth ring. I asked if Mr Hodpepper was in, and she said I had the wrong number, but that's what she thought.

I stopped at a florist on Seventy-second and picked up an assortment for $4.98. It struck me, as it has often struck me in the past, that flowers haven't gone up much in price over the years, to the point where they're one of the few things left that give you your money's worth.

I asked for a small blank card, wrote *Leona Tremaine* on the envelope, and inscribed the card *Fondly, Donald Brown.* (I thought of signing it Howard Hodpepper but sanity prevailed, as it now and then does.) I paid for the flowers, taped the card to the wrapping paper, and went outside to hail a cab.

It dropped me on Madison Avenue around the corner from the Charlemagne. A florist's delivery boy does not, after all, arrive by taxi. I walked to the building's front entrance and moved past the doorman to the concierge.

'Got a delivery,' I said, and read from the card. 'Leona Tremaine, it says.'

'I'll see she gets them,' he said, reaching for the bouquet. I drew it back.

'I'm supposed to deliver 'em in person.'

'Don't worry, she'll get 'em.'

'Case there's a reply,' I said.

'He wants his tip,' the doorman interposed. 'That's all he wants.'

'From Tremaine?' the concierge said, and he and the doorman

exchanged smiles. 'Suit yourself,' he told me, and picked up the inter-com phone. 'Miz Tremaine? Delivery for you, looks like flowers. The delivery boy's bringing them up. Yes, ma'am.' He hung up and shook his head. 'Go on up,' he said. 'Elevator's over there. It's apartment 9-C.'

I glanced at my watch in the elevator. The timing, I thought, could not have been better. It was three-thirty. The doorman, the concierge and the elevator operator were not the crew who'd seen me enter last night, nor had they been around when I left with Appling's stamps in my attaché case. And in half an hour they'd go off duty, before they'd had a chance to wonder why the kid with the flowers was spending so much time in Ms Tremaine's apartment. The crew that relieved them wouldn't realize I'd come delivering flowers and would assume I'd had legitimate business with some other tenant. Anyway, they don't hassle you as much on the way out, assuming you must have been okay to get past their security the first time around. It's different if you try to carry out the furniture, of course, but generally speaking getting in's the hard part.

The elevator stopped on Nine and the operator pointed at the ap-propriate door. I thanked him and went and stood in front of it, waiting for the sound of the door closing. It didn't close. Of course it didn't. They waited until the tenant opened the door. Well, she was expecting the flowers anyway, so what was I waiting for?

I poked the doorbell. Chimes sounded within, and after a moment the door opened. The woman who answered it had improbable auburn hair and a face that had fallen one more time than it had been lifted. She was wearing a sort of dressing gown with an oriental motif and she had a look about her of someone who had just smelled something unseemly.

'Flowers,' she said. 'Now are you quite sure those are for me?'

'Ms Leona Tremaine?'

'That's correct.'

'Then they're for you.'

I was still listening for the sound of the elevator door, and I was beginning to realize I wasn't going to hear it. And why should I? He wasn't going anywhere, he'd wait right there until she'd taken the flowers and given me my tip, and then he'd whisk me downstairs again. Terrific. I'd found a way to get into the Charlemagne but I still needed a way to stay there.

'I can't think who'd send me flowers,' she said, taking the wrapped bouquet from me. 'Unless it might be my sister's boy Lewis, but why would he take a notion of sending me flowers? There must be some mistake.'

'There's a card,' I said.

'Oh, there's a card,' she said, discovering it for herself. 'Just wait a moment. Let me see if there hasn't been some mistake here. No, that's my name, Leona Tremaine. Now let me open this.'

Didn't anyone else in the goddamned building want the elevator? Would nothing summon this putz out of his reverie and float him away to another floor?

' "Fondly, Donald Brown," ' she read aloud. 'Donald Brown. Donald. Brown. Donald Brown. Now who could that be?'

'Uh.'

'Well, they're perfectly lovely, aren't they?' She sniffed industriously, as if determined to inhale not merely the bouquet but the petals as well. 'And fragrant. Donald Brown. It's a familiar name, but – well, I'm sure there's been a mistake, but I'll just enjoy them all the same. I'll have to get down a vase, I'll have to put them in water—' She broke off suddenly, remembering that I was there. 'Is there something else, young man?'

'Well, I just—'

'Oh, for heaven's sake, I'm forgetting you, aren't I? Just one moment, let me get my bag. I'll just put these down, here we are, here we are, and thank you very much, and my thanks to Donald Brown, whoever he may be.'

The door closed.

I turned and there was the goddamned elevator, waiting for to carry me home. The attendant wasn't exactly smiling but he did look amused. I rode down and walked through the lobby. The doorman grinned when he saw me coming.

'Well,' he said. 'How'd you make out, fella?'

'Make out?'

'She give you a good tip?'

'She gave me a quarter,' I said.

'Hey, cheer up, that's not bad for Tremaine. She doesn't part with a nickel all year round and then at Christmas she tips the building staff five bucks a man. That's ten cents a week. Can you believe it?'

'Sure,' I said. 'I can believe it.'

7

I didn't keep Leona Tremaine's quarter for very long. I walked around the corner, passed a watering hole called Big Charlie's, and had a cup of coffee at a lunch counter on Madison Avenue, where I left the quarter as a tip, hoping it would delight the waitress as much as it had delighted me. I got out of there and started walking uptown until I came to a florist.

It was past four. The shift would have changed by now, unless someone was late. Still, it would probably be easier getting past a crew who'd seen me last night than convincing the doorman and concierge I wanted to make another in-person delivery.

I went in and paid $7.98 for essentially the same assortment that had set me back $4.98 on the West Side. Ah, well. No doubt this chap had higher rent to pay. In any event, I might get another quarter from Ms Tremaine, and that would offset some of my expenses.

Leona Tremaine, I wrote once more on the outside of the envelope. And, on the card, *Won't you say I'm forgiven? Donald Brown.*

The staff had turned over at the Charlemagne. I recognized the concierge and the doorman from the night before, but if my face was familiar they didn't remark on it. Last night I'd been a guest of a tenant, all decked out in suit and tie, while today I was a short-sleeved member of the working class. If either of them recognized me, he probably assumed he'd seen me delivering flowers another time.

Again the concierge offered to see that the flowers were delivered, and again I insisted on making the delivery in person, and again the doorman snickered, guessing that I wanted my tip. It was nice to see they all had their lines down pat. The concierge announced me on the intercom and Eduardo took me up to the ninth floor, where Ms Tremaine was waiting in the doorway of her apartment.

'Why, it's you again,' she said. 'I can't understand this at all. Are you *sure* these flowers are for me?'

'The card says—'

'The card, the card, the card,' she said, and opened its envelope. '"Won't you say I'm forgiven? Donald Brown." What a curious sentiment. More specific than *fondly*, I daresay, but rather more baffling. Who is this Donald Brown and why am I to forgive him?'

The elevator had not gone away.

'I'm supposed to ask if there's a reply,' I said.

'A reply? A reply? To whom am I supposed to address this reply? It's quite clear to me that I'm not the intended recipient of these flowers, and yet how could such a mistake have been made? I no more know of another Leona Tremaine than I know any Donald Brown. Unless it's someone I knew years ago whose name has apparently slipped my recollection.' Her hands, tipped with persimmon-colored nails, unwrapped the elusive Mr Brown's offering. 'Lovely,' she said. 'Lovelier than the last, but I don't understand why they've been given to me. I don't begin to understand it.'

'I could call the store.'

'I beg your pardon?'

'I could call the flower shop,' I suggested. 'Could I use your phone? If there's a mistake I'll get in trouble, and if there's no mistake maybe they can tell you something about the person who sent you the flowers.'

'Oh,' she said.

'I really better call,' I said. 'I don't know if I should leave the flowers without calling in.'

'Well,' she said. 'Well, yes, perhaps you'd better call.'

She led me inside, drew the door shut. I tried to hear the elevator going off on other business, but of course I couldn't hear anything. I followed Leona Tremaine into a thickly carpeted living room filled with more furniture than it needed, the bulk of it French Provincial. The chairs and sofa were mostly tufted and the colors ran to a lot of pink and white. A cat displayed himself on what looked to be the most comfortable of the chairs. He was a snow-white Persian and his whiskers were intact.

'There's a telephone,' she said, pointing to one of those old French-style instruments trimmed out in gold and white enamel. I lifted the receiver to my ear and dialed Onderdonk's number. The line was busy.

'It's busy,' I said. 'People phone in orders all the time. You know how it is.' Why was I running off at the mouth like this? 'I'll try again in a minute.'

'Well.'

Why was Onderdonk's line busy? He'd been out earlier. Why couldn't he stay out, now that I'd finally gotten into his building? I couldn't leave now, for God's sake. I'd never get back in again.

I picked up the phone and called Carolyn Kaiser. When she answered I said, 'Miz Kaiser, this is Jimmie. I'm up at Miz Tremaine's at the Charlemagne.'

'You got the wrong number,' my quick-witted henchperson said. 'Wait a minute. Did you say – Bernie? Is that you?'

'Right, the delivery,' I said. 'Same as before. She says she don't know any Donald Brown and she don't think the flowers are for her. Right.'

'You're calling from somebody's apartment.'

'That's the idea,' I said.

'Is she suspicious of you?'

'No, the thing is she doesn't know who this guy is.'

'What's it all about, Bern? Are you just killing time?'

'Right.'

'You want me to talk to her? I'll tell her What's-his-face paid cash and he gave her name and address. Gimme the names again.'

'Donald Brown. And she's Leona Tremaine.'

'Gotcha.'

I handed the phone to Ms Tremaine, who'd been hovering. She said, 'Hello? To whom am I speaking, please?' and then she said things like 'Yes' and 'I see' and 'But I don't—' and 'It's so mysterious.' And then she gave the phone back to me.

'Someday,' said Carolyn, 'all of this will be crystal clear to me.'

'Sure thing, Miz Kaiser.'

'Same to you, Mr Rhodenbarr. I hope you know what you're doing.'

'Yes, ma'am.'

I hung up. Leona Tremaine said, ' "Curiouser and curiouser, said Alice." Your Donald Brown is a tall, gray-haired gentleman, elegantly dressed, who carried a cane and paid for both deliveries with a pair of crisp twenty-dollar bills. He did not give his address.' Her face softened. 'Perhaps it's someone I knew years ago,' she said quietly. 'Under another name, perhaps. And perhaps I'll hear further from him. I'm sure to hear further from him, wouldn't you say?'

'Well, if he went to all this trouble—'

'Exactly. He would scarcely go to such lengths merely to remain forever mysterious. Oh, dear,' she said, and fluffed her auburn hair. 'Such unaccustomed excitement.'

I edged toward the door. 'Well,' I said. 'I guess I'd better be going.'

'Yes, well, you've been very kind, making that phone call.' We walked together toward the door. 'Oh,' she said, remembering. 'Just let me get my bag and I'll give you something for your trouble.'

'Oh, that's all right,' I said. 'You took care of me before.'

'That's right,' she said. 'I did, didn't I? It slipped my mind. It's good of you to remind me.'

If the elevator's there, I thought, I'll just give up. But it wasn't. The floor indicator showed it on Three, and as I watched it moved to Four. Maybe Eduardo had forgotten about me. Then again, maybe he was on his way back.

643

I opened the fire door and went out onto the stairs.

Now what? Onderdonk's line was busy. I'd dialed the number from memory and I could have gotten it wrong, or it could have been busy because someone else had dialed the same number a few seconds before I did. Or he could be home.

I couldn't chance breaking in if anybody was home. And I couldn't knock on the door first, either. And I couldn't spend eternity on the stairs, because while it was possible the concierge and elevator operator and doorman would forget all about me, it was also possible they would not. A call on the intercom would establish that I'd left the Tremaine apartment, at which point they could either assume I'd left via the stairs (or even on the elevator) without anyone's noting the fact or else they'd figure I was still in the building.

In which case they might start looking for me.

Even if they didn't, the stairway was no place to be. I had to be able to establish via the telephone that Onderdonk's apartment was empty before I could enter it. And, once I'd entered it, I had to wait until midnight before I left with the painting in tow. Because the staff that was on duty now would certainly remember me, no matter what I did, and what kind of florist's delivery boy leaves a building an hour after he brings the flowers? I could perhaps get away with it, merely sullying Ms Tremaine's reputation a bit, letting them assume we'd passed the time in amorous dalliance, but if they'd checked with her in the meanwhile and already *knew* I'd left—

I climbed two flights of stairs. I loided the fire door, checked the hallway, found it empty, and did the only sensible thing I could think of. Without bothering to put on my gloves, without even taking the obvious precaution of ringing the bell, and certainly without wasting a moment on the mock burglar alarm, I whipped out my ring of picks and probes and let myself into John Charles Appling's apartment.

8

For a moment I thought I'd made a horrible mistake. The apartment
was brighter by day than it had been on my last visit. Even with the
drapes drawn a certain amount of daylight filtered in, and I thought
there were lights on, indicating someone's presence. My heart stopped
or raced or skipped a beat or whatever it does at such times, and then it
calmed down and so did I. I put on my rubber gloves and locked the
door and took a deep breath.

It felt very odd being back in the Appling place. There was once again
the thrill of illicit entry, but it was diminished by the fact that I'd been
here before. You can get as much pleasure the second or third or
hundredth time you make love to a particular woman – you can get
more, actually – but you can't get that triumphant sense of conquest
more than once, and so it is too with the seduction of locks and the
breaching of thresholds. On top of that, I hadn't broken in this time to
steal anything. I was just looking for sanctuary.

And that was strange indeed. Less than twenty-four hours earlier I'd
been in a state of high tension that didn't begin to dissipate until I left
this apartment. Now I'd had to break into it all over again just to feel
safe.

I went to the phone, picked it up. But why call Onderdonk now? I
didn't want to leave the building until midnight, so why break into
his place before then? I could go now, of course, if he was out. I could
snatch the Mondrian and bring it back downstairs to the Appling
apartment, and I could wait there until it was after midnight and safe
to leave.

But I didn't want to. Better to stay where I was and call Onderdonk
around midnight, and if he was out I could break and enter and leave in
a hurry, and if he was in I could say, 'Sorry, wrong number,' and give
him three or four or five hours to go to sleep, and then do my breaking
and entering while he lay snug in his bed. I'd rather not hit a dwelling
while its occupants are at home, intent as I am on avoiding human
contact while I work, but the one advantage of visiting them when
they're already at home is you don't have to worry about their coming
home before you're done. In this case I wanted one thing and one thing

only and I didn't have to search for it. It was right out there in the living room, and if he was asleep in the bedroom I wouldn't have to go anywhere near him.

I dialed the number anyway. It rang half a dozen times and I hung up. I'd have let it ring longer, but since I wasn't going in anyway, not for at least seven hours, why bother?

I crossed the living room, edged the drapery aside with a rubber-tipped finger. The window looked out on Fifth Avenue, and from where I stood I had a fairly spectacular view of Central Park. I also had no need to worry about anyone looking in, unless someone was perched half a mile away on Central Park West with a pair of binoculars and a whole lot of patience, and that didn't seem too likely. I drew the drapes and pulled up a chair so that I could look out at the park. I picked out the zoo, the reservoir, the band shell, and other landmarks. I could see plenty of runners, on the circular drive and the bridal path and the running track around the reservoir. Watching them was like observing highway traffic from an airplane.

Too bad I couldn't be out there with them. It was a perfect day for it.

I got restless after a while and moved around the apartment. In Appling's study I took down a stamp album and paged idly through it. I saw a number of things I really should have taken on my last visit but I didn't even consider taking them now. Before I'd been a burglar, a predator on the prowl. This time around I was a guest, albeit uninvited, and I could hardly so abuse my host's hospitality.

I did enjoy looking at his stamps, though, without being under any obligation to make them my own. I sat back and let myself relax in the fantasy that this was my apartment and my stamp collection, that I had located and purchased all those little perforated rectangles of colored paper, that my fingers had delighted in fitting them with mounts and affixing them in their places. Most of the time I have trouble imagining why anyone would want to devote time and money to pasting postage stamps in a book, but now I sort of got into it, and I even felt a little guilt about having looted such a labor of love.

I'll tell you, it's a good thing I didn't have his stamps with me. I might have tried putting them back.

Time crawled on by. I didn't want to turn on the television set or play a radio, or even walk around too much, lest a neighbor wonder at sounds issuing from a supposedly empty apartment. I didn't have the concentration for reading, and there's something about holding a book in gloved hands that keeps one from getting caught up in the story. I went back to my chair by the window and watched the sun drop behind the buildings on the west side of the park, and that was about it, entertainment-wise.

I got hungry sometime around nine and rummaged around the

kitchen. I filled a bowl with Grape-Nuts and added some suspicious milk. It probably would have curdled in a cup of coffee but it was all right in the cereal. Afterward I washed my bowl and spoon and put them where I'd found them. I went back to the living room and took off my shoes and stretched out on the rug with my eyes closed. My mind's eye gave itself over to a vast expanse of white, and while I was observing its pure perfection – virgin snow, I thought, or the fleeces of a million lambs – while I was thus waxing poetic, black ribbons uncurled and stretched themselves across the white expanse, extending from top to bottom, from left to right, forming a random rectangular grid. Then one of the enclosed spaces of white blushed and reddened, and another spontaneously took on a faint sky tint that deepened all the way to a rich cobalt blue, and another red square began to bleed in on the lower right, and—

By God, my mind was painting me a Mondrian.

I watched as the pattern changed and re-formed itself, working variations on a theme. I'm not sure just what consciousness is and is not, but at one point I was conscious and at another I wasn't, and then there came a moment when I caught hold of myself and shook myself loose of something. I sat up, looked at my watch.

Seven, eight minutes past twelve.

I took another few minutes making sure I left Appling's apartment as I'd found it. I'd slept in my rubber gloves and my fingers were damp and clammy. I stripped off the gloves, dried the insides of the fingers, washed and dried my hands, and put them back on again. I straightened this and tidied that, drew the drapes, put back the chair I'd moved. Then I picked up the phone, checked Onderdonk's number in the book to make sure I got it right, dialed it, and let it ring an even dozen times.

I turned off the one light I'd had on, let myself out, locked the door after me and wiped the knob and the surrounding area and the doorbell. I hurried through the fire door and up four flights to Sixteen, let myself into the hallway, crossed over to Onderdonk's door and rang his bell. I waited for a moment, just in case, said a fervent if hurried prayer to Saint Dismas, and knocked off a four-tumbler Segal drop-bolt lock in not much more time than I'd spent pouring the milk over the Grape-Nuts.

Darkness within. I slipped inside, drew the door shut, breathed slowly and deeply and let my eyes adjust. I put my ring of picks back in my pocket and fumbled around for my penlight. I already had my gloves on, not having bothered to remove them for the quick run upstairs. I oriented myself in the darkness, or tried to, and I raised my penlight, pointed it to where the fireplace ought to be, and switched it on.

The fireplace was there. Above it was an expanse of white, just what I'd envisioned on Appling's floor before the black lines insinuated themselves across its length and breadth. But where were the black lines now? Where were the rectangles of blue and red and yellow?

Where, for that matter, was the canvas? Where was the aluminum frame? And why was there nothing above Onderdonk's fireplace but a blank wall?

I flicked off my light, stood again in darkness. The familiar thrill of burglary took on the added element of panic. Was I, for heaven's sake, in the wrong apartment? Had I, for the love of God, climbed one too few or one too many flights of stairs? Leona Tremaine was on Nine, and I'd gone up two flights to Eleven, where I'd been a guest of the Applings. From Eleven to Sixteen was four flights, but had I counted flights as I went and included the nonexistent thirteenth?

I flicked the light on. It was likely that all of the apartments in the B line had the same essential layout, and each would have a fireplace in that particular spot. But would other apartments have bookcases flanking the fireplace? And these were familiar shelves, and I could even recognize some of the books. There was the leatherbound Defoe. There were the two volumes, boxed, of Stephen Vincent Benét's selected prose and selected poetry. And there, faintly discernible in that expanse of white, looking almost like the negative image of an Ad Reinhardt black-on-black canvas, was the slightly lighter rectangle where the Mondrian had lately hung. Time and New York air had darkened the surrounding wall, leaving a ghost image of the painting I'd come to steal.

I lowered the light to the floor, made my way into the room. The picture wasn't there and the picture should have been there and something didn't compute. Was I still asleep? Was I dozing on Appling's floor, and had I merely dreamed the part about waking up and going upstairs? I decided I had, and I gave a mental yank to pull myself out of it, and nothing happened.

Something felt wrong, and I was feeling more than the unexpected absence of the painting. I moved farther into the room and played my light here and there. If anything else was missing, I didn't notice it. The Arp painting still hung where I'd seen it on my first visit. Other paintings were where I remembered them. I turned and swung the flashlight around, and its beam showed me a bronze head, Cycladic in style, on a black lucite plinth. I remembered the head from before, though I'd paid it little attention then. I continued to move the light around in a slow circle, and I may have heard or sensed an intake of breath, and then the flashlight's beam was falling full upon a woman's face.

Not a painting, not a statue. A woman, positioned between me and the door, one small hand held at waist level, the other poised at shoulder height, palm out, as if to ward off something menacing.

'Oh, my God,' she said. 'You're a burglar, you're going to rape me, you're going to kill me. Oh, my God.'

Be a dream, I prayed, but it wasn't and I knew it wasn't. I was caught in the act, I had a pocket full of burglar's tools and no right to be where I was, and a search of my apartment would turn up enough stolen stamps to start a branch post office. And she was between me and the door, and even if I got past her she could call downstairs before I could get anywhere near the lobby, and her mouth was ajar and any second now she was going to scream.

All for the sake of some goddamn cat with a clever name and an assertive personality. Six days a week the ASPCA's busy putting surplus cats to sleep, and I was going to wind up in slam trying to ransom one. I stood there, holding the light in her eyes as if it might hypnotize her, like a deer in a car's headlights. But she didn't look hypnotized. She looked terrified, and sooner or later the terror would ease up enough for her to scream, and I thought about that and thought about stone walls.

Stone walls do not a prison make, according to Sir Richard Lovelace, and I'm here to tell you the man was whistling in the dark. Stone walls make a hell of a prison and iron bars make a perfectly adequate cage, and I've been there and I don't ever want to go back.

Just get me out of this and I'll—

And I'll what? And I'll probably do it again, I thought, because I'm evidently incorrigible. But just get me out of it and we'll see.

'Please,' she said. 'Please don't hurt me.'

'I'm not going to hurt you.'

'Don't kill me.'

'Nobody's going to kill you.'

She was about five-six and slender, with an oval face and eyes a spaniel would have won Best of Breed with. Her hair was dark and shoulder-length, drawn back from a sharp widow's peak and secured in unbraided pigtails. She was wearing oatmeal jeans and a lime polo shirt with a real alligator on it. Her brown suede slippers looked like something a Hobbit would wear.

'You're going to hurt me.'

'I never hurt anyone,' I told her. 'I don't even kill cockroaches. Oh, I put boric acid around, and I guess that's the same thing from a moral standpoint, but as far as hauling off and swatting 'em, that's something I never do. And not just because it makes a spot. See, I'm basically nonviolent, and—'

And why was I running off at the mouth like this? Nerves, I suppose, and the premise that she'd be polite enough not to scream while I was talking.

'Oh, God,' she said. 'I'm so frightened.'

649

'I didn't mean to frighten you.'

'Look at me. I'm shaking.'

'Don't be afraid.'

'I can't help it. I'm scared.'

'So am I.'

'You are?'

'You bet.'

'But you're a burglar,' she said, frowning. 'Aren't you?'

'Well—'

'Of course you are. You've got gloves on.'

'I was doing the dishes.'

She started to laugh, and the laughter slipped away from her and climbed toward hysteria. She said, 'Oh, God, why am I laughing? I'm in danger.'

'No, you're not.'

'I am, I am. It happens all the time, a woman surprises a burglar and she gets raped and killed. Stabbed to death.'

'I don't even have a penknife.'

'Strangled.'

'I don't have any strength in my hands.'

'You're making jokes.'

'You're sweet to say so.'

'You're – you seem nice.'

'That's exactly it,' I said. 'You hit it. What I am, I'm your basic nice guy.'

'But look at me. I mean don't look at me. I mean – I don't know what I mean.'

'Easy. Everything's going to be all right.'

'I believe you.'

'Of course you do.'

'But I'm still frightened.'

'I know you are.'

'And I can't help it. I can't stop trembling. On the inside it feels like I'm going to shake myself to pieces.'

'You'll be okay.'

'Could you—'

'What?'

'This is crazy.'

'It's all right.'

'No, you're going to think I'm crazy. I mean, you're the one I'm afraid of, but—'

'Go ahead.'

'Could you just hold me? Please?'

'Hold you?'

'In your arms.'

650

'Well, uh, if you think it'll help—'

'I just want to be held.'

'Well, sure.'

I took her in my arms and she buried her face in my chest. Our polo shirts pressed together and became as one. I felt the warmth and fullness of her breasts through the two layers of fabric. I stood there in the dark – my penlight was back in my pocket – and I held her close, stroking her silky hair with one hand, patting her back and shoulder with the other, and saying 'There, there,' in a tone that was meant to be reassuring.

The awful tension went out of her. I kept holding her and went on murmuring to her, breathing in her scent and absorbing her warmth, and—

'Oh,' she said.

She lifted up her head and our eyes met. There was enough light for me to stare into them and they were deep enough to drown a man. I held her and looked at her and Something Happened.

'This is—'

'I know.'

'Crazy.'

'I know.'

I let go of her. She took her shirt off. I took my shirt off. She came back into my arms. I was still wearing those idiot gloves, and I tore them off and felt her skin under my fingers and against my chest.

'Gosh,' she said.

9

'Gosh,' she said again some minutes later. Our clothing was on the floor in a heap and so, in another heap, were we. Given a choice, I suppose I'd have gone for, say, a platform bed with an inner-spring mattress and Porthault sheets, but we'd done remarkably well on an Aubusson carpet. The sense of dreamlike unreality that had begun with the mysterious disappearance of the Mondrian was getting stronger every minute, but I'll tell you, I was beginning to like it.

I ran a lingering hand over an absolutely marvelous curved surface, then got to my feet and groped around in the dimness until I found a table lamp and switched it on. She instinctively covered herself, one hand at her loins, the other across her breasts, then caught herself and laughed.

She said, 'What did I tell you? I knew you were going to rape me.'

'Some rape.'

'I'm just grateful you took those gloves off. I'd have felt as if I'd dropped in for a Pap smear.'

'Speaking of which, why did you?'

'Why did I what?'

'Drop in.'

She tilted her head to the side. 'Shouldn't I be asking you that question?'

'You already know why I'm here,' I said. 'I'm a burglar. I came here to steal something. What about you?'

'I live here.'

'Uh-uh. Onderdonk's been alone since his wife died.'

'He's been alone,' she said, 'but he hasn't been *alone*.'

'I see. You and he have been—'

'Are you shocked? I just did it with you on the living room rug so you must have figured out I wasn't a virgin. Why shouldn't Gordon and I be lovers?'

'Where is he?'

'He's out.'

'And you were waiting for him to come back.'

'That's right.'

'Why didn't you answer the phone a few minutes ago?'

'Was that you? I didn't answer it because I never answer Gordon's phone. After all, I don't officially live here. I just stay over sometimes.'

'Don't you answer the bell, either?'

'Gordon always uses his key.'

'So when he used it this time you turned off the lights and stood with your back against the wall.'

'I didn't turn off the lights. They were already off.'

'You were just sitting here in the dark.'

'I was lying on the couch, actually. I was reading and I dozed off.'

'Reading in the dark and you dozed off.'

'I felt drowsy so I switched off the light, and *then* I dozed off in the darkness. And because I was half asleep I reacted slowly and perhaps illogically when you rang the bell and then opened the door. Satisfied?'

'Deeply satisfied. Where's the book?'

'The book?'

'The one you were reading?'

'Maybe it dropped to the floor and wound up under the couch. Or maybe I put it back on the shelf when I turned the light off. What difference does it make, anyway?'

'No difference.'

'I mean, you're a burglar, right? You're not Mr District Attorney, asking me where I was on the night of March twenty-third. I should be asking the questions. How did you get past the front desk? There's a good question.'

'It's a great one,' I agreed. 'I landed on the roof with a helicopter and let myself down by rope and got into a penthouse apartment through the door from the terrace. Then I walked down a few flights of stairs and here I am.'

'Didn't you steal anything in the penthouse?'

'They didn't have anything. I guess they were house-poor, you know? Spent all their money on the apartment.'

'I suppose that happens all the time.'

'You'd be surprised. How did *you* get past the desk?'

'Me?'

'Uh-huh. You don't officially live here. Why would they let you up when Onderdonk was out?'

'He was here when I came. Then he went out.'

'And left you here in the dark.'

'I told you I—'

'Right. You turned the light off when you got drowsy.'

'Didn't that ever happen to you?'

'I never get drowsy. What's the capital of New Jersey?'

'New Jersey? The capital of New Jersey?'

'Right.'

'Is this some kind of a trick question? The capital of New Jersey. It's Trenton, isn't it?'

'That's right.'

'What does that have to do with anything?'

'Not a thing,' I admitted. 'I just wanted to see if your face changed when you told the truth. The last honest thing you said was "Gosh." You cut the lights when you heard me coming and you tried to melt into the wall. You were scared to death when you saw me but you'd have been scared clear into the next world if it had been Onderdonk. Why don't you tell me what you came to steal and whether or not you found it yet? Maybe I can help you look.'

She just looked at me for a moment and her face went through some interesting changes. Then she sighed and rummaged around in the heap of clothing.

'I'd better get dressed,' she said.

'If you feel you must.'

'He'll be back soon. Or at least he might. Sometimes he stays the night but he'll probably be back around two. What time is it?'

'Almost one.'

We sorted out our clothes and began getting into them. She said, 'I haven't stolen anything. You're welcome to search me if you don't believe me.'

'Good idea. Strip.'

'But I just – for a second I thought you were serious.'

'Just my little joke.'

'Well, you had me going there.' She thought for a moment. 'Maybe I should just tell you why I'm here.'

'Maybe you should.'

'I'm married.'

'Not to Onderdonk.'

'God, no. But Gordon and I – let's say I was indiscreet.'

'On this very rug?'

'No, this was a first for me. You were my first burglar and my first romp on a carpet.' She grinned suddenly. 'I always had fantasies of being taken passionately and abruptly by a stranger. Not of being raped, exactly, but of being, oh, carried away. Transported by desire.'

'I hope I didn't ruin your fantasies for you.'

'*Au contraire*, darling. You brought them to life.'

'Shall we get back to Onderdonk? You were indiscreet.'

'Very, I'm afraid. I wrote him some letters.'

'Love letters?'

'Lust letters is more like it. "I wish I had your this in my that. I'd like to verb your noun until you verb." That sort of thing.'

'I bet you write a terrific letter.'

654

'Gordon thought so. After we stopped seeing each other – we broke it off weeks ago – I asked for my letters back.'

'And he refused?'

'"They were written to me," he said. "That makes them my property." He wouldn't give them back.'

'And he was using them to blackmail you?'

Her eyes widened. 'Why would he do that? Gordon's rich, and I don't have any money of my own.'

'He could have blackmailed you for something besides money.'

'Oh, you mean sex? I suppose he could have but he didn't. The affair ended by mutual consent. No, he simply wanted to retain the letters as a way of keeping the affair's memory fresh. He said once that he intended to save them for his old age. Something to read when reading was the only thing left for him.'

'I suppose it beats Louis Auchincloss.'

'I beg your pardon?'

'Nothing. So he kept your letters.'

'And the photographs.'

'Photographs?'

'He took pictures a couple of times.'

'Pictures of you?'

'Some of me and some of both of us. He has a Polaroid with a cable shutter release.'

'So he could get some good shots of you verbing his noun.'

'He could and did.'

I straightened up. 'Well, we've still got a few minutes,' I said, 'and I'm pretty good at search-and-destroy missions. If the letters and photos are in this apartment, I bet I can find them.'

'I already found them.'

'Oh?'

'They were in his dresser and it was almost the first place I looked.'

'And where are they now?'

'Down the incinerator.'

'Dust to dust, ashes to ashes.'

'You have a way with words.'

'Thank you. Mission accomplished, eh? You found the letters and pictures, sent them down to be burned or compacted or whatever they do at the Charlemagne, and then you were on your way.'

'That's right.'

'So how come you were still here when I let myself in?'

'I was on my way out,' she said. 'I was heading for the door. I had my hand on the knob when you rang the bell.'

'Suppose it had been Onderdonk.'

'I thought it was. Not when I heard the bell, because why would he ring his own door? Unless he knew I was in his apartment.'

'How'd you get in?'

'He never double-locks the door. I opened it with a credit card.'

'You know how to do that?'

'Doesn't everybody? All you have to do is watch television and you see them doing it. It's educational.'

'It must be. The door was double-locked when I tried it. I had to pick the tumblers.'

'I turned the bolt from inside.'

'Why?'

'I don't know. Reflex, I guess. I should have put the chain on while I was at it. Then you'd have known somebody was here and you wouldn't have come in, would you?'

'Probably not, and you wouldn't have had a chance to bring your fantasy to life.'

'That's a point.'

'But suppose instead of me it had been Onderdonk. Would you have verbed him on the carpet or hauled him off to the bedroom?'

She sighed. 'I don't know. I guess I would have told him what I'd done. I think he probably would have laughed about it. As I said, we parted on good terms. But he was a big man and he had a temper, and that's why I was scrunched up against the wall hoping for a way to get out without being seen. And knowing it was impossible, but not knowing what else to do.'

'What happened to the painting?'

She blinked at me. 'Huh?'

'There. Over the fireplace.'

She looked. 'He had a painting hanging there, didn't he? Of course he did. You can see the outline.'

'A Mondrian.'

'Of course, what am I thinking of. His Mondrian. *Oh.* You came here to steal his Mondrian!'

'I just wanted to look at it. The museums all close around six and I had a sudden urge to bask in the inner glow of great art.'

'And here I thought you just hit this apartment at random. But you were here for the Mondrian.'

'I didn't say that.'

'You didn't have to. You know, he said something about that painting. It was a while ago. I wonder if I can remember what it was.'

'Take your time.'

'Isn't there an exhibition forming of Mondrian's work? Either Mondrian or the whole De Stijl school of abstract painting. They wanted Gordon to lend them his Mondrian.'

'And they picked it up this afternoon?'

'Why, is that when it left its spot on the wall? If you knew it was gone this afternoon, why did you come for it tonight?'

'I don't know when it left. I just know it was here yesterday.'

'How do you know that? Never mind, I don't think you want to tell me that. I may not remember this correctly – I wasn't paying too much attention – but I think Gordon was having the painting reframed for the exhibition. He had it framed in aluminum like the rest of the ones here and he wanted some other kind of frame that would enclose the canvas without covering up its edges. Mondrian was one of those painters who continue the design of the painting right around the sides of the canvas, and Gordon wanted that part to show because it was technically part of the work, but he didn't want to display a completely unframed canvas. I don't know how he was going to have it done, but, well, I wouldn't be surprised if that's what happened to the painting. What time is it?'

'Ten minutes past one.'

'I have to go. Whether he's coming back or not, I have to go. Are you going to steal anything else? Other paintings or anything else you can find?'

'No. Why?'

'I just wondered. Do you want to leave first?'

'Not particularly.'

'Oh?'

'It's my chivalrous nature. Not just the old principle of ladies first, but I'd worry about you forever if I didn't know you got out safely. How are you going to get out, by the way?'

'I won't even need my credit card. Oh, you mean how'll I get out of the building? The same way I got in. I'll ride down in the elevator, smile sweetly, and let the doorman get me a cab.'

'Where do you live?'

'A cab ride away.'

'So do I, but I think we should take separate cabs. You don't want to tell me where you live.'

'Not really, no. I don't think it's a good idea to tell burglars my home address. You might make off with the family silver.'

'Not since the price drop. It's barely worth stealing these days. Suppose I wanted to see you again?'

'Just keep opening doors. You never know what you'll find on the other side.'

'Isn't that the truth. Could be the lady, could be the tiger.'

'Could be both.'

'Uh-huh. You've got sharp claws, incidentally.'

'You didn't seem to mind.'

'I wasn't objecting, just commenting. I don't even know your name.'

'Just think of me as the Dragon Lady.'

'I didn't notice anything draggin'. My name is Bernie.'

She cocked her head, gave the matter some thought. 'Bernie the

Burglar. I don't suppose there's any harm in your knowing my first name, is there?'

'Besides, you could always make one up.'

'Is that what you just did? But I couldn't. I never lie.'

'I understand that's the best policy.'

'That's what I've always heard. My name is Andrea.'

'Andrea. You know what I'd like to do, Andrea? I'd like to throw you right back down on the old Aubusson and have my way with you.'

'My, that doesn't sound bad at all. If we had world enough and time, but we really don't. *I* don't, anyway. I have to get out of here.'

'It would be nice,' I said, 'if there were a way I could get in touch with you.'

'The thing is I'm married.'

'But occasionally indiscreet.'

'Occasionally. But discreetly indiscreet, if you get my drift. Now if you were to tell *me* how to get in touch with *you*—'

'Uh.'

'You see? You're a burglar and you don't want to run the risk that I'll get an attack of conscience or catch a bad case of the crazies and go to the police. And I don't want to run a similar sort of risk. Maybe we should just leave it as is, ships that pass in the night, all that romantic stuff. That way we're both safe.'

'You could be right. But sometime down the line we might decide the risk's worth running, and then where would we be? You know what the saddest words of tongue or pen are.'

' "It might have been." You're witty, but John Greenleaf was Whittier.'

'My God, you read poetry and you're a smartass and you can verb like a mink. I can't let you get away altogether. I know.'

'You know what?'

'Buy the *Village Voice* every week and read the personals in the "Village Bulletin Board" section. Okay?'

'Okay. You do the same.'

'Faithfully. Can a burglar and an adulteress find happiness in today's world? We'll just have to see, won't we? Go ahead, you ring for the elevator.'

'You don't want to ride down with me?'

'I want to tidy up here a little. And I'll hang around so that we leave the building a few minutes apart. If I get in any trouble, you don't want to get hooked into it.'

'Will you get in trouble?'

'Probably not, because I'm not stealing anything.'

'That's what I was asking, really. I mean, I shouldn't care if you steal anything, including the carpet we verbed on, but evidently I do. Bernie, would you hold me?'

'Are you scared again?'

'Nope. I just like the way you hold me.'

I put my gloves on and waited with the door a few inches ajar until I saw her ring for the elevator. Then I drew the door shut, turned the bolt, and gave the apartment a very quick look-see, just to make sure there was nothing I should know about in any of the other rooms. I didn't open a drawer or a closet, just ducked into each room and flicked the lights on long enough to establish that there were no signs of Andrea's presence. No drawers pulled out and dumped, no tables over-turned, no signs that the apartment had been visited by a burglar or a cyclone or any comparable unwelcome phenomenon.

And no dead bodies in the bed or on the floor. Not that one goes around expecting that sort of thing, but I was once caught in the act of burgling the apartment of a man named Flaxford, and Mr F. himself was dead in another room at the time, a fact which became known to the police before it joined my storehouse of information. So I gave a quick look-see here and there, and if I'd come across the Mondrian, leaning against the wall or perhaps wrapped in brown paper and waiting for the framer, I'd have been roundly delighted.

No such luck, nor did I spend much time looking. I did all of this reconnaissance rather more quickly than it takes to tell about it, as a matter of fact, and when I was out in the hallway the elevator was on its way up.

Was it swarming with boys in blue? Had I, like Samson and Lord Randall and the Bold Deceiver before me, been done in by a woman's treachery? No point, surely, in sticking around to find out. I ducked through the fire door and waited for the elevator to stop on Sixteen.

But it didn't. I peeked through the open fire door, and I listened carefully, and the cage went on past Sixteen, stopped, waited, and went on down, passing Sixteen in its descent. I returned to the hallway, picked the tumblers to lock Onderdonk's door, recalled that Andrea'd said he never double-locked it, picked it again to leave it on the spring-lock as he was said to have done, sighed heavily at all of this wasted time and effort, stripped off my silly rubber gloves, put them in a pocket, and rang for the elevator.

No cops in the elevator. No cops in the lobby or out on the street. No hassle from the elevator operator, the concierge or the doorman, even when I refused the last-named chap's offer to hail me a taxi. I said I felt like walking, and I walked three blocks before hailing a cab myself. That way I didn't have to switch to some other cab a few blocks away. I could just ride straight home, and that's what I did.

Once there, I would have liked to go straight to bed. But I had J. C. Appling's stamps to worry about and I was worried. I'd have taken a chance and left the job unfinished, but not after all I'd gone through at the Charlemagne in the past ten hours. I'd had far too many human contacts, enough so that I stood a chance of attracting police attention. I hadn't done anything in Onderdonk's apartment, hadn't stolen anything at all but Appling's stamps (and those earrings, mustn't forget those earrings) but I certainly didn't want those stamps sitting around if someone with a tin shield and a warrant came knocking on my door.

I was up all night with the damned stamps. I swear you never have that problem with cash; you just spend it at leisure. I got all the stamps into glassine envelopes and all of Appling's album pages into the incinerator, and then I fitted the envelopes into a hidey-hole I probably shouldn't tell you about, but what the hell. There's a baseboard electrical outlet that's a phony, with no BX cable feeding into an aluminum box at its rear. It's just a plate and a couple of receptacles, mounted to the baseboard with a pair of screws, and if you undo the screws and remove the plate you can reach your hand into an opening about the size of a loaf of bread. (Not the puffy stuff but a nice dense loaf from the health food store.) I keep contraband there until I can unload it, and I also stow burglar tools there. (Not all of them because some of them are innocent enough out of context. You can keep a roll of adhesive tape in the medicine chest and a penlight in the hardware drawer and feel secure about it. Picks and probes and prybars, however, are another story, incriminating in or out of context.)

There's another hidey-hole, similar in nature, where I keep my mad money. I even have a radio plugged into one of its receptacles, and the radio even works, running on batteries since its dummy cord is plugged into thin air. I've got a few thousand dollars there in untraceable fifties and hundreds, and it'll do to bribe a cop or post a bond or, if things ever get that desperate, pay my way to Costa Rica. And I hope to God it never comes to that because I'd go nuts there. I mean who do I know in Costa Rica? What would I do if I got a craving for a bagel or a slice of pizza?

I never did get to sleep. I showered and shaved and put on clean clothes. I went out and had a bagel (but not a slice of pizza) and a plate of eggs and bacon and a lot of coffee at the Greek place a block from my door. I sipped the coffee and my mind, exhausted and overamped from too many hours awake and too much concentration on itty bitty squares of colored paper, slipped a few hours into the past. I remembered eager hands and smooth skin and a warm mouth, and I wondered if there was any truth mixed in with the lies she'd told me.

There was that sweet magic between us, the physical magic and the mental magic, and I was tired enough to drop my guard and let her in. It would be easy, I thought, to let go a little bit more and fall in love with her.

And it wouldn't be *that* dangerous, I decided. Not much worse than hang-gliding blindfolded. Safer on balance than swimming with an open wound in shark-infested waters, or playing catch with a bottle of nitroglycerine, or singing *Rule, Brittania* at Carney's Emerald Lounge in Woodside.

I paid the check and overtipped, as lovers are wont to do. Then I walked over to Broadway and caught a train heading downtown.

10

I unlocked the steel gates, opened the door, scooped up the mail and tossed it on the counter, shlepped the bargain table outside and turned the sign in the window from *Sorry . . . We're CLOSED* to *OPEN . . . Come in!* By the time I was perched on my stool behind the counter I had my first browser of the day. He was a round-shouldered gentleman in a Norfolk jacket and he was taking a mild interest in the shelves of General Fiction while I was taking about as much interest in the mail. There were a couple of bills, quite a few book catalogs, a postcard asking if I had the Derek Hudson biography of Lewis Carroll – I didn't – and a government-franked message from some clown who hoped he could continue representing me in Congress. An understandable desire. Otherwise he'd have to start paying his own postage.

While the chap in the Norfolk jacket was paging through something by Charles Reade, a sallow young woman with teeth like a beaver bought a couple of things from the bargain table. The phone rang and it was someone wanting to know if I had anything by Jeffery Farnol. Now I've had thousands of phone calls and I swear no one ever asked me that before. I checked the shelves and was able to report that I had clean copies of *Peregrine's Progress* and *The Amateur Gentleman.* My caller wondered about *Beltane the Smith.*

'Not unless he's under the spreading chestnut tree,' I said. 'But I'll have a look.'

I agreed to put the other two titles aside, not that anyone else was likely to snatch them up meanwhile. I took them from the shelves, ducked into my back room, placed them on my desk where they could bask in the illumination of the portrait hanging over the desk (St John of God, patron saint of booksellers), and came back to confront a tall and well-fed man in a dark suit that looked to have been very meticulously tailored for someone else.

'Well, well, well,' said Ray Kirschmann. 'If it ain't Miz Rhodenbarr's son Bernard.'

'You sound surprised, Ray,' I said. 'This is my store, this is where I work. I'm here all the time.'

'Which is why I came here lookin' for you, Bern, but you were in back and it gave me a turn. I figured somebody snuck in and burgled you.'

I looked over his shoulder at the fellow in the Norfolk jacket. He'd gone on from Charles Reade to something else, but I couldn't see what.

'Business pretty good, Bern?'

'I can't complain.'

'It's holdin' up, huh? Except you were never a one for holdups, were you? Makin' ends meet?'

'Well, there are good weeks and bad weeks.'

'But you get by.'

'I get by.'

'And you got the satisfaction of treadin' the straight an' narrow path between right an' wrong. That's gotta be worth somethin'.'

'Ray—'

'Peace of mind, that's what you got. It's worth a lot, peace of mind is.'

'Uh—'

I nodded in the direction of the browser, who had assumed the unmistakable stance of a dropper of eaves. Ray turned, regarded my customer, and pinched his own abundant chin between thumb and forefinger.

'Oh, I get your drift, Bern,' he said. 'You're worried this gentleman here'll be taken aback to learn about your criminal past. Is that it?'

'Jesus, Ray.'

'Sir,' Ray announced, 'you may not realize this, but you're gonna have the privilege of buyin' a book from a former notorious criminal. Bernie here was once the sort'd burgle you outta house an' home, and now he's a walking testimony to criminal rehabilitation. Yessir, I'll tell you, all of us in the NYPD think the world of Bernie here. Say, mister, you're welcome to hang around an' browse. Last thing I want to do is chase you.'

But my customer was on his way, with the door swinging shut behind him.

'Thanks,' I said.

'Aw, he was a stiff anyway, Bern. Never woulda bought that book. Guys like him, treat the place like a library. How you gonna make a dime on a bum like that?'

'Ray—'

' 'Sides, he looked shifty. Probably woulda stole the book if he had half the chance. An honest guy like yourself, you don't realize how many crooked people there are in the world.'

I didn't say anything. Why encourage him?

'Say, Bern,' he said, leaning a heavy forearm on my glass counter. 'You're around books all the time, you're all the time readin'. What I want to do is read somethin' to you. You got a minute?'

'Well, I—'

'Sure you do,' he said, and reached into his inside jacket pocket, and just then the door burst open and Carolyn exploded through it. 'There you are,' she cried. 'I called and you didn't answer, and then I called and the line was busy, and then I – Oh, hi, Ray.'

'"Oh, hi, Ray,"' he echoed. 'Say it like you're glad to see me, Carolyn. I'm not some dog that you gotta give me a bath.'

'I'm going to leave that line alone,' she said.

'Thank God,' I said.

'You called and he wasn't here,' Ray said, 'and then you called and the line was busy, and then you ran over here. So you got somethin' to say to him.'

'So?'

'So say it.'

'It'll keep,' she said.

'Then maybe you oughta run along, Carolyn. Go get your vacuum cleaner and suck the ticks off a bloodhound.'

'I could make you the same suggestion,' she said sweetly, 'but without the vacuum cleaner. Why don't you go solicit a bribe, Ray? I got business with Bernie.'

'So do I, sweetie. I was just lookin' for a literary opinion from him. The hell, I don't guess it'd hurt you to hear what I gotta read to him.'

He drew a little card from his pocket. '"You have the right to remain silent,"' he intoned. '"You have the right to consult an attorney. If you do not have legal counsel, you have the right to have counsel provided for you."' There was more, and the wording wasn't exactly the way I remembered it, but I'm not going to look it up and reproduce the whole thing here. If you're interested, go throw a rock through a precinct house window. Somebody'll come out and read it to you word for word.

'I don't get it,' I said. 'Why are you reading me that?'

'Aw, Bernie. Lemme ask you a question, okay? You know an apartment building called the Charlemagne?'

'Sure. On Fifth Avenue in the Seventies. Why?'

'Ever been there?'

'As a matter of fact I was there the night before last.'

'No kiddin'. Next you're gonna tell me you've heard of a man named Gordon Onderdonk.'

I nodded. 'We've met,' I said. 'Once here, in the store, and again two nights ago.'

'At his apartment at the Charlemagne.'

'That's right.' Where was he going with all this? I hadn't stolen anything from Onderdonk, and the man would hardly have reported me to the police for lifting his letters from Andrea. Unless Ray was taking an elaborate windup before delivering the pitch, and all this Onderdonk stuff was prelude to some more incisive questions about J. C. Appling's stamp collection. But the Applings hadn't even returned to the city as of midnight, so how could they have discovered the loss and reported it, and how could Ray have already tied it to me?

'I went there at his invitation,' I said. 'He wanted an appraisal of his personal library, although he's not likely to be selling it. I spent some time going through his books and came up with a figure.'

'Decent of you.'

'I got paid for my time.'

'Oh, yeah? Wrote you out a check, did he?'

'Paid me in cash. Two hundred dollars.'

'Is that a fact. I suppose you'll report the income on your tax return, a good law-abidin' reformed citizen like yourself.'

'What's all this sarcasm about?' Carolyn demanded. 'Bernie didn't do anything.'

'Nobody ever did. The prisons are full of innocent guys who got railroaded by corrupt police.'

'God knows there are enough corrupt police to go around,' Carolyn said, 'and if they're not railroading innocent people, what are they doing?'

'Anyway, Bern—'

'Besides eating in restaurants and not paying for their meals,' she went on. 'Besides swapping jokes on street corners while old ladies get mugged and raped. Besides—'

'Besides puttin' up with insults from some little dyke who needs a rabies shot an' a muzzle.'

I said, 'Get to the point, Ray. You just read me my rights and it says I don't have to answer questions, so you can stop asking them. I'll ask you one. What's this circus about?'

'What's it about? What the hell do you think it's about? You're under arrest, Bernie. Why else'd I read you your Miranda?'

'Under arrest for what?'

'Aw, Jesus, Bern.' He sighed and shook his head, as if his pessimistic view of human nature had once again been confirmed. 'This guy Onderdonk,' he said. 'They found him in his bedroom closet, bound and gagged with his head bashed in.'

'He's dead?'

'Why, was he breathin' when you left him like that? Inconsiderate of the bastard to die, but that's what he did. He's dead, all right, and what I gotta bring you in for is murder.' He showed me a pair of handcuffs. 'I gotta use these,' he said. 'Regulations which they're enforcin' again these days. But take your time first and close up, huh? And do a good job. Place might wind up stayin' closed for a while.'

I don't think I said anything. I think I just stood there.

'Carolyn, whyntcha hold the door and me'n Bern'll bring in the table. You don't want to leave it out there. They'll steal it empty in an hour and then somebody'll walk off with the table. Aw shit, Bern, what's the matter with you, anyway? You were always a gentle guy. Stealin's stealin', but what'd you go an' kill him for?'

11

'What gives me the most trouble,' Wally Hemphill said, 'is finding the time to fit in the miles. Of course what really helps is if I got a client who's a runner himself. You know how some people'll do their business over nine holes of golf? "Suit up," I'll say, "and we'll lope around the reservoir and see where we stand on this." You think we could pick up the pace a little, Bernie?'

'I don't know. This is pretty fast, isn't it?'

'I'd judge we're doing a 9:20 mile.'

'That's funny. I could have sworn we were going faster than sound.'

He laughed politely and picked up the pace and I sucked air and stayed with him. Gamely, you might say. It was still Thursday and I still hadn't been to bed, and it was now around six-thirty in the evening and Wally Hemphill and I were making a counterclockwise circuit of Central Park. The circular park drive was closed to cars throughout its six-mile loop, and runners beyond number were out taking the air and turning its oxygen into carbon dioxide.

'Call Klein,' I'd told Carolyn when I left the store in handcuffs. 'Tell him to come collect me. And pick up some cash from my place and bail me out.'

'Anything else?'

'Have a nice day.'

As Ray and I walked in one direction and Carolyn walked in the other, I thought how Norb Klein had represented me several times over the years. He was a nice little guy who looked sort of like a fat weasel. He had an office on Queens Boulevard and a small-time criminal practice that never got him any headlines. He wasn't very impressive in court but he handled himself nicely behind the scenes, knowing which judge would be sympathetic to the right approach. I was trying to remember when I'd seen Norb last when Ray said, conversationally, 'You didn't hear, Bern? Norb Klein's dead.'

'What?'

'You know what a skirt chaser he was, and he never had a hooker for a client that he didn't sample the merchandise, and how'd he wind up goin' out? He was bangin' his secretary on his office couch, same girl's been with him eight, ten years, and his ticker blows out on him. Massive whatchacallit, coronary, an' he's dead in the saddle. Girl said she tried everythin' to revive him, and I just bet she did.'

'Jesus,' I said. 'Carolyn!'

So we'd had a hurried conference on the street, and the only name I could think of was Wally Hemphill's, who was ensuring himself against Norb Klein's fate by training for the upcoming marathon. His was a general legal practice, running to divorces and wills and partnership agreements and such, and I had no reason to believe he knew his way around what people persist in calling the criminal justice system. But he'd come when called, God love him, and I was out on bail, and I'd declined on the advice of my attorney to answer any and all questions put to me by the police, and if I just survived the trek around the park I might live forever.

'It's funny,' Wally said now, leading our charge up a hill as if he thought he was Teddy Roosevelt. 'We'd see each other in Riverside Park, we'd do a few easy miles together, and I always thought of you as a runner.'

'Well, I rarely go more than three miles, see, and I'm not used to hills.'

'No, you didn't let me finish. I'm not knocking your running, Bernie. I thought of you as a runner and it never occurred to me that you might be a burglar. I mean you don't think of burglars as regular-type guys who talk about Morton's Foot and shin splints. You know what I mean?'

'Try to think of me as a guy who runs a secondhand book store.'

'And that's why you were at Onderdonk's apartment.'

'That's right.'

'At his invitation. You went over the night before last, that was Tuesday night, and you appraised his library.'

'Uh-huh.'

'And he was alive when you left.'

'Of course he was alive when I left. I never killed anybody in my life.'

'You left him tied up?'

'No, I didn't leave him tied up. I left him hale and hearty and saying goodbye to me at the elevator. No, come to think of it, he ducked back into his apartment to answer the phone.'

'So the elevator operator didn't actually see him there when he took you out of the building.'

'No.'

'What time was that? If he was talking to somebody on the phone, and if we can find out who—'

'It was probably around eleven. Something like that.'

'But the elevator operator who took you down went on after midnight, didn't he? And the doorman and the whatchamacallit—'

'The concierge.'

667

'Right. They changed shifts at midnight, and they identified you, said they let you out of the building around one. So if you left Onderdonk at eleven—'

'It could have been eleven-thirty.'

'I guess you had a long wait for the elevator.'

'They're like the subways, you miss one at that hour and you can wait forever for the next one.'

'You had another engagement in the building.'

I don't think Norb Klein would have figured it out any faster. 'Something like that,' I agreed.

'But then you went back again last night. Without using Onderdonk to get you into the building. The after-midnight staff said you left the building late two nights running, and both times the elevator operator swears he picked you up at Onderdonk's floor. Did he?'

'Uh-huh.'

'And the other staff people say you managed to get in delivering sandwiches from the deli.'

'It was flowers from the florist, which shows how reliable eye-witnesses are.'

'I think they said flowers, as a matter of fact.'

'From the deli?'

'I think they said flowers from the florist, and I think my memory changed it to sandwiches from the deli, and I think you're fooling yourself if you think those witnesses aren't going to be good ones. And the medical evidence isn't good.'

'What do you mean?'

'According to what I managed to learn, Onderdonk was killed by a blow to the head. He was hit twice with something hard and heavy, and the second shot did it. Fractured skull, cerebral hematoma, and I forget the exact language but what it amounts to is he got hit and he died of it.'

'Did they fix the time?'

'Roughly.'

'And?'

'According to their figures, he died sometime between when you arrived at the Charlemagne and when you left.'

'When I left the second time,' I said.

'No.'

'No?'

'You went up to Onderdonk's apartment Tuesday night, right? And left a little before one Wednesday morning, something like that.'

'Something like that.'

'Well, that's when he died. Now that's give or take a couple of hours, that's for sure, because they're just not that accurate when another

668

twenty-four hours has gone by before the body's discovered. But he definitely got it that night. Bernie? Where are you going?'

Where I was going was over the 102nd Street cutoff, which trims a full mile off the six-mile circuit and avoids the worst hill. Wally wanted the extra mile and the hill training that went with it, but I just kept trotting doggedly west on the cutoff road and all he could do was run alongside arguing.

'Listen,' he said, 'in a couple of years you'll be begging for some hill training. Those prison yards, you get plenty of time to run but it's all around a flat tenth-of-a-mile track. Even so, I got a client up at Green Haven who's doing upwards of a hundred miles a week. He just goes out there and runs for hours. It's boring, but it has its advantages.'

'He probably doesn't have too much trouble remembering the route.'

'There's that, and he's averaging something like fifteen miles a day. You can imagine the kind of shape he'll be in when he gets out.'

'When'll that be?'

'Oh, that's hard to say. But he should be coming up for parole in a couple of years, and he'll have a very good chance if he behaves himself between now and then.'

'What did he do?'

'Well, he had a girlfriend and she had a boyfriend and he found out, and he sort of cut them a little.'

'Socially?'

'With a knife. They, uh, died.'

'Oh.'

'These things happen.'

'Like clockwork,' I said. 'Wally, ease up. These uphills cut the legs out from under me.'

'You gotta charge the hills, Bernie. That's how you develop your quads.'

'It's how I develop angina. How could he have been dead before I left the building?'

He didn't say anything for a moment, and we ran along in a companionable silence. Then he said, without looking my way, 'Bernie, I could see how it could happen accidentally. He was a big, powerful guy and you had to knock him out and tie him up to rob him. You knocked him cold and tied him up and he was alive at that point, and then some leakage inside his head or something murky along those lines, it killed him and you didn't even know it. Because obviously you wouldn't go back to the building the next day if you knew he was dead. Except wait a minute. If you thought you left him tied up and alive, why would you go back to the building? You wouldn't want to show your face within a mile of that building, would you?'

'No.'

'You didn't kill him.'

'Of course not.'

'Unless you killed him and you knew he was dead, and you went back – to what?'

'I didn't hit him or steal from him, let alone kill him, Wally, so that makes the question a hard one to answer.'

'Forget Onderdonk for a minute. Why did you go back to the Charlemagne? You'd already committed a burglary there the night before. That's what you did, right? Stole something from somebody after you left his apartment?'

'Right.'

'So why'd you go back? Don't tell me the building was such a soft touch because I won't believe it.'

'No, it's worse than Fort Knox. Shit.'

'It's easier if you level with me, Bernie. And anything you tell me is privileged. I can't reveal it.'

'I know that.'

'So?'

'I went back to Onderdonk's apartment.'

'To Onderdonk's apartment.'

'Right.'

'You had another appointment with him? No, because you used the scam with the sandwiches to get in the door.'

'Flowers.'

'Did I say sandwiches again? I meant flowers. You went back there knowing he was dead?'

'I went back there knowing he was out because he didn't answer his goddamn phone.'

'You called him? Why?'

'To establish that he was out so I could go back.'

'What for?'

'To steal something.'

Left foot, right foot, left foot, right foot. 'Something caught your eye when you were appraising his library.'

'That's right.'

'So you thought you'd drop in and lift it.'

'It's more complicated than that, but that's the idea, yes.'

'It's getting harder to think of you as a bookseller and easier to think of you as a burglar. What the papers call an unrepentant career criminal, but this bit makes you sound like a kleptomaniac with foresight. You went back to an apartment that you'd already left your fingerprints all over the night before? And where you'd already given your right name to get into the building?'

'I'm not saying it was the smartest move I ever made.'

'Good, because it wasn't. I don't know, Bernie. I'm not sure hiring me was the smartest move you ever made, either. I'm a pretty decent attorney but my criminal experience is limited, and I can't say I did a hell of a lot for the client who cut those two people, but then I didn't knock myself out because I figured we'd all sleep better with him running around the yard at Green Haven. But you need someone who can work a combination of bribery and plea bargaining, if you want my honest opinion, and I don't have the moves for that.'

'I'm innocent, Wally.'

'I just can't understand why you hit the building again yesterday.'

'It seemed like a good idea at the time, okay? Wally, I didn't get any sleep last night and I never run more than four miles tops. I've got to stop.'

'We can slow down a little.'

'Good.' I kept moving my feet. 'What difference did the second visit make?' I asked him. 'I'd be in the same trouble anyway, with my prints all over the apartment and the staff remembering me, and if they really figure the time of death the way you said, the second visit is redundant.'

'Uh-huh. Except it makes it much harder in court to argue that you were never there in the first place.'

'Oh.'

'You were there for over eight hours yesterday, Bernie. That's another thing I don't understand. You spent eight hours in an apartment with a dead man and you say you didn't even know he was dead. Didn't he strike you as a little unresponsive?'

'I never saw him, Wally.' Puff, puff. 'Ray Kirschmann said the body was discovered in the bedroom closet. I checked all the rooms but I didn't go into the closets.'

'What did you take from his apartment?'

'Nothing.'

'Bernie, I'm your lawyer.'

'And here I thought you were my coach. It doesn't matter. Even if you were my spiritual adviser the answer would be the same. I didn't take anything from Onderdonk's apartment.'

'You went there to steal something.'

'Right.'

'And you left there without it.'

'Right again.'

'Why?'

'It was gone when I got there. Somebody'd already hooked it.'

'So you turned around and went home.'

'That's right.'

'But not for eight hours or so. Something on television you didn't want to miss? Or were you reading your way through his library?'

'I didn't want to leave the building until the shift changed. And I

671

didn't spend eight hours in Onderdonk's apartment. I stayed in another apartment, an empty one, until after midnight.'

'There's things you're not telling me.'

'Maybe a couple.'

'Well, that's okay, I guess. But you haven't done much direct lying to me, have you?'

'No.'

'You're sure about that?'

'Positive.'

'And you didn't kill him.'

'God, no.'

'And you don't know who did. Bernie? *Do* you know who killed him?'

'No.'

'Got an idea?'

'Not a clue.'

'Once more around? We'll take the Seventy-second Street cutoff, do a nice easy four-mile loop. Okay?'

'No way, Wally.'

'C'mon, take a shot at it.'

'Not a chance.'

'Well,' he said, chest heaving, arms pumping, 'I'll catch you later, then. I'm gonna go for it.'

12

'She must have killed him,' Carolyn said. 'Right?'

'You mean Andrea?'

'Who else? That'd be one reason why she was scared shitless when you walked in on her. She was afraid you'd discover the skeleton in her closet. Of course it wasn't her closet and he wasn't a skeleton yet, but—'

'You figure she overpowered him and tied him up and killed him? She's just a girl, Carolyn.'

'That's a real pig remark, you know that?'

'I mean in terms of physical strength. Maybe she could hit him hard enough to knock him out, maybe even hard enough to kill him, and maybe she could even drag him into the closet when she was done, but somehow I can't believe she did any of those things. Maybe she went there to look for her letters, just as she said.'

'Do you believe it?'

'Somehow I don't. But I'm willing to believe she went there looking for something.'

'The Mondrian.'

'And then what did she do, smuggle it past me secreted in her bodily cavities?'

'Not likely. You'd have found it.'

I gave her a look. It was morning, Friday morning, and if I didn't feel like a new man, I at least felt like a secondhand one in excellent shape. I'd left Wally Hemphill in the park and went straight home to a shower and a hot toddy and a full ten hours of sleep with the door double-bolted and the blinds shut and the phone unplugged. I'd come down-town early and tried Carolyn at the Poodle Factory every ten minutes or so, and when she answered I hung the *Back in Ten Minutes* sign in the window and went outside and pulled the door shut.

Across the street, a couple of shaggy guys lurking in a doorway shrank into the shadows when I glanced their way. They looked like a bottle gang without a bottle, and I had second thoughts about leaving my bargain table on the street, but what could they steal? My books on home winemaking were all safe inside the store. I left the table where it was and picked up two cups of coffee around the corner, then took them to Carolyn's canine beauty parlor.

She was clipping a Bichon Frise when I got there. I mistook it at first for a snow-white poodle, and Carolyn was quick to point out why it didn't look at all like a poodle, and after a couple of paragraphs of American Kennel Club lore I cut her off in midsentence and brought her up to date. The visit to the Charlemagne, the bit with the flowers, the incident in Onderdonk's apartment, the conversation with Wally Hemphill. Everything.

Now she said, 'How bad is it, Bernie? Are you in deep shit or what?'

'Let's call it chest high and rising.'

'It's my fault.'

'What do you mean?'

'Well, it's my cat, isn't it?'

'They kidnapped Archie to get at me, Carolyn. If you hadn't had a cat they'd have found some other way to put pressure on me. All to get a picture off a museum wall, and that's as impossible as it ever was. You asked if Andrea killed him. That was my first thought, but the times are all wrong. Unless the Medical Examiner's crazy, Onderdonk was killed while I was stealing Appling's stamps.'

'He was alone when you left him.'

'As far as I know.'

'And someone else dropped in on him, beat his head in, tied him up, and stuffed him in the closet. And stole the painting?'

'I suppose so.'

'Isn't it interesting that someone just happens to kill a guy and steal a painting from him, and we're supposed to steal a painting by the same artist in order to get my cat back?'

'The coincidence struck me, too.'

'Uh-huh. You get this coffee at the felafel joint?'

'Yeah. Not very good, is it?'

'It's not a question of good or bad. It's a matter of trying to figure out what they put in it.'

'Chickpeas.'

'Really?'

'Just a guess. They put chickpeas in everything. I must have lived the first twenty-five years of my life without knowing what a chickpea was, and all of a sudden they're inescapable.'

'What do you figure caused it?'

'Probably nuclear testing.'

'Makes sense. Bern, why tie Onderdonk up and stuff him in the closet? Let's say they killed him in order to get away with the painting.'

'Which is crazy, because it didn't look as though anything else was taken. The other art was worth a fortune but the place didn't even look as though it had been searched, let alone stripped.'

'Maybe somebody just needed the Mondrian for a specific purpose.'

'Like what?'

'Like ransoming a cat.'

'Didn't think of that.'

'The point is – next time get the coffee at the coffee shop, okay?'

'Sure.'

'The point is, why tie him up and why put him in the closet? To keep the body from being discovered? Makes no sense, does it?'

'I don't know.'

'Did whatsername, Andrea, did she know he was in the closet?'

'Maybe. I don't know.'

'She was pretty cool, wasn't she? She's in an apartment with a dead guy in the closet and a burglar walks in on her and what does she do? Rolls around on the oriental rug with him.'

'It was an Aubusson.'

'My mistake. What do we do now, Bern? Where do we go from here?'

'I don't know.'

'You didn't tell the police about Andrea.'

I shook my head. 'I didn't tell them anything. It's not as if she could give me an alibi. I could try telling them that I was in the Appling apartment while somebody was killing Onderdonk, but where would that get me? Just charged with another burglary, and even if I showed them the stamps I couldn't prove I hadn't killed Onderdonk before or after I performed philately on Appling's collection. Anyway, I don't know her name or where she lives.'

'You don't think her name's Andrea?'

'Maybe. Maybe not.'

'You could run an ad in the *Voice*.'

'I could.'

'What's the matter?'

'Oh, I don't know,' I said. 'I, oh, I sort of liked her, that's all.'

'Well, that's good. You wouldn't want to caper on the carpet with someone you hated.'

'Yeah. The thing is, I sort of thought I might get together with her again. Of course she's a married woman and there's no future in that sort of thing, but I thought—'

'You had romantic feelings.'

'Well, yeah, Carolyn, I guess I did.'

'That's not a bad thing.'

'It isn't?'

'Of course not. I have them myself. Alison came over last night. We met for a drink, and then I explained I didn't want to miss an important phone call so we went back to my place. The phone call I was talking about was about the cat, but it never came, and we just sat around and listened to music and talked.'

'Did you get lucky?'

'Bern, I didn't even try. It was just sort of peaceful and cozy, you know what I mean? You know how standoffish Ubi can be, and he's especially whacko with Archie gone, but he came over and curled up in her lap. I told her about Archie.'

'That he was missing?'

'That he'd been kidnapped. The whole thing. I couldn't help it, Bernie. I had to talk about it.'

'It's okay.'

'Romance,' she said. 'It's what makes the world go round, isn't it, Bern?'

'So they say.'

'You and Andrea, me and Alison.'

'Andrea's about five-foot-six,' I said. 'Slender, narrow at the waist. Dark hair to her shoulders, and she was wearing it in pigtails when I saw her.'

'Alison's slim, too, but she's not that tall. I'd say five-four. And her hair's light brown and short, and she doesn't wear any lipstick or nail polish.'

'She wouldn't, not if she's a political and economic lesbian. Andrea wears nail polish. I can't remember about the lipstick.'

'Why are we comparing descriptions of our obsessions, Bern?'

'I just had this dumb idea and I wanted to make sure it was a dumb idea.'

'You thought they were the same girl.'

'I said it was a dumb idea.'

'You're just afraid to let yourself have romantic feelings, that's all. You haven't been involved with anybody that way in a long time.'

'I guess.'

'Years from now,' she said, 'when you and Andrea are old and gray, nodding off together before the fire, you'll look back on these days and laugh quietly together. And neither of you will have to ask the other why you're laughing, because you'll just know without a word's being spoken.'

'Years from now,' I said, 'you and I will be having coffee somewhere, and one of us will puke, and without a word's being spoken the other'll immediately think of this conversation.'

'And this lousy coffee,' said Carolyn.

676

13

When I got back to my shop the phone was ringing, but by the time I got inside it had stopped. I thought I'd just pulled the door shut, letting the springlock secure it, but evidently I'd taken the time to lock it with the key because now I had to unlock it with the key, and that gave my caller the extra few seconds needed to hang up before I could reach the phone. I said the things one says at such times, improbable observations on the ancestry, sexual practices and dietary habits of whoever it was, and then I bent down to pick a dollar bill off the floor. A scrap of paper beside it bore a penciled notation that the payment was for three books from the bargain table.

That happens sometimes. No one has yet been so honest as to include the extra pennies for sales tax, and if that ever happens I may find myself shamed out of crime altogether. I put the dollar in my pocket and settled in behind the counter.

The phone rang again. I said, 'Barnegat Books, good morning,' and a man's voice, gruff and unfamiliar, said, 'I want the painting.'

'This is a bookstore,' I said.

'Let's not play games. You have the Mondrian and I want it. I'll pay you a fair price.'

'I'm sure you will,' I said, 'because you sound like a fair guy, but there's something you're wrong about. I haven't got what you're looking for.'

'Suit yourself. Do yourself a favor, eh? Don't sell it to anyone else without first offering it to me.'

'That sounds reasonable,' I said, 'but I don't know how to reach you. I don't even know who you are.'

'But I know who *you* are,' he said. 'And I know how to reach *you*.'

Had I been threatened? I was pondering the point when the phone clicked in my ear. I hung up and reviewed the conversation, searching for some clue of my caller's identity. If there was one present, I couldn't spot it. I guess I got a little bit lost in thought, because a moment or two down the line I looked up to see a woman approaching the counter and I hadn't even heard the door open to let her into the store.

She was slender and birdlike, with large brown eyes and short brown hair, and I recognized her at once but couldn't place her right away. She had a book in one hand, an oversized art book, and she placed the other hand on my counter and said, 'Mr Rhodenbarr? "Euclid alone has looked on Beauty bare." '

I'd heard the voice before. When? Over the phone? No.

'Ms Smith of the Third Oregon,' I said. 'That's not Mary Carolyn Davies you're quoting.'

'Indeed it's not. It's Edna St Vincent Millay. The line came to mind when I looked at this.'

She placed the book on the counter. It was a survey volume covering modern art from the Impressionists to the current anarchy, and it was open now to a color plate which showed a geometrical abstract painting. Vertical and horizontal black bands divided an off-white canvas into squares and rectangles, several of which were painted in primary colors.

'The absolute beauty of pure geometry,' she said. 'Or perhaps I mean the pure beauty of absolute geometry. Right angles and primary colors.'

'Mondrian, isn't it?'

'Piet Mondrian. Do you know much about the man and his work, Mr Rhodenbarr?'

'I know he was Dutch.'

'Indeed he was. Born in 1872 in Amersfoort. He began, you may recall, as a painter of naturalistic landscapes. As he found his own style, as he grew artistically, his work became increasingly abstract. By 1917 he had joined with Theo van Doesburg and Bart van der Leck and others to found a movement called *De Stijl*. It was an article of faith for Mondrian that the right angle was everything, that vertical and horizontal lines intersected space in such a way as to make an important philosophical statement.'

There was more. She gave me the four-dollar lecture, declaiming it as fervently as she'd read about poor Smith a couple of days earlier. 'Piet Mondrian held his first exhibition in America in 1926,' she told me. 'Fourteen years later he moved here. He'd gone to Britain in 1939 to get away from the war. Then, when the Luftwaffe started bombing London, he came here. New York fascinated him, you know. The grid pattern of the streets, the right angles. That was the beginning of his boogie-woogie period. You look confused.'

'I didn't know he was a musician.'

'He wasn't. His painting style changed, you see. He was inspired by the traffic in the streets, the elevated railways, the yellow cabs, the red lights, the jazzy pulsebeat of Manhattan. You're probably familiar with *Broadway Boogie Woogie* – that's one of his most famous canvases. It's in the Museum of Modern Art. There's also *Victory Boogie Woogie* and, oh, several others.'

In several other museums, I thought, where they were welcome to remain.

'I see,' I said, which is something I very often say when I don't.

'He died on February 1, 1944, just six weeks before his seventy-second birthday. I believe he died of pneumonia.'

'You certainly know a great deal about him.'

Her hands moved to adjust her hat, which didn't really need adjusting. Her eyes aimed themselves at a spot just above and to the left of my shoulder. 'When I was a little girl,' she said evenly, 'we went to my grandmother's and grandfather's every Sunday for dinner. I lived with my parents in a house in White Plains, and we came into the city where my grandparents had a huge apartment on Riverside Drive, with enormous windows overlooking the Hudson. Piet Mondrian had stayed at that apartment upon arriving in New York in 1940. A painting of his, a gift to my grandparents, hung over the sideboard in the dining room.'

'I see.'

'We always had the same seating arrangement,' she said, and closed her big eyes. 'I can picture that dinner table now. My grandfather at one end, my grandmother at the other near the door to the kitchen. My uncle and aunt and my younger cousin on one side of the table, and my mother and father and me on the other. All I had to do was gaze above my cousin's head and I could look at the Mondrian. I had it to stare at almost every Sunday night for all of my childhood.'

'I see.'

'You'd think I'd have tuned it out as children so often do. After all, I'd never met the artist. He died before I was born. Nor was I generally responsive to art as a child. But that painting, it evidently spoke to me in a particular way.' She smiled at a memory. 'When I was in art class, I always tried to produce geometrical abstracts. While the other children were drawing horses and trees, I was making black-and-white grids with squares of red and blue and yellow. My teachers didn't know what to make of it, but I was trying to be another Mondrian.'

'Actually,' I said tentatively, 'his paintings don't look all that hard to do.'

'He thought of them first, Mr Rhodenbarr.'

'Well, there's that, of course, but—'

'And his simplicity is deceptive. His proportions are quite perfect, you see.'

'I see.'

'I myself had no artistic talent. I wasn't even a fair copyist. Nor did I have any true artistic ambitions.' She cocked her head again, probed my eyes with hers. 'The painting was to be mine, Mr Rhodenbarr.'

'Oh?'

'My grandfather promised it to me. He was never a wealthy man. He and my grandmother lived comfortably but he never piled up riches. I don't suppose he had much idea of the value of Mondrian's painting. He knew its artistic worth, but I doubt he would have guessed the price it would command. He never collected art, you see, and to him this painting was nothing more or less than the valued gift of a treasured friend. He said it would come to me when he died.'

'And it didn't?'

'My grandmother was the first to die. She contracted some sort of viral infection which didn't respond to antibiotics, and within a month's time she was dead of kidney failure. My parents tried to get my grandfather to live with them after her death but he insisted on staying where he was. His one concession was to engage a live-in housekeeper. He never really recovered from my grandmother's death, and within a year he too was dead.'

'And the painting—'

'Disappeared.'

'The housekeeper took it?'

'That was one theory. My father thought my uncle might have taken it, and I suppose Uncle Billy thought the same of my father. And everyone suspected the housekeeper, and there was some talk of an investigation, but I don't think anything ever came of it. The family came to some sort of agreement that there'd been a burglary, because there were other things missing, some of the wedding silver, and it was easier to attribute it to some anonymous burglar than for us to make a thing of suspecting each other.'

'And I suppose the loss was covered by insurance.'

'Not the painting. My grandfather had never taken out a floater policy on it. I'm sure it never occurred to him. After all, it had cost him nothing, and I'm sure he never thought it might be stolen.'

'It was never recovered?'

'No.'

'I see.'

'Time passed. My own father died. My mother remarried and moved across the country. Mondrian remained my favorite painter, Mr Rhodenbarr, and whenever I looked at one of his works in the Modern or the Guggenheim I felt a strong primal response. And I felt a pang, too, for *my* painting, *my* Mondrian, the work that had been promised to me.' She straightened up, set her shoulders. 'Two years ago,' she said, 'there was a Mondrian retrospective at the Vermillion Galleries. Of course I went. I was walking from one painting to another, Mr Rhodenbarr, and I was breathless as I always am in front of Mondrian's work, and then I stepped up to one painting and my heart stopped. Because it was my painting.'

'Oh.'

'I was shocked. I was stunned. It was my painting and I would have known it anywhere.'

'Of course you hadn't seen it in ten years,' I said thoughtfully, 'and Mondrian's paintings do have a certain sameness to them. Not to take away anything from the artist's genius, but—'

'It was my painting.'

'If you say so.'

'I sat directly across from that painting every Sunday night for years. I stared at it while I stirred my green peas into my mashed potatoes. I—'

'Oh, did you do that, too? You know what else I used to do? I used to make a potato castle and then make a sort of moat of gravy around it, and then I'd have a piece of carrot for a cannon and I'd use the green peas for cannonballs. What I really wanted was some way to catapult them into the brisket, but that was where my mother drew the line. How did your painting get to the Vermillion Galleries?'

'It was on loan.'

'From a museum?'

'From a private collection. Mr Rhodenbarr, I don't care how the painting got into the private collection or how it got out of it. I just want the painting. It's rightfully mine, and at this point I wouldn't even care if it weren't rightfully mine. It's been an overwhelming obsession ever since I saw it at the retrospective. I have to have it.'

What was it about Mondrian, I wondered, that appealed so strongly to crazy people? The catnapper, the man on the phone, Onderdonk, Onderdonk's killer; and now this ditsy little lady. And, come to think of it, who was she?

'Come to think of it,' I said, 'who are you?'

'Haven't you been listening? My grandfather—'

'You never told me your name.'

'Oh, my name,' she said, and hesitated for only a second. 'It's Elspeth. Elspeth Peters.'

'Lovely name.'

'Thank you. I—'

'I suppose you think I stole the painting from your grandfather's house lo these many years ago. I can understand that, Ms Peters. You bought a book in my shop and my name stuck in your mind. Then you read something or heard something to the effect that I had a minor criminal career years ago before I became an antiquarian bookman. You made a mental connection, which I suppose is understandable, and—'

'I don't think you stole the painting from my grandfather.'

'You don't?'

'Why, did you?'

'No, but—'

'Because I suppose it's possible, although you would have been a fairly young burglar yourself at the time, wouldn't you? Personally I've always thought that my father was right and Uncle Billy took it, but for all I know Uncle Billy was right and my father took it. Whoever took it sold it, and do you know who bought it?'

'I could take a wild guess.'

'I'm sure you could.'

'J. McLendon Barlow.'

That was news to her. She stared at me. I repeated the name and it still didn't seem to mean anything to her. 'That was the man who loaned it to the Vermillion Galleries,' I said, 'and later on he donated it to the Hewlett Collection. Remember?'

'I don't know what you're talking about,' she said. 'The painting – *my* painting – was on loan from the collection of a Mr Gordon Kyle Onderdonk.'

'Oh,' I said.

'And I read newspapers, Mr Rhodenbarr. That minor criminal career of yours doesn't seem to have ceased with your entry into the book business. If the papers are to be believed, you were arrested for Mr Onderdonk's murder.'

'I suppose that's technically true.'

'And now you're out on bail?'

'More or less.'

'And you stole the painting from his apartment. My painting, my Mondrian.'

'Everyone seems to think that,' I said, 'but it's not true. The painting's gone, I'll admit that, but I never laid a glove on it. There's some sort of traveling exhibit coming up and Onderdonk was going to lend them his painting. He sent it out for reframing.'

'He wouldn't do that.'

'He wouldn't?'

'The sponsors of the show would attend to that, if they felt the work needed reframing. I'm positive you took the painting.'

'It was gone when I got there.'

'That's very difficult to believe.'

'I had trouble believing it myself, Ms Peters. I still have trouble, but I was there and saw for myself. Or didn't see for myself, since there was nothing to see except an empty space where a picture had been.'

'And Onderdonk told you he'd sent the picture out for framing?'

'I didn't ask him. He was dead.'

'You killed him before you noticed the painting was gone?'

'I didn't get a chance to kill him because somebody beat me to it. And I didn't know he was dead because I didn't look in the closet for his body, because I didn't know there was a body to look for.'

'Someone else killed him.'

'Well, I don't think it was suicide. If it was, it's the worst case of suicide I ever heard of.'

She looked off into the middle distance and a couple of frown lines clouded her brow. 'Whoever killed him,' she said, 'took the painting.'

'Could be.'

'Who killed him?'

'I don't know.'

'The police think you did it.'

'They probably know better,' I said. 'At least the arresting officer does. He's known me for years, he knows I don't kill people. But they can prove I was in the apartment, so I'll do for a suspect until they come up with a better one.'

'And how will that come about?'

I'd already thought of this. 'Well, if I can figure out who did it, I suppose I could pass the word.'

'So you're trying to learn the identity of the killer.'

'I'm just trying to get through the days one at a time,' I said, 'but I'll admit I'm keeping my eyes and ears open.'

'When you find the killer, you'll find the painting.'

'It's not when, it's if. And even so, I may or may not find the painting at the same time.'

'When you do, I want it.'

'Well—'

'It's rightfully mine. You must realize that. And I mean to have it.'

'You just expect me to hand it over to you?'

'That would be the smartest thing you could do.'

I stared at this delicate creature. 'Good grief,' I said. 'Was that a threat?'

She didn't draw her eyes away, and what big eyes they were. 'I would have killed Onderdonk,' she said, 'to get that painting.'

'You're really obsessed.'

'I'm aware of that.'

'Listen, this may strike you as a wild idea, but have you ever thought about therapy? Obsessions just keep the focus off our real problems, you know, and if you could have the obsession lifted—'

'When I have my hands on my painting, the obsession will be lifted.'

'I see.'

'I could be a good friend to you, Mr Rhodenbarr. Or I could be a dangerous enemy.'

'Suppose I did get the painting,' I said carefully.

'Does that mean you already have it?'

'No, it means what I just said. Suppose I get it. How do I get hold of you?'

She hesitated for a moment, then opened her bag and took out a fine-line felt tip pen and an envelope. She held the envelope upside-down and tore off a piece of its flap, returned the rest of the envelope to her

683

purse, and wrote a telephone number on the scrap. Then she hesitated for another beat and wrote *E. Peters* beneath the number.

'There,' she said, setting the slip on the counter beside the open art book. She capped her pen, put it back in her purse, and seemed about to say something when the door opened and the tinkling of bells announced a visitor.

The visitor in turn announced herself. It was Carolyn, and she said, 'Hey, Bern, I got another phone call and I thought—' Then Elspeth Peters turned to face Carolyn, and the two women looked at each other for a moment, and then Elspeth Peters walked past her and on out the door.

14

'Don't fall in love with her,' I told Carolyn. 'She's already in the grip of an obsession.'

'What are you talking about?'

'The way you stared at her. I figured you were falling in love, or perhaps in lust. Which is understandable, but—'

'I thought I recognized her.'

'Oh?'

'I thought for a minute she was Alison.'

'Oh,' I said. 'Was she?'

'No, of course not. I'd have said hello if she was.'

'Are you sure?'

'Of course I'm sure. Why, Bern?'

'Because she said her name was Elspeth Peters, and I don't believe her. And she's tied into the Mondrian business.'

'So? Alison's not, remember? Alison's tied into me.'

'Right.'

'There's a strong resemblance, but that's all it is, a resemblance. How's she tied in?'

'She thinks she's the painting's rightful owner.'

'Maybe she stole the cat.'

'Not that painting. Onderdonk's painting.'

'Oh,' she said. 'There's too many paintings, you know that?'

'There's too much of everything. You just had a phone call, you started to say. From the Nazi?'

'Right.'

'Well, it couldn't have been Peters. She was here with me.'

'Right.'

'What did she want?'

'Well, she sort of put my mind at rest,' Carolyn said. 'She said the cat was alive and well and nothing bad would happen to him as long as I cooperated. She said I didn't have to worry about them cutting off an ear or a foot or anything, that the bit with the whiskers was to show they meant business but they wouldn't hurt him or anything. And she

685

said she knew the painting was going to be difficult to get but she was sure we could do it if we put our minds to it.'

'It sounds as though she was trying to comfort you.'

'Well, it worked, Bern. I feel a lot better about the cat. I still don't know if I'm ever gonna see him again, but I'm not crazy the way I was. Talking with Alison about it last night helped a lot, and now the phone call. Just so I know nothing terrible's gonna happen to the cat—'

I barely heard the door, but I did look up and see him, and as he approached I sshhhed Carolyn, and she broke off in the middle of a sentence and turned to see why I was interrupting her.

'Shit,' she said. 'Hello, Ray.'

'Hello yourself,' said the best cop money can buy. 'You know, you find out who your friends are in this business. Here's a couple of people I know for years, and all I gotta do is walk in the room and one says sshhh and the other says shit. What's gonna happen to the cat, Carolyn?'

'Nothing,' she said. Years ago she'd heard somewhere that the best defense is a good offense, and she'd never forgotten it. 'The real question is what's gonna happen to Bernie if his so-called old friends keep arresting him every time he turns around. You ever hear of police harassment, Ray?'

'Just be grateful I never heard of police brutality, Carolyn. Whyntcha take a hike, huh? Stretch your legs. They could use it.'

'If you're gonna do short jokes, Ray, I'll do asshole jokes, and where'll that leave you?'

'Jesus, Bern,' he said. 'Can't you get her to act like a lady?'

'I've been working at it. What do you want, Ray?'

'About three minutes of conversation. Private conversation. If she wants to stick around, I suppose we could go in your back room.'

'No, I'll go,' Carolyn said. 'I gotta use the bathroom anyway.'

'Now that you mention it, so do I. No, you go ahead, Carolyn. Bernie an' I'll talk, so you take your time in there.' He waited until she had left the room, then laid a hand on the art book that Elspeth Peters had left on my counter. It was closed now, no longer open to the Mondrian reproduction. 'Pictures,' he said. 'Right?'

'Very good, Ray.'

'Like the one you lifted from Onderdonk's place?'

'What are you talking about?'

'A guy named Mondrian,' he said, except he pronounced it *Moon-drain*. 'Used to hang over the fireplace and covered by $350,000 insurance.'

'That's a lot of money.'

'It is, isn't it? Far as they can tell so far, that's the only thing that was stolen. Pretty good-sized paintin', white background, black lines criss-crossin', a little color here an' there.'

'I've seen it.'

'Oh? No kiddin'.'

'When I appraised his library. It was hanging over the fireplace.' I thought for a moment. 'I think he said something about sending it out for framing.'

'Yeah, it needed a new frame.'

'How's that?'

'I'll tell you how it is, Bernie. The picture frame from the Moondrain was in the closet with Onderdonk's body, all broken into pieces. There was the aluminum frame, pulled apart, and there was what they call the stretcher that the canvas is attached to, except it wasn't.'

'It wasn't? It wasn't what?'

'Attached. Somebody cut the paintin' off the stretcher, but there was enough left so that a guy from the insurance company only had to take one look to know it was the Moondrain. To me it didn't look like much. Just about an inch-wide strip of canvas all the way around, white with black dashes here and there like Morse code, and I think one strip of red. My guess is you rolled it and wore it out of the buildin' under your clothes.'

'I never touched it.'

'Uh-huh. You musta been in some kind of rush to cut it out of the frame instead of takin' the time to unfasten the staples. That way you coulda got the whole canvas. I don't figure you killed him, Bern. I been thinkin' about that, and I don't think you did it.'

'Thanks.'

'But I know you were there and you musta got the paintin'. Maybe you heard somebody comin' and that's why you rushed and cut it outta the frame. Maybe you left the frame hangin' on the wall an' left Onderdonk tied up, and somebody else stuck the frame in the closet and killed him while they were at it.'

'Why would anybody do that?'

'Who knows what people'll do? This is a crazy world with crazy people in it.'

'Amen.'

'The point is, I figure you got the Moondrain.'

'Mondrian. Not Moondrain. Mondrian.'

'What's the difference? I could call him Pablo Fuckin' Picasso and we'd still know who we were talkin' about. I figure you got it, Bern, and if you haven't got it I figure you can get it, and that's why I'm here on my own time when I oughta be home with my feet up and the TV on.'

'Why's that?'

'Because there's a reward,' he said. 'The insurance company's a bunch of cheap bastards, the reward's only ten percent, but what's ten percent of $350,000?'

'Thirty-five thousand dollars.'

'Bookstore goes under, Bern, you can always become an accountant. You're gonna need some cash to get out from under this murder rap, right? Money for your lawyer, money for costs. The hell, everybody needs money, right? Otherwise you wouldn't have to go out stealin' in the first place. So you come up with the paintin' and I haul it in for the reward and we split.'

'How do we split?'

'Bern, was I ever greedy? Fifty-fifty's how we split an' that way everybody's happy. You wash my hand, I'll scratch your back, you know what I mean?'

'I think so.'

'So we're talkin' seventeen-five apiece, and I'll tell you, Bern, you're not gonna beat that. All this publicity, a murder and all, you can't run out and find a buyer for it. And forget about workin' a deal where you sell it back to the insurance company, because these bastards set traps and all you'll wind up with is your tit in a wringer. Of course maybe you stole it to order, maybe you got a customer waitin', but can you take a chance with him? In the first place he could cross you, and in the second place you can take some of the pressure off your own self if the insurance company gets the picture back.'

'You've got it all worked out.'

'Well,' he said, 'a man's got to think for himself. Another thing is maybe you already fenced it, stole it to order and turned it over the same night.' He shifted his weight from one foot to the other. 'Say, what's she doin' in there, Bernie?'

'Answering a call of nature, I suppose.'

'Yeah, well, I wish she'd shit or get off the pot. My back teeth are floatin'. What I was sayin', if you already offed the Moondrain, what you got to do is steal it back.'

'From the person I sold it to?'

'Or from the person *he* sold it to, if it passed on down the line. I'm tellin' you, Bernie, this case'll quiet down a lot if the Moondrain gets recovered. That'll tend to separate the burglary aspect from the murder aspect, and maybe it'll get people lookin' elsewhere than yourself for the killer.'

'It'll also put half of thirty-five thousand dollars in your pocket, Ray.'

'And the other half in yours, and don't forget it. What the hell happened to Carolyn? Maybe I better go see if she fell in.'

Whereupon my favorite dog groomer burst breathless into the room, hitching at the belt of her slacks with one hand, holding the other up with the palm facing toward us.

She said, 'Bernie, there's been a disaster. Ray, don't go in there, don't even think about it. Bernie, what I did, I flushed a bloody tampon. I thought it'd be all right, and everything blocked up and backed up and there's shit all over the floor and it's still running. I tried to clean up

688

but I only made it worse. Bernie, can you help me? I'm afraid it's gonna flood the whole store.'

'I was just leavin',' Ray said, backing off. His face had a greenish tinge and he didn't look happy. 'Bern, I'll be in touch, right?'

'You don't want to give us a hand?'

'Are you kiddin'?' he said. 'Jesus!'

I was around the counter before he was out the door, and he wasn't taking his time, either. I went through toward the back room and ducked into the john, and there was nothing on the floor but red and black vinyl tiles in a checkerboard pattern. They were quite dry, and about as clean as they generally are.

There was a man sitting on my toilet.

He didn't look as though he belonged there. He was fully dressed, wearing gray sharkskin trousers with a gray glen-plaid suit jacket. His shirt was maroon and his shoes were a pair of scuffed old wingtips, somewhere between black and brown in hue. He had shaggy rust-brown hair and a red goatee, ill-trimmed and going to gray. His head was back and his jaw slack, showing tobacco-stained teeth that had never known an orthodontist's care. His eyes, too, were open, and they were of the sort described as guileless blue.

'Well, I'll be damned,' I said.

'You didn't know he was in here?'

'Of course not.'

'That's what I figured. You recognize him?'

'The artist,' I said. 'The one who paid a dime at the Hewlett Collection. I forget his name.'

'Turner.'

'No, that's another artist, but it's close. The guard knew his name, called him by name. Turnquist.'

'That's it. Bernie, where are you going?'

'I want to make sure there's nobody in the store,' I said, 'and I want to turn the bolt, and I want to change the sign from *Open* to *Closed*.'

'And then what?'

'I don't know yet.'

'Oh,' she said. 'Bernie?'

'What?'

'He's dead, isn't he?'

'Oh, no question,' I said. 'They don't get much deader.'

'That's what I thought. I think I'm gonna be sick.'

'Well, if you have to. But can't you wait until I get him off the toilet?'

15

'You can rent 'em for only fifty bucks a month,' she said. 'That's a pretty good deal, isn't it? Comes to less than two dollars a day. What else can you get for less than two dollars a day?'

'Breakfast,' I said, 'if you're a careful shopper.'

'And a lousy tipper. The only thing is they got a one-month minimum. Even if we bring the thing back in an hour and a half, it's the same fifty bucks.'

'We might not bring it back at all. How much of a deposit did you have to leave?'

'A hundred. Plus the first month's rental, so I'm out a hundred and a half. But the hundred comes back when we return the thing. *If* we return the thing.'

We paused at the corner of Sixth Avenue and Twelfth Street, waiting for the light to change. It changed and we headed across. At the opposite side Carolyn said, 'Didn't they pass a law? Aren't there supposed to be access ramps at all corners?'

'That sounds familiar.'

'Well, do you call this a ramp? Look at this curb, will you? You could hang-glide off of it.'

'You push down on the handles,' I said, 'and I'll lift. Here we go.'

'Shit.'

'Easy does it.'

'Shit with chocolate sauce. I mean we can manage it, even a steep curb, but what's a genuinely handicapped person out on his own supposed to do, will you tell me that?'

'You've been asking that question once a block.'

'Well, my consciousness is being raised every time we have to shlep this damned thing up another curb. It's the kind of cause I could get worked up about. Show me a petition and I'll sign it. Show me a parade and I'll march. What's so funny?'

'I was picturing the parade.'

'You've got a sick sense of humor, Bernie. Anyone ever tell you that? Help me push – I'm giving our friend here a bumpy ride.'

Not that our friend was apt to complain. He was the late Mr

Turnquist, of course, and the thing we were pushing, as you've probably figured out, was a wheelchair, leased from Pitterman Hospital and
Surgical Supply on First Avenue between Fifteenth and Sixteenth
Streets. Carolyn had gone there, rented the contraption, and brought
it back in the trunk of a cab. I'd helped her get it into the bookstore,
where we'd unfolded it and wrestled Turnquist into it.

By the time we left the store he looked natural enough sitting there,
and a lot better than he'd looked on the throne in my john. There was a
leather strap that fastened around his waist, and I'd added a couple of
lengths of old lamp cord to secure his wrists to the chair's arms and his
ankles to an appropriately positioned rail. A lap robe – an old blanket,
really, slightly mildewed – covered him from the neck down. A pair of
Foster Grants hid his staring blue eyes. A peaked tweed cap that had
been hanging on a nail in my back room since March, waiting for its
owner to reclaim it, now sat on Turnquist's head, doing its best to
make him a shade less identifiable. And in that fashion we made our
way westward, trying to figure out what the hell was happening, and
getting distracted once a block when Carolyn started bitching about
the curbs.

'What we're doing,' she said. 'Transporting a dead body. Is it a felony
or a misdemeanor?'

'I don't remember. It's a no-no, that's for sure. The law takes a dim
view of it.'

'In the movies, you're not supposed to touch anything.'

'I never touch anything in the movies. What you're supposed to do is
report dead bodies immediately to the police. You could have done
that. You could have come right out of the john and told Ray there
was a corpse sitting on the pot. You wouldn't have even had to make a
phone call.'

She shrugged. 'I figured he'd want an explanation.'

'It's likely.'

'I also figured we didn't have one.'

'Right again.'

'How'd he get there, Bernie?'

'I don't know. He felt fairly warm to the touch but I haven't touched
a whole lot of dead people in my time and I don't know how long it
takes them to cool off. He could have been in the store yesterday when
I locked up. I closed the place in a hurry, remember, because I'd just
been arrested and that kept me from concentrating fully upon my usual
routine. He could have been browsing in the stacks, or he could have
slipped into the back room and hidden out on purpose.'

'Why would he do that?'

'Beats me. Then he could have been there and sometime in the
course of the night or morning he could have gone to the john, sat
down on it without dropping his pants, and died.'

691

'Of a heart attack or something?'

'Or something,' I agreed, and the wheelchair hit a bump in the sidewalk. Our passenger's head flopped forward, almost dislodging cap and sunglasses. Carolyn straightened things out.

'He'll sue us,' she said. 'Whiplash.'

'Carolyn, the man's dead. Don't make jokes.'

'I can't help it. It's a nervous reaction. You think he just died of natural causes?'

'This is New York. Murder's a natural cause in this city.'

'You think he was murdered? Who could have murdered him?'

'I don't know.'

'You think somebody else was in the store with him? How did they get out?'

'I don't know.'

'Maybe he committed suicide.'

'Why not? He was a Russian agent, he had a cyanide capsule in a hollow tooth, and he knew the jig was up, so he let himself into my store and bit down on the old bicuspid. It's natural enough that he'd want to die in the presence of first editions and fine bindings.'

'Well, if it wasn't a heart attack or suicide—'

'Or herpes,' I said. 'I understand there's a lot of it going around.'

'If it wasn't one of those things, and if somebody killed him, how did they do it? You think you locked two people in the store last night?'

'No.'

'Then what?'

'He could have slipped in when I opened up this morning. I might not have noticed. Then, while I was picking up coffee and taking it to your place—'

'That rotten coffee.'

'—he could have gone into the john and died. Or if there was someone with him that person could have killed him. Or if he came alone, and then someone else came along, he could have opened the door for that person, and then the person could have killed him.'

'Or the murderer managed to get locked in the store either last night or this morning, and when Turnquist showed up the murderer let him in and murdered him. Could either one of them let the other in without a key?'

'No problem,' I said. 'I didn't do much of a job of locking up when I went for coffee. I left the bargain table outside and just pressed the button so the springlock would work. I don't even remember double-locking the door with the key.' I frowned, remembering. 'Except I must have, because it was bolted when I came back. I had to turn the key in the lock twice to turn both the bolt and the springlock. Shit.'

'What's the matter?'

'Well, that screws it up,' I said. 'Say Turnquist let the killer in, which

692

he could have done from inside just by turning the knob. Then the killer left Turnquist dead on the potty and went out, but how did he lock the door?'

'Don't you have extra keys around somewhere? Maybe he found them.'

'You'd really have to look for them, and why would he bother? Especially when I didn't have the door double-locked in the first place.'

'It doesn't make sense.'

'Hardly anything does. Watch the curb.'

'Shit.'

'Watch that, too. People seem to have stopped picking up after their dogs. Walking's becoming an adventure again.'

We managed another curb, crossed another street, scaled the curb at the far side. We kept heading west, and once we got across Abingdon Square, the traffic, both automotive and pedestrian, thinned out considerably. At the corner of Twelfth and Hudson we passed the Village Nursing Home, where an old gentleman in a similar chair gave Turnquist the thumbs-up sign. 'Don't let these young people push you around,' he counseled our passenger. 'Learn to work the controls yourself.' When he got no response, his eyes flicked to me and Carolyn. 'The old boy a little bit past it?' he demanded.

'I'm afraid so.'

'Well, at least you're not dumping the poor bastard in a home,' he said, with not a little bitterness. 'He ever comes around, you tell him I said he's damn lucky to have such decent children.'

We walked on across Greenwich Street, took a left at Washington. A block and a half down, between Bank and Bethune, a warehouse was being transmuted into co-op living lofts. The crew charged with performing this alchemy was gone for the day.

I braked the wheelchair.

Carolyn said, 'Here?'

'As good a place as any. They angled a plank over the steps for the wheelbarrows. Make a good ramp for the chair.'

'I thought we could keep on going down to the Morton Street Pier. Send him into the Hudson, chair and all.'

'Carolyn—'

'It's an old tradition, burial at sea. Davy Jones's Locker. "Full fathom five my father lies—"'

'Want to give me a hand?'

'Oh, sure. Nothing I'd rather do. "Well, at least you're not dumping the poor bastard in a home." Hell no, old timer. We're dumping the old bastard in a seemingly abandoned warehouse where he'll be cared for by the Green Hornet and Pluto.'

'Kato.'

693

'Whatever. Why do I feel like Burke and Hare?'

'They stole bodies and sold them. We're just moving one around.'

'Terrific.'

'I told you I'd do this myself, Carolyn.'

'Oh, don't be ridiculous. I'm your henchperson, aren't I?'

'It looks that way.'

'And we're in this together. It's my cat that got us in this mess. Bern, why can't we leave him here, chair and all? I honest to God don't care a rat's ass about the hundred dollars.'

'It's not the money.'

'What is it, the principle of the thing?'

'If we leave the chair,' I said, 'they'll trace it.'

'To Pitterman Hospital and Surgical Supply? Big hairy deal. I paid in cash and gave a phony name.'

'I don't know who Turnquist was or how he fits into this Mondrian business, but there has to be a connection. When the cops tie him to it they'll go to Pitterman and get the description of the person who rented the chair. Then they'll take the clerk downtown and stick you in front of him in a lineup, you and four of the Harlem Globetrotters, and who do you figure he'll point to?'

'I expect short jokes from Ray, Bernie. I don't expect them from you.'

'I was just trying to make a point.'

'You made it. I thought it would be more decent to leave him in the chair, that's all. Forget I said anything, okay?'

'Okay.'

I got the wire off his wrists and ankles, unstrapped the belt from around his waist, and managed to stretch him out on his back on a reasonably uncluttered expanse of floor. I retrieved the cap and sunglasses and blanket.

Back on the street I said, 'Hop on, Carolyn. I'll give you a ride.'

'Huh?'

'Two people pushing an empty wheelchair are conspicuous. C'mon, get in the chair.'

'You get in it.'

'You weigh less than I do, and—'

'The hell with that noise. You're taller than I am and you're a man, so if one of us has to play Turnquist you're a natural choice for the role. Get in the chair, Bern, and put on the cap and the glasses.' She tucked the blanket around me and the mildew smell wafted to my nostrils. With a sly grin, my henchperson released the handbrake. 'Hang on,' she said. 'And fasten your seat belt. Short jokes, huh? We may hit a few air pockets along the way.'

16

Back at the store, I checked the premises for bodies, living or dead, before I did anything else. I didn't find any, nor did I happen on any clues as to how Turnquist had gotten into my store or how he'd happened to join his ancestors in that great atelier on high. Carolyn wheeled the chair into the back room and I helped her fold it. 'I'll take it back in a cab,' she said, 'but first I want some coffee.'

'I'll get it.'

'Not from the felafel joint.'

'Don't worry.'

When I got back with two coffees she said the phone had rung in my absence. 'I was gonna answer it,' she said, 'and then I didn't.'

'Probably wise.'

'This coffee's much better. You know what we oughta do? In either your place or my place we oughta have one of those machines, nice fresh coffee all day long. One of those electric drip things.'

'Or even a hotplate and a Chemex pot.'

'Yeah. Of course you'd be pouring coffee for customers all day long, and you'd never get rid of Kirschmann. He'd be a permanent guest. I really grossed him out, didn't I?'

'He couldn't get out of here fast enough.'

'Well, that was the idea. I figured the more disgusting I made it, the faster he'd split. I was trying to wait him out, you know, figuring he might leave if I stayed out of the room long enough, but it looked as though he wasn't gonna leave without peeing, so—'

'I almost left myself. He's not the only one you grossed out.'

'Oh, right. You didn't know I was faking it.'

'Of course not. I didn't know there was a dead man in there.'

'Maybe I went into too much detail.'

'Don't worry about it,' I said, and the phone rang.

I picked it up and Wally Hemphill said, 'You're a hard man to get hold of, Bernie. I was thinking you'd jumped bail.'

'I wouldn't do that. I don't know anybody in Costa Rica.'

'Oh, a guy like you would make friends anywhere. Listen, what do you know about this Mondrian?'

'I know he was Dutch,' I said. 'Born in 1872 in Amberfoot or something like that. He began, you may recall, as a painter of naturalistic landscapes. As he found his own style he grew artistically and his work became increasingly abstract. By 1917—'

'What's this, a museum lecture? There's a painting missing from Onderdonk's apartment worth close to half a million dollars.'

'I know.'

'You get it?'

'No.'

'It might be useful if you could come up with it. Give us a bargaining chip.'

'Suppose I gave them Judge Crater,' I said, 'or a cure for cancer.'

'You really haven't got the painting?'

'No.'

'Who got it?'

'Probably the person who killed him.'

'You didn't kill anybody and you didn't take anything.'

'Right.'

'You were just there to leave fingerprints.'

'Evidently.'

'Nuts. Where do you go from here, Bernie?'

'Around in circles,' I said.

I got off the phone and went in back, with Carolyn trailing after me. There's a sort of cupboard next to the desk, filled with things I haven't gotten around to throwing out, and I keep a sweat shirt and some other running gear there. I opened it, took inventory, and removed my shirt.

'Hey,' she said. 'What are you doing?'

'Getting undressed,' I said, unbelting my pants. 'What's it look like?'

'Jesus,' she said, turning her back on me. 'If this is a subtle pass, I pass on it. In the first place I'm gay and in the second place we're best friends and in the third place—'

'I'm going for a run, Carolyn.'

'Oh. With Wally?'

'Without Wally. A nice lope around Washington Square until my mind clears up. There's nothing in it now but false starts and loose ends. People keep coming out of the woodwork asking me for a painting I never even had my hands on. They all want me to have it. Kirschmann smells a reward and Wally smells a fat fee and I don't know what all the other people smell. Oil paint, probably. I'll run and work the kinks out of my mind and maybe all of this will start to make sense to me.'

'And what about me? What'll I do while you're doing your Alberto Salazar impression?'

'You could take the wheelchair back.'

'Yeah, I have to do that sooner or later, don't I? Bern? I wonder if any of the people who saw you in the wheelchair will recognize you jogging around Washington Square.'

'Let's hope not.'

'Listen,' she said, 'anybody says anything, just tell 'em you've been to Lourdes.'

Washington Square Park is a rectangle, and the sidewalk around it measures just about five-eighths of a mile, which in turn is just about a kilometer. It's flat if you're walking, but when you run there's a slight slope evident, and if you run counterclockwise, as almost everybody does, you feel the incline as you run east along the southern border of the park. I felt it a lot on the first lap, with my legs still a little achey from the previous day's ordeal in Central Park, but after that it didn't bother me.

I was wearing blue nylon shorts and a ribbed yellow tank top and burgundy running shoes, and there was a moment when I found myself wondering whether Mondrian would have liked my outfit. Scarlet shoes would have suited him better, I decided. Or vermillion, like the galleries.

I took it very slow and easy. A lot of people passed me, but I didn't care if old ladies with aluminum walkers whizzed by me. I just put one wine-colored foot after the other, and somewhere around the fourth lap my mind started to float, and I suppose I ran three more laps after that but I wasn't keeping score.

I didn't think about Mondrian or his paintings or all the crazy people who wanted them. I didn't really think about anything, and after my close to four miles I picked up the plastic bag of stuff I'd left with one of the chessplayers at the park's southwest corner. I thanked him and trotted west to Arbor Court.

Carolyn wasn't home, so I used the tools I'd brought along to let myself into her building and then her apartment. The vestibule lock was candy but the others were not, and I wondered what curious villain had picked those locks without leaving a hint of his presence, and why he couldn't use the same talents to hook the Mondrian out of the Hewlett Collection all by his own self.

I got in, locked up, stripped and showered, the last-named act being the reason I'd come to Arbor Court. I dried off and put on the clothes I'd been wearing earlier and hung my sopping shorts and tank top over the shower curtain rod. Then I looked in the fridge for a beer, made a face when I failed to find one, and fixed some iced tea from a mix. It tasted like what you would expect.

I made a sandwich and ate it and made another sandwich and started eating it, and some clown outside slammed on his brakes and hit his horn, and Ubi hopped onto the window ledge to investigate. I watched him stick his head through the bars, the tips of his whiskers just

697

brushing the bars on either side, and I thought of Archie's whiskers and found myself feeling uncommonly sorry for the poor cat. There were two people dead already and I was charged with one murder and might very well be charged with the other, and all I could think of was how forlorn Carolyn's cat must be.

I looked up a number, picked up the phone and dialed it. Denise Raphaelson answered on the third ring and I said, 'This is Bernie, and we never had this conversation.'

'Funny, I remember it as if it were yesterday.'

'What do you know about an artist named Turnquist?'

'That's why you called? To find out what I know about an artist named Turnquist?'

'That's why. He's probably crowding sixty, reddish hair and goatee, bad teeth, gets all his clothes from the Goodwill. Sort of a surly manner.'

'Where is he? I think I'll marry him.'

Denise was a girlfriend of mine for a while, and then she rather abruptly became a girlfriend of Carolyn's, and that didn't last very long. She's a painter, with a loft on West Broadway called the Narrowback Gallery where she lives and works. I said, 'Actually, it's a little late for that.'

'What's the matter with him?'

'You don't want to know. Ever hear of him?'

'I don't think so. Turnquist. He got a first name?'

'Probably. Most people do, except for Trevanian. Maybe Turnquist's his first name and he doesn't have a last name. There are a lot of people like that. Hildegarde. Twiggy.'

'Liberace.'

'That's his last name.'

'Oh, right.'

'Does Turnquist ring a bell?'

'Doesn't even knock softly. What kind of painter is he?'

'A dead one.'

'That's what I was afraid of. Well, he's in good company. Rembrandt, El Greco, Giotto, Bosch – all those guys are dead.'

'We never had this conversation.'

'What conversation?'

I hung up and looked up Turnquist in the Manhattan book, and there was only one listing, a Michael Turnquist in the East Sixties. Things are never that easy, and he certainly hadn't dressed to fit that address, but what the hell. I dialed the number and a man answered almost immediately.

I said, 'Michael Turnquist?'

'Speaking.'

'Sorry,' I said. 'I must have the wrong number.'

The hell with it. I picked up the phone again and dialed 911. When a woman answered I said, 'There's a dead body at a construction site on Washington Street,' and gave the precise address. She started to ask me something but I didn't let her finish her sentence. 'Sorry,' I said, 'but I'm one of those people who just don't want to get involved.'

I was lost in something, possibly thought, when a key turned in one of the locks. The sound was repeated as someone opened the other two locks in turn, and I spent a couple of seconds trying to decide what I'd do if it wasn't Carolyn. Suppose it was the Nazi, coming to swipe the other cat. I looked around for Ubi but didn't see him, and then the door swung inward and I turned to look at Carolyn and Elspeth Peters.

Except it wasn't Elspeth Peters, and all it took was a second glance to make that clear to me. But I could see why my henchperson had taken a second glance at the Peters woman, because the resemblance was pronounced.

I could also see why she'd taken more than a couple glances at this woman, who obviously had to be Alison the tax planner. She was at least as attractive as Elspeth Peters, and the airy quality of Ms Peters that went so well with old-timey lady poets and secondhand books was replaced in Alison by an earthy intensity. Carolyn introduced us – 'Alison, this is Bernie Rhodenbarr. Bernie, this is Alison Warren' – and Alison established her credentials as a political and economic lesbian with a firm no-nonsense handshake.

'I didn't expect you,' Carolyn said.

'Well, I stopped in to use the shower.'

'Right, you were running.'

'Oh, you're a runner?' Alison said.

We got a little mileage out of that, so to speak, and Carolyn put some coffee on, and Alison sat down on the couch and Ubi turned up and sat in her lap. I went over to the stove, where Carolyn was fussing with the coffee.

'Isn't she nice?' she whispered.

'She's terrific,' I whispered back. 'Get rid of her.'

'You've got to be kidding.'

'Nope.'

'Why, for Christ's sake?'

'We're going to the museum. The Hewlett.'

'Now?'

'Now.'

'Look, I just got her here. She's all settled in with a cat on her lap. The least I can do is give her a cup of coffee.'

'Okay,' I said, still whispering. 'I'll split now. Get away as soon as you can and meet me in front of the Hewlett.'

*

699

When I handed over my two singles and two quarters, the attendant at the Hewlett was nice enough to point out that the gallery would be closing in less than an hour. I told him that was all right and accepted my lapel pin in return. The whole exchange brought the late Mr Turnquist to life for me, and I remembered the fierce animation with which he'd lectured to us about art. I suppose I'd depersonalized the man in order to drag his body across town and dump him, and I guess it had been necessary, but now I saw him again as a person – quirky and abrasive and vividly human – and I felt sorry he was dead and sorrier that I'd used him after death as a prop in a macabre farce.

The feeling was a dismal one and I shook it off as I made my way to the upstairs gallery where the Mondrian was on display. I entered with a perfunctory nod at the uniformed guard. I half expected to find a blank spot on the wall where *Composition With Color* had lately hung, or another painting altogether, but Mondrian was right where he belonged and I was glad to see him again.

Half an hour later a voice at my elbow said, 'Well, it's good, Bernie, but I don't think it would fool many people. It's hard to make a pencil sketch look like an oil painting. What are you doing?'

'Sketching the painting,' I said, without looking up from my notebook. 'I'm guessing at the measurements.'

'What are the initials for? Oh, the colors, right?'

'Right.'

'What's the point?'

'I don't know.'

'The guy downstairs didn't want to take my money. The place is gonna close any minute. What I did, I gave him a dollar. Are we gonna steal the painting, Bernie?'

'Yes.'

'Now?'

'Of course not.'

'Oh. When?'

'I don't know.'

'I don't suppose you know how we're gonna do it, either.'

'I'm working on it.'

'By drawing in your notebook?'

'Shit,' I said, and closed the notebook with a snap. 'Let's get out of here.'

'I'm sorry, Bern. I didn't mean to hassle you.'

'It's okay. Let's get out of here.'

We found a bar called Gloryosky's a couple of blocks up Madison. Soft lighting, deep carpet, chrome and black formica, and some Little Orphan Annie murals on the walls. About half the patrons were gulping their first après-work drinks while the rest looked as though they hadn't made it back from lunch. Everybody was thanking God that it was Friday.

'This is nice,' Carolyn said as we settled into a booth. 'Dim lights, gaiety, laughter, the clink of ice cubes and a Peggy Lee record on the jukebox. I could be happy here, Bernie.'

'Cute waitress, too.'

'I noticed. This joint has it all over the Bum Rap. It's a shame it's so far from the store.' The waitress appeared and leaned forward impressively. Carolyn gave her a full-tilt smile and ordered a martini, very cold, very dry, and very soon. I asked for Coca-Cola and lemon. The waitress smiled and departed.

'Why?' Carolyn demanded.

'Pardon?'

'Why Coke with lemon?'

'It cuts some of the sugary taste.'

'Why Coke in the first place?'

I shrugged. 'Oh, I don't know. I guess I'm not in the mood for Perrier. Plus I figure I can use a little sugar rush and a caffeine hit.'

'Bern, are you being willfully obtuse?'

'Huh? Oh. Why no booze?'

'Right.'

I shrugged again. 'No particular reason.'

'You're gonna try breaking into the museum? That's crazy.'

'I know, and I'm not going to try. But whatever I do I've got a complicated evening coming up and I guess I want to be at the top of my form. Such as it is.'

'Myself, I figure I'm better with a couple of drinks.'

'Maybe you are.'

'Not to mention the fact that I couldn't survive another ten minutes without one. Ah, here we are,' she said, as our drinks appeared. 'You can tell him to start mixing up another of these,' she told the waitress, 'because I wouldn't want to get too far out in front of him.'

'Another round.'

'Just another martini,' she said. 'He's got to sip that. Didn't your mother ever tell you? Never gulp anything fizzy.'

I squeezed the lemon into the Coke, stirred and sipped. 'She's got a great laugh,' Carolyn said. 'I like a girl with a nice sense of humor.'

'And a nice set of—'

'Those too. There's a lot to be said for curves, even if your buddy Mondrian didn't believe in them. Straight lines and primary colors. You think he was a genius?'

'Probably.'

'Whatever genius is. As far as having something to hang on the wall, I'm a lot happier with my Chagall litho.'

'That's funny.'

'What is?'

'Before,' I said. 'Standing in front of the painting, I was thinking how great it would look in my apartment.'

'Where?'

'Over the couch. Sort of centered over the couch.'

'Oh yeah?' She closed her eyes, trying to picture it. 'The painting we just saw? Or the one you saw in Onderdonk's apartment?'

'Well, the one we just saw. But the other was the same idea and the same general proportions, so it would do, too.'

'Over the couch.'

'Right.'

'You know, it might look kind of nice in your place,' she said. 'Once all this mess is cleared away, you know what you'll have to do?'

'Yeah,' I said. 'Something like one-to-ten.'

'One-to-ten?'

'Years.'

'Oh,' she said, and dismissed the entire penal system with an airy wave of her hand. 'I'm serious, Bern. Once everything's cleared up, you can sit down and paint yourself a Mondrian and hang it over the couch.'

'Oh, come on.'

'I mean it. Face it, Bern. What old Piet did back there doesn't look all that hard to do. Okay, he was a genius because he thought of it first, and his proportions and colors were brilliant and perfect and fit into some philosophical system, whatever it was, but so what? If all you're looking to do is make a copy for your own place, how hard could it be to follow his measurements and copy his colors and just paint it? I mean there's no drawing involved, there's no shading, there's no changes in texture. It's just a white canvas with black lines and patches of color. You wouldn't have to spend ten years at the Art Students League to do that, would you?'

'What a thought,' I said. 'It's probably harder than it looks.'

'Everything's harder than it looks. Grooming a Shih Tzu's harder than it looks, but you don't have to be a genius. Where's that sketch you made? Couldn't you follow the dimensions and paint it on canvas?'

'I can paint a wall with a roller. That's about it.'

'Why'd you make the sketch?'

'Because there's too many paintings,' I said, 'and unless they're side by side I couldn't tell them apart, Mondrian being Mondrian, and I thought a sketch might be useful for identification purposes. If I ever see any picture besides the one in the Hewlett. I couldn't do it.'

'Couldn't do what?'

'Paint a fake Mondrian. I wouldn't know what to do. All the black bands are straight like a knife edge. How would you manage that?'

'I suppose you'd need a steady hand.'

'There must be more to it than that. And I wouldn't know how to buy paints, let alone mix colors.'

'You could learn.'

'An artist could do it,' I said.

'Sure. If you knew the technique, and—'

'It's a shame we didn't get to Turnquist before he died. He was an artist and he admired Mondrian.'

'Well, he's not the only artist in New York City. If you want a Mondrian for over the couch and you don't want to try painting it yourself, I'm sure you could find someone to—'

'I'm not talking about a Mondrian for my apartment.'

'You're not? Oh.'

'Right.'

'You mean—'

'Right.'

'Where's the waitress, dammit? A person could die of thirst around here.'

'She's coming.'

'Good. I don't think it'll work, Bern. I was talking about making something that'd look good over your couch, not something that would fool experts. Besides, where would we find an artist we could trust?'

'Good point.'

The waitress arrived, setting a fresh martini in front of Carolyn and having a look at my Coke, which was still half full. Or half empty, if you're a pessimist.

'That's perfect,' Carolyn told her. 'I bet you used to be a nurse, didn't you?'

'That's nothing,' she said. 'It's supposed to be a secret, but I just know you won't tell anyone. The bartender used to be a brain surgeon.'

'He hasn't lost his touch. It's a good thing I've got Blue Cross.'

The waitress did her exit-laughing number, taking Carolyn's eyes with her. 'She's cute,' said my partner in crime.

'A shame she's not an artist.'

'Clever repartee, a great personality, and a nifty set of wheels. You figure she's gay?'

'Hope does spring eternal, doesn't it?'

'That's what they tell me.'

'Gay or straight,' I said, 'what we really need is an artist.'

The whole room seemed to go silent, as if someone had just mentioned E. F. Hutton. Except that other conversations were still going on. It's just that we stopped hearing them. Carolyn and I both froze, then turned our eyes slowly to meet one another's exophthalmic gazes. After a long moment we spoke as if in a single voice.

'Denise,' we said.

17

'Hold this,' Denise Raphaelson said. 'You know, I can't remember the last time I stretched a canvas. Who bothers nowadays? You buy a stretched canvas and save yourself the aggravation. Of course I don't usually get customers who specify the size they want in centimeters.'

'It's becoming a metric universe.'

'Well, you know what I always say. Give 'em a gram and they'll take a kilo. This should be close, Bernie, and anybody who takes a yardstick to this beauty will already have six other ways to tell it's not the real thing. But the measurements'll be very close. Maybe it'll be a couple millimeters off. Remember that cigarette that advertised it was a silly millimeter longer?'

'I remember.'

'I wonder whatever happened to it.'

'Somebody probably smoked it.'

Denise was smoking one of her own, or letting it burn unattended in a scallop shell she used as an ashtray. We were at her place and we were stretching a canvas. *We* meant Denise and me. Carolyn had not accompanied me.

Denise is long limbed and slender, with dark brown curly hair and fair skin lightly dusted with freckles. She is a painter, and she does well enough at it to support herself and her son Jared, with the occasional assistance of a child-support check from Jared's father. Her work is abstract, very vivid, very intense, very energetic. You might not like her canvases but you'd be hard put to ignore them.

And, come to think of it, you could say much the same of their creator. Denise and I had kept occasional company over a couple of years, sharing a fondness for ethnic food and thoughtful jazz and snappy repartee. Our one area of disagreement was Carolyn, whom she affected to despise. Then one day Denise and Carolyn commenced to have an affair. That didn't take too long to run its course, and once it was over Carolyn didn't see Denise anymore, and neither did I.

I could say I don't understand women, but what's so remarkable about that? Nobody does.

*

'This is gesso,' Denise explained. 'We want a smooth canvas so we put this on. Here, take the brush. That's right. A nice even coat. It's all in the wrist, Bernie.'

'What does this do?'

'It dries. It's acrylic gesso so it'll dry in a hurry. Then you sand it.'

'I sand it?'

'With sandpaper. Lightly. Then you do another coat of the gesso and sand it again, and a third coat and sand it again.'

'And you on the opposite shore will be?'

'That's it. Ready to ride and spread the alarm through every something village and farm.'

'Every Middlesex village and farm,' I said, which was the way Longfellow had put it. *Middlesex* sort of hung in the air between us. 'It comes from Middle Saxons,' I said. 'According to where they settled in England. Essex was the East Saxons, Sussex was the South Saxons, and—'

'Leave it alone.'

'All right.'

' "Every bisexual village and farm." I suppose No Sex was the North Saxons, huh?'

'I thought we were going to leave it alone.'

'It's like a scab, it's irresistible. I'm going to see if I can't find a book with the painting reproduced. *Composition With Color*, 1942. God knows how many paintings he did with that title. There's a minimalist I know on Harrison Street who calls everything he paints Composition #104. It's his favorite number. If he ever amounts to anything, the art historians are going to go batshit trying to straighten it all out.'

I was sanding the third coat of gesso when she returned with a large book entitled *Mondrian and the Art of De Stijl*. She flipped it open to a page near the end, and there was the painting we'd seen in the Hewlett. 'That's it,' I said.

'How are the colors?'

'What do you mean? Aren't they in the right place? I thought you took my sketch along.'

'Yes, and it's a wonderful sketch. Burglary's gain was the art world's loss. Books of reproductions are never perfect, Bernie. The inks never duplicate the paint a hundred percent. How do these colors compare to what you saw in the painting?'

'Oh,' I said.

'Well?'

'I don't have that kind of an eye, Denise. Or that kind of a memory. I think this looks about right.' I held the book at arm's length, tilted it to catch the light. 'The background's darker than I remember it. It was whiter in – I want to say real life, but that's not what I mean. You know what I mean.'

She nodded. 'Mondrian used off-whites. He tinted his white with a little blue, a little red, a little yellow. I can probably make up something that looks sort of all right. I hope this isn't going to have to fool an expert.'

'So do I.'

'Let me see how you did with the gesso. That's not bad. I think what we want now is a coat or two of white, just to get that smooth canvas effect, and then a coat of tinted white, and then – I wish I could have like two weeks to work on this.'

'So do I.'

'I'm going to use acrylics, obviously. Liquid acrylics. He used oils but he didn't have some lunatic at his elbow who wanted the finished painting in a matter of hours. Acrylics dry fast but they're not oils and—'

'Denise?'

'What?'

'There's no point making ourselves crazy. We'll just give it our best shot. Okay?'

'Okay.'

'I've got a few things to do, but I can come back after I do them.'

'I can handle this myself, Bernie. I don't need help.'

'Well, I was thinking while I was putting the gesso on the canvas. There are a few things I can be doing at the same time.'

'Only one person can work on a canvas at a time.'

'I know that. See how this sounds to you.'

I told her what I had in mind. She listened and nodded, and when I finished she didn't say anything but stopped to light a cigarette. She smoked it almost to the filter before she spoke.

'Sounds elaborate,' she said.

'I guess it is.'

'Complicated. I think I see what you're getting at, but I've got the feeling I'm better off not knowing too much. Is that possible?'

'It's possible.'

'I think I want music,' she said, and lit another cigarette and switched on her radio, which was tuned to one of the FM jazz stations. I recognized the record they were playing, a solo piano recording of Randy Weston's.

'Brings back memories,' I said.

'Doesn't it? Jared's over at a friend's house. He'll be home within the hour. He can help.'

'Great.'

'I love the Hewlett Collection. Of course Jared had a fierce resentment against the place.'

'Why?'

'Because he's a kid. Kids aren't allowed, remember?'

'Oh, right. Not even accompanied by an adult?'

'Not even accompanied by the front four of the Pittsburgh Steelers. Nobody under sixteen, no exceptions, nohow.'

'That does seem a little high-handed,' I said. 'How's a kid supposed to develop an appreciation for art in this town?'

'Oh, it's real tough, Bernie. Outside of the Met and the Modern and the Guggenheim and the Whitney and the Museum of Natural History and a couple of hundred private galleries, a young person in New York is completely bereft of cultural resources. It's really hell.'

'If I didn't know better, I'd swear you were being sarcastic.'

'Me? Not in a million years.' She sucked on her cigarette. 'I'll tell you, it's a pleasure to go in there and not have eight million kids bouncing off the walls. Or class groups, with some brain-damaged teacher explaining at eighty decibels what Matisse had in mind while thirty kids fidget around, bored out of their basketball sneakers. The Hewlett's a museum for grownups and I love it.'

'But Jared doesn't.'

'He will the day he turns sixteen. Meanwhile it has the lure of forbidden fruit. I think he must be convinced it's the world's storehouse of erotic art and that's why he's not allowed in it. What *I* like about the place, aside from the childless aspect and the quality of the collection, is the way the paintings are hung. Hanged? Hung?'

'Whatever.'

'Hung,' she said decisively. 'Murderers are hanged, or they used to be. Paintings and male models are hung. There's plenty of space between the paintings at the Hewlett. You can look at them one at a time.' She looked meaningfully at me. 'What I'm trying to say,' she said, 'is I have a special feeling for the place.'

'I understand.'

'Assure me once more that this is in a good cause.'

'You'll be helping to ransom a cat and keep an antiquarian bookman out of jail.'

'Screw the bookman. Which cat is it? The Siamese?'

'You mean Burmese. Archie.'

'Right. The friendly one.'

'They're both friendly. Archie's just more outgoing.'

'Same difference.'

Randy Weston had given way to Chick Corea, and now that record had also ended and a young man with an untrained voice was bringing us the news. The first item had to do with progress in some arms-limitations talks, which may have had global importance but which I must admit I didn't pay heed to, and then the little big mouth was telling us that an anonymous tip had led police to the body of a man identified as Edwin P. Turnquist in a West Village warehouse. Turnquist had been stabbed in the heart, probably with an icepick. He was an artist and a latter-day bohemian who'd hung out with the early Abstract Expressionists at the old Cedar Tavern, and who'd been living at the time of his death in an SRO rooming house in Chelsea.

That would have been plenty, but he wasn't finished. Prime suspect in the case, he added, was one Bernard Rhodenbarr, a Manhattan bookseller with several arrests for burglary. Rhodenbarr was out on bail after having been charged with homicide in the death of Gordon Kyle Onderdonk just days ago at the fashionable and exclusive Charlemagne Apartments. Onderdonk was presumed to have been murdered in the course of a burglary, but Rhodenbarr's motive for the murder of Turnquist had not yet been disclosed by police sources. 'Perhaps,' the little twerp suggested, 'Mr Turnquist was a man who knew too much.'

I went over and turned off the radio, and the ensuing silence stretched out like the sands of the Sahara. It was broken at length by the flick of a Bic as Denise kindled yet another cigarette. Through a cloud of smoke she said, 'The name Turnquist rings a muted bell.'

'I thought it might.'

'What was his first name – Edwin? I still never heard of him. Except in that conversation we never had.'

'Uh.'

'You didn't kill him, did you, Bernie?'

'No.'

'Or that other man? Onderdonk?'

'No.'

'But you're in this up to your eyeballs, aren't you?'

'Up to my hairline.'

'And the police are looking for you.'

'So it would seem. It would be, uh, best if they didn't find me. I used up all my cash posting a bond the other day. Not that any judge would let me out on bail this time around.'

'And if you're in a cell on Rikers Island, how can you right wrongs and catch killers and liberate pussycats?'

'Right.'

'What do they call what I am? Accessory after the fact?'

I shook my head. 'Unwitting accomplice. You never turned the radio on. If I get out of this, there won't be any charges, Denise.'

'And if you don't?'

'Er.'

'Forget I asked. How's Carolyn holding up?'

'Carolyn? She'll be okay.'

'Funny the turns human lives take.'

'Uh-huh.'

708

She tapped the canvas. 'The one in the Hewlett's not framed? Just a canvas on a stretcher?'

'Right. The design continues around the edge.'

'Well, he painted that way sometimes. Not always but sometimes. This whole business is crazy, Bernie. You know that, don't you?'

'Yeah.'

'All the same,' she said, 'it just might work.'

18

It was somewhere around eleven when I left the Narrowback Gallery. Denise had offered me the hospitality of the couch but I was afraid to accept it. The police were looking for me and I didn't want to be any-place they might think of looking. Carolyn was the only person who knew I'd gone to Denise's, and she wouldn't talk unless they lit matches underneath her fingernails, but suppose they did? And she might let it slip to a friend – Alison, for instance – and the friend might prove less closemouthed.

For that matter, the police might not need a tip. Ray knew Denise and I had kept company in the past, and if they went through the routine of checking all known associates of the suspect, the fat would be in the fire.

Meanwhile it was in the frying pan and I was on the street. In an hour or so the bulldog edition of the *Daily News* would also be on the street, and it would very likely have my picture in it. For the time being I was my usual anonymous self, but I didn't feel anonymous; walking through SoHo, I found myself seeking shadows and shrinking from the imagined stares of passersby. Or perhaps the stares weren't imagined. Spend enough time shrinking in shadows and people are apt to stare at you.

On Wooster Street I found a telephone booth. A real one, for a change, with a door that drew shut, not one of those new improved numbers that leaves you exposed to the elements. Such booths have become rare to the point that some citizen had failed to recognize this particular one for what it was, mistaking it instead for a public lavatory. I chose privacy over comfort and closed myself within.

When I did this, a little light went on – literally, not figuratively. I loosened a couple of screws in the overhead fixture, took down a sheet of translucent plastic, and unscrewed the bulb a few turns, then put the plastic back and tightened the screws. Now I was not in the spotlight, which was fine for me. I called Information, then dialed the number the operator gave me.

I got the precinct where Ray Kirschmann hangs his hat, except that he doesn't, given as he is to wearing it indoors. He wasn't there. I called

Information again and reached him at his house in Sunnyside. His wife answered and put him on without asking my name. He said 'Hello?' and I said, 'Ray?' and he said, 'Jesus. The man of the hour. You gotta stop killin' people, Bernie. It's a bad habit and who knows what it could lead to, you know what I mean?'

'I didn't kill Turnquist.'

'Right, you never heard of him.'

'I didn't say that.'

'Good, because he had a slip of paper with your name and the address of your store in his pocket.'

Could it be? Had I overlooked something that incriminating in my search of the dead man's pockets? I wondered about it, and then I remembered something and closed my eyes.

'Bernie? You there?'

I hadn't searched his pockets. I'd been so busy getting rid of him I hadn't taken five minutes to go through his clothes.

'Anyway,' he went on, 'we found one of your business cards in his room. And on top of that we got a phone tip shortly after the body was discovered. What we got, we got two phone tips, and I wouldn't be surprised if they were the same person. First one told us where the body was, second said that if we wanted to know who killed Turnquist we should ask a fellow named Rhodenbarr. So what the hell, I'm askin'. Who killed him, Bern?'

'Not me.'

'Uh-huh. We let guys like you out on bail and what do you do but commit more crimes? I can see gettin' carried away with a big hulk like Onderdonk, havin' to hit him and hittin' too hard. But shovin' an icepick in a shrimp like Turnquist, that's a pretty low thing to do.'

'I didn't do it.'

'I suppose you didn't search his room, either.'

'I don't even know where it is, Ray. One of the reasons I called you was to get his address.'

'He had ID in his pocket. You coulda got it off that.'

Shit, I thought. Everything had been in Turnquist's pockets but my two hands.

'Anyway,' he said, 'why'd you want his address?'

'I thought I might—'

'Go search his room.'

'Well, yes,' I admitted. 'To find the real killer.'

'Somebody already turned his room inside out, Bernie. If it wasn't you, then it was somebody else.'

'Well, it certainly wasn't me. You found my card there, didn't you? When I search dead men's rooms I don't make a point of leaving a calling card.'

'You don't make a point of killin' people, either. Maybe the shock left you careless.'

'You don't believe that yourself, Ray.'

'No, I don't guess I do. But they got an APB out on you, Bernie, and your bail's revoked, and you better turn yourself in or you're in deep shit. Where are you now? I'll come get you, make sure you can surrender yourself with no hassles.'

'You're forgetting the reward. How can I come up with the painting if I'm in a cell?'

'You think you got a shot at it?'

'I think so, yes.'

There was a lengthy pause, as pride warred with greed while he weighed an impressive arrest against a highly hypothetical $17,500. 'I don't like telephones,' he said. 'Maybe we should talk it over face to face.'

I started to say something but a recording cut in to tell me my three minutes were up. It was still babbling when I broke the connection.

There wasn't a single acceptable movie on Forty-second Street. There are eight or ten theaters on the stretch between Sixth and Eighth Avenues and the ones that weren't showing porn featured epics like *The Texas Chain-Saw Massacre* and *Eaten Alive by Lemmings*. Well, it figured. Get rid of sex and violence and how would you know Times Square was the Crossroads of the World?

I settled on a house near Eighth Avenue where a pair of kung fu movies were playing. I'd never seen one before, and all along I'd had the right idea. But it was dark inside, and half empty, and I couldn't think of a safer place to pass a few hours. If the cops were really working at it, they'd have circulated my picture to the hotels. The papers would be on the street any minute. A person could sleep on the subway, but transit cops tend to look at you, and even if they didn't I'd have felt safer curling up on the third rail.

I took a seat off to one side and just sat there looking at the screen. There wasn't much dialogue, just sound effects when people got their chests kicked in or fell through plate glass windows, and the audience was generally quiet except for murmurs of approval when someone came to a dramatically bad end, which happened rather often.

I sat there and watched for a while. At some point I dozed off and at another I woke up. The same movie may have been playing, or it might have been the other one. I let the on-screen violence hypnotize me, and before I knew it I was thinking about everything that had happened and how it had all started with a refined gentleman turning up at my shop and inviting me to appraise his library. What a civilized incident, I thought, with such a brutal aftermath.

Wait a minute.

712

I sat up straighter in my seat and blinked as a wild-eyed Oriental chap on the screen smashed a woman's face with his elbow. I scarcely noticed. Instead, in my mind I saw Gordon Onderdonk greeting me at the door of his apartment, unfastening the chain lock, drawing the door wide to admit me. And other images played one after another across the retina of the mind, while snatches of a dozen different conversations echoed in accompaniment.

For a few minutes there my mind raced along as though I'd just brewed up a whole potful of espresso and injected it straight into a vein. All of the events of the past few days suddenly fell into place. And, on the screen in front of me, agile young men made remarkable leaps and stunning pirouettes and kicked and slashed and chopped the living crap out of each other.

I dozed off again, and in due course I awoke again, and after sitting up and blinking a bit I remembered the mental connections I'd made. I thought them through and they still made as much sense as ever, and I marveled at the way everything had come to me.

It struck me, on my way up the aisle to the exit, that I might have dreamed the whole solution. But I couldn't really see that it made very much difference. Either way it fit. And either way I had a lot to do.

19

I stood in a doorway on West End Avenue and watched a couple of runners on their way to the park. When they'd cantered on by I leaned out a ways and fixed an eye on the entrance to my building. I kept it in view, and after a few minutes a familiar shape emerged. She walked to the curb, the ever-present cigarette bobbing in the corner of her mouth. At first she started to turn north, and I started to wince, and then she turned south and walked half a block and crossed the street and made her way to me.

She was Mrs Hesch, my across-the-hall neighbor, an ever-available source of coffee and solace. 'Mr Rhodenbarr,' she said now. 'It's good you called me. I was worried. You wouldn't believe the things those *momsers* are saying about you.'

'Just so you don't believe them, Mrs Hesch.'

'Me? God forbid. I know you, Mr Rhodenbarr. What you do is your business – a man has to make a living. And when it comes to neighbors you can't be beat. You're a nice young man. You wouldn't kill any-body.'

'Of course I wouldn't.'

'So what can I do for you?'

I gave her my keys, explained which one went in which lock, and told her what I needed. She was back fifteen minutes later with a shopping bag and a word of caution. 'There's a man in the lobby,' she said. 'Regular clothes, no uniform, but I think he's an Irisher and he looks like a cop.'

'He's probably both of those things.'

'And there's two men, also looking like cops, in that dark green car over there.'

'I already spotted them.'

'I got the suit you told me and a clean shirt, and I picked you out a nice tie to go with it. Also socks and underwear which you didn't mention but I figure what does it hurt? Also the other things which I don't have to know what they are, and how you use them to open locks I don't want to know, but it's clever where you keep them, behind the

714

fake electric outlet. You could fix me a place like that to keep things in?'

'First thing next week, if I can just stay out of jail.'

'Because the burglaries lately have been something awful. You put on that good lock for me, but even so.'

'I'll fix you up with a hidey hole first chance I get, Mrs Hesch.'

'Not that I got the Hope Diamond upstairs, but why take chances? You're all right now, Mr Rhodenbarr?'

'I think so,' I said.

I changed clothes in a coffee shop lavatory, tucked my burglar's tools into various pockets, and left my dirty clothes in the wastebasket. The British would have called it a dustbin, and who had told me so recently? Turnquist, and Turnquist was dead now, with an icepick in his heart.

I bought a disposable razor in a drugstore, made quick use of it in another coffee shop restroom, and promptly disposed of it. The same drugstore sold me a pair of sunglasses rather like the ones Turnquist had worn when we wheeled him across town. I'd worn them myself on the way back to the store, and they were there now on a shelf in my back room, and it struck me as curious that I'd bought two pairs of drugstore sunglasses in as many days. In the ordinary course of things, years would go by before I bought a pair of sunglasses.

The day was overcast and I wasn't sure the sunglasses helped; they might hide my eyes, but at the same time they drew a certain amount of attention. I wore them for the time being and rode the subway downtown to Fourteenth Street. Between Fifth and Seventh Avenues there are schlock stores of every description, selling junk at cut-rate prices, their wares spilling out onto the sidewalk. One had a table piled high with clear-lensed sunglasses. People who wanted to save an optician's fee could try on pair after pair until they found something that seemed to help.

I tried on pair after pair until I found a heavy horn-rimmed pair that didn't seem to distort things at all. Nonprescription glasses always look like stage props because of the way the light glints off them, but these glasses would disguise my appearance reasonably well without looking like a disguise. I bought them, and a few doors down the street I tried on hats until I found a dark gray fedora that looked and felt right.

I bought a knish and a Coke from a Sabrett vendor, tried to tell myself I was eating breakfast, made a couple of phone calls, and was at the corner of Third Avenue and Twenty-third Street when a rather battered Chevy pulled up. The way the man steals, you'd think he could afford a flashier automobile.

'I looked right at you an' didn't recognize you,' he said as I got into the front seat next to him. 'You oughta put on a suit more often. It

715

looks nice. Of course you ruin the whole effect wearin' runnin' shoes with it.'

'Lots of people wear running shoes with a suit these days, Ray.'

'Lotsa guys eat peas with a knife but that don't make it right. The hat an' the glasses, you look like a tout at Aqueduct. What I oughta do, Bern, I oughta take you in. You'll be outta trouble and I'll wind up with a citation.'

'Wouldn't you rather wind up with a reward?'

'You call it a reward and I call it two in the bush.' He sighed the sigh of the long-suffering. 'This is crazy, what you're askin'.'

'I know.'

'But I played along with you in the past, and I gotta admit it paid off more'n it didn't.' He looked at the hat, the glasses, the running shoes, and he shook his head. 'I wish you looked a little more like a cop,' he said.

'This way I look like a cop wearing a disguise.'

'Well, it's some disguise,' he said. 'It'd fool anybody.'

He left the car in a no-parking zone and we walked up a flight of stairs and down a corridor. Periodically Ray pulled out his shield and showed it to somebody who passed us on through. Then we took an elevator down to the basement.

When you're a civilian and you show up to identify a body, you wait on the first floor and they bring up the late lamented on an elevator. When you're a cop they save time and let you go down to the basement, where they pull out a drawer and give you a peek. The attendant, a whey-faced little man who hadn't seen the sun since he posed for Charles Addams, pulled a card from a file, led us across a large and silent room, and opened a drawer for us.

I took one look and said, 'This isn't the right one.'

'Gotta be,' the attendant said.

'Then why does the toe tag say *Velez, Concepción?*'

The attendant examined it himself and scratched his head. 'I don't get it,' he said. 'This is 228-B and right here on the card it says—' he looked at us accusingly '—it says 328-B.'

'So?'

'So,' he said.

He led the way and pulled out another drawer, and this time the toe tag said *Onderdonk, Gordon K*. Ray and I stood looking in companionable silence. Then he asked me if I'd seen enough, and I said I had, and he spoke to the attendant and told him to close the drawer.

On the way upstairs I said, 'Can you find out if he was drugged?'

'Drugged?'

'Seconal or something. Wouldn't it show in an autopsy?'

'Only if somebody went looking for it. You come across a guy with

716

his head beaten in, you examine him and determine that's what killed him, hell, you don't go an' check to see if he also had diabetes.'

'Have them check for drugs.'

'Why?'

'A hunch.'

'A hunch. I'd feel better about your hunches if you didn't look like a racetrack tout. Seconal, huh?'

'Any kind of sedative.'

'I'll have 'em check. Where do we go from here, Bernie?'

'Separate ways,' I said.

I called Carolyn and let her carry on for a few minutes until her panic played itself out. 'I'm going to need your help,' I said. 'You're going to have to create a diversion.'

'That's my specialty,' she said. 'What do you want me to do?'

I told her and went over it a couple of times, and she said it sounded like something she could handle. 'It would be better if you had help,' I said. 'Would Alison help you?'

'She might. How much would I have to tell her?'

'As little as possible. If you have to, tell her I'm going to be trying to steal a painting from the museum.'

'I can tell her that?'

'If you have to. In the meantime – I wonder. Maybe you should close the Poodle Factory and go over to her house. Where does she live, anyway?'

'Brooklyn Heights. Why should I go there, Bern?'

'So you won't be where the cops can hassle you. Is Alison with you now?'

'No.'

'Where is she, at home?'

'She's at her office. Why?'

'No reason. You don't happen to know her address in Brooklyn Heights, do you?'

'I don't remember it, but I know the building. It's on Pineapple Street.'

'But you don't know the number.'

'What's the difference? Oh, I bet you're looking for a place to hole up, aren't you?'

'Good thinking.'

'Well, her place is nice. I was there last night.'

'So that's where you were. I tried you early this morning and I couldn't reach you. Wait a minute. You were at Alison's last night?'

'What's the matter with that? What are you, the Mother Superior, Bern?'

'No, I'm just surprised, that's all. You'd never been there before, had you?'

'No.'

'And it's nice?'

'It's very nice. What's so surprising about that? Tax planners make a decent living. Their clients tend to have money or else they wouldn't have to worry about taxes.'

'It seems to me everybody has to worry about taxes. You saw the whole apartment? The, uh, bedroom and everything?'

'What the hell is that supposed to mean? There's no bedroom, what she's got is a giant studio. It's about eight hundred square feet but it's all one room. Why?'

'No reason.'

'Is this a roundabout way of asking me if we slept together? Because that's none of your business.'

'I know.'

'So?'

'Well, you're right about it being none of my business,' I said, 'but you're my best friend and I don't want to see you get hurt.'

'I'm not in love with her, Bern.'

'Good.'

'And yes, we slept together. I figured she was used to men hassling her and conning her and trying to exploit her, so I picked my strategy accordingly.'

'What did you do?'

'I told her I'd only put the tip in.'

'And now you're at the Poodle Factory.'

'Right.'

'And she's at her office.'

'Right.'

'And I'm wasting my time worrying about you.'

'Listen,' she said, 'I'm touched. I really am.'

I cabbed down to the Narrowback Gallery, wearing the sunglasses so that the driver wouldn't see anything recognizable in his rear-view mirror. When I got out I switched to my other glasses so I'd be less conspicuous. I was still wearing the hat.

Jared opened the door, took in the glasses and the hat, then looked down at what I was carrying. 'That's pretty neat,' he said. 'You can carry anything in there and people figure it's an animal. What have you got in there, burglar tools?'

'Nope.'

'I bet it's swag, then.'

'Huh?'

'Swag. Loot. Plunder. Can I see?'

718

'Sure,' I said, and opened the clasps and lifted the hinged top.

'It's empty,' he said.

'Disappointing, huh?'

'Very.' We moved on into the loft, where Denise was touching up a canvas. I examined what she'd done in my absence and told her I was impressed.

'You ought to be,' she said. 'We worked all night, both of us. I don't think we got an hour's sleep between us. What have you been doing in the meantime?'

'Staying out of jail.'

'Well, keep on doing it. Because when all of this is history I expect a substantial reward. I won't settle for a good dinner and a night on the town.'

'You won't have to.'

'You can throw in dinner and a night out as a bonus, but if there's a pot of gold at the end of this rainbow, I want a share.'

'You'll get it,' I assured her. 'When will all this stuff be ready?'

'Couple hours.'

'Two hours, say?'

'Should be.'

'Good,' I said. And I called Jared over and explained what I had in mind for him. A variety of expressions played over his face.

'I don't know,' he said.

'You could organize it, couldn't you? Get some of your friends together.'

'Lionel would go for it,' Denise suggested. 'And what about Pegeen?'

'Maybe,' he said. 'I don't know. What would I get?'

'What do you want? Your pick of every science fiction book that comes through my store for the next – how long? The next year?'

'I don't know,' he said. He sounded about as enthusiastic as if I'd offered him a lifetime supply of cauliflower.

'Make sure you get a good deal,' his mother told him. 'Because you'll have a lot to handle. I wouldn't be surprised if there's a TV news crew. If you're the leader you'll be the one they interview.'

'Really?'

'Stands to reason,' she said.

He thought about it for a moment. I started to say something but Denise silenced me with a hand. 'If somebody made a couple of phone calls,' Jared said, 'then they'd know to have camera crews there.'

'Good idea.'

'I'll get Lionel,' he said. 'And Jason Stone and Shaheen and Sean Glick and Adam. Pegeen's at her father's for the weekend, but I'll get – I know who I'll get.'

'All right.'

'And we'll need signs,' he said. 'Bernie? What time?'

'Four-thirty.'

'We'll never make the six o'clock news.'

'You'll make the eleven o'clock.'

'You're right. And not that many people watch the six o'clock on Saturday anyway.'

He tore off down the stairs. 'That was terrific,' I told Denise.

'It was wonderful. Look, if you can't manipulate your own kid, what kind of a parent are you?' She moved in front of one of the canvases, frowned at it. 'What do you think?'

'I think it looks perfect.'

'Well, it doesn't look perfect,' she said, 'but it doesn't look bad, does it?'

20

It was lunch hour when I hit the downtown financial district. The narrow streets were full of people. Stock clerks and office girls, those vital cogs in the wheel of free enterprise, passed skinny cigarettes from hand to hand and smoked their little capitalist brains out. Older men in three-piece suits shook their heads at all of this and dove into bars for sanctuary and solace.

I made a phone call. When no one answered I joined the take-out line at a luncheonette and emerged with two sandwiches and a container of coffee in a brown paper bag. I carried it into the lobby of a ten-story office building on Maiden Lane. I was still wearing the hat and the horn-rimmed glasses and carrying the pet carryall that Jared had found so disappointingly empty. I stopped on my way to the elevator to sign *Donald Brown* on the log sheet, entering my destination *(Rm. #702)* and my time of arrival *(12:18)*. I took the elevator to the seventh floor and then walked up a flight, having prevaricated about everything but the time. I found the office I was looking for. The lock on the door was rather less challenging than Rubik's Cube. I set down the pet carrier but held the lunch bag in one hand while I opened the door with the other.

Inside the office I sat down at one of those metal desks with a fake wood-grain top and unpacked my lunch. I opened up one sandwich, removed the slices of pastrami and turkey, tore them into small pieces, and arranged them in a pile on the desk top. I ate the other sandwich and drank the coffee, looked up something in the Manhattan phone book, and dialed a number. A woman answered. The voice was familiar but I wanted to be absolutely certain, so I asked to speak to Nathaniel. The voice told me that I had the wrong number.

I made a couple of other calls and talked to some people, and then I dialed 0 and said, 'This is Police Officer Donald Brown, my shield number's 23094, and I need you to get an unlisted number for me.' I told her the name and read off the number I was calling from. She called back less than a minute later and I wrote down the number she gave me. I said, 'Thanks. Oh, and what's the address on that?' and she told me the address. I didn't have to write it down.

I dialed the number. A woman answered. I said, 'This is Bernie. You wouldn't believe how I've missed you.'

'I don't know what you're talking about,' she said.

'Ah, darling,' I said. 'I can't eat, I can't sleep—'

The phone clicked in my ear.

I sighed and dialed another number. I went through channels and then a familiar voice came on the line. 'Okay, give,' it said. 'How'd you know?'

'They found Seconal?'

'Chloral hydrate, the ever-popular Mickey Finn. How'd you take one look at a dead man with his head beaten in and figure drugs? Even on *Quincy* they gotta run tests and stick things in microscopes.'

'I'm working up a new series. *Bernie Rhodenbarr, Psychic Pathologist.*'

We said a few more reasonably pleasant things to one another. I hung up and made a couple more calls, rummaged in some desk drawers and pawed through a filing cabinet. I left the contents of drawers and cabinet as I'd found them. Then I dropped the lunch bag and wrappings in the wastebasket, along with the bread from the pastrami-and-turkey sandwich and the empty coffee container. I opened the case I'd brought along, and a few minutes later I closed it and fastened its clasps.

'Off we go,' I said.

On the way out I checked my watch and entered *12:51* under time of departure.

The sun was out so I switched to sunglasses and caught a cab at the corner of Broadway and John Street. I gave the driver a West Village address. He was a recent arrival from Iran with uncertain English and a very vague sense of the geography of Manhattan, so I guided him and we both got lost. But we wound up on a familiar street and I paid him off and sent him on his way.

I entered a building I'd never been in before, carding my way past the locked vestibule door. I walked through the building to another locked door which led to a rear courtyard. The lock wasn't a problem, and I left part of a toothpick jammed up against the springbolt so it would be even less of a problem on the way back.

The courtyard held some garbage cans and a neglected garden. I crossed it and clambered over a concrete-block fence leading to another courtyard, where I peered into a window, then opened it, and then closed it. I retraced my steps, case in hand, scaling the block fence, retrieving my broken toothpick as I reentered the building, finally emerging on the street and walking a few blocks and catching another cab.

*

Back at the Narrowback Gallery, Jared let me in and eyed the case I was carrying. 'You've still got it,' he said.

'Right you are.'

'*Now* is it filled with swag?'

'See for yourself.'

'Still empty.'

'Uh-huh.'

'What are you going to do with it?'

'Nothing,' I said.

'Nothing?'

'Nothing. You keep it. I'll tell you, I'm sick of carrying the damn thing around.' I walked over to where his mother was eyeing a canvas. 'Looks good,' I said.

'You bet it does. We're lucky Mondrian didn't have acrylics to play with. He could have painted five hundred pictures a year.'

'You mean he didn't?'

'Not quite.'

I extended a finger, touched paint. 'Dry,' I said.

'And as ready as they'll ever be.' She sighed and picked up a menacing-looking implement with a curved blade. I think it's a linoleum knife. I'm not made of linoleum, but I'd certainly hate to irritate somebody who had one of them in his hand. Or her hand, for that matter.

'This goes against the grain,' Denise said. 'You're sure about this?'

'Positive.'

'About an inch? Like about so?'

'That looks good.'

'Well, here goes,' she said, and she began cutting the canvas off the stretcher.

I watched the process. It was unsettling. I'd watched her paint the thing, and I'd painted part of it myself, affixing masking tape to the primed canvas, filling in the lines, peeling off the tape when the quick-drying paint had set. So I knew Mondrian had been no closer to the thing than, say, Rembrandt. Even so, I got a funny feeling in the pit of my stomach as the knife slashed through it as if it were, well, linoleum.

I turned away and went over to where Jared lay stretched out on the floor, writing *UNFAIR!* on a large square of cardboard with an El Marko marking pen. Several completed signs, neatly tacked to strips of wooden lath, leaned up against a metal table. 'Good work,' I told him.

'They should show up well,' he said. 'The media's been alerted.'

'Great.'

'Performance art,' Denise was saying. 'First you paint a picture and then you destroy it. Now all we need is Christo to wrap it in aluminum foil. Shall I wrap it up or will you eat it here?'

'Neither,' I said, and began removing my clothes.

I got to the Hewlett Gallery a few minutes after three, walking a little stiffly in my suit. I was wearing the hat and the clear-lensed horn-rimmed glasses, the latter of which had begun giving me a headache an hour or so earlier. I handed over my suggested contribution of $2.50 without a murmur and went through the turnstile and up a flight of stairs to my favorite gallery.

I'd managed to work up a certain amount of anxiety over the possibility of the Mondrian's having been moved, or removed altogether for loan to the exhibit that was being organized, but *Composition With Color* was right where it was supposed to be. The first thing I thought was that it didn't look anything like what we'd thrown together in Denise's loft, that the proportions and colors were completely wrong, that we'd produced something on a par with a child's crayon copy of the *Mona Lisa*. I looked again and decided that legitimacy, like beauty, is largely in the eye of the beholder. The one on the wall looked right because it was there on the wall, with a little brass plaque by its side to attest to its noble origins.

I just studied it for a while. Then I wandered a bit.

Back on the ground floor, I walked through a room full of Eighteenth-Century French canvases, Boucher and Fragonard, idealized bucolic scenes of fauns and nymphs, shepherds and Bo-Peeps. One canvas showed a pair of barefoot rustics picnicking in a sylvan glade, and studying that canvas under a uniformed guard's watchful gaze were Carolyn and Alison.

'You'll notice,' I murmured to them, 'that both of those little innocents have Morton's Foot.'

'What's that mean?'

'It means their second toes are longer than their big toes,' I said, 'and they'll need special orthotic implants if they're planning to run marathons.'

'They don't look like runners to me,' Carolyn said. 'They look horny as toads, as a matter of fact, and the only kind of marathon they're likely to be in is—'

'Jared and his friends are in position outside,' I cut in. 'Give them five minutes to get started. Okay?'

'Okay.'

In a stall in the men's room I took off my jacket and shirt, then put them on again and walked somewhat less stiffly to the gallery where the Mondrian was hanging. No one paid me any attention because there was a lot of noise and commotion out in front of the building and people were drifting toward the entrance to see what was going on.

The sound of rhythmic chanting rose to my ears. '*Two, four, six, eight! We need art to appreciate!*'

I stepped closer to the Mondrian. Time crawled and the kids went on chanting and I glanced for the thousandth time at my watch and started wondering what they were waiting for when suddenly all hell broke loose.

There was a loud noise like a clap of thunder, or a truck backfiring, or a bomb going off, or, actually, rather like a cherry bomb left over from the Fourth of July. And then, from another direction there was a great deal of smoke and cries of *'Fire! Fire! Run for your lives!'*

Smoke positively billowed. People bolted. And what did I do? I grabbed the Mondrian off the wall and ran into the men's room.

And caromed off a balding fat man who was just emerging from a stall. 'Fire!' I shouted at him. 'Run! Run for your life!'

'My word,' he said, and away he went.

A few minutes later, so did I. I left the men's room and hastened down a flight of stairs and out the main entrance. Fire trucks had drawn up and police were everywhere and Jared and his troops brandished their signs, dodging cops and throwing themselves in front of portable TV cameras. Throughout it all, the Hewlett's security staff kept a tight rein on things, making sure no one walked off with a masterpiece.

I perspired beneath my hat, blinked behind my glasses, and walked right past all of it.

I caught the six o'clock news in a dark and dingy tavern on Third Avenue, and there was young Jared Raphaelson, angrily asserting Youth's right of access to great public art collections, then quickly disclaiming all responsibility for the terrorist assault on the Hewlett and the mysterious disappearance of Piet Mondrian's masterpiece, *Composition With Color.*

'We don't think the kids are directly involved,' a police spokesman told the camera. 'It's a little early to tell yet, but it looks as though some quick-witted thief took the opportunity to cut the painting from its frame. We found the frame itself, all broken and with shreds of canvas adhering to it, in the second-floor washroom. Now it looks as though the kids must be responsible for the fire, although they deny it. What happened was somebody tossed an explosive device called a cherry bomb of the type used to celebrate Independence Day, and it happened to go off in a wastebasket in which some tourist had evidently discarded a few rolls of film, and what would have been a big bang turned into a full-scale trash fire. The fire itself didn't cause any real damage. It put out a lot of smoke and shook people up some, but it didn't amount to anything except to provide cover to the thief.'

Ah, well, I thought. Accidents will happen. And I kept a close eye on the screen, looking for a sign of the quick-witted opportunistic thief. But I didn't see him. Not on that channel, at any rate.

A museum official expressed chagrin at the loss of the painting. He talked about its artistic importance and with some reluctance estimated its value at a quarter of a million dollars. The announcer mentioned the recent robber-cum-murder at the Charlemagne, in which another Mondrian was taken, and wondered whether press coverage of that theft might have led the present thief to pick Mondrian rather than some other masterpiece.

The museum official thought that was highly possible. 'He might have taken a van Gogh or a Turner, even a Rembrandt,' he said. 'We have paintings worth ten or more times what the Mondrian might bring. That's why this strikes me as an impulsive, spur-of-the-moment act. He knew the Mondrian was valuable, he'd heard what the Onderdonk Mondrian was valued at, and when the opportunity presented itself he acted swiftly and decisively.'

They cut for a commercial. In Carney's Bar and Grill, an impulsive, spur-of-the-moment guy in horn rims and a fedora picked up his glass of beer and swiftly and decisively drank it down.

21

'What you got in there?' the child demanded. 'Fission poles?'

Fission poles?

'Andrew, don't bother the man,' said its mother, and flashed me a brave smile. 'He's at that age,' she said. 'He's learned how to talk, and he hasn't learned how to shut up.'

'Man goin' fishin',' said Andrew.

Oh. *Fishin'* poles.

Andrew and Andrew's mother and I, along with perhaps four other people, were sheltering ourselves behind a transparent barrier designed to protect bus passengers from the elements, even as its construction had enriched several public officials a few scandals ago. I had one arm around a cylindrical cardboard tube which stood five feet tall and ran about four inches in diameter. I forebore advising Andrew that it did not contain fishing poles. It contained – what? Bait?

Something like that.

Two buses came. They're like cops in bad neighborhoods; they travel in pairs. Andrew and his mother got on one of them, along with our other companions in the shelter. I remained behind, but there was nothing remarkable in this. A variety of buses travel south on Fifth Avenue, bound for a variety of destinations, so I merely seemed to be waiting for another bus.

I don't know what I was waiting for. Divine intervention, perhaps.

Across the street and a little to my left loomed the massive bulk of the Charlemagne, as fiercely impregnable as ever. I'd breached its portals three times, once at Onderdonk's invitation, twice bearing flowers, and in fairy tales the third time is the charm. But now I had to get in there a fourth time, and everyone who worked for the building knew me by now, and you couldn't get into the goddamned building even if nobody knew you from Adam.

There's always a way, I told myself. What little story had I made up for Andrea? Something about a helicopter to the roof? Well, that was fanciful, surely, but was it absolutely out of the question? There were private helicopter services. They'd take you up for a couple of hours of soaring over the city for a fee. For a considerably higher fee, one such bold entrepreneur would no doubt drop you off on a particular roof, especially if he weren't required to stand by and lift you off again.

There were problems, however. I didn't have the money to hire a limousine, let alone a helicopter, and I hadn't the faintest idea where to find an avaricious helicopter pilot, and I rather suspected they didn't do business at night anyway.

Hell.

The buildings that adjoined the Charlemagne were no help, either. All were significantly lower than their neighbor, by a minimum of four floors. It was theoretically possible to outfit oneself with Alpine climbing gear and proceed from the roof of one of those buildings, sinking pitons into the mortar between the Charlemagne's bricks, clambering hand over hand to the top of the Charlemagne's roof, and getting in that way. It was also theoretically possible to master the lost art of levitation and float halfway to heaven, and this struck me as a little easier than pretending the Charlemagne was the Matterhorn.

Besides, I had no reason to think I could crack the security of one of the neighboring buildings, either. They'd have security-conscious doormen and concierges of their own.

Flowers wouldn't work, not for Leona Tremaine, not for anyone else. Other things get delivered to buildings – liquor, ice, anchovy pizza – but I'd used the deliveryman number and I was sure I couldn't get by with it again. I thought of various disguises. I could be a blind man. I already had the dark glasses; all I'd need would be a white cane. Or I could be a priest or a doctor. Priests and doctors can get in anywhere. A stethoscope or a Roman collar will get you in places you can't even crack with a clipboard.

But not here. They'd phone upstairs, whoever I said I was, whoever I was presumably visiting.

A blue-and-white patrol car cruised slowly down the avenue. I turned a little to the side, putting my face in shadow. The car coasted through a red light and kept going.

I couldn't just stand there, could I? And I'd be more comfortable inside than out, sitting than standing. And, since there didn't seem to be any way I could work that night, there was no real reason to abstain from strong drink.

I crossed the street and went around the corner to Big Charlie's.

It was a much more opulent establishment than the name would have led you to expect. Deep carpet, recessed lighting, banquette tables in dark corners, a piano bar with well-padded and backed barstools. Waitresses in starched black-and-white uniforms and a bartender in a tuxedo. I was glad I was wearing a suit and I felt deeply ashamed of the sneakers and the fedora.

I doffed the latter and tucked the former beneath one of the banquettes. I ordered a single-malt Scotch with a splash of soda and a twist of lemon peel, and it came in a man-sized cut glass tumbler that looked and felt like Waterford. And perhaps it was. Stores sold a whole pint of whiskey for what this place charged for a drink, so Big Charlie ought to be able to spend a fair amount on glassware.

Not that I begrudged him a cent. I sipped and thought and sipped and thought, and a pianist with a touch like a masseuse and a voice like melted butter worked her way through Cole Porter, and I sent my mind around the corner to the Charlemagne and looked for a way in.

There's always a way in. Somewhere in the course of my second drink I thought of phoning in a bomb scare. Let 'em evacuate the building. Then I could just mingle with the crowd and wander back in. If I was wearing pajamas and a robe at the time of mingling, who'd think for a moment that I didn't belong there?

Now where was I going to get pajamas and a robe?

I found some interesting answers to that question, the most fanciful of which involved a daring burglary of Brooks Brothers, and I was just finishing my third drink when a woman came over to my table and said, 'Well, which are you? Lost or stolen or strayed?'

'A. A. Milne,' I remembered.

'Right!'

'Somebody's mother. James James Morrison Morrison—'

'Weatherby George Dupree,' she finished for me. 'Now how did I know that you would know? Perhaps it's because you look so soulful. And so lonely. It's said that loneliness cries out to loneliness. I don't know who said that, but I don't believe it was Milne.'

'Probably not,' and there was a silence, and I should have invited her to join me. I didn't.

No matter. She sat down beside me anyhow, a supremely confident woman. She was wearing a low-cut black dress and a string of pearls and she smelled of costly perfume and expensive whiskey, but then that last was the only kind Big Charlie sold.

'I'm Eve,' she said. 'Eve DeGrasse. And you are—'

I very nearly said Adam. 'Donald Brown,' I said.

'What's your sign, Donald?'

'Gemini. What's yours?'

'I have several,' she said. She took my hand, turned it, traced the lines in my palm with a scarlet-tipped index finger. ' "Yield" is one of them. "Slippery When Wet" is another.'

'Oh.'

The waitress, unbidden, brought us both fresh drinks. I wondered how many it would take before this woman looked good to me. It wasn't that she was unattractive, exactly, but that she was a sufficient number of years older than I to be out of bounds. She was well built and well coiffed, and I suppose her face had been lifted and her tummy tucked, but she was old enough to be – well, not my mother, maybe, but perhaps my mother's younger sister. Not that my own mother actually *had* a younger sister, but—

'Do you live near here, Donald?'

'No.'

'I didn't think so. You're from out of town, aren't you?'

'How did you know?'

'Sometimes one can sense these things.' Her hand dropped to my thigh, gave a little squeeze. 'You're all alone in the big city.'

'That's right.'

'Staying in some soulless hotel. Oh, a comfortable room, I'm sure of that, but lifeless and anonymous. And so lonely.'

'So lonely,' I echoed, and drank some of my Scotch. One or two more drinks, I thought, and it wouldn't much matter where I was or who I was with. If this woman had a bed, any sort of a bed, I could pass out in it until daybreak. I might not win any points for gallantry that way, but I'd at least be safe, and God knew I was in no condition to wander the streets of New York with half the NYPD looking for me.

'You don't have to stay in that hotel room,' she purred.

'You live near here?'

'Indeed I do. I live at Big Charlie's.'

'At Big Charlie's?'

'That's right.'

'Here?' I said stupidly. 'You live here in this saloon?'

'Not here, silly.' She gave my leg another companionable squeeze. 'I live at the real Big Charlie's. The big Big Charlie's. Oh, but you're from out of town, Donald. You don't know what I'm talking about, do you?'

'I'm afraid not.'

'Charlemagne equals Charles the Great equals Big Charlie. That's how they named this place, because the owner's a couple of fags named Les and Maurie, and they could have called it More or Less, only they didn't. But you're from out of town so you don't know there's an apartment building around the corner called the Charlemagne.'

'The Charlemagne,' I said.

'Right.'

'An apartment house.'

'Right.'

'Around the corner. And you live there.'

'Right you are, Donald Brown.'

'Well,' I said, setting my glass down unfinished. 'Well, what are we waiting for?'

I recognized the doorman and the concierge and Eduardo, the kindly elevator operator. None of them recognized me. They didn't even take a second glance at me, perhaps because they didn't take a first glance at me, either. I could have been wearing a gorilla suit and they'd have been just as careful to avert their eyes. Ms DeGrasse was, after all, a tenant, and I don't suppose I was the first young man she'd ever pulled out of Big Charlie's and brought on home, and the staff was no doubt well tipped to keep their eyes in their sockets where they belonged.

We rode the elevator clear to the fifteenth floor. I'd gulped air furiously as we walked from the bar to the building, but it takes more than a few lungfuls of New York's polluted atmosphere to counteract the effects of three and a half large whiskeys, and I felt a little woozy in the elevator. The light in there, unkind as it was to my companion, didn't help either. We walked to her door, and she had more trouble opening it with the key than I generally have without one, but I let her do the honors and she got it open.

Inside, she said, 'Oh, Donald!' and swept me in her arms. She was almost my height, and there was quite a bit of her. She wasn't fat or blowsy or anything. There was just a lot of her, that's all.

I said, 'You know what? I think we could both use a drink.'

We used three. She drank hers and I dumped mine in an areca palm that looked as though it was going to die soon anyway.

Perhaps it was just intimidated by its surroundings. The apartment looked like a spread in *Architectural Digest*, with not much furniture and a lot of carpeted platforms and such. The only picture on the wall was a mural and it was all loops and swirls without a single right angle to be found in it. Mondrian would have hated it, and you'd have had to take the whole wall to steal it.

'Ah, Donald—'

I'd hoped she might dim out with all that whiskey, but it didn't seem to be affecting her at all. And I wasn't getting a whole lot more sober with the passage of time. I thought, *Oh, what the hell*, and I said, 'Eve!' and we went into a clinch.

There was no bed in her bedroom, just another carpeted platform with a mattress on it. It did the job. And so, much to my surprise, did I.

It was odd. At first I just concentrated on not thinking about my mother's younger sister, which should have been a cinch in view of the fact that she'd never had one. Then I tried to build a fantasy incorporating our age differences, imagining myself as an eager youth of seventeen and Eve as a ripe, knowing woman of thirty-six. That didn't work too well because I imagined myself right back into a state of coltish clumsiness and embarrassment.

Finally I just gave up and forgot who either of us was, and that worked. I don't know if the whiskey helped or hindered, but one way or another I stopped thinking about what was going on and just let it happen, and damned if it didn't.

Go figure.

22

Afterward, the hardest part was staying awake long enough for her to fall asleep. I kept catching myself just as my mind was starting to drift, following some abstruse line of thought along one of those tangled paths that lead to Dreamland. Each time I yanked myself conscious, and each time it felt like a narrow escape.

When her breathing changed I stayed put for a minute or two, then slipped off the mattress and dropped from the sleeping platform to the floor. The carpet was deep and I padded silently across it, reclaimed my clothes, and put them on in the living room. I was almost to the door when I remembered my five-foot tube and went back for it. 'I'll bet you're an architect,' Eve had said, 'and I'll bet you've got blueprints in there.' I'd asked her how she'd guessed. 'Those glasses,' she said, 'and that hat. And those sensible sensible shoes. Hell, Donald, you *look* like an architect.'

I squinted through the judas, unlocked the door, cracked it and checked the hallway. Outside, I thought of using my picks to lock the door behind me and decided against it. Eve's life-style was such that she probably slept behind unlocked doors as a regular thing. For that matter, it wasn't inconceivable that departing guests often went through her purse on the way out, or that she considered such actions not theft but a quid pro quo. A fair exchange, they say, is no robbery.

I used the fire stairs to reach the eleventh floor. For a moment I couldn't remember which door led to the Appling apartment, and then I spied the telltale burglar alarm keyhole, the one to which no alarm system was attached. I had my ring of picks in hand and one slim piece of steel probing the innards of the Poulard lock when something stopped me.

And a good thing, too, because there were people inside that apartment. I must have heard something that made me put my ear to the door, and when I did that I heard what must have been the laugh track of a television situation comedy. I put my eye where my pick had been, and, surprise! Light showed through the keyhole.

The Applings were home. Even now, as I stood lemminglike on the brink of their apartment, Mr A. might be paging idly through his plundered stamp collection. At any moment he might let out a great bellow, doubtless startling his wife and driving Mary Tyler Moore reruns clear out of her head. Whereupon he might reflexively dash to the door, yank it open, and find – what?

An empty hallway, because by the time I'd reached this stage in my thoughts I was already through the fire door and on the stairs again. I climbed three flights, which put me back on Fifteen where I'd left Eve DeGrasse, hesitated for a moment in front of the fire door, then climbed another flight of stairs and opened the door with my picks.

There was an argument going on behind a closed door, but it was another door than Onderdonk's. His had a piece of paper taped to it proclaiming that the premises within were ordered sealed by the New York Police Department. The seal was symbolic rather than literal; Onderdonk's lock provided the only tangible barrier to Onderdonk's apartment. It was a Segal drop-bolt, a good enough lock, but I'd already picked it open once and it held no secrets for me.

But I didn't open it at once. First I listened, ear to door, and then I put my eye to the keyhole and stooped lower to see if any light issued forth from beneath the door. Nothing, no light, no sound, nothing.

I let myself in.

Other than mine, there were no bodies, living or otherwise, in the Onderdonk apartment. I checked everywhere, even the kitchen cupboards, to establish as much. Then I let the tapwater run until it was hot enough to make instant coffee. The resultant beverage wouldn't have thrilled El Exigente, nor would it get me sober, but at least I'd be a wide-awake drunk instead of a falling-down one.

I drank it, shuddering, and then I got on the phone.

'Bernie, thank God. I was worried sick. I was afraid something happened. You're not calling from jail, are you?'

'No.'

'Where are you?'

'Not in jail. I'm all right. You and Alison got out okay?'

'Sure, no problem. What a scene! I think we coulda grabbed the *Mona Lisa* on the way out, except it's in the Louvre. But I've gotta tell you the big news – the cat's back!'

'Archie?'

'Archie. We went and had a drink, and then we had another drink, and then we came home and Ubi rushed over to be petted, which isn't like him, and I was petting him and I looked up and there was Ubi on the other side of the room, so I looked down at the cat I was petting and damned if it wasn't old Archie Goodwin himself. Whoever broke in to take him broke in again to return him, and left the locks just the way I left them, same as the other time.'

'Amazing. The Nazi kept her word.'

'Kept her word?'

'I gave her the painting and she returned the cat.'

'How'd you find her?'

'She found me. It's too complicated to explain right now. The important thing is he's back. How are his whiskers?'

'Gone on one side. His balance is sort of weirded out, like he's very
unsure of himself when it comes to leaps and pounces. I can't make up
my mind whether to trim 'em on the other side or just wait for 'em to
grow back in.'

'Well, take your time deciding. You don't have to do anything
tonight.'

'Right. Alison was amazed to see him. I think she was as amazed as I
was.'

'I can believe it.'

'Bernie, what do you think you're doin', collectin' Moondrains? Because
I understand they got a couple at the Guggenheim and I wondered if
that's where you're gonna strike next.'

'Always a pleasure to talk to you, Ray.'

'The pleasure's mine. Are you crazy or somethin'? And don't tell me
it wasn't you because I saw you on television. That's about the
dumbest lookin' hat I ever saw in my life. I think I recognized the hat
more'n I recognized you.'

'Makes a good disguise, doesn't it?'

'But you weren't carryin' anythin', Bern. What did you do with the
Moondrain?'

'Folded it very small and tucked it inside my hat.'

'What I figured. Where are you?'

'In the belly of the beast. Listen, I've got a job for you, Ray.'

'I already got a job, remember? I'm a police officer.'

'That's not a job, it's a license to steal. What's that line in *Casa-
blanca*.'

' "Play it again, Sam." '

'Actually he never says it exactly that way. It's "Play it, Sam," or
"Play the song, Sam," or some variation like that, but he never says,
"Play it again, Sam." '

'That's really fascinatin', Bern.'

'But that wasn't the line I meant. "Round up the usual suspects."
That's the line I meant. And that's what I want you to do.'

'I don't get it.'

'You will when I explain.'

'Bernie, it's been a madhouse here. Things are just starting to settle
down. How about that kid of mine, huh?'

'He's a trouper.'

'His fathead of a father called up. How could I allow such a thing, and he's thinking seriously of instituting a custody suit, unless of course I agree to a reduction in alimony and child support payments, blah blah blah. Jared says he'll live at the Hewlett before he lives with his old man. You think he's got a case?'

'I don't even think he thinks he's got a case, but I'm not a lawyer. How's Jared holding up under questioning?'

'His answers turn into political speeches. Don't worry. He hasn't mentioned you.'

'What about his buddies?'

'You mean the other members of his cadre? They couldn't mention you if they wanted to. Jared's the only one who knows this afternoon's incident was anything other than a political action of the Young Panthers.'

'Is that what they're calling themselves?'

'I think it's a media invention, but I also think it might stick. Jared's friend Shaheen Vladewicz suggested Panther Cubs, but his other friend Adam informed them that panthers don't have cubs, they have kittens, and Panther Kittens was rejected as insufficiently militant. Anyway, our secret's safe. I think Jared's beginning to believe he thought up the whole thing and you cashed in on it at the last minute.'

'A quick-witted opportunist of a thief.'

'Well, if the shoe fits. Incidentally, you left that case here. That cat carrier or whatever it is.'

'Well, give it to someone with a cat. I won't be needing it. Carolyn got her cat back.'

'No shit?'

'Only in the litter box.'

'She really got the cat back?'

'So she tells me.'

'And the Hewlett? Are they going to get their Mondrian back?'

'What Mondrian?'

'Bernie—'

'Don't worry, Denise. Everything's going to work out fine.'

'Everything's going to work out fine.'

'Gee, I hope you're right, Bernie. I don't know, though. I went out this morning figuring to do fifteen miles, and after ten miles I started to get this funny feeling on the inside of my right knee. Not a pain exactly but a feeling, a sensitivity, you know what I mean? Now what they say is you run *to* pain but not *through* pain, but what do you do about sensitivity? I figured as soon as it became pain I'd stop, but it just stayed sensitive and got a little *more* sensitive, and I did my fifteen miles and then did three miles on top of it, eighteen miles altogether, and I came home and took a shower and lay down, and now my knee's throbbing like a bastard.'

'Can you walk on it?'

'I could probably run another eighteen miles on it. It's throbbing with sensitivity, not with pain. It's crazy.'

'Well, it'll work out. Wally, there was an incident at a museum this afternoon—'

'Jesus Christ, I almost forgot. I don't even know if I should be talking to you. Were you involved in that?'

'Of course not. But the leader of the kids' protest is the son of a friend of mine, and—'

'Oh, here we go.'

'Wally, how'd you like to make a name for yourself representing the Young Panthers? I don't think anybody's going to bring charges against them, but there'll be reporters wanting interviews and there might even be a book or a movie in the thing, and Jared's going to need someone to look out for his interests. And his father's talking about a custody suit, so Jared's mother's going to need somebody looking out for her interests, and—'

'You got an interest in the mother?'

'We're just good friends. As a matter of fact, Wally, I think you might like the mother. Denise, her name is.'

'Oh?'

'Got a pencil? Denise Raphaelson, 741–5374.'

'And the kid's name is Jason?'

'Jared.'

'Same difference. When should I call her?'

'In the morning.'

'It's already morning, for Christ's sake. Do you know what time it is?'

'I don't call my lawyer to find out the time. I call my lawyer when there's something I want him to do for me.'

'Is there something you want me to do for you?'

'Thought you'd never ask.'

'Miss Petrosian? "I sing of sorrow / I sing of weeping / I have no sorrow. / I only borrow—" '

'Who is this?'

' "I only borrow / From some tomorrow / Where it lies sleeping / Enough of sorrow / To sing of weeping." It's Mary Carolyn Davies, Miss Petrosian. Your old favorite.'

'I don't understand.'

'What's to understand? It's a nice straightforward poem, it seems to me. The poet's saying that she draws against a store of future miseries in order to write about a depth of emotion she hasn't yet experienced.'

736

'Mr Rhodenbarr?'

'The same. I have your painting, Miss Petrosian, and you have only to come and collect it.'

'You have—'

'The Mondrian. It's yours for a thousand dollars. I know that's no money, a ridiculous sum, but I have to get out of town fast and I need every cent I can raise.'

'I can't get to the bank until Monday and—'

'Bring what cash you can and a check for the balance. Get a pencil and write down the address and time. And don't be early or late, Miss Petrosian, or you can forget all about the painting.'

'All right. Mr Rhodenbarr? How did you find me?'

'You wrote down your name and number for me. Don't you remember?'

'But the number—'

'Turned out to be that of a Korean fruit store on Amsterdam Avenue. I was disappointed, Miss Petrosian, but not surprised.'

'But—'

'But you're listed in the book, Miss Petrosian. The Manhattan phone book, the white pages. I can't be the first person to have called the fact to your attention.'

'No, but – but I didn't give you my name.'

'You said Elspeth Peters.'

'Yes, but—'

'Well, with all due respect, Miss Petrosian, I wasn't fooled. The way you hesitated when you gave your name, and then the wrong number, well, it was a dead giveaway.'

'But how on earth did you know my real name?'

'A bit of deduction. When amateurs select an alias, they almost always keep the same initials. And they very frequently choose as a last name some form of modified first name. Jackson, Richards, Johnson. Or Peters. I guessed that your real name began with a P, and that it very likely had the same root as Peters. Something about your features suggested further that you might be of Armenian descent. I pulled out the phone book, turned to the P-e-t's, and looked for an Armenian-sounding name with the initial E.'

'But that's extraordinary.'

'The extraordinary is only the ordinary, Miss Petrosian, with the addition of a little extra. That's not mine, by the way. A grade-school teacher of mine used to say that. Isabel Josephson was her name, and as far as I know it was not an alias.'

'I'm only a quarter Armenian. And I'm said to take after my mother's side of the family.'

'I'd say there's a distinct Armenian cast to your features. But perhaps

737

I just had one of those psychic flashes people are subject to now and then. It hardly matters. You want that painting, don't you?'

'Of course I want it.'

'Then write this down . . .'

'Mr Danforth? My name is Rhodenbarr, Bernard Grimes Rhodenbarr. I apologize for the lateness of the call, but I think you'll excuse the intrusion when you've heard what I have to say. I have a couple of things to tell you, sir, and a question or two to ask you, and an invitation to extend . . .'

Phone calls, phone calls, phone calls. By the time I was done my ears ached from taking their turns pressed against the receiver. If Gordon Onderdonk knew what I was doing with his message units, he'd turn over in his drawer.

When I was finished I made another cup of coffee and found a Milky Way bar in the freezer and a package of Ry-Krisp in a cupboard. It made a curious meal.

I ate it anyway, went back to the living room and killed a little time. It was late but not late enough. Finally it *was* late enough, and I let myself out of Onderdonk's apartment, leaving the door unlocked. I walked all the way down to the fifth floor, smiling as I passed the sleeping Ms DeGrasse on Fifteen, sighing as I passed the Applings on Eleven, shaking my head as I passed Leona Tremaine on Nine. I had a bad moment getting through the fire door lock on Five. I don't know why. It was the same simple proposition as all the other fire door locks, but perhaps my fingers were stiff from dialing the telephone. I unlocked the door, and I crossed the hallway to another door, and after a careful look and listen I opened the door.

I was as quiet as a mouse. There were people asleep within and I didn't want to wake them. And I had a great many things to do.

And, finally, they were all done. I slipped ever so quietly out of that fifth-floor apartment, locked the locks after me, and went up the stairs again to Sixteen.

You know, I think that was the worst part of it. Climbing stairs is hard work, and climbing ten flights of stairs (there was still, thank God, no thirteenth floor) was very hard work. The New York Road Runners Club has a race each year up eighty-six flights of stairs to the top of the Empire State Building, and some lean-limbed showoff wins it every time, and he's welcome to it. Ten flights of stairs was bad enough.

I let myself into Onderdonk's apartment once again, closed the door, locked it, and took a little time to catch my breath.

23

'Oh, great,' I said. 'Everybody's here.'

And indeed everybody was. Ray Kirschmann had shown up first, flanked by a trio of fresh-faced young lads in blue. He talked to someone downstairs, and a couple of building employees came up to the Onderdonk apartment and set up folding chairs to supplement the Louis Quinze pieces that were already on hand. Then the three uniformed cops stuck around, one upstairs, the others waiting in the lobby to escort people up as they arrived, while Ray went out to pick up some of the other folks on the list.

While all this was going on, I stayed in the back bedroom with a book and a thermos of coffee. I was reading Defoe's *The History of Colonel Jack*, and the man lived seventy years without ever writing a dull sentence, but I had a little trouble keeping my mind on his narrative. Still, I bided my time. A man likes to make an entrance.

Which I ultimately did, saying, *Oh, great. Everybody's here.* It was comforting the way every head turned at my words and every eye followed me as I skirted the semicircular grouping of chairs and dropped into the leather wing chair facing them. I scanned the little sea of faces – well, call it a lake of faces. They locked back at me, or at least most of them did. A few turned their eyes to gaze over the fireplace, and after a moment so did I.

And why not? There was Mondrian's *Composition With Color*, placed precisely where it had been on my first visit to the Charlemagne, and positively glowing with its vivid primary colors and sturdy horizontal and vertical lines.

'Makes a powerful statement, doesn't it?' I leaned back, crossed my legs, made myself comfortable. 'And of course it's why we're all here. A common interest in Mondrian's painting is what binds us all together.'

I looked at them again, not as a group but as individuals. Ray Kirschmann was there, of course, sitting in the most comfortable chair and keeping one eye on me and another on the rest of the crowd. That sort of thing can leave a man walleyed, but he was doing a good job of it.

Not far from him, in a pair of folding chairs, were my partner in crime and her partner in lust. Carolyn was wearing her green blazer and a pair of gray flannel slacks, while Alison wore chinos and a striped Brooks Brothers shirt with the collar buttoned down and the sleeves roiled up. They made an attractive couple.

Not far from them, seated side by side on a six-foot sofa, were Mr and Mrs J. McLendon Barlow. He was a slender, dapper, almost elegant man with neatly combed iron gray hair and a military bearing; with his posture he could have been just as comfortable on one of the folding chairs and left the sofa for somebody who needed it. His wife, who could have passed for his daughter, was medium height and slender, a large-eyed creature who wore her long dark hair pinned up in what I think they call a chignon. I know they call something a chignon, and I think that's what it is. Was. Whatever.

Behind and to the right of the Barlows was a chunkily built man with the sort of face Mondrian might have painted if he'd ever gotten into portrait work. It was all right angles. He was jowly and droopy eyed, and he had a moustache that was graying and tightly curled hair as black as India ink, and his name was Mordecai Danforth. The man sitting next to him looked about eighteen at first glance, but if you looked closer you could double the figure. He was very pale, wore rimless spectacles and a dark suit with an inch-wide black silk tie, and his name was Lloyd Lewes.

A few feet to Lewes's right, Elspeth Petrosian sat with her hands folded in her lap, her lips set in a thin line, her head cocked, her expression one of patient fury. She was neatly dressed in Faded Glory jeans and a matching blouse, and was wearing Earth Shoes, with the heel lower than the toe. Those were all the rage a few years back, with ads suggesting that if everybody wore them we could wipe out famine and pestilence, but you don't see them much anymore. You still see a lot of famine and pestilence, though.

To the right and to the rear of Elspeth, in another of the folding chairs, was a young man whose dark suit looked as though he only wore it on Sundays. Which was fine, because that's what day it was. He had moist brown eyes and a slightly cleft chin, and his name was Eduardo Melendez.

On Eduardo's left was another young man, also in a suit, but with a pair of New Balance 730s on his feet instead of the plain black oxfords Eduardo favored. I could see the top of one shoe and the sole of the other, because he was sitting on an upholstered chair with his right leg up on one of the folding chairs. He was Wally Hemphill, of course, and I guessed that his knee had finally made it from sensitivity to pain.

Denise Raphaelson was sitting a couple of yards from Wally. There were paint smears on her dungarees and her plaid shirt was starting to go in the elbow, but she looked all right to me. She evidently looked not bad to Wally, too, and the feeling seemed to be mutual, judging from the glances they kept stealing at one another. Well, why not?

Four more men filled out the audience. One had a round face and a high forehead and looked like a small-town banker in a television commercial, eager to lend you money so that you could fix up your home and make it an asset to the community you lived in. His name was Barnett Reeves. The second was bearded and booted and scruffy, and he looked like someone who'd approach the banker and ask for a college loan. And be turned down. His name was Richard Jacobi. The third was a bloodless man in a suit as gray as his own complexion. He had, as far as I could tell, no lips, no eyebrows, and no eyelashes, and he looked like the real-life banker, the one who approved mortgages in the hope of eventual foreclosure. His name was Orville Widener. The fourth man was a cop, and he wore a cop's uniform, with a holstered pistol and a baton and a memo book and handcuffs and all that great butch gear cops get to carry. His name was Francis Rockland, and I happened to know that he was missing a toe, but offhand I couldn't tell you which one.

I looked at them and they looked at me, and Ray Kirschmann, who I sometimes think exists just to take the edge off moments of high drama, said, 'Quit stallin', Bernie.'

So I quit stalling.

I said, 'I'd say I suppose you're wondering why I summoned you all here, but you're not. You know why I summoned you here. And, now that you're here, I'll—'

'Get to the point,' Ray suggested.

'I'll get to the point,' I agreed. 'The point is that a man named Piet Mondrian painted a picture, and four decades later a couple of men got killed. A man named Gordon Onderdonk was murdered in this very apartment, and another man named Edwin Turnquist was murdered in a bookstore in the Village. *My* bookstore in the Village, as it happens, and along with Mondrian I seem to be the common denominator in this story. I left this apartment minutes before Onderdonk was killed, and I walked into my own store minutes after Turnquist was killed, and the police suspected me of having committed both murders.'

'Perhaps they had good reason,' Elspeth Petrosian suggested.

'They had every reason in the world,' I said, 'but I had an edge. I knew I hadn't killed anybody. Beyond that, I knew I'd been framed. I'd been led to this apartment on the pretext that its owner wanted his library appraised. I spent a couple of hours examining his library, came up with a figure and accepted a fee for my work. I walked out with my fingerprints all over the place, and why not? I hadn't done anything wrong. I didn't care if I left my fingerprints on the coffee table or my name with the concierge. But it was crystal clear to me that I'd been invited here for the sole purpose of establishing my presence here, so that I could take the rap for burglary and homicide, the theft of a painting and the brutal slaying of its rightful owner.'

I took a breath. 'I could see that much,' I went on, 'but it didn't make sense. Because I'd been framed not by the murderer but by the victim, and where's the sense in that? Why would Onderdonk wander into my shop with a cock-and-bull story, lure me up here, get me to leave my prints on every flat surface that would take them, and then duck into the other room to get his head beaten in?'

'Maybe the murderer capitalized on an opportunity,' Denise said. 'The way some quick-witted thief seized a chance to steal a painting yesterday afternoon.'

'I thought of that,' I said, 'but I still couldn't figure Onderdonk's angle. He'd had me up here to frame me for something, and what could it be if it wasn't his murder? The theft of the painting?

'Well, that seemed possible. Suppose he decided to fake a burglary in order to stick it to his insurance company. Why not add verisimilitude by having the fingerprints of a reformed burglar where investigators could readily find them? It didn't really make sense, because I could justify my presence, so framing me would only amount to an unnecessary complication, but lots of people do dumb things, especially amateurs dabbling at crime. So he could have done that, and then his accomplice in the deal could have double-crossed him, murdered him, and left the reformed burglar to carry the can for both the burglary and the murder.'

'Reformed burglar,' Ray grunted. 'I could let that go once, but that's twice you said it. Reformed!'

I ignored him. 'But I still couldn't make sense out of it,' I said. 'Why would the murderer tie Onderdonk up and stuff him in a closet? Why not just kill him and leave him where he fell? And why cut the Mondrian canvas from its stretcher? Thieves do that in museums when they have to make every second count, but this killer figured to have all the time in the world. He could remove the staples and take the painting from the stretcher without damaging it. For that matter, he could wrap it in brown paper and carry it out with the stretcher intact.'

'You said he was an amateur,' Mordecai Danforth said, 'and that amateurs do illogical things.'

'I said dumb things, but that's close enough. Still, how many dumb things can the same person do? I kept getting stuck on the same contradiction. Gordon Onderdonk went to a lot of trouble to frame me, and what he got for his troubles was killed. Well, I was missing something, but you know what they say – it's hard to see the picture when you're standing inside the frame. I was inside the frame and I couldn't see the picture, but I began to get little flashes of it, and then it became obvious. The man who framed me and the murder victim were two different people.'

Carolyn said, 'Slow down, Bern. The guy who got you over here and the guy who got his head bashed in—'

'Were not the same guy.'

'Don't tell me that's not Onderdonk down there in the morgue,' Ray Kirschmann said. 'We got a positive ID from three different people. That's him, Gordon Kyle Onderdonk, that's the guy.'

'Right. But somebody else came into my shop, introduced himself as Onderdonk, invited me up here, opened the door for me, paid me two hundred dollars for looking at some books, and then beat the real Onderdonk's brains out as soon as I walked out the door.'

'Onderdonk himself was here all the time?' This from Barnett Reeves, the jolly banker.

'Right,' I said. 'In the closet, all trussed up like a chicken and with enough chloral hydrate in his bloodstream to keep him quiet as an oiled hinge. That's why he was out of sight, so I wouldn't step on him if I took a wrong turn on my way to the bathroom. The murderer didn't want to risk killing Onderdonk until he had the frame perfectly fitted around me. That way, too, he could make sure the time of death coincided nicely with my departure from the building. Medical examiners can't time things to the minute – it's never that precise – but he couldn't go wrong timing things as perfectly as possible.'

'You're just supposing all this, aren't you?' Lloyd Lewes piped up. His voice was reedy and tentative, a good match for his pale face and his narrow tie. 'You're just creating a theory to embrace some inconsistencies. Or do you have additional facts?'

'I have two fairly substantial facts,' I said, 'but they don't prove much to anyone but me. Fact number one is that I've been to the morgue, and the body in Drawer 328-B—' now how on earth did I remember that number? '—isn't the man who wandered into my bookstore one otherwise fine day. Fact number two is that the man who called himself Gordon Onderdonk is here right now, in this room.'

I'll tell you, when everybody in a room draws a breath at the same moment, you get one hell of a hush.

Orville Widener broke the silence. 'You have no proof for that,' he said. 'We have just your word.'

'That's right, that's what I just told you. For my part, I suppose I should have guessed early on that the man I met wasn't Gordon Onderdonk. There were clues almost from the beginning. The man who let me into this apartment – I can't call him Onderdonk anymore so let's call him the murderer – he just opened the door an inch or two before he let me in. He kept the chain lock on until the elevator operator had been told it was okay. He called me by name, no doubt for the operator's benefit, but he fumbled with the lock until the elevator had left the floor.'

'Is true,' Eduardo Melendez said. 'Mr Onderdonk, he alla time comes into the hall to meet a guest. This time I doan see him. I think notheen of it at the time, but is true.'

'I thought nothing of it myself,' I said, 'except that I wondered why a man security-conscious enough to keep a door on a chainlock when an announced and invited guest was coming up wouldn't have more than one Segal dropbolt lock on his door. I should have done some wondering later on, when the murderer left me to wait for the elevator alone, dashing back into his apartment to answer a phone that I never heard ringing.' I hadn't questioned that action, of course, because it had been a response to a fervent prayer, allowing me to dash down the stairs instead of getting shunted back onto the elevator. But I didn't have to tell them that.

'There was another thing I kept overlooking,' I went on quickly. 'Ray, you kept referring to Onderdonk as a big hulk of a man, and you made it sound as though clouting him over the head was on a par with felling an ox with a single blow. But the man who called himself Onderdonk wasn't anybody's idea of a hulk. If anything he was on the slight side. That should have registered, but I guess I wasn't paying attention. Remember, the first time I ever even heard the name Onderdonk was when the killer came into my bookshop and introduced himself to me. I assumed he was telling the truth, and I took a long time to start questioning that assumption.'

Richard Jacobi scratched his bearded chin. 'Don't keep us in suspense,' he demanded. 'If one of us killed Onderdonk, why don't you tell us who it is?'

'Because there's a more interesting question to answer first.'

'What's that?'

'Why did the killer cut *Composition With Color* out of its frame?'

'Ah, the painting,' said Mordecai Danforth. 'I like the idea of discussing the painting, especially in view of the fact that it seems to have been miraculously restored. There it reposes on the wall, a perfect example of Mondrian's mature style. You'd never know some foul fiend cut it from its stretcher.'

'You wouldn't, would you?'

'Tell us,' said Danforth. 'Why did the killer cut the painting?'

'So everyone would know it had been stolen.'

'I don't follow you.'

Neither, from the looks on their faces, did most of his fellows. 'The killer didn't just want to steal the painting,' I explained. 'He wanted the world to know it was gone. If he just took it, well, who would realize it was missing? Onderdonk lived alone. I suppose he must have had a will, and his worldly goods must go to somebody, but—'

'His heir's a second cousin in Calgary, Alberta,' Orville Widener cut in. 'And now we're coming to my part of the field. My company underwrote Onderdonk's insurance and we're on the hook for $350,000. I gather the painting was stolen so that we'd have to pay, but what we ask in a situation like that is *Cui bono?* I'm sure you know what that means.'

'Cooey Bono,' Carolyn said. 'That was Sonny's first wife, before he was married to Cher. Right?'

Widener ignored her. which I thought showed character. 'To whose good?' he said, translating the Latin himself. 'In other words, who benefits? The policy's payable to Onderdonk, and in the event of his death it becomes part of his estate, and his estate goes to somebody in western Canada.' His eyes narrowed, then turned toward Richard Jacobi. 'Or is that Canadian relative actually among those present?'

'He's in Canada,' Wally Hemphill said, 'because I spoke to him at an hour that was equally uncivilized in either time zone. He's empowered me to look out for his interests in this matter.'

'Indeed,' said Widener:

It was my turn. 'The cousin never left Calgary,' I said. 'The painting was stolen not for the insurance, considerable though it may be. The painting was stolen for the same reason its owner was murdered. Both acts were committed to conceal a crime.'

'And what crime was that?'

'Well, it's a long story,' I said, 'and I think we should make ourselves comfortable and have a cup of coffee. Now how many of you want cream and sugar? And how many just cream? And how many just sugar? And the rest of you want it all the way black? Fine.'

I don't think they really wanted coffee, but what I wanted was a breathing spell. When Carolyn and Alison had served the nasty stuff all around the room, I sipped some of mine, made a face, and started in.

'Once upon a time,' I said, 'a man named Haig Petrosian had a painting in his dining room. It would later be called *Composition With Color*, but Petrosian probably didn't call it anything but "My friend Piet's picture," or words to that effect. Whatever he called it, it disappeared around the time of his death. Maybe a family member spirited it away. Maybe a servant made off with it, perhaps acting on the belief that the old man wanted her to have it.'

'Perhaps Haig Petrosian's son William stole it,' Elspeth Petrosian said, with a sharp glance to her right and another sharp glance at me.

'Perhaps,' I said agreeably. 'Whoever took it, it wound up in the possession of a man who found a wonderful way to make money. He bought paintings and gave them away.'

Carolyn said, 'That's a way to make money?'

'It is the way this fellow did it. He would buy a painting by an important artist, a genuine painting, and he would lend it to a show or two in order to establish its provenance and his history as its owner. Then a talented if eccentric artist would be engaged to produce a copy of the painting. The owner would let himself be persuaded to donate the painting to a museum, but in the course of things it would be the copy that wound up getting donated. Further on down the line, he'd donate the painting to another institution in another part of the country, and once again it would be a copy that changed hands. Occasionally he might vary the pitch by selling the painting to a collector, picking someone who wouldn't be likely to show it. In the course of a decade, he could sell or donate the same painting five or six times, and if he stuck to abstract artists like Mondrian and had his wacky painter vary the precise design a bit from one canvas to the next, he could get away with it forever.

'And the richer you are to start with, the more profitable it is. Donate a painting appraised at a quarter of a million dollars and you can save yourself over a hundred thousand dollars in taxes. Do that a couple of times and you've more than paid for the painting, and you've still got the original painting yourself. There's only one problem.'

'What's that?' Alison asked.

'Getting caught. Our killer found out that Mr Danforth was putting together a retrospective exhibit of Piet Mondrian's works, which in and of itself was no cause for alarm. After all, his fake paintings had survived such exposure in the past. But it seemed that Mr Danforth was aware that there were far more Mondrians in circulation than Mondrian ever painted. What is it they used to say about Rembrandt? He painted two hundred portraits, of which three hundred are in Europe and five hundred in America.'

'Mondrian's not been counterfeited on that grand a scale,' Danforth said, 'but in the past few years there have been some disconcerting rumors. I decided to combine the retrospective with an exhaustive move to authenticate or denounce every Mondrian I could root out.'

'And toward that end you enlisted the aid of Mr Lewes.'

'That's right,' Danforth said, and Lewes nodded.

'Our killer learned as much,' I said, 'and he was scared. He knew Onderdonk intended to put his painting in the show, and he wasn't able to talk him out of it. He couldn't let on that the painting was a fake, not after he'd sold it to Onderdonk himself, and perhaps Onderdonk began to suspect him. That's supposition. What was clear was that Onderdonk had to die and the painting had to disappear, and it had to be a matter of record that the damned thing disappeared. All he had to do was frame me for the theft and murder and he was home free. It didn't matter if the charges stuck. If I went up for the job, fine. If not, that was fine, too. The cops wouldn't look for someone with a private motive for Onderdonk's death. They'd just decide I was guilty even if they couldn't make the charges stick, and they'd let the case go by the boards.'

'And we'd pay the cousin in Calgary $350,000 for a fake painting,' Orville Widener said.

'Which wouldn't affect the killer one way or the other. His interest was self-preservation, and that's a pretty good *cui bono* six days out of seven.'

Ray said, 'Who did it?'

'Huh?'

'Who sold the fake paintings and killed Onderdonk? Who did it?'

'Well, there's really only one person it could be,' I said, and turned toward the little sofa. 'It's you, isn't it, Mr Barlow?'

We had another one of those hushes. Then J. McLendon Barlow, who'd been sitting up very straight all along, seemed to sit up even straighter.

'Of course that's nonsense,' he said.

'Somehow I thought you might deny it.'

'Palpable nonsense. You and I have never met before today, Mr Rhodenbarr. I never sold a painting to Gordon Onderdonk. He was a good friend and I deeply regret his tragic death, but I never sold him a painting. I defy you to prove that I did.'

'Ah,' I said.

'Nor did I ever visit your shop, or represent myself to you or to anyone else as Gordon Onderdonk. I can understand your confusion, since it is a matter of record that I did in fact donate a painting of Mondrian's to the Hewlett Gallery. I'd hardly be inclined to deny it; there's a plaque on the gallery wall attesting to the fact.'

'Unfortunately,' I murmured, 'the painting seems to have disappeared from the Hewlett.'

'It's clear that you arranged its disappearance in preparing this farce. I certainly had nothing to do with it, and can provide evidence of my whereabouts at all times yesterday. Furthermore, it's to my disadvantage that the painting has disappeared, since it was unquestionably genuine.'

I shook my head. 'I'm afraid not,' I said.

'One moment.' Barnett Reeves, my jolly banker, looked as though I'd offered a dead rat as collateral. 'I'm the curator of the Hewlett, and I'm quite certain our painting is genuine.'

I nodded at the fireplace. 'That's your painting,' I said. 'How positive are you?'

'That's not the Hewlett Mondrian.'

'Yes it is.'

'Don't be a fool. Ours was cut from its stretcher by some damned vandal. That painting's intact. It may well be a fake, but it certainly never hung on our walls.'

'But it did,' I said. 'The man who stole it yesterday, and I'd as soon let him remain anonymous, was by no means a vandal. He wouldn't dream of slashing your painting, genuine or false. He went to the Hewlett carrying a bit of broken stretcher with the outside inch of canvas of a homemade fake Mondrian. He dismantled the stretcher on our specimen, opening the staples and hiding the canvas under his clothing. He hung the pieces of stretcher down his trouser legs. And he left evidence behind to make you assume he'd cut the painting from its mounting.'

'And that painting over the fireplace—'

'Is your painting, Mr Reeves. With the stretcher reassembled and the canvas reattached to it. Mr Lewes, would you care to examine it?'

Lewes was on his way before I'd finished my sentence. He whipped out a magnifying glass, took a look, and drew back his head almost at once.

'Why, this is painted with acrylics!' he said, as if he'd found a mouse turd on his plate. 'Mondrian never used acrylics. Mondrian used oils.'

'Of course he did,' said Reeves. 'I told you that wasn't ours.'

'Mr Reeves? Examine the painting.'

He walked over, looked at it. 'Acrylics,' he agreed. 'And not ours. What did I tell you? Now—'

'Take it off the wall and look at it, Mr Reeves.'

He did so, and it was painful to watch the play of expression across the man's face. He looked like a banker who'd foreclosed on what turned out to be swampland. 'My God,' he said.

'Exactly.'

'Our stretcher,' he said. 'Our stamp incused in the wood. That paint-ing was hanging in the Hewlett where thousands of eyes looked at it every day and nobody ever noticed it was a fucking acrylic copy.' He turned, glared furiously at Barlow. 'You damned cad,' he said. 'You filthy murdering bounder. You fucking counterfeit.'

'It's a trick,' Barlow protested. 'This burglar pulls fake rabbits out of fake hats and you fools are impressed. What's the matter with you, Reeves? Can't you see you're being flimflammed?'

'I was flimflammed by you,' Reeves said, glowering. 'You son of a bitch.'

Reeves took a step toward Barlow, and Ray Kirschmann was sud-denly on his feet, with a hand on the curator's forearm. 'Easy,' he said.

'When this is all over,' Barlow said, 'I'll bring charges against you, Rhodenbarr. I think any court would call this criminal libel.'

'That's really a frightening prospect,' I said, 'to someone who's cur-rently wanted for two murders. But I'll keep it in mind. You won't be pressing any charges, though, Mr Barlow. You'll be upstate pressing license plates.'

'You've got no evidence of anything.'

'You had easy access to this apartment. You and your wife live on the fifth floor. You didn't have the problem of getting in and out of a high-security building.'

'A lot of people live here. That doesn't make any of us murderers.'

'It doesn't,' I agreed, 'but it makes it easy to search your apartment.' I nodded at Ray, and he in turn nodded at Officer Rockland, who went to the door and opened it. In marched a pair of uniformed officers carrying yet another Mondrian. It looked for all the world just like the one Lloyd Lewes had just damned as an acrylic fake.

'The genuine article,' I said. 'It almost glows when it's in the same room with a copy, doesn't it? You might have carved up the painting you palmed off on Onderdonk, but you took good care of this one, didn't you? It's the real thing, the painting Piet Mondrian gave to his friend Haig Petrosian.'

'And we had a warrant,' Ray said, 'in case you were wondering. Where'd you boys find this?'

'In a closet,' one said, 'in the apartment you said on the fifth floor.'

Lloyd Lewes was already holding his glass to the canvas. 'Well, this is more like it,' he said. 'It's not acrylic. It's oil paint. And it certainly looks to be genuine. Quite a different thing from that, that specimen over there.'

'Now there's been some mistake,' Barlow said. 'Listen to me. There's been some mistake.'

'We also found this,' the cop said. 'In the medicine cabinet. No label, but I tasted it, and if it ain't chloral hydrate it's a better fake than the painting.'

'Now that's impossible,' Barlow said. 'That's impossible.' And I thought he was going to explain why it was impossible, that he'd flushed all the extra chloral hydrate down the john, but he caught himself in time. Listen, you can't have everything.

'You have the right to remain silent,' Ray Kirschmann told him, but I'm not going to go through all that again. Miranda-Escobedo's a good or a bad thing, depending on whether or not you're a cop, but who wants to put it down word for word all the time?

24

After a few urgent words to his wife, something about which lawyer to call and where to reach him, two of the uniformed police officers led J. McLendon Barlow off in handcuffs. Francis Rockland stayed behind, and so did Ray Kirschmann.

There was a respectful silence, broken at length by Carolyn Kaiser. 'Barlow must have killed Turnquist,' she said, 'because Turnquist was the artist he used, and Turnquist could expose him. Right?'

I shook my head. 'Turnquist was the artist, all right, and Barlow might have killed him sooner or later if he felt he had to. But he certainly wouldn't have come down to my bookstore to do it. Remember, I'd met Barlow as Onderdonk, and all I had to do was catch sight of him walking around hale and hearty and the whole scheme would collapse. It's my guess that Barlow never even left his apartment after the murder. He wanted to stay out of sight until I was behind bars where I couldn't get a look at him. Isn't that right, Mrs Barlow?'

All eyes turned to the woman who now sat alone on the couch. She cocked her head, started to say something, then simply nodded.

'Edwin P. Turnquist was an artist,' I said, 'and a fervent admirer of Mondrian's. He never considered himself a forger. God knows how Barlow got hold of him. Turnquist talked to total strangers in museums and galleries, and perhaps that's how they first made one another's acquaintance. At any rate, Barlow latched on to Turnquist because he could use him. He got the man to copy paintings, and Turnquist derived great satisfaction from looking at his own work in respected museums. He was a frequent visitor to the Hewlett, Mr Reeves. All the attendants knew him.'

'Ah,' said Reeves.

'He only paid a dime.'

'And quite proper,' Reeves said. 'We don't care what you pay, but you must pay something. That's our policy.'

'That and exclusion of the young. But no matter. When Barlow began to panic about your forthcoming retrospective exhibition, Mr Danforth, he paid a call on Edwin Turnquist. I suppose he urged him to keep out of sight. The substance of their conversation is immaterial. More to the point, Turnquist realized that all along Barlow had not merely been playing a joke on the art world. He'd been making great sums of money at it, and Turnquist's idealism was outraged. He'd been satisfied with the subsistence wages he made as Barlow's forger. Art for art's sake was fine with him, but that Barlow should profit from the game was not.'

I looked at the bearded man with the lank brown hair. 'That's where you came into it, isn't it, Mr Jacobi?'

'I never really came into it.'

'You were Turnquist's friend.'

'Well, I knew him.'

'You had rooms on the same floor in the same Chelsea rooming house.'

'Yeah. I knew him to talk to.'

'You teamed up with Turnquist. One or the other of you followed Barlow to my shop. After that, and just hours before I came up here to appraise the books, you came to my shop alone and tried to sell me a book you'd stolen from the public library. You wanted me to buy it knowing it was a stolen book, and you figured I would because you thought I was an outlet for faked or stolen art. You thought that would give you some kind of an opening, some kind of hold on me, but when I wouldn't bite you didn't know what to do next.'

'You make it sound pretty sinister,' Jacobi said. 'Eddie and I didn't know how you fit into the whole thing and I wanted to dope it out. I thought if I sold you the butterfly book you'd let something slip. But you didn't.'

'And you didn't pursue it.'

'I figured you were too honest. Any book dealer who'd turn down a deal like that wouldn't be into receiving stolen works of art.'

'But Friday morning you evidently changed your mind. You and Edwin Turnquist came to my shop together. By then I'd been arrested for Onderdonk's murder and released on bail, and you figured I was tied in somehow. Turnquist, meanwhile, wanted to let me know what Barlow was up to. He probably guessed I'd been framed and wanted to help me clear myself.'

I took a sip of coffee. 'I opened the store and then went two doors down the street to visit a friend of mine. Maybe you two got there after I'd left. Maybe you were the bums I saw lurking in a doorway, and maybe you purposely dawdled across the street until you saw me leave. In either event, the two of you let yourselves in. I just left the door on the springlock, and that wouldn't present any great problem for a man who can spirit large illustrated books out of libraries.'

'Hell, I'm not a real book thief,' Jacobi protested. 'That was just to get your interest.'

I let that pass for the time being. 'Once inside,' I said, 'you turned the bolt so no one else would walk in and interrupt you. You led your good friend Turnquist to the back of the store where nobody could see you, and you stuck an icepick in his heart and left him sitting on the toilet.'

'Why would I do that?'

'Because there was money to be made and he was screwing it up. He had a batch of forged canvases he'd painted in his spare time and he was planning to destroy them. You figured they were worth money, and you were probably right. For another, he had the goods on Barlow. Once I was safely behind bars, you could put the screws on Barlow and bleed him forever. If Turnquist talked, to me or to anybody else, he was taking away your meal ticket. You made up your mind to kill him, and you knew that if you killed him in my store I'd very likely get tagged with his murder, and that would get me out of the picture. Which would make it that much easier for you to turn up the heat under Barlow.'

'So I killed him right there in your store.'

'That's right.'

'And then walked out?'

'Not right away, because you were still there when I came back. The door was bolted when I came back and I'd left it on the springlock, and if it was bolted that meant you were still inside. I guess you must have hidden in the stacks or in the back room, and after I opened up you slipped out. That had me confused for a while, because I had a visitor shortly after I opened up—' I glanced significantly at Elspeth Petrosian '—and I never even noticed her come in. At first I suspected she'd been the one hiding in the back room and that she had murdered Turnquist, but I couldn't make sense out of that. You probably left just as she was walking in, or else you slipped out during my conversation with her. It was a lengthy and intense conversation, and I'm sure you could have departed without either of us having noticed.'

He got to his feet, and Ray Kirschmann stood up immediately. Francis Rockland was already standing; he'd moved to within arm's reach of Jacobi.

'You can't prove any of this,' Jacobi said.

'Your room was searched,' Ray told him pleasantly. 'You got enough city-owned books in there to start a branch library.'

'So? That's petty theft.'

'It's about eight hundred counts of petty theft. Tack all those short sentences together, you got yourself a pretty good-sized paragraph.'

'Kleptomania,' Jacobi said. 'I have a compulsion to steal library books. It's harmless, and I eventually return them. It hardly qualifies me as a murderer.'

'There were some pictures in there too,' Ray said. 'Fakes, I suppose, but you couldn't prove it by me. Mr Lewes here's the expert, but all I can tell is they're paintin's without frames, and what do you bet they turn out to be the work of your buddy Turnquist?'

'He gave them to me. They were a gift of friendship, and I'd like to see you prove otherwise.'

'We got a guy goin' door-to-door at your roomin' house, and what do you bet we turn up somebody who saw you carryin' those canvases from his room to yours? And that woulda been after he was killed an' before the body was discovered, and let's hear you explain that one away. Plus we got a note in his room, Turnquist's room, with Bernie's name and address, same as the note we found on the body. You want to bet they turn out to be your handwritin' and not his?'

'What does that prove? So I wrote down a name and address for him.'

'You also phoned in a tip. You said if we wanted to know who killed Turnquist we should ask Bernie Rhodenbarr.'

'Maybe somebody called you. It wasn't me.'

'Suppose I told you that all incomin' calls are recorded? And suppose I told you that voiceprint identification is as good as fingerprints?'

Jacobi was silent.

'We found somethin' else in your room,' Ray said. 'Show him, Francis.'

Rockland reached into a pocket and produced an icepick. Richard Jacobi stared at it – hell, so did everybody else in the room – and I thought he was going to fall over in a faint. 'You planted that,' he said.

'Suppose I told you there were blood traces on it? And suppose I told you the blood type's the same as Turnquist's?'

'I must have left it in the bookshop,' Jacobi blurted. 'But that's impossible. I threw it in a Dempsey dumpster. Unless I'm wrong and I dropped it in the store, but no, no, I remember I had it in my hand on the way out.'

'So you could stab me if I challenged you,' I put in.

'You never even knew I was there. And you didn't follow me. Nobody followed me. Nobody even knew I left, and I went around the corner with the icepick hidden under my jacket and I went up Broadway and dumped it in the first dumpster I came to, and you couldn't possibly have gotten it out of there.' He drew himself triumphantly to his full height. 'So it's a bluff,' he told Ray. 'If there's any blood on that thing it's not Eddie's. Somebody planted that icepick and it wasn't the murder weapon in the first place.'

'I guess it was just another icepick that happened to be in your room,' Ray said. 'But now that you've told us where to look for the other one, I don't think we'll have a whole lot of trouble finding it. Should be easier than a needle in a haystack, anyway. What else do you want to tell us?'

'I don't have to tell you anything,' Jacobi said.

'Now you're absolutely right about that,' Ray said. 'As a matter of fact, you have the right to remain silent, and you have the right to—'

Di dah di dah di dah.

753

After Rockland had led him away, Ray Kirschmann said, 'Now we come to the best part.' He went into the kitchen and returned with my five-foot cylindrical tube, uncapped it and drew out a rolled canvas. He unrolled it, and damned if it didn't look familiar.

Barnett Reeves asked what it was.

'A paintin',' Ray told him. 'Another of the Moondrains, except it's a fake. Turnquist painted it for Barlow and Barlow sold it to Onderdonk and stole it back after he killed him. It's a perfect match for the broken frame and bits of canvas we found with Onderdonk's body in the bedroom closet.'

'I can't believe it,' Mrs Barlow said. 'Do you mean to say my husband carried that thing off and didn't have the brains to destroy it?'

'He probably didn't have the opportunity, ma'am. What was he gonna do, drop it down the incinerator? Suppose it was recovered? He put it where he thought it would be safe and intended to destroy it at leisure. But acting on my own initiative I discovered it through the use of established police investigative techniques.'

Oh, God.

'Anyway,' he went on, presenting it to Orville Widener, 'here it is.'

Widener looked as though his dog had just brought home carrion. 'What's this?' he said. 'Why are you giving it to me?'

'I just told you what it is,' Ray said, 'and I'm givin' it to you on account of the reward.'

'What reward?'

'The thirty-five grand reward your company's gonna shell out for the paintin' they insured. I'm handin' you the paintin' in front of witnesses and I'm claimin' the reward.'

'You must be out of your mind,' Widener snapped. 'You think we're going to pay that kind of money for a worthless fraud?'

'It's a fraud, okay, but it's a long ways from worthless. You can pay me the thirty-five grand and say thank you while you do it, because otherwise you'd be ponyin' up ten times as much to the cousin in Calgary.'

'That's nonsense,' Widener said. 'We don't have to pay anything to anybody. The painting's a fake.'

'Doesn't matter,' Wally Hemphill said, one hand on his wounded knee. 'Onderdonk paid the premiums and you people took them. The fact that it was a fake and was overinsured doesn't alter your responsibility. The insured acted in good faith – he certainly believed it to be authentic and he had paid a price for it commensurate with the coverage he took out on it. You have to restore the insured painting to my client in Calgary or else reimburse him for a loss in the amount of $350,000.'

'I'll see what our own legal people have to say about that.'

'They'll say just what I just got through telling you,' Wally said, 'and I don't know what you're in a huff about. You're getting off cheap. If it weren't for Detective Kirschmann here, you'd pay the full insured value.'

'Then Detective Kirschmann's costing your client money, isn't he, counselor?'

'I don't think so,' Wally said, 'because we need the fake in order to substantiate our suit against Barlow. Barlow's got money, and he got some of it from my client's deceased uncle, and I intend to bring suit to recover the price paid for the spurious Mondrian. And I'm also representing Detective Kirschmann, so don't think you can weasel out of paying him his reward.'

'We're a reputable company. I resent your use of the word "weasel." '

'Oh, please,' Wally said. 'You people invented the word.'

Barnett Reeves cleared his throat. 'I have a question,' he said. 'What about the real painting?'

'Huh?' somebody said. Probably several people, actually.

'The real painting,' Reeves said, pointing to the canvas that Lloyd Lewes had authenticated several revelations ago. 'If there's no objection, I should like to take that back to the Hewlett Gallery, where it belongs.'

'Now wait a minute,' Widener said. 'If my people are coming up with $35,000—'

'That's for that thing,' Reeves said. 'I want my painting.'

'And you'll get yours,' I said, gesturing toward the acrylic hanging over the fireplace. 'That's the painting that was on display in your gallery, Mr Reeves, and that's the painting you'll take back with you.'

'We never should have had it in the first place. Mr Barlow donated a genuine Mondrian—'

'Nope,' I said. 'He donated a fake, and he didn't even cheat you by doing it. Because it never cost you people a penny. He defrauded the Internal Revenue Service, and they'll probably have words with him on the subject, but he didn't defraud you beyond making a horse's ass out of you, and what's the big deal about that? A bunch of school kids made a horse's ass out of you just yesterday afternoon. You've got no claim on the painting.'

'Then who does?'

'I do,' Mrs Barlow said. 'The police officers took it from my apartment, but that doesn't mean my husband and I relinquish title to it.'

'You don't have title,' Reeves said. 'You gave title to the museum.'

'Not true,' Wally said. 'My client in Calgary should get the painting. It should have passed to Onderdonk, and so it now passes in fact to Onderdonk's heirs.'

'That's all nonsense,' Elspeth Petrosian cried. 'That thief Barlow never had clear title to it in the first place. The painting belongs to

755

me. It was promised to me by my grandfather, Haig Petrosian, and someone stole it before his wishes could be carried out, I don't care what Barlow paid for it or who he did or didn't sell it to. He never dealt with a rightful owner in the first place. That's my painting.'

'I'd love to include it in the retrospective,' Mordecai Danforth said, 'while all of this is being sorted out, but I suppose that's out of the question.'

Ray Kirschmann went over and put a hand on the painting. 'Right now this paintin's evidence,' he said, 'and I'm impoundin' it. The rest of you got your claims and notions and you can fight it out, but the paintin' goes downtown while you drag each other through the courts, and once the lawyers get started it could go on for a good long while.' To Reeves he said, 'If I was you, I'd take that other one downtown and hang it back where it was. By the time the papers write this up, half the city's gonna want to look at it, fake or no. You can waste time worryin' about lookin' like a horse's ass, but that'd just make you more of a horse's ass, because whatever you look like they're gonna be lined up around the block to look at this thing, and what's so bad about that?'

25

'This is a nice place,' Carolyn said, 'and they make a hell of a drink, even if they do charge twice as much as they should for it. Big Charlie's, huh? I like it.'

'I thought you would.'

'I like the girl playing piano, too. I wonder if she's gay.'

'Oh, God.'

'What's wrong with wondering?' She took a sip, set down her glass. 'You left some things out,' she said. 'Explaining everything and making all the bits and pieces fit together, you left a few things out.'

'Well, it was confusing enough as it was. I didn't want to make it impossible for people to follow.'

'Uh-huh. You're a considerate guy. You left out the bit about the cat.'

'Oh, come on,' I said. 'Two men had been murdered and a couple of paintings had been stolen. I couldn't waste people's time talking about a kidnapped cat. Anyway, he'd been ransomed and returned, so what was the point?'

'Uh-huh. Alison was Haig Petrosian's other granddaughter, wasn't she? The other one at the dining room table on Riverside Drive. She's Elspeth's cousin, and her father was Elspeth's Uncle Billy.'

'Well, the resemblance was striking. Remember how you stared at Elspeth in my shop? The funny thing is at first I thought Andrea was the missing cousin, because she and Elspeth both have this habit of cocking their heads to the side, but that was just coincidence. The minute I saw Alison I knew she was the cousin and not Andrea.'

'Andrea Barlow.'

'Right.'

'You left her out, too, didn't you? You didn't mention running into her in Onderdonk's apartment, let alone rolling around on the rug with her.'

'Well, certain things ought to stay private,' I said. 'One thing she told me was true enough. She had been having an affair with Onderdonk, and as it happens her husband knew about it, which probably added to the zest with which he killed the man. Then he must have gloated over the man's death, and Andrea had visions of a police search of the

757

premises uncovering some pictures Onderdonk had taken of the two of them with a time-release Polaroid. She went back for them, found them or didn't find them, who the hell knows, and then I walked in on her. No wonder she was terrified. She must have already found Onderdonk's body in the closet, so she knew it wasn't him, but who could it be? Either the police, in which case she had some fancy explaining to do, or her murderous husband coming to kill her and leave her there with her dead lover. Either way she was in deep trouble.'

'And she was so relieved it was you that she was overcome with passion.'

'Either that or she figured it made sense to screw her way to safety,' I said, 'but I'm inclined to give her the benefit of the doubt. But why mention all of that to the police?'

'Especially since you'd like to verb her again.'

'Well—'

'And why not? She's got a nifty pair of nouns. I think I need another one of these, and don't you just love the little getups the waitresses wear? Let's order another round, and then you can tell me what really happened with the paintings.'

'Oh, the paintings.'

'Yeah, the paintings. This one's from here and that one's from there and this one's cut out of the frame and that one isn't and who can keep it all straight? I know some of what you said was true and I know some of it wasn't, and I want the whole story. But first I want another of these.'

Who could deny her anything? She got what she wanted, first the drink and then the explanation.

'The painting Ray gave back to Orville Widener, the insurance guy, was one that Denise and I painted,' I said. 'Naturally Barlow destroyed the canvas he took from the Onderdonk apartment. All he had to do was slash it to ribbons and put it down the incinerator, and I'm sure he did just that. The canvas I gave to Ray, which he in turn gave to Widener, was the portion I cut out of the frame that I left at the Hewlett. And it doesn't matter if it doesn't match the piece of frame that was left in the closet with Onderdonk's corpse, because that frame will get conveniently lost. Ray'll see to that.'

'What about the painting Reeves took back with him? Was that the one you took from the Hewlett? Did they have an acrylic fake on display all along?'

'Of course not. Turnquist was an artist and he wasn't in a hurry. He didn't use acrylics. He used oil paints, same as Mondrian, and the painting in the Hewlett was one of his.'

'But what Reeves took back with him—'

'Was a second fake that Denise and I did, tacked to the stretcher from the Hewlett. Remember, it was the incused mark on the stretcher that convinced him. I'd already unstapled the canvas and taken the frame apart to get the painting out of the museum. When I put it back together, I just tacked the acrylic fake to the Hewlett frame.'

'And Reeves thinks that's what he had all along.'

'So it would appear, and what's the difference? A fake is a fake is a fake is a fake.'

'I didn't know Denise painted more than one fake.'

'Actually she painted three of them. One got cut up, with the frame and some fragments left at the Hewlett and the rest of it returned to Orville Widener. The other went back to the Hewlett with Reeves.'

'And the third?'

'Is hanging on a wall in the Narrowback Gallery, and it's a little different from the others in that the signature monogram is DR instead of PM. She's pretty proud of it, although I had a hand in it myself, and so did Jared.'

'She painted three fakes and Turnquist painted two. You said Barlow destroyed one of the Turnquist fakes. What happened to the other one? The one you lifted out of the Hewlett.'

'Ah,' I said. 'It's been impounded.'

'Jesus. Bern. That was the *real* real one that was impounded, the one Mondrian himself painted, remember? Everybody's claiming it and there'll be court cases for years and – oh.'

I guess I must have smiled.

'Bern, you didn't.'

'Well, why not? You heard what Lloyd Lewes said. He looked at the canvas the two cops brought in and said it was an oil painting and it looked right. Why shouldn't it look right? After all, it sat in the Hewlett for years and nobody suspected a thing. Now it can sit in a locked closet at Number One Police Plaza for a few more years and nobody'll suspect a thing there, either. I took it along with me when I let myself into the Barlow apartment last night, stapled it to a stretcher and left it where the cops would find it.'

'And the real Mondrian?'

'It was in the Barlow apartment when I got there, of course. I took it off its stretcher and stapled Turnquist's fake in its place. I had to have a stretcher for the Turaquist canvas, remember.'

'Because you used the stretcher it was on in the Hewlett for one of Denise's fakes.'

'Right.'

'You know what the trouble is, Bern? There's too many Mondrians. It sounds like a Nero Wolfe novel, doesn't it? *Too Many Cooks, Too Many Clients, Too Many Detectives, Too Many Women.* And *Too Many Mondrians.*'

'Right.'

'Denise painted three acrylic fakes, Turaquist painted two oil fakes, and Mondrian painted one. Except his was a real one, and are you gonna keep me in suspense forever, Bern? What happens to the real one?'

'It's going to go to the rightful owner.'

'Elspeth Petrosian? Or Alison? She's got as much real claim on it as her cousin.'

'Speaking of Alison—'

'Yeah,' she said heavily. 'Speaking of Alison. When you figured they were cousins, that was how you knew Elspeth Peters was Armenian. And you looked through the phone book and—'

'Not quite. I looked through papers in Alison's office and found out her maiden name. That's a little simpler than reading the phone book.'

'Is that where you got the cat?' She put a hand on mine. 'I couldn't help figuring it out, Bernie. She took my cat, didn't she? And that's why she used the Nazi voice when she talked with me, because I would have recognized her real voice. She talked normally with you because she'd never met you. And she was nervous when we got to my place and you were there, because she thought you might recognize her voice from over the phone. Did you?'

'Not really. I was too busy recognizing the resemblance between her and her cousin Elspeth.'

'She wasn't really that bad,' Carolyn said thoughtfully. 'She didn't hurt Archie, except for cutting his whiskers, and that's a far cry from mutilating him. And the closer she and I got, the more reassuring the Nazi became over the phone, until there was a point where I pretty much stopped worrying about the cat. You know something? When we got back to the apartment and the cat was there, I think she was as relieved as I was.'

'I wouldn't be surprised.'

She sipped her drink. 'Bern? How'd she get past my locks?'

'She didn't.'

'Huh?'

'Your cats liked her, remember? Especially Archie. She went through another building into the courtyard and coaxed him through the bars of the window. A person couldn't get in, but a cat could get out. That's one reason there were no traces of her visit inside the apartment. She never went inside the apartment except when she was with you. She didn't have to. The cat walked right out into her arms.'

'When did you dope that out?'

'When I saw Ubi measuring the distance between the bars with his whiskers. They fit, which meant his head would fit, which meant his whole body would fit, and I knew that's how it was done. Which meant it had to be done by somebody the cat liked, and you told me early on how much the cat liked Alison.'

'Yeah, animals are great judges of character. Bernie, were you gonna tell me all this?'

'Well—'

'Either you were or you weren't.'

'Well, I wasn't sure. You seemed to be having a good time with Alison and I figured I'd let the relationship run its course before I said anything.'

'I think it's run its course.' She knocked back the rest of her drink and sighed philosophically. 'Listen, I got my cat back,' she said, 'and I had a little excitement, and Alison was a big help at the Hewlett. I don't know if I could have managed the firecracker and the fire and everything without her. And I got laid, so why should I hold a grudge?'

'That's about how I felt about Andrea.'

'Plus I might want to see her again.'

'That's exactly how I felt about Andrea.'

'Right. So I came out of it okay.'

'Don't forget the reward.'

'Huh?'

'From the insurance company. The $35,000. Ray's getting half of what's left after Wally takes his fee, and the rest gets cut up between you and Denise.'

'Why?'

'Because you both worked for it. Denise labored like Michelangelo on the Sistine Chapel, and you risked arrest at the Hewlett, and for that you get rewarded.'

'What about you, Bern?'

'I've got Appling's stamps, remember? And his wife's ruby earrings, except I don't think they're rubies. I think they're spinels. And it's funny, I almost feel bad about keeping them, but how could I put them back? If there's one thing I'm sure of it's that I'm never going to break into the Charlemagne again.'

'I forgot about the stamps.'

'Well, I'm going to sell them,' I said, 'and then we can all forget about them.'

'Good idea.' Her fingers drummed the tabletop. 'You stole those stamps before any of this happened,' she said. 'Well, almost. While you were breaking into Appling's apartment, Barlow was murdering Onderdonk. That gives me a chill to think about.'

'Me too, when you put it that way.'

'But most of what happened came after you took the stamps, and you didn't get anything for that part of it. You just spent a lot of money and had to post bond.'

'I'll get the bond back. I'll have paid a fee to the bondsman, but that's no big deal. Wally won't charge me anything, not with all the business I threw his way. And I had a few incidental expenses, from cab rides to the icepick I planted in Jacobi's room.'

'And the chloral hydrate you planted in Onderdonk's apartment.'

'That wasn't chloral hydrate. That was talcum powder.'

'The cop said it tasted like chloral hydrate.'

'And Ray said there was a voiceprint record of Jacobi's telephone tip, and that there was blood on the icepick. This may come as a shock, Carolyn, but cops have been known to tell lies.'

'It's a shock, all right. Anyway, you had expenses, and all you get is your freedom.'

'So?'

'So don't you want part of the reward? Thirty-five thousand less Wally's fee'll be what? Thirty thousand?'

'Call it that. I don't know if he'll dare grab off that much, but lawyers are hard to figure.'

'Thirty grand less half to Ray leaves fifteen, and if we cut that three ways it's five apiece, and that's plenty. Why don't you take a third, Bern?'

I shook my head. 'I got the stamps,' I said, 'and *that's* plenty. And I got something else, too.'

'What? A shot at Andrea and a shot at Eve DeGrasse? Big deal.'

'Something else.'

'What?'

'I'll give you a hint,' I said. 'It's all right angles and primary colors, and I'm going to hang it over my couch. I think that's the best place for it.'

'Bernie!'

'I told you,' I said. 'The Mondrian's with its rightful owner. And who do you know who's got a better right to it?'

And I'll tell you something. It looks gorgeous there.